Adventures of the First Woman Mountie

Omnibus Volume 1

LAURIE SCHRAMM

Adventures of the First Woman Mountie. Omnibus Volume 1

An Inconvenient Mountie. Book 1
An Inconspicuous Mountie. Book 2
An Indestructible Mountie. Book 3
An International Mountie. Book 4

Print ISBN: 978-1-9994940-8-7
ePub ISBN: 978-1-9994940-9-4

Laurie Schramm

DEDICATION

Dedicated to the present and past Members of the Royal Canadian Mounted Police and its forebears, the Royal North-West Mounted Police and the North-West Mounted Police.

Laurie Schramm

CONTENTS

Laurie Schramm

ACKNOWLEDGMENTS

I am extremely grateful to the growing number of friendly readers that that have provided encouragement, comments, and suggestions based on drafts of these books: Ann Marie, Victoria, Katherine, William, Dawson, Al, Moira, Jayme, Karen, and Ernie.

Special thanks also to three real-life veterans of the RCMP, all of whom have supplemented their encouragement with numerous background and factual reference materials on the Force: Chief Superintendent William Schramm (Ret.), who also kindly allowed my main character to borrow his Regimental Number, Assistant Commissioner Dawson Hovey (Ret.), and Staff Sergeant Al Lund (Ret., author of *Mounties on the Cover* and probably the world's leading authority on Mountie fiction).

Laurie Schramm

A journey of a thousand miles begins with a single step.

Tao Te Ching, *circa* 5th century BCE,
Laozi ("Lao-tzu") a legendary Chinese philosopher

Laurie Schramm

An Inconvenient Mountie

Adventures of the First Woman Mountie. Book 1

LAURIE SCHRAMM

Laurie Schramm

M
0535 EST+
RCMP PR ALBERT
V
VIA WUI+
RCMP PR ALBERT

RCMP RADCITY

PRIORITY

FM: RADIUM CITY DET.
TO: PR ALBERT S/DIV
BT
UNCLAS

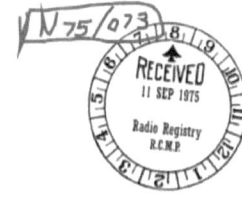

MISSING PERSON REPORTED BY RUBY GILLESPIE, AGE 45, APPEARS TO
BE SINCERE. REPORTED MISSING IS NORMAN VINCENT POOLE, AGE 40,
AKA NORM, RESIDENT OF RADIUM CITY. LAST SEEN R. CITY, ON 9
SEPT, AT 11 AM. INVESTIGATING.
ELS.
+
RCMP PR ALBERT

RCMP RADCITY
VVV

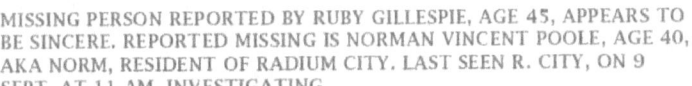

Laurie Schramm

DEDICATION

To Ally.

Laurie Schramm

BOOK 1 CONTENTS

Laurie Schramm

LIST OF CHARACTERS
(IN ORDER OF APPEARANCE)

- Constable Alexandra (Alex) Houston, RCMP
- Norm Poole, Hunting and Fishing Guide
- Assistant Commissioner George MacLeod, RCMP 'Depot' Division, Regina
- Horace Best, Mayor, Radium City
- Sergeant Major R. Walsh, RCMP 'Depot' Division, Regina
- Fred Hoskins, a fellow recruit in RCMP training
- Corporal Mike Morrison, RCMP, Radium City Detachment
- Ruby Gillespie, Coffee Shop Owner/Manager, Radium City
- Jim Dumont, Hunting and Fishing Guide
- Dr. Evans, a physician
- Vern Schriver, a retired commercial airline pilot
- Jennifer Stone, part-time helper, RCMP, Radium City Detachment
- Lucy Weaver, Bookstore Owner, Radium City
- Ron McGee, a prospector
- Ally, a cat
- Jack McDonald, a fellow recruit in RCMP training, Regina
- Andrew Fielding, Bank Manager, Radium City
- Silver, an Alaskan Malamute
- Mervyn J. Crowe, a lawyer
- Franklin P. Heath, a lawyer

Cst. Alexandra Houston

1 AN UNEXPECTED MEETING

"IT'S NOT HALLOWEEN IS IT?"

It was June 1975, and that was my greeting as I stepped off the de Havilland Twin Otter aircraft at the airport (more like a small airstrip, really) in Radium City, Saskatchewan. I knew what was coming next and as my inner voice reminded me to keep a straight face, I said: "No, not yet."

It was, in fact, only June but as I say, I knew what was coming next.

"If it isn't Halloween, then why are you dressed up like a Mountie?" asked the man who was helping unload the modest cargo of luggage, mail bags, and supplies for the town's store. He seemed both forceful and slightly sneaky in demeanour, a bit larger than average height and build, but slightly stooped in posture. I later discovered him to be a hunting and fishing guide named Norm Poole.

"It's because I really am a Mountie," I said, deciding to play it straight and wait for the inevitable response.

"Well, if you are, then you're the first I've ever heard of," said Norm. "What'll they think of next?"

I kept to my standard script, and simply said: "Yes, one of the first." In fact, I really was the first woman Mountie, but I didn't feel the need to tell him that. I hadn't even intended for it to happen at all. It came and found me.

***

There had been women police officers in Canada since about 1830 in Annapolis Royal, Nova Scotia, or 1912 in Vancouver or Edmonton, depending on who you listened to. I had always wanted to become a police officer of some kind, and I admit that I even harboured a secret admiration for the Mounties in the old classics my parents would wake me up to watch when they came on late night television. **Rose Marie**, with Jeanette MacDonald and Nelson Eddy, and **Susannah of the Mounties**, with Shirley Temple and Randolph Scott, inspired in me a fascination with the notion of becoming a police officer of some kind.

They say you should be careful what you wish for.

I did become a police officer of 'some kind.' Appointment of female police officers dated back to the beginning of the 20th century, it had only been in recent years that women officers had been allowed to become 'real' officers, as in allowed to carry guns and do 'real' policing – at least theoretically. In 1972 I had graduated from training and become a Constable in the Metropolitan Toronto Police force ('Metro'). My two years since then had mostly consisted of such critical policing tasks as desk-duty, matron-duty (searching female prisoners), and traffic-duty. Not that there's anything wrong with those jobs, they're important, and they need to be done well. But, for me, they didn't fit the Hollywood vision I had developed, and I wasn't finding them to be very challenging.

All of that changed with an unexpected meeting in 1974.

I had been called in by my Captain and ordered to go and see a Royal Canadian Mounted Police (RCMP) officer that wanted to meet me. My reaction to this was apprehension. I wondered what I had done wrong. I probably could have asked my Captain, but it was only my second year on the force, I was insecure in my position, and I was still a bit afraid of him. I knew how to take orders though, so I went to the meeting, which was arranged for a quiet downtown coffee shop.

Walking into the coffee shop, I was immediately waved to a corner table by an older man (these things are relative), with short greying hair, and wearing civilian clothes. I didn't recognize him but he obviously recognized me. He introduced himself as Assistant Commissioner George MacLeod and explained that he was the Commanding Officer (CO) of the RCMP's 'Depot' Division training centre and that he was an old friend of my Captain.

He'd already ordered a pot of coffee and launched straight into a volley *of questions that ranged all over the map. He asked about my preferences for dealing with tense situations and volatile people, and I explained that I preferred to engage in discussions with people over brute force. He asked how I felt about Aboriginal people, immigrants, and visible minorities. I replied that I thought any police force should be representative of the population that it serves, and related an experience I'd had patrolling in 'Chinatown' with a fellow Constable who was of Asian descent. I was just about to launch into a full-out discourse on the merits of diversity when he cut me off and jumped to his next question. With each question, he'd let me talk a bit and then cut me off and move to the next question. He asked about my girlhood, education, training in the Metro force, and my duties over the preceding two years. I eventually realized that I was being interviewed for something.*

Finally, he leaned back in his chair, looked at me broodingly, and got to the point. He had asked my Captain, his friend, to recommend one of his young officers for a special pilot project he had in mind. He wanted someone who wanted to accomplish things, someone eager and tenacious, someone chomping at the bit to be allowed to do some 'real' police work, and ... someone female. At this point, he shed his stern 'Mountie Look,' relaxed his entire body, chuckled, and said that my Captain had recommended the "biggest pain in the butt" in his Division - me.

Seeing my obvious confusion, he moved on. "The Force has fallen behind the times," he said, "it's becoming embarrassing, with political pressure for change mounting, but some of us have a genuine desire to catch up and build a more diverse police force."

"We're going to be recruiting immigrants, visible minorities, maybe even people with some kinds of disabilities as well, but we have to start somewhere, and that somewhere is by engaging women"

He went on to explain that as CO of the training centre he was ready to try a first "pilot test" with a woman, but that the pilot test had to succeed as it would pave the way for an entire first troop of policewomen that would follow[1]. He had thought of using someone that had already qualified as a policewoman, and simply re-train them in the "RCMP way."

That brought me up to full attention. "Wait a minute! Do basic training all over again?"

"Yes!" he replied, "that's the only way you can possibly succeed. In the

old days of the Northwest Mounted Police, a person could get appointed straight into the Force, even as a commissioned officer, if they had the right political connections. No more. Now everyone starts out the same way, as a Constable, and by going through the same basic training. If you want to have any hope of being accepted, much less respected, that's how you have to begin."

"Will you do it?"

***

Radium City, Canada

Two years later, I'd arrived at the Radium City airport and played out the "IT'S NOT HALLOWEEN IS IT?" scene as part of my first introduction to a local resident, Norm.

As I collected my luggage, I was eagerly looking forward to doing some "real" police work. There was a large van serving as the airport shuttle for the four-mile trip into town, driven by – Norm, again. Although he had given me a hard time, the others taking the shuttle seemed nice enough.

Despite the name, Radium City is actually a town, not a city. It is located on the northern shore of Lake Athabasca, the 22nd largest lake in the world (8th largest in Canada), in the extreme northwestern corner of Saskatchewan, one of Canada's prairie provinces.

When we reached the centre of town, I took in a fairly typical small-town Canadian scene: a long, main street accommodating most of the key stores and offices, with several back streets radiating out to each side. One block back from the main street was the RCMP Detachment, a standard one-and-a-half story brown building of the same architecture that characterized hundreds of small RCMP detachments across the country. That's where I headed.

When I arrived, I was greeted by a locked door with a typed notice taped to it, saying "Gone fishing. For emergencies, contact the Mayor's Office. Otherwise, leave a note." I noticed that the door also had a notebook and pen hanging from a string. I wrote: "Cst. A. Houston reporting. Just arrived. Will report back tomorrow am," and went off to check-in to the one hotel.

It was late afternoon by the time I had settled into the hotel, so I tried the Mayor's Office. I found the Mayor, Horace Best, was in and was eager to welcome me to the community. Horace was about average in height and build, with thick blond hair, and lively blue eyes. I found him to be instantly engaging. He would lean forward and look directly at me with a smile on his face and a twinkle in his eye. Obviously relishing the opportunity to speak to an eager listener, he soon launched into a sketch of Radium City's history.

I already knew some of the histories, having looked-up what I could in the City of Regina's library. I knew that Lake Athabasca was originally spelled "Athabaska," from a Cree word meaning "the place where there are reeds," referring to a reedy delta where the Athabasca River flows into the big lake. I also knew that Radium City had gone through a boom and bust cycle, and was now continuing to decline. Horace brought it all alive.

There had been mineral exploration activities in the area since the early 1900s, with prospectors looking for everything from iron, to gold, to radium. There hadn't been much development though, as the ore bodies discovered had been small, or the market timing was off, or both. Then, in the late 1940s, government interest in finding and stockpiling uranium for atomic weapons created an exploration rush in the region. By 1950, uranium prices had risen sharply, and prospectors' "tent cities" had begun to spring up around numerous mine sites in the area. By 1950, thousands of radioactive "surface showings" had been discovered. In response, the Saskatchewan government established the community of Radium City, in 1951, with the aim of serving the entire region.

Apparently, the city had been named after the "Radium Ore," everyone was prospecting for, this being the old term for the uranium mineral pitchblende. Horace chuckled, "The irony is that this radium ore was the same mineral prospectors had searched for in the 1920s and '30s, as an indicator of radium potential, but back then, the uranium itself was thought to be worthless and no one bothered to take much notice of it."

"Those were the days," he mused dreamily. In 1952, the government changed the regulations, making it more attractive for prospectors to explore and stake claims in the Lake Athabasca region. This even made it attractive for amateurs to prospect for uranium. The result was a massive uranium exploration and claim-staking rush that helped Canada build an international position as a uranium producer. "For a while, anyone with a rucksack and a Geiger Counter could become a prospector," Horace Explained, "and for a few years, the place was crawling with them." He showed me a scrapbook of newspaper and magazine clippings from publications like the New York Times, Maclean's, and Life Magazine, with headlines like "*Uranium - Canada Maintains Place in Frantic World Production Race.*"

Several large uranium mines were established near the town, with the Rix Athabasca and Eldorado mines starting-up in 1953, followed by Cayzor Athabasca in 1954, Cinch Lake in 1955, Gunnar in 1955, and Lorado in 1956. With all this activity, Radium City grew from about 1,500 people in 1953 to nearly 5,000 by 1957. "They even made documentary movies[2] about us," Horace gushed, "like *The Birth of a Great Uranium Area* in 1953, and *The Road to Uranium* in 1957, and those movies were shown all over the world!"

"And the money flowed like water for a while," Horace concluded. Apparently, by 1960 the twelve mines and three mills operating in the Radium City area had produced about $300 million worth of uranium. This was big money in those days, and uranium was Canada's number one mineral export (ahead of aluminum, iron, and nickel).

"Of course, it had to end someday," Horace sighed, "We knew, or we should have known. But no one talked about it; no one wanted to think about it." By 1961, some of the mines had run out of ore and closed. By 1963 Canada, the U.S., and Great Britain had accumulated enough uranium, and they stopped buying.

"The next thing you know, uranium was a glut on the market, and the price collapsed." As the price collapsed, so did the exploration, mining, and milling activities, and the number of active mines shrunk to only two, the Eldorado and Gunnar mines.

"By 1964, Radium City population was 1,500 again, right back where we started, and it's still shrinking. Ten years later, and we're now down to about 1,000." To hear Horace tell it, Radium City was once a wild, frontier town, but that was in the past. With the boom and bust years well behind, it sounded like the town had eased into a nice, quiet life. There was a two-person RCMP Detachment, and Horace thought I'd find it nice and relaxing because, he said, "Nothing exciting happens around here anymore."

Horace was wrong.

RCMP 'Depot' Division, Regina

2 A NEW BEGINNING

"WHAT THE HELL ARE YOU DOING HERE?"
I had heard that before.

***

Having been sworn-in in Toronto, and given my permanent Regimental Number of 15425, I had travelled to the RCMP's training centre in Regina, which was called 'Depot' Division. It looked like a military base, with a big Canadian flag flying from a tall flagpole in the centre of a huge parade square that was decorated with monuments and old cannon, and surrounded by large, sprawling brown brick buildings.

Locating the Guardroom, I checked in – or tried to. The Constable on duty read the engagement card I had been given: "Houston, A., Reg.#15425."

"This is you?" he asked.

"This is me," I replied.

"But you're a girl!" he exclaimed.

Fearing that we were about to perform an Abbott and Costello skit, I quickly explained that I was a new pilot project of the CO's. This set him back a bit, but then he suddenly grinned conspiratorially and pointed down the hallway. "You'd better go see the Sergeant Major."

Reading the nameplates on the doors as I walked down the indicated hallway, I came to an old-looking, wood-framed door bearing a sign marked "Senior Training Officer, S/M R. Walsh," at the very end of the hall. My knock on the door was meet with a sharp, booming command,

"Enter!"

Seated inside, behind a large government-issue wooden desk, was a square-jawed poster-image of a Hollywood-style Mountie. Expecting to repeat the dance that had begun with the duty Constable, I entered, handed the engagement card across his desk, and stood to attention. Without even looking at the card, he simply stared me up and down for a moment. "This is someone that doesn't miss much," I thought.

"So you're Houston are you?" he asked. Before I could answer he went on, "Heard about you from the CO. The CO wants to start diversifying the force, beginning with women, and then moving on to others, ..., visible minorities, immigrants, ... God alone knows what else, ... and DO YOU KNOW WHAT I THINK ABOUT IT?" He paused for a breath, but once again, before I could say anything, he went on, "I think it's about bloody time, that's what I think."

Sensing that there was more to come I remained silent.

"I see that you know how to stand to attention, and keep your mouth shut, so there may be some hope for you," he went on, in just slightly less than parade-ground volume. "I've read your file. I know that you're the CO's pilot project, and I know that you've come from the Metro Toronto Force, so you have some training."

"You're going to have to unlearn some of your training because we do things a bit differently in the Force (he said it like "IN THE FORCE"). He reiterated that he fully supported the idea of women becoming Mounties - "We need to be representative of the people we exist to serve" - but that I should expect no special treatment. He expected a high standard of work performance from everyone, in everything they do, and that in my case I'd quite likely have to do everything as well or better than the men.

"You're assigned to 'M Troop.' The rest of your troop will be straggling in over the next few days, so you'll have time to get to know the base. Your troop will all be staying in 'B' Block, but we can't put you in there as we don't have separate facilities yet. There's an office with a bed next door to the Guardroom you came in through, and there's a bathroom with a shower across the hall from it that will be reserved for you. You'll eat in the Mess and do everything else with the rest of your troop." He then gave me a long list of places to go and people to see for uniforms, schedules, textbooks, and regulations.

"Come and see me anytime," he concluded, "but don't come crying to

me saying something 'isn't fair,' because I'm going to agree with you – 'it isn't fair.' Deal with it!"

My initial impressions, having gotten somewhat over the shock of his parade-ground voice, were that he was probably highly intelligent, far more-broad minded than his outward appearance would suggest (playing a role perhaps?), possibly fair, but tough - someone whose bark could actually be worse than his bite. I made a mental note to stay out of his "Bad Book."

As my troop came together, and we started our busy schedule I found that my training for the Metro Toronto force had prepared me well for some things, but I wasn't prepared for how regimented things were, nor for the almost fanatical emphasis on neatness and physical fitness. For example, we ran everywhere. We even ran to our PT[3] and swimming classes, in troop formation, with the cadence called-out by our Right Marker[4] - all 32 of us dressed in the same T-shirts, shorts, socks, and shoes, and everyone carrying their bathing suit wrapped tightly inside a perfectly rolled white towel.

One difference was that the male recruits all got the brush cuts of the century. I wondered at first if the barbers had used an electric razor rather than scissors on them, and then learned that truth can be stranger than fiction – because that's exactly what had been used! They weren't sure what to do with me but settled on cutting my hair short enough that I could just barely tie it into a ponytail and push the end through the back of the baseball-type cap we sometimes wore, or up and inside of my forage cap. Anyway, we ran to the Mess, ran from the Mess, ran to class, ran from class, ran to Fatigues, ran from Fatigues.

Fatigues ...

"Fatigues" were named for the brown uniform pants and jackets that we wore while doing what on a farm would be called "chores." We had Fatigues every day, and we cleaned everything, our rooms, our building, other buildings, and of course, the stables. The term "Fatigues" came from the French word 'fatigue,' meaning 'duty that causes weariness.' They got that right! I was torn between judging that we were being put through all this to develop discipline and camaraderie, and my suspicion that they had an obsessive aversion to letting us have any idle time. I eventually concluded that it was both.

Hazing...

There was the mild hazing all newcomers received. It was all very *juvenile, mostly just silly, and not very much different from the hazing most students received in their first week of high school in those days. There was also the give and take of any new bunch of strangers that are thrown together in close, repeated proximity. Everyone was trying to get to know each other and look out for potential friends or threats. Naturally, there was an occasional incident that was more specific to gender. It would have been naive to expect otherwise.*

One of our lecturers was a Corporal. I really don't remember his name anymore, or even what he was supposed to be lecturing to us about, which may say something about his abilities as an instructor. But, I do remember our first day in his classroom. As we were settling into our desks and getting our binders out, he stalked into the room and took a look around at all the new recruits with a rather bemused, almost paternal expression on his face. That is, paternal until his gaze landed on me and he called out in yet another parade-ground voice: "WHAT THE HELL ARE YOU DOING HERE?"

"I'm here to learn, Sir," I replied in a neutral tone.

"Name?" he barked. I supplied it. Checking his class list, he seemed surprised to find my name on it. "Well, Houston," he continued, "someone seems to have let a girl in here. There's a sewing class right down the hall, are you sure you wouldn't rather be there?"

I heard a few low chuckles from people seated behind me.

"No Sir, this is where I want to be, Sir."

"Hmmm" was his only response, and then he singled out the smallest person in the class and proceeded to embarrass and harass him. Being, for the moment, out of the spotlight, I felt uncharitably thankful for not also being the smallest person in our troop."

Most episodes, like this one with the Corporal, were pretty standard fare – everyone was singled out for verbal abuse from our instructors at one time or another, and to be fair our other instructors treated me just like any other recruit, no better, and no worse.

The most serious incident involved a fellow recruit. It happened one Sunday afternoon, when a troop-mate named Fred Hoskins and I were working in the stables[5], him brushing down a horse in its stall, and me mucking out an empty stall nearby. It was inevitable that our paths should cross, and on one such occurrence he reached over and grabbed my left buttock. This wasn't a casual, friendly touch like guys might hand out after a good volley in a racquetball game or a good play in a football game - this was a full-out grab.

I suppose that I should have handled it differently, but I was hot and tired. I was also probably feeling a bit cranky, as I'd been unsuccessfully trying to work out how cleaning the stables was going to make me a good policewoman. I'd also had just about enough of jokes and put-downs with regard to being a woman and having red hair, so without thinking I just swung around to my left and kneed him right dead-center in the crotch. I don't know which of us was more surprised, but it didn't last long as his eyes rolled up, his head and shoulders slumped forward, and he dropped to the floor like a sack of flour, unconscious.

Now what? It was Sunday, and there was no one else around in the stables, the rest of our troop having been assigned to a myriad of other duties. But, I had a wheelbarrow right there with me, so I pulled him up onto it and wheeled him over to the Post Hospital. I told the Hospital Steward that "one minute he was brushing the horse's tail, and the next minute he was lying on the ground," which was true but incomplete. These circumstances plus the location of Fred's obvious swelling led them to the obvious but incorrect conclusion that "the poor horse must have done it." Apparently, this kind of thing had actually happened to other recruits in the past. I didn't correct them about this one.

The incident was never spoken of again - not by Fred, not by me, not by anyone. On the other hand, it might have been my imagination, but over the next week or so there did seem to be a number of knowing glances, smiles, and the occasional reference to the legendary temper of red-heads. Nothing specific mind you, but it seemed that my colleagues approved. Perhaps it was all for the best, as no one else tried making a pass at me for the rest of my time at Depot. Fred later got into other troubles and either quit or was dropped from the program. I didn't ever hear which.

The only direct reference to the incident came when training was finally over and we were preparing for graduation. I was back in the Sergeant Major's office, meeting with him about something or other, and as I was starting to rise up from my chair to leave, he stopped me cold with his signature parade-ground voice: "Anything you want to tell me about young Hoskins and the horse?"

I sat back down, paused, looked directly at him, and in a firm, clear voice answered "No sir."

"Hmmm," he said, rubbing his chin. "Well, sometimes constables need to trust to their own initiative. Carry on."

My last meeting at Depot Division involved being called in to see the CO, Assistant Commissioner George MacLeod, whom I hadn't seen since our meeting in Toronto. He said he was pleased that I'd survived training, but that the real challenges lie ahead.

"Some of your colleagues want to get posted to the Musical Ride, or to a Traffic Section where they can wear big sunglasses and ride motorcycles, or to Ottawa to join the race for promotions," he said. "I don't want to wave you like a flag, and I certainly don't want you sent to a big city, or even to a large detachment - as you'll just end up being assigned to routine duties like you've already had in Toronto. I've recommended that you be transferred to one of our smaller, more remote detachments, preferably a "two-man" detachment. You won't be alone but you'll get a taste of doing everything yourself."

"Your colleagues will think you're being punished, but you're not," he added. "You want the full policing experience - a small remote detachment is the place to get it, and that's where you're going."

***

"WHAT THE HELL ARE YOU DOING HERE?"

Here we go again, I thought.

It was my second day in Radium City and as promised, I had presented myself at the Detachment Office promptly at 8 am. This time the door opened easily and I stepped into the office, where a Corporal sat sternly behind a ubiquitous large wooden desk. My orders said to report to the NCO IC[6], and this was he. He was alternately frowning at me and two papers held in his left hand. One was my note from yesterday and the other was a telex[7] form.

"Houston, A., Reg.#15425," he read. "what's the 'A' stand for?"

"Alexandra, Sir, … Alex," I promptly replied. In training, we had been taught to look up to Corporals like gods. Angry gods, to be sure, but gods nonetheless.

Seeing that he was still scowling, I added, "Alexandra, Sir."

There was a pause, during which he looked back and forth between me and the papers in his hand as if he couldn't believe what was happening. Eventually, though, he crossed some kind of decision point and with a growling "Hrrumph," he dropped the papers to the desk, leaned back in his large wooden swivel chair, introduced himself as Cpl. Morrison and said, "Take a seat Houston."

For the next hour, he described the area for which we were responsible. It was not just Radium City, but a huge area of land bounded by the southern shore of Lake Athabasca, all the way to Camsell Portage to the east, Fond-du-Lac to the west, and the border with the Northwest Territories, which is 70 miles to the north. Less than two thousand people, but some of them widely scattered, and over a geographical area of nearly two thousand square miles.

From there he went on to summarize our duties, which comprised upholding not only federal laws but also provincial and municipal laws. As was common in Western Canada, the RCMP had been contracted to conduct provincial and municipal policing in this area. It made sense, really, as we had to be there anyway, and the cost of additional police to cover the other laws only made sense in heavily populated areas in central Canada and in big cities like Toronto, where I had started out.

Beyond that, as a small Detachment in a remote area, we were expected to assist our fellow citizens with a bewildering array of other things, from administering drivers' license exams to witnessing government and legal documents, to assisting with the delivery of babies when there was no one else around to help. He looked at me, and I waited for the predictable crack about me being at least suitable for helping to deliver babies. I could see the thought pass through his mind, as he looked at me with hooded eyes, but he surprised me by letting the thought go unspoken and instead talked about how it was vital that we quickly come together as a team.

He explained that there were only the two of us, with more work than two people could possibly handle, so we would have to learn to work together, help each other, and cover each other's backs. As he started to explain my essential duties, he increasingly lapsed into extolling the virtues of Allan.

Allan, it developed, was my predecessor, Cst. Allan Sharpe. Clearly, Allan had been a miracle worker. Allan had done this, Allan had done that, Allan had done... everything. This Allan person was coming across like Dudley Doright (who was NOT one of my Hollywood Mountie heroes). *No wonder that 'Gone fishing' note had looked so well worn*, I thought to myself – with Allan here, who needed the Corporal? As Cpl. Morrison continued to extoll Allan's virtues, it seemed that my departed predecessor could do no wrong.

Contrary to popular belief, some police officers have a sense of humour. Trying to at least look attentive and keep a straight face, I was reminded of a satirical performance review that had circulated near the end of my training days. The highest performance-rating column was filled with assessments like: "*Stronger than a locomotive; Faster than a speeding bullet; Leaps tall buildings with a single bound; Speaks with the angels; Walks on water...*"

Finally running out of steam, Cpl. Morrison summarized Allan's exploits with a few more examples of how indispensable he had become. There was a pause, and then he looked back across the desk at me,

"... and now I have... you."

With a huge sigh of resignation and the look of a martyr in his eye, he stroked his huge handlebar mustache and said, "We'll just have to make the best of it."

Seeing the look on my face (my jaw must have dropped a bit), he relented a bit and said, "Don't take it so hard Houston. Fortunately, nothing interesting ever happens around here."

Prophetic sounding words but, like Horace, he was wrong.

3 RADIUM CITY

My first task was to get my things and settle-in to the detachment. Our building had originally been built to house the larger police presence needed for a larger town, so there was quite a bit of extra space available. The upper half-floor containing three bedrooms and a large bathroom was vacant and unlikely to be filled up anytime soon, so I had the whole thing to myself.

The next few days, involved getting acquainted with the town and its people. My first stop was the Coffee Shop, which I quickly learned was the hub of the community. Having introduced myself to Ruby, the owner/manager, and settled in with a cup of coffee, I noticed that everyone seemed to drop by at one time or another. Some would come for a drink or a meal, of course, but many others came to cash cheques, use the pay telephone, watch the television that was mounted up high in a corner, purchase small incidentals, or – and this seemed to be the café's main function – gather to chat and gossip. As I later commented to Cpl. Morrison (first name still to be determined), the simplest way to get introduced to Radium City residents would be to just sit at Ruby's all day and wait for them all to pass by.

Norm Poole, to whom I had already been introduced as our aircraft baggage handler and airport shuttle driver, turned out to be something of a *Jack of all trades* who did odd jobs for other businesses in town as well.

Norman Poole

In one of the furthest corners of town, I was intrigued to encounter a ramshackle house on a huge lot that seemed to be home to several boats, none of which looked seaworthy, and a large pack of dogs of varying breeds. This was Norm's place.

It turned out that the dogs were sled dogs. There was an assortment of dog houses on one side of the property, each slightly different in appearance and seemingly built from salvaged lumber, and each having a flat roof that projected over the entrance. In this way, the projecting roof provided some shelter for the entrance, and the flat rooves provided places for the dogs to sit and survey the area. The dogs must have liked this arrangement, because most of them were lying down, lounging on the tops of their dog houses.

Although still a bit rough around the edges, Norm became more talkative when I showed interest in everything. The house, he explained proudly, came from four houses that he had dragged across the ice from the camp of a former Eldorado mine. He had essentially cut some of the walls away, butted-up the four houses together, and then connected everything to make one single house that was much more spacious on the inside than it had appeared from the exterior.

"Didn't cost me much more than the fuel for the truck to do the dragging," said Norm proudly. "I even scavenged the nails!"

The first thing I noticed on entering was the smell. Not the unwashed, hermit living-alone smell that you're probably imagining, although there was that too. The strongest smell reminded me of the section in most northern general stores where hand-made fur and leather goods were displayed. It turned out that Norm was also a trapper and amateur taxidermist. The unique smell of his house came from the odour of tanning fluids mixed with whatever he used in his taxidermy.

Norm explained that he was of Métis descent and that he had learned to trap, and its grounding in traditional knowledge, from his father and grandfather. He had learned taxidermy from an uncle who lived in Prince Albert and had a taxidermy business and display store there.

Seemingly, every room in the house displayed realistically posed, stuffed creatures. It was as if Norm had an entire family of forest creatures, all frozen in an instant of time while they had been going about their normal lives in the wild. I commented that I was used to seeing the occasional stuffed animal head on a wall.

"Sport hunters!" scoffed Norm, who warmed-up considerably as my interest in these became apparent. "Some people just want trophies to display," he said, "and I give them what they want – it helps pay the bills."

He explained that he ran trap-lines in the winter, and sold the pelts to the local general store. "Some animals, I keep for myself though," he said, as I was admiring a stuffed Marten that had arched-up on its hind legs and was looking ahead with its eyes bright and it's forepaws at the ready. It was mounted on a stand together with small shrubs and bunches of grasses. It had been made so realistically that you could imagine it was almost alive. All of his other household animals were similarly mounted, in lifelike poses, framed with several bits of realistic branches and flora. Norm had stories for each such animal, that were grounded in aboriginal traditional knowledge, respect for *"Mother Earth,"* and historical stories from his ancestors. Between the lifelike animals, their realistic mountings, and his stories about them, I found myself captivated. I began to perceive that there were hidden depths to Norm's rough exterior.

Norm was also full of other surprises. It developed that he was a hunting and fishing guide in the spring through fall seasons, which partly explained his yard full of semi-derelict boats – although he was quick to reassure me that his work-boat was very capable and safe. I later learned that, like many others in this remote community, he might "walk a mile to save a penny" in most things, but he spared no expense when it came to his boat and his truck.

Between his collections and his many careers my "few minutes to get acquainted" turned into an entire morning – a pattern that would recur as I introduced myself to other inhabitants of the town.

Driving down to the town's marina, I tried wandering around there. I was again surprised at the size of things but realized that, like much of the town's infrastructure, it had evolved to meet the needs of a community that was nearly four times larger than its current population.

At one of the jetties, another of the local hunting and fishing guides, Jim Dumont seemed happy to get an excuse to stop working on his boat and talk. If his profession was similar to Norm's, his manner certainly was not. I found Jim to be extremely outgoing and friendly by nature, and almost always with a smile on his face. As we chatted, it became obvious that he loved to talk, and was an inveterate storyteller – or perhaps I should say - anecdote teller. Thus, I quickly learned that Jim also had deep roots in the area, and was a fountain of knowledge about Radium City, its people, and the surrounding area.

It occurred to me that I could learn a lot from Jim, and as I turned to continue on with my explorations, I mentioned that I'd like to hear more of his stories sometime. I was brought up short by his immediate rejoinder of "It'll cost you!"

Jim was pretty perceptive. Immediately noticing the early warning signs of a bristle on my part, he quickly added, "A cup of coffee I mean. It'll cost you a cup of coffee."

Relaxing, I laughed, "Sounds like a good deal to me. You're on!" Although always ready with a joke of some kind, I would learn in time that Jim had an obsession with money, and did virtually nothing for free.

> Any complex organization must have administrative machinery to function properly, and the Force is no exception. A detachment member's ability to perform administrative duties is equally as important to the successful operation of the Force as is a well-founded knowledge of criminal investigation. Both these aspects of police work are dependent on one another.
>
> ATTRIBUTES. "RCMP CONSTABLES' MANUAL." OTTAWA

I found small-town police work to be quite different from my experiences with the Metro Toronto force. Not everything was different, of course. Like police officers everywhere, we rated police responses to the urgent summons as our highest priority, regardless of whether these were from a criminal or public safety nature. But other aspects were definitely different.

The work-load was heavier because there were only two of us to cover a wide geographical region. This meant that response times were longer than would be considered acceptable in a large city. Fortunately, as Cpl. Morrison had wryly pointed out, there was rarely any serious crime to contend with.

Nevertheless, the detachment would get its share of calls. Our citizens had the option of calling our detachment directly (during regular office hours) or else to a dispatcher in Prince Albert (during evenings and weekends). The nature of the responses would vary. Some calls need only a short, quick response, while others might need investigation. These latter would generate official files. A typical day could easily involve see-sawing back and forth between responding to a call, returning to the detachment, continuing work on an interrupted file investigation, responding to another call, and so on *ad infinitum*.

Many, almost most, of the calls would turn out to be matters that would not normally be considered to be proper "police business," but we would usually respond to these anyway, seeing it as a way to serve the community, and build good community relations. I say "we," but that's really just a nice way of saying "I," as Cpl. Morrison would normally send me out to make the responses. As the rookie in town, and Cpl. Morrison's only staff, I accepted this as the normal way of things.

In larger detachments, and certainly in the cities, the Force would have civilian employees serving as dispatchers, and part of their job would be to screen-out most of the "non-police business" calls. In our case, however, during regular office hours, we would take the calls. It was a blessing to have the Prince Albert dispatchers take such calls on evenings and weekends though, otherwise, we'd have never been able to sleep or even take a break. But we would still review the logged calls the next day and generally follow-up on them when we had time.

A good example of a non-police business call came in early one Tuesday morning. Cpl. Morrison took the call and decided to send me out to deal with it.

"I've got a 'live one' here for you Houston. Dr. Evans has been called out to help a pregnant woman who's broken a leg, or something. It must be Mrs. Smith, … apparently, she's fallen into the river on the edge of town and gotten stuck in the mud. One of the local kids ran into town to report it. Doc Evans is on his way but he wants help."

Dr. Evans was our only town physician. I knew him to see him but we hadn't become acquainted yet. Taking our detachment's truck, I was able to easily find the river on the edge of town and then drive cautiously off-road along the riverbank to the location of the stuck woman, at just about the same time that Dr. Evans had done basically the same thing in his big, bright red Suburban SUV.

Introducing myself to Mrs. Smith, whom I also hadn't met before, Dr. Evans and I were able to extract her from where she'd become stuck in the mud between some large rocks. She'd been taking a short-cut across the river, lost her balance, and fallen and twisted her leg between the two large rocks. She hadn't been in danger of drowning but, between her twisted leg and being nearly nine months pregnant, she hadn't been able to rescue herself either. Examining her *in situ*, Dr. Evans judged that her leg was more likely badly sprained than broken, but her water had broken, and contractions had begun. Between the two of us, we were able to free her from the mud and rocks and carry her to shore. After another quick examination, Dr. Evans decided that it was safe to move her to the hospital, so we loaded her into the back of his SUV and I escorted them to the hospital. As I say, not exactly police business, but a worthwhile public service response with a happy ending (she eventually delivered a pair of healthy twin girls; just over six pounds each).

Another category of calls was the civil but not criminal incidents. A few days after the pregnant Mrs. Smith incident, I was sent out to respond to a complaint from one of our downtown store-owners. Videocassette recorders, VCRs, had come onto the market spawning a rising business in rentals of both the VCR machines and the movie tapes. In this case, the owner was upset that a customer had returned a rented VCR machine that had been damaged. The customer was claiming that it had been an accident and was refusing to pay extra for the damage, while the owner argued that it was the customer's responsibility and wanted either extra payment or charges laid. Hearing them both out, it seemed to me that there was no reason to believe that the damage had been caused intentionally. I explained to both that this was really a civil matter rather than criminal, and that it was up to them, but that the customer might consider offering some compensation for the damage that was incurred while the VCR machine was in his care, and that the store owner should recognize that he hadn't made it clear to the customer what the consequences of damage to the machine would be. I further suggested to the store owner, who was new to renting as opposed to selling things, that he might consider taking the experience as a valuable lesson and seek legal advice on modifying his standard rental contract to make it more clear who was responsible for what, and perhaps consider demanding a damage deposit be placed by customers in advance of future rentals. This mediation approach, involving taking the heat out of the arguments, explaining the law, and suggesting possible solutions, turned out to be effective in this case. Neither party wanted to see the matter go to small claims court, which would have been expensive in time and travel (since they would have had to fly to Prince Albert for this), and they both readily accepted my suggested compromises.

Slightly more serious, but still minor incidents would include something like a store owner receiving a bad cheque. In a small town, where everyone (but me) knew each other the likelihood of outright fraud was extremely low, and such cases invariably turned out to be the result of customers simply not realizing that their bank account had insufficient funds when they wrote the cheque. In such cases, Cpl. Morrison correctly predicted that the appearance of a "Mountie," in uniform, appearing on their doorstep was sufficient to prompt such careless cheque-writers to make amends. Police officers acting as "collection agents" was certainly not something we were taught in basic training in either the Toronto force or the RCMP!

Moving up the seriousness scale, our principal areas of actual law enforcement activity were: the Motor Vehicle Act, and the Liquor Control Act. In the case of the Motor Vehicle Act, there wasn't a lot for us to do. Radium City had a main street and a grid of secondary streets and avenues, plus a number of roads radiating out of town, and one short stretch of highway. The highway was interesting in that it was an official Saskatchewan provincial highway, but its nominal length was only 25 miles, stretching in one direction from the town to a dead end near Beaverdam Lake, and in another direction from the town to Lake Athabasca. I say "nominal length," because at the Lake Athabasca end it matches up with a winter ice road that is plowed every year, and which connects to the community of Fond-du-Lac, and from there to other northeastern communities. Along its short, year-round distance, the highway passes by the abandoned community of Eldorado, and several branch roads connect to the airport, the marina, and to various nearby abandoned mine sites. Summing it all up, Cpl. Morrison had explained that there weren't many roads, there weren't many vehicles, parking was pretty much a free-for-all, and people in town were seldom in a big hurry to get anywhere, so there was little in the way of traffic violations to worry about.

"Even vehicular accidents are rare, quite rare," he explained, and then after a pause, "at least multiple vehicle accidents are rare, single vehicle accidents are actually quite common."

"Common?" I asked, raising my eyebrows.

"Common when people have been drinking too much."

This brings me to the one area in which we did have enforcement problems – liquor. It wasn't so much Liquor Control Act violations per se, although Cpl. Morrison was apparently engaged in a never-ending game of cat and mouse with the town bootlegger, Barney. For some reason, every small town in Canada seems to have a bootlegger (or more), and Radium City was apparently no exception.

Although the government liquor store has closed up when the size of the town so dramatically shrunk years earlier, there was a bar in the town's hotel, and two of the restaurants were licenced, but apparently, there was still a demand for Barney the bootlegger's services as well.

In any case, the problems with liquor weren't so much illegal sales, but overconsumption leading to occasions of fighting, property damage, and impaired driving of seemingly anything that moved, including cars, trucks, snowmobiles, boats, and even bicycles!

This brings me to serious crime. According to Cpl. Morrison, there simply wasn't any. He expressed this in tones that suggested extreme regret. When he'd told me at our first meeting that "… nothing interesting ever happens around here," he was mostly referring to the virtual absence of serious crime. I could understand his disappointment. Not that any police officer likes to see crimes being committed, especially those involving harm to innocent people, an occupational hazard for us all was to view serious crime and the need for criminal investigation as the "Holy Grail" of "real" police work.

"Not for us, the systematic process of investigation that begins with an incident or public complaint, requires a thorough and wide-ranging investigation, the arrest, possibly following a dangerous pursuit, and culminating in an arrest and a court hearing," he would say, leaning back in his chair, with his hands and fingers steepled over his chest. "In a regular detachment, Members[8] are required to be constable-generalists and might have to manage as many as 30 or 40 open files[9] at the same time, requiring them to spend as much as 60% of their time on criminal investigative work... but not in Radium City."

I quickly discovered two more things about Cpl. Morrison: he strongly believed in the relatively new concept of community-based policing, and he had a very clear policy on how it should be carried out. The concept, of course, is that police visibility and the appearance of almost constant police presence is, by itself, believed to provide a deterrent to crime. Secondly, highly frequent and visible police patrols are, for obvious reasons, very highly regarded and vocally supported by business owners and resident alike, both of whom have a vested interest in feeling that their businesses, personal property, and community as a whole are being kept safe. Naturally, in a small town like ours, Cpl. Morrison felt that such frequent, visible, and almost continuous patrols were best carried out ... on foot.

"In the big cities," Cpl. Morrison would say, shifting smoothly into speech-giving mode, "roving patrols are looked-down upon by most officers as being essentially 'security work,' or simply 'waving the flag,' and therefore beneath the dignity of 'real' police officers. But in these small towns...," he said, his voice rising to parade-square volume, "in these small towns, we need to be visible, our citizens see this as possibly the most important service that we can provide to them, and it is a duty we must take seriously."

I mentioned that he had a very clear policy on how this should be carried out, and he did. This was the province of the junior member of the detachment. In other words... me.

My next introduction unexpectedly led to an opportunity to get a physical sense of the size and beauty of our entire area of responsibility. On about my fifth day in Radium City, I had gone back to the airport and discovered that one of the old aircraft hangers was still being maintained, and was still in active use, housing a single-engine bush plane of some kind. I found our local pilot busy taking removable seats out of the back of this plane.

Vern Schriver turned out to be a very pleasant, but somewhat reserved, former pilot from one of the large American airlines. He explained that he had retired early from his airline job, and retired "way up here" to get away from his fast-paced, highly organized and regimented former life. He hadn't turned away from his passion for flying, however, he'd simply traded-in flying big, Boeing 727 tri-jet airliners for his own personal plane.

Not really knowing what I was talking about, I asked whether he'd become a bush pilot.

"Well, yes!" he laughed, "Bush flying means any kind of flying that's done in rugged and remote parts of northern Canada and Alaska, so anyone that flies up here is a "bush pilot."

Vern Schriver's de Havilland DHC-2 Beaver

Vern went on to explain that he didn't fly for a living anymore, although he would take on paying flights if and when it suited him, which included anything that was particularly interesting from a pilot's point of view. He said that he would fly to Fort McMurray once in a while, partly just to be able to fly, and partly to pick up groceries when the local barge was late or undergoing repairs, and that in such cases he'd often volunteer to pick up supplies for other townspeople as well.

"Isn't that a long way to go?" I asked.

"Well, our options for getting supplies in the summer and early fall are boat, barge, or plane. The barge is the most economical when it's running. It's a long haul in a small boat, and commercial air cargo rates are pretty high, so sometimes a small plane is the best option."

Then, realizing what I was thinking, he said: "You meant, why fly all the way to Alberta instead of simply flying south?"

I nodded.

"Ah Ha. Well the nearest city with big stores, good prices, and lots of selection, are Prince Albert to the south, and Fort McMurray to the west. Depending on the route and weather, the flying time to

Fort McMurray is a little over two hours; the time to Prince Albert is twice that."

"Wow, I guess we're further north than I realized."

"Right. It took me a while to get used to it too."

Vern didn't look the least bit like my conception of the stereotypical bush pilot. Rather than being tall and heavy-set, with a haggard, unshaved face, he was slender, medium-height, and clean-shaven, with piercing blue eyes. I mentioned that he'd initially seemed somewhat reserved, but that didn't last long. If the secret to getting people like Norman Poole and James Dumont to open-up was to ask about their boats, then asking about flying, or more specifically, his plane was the key to Vern Schriver. I asked about his plane.

"This here's what we call a "Beaver." It was designed and built by de Havilland Canada just after World War II. They wanted to keep building airplanes after the war but needed some civilian plane designs that people would buy, so they came up with some planes that could easily switch from wheels to floats, to skis. They liked naming their planes after animals and called the single-engine one the Beaver, and the twin-engine one the Otter. This one is a Beaver"

"And it was made just after World War II?"

"Not this one. Some were. The first one was built in 1947, and they kept on building them up until 1967. Hundreds of them are still flying."

"Isn't that dangerous?"

"Not if the airframe is still sound, and if they're properly maintained and regularly checked. This one was built in 1967, and has been almost completely rebuilt over the years, plus has had all of its electronic, communication, and navigation systems upgraded to modern standards."

"Wouldn't it be simpler to just buy a modern aircraft?" I asked, starting to get interested myself, now.

"Simpler, yes. Better, no. It's probably un-American of me to say this, but the Beaver is probably the best bush plane ever designed. It's rugged, powerful, pretty easy to fly, and can land and take-off again in really short distances, on land, water, snow, or ice. Up here, that's awfully hard to beat. That's why they've been used for so many things, '*The Workhorse of the North*,' as people say – surveying, prospecting, hunting, aerial photography, passengers, mail, and supply services – you name it."

"What are you doing with the seats?" I asked.

"Well, as you can see from these big doors on the side, it's been built so that you can easily shift back and forth between cargo and passengers, and I'm right now pulling out the rear seats to shift it from passengers back to cargo. It's wide enough for a full-sized 44-gallon drum to be rolled-up inside, but I'm just getting ready for a supply trip to Fort McMurray tomorrow." Then, looking at me more closely, he said: "I take it you're not very familiar with the north."

"No," I laughed, "I'm a big-city girl from southern Ontario. Most of my life, I've lived in Ottawa and Toronto."

"Hmmm, so you don't really have a feeling for the country up here then," he mused. "Why don't you come along with me tomorrow, we can get my work done in Fort McMurray and I'll take a slightly different flight path each way so you can see some of the country from the air. I think you'll be surprised."

"Sounds fantastic," I said. Let me just check with my boss to make sure I can take the day off and I'll get back to you.

"Sure thing, just call for me at the commercial air service office and they'll get the message over to me."

Promising to do that right away, I headed back into town. I expected Cpl. Morrison to take a dim view of traipsing off sightseeing after only being on the job for five days, but he surprised me.

"Great idea," he said, "It will give you some perspective on the size of the territory we're responsible for and help you lock-in some of the local landmarks."

"And Vern?" I asked.

"You'll have a hard time finding a more skilled pilot or a more reliable person than Vern," he laughed, "and he's like a walking encyclopedia. If you keep your eyes and ears open, you'll end the day feeling like you've been drinking from a fire hose."

The next day, I met Vern at the airport and we headed out in his Beaver. Since there were just the two of us, I was able to sit in the right-hand, co-pilot's seat, so I had an excellent view, and he offered me a set of headphones with a boom microphone so we were able to speak to each other over the roar of the engine.

On my original flight into Radium City, I had seen some of the rich mixtures of lakes, islands, rock, and forests, and I once again marvelled at just how huge Lake Athabasca seemed to be.

"It's like another Great Lake," I said, referring to the famous

Great Lakes that bordered southern Ontario.

"Yes, it's not really as big," Vern said, "but it's going to feel like it in a moment as we fly across it."

Sure enough, as we turned south and flew straight across the lake there came a point where I could barely see the shore in either direction.

"Isn't Fort McMurray to the west?" I asked.

"Actually, it's almost exactly south-west of here. I like to cut across the lake first and get it behind us. When we reach the southern shore, we'll turn harder to the west than we need to because I want to show you something that you won't believe unless you see it for yourself."

He didn't elaborate, so I contented myself with looking at the broad expanse of the lake below us. Once again, it brought home how isolated we really were, as in the entire flight to Fort McMurray and back I didn't see a single boat out on the water.

Watching the southern shore, I noticed that it seemed to be a greyish-brown colour, rather than the greys and greens of rock and trees that I was used to seeing. Looking over, I saw Vern watching me and he nodded.

"Keep watching the shore," he said.

As we approached ever closer, my eyes widened. "Sand," I said.

"Not just sand. Lots of sand!" he said, "keep watching."

Like he said, not just sand, but rolling sand dunes that seemed to go on forever. Once we were over the sand I exclaimed, "It's like looking a desert. How could a desert be all the way up here?"

"Not exactly a desert in this climate," Vern corrected, "but these are the Athabasca Sand Dunes – they are the most northerly and active sand dunes in the world."

"Active?"

"Active, because they are constantly shifting and changing due to the winds, just like in Africa."

"Where did they come from?" I asked, and then I answered my own question. "They must have been left here by the glaciers after the last ice age, but what an unusual formation to have in Canada!"

"That's right," Vern said, "The way it was explained to me, is that when the glaciers pulled away, huge amounts of sand, and silt, and whatever were washed into the basin that became Lake Athabasca. Apparently, 8,000 years ago the water level in the lake was much higher, so what we're looking at used to be the sandy bottom of part of the lake. When the water level dropped, this part of the lake bottom was exposed and there we are. But look at the scale of it all - some of those sand dunes are a hundred feet high!"

"Does anything live there?"

"There's lots of water underneath the sand, fed by the lake, and I gather that the scientists have found some rare plants growing there. Between the rare plants and how unique this whole thing is, the government in Regina is talking about making it a protected area so it can be preserved[10]," he said.

The rest of the trip was fun, but seeing the lake and sand dunes up close were by far the highlights. On the return trip, I remembered my primary mission of getting a sense of the size and geography of the area for which we were responsible and I marvelled, not just at the size of it all, but of how natural and unspoiled it all was. As we approached Radium City I did, this time, spot a couple of small boats out on the lake, and the occasional cabin on a point of land or small island. I thanked Vern more than once for this eye-opening adventure and offered to pay for his fuel. He had graciously allowed me to buy him lunch in Fort McMurray but refused to take anything else, saying that it was nice to have had the company and fun showing me some of the sights.

Over the next few days, I got to know the town quite well and was ready to see more of the surrounding areas.

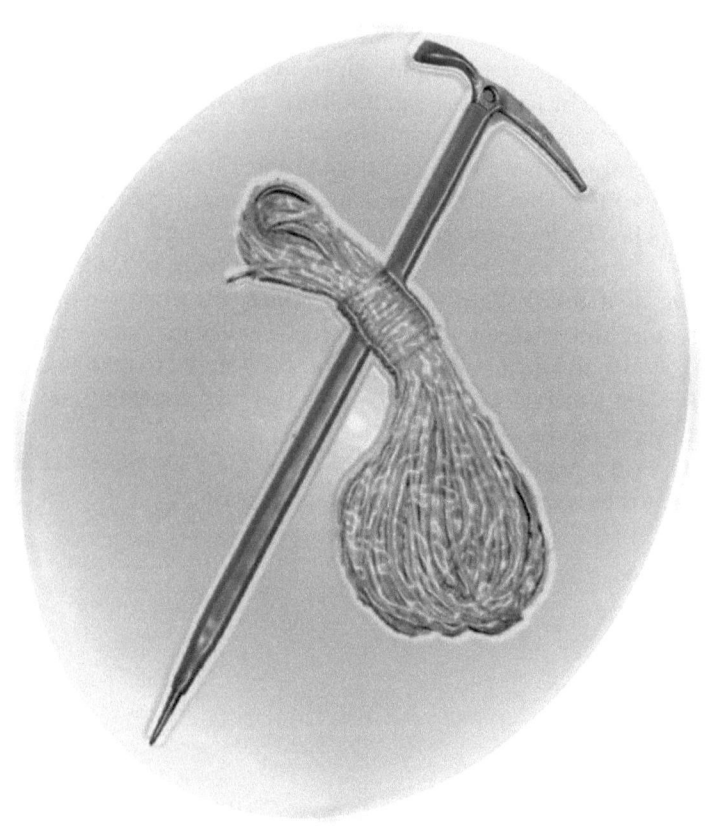

4 URANIUM MINES

I DON'T HAVE THE RIGHT EQUIPMENT FOR THIS!
I get *déjà vu* a lot.

* * *

It was 1972. I had been mountaineering with a cousin in the mountains near Jasper, Alberta. We had been hiking along a trail on a very steep slope, following a fairly clear game trail. The trail was probably one of many that were used daily by Mule Deer in the area. Then, suddenly, we lost the trail. All we could see was rock, long grasses, and some short trees. By itself, this was only inconvenient, as we could always retreat back the way we had come, except that we had noticed storm clouds working their way down the valley towards us.

When we had taken our mountaineering – rock climbing course the year before, our Mountain Guide/Instructor had warned of how quickly a storm could roll down the valley, and the danger from lightning if caught up high, especially on an exposed rock face. We were not terribly high up, nor on an absolutely sheer rock face, but we were high up enough, and exposed enough, to have become concerned. Now we need to get off such an exposed slope, and down to a lower elevation, and quickly. Retreating the way we had come was feasible but very time-consuming. Much better would be to simply descend directly down the slope from our existing position.

The problem was that the slope was too steep for us to walk or slide down without losing control and falling the rest of the way. Looking ahead, we noticed that there was a solid-looking tree not too far away that, when we got to it, exhibited bits of frayed nylon webbing lying at its base. This suggested that previous climbers had used the tree as an anchor point for rappelling down.

The frayed pieces of webbing all looked too old and frayed to trust, and I remember thinking, "I don't have the right equipment for this!"

*We had brought minimal climbing equipment with us because we had only planned to practice rock climbing on short faces, climbing one at a time, while the other belayed from above. We had climbing harnesses, a 50 m length of 9mm climbing rope, a couple of slings, an alloy Figure 8 self-belay device[11], and our gloves. We tied our two slings together so that they would reach around the tree leaving a loop hanging around each side, then fed our rope exactly half-way through both loops. Our 50 m rope was now only 25 m long. Allowing for the rope that had to be bent around the Figure-8, and a bit of a gap from the rock slope, that gave us about 80 feet of coverage. Looking down, the next level that seemed to have a bit of path or at least a lot of rocky protrusions looked like it **might not** be more than 80 feet down. It was hard to be sure.*

With the storm advancing rapidly, we decided to give it a try. We attached the Figure-8 to the rope and my harness, knotted the two free ends together to prevent inadvertently rappelling right off the ends of the rope, and threw the knotted end out and down the face. I started rappelling down. As I worked my way down, it was still hard to judge the conditions at the bottom of the rope, but it didn't look too bad. As I neared the end of the twinned rope, I found that I could securely stand on some rock protrusions, and as I looked around, I could see another game trail that seemed to angle downwards. Breathing a sigh of relief, I slipped the rope off the Figure-8. It was fortunate that I didn't lose my one-handed grip on the rope because as it came away from the Figure-8 there was a strong upwards pull. At first, I thought it was my cousin but then realized that it was the slight elastic stretch in the rope. Climbing ropes are designed to stretch a bit in order to absorb some of the shocks should a climber fall. Had it not been for the stretch in the rope I'm not sure that I would have been able to get my boots anchored and the rope off – a close call.

I'm not particularly religious, but I wondered for a moment whether to offer a prayer of thanks to St. Bernard of Montjoux, the patron saint of mountaineers, or possibly St. Simeon of Emesa, the patron saint of fools.

The rest was pretty easy. I tied the Figure-8 into the rope, called upwards "Off belay!" and my cousin pulled the rope up, retrieved the Figure-8, reset the rope and rappelled down. We reclaimed the rope and Figure-8 but had to leave our two slings behind on the tree up above, a sacrifice we were happy to make, and we followed the new game trail down the slope just as the lightning was beginning to flash and rain began to pour down.

> As in life generally, problems that cannot be solved by predetermined rules continually arise in police work. In addition, the nature of some situations demand immediate action … the Constable who is confronted with such a situation … must display a high degree of initiative and at times take a calculated risk.
>
> ATTRIBUTES. "RCMP CONSTABLES' MANUAL." OTTAWA

* * *

Cpl. Morrison had offered to drive me around some of the roads radiating outwards from Radium City. Other than the roads to the airstrip, marina, and a couple of isolated picnic- and boat launch sites, these seemed to comprise mostly roads to abandoned uranium mines. We didn't go to all of them, but occasionally we'd stop where a road would vanish into the rock, grasses, and scrub, and then get out and walk to an old mine.

In most cases, the only remaining evidence of a former mine would be some cement slabs in the ground (covering rises), or a cave-like entrance set into the side of a hill and covered by a rusty steel grate or some piled-up boulders. Here and there would be odd relics from the mines former lives: often just rusty bits of odd-shaped iron that looked like junk to me, but sometimes there would be ring-bolts in large rocks, broken heavy timbers with big nails or spikes sticking out, thick wire rope cables, and, of course, beer bottles. Every site we visited seemed to have its own unique scattering of old beer bottles. Judging from the shapes of the more-or-less unbroken ones they were of both recent and quite old origin, and I gathered that the roads leading to these old sites had provided people with convenient hiking, picnicking, and hunting trails.

Once we'd seen a couple of these old sites, I was beginning to detect a familiar pattern and Cpl. Morrison said, "Just one more, it's kind of unique." We drove along another road, that led to yet another hill. As the road suddenly turned into a path, we parked and walked a ways around the hill. After looking at yet another iron grate covered mine entrance, I looked quizzically at Cpl. Morrison, who only said, "Patience is a virtue." We had walked partly back along the path when the Corporal stopped and pointed out a slight depression in the pathway just ahead, that hadn't been as easy to discern when we had walked from the other direction.

Saying, "Wait here," he walked onto the centre of the depression, paused for effect, and then stamped his boot on the ground several times. Amazingly, each stamp of his boot produced a hollow-sounding echo. He explained that there were places where old underground mine workings went off in odd-seeming directions, as the miners had tried to follow the ore-bearing veins wherever they might lead. In some places, this led them to mine underneath roadways, pathways, and even ponds and rivers. Getting into the spirit of the thing, he then tried jumping up into the air and coming down, hard, with his two boots together. That was a mistake!

If there was a hollow sound this time, it was completely drowned out by the sound made by the ground and pathway immediately giving way beneath him. In a flash, he simply dropped straight down and out of sight.

I rushed-up, then slowed to a crawl realizing that more of the ground might be unstable enough to give way. Stretching my body out lengthwise, I peeked carefully over the edge and saw – nothing. Peering into the dark and the still-disturbed dust in the air, I called out "Are you OK?"

This was met with a moderately loud groan, and a growly "Yes, but be careful."

"Can you get out on your own?" I called down.

"I don't think so, I don't seem to be able to move my legs."

"OK," I responded, "Wait here. I'll be back in less than fifteen minutes." Running back to the police truck, which thankfully had the keys still in the ignition, I did a quick inventory. Standard equipment included a First Aid kit, a flashlight, a blanket, our VHF radio, and a body bag – I would need the first three, there was no one to call with the fourth, and I hoped not to need the fifth. The truck also had an electric winch on the front bumper, a long-handled shovel, a 30-foot tow-strap (for vehicle recoveries), plus electric jumper cables and tire chains (for use in the winter).

My first reaction was, *I DON'T HAVE THE RIGHT EQUIPMENT FOR THIS!* – but it would have to be enough until I could better assess the situation.

Starting the truck, I drove it carefully along the pathway. I had to drive slowly, and navigate around numerous rocks and exposed tree roots, but got to the cave-in in pretty good time. I parked the truck as close as I dared to the hole, then, having verified that Cpl. Morrison was still conscious and seemingly no worse off, I tied the tow-strap to the front bumper of the truck and eased the rest of it down the hole. "Can you see the tow-strap?" I called down.

"Yes, it reaches the bottom, I'm probably about 20 feet down and I'm lying in an old mine shaft so the floor seems stable."

Grabbing the First Aid kit and flashlight, shoving them inside my uniform shirt, I used the tow-strap like a climbing rope, except that with no belay device I had to rely on my hands on the rope and boots scraping along the wall, to guide my way down.

Cpl. Morison was lying where he had fallen. We had been taught First Aid as recruits, in both the Metro Toronto force and the RCMP, and I tried to remember our lessons. He was conscious and didn't seem concussed, but he was very pale and was lying at an unnatural angle. Clearly, shock was setting in. I asked about injuries and he said that everything felt OK except that he was woozy and couldn't move his legs. There was nothing obviously trapping his legs, so I tried gently exploring his lower limbs, then slightly moving one leg. Even a tiny leg movement produced an immediate gasp from him. I tried gently moving the other leg. This produced a louder gasp and his pallor went from pale to sheet-white.

"OK," I said, "Looks like you've broken some bones, one or both legs, and I'm a bit worried about your pelvis. Must have been the combination of the fall plus the rocks ... What do you think about waiting here while I drive back to town and round-up some help? I can try to find our doctor or at least one of our nurses."

Cpl. Morrison really didn't like the idea of being left behind. I really didn't like the idea of trying to move him myself and risk doing more harm. In the end, we sort of compromised. He ordered me flat-out to do whatever it took to get him out of that "Damn hole," and I agreed to give it a try, but insisted that I intended to disobey orders if it looked like I was going to cause more damage in the attempt.

So, using the tow-strap again for support, I climbed up out of the hole. It sounds easy but it was slow going, and when I reached the surface, I was exhausted, and I'd had to rest a bit and catch my breath before collecting up the shovel, tire chains, and jumper cables. Using one of the jumper cables to tie them all into a bundle, as best I could, I attached the bundle to the hook on the wire rope from the electric winch and then used the winch to lower it down the hole. Then I tossed the blanket down and, for the second time, I used the tow-strap to climb back down myself.

I placed the long-handled shovel between his legs, explaining that I intended to use it as a splint, and then wrapped the blanket around the combination of both legs plus the shovel. Of course, to get the blanket under his legs I had to lift them slightly, producing more waves of pain. These waves were repeated as I started to wrap the first tire chain around the blanket.

Not knowing what else to say, and hoping to distract him, I said, "Now that we are working so closely together are you able to divulge your first name?"

"Mike," he growled. I knew he wasn't really growling at me, it was the pain, so I kept up some kind of feeble chatter as I continued to tie the remaining tire chains, in turn, around the bundle and then used the two jumper cables.

Standing up to stretch my back and view my handiwork with its bizarre accoutrements, in the soft glow of the flashlight, I started to chuckle.

"What?" growled Mike.

"Have you ever seen the old movie called 'The Mummy' with Boris Karloff?"

He tried to laugh, but it was cut off with another spasm of pain.

"OK," I said, "no more jokes. Let's both take a minute, and then I'm going to wrap the winch-rope under your armpits, climb back up, and winch you up. Are you OK with that?"

"Do it," was all he said.

"Here goes," I said. I removed my boots and began to pull off my uniform pants. As he stared in surprise, I said, "No jokes, and no leering – got it?" He just nodded as I wrapped my pants under his armpits from behind and then up and over his shoulders. Tying the smallest loop that I could into the winch rope, I passed the free end along and under the pants, and then clipped it to the loop so that under stress it would not turn into a noose and choke him, or worse.

Then, having replaced my boots and provided another reminder about not joking or leering, I grabbed the tow-strap and climbed one last, paralyzing time, up and out of what I also now thought of as *that damn hole.*

Activating the winch, I wound-in the wire-rope in short bursts, to allow Mike to use his arms and hands to guide his body to the nearest wall… then again to get him up to a vertical position… and then once more to lift him up to the surface. At that point, I was able to offer an arm and hand of my own to help get him up and over the edge.

"Very nice, Alex… ," he said, and before I could decide whether he was referring to the winch-trip, or his ring-side view of my panty-clad bottom climbing up and out of the hole, he fainted.

It was just as well, I decided, as I unwound the winch-rope, recovered and restored my pants. Just as well because I next had to drag him over to the truck, and then up and into the box at the back. I left the makeshift splint on him and checked his breathing. Still OK, but he was still out cold. It occurred to me that I was developing a pattern of rendering men unconscious.

"Make haste slowly," my Mountain-Guide/Instructor used to say, and this pithy saying came back to me now as I tried to drive as quickly as I could without causing too much bouncing and jarring, all the way back to our town's small hospital.

Cpl. Mike Morrison

5 MORE CHALLENGES

We had a small, but pretty well set-up hospital in Radium City, with one doctor (the Dr. Evans I helped with the pregnant Mrs. Smith), two nurses, a few other staff, two examination rooms, an X-ray machine, multi-purpose surgery, and two six-bed wards.

Dr. Evans found broken bones in both legs and a fractured pelvis. He assured me that jury-splinting his legs and getting him in right away was the best thing I could have done in the circumstances and that while the bouncing around in the truck hadn't done his fractures any good, it was far preferable to the alternatives.

This left Cpl. Morrison (I had mentally reverted to our formal form of address) lying in bed, in traction, with both legs elevated and in casts. Dr. Evans explained that some of the bone had been torn away from the pelvis and that he couldn't be certain, but it could take as much as 6 weeks before he could graduate to limited mobility with crutches.

Correctly interpreting my slightly horrified expression, he relented a bit. "Maybe less could be four weeks... we'll have to see."

Learning that I wouldn't be able to talk to Cpl. Morrison until the next morning, I left for the Detachment to file a report.

Prince Albert Sub-Division, I thought, was going to love this.

An hour later, having sent a brief report by telex, I crawled into bed and fell instantly asleep.

The next morning, there was a reply waiting for me in the teletype machine:

FM: **PR ALBERT S/DIV**
TO: **RADIUM CITY DET.**
BT
UNCLAS

UNFORTUNATE CPL. M. INJURED. NO REPLACEMENT AVAILABLE AT PRESENT. HOLD THE FORT. ELS.

In other words: I was on my own until further notice.

My first stop was the hospital, but Cpl. Morrison was too heavily sedated to do much more than wave at me in dim recognition. Things were quiet in town, so I continued exploring and meeting the residents.

By the evening of his second day in the hospital, Cpl. Morrison was much more alert, and the two of us held Dr. Evans spellbound as we compared our recollections of the events and emotions of our recent wilderness experience. After an hour of this, and worried that I was tiring Cpl. Morrison out, I got up to take a tour around town and had made it partway through the door when his gruff "Constable Houston!" caught me in mid-stride. Turning, I straightened up and said, "Yes, Sir?"

"Permission granted to continue referring to me as 'Mike' ..."

Were the corners of his mouth turning up ever so slightly?

"Yes, Sss... Mike," I replied, and walked out feeling just a bit taller than when I had first arrived in Radium City.

As the days went by, we settled into a pattern of regular morning and evening visits.

To my surprise, his initially gruff and grudging acceptance of his fate in having been "saddled" with me had been completely replaced with the manner of a teacher, and then, sometime later, ... a coach.

Mike felt that we should get some local part-time help to cover the bulk of the non-policing, administrative tasks around the detachment like office reception, logging citizen queries and complaints, answering the phone, watching the teletype machine, and so on. To this end, he told me to send a telex to Prince Albert Sub-Division requesting permission to hire some local part-time help until either they were able to send a replacement, or else Mike was released for duty by Dr. Evans.

My experience on the Metro Toronto police force had left me with a low opinion of any big-system bureaucracy's willingness to spend unbudgeted money, but Mike simply said: "Give it a try."

Sure enough, the next day the office teletype rattled away and the keys typed out a reply:

APPROVE HIRING LOCAL HELP FOR ADMIN DUTIES. MINIMIZE COST.

That, of course, meant find a great person that would work long hours and do a great job, for not much pay. Chuckling at my interpretation, Mike then suggested a few people in town that he thought might be willing, available, and suitable for this work, but he left it up to me to meet and interview them, make the decisions, and engage them under contract to the Force.

In the end, I hired Jennifer Stone, Ruby Gillespie's niece. Jennifer was nineteen years old, had just graduated from high school, and was trying to decide what to do next in life. While pondering this, she had been working part-time at the coffee shop, but Ruby really only needed her for the peak lunch and dinner meal hours. This meant that, for most of the mornings and afternoons, Jennifer could watch over our phone and teletype machine, and handle walk-in inquiries. She was a quick study and a hard worker. Having mastered the phone and telex in a matter of minutes, she was eager for more and, wonder of wonders, she could type! A single demonstration proved that she could not only type, but faster than I could. I quickly sorted our piles of hand-written files and notes into two piles: confidential and non-confidential. Extracting a promise from her to stay out of the former, I turned her loose on the latter.

Meanwhile, my meetings with Mike settled into a pattern. He would explain what needed to be done, make a few suggestions to get me started, and then leave me to do the rest – try things, make decisions, succeed or fail, and report back. In the evenings, we'd discuss what, if anything, I'd learned from each and every new experience. His breadth and depth of knowledge and experience were formidable, but I think I was most impressed with how personally committed he obviously was to the job. It didn't seem possible, but he appeared to have both studied and built relationships with almost every one of our town's four hundred or so adults. I had expected that having spent some time in the community that he would know almost everyone "by sight," he seemed to know them all by name. Every time I related a fresh meeting with a resident, and my impressions, he would add his own perspectives and we would discuss them. I was never able to figure out how he managed to get to know so much about virtually everyone in town, seemingly without having expended much effort!

My own routine also settled into a pattern. On a typical day, I would go for a morning jog, have breakfast, do some cleaning up and maintenance around the detachment (fatigues), and spend the rest of the morning on administrative tasks, including the endless series of reports that always needed to be prepared, updated, and filed. After lunch, I would work on our active case files. When I needed a break, whether morning or afternoon, I would drive around a bit, following random routes around town and the surrounding areas. Following supper, I would do an early- or late-evening foot patrol around town.

Despite the tedium of some of the administrative work and the mundane nature of some of the calls, overall, it was frightening, stretching, rewarding, exhausting, and fun – all at the same time. I think I learned more in the next three weeks than in any other three-week period of my life.

I suppose it couldn't have lasted forever. In week number four, things changed.

6 THE BOOKSTORE

I CAN'T BREATHE!

∗∗∗

I've read that everyone has natural talents for some things. If so, the converse is probably true as well. Wrestling, for example, is not one of my talents.

In training, they had started us off with wrestling, as a prelude to self-defence training. I hadn't been good at wrestling when I trained for the Metro Toronto force, and I wasn't good at it in Depot Division training either.

They would demonstrate a move or two, then have us try it in turns. One day, when my turn came up, I'd been partnered with a recruit that was quite a bit larger, and heavier than I am. This didn't seem fair to me at the time, and I wondered whether it was a case of being mean or discriminatory on the part of my instructor. I'm glad that I didn't make an issue of it though because looking back on it, I realized that it was realistic, and good preparation for real-life situations that could come up later.

We hadn't jostled for grips and positioning very long before I found that my legs had been cut out from under me and I'd been driven face-down to the floor, ... and I mean well pinned, flat on the floor, with my arms and legs stretched straight out.

My wrestling partner was not only heavier, but stronger and more skilled, and I found that I couldn't break his holds, nor slither forwards, backward, or to either side. Having tried all of these in turn, I was tiring quickly and finding it more and more difficult to get air into my lungs. I had just enough time for the left (logical/rational) side of my brain to think, "Great!" before the right (emotional/intuitive) side started sending an emergency "I can't breathe!" message that was impossible to ignore.

What happened next came from instinct, not thought or planning.

I took a long slow breath, gritted my teeth, and eased slowly up onto my knees and put everything I had into my arms, back, and legs, to rise up on my forearms. My partner kept his holds in place and perfectly maintained his balance on top of me. He seemed inclined to simply wait for me to inevitably tire and drop back down again. Taking another deep breath, I again put everything I had into my arms, back, and legs, but this time focused all my energy on levering my back upright. I had underestimated my strength, and rather than simply rising up, I snapped up so quickly that my partner was thrown up and off me. As he crashed down to the floor, I looked over, and I don't know who was the more surprised, him, me, or our instructor.

Our instructor said, "Unusual, but effective ... nice!" I seemed to have earned some approval from my troop-mates as well because as we later headed for our respective shower-rooms, there was a loud "Crack!," as the tip of an accurate towel-snap just made contact with my butt, followed by someone saying, sotto voce, "Nice job, Red."

Although I certainly have the hair for it, I've never liked being called "Red." In this case, however, I was relieved and pleased, rather than offended, and I gratefully accepted it all in the spirit with which it had been delivered.

***

Now I was experiencing the same thing all over again, this time in Radium City.

I had been doing my last walking patrol around the streets of the town. It was late, probably near midnight, and the cool night air contributed to an eerie atmosphere as I listened to the sound of my boots on the boardwalk. I tested the doorknobs of the shops as I walked along. They were all locked, but as I tested the door of the bookstore, I thought I detected something move in the grey darkness near the back of the store. Peripheral vision isn't always very reliable, but I decided to walk around the back of the store, just to be sure.

Having made my way down the next lane and around the back, sure enough, the back door was unlocked and slightly ajar. This wasn't a rare occurrence. Small town residents didn't usually lock the doors of their houses or even their vehicles for that matter. Shopkeepers were usually a bit more careful, however, for obvious reasons, but even they tended towards complacency, secure in the knowledge that "nothing ever happens around here."

As I went into the back of the store, my adrenalin was up a bit and I was careful to be quiet, but I wasn't overly concerned. I had just made my way through the back storeroom and was stepping into the main part of the store when I felt a huge weight on my back as someone jumped from somewhere above and behind me onto my back, pushing me forward and driving me face-down to the floor.

Whomever it was had the advantage of greater weight and must have had some experience wrestling, as I soon found that I was fully pinned down and could barely move. I couldn't effectively grab anything for leverage, and I was having trouble getting enough air into my lungs to be able to try much else. *Damn it all, it's happening again*, I thought, as I flashed back to my training days.

Sometimes you rely on your training, sometimes on your experiences.

In this case, the same old instinct from before kicked-in. I took a long slow breath. Just like in training, again, I eased slowly up onto my knees and put everything I had into my arms, back, and legs, to rise up on my forearms. My assailant stayed in place and seemed more intent on maintaining the *status quo* than on trying anything new. Having taken another long slow breath, I again put everything I had into my back and legs, and this time focused all my energy on using my back to lever myself straight up – as quickly as I possibly could. For a wonder, it worked again.

Like in training, I don't know which of us was more surprised, but my assailant was thrown up, backward and to my left side. As we went down, he kicked out, pushing me over to my right side and back down to the floor. This time, however, his mind was on flight, and he scrambled to his feet and immediately ran off towards the back of the store. He must have had some familiarity with the layout of the store's bookcases because he didn't waste any time getting out. I'm saying "he" because I had the impression that my assailant was male, although I wasn't sure.

Despite getting up as quickly as I could and launching out in pursuit, a combination of darkness and my own unfamiliarity with the store had me stumbling into chairs and bookcases. The result was that by the time I reached the back of the store and out into the back lane, there was nothing to see. Not hearing any telltale sounds, I chose to jog to the right, down the lane and out onto the nearest cross-street, but I was not able to see or hear anything useful. Thinking it would be futile, but not wanting to give up, I ran back the other way, checking the lane and into its cross-street, but with no better results.

It seemed pointless to search the streets any further, so I went back to the bookstore to see if I could learn anything about what the intruder might have been doing. Reaching the store and turning all the lights on, I looked around. Although I did not know my way around the store, the only thing that looked out of place was a pile of books lying in disarray near the aisle in which I had been jumped earlier.

Someone seemed to have pulled out nearly a shelf-full of books and left them scattered as if they had been flipping through them looking for something and then discarding them haphazardly afterward. There was a flashlight lying near the pile.

Everything in the pile seemed to have something to do with prospecting or early mine developments in the Radium City area. Three of the books were histories of the larger mines that had once operated nearby, Eldorado, Gunnar, and Lorado. Several other books contained collections of old prospecting stories, with references to small mines that had been developed, or not, in the past. Aside from some bundles of old maps, the rest seemed to be leather-bound daily journals that once belonged to prospectors looking for radioactivity. Flipping through the journals I found that some were basically illegible, some simply contained dates and cryptic notes about locations and plans, while a few contained quite detailed accounts of dates, places, plans, things they encountered, and their thoughts about it all. It wasn't obvious to me whether the prospectors had been looking for radium or uranium.

As I locked-up the store, several things ran through my mind:

1. Why covertly search a bookstore at night? Was it an attempt to maintain secrecy? I had clearly surprised the intruder in the act, otherwise, he surely would have replaced the books on the shelves.
2. Did the intruder know he had attacked a police officer or was he just trying not to be "caught in the act" by anyone?
3. What could possibly be so important about a bunch of old books about prospecting and early mine development? Was he trying to steal something, or was he trying to discover something?

It was late. Since the store didn't seem to be damaged, I decided not to bother the owner about it in the middle of the night.

The next morning, I met the bookstore's owner, Lucy Weaver. She reminded me of my high school librarian – middle-aged, willowy, with thin brown hair tied up in a rather severe bun. Another thing they had in common was a complete personality change from reserved and rather formal at first, to outgoing and excited when the conversation turned to the subject of books.

Lucy judged, with obvious relief, that nothing had been stolen. She was adamant that the old books and journals, that had obviously been searched, contained a treasure trove of important historical information, but not in monetary terms. She said that they'd languished on her shelves for many years as she patiently waited for just the right collector to show up and buy them – but even then, she didn't expect to get much money for them. Although she was quite firm in asserting that, "*Anyone* would naturally find them highly interesting," she "really could not imagine why anyone would want to do so in secret, especially when the whole lot could have simply been purchased for less than $50." I asked her to consider locking the rifled materials away in a safe place for now.

As I walked out, I wondered what it was about a bunch of mine histories or prospectors' journals that could be so important and require such secrecy that someone was willing to break-and-enter, and possibly steal. If it was something on the maps, they could have simply been purchased. In fact, they could have simply bought everything for such a low price.

That evening I related to Mike my experiences of the previous night and my meeting with Lucy. Mike also thought that the whole thing was very strange, but his main advice was to stay vigilant. I thought that was pretty funny, considering that three weeks of policing the town solo still had me looking over my shoulder and jumping at shadows at the best of times. Mike also had a specific suggestion, which was that I have a chat with "Prospector McGee."

The next morning, I headed out to meet Ron McGee, who lived outside of town on the edge of Nero Lake. I'd started out driving on a fairly rough, paved road, that was officially one of the province's secondary highways. After about half an hour, the rough road became a gravel road, and then something more like sand. Continuing along, I passed a number of derelict buildings that clearly represented yet another old mine site, although this one obviously had a complete processing facility, or mill, associated with it. I realized then that I must be driving on the old mine tailings, which I could see extended from the mill buildings all the way down to the lake shore.

Who would build a provincial highway across old mine tailings? I wondered. It occurred to me to wonder whether this had been a uranium mine and whether I was driving on radioactive tailings (I later learned that the answers were yes and yes).

Eventually, I came to a fork in the road and turned left, towards the lake. A short distance down the lane I came to a large log cabin that looked like a Hollywood image of an old trapper's cabin. It looked very old, was sagging a bit in a few places, and even had old-style wooden snowshoes and a rack of deer antlers hung-up on the outer walls.

The resident had obviously heard the sound of my truck approaching because I no sooner turned off the engine than the front door opened and a wizened old man came out to see who I was. He certainly looked like a prospector to me, with greying, longish hair, and the grizzled look that comes from not having shaved for a week or so. He peered out at me with penetrating eyes and bushy eyebrows. His eyebrows reminded me of Mike's.

I identified myself as a police officer and asked if I could come in and ask him a few questions related to an investigation that I was conducting.

He was quite taken with the fact that I was a woman Mountie. "But you're a girl!" was his first statement.

Sigh.

I explained the whole being a woman thing, and he took a moment to get it all clear in his mind.

"Well, isn't that the durndest thing? ... Whatever will they think up next?" he exclaimed.

These seemed like rhetorical questions, so I moved on to explain that I was investigating a mysterious break-in that had happened in town, that it seemed to have something to do with old mines and prospecting, and that my boss had suggested that he might be able to help me.

Seeming satisfied, he introduced himself as Ron McGee and confirmed that he was a part-time prospector. When I mentioned that his home looked more like a trapper's cabin than a prospector's, he chuckled.

"I'm also a part-time trapper," he explained in a deep Scottish accent. Then, with a sly expression, he confided that he wasn't a very good trapper, but that under an old provincial law, trappers of Aboriginal heritage were allowed to live on government-owned land in order to pursue trapping on traditional hunting grounds.

"I'm only allowed to live here temporarily, and only as long as I spend some of my time trapping around here, but it's free and that's tough to beat don't you think?"

Starting to get the joke, I asked him how long he'd been living there.

He'd originally worked as a conductor for CP Rail, travelling all across Canada, he said, but had retired from that after 35 years of "riding the rails." Now he just wanted to be away from cities and their crowds and had moved to Radium City to "get away from it all."

"I've been here for five years now," he said, "and I'll continue on here until the day I die, but that's only living temporarily – isn't it?"

Laughing, I agreed that life was temporary. I asked him about the highway and the old mine and mill site that I'd come across.

"That's the old Lorado mine," he explained. "It was one of the larger uranium mines around here during the Cold War, but it closed-up in 1960 and it's been abandoned ever since. The highway was built to connect the town to the mine and mill, but a lot of it's covered in tailings now."

"Are the tailings radioactive, then?" I asked.

"Sure they are!" Ron exclaimed, "but the radiation level isn't very high." Then, seeing my frown, he added, "but you don't have to worry as long as you don't live on them full-time like I do."

I wasn't sure whether he was entirely serious, but I let it go and asked how many other people lived in the area.

"Just me," he said.

"You mean the province maintains the whole road out here just for you?" I asked, incredulously.

"Well, I sure don't think they do a very good job of maintaining the highway. You saw how rough it is coming out here. But, yeah, I imagine they'll have to keep the road open as long as I'm still alive – and I intend on living another forty years out here!"

Mentally placing him at about sixty, I didn't doubt him. Although he moved slowly, and with his shoulders hunched over a bit, he reminded me of a Mountain Goat and I suspected that when he was out prospecting, he could probably out-hike me without breaking into a sweat.

Ron explained that he liked his solitude and didn't have much interest in people. I found him easy to talk to, however, and he actually warmed up when he introduced me to his cat, Ally. Ally was a black and white American short-hair, and I would later discover that she and he were constant companions.

I didn't dwell on the cat, though, as I wanted to shift the conversation to old mines and prospecting. I told him about the break-in and what I'd found in the mess left behind in the bookstore.

Ron seemed surprised about the break-in but didn't see anything unusual in someone being interested in old mines. Ron himself prowled around the old mines, he said, looking for overlooked deposits of uranium. "There was such a frenzy in the 1950s that sometimes they overlooked things in their rush to find the big deposits," he explained. It was the small deposits that Ron was hunting for. These could still pay off for an independent prospector, he said, especially since uranium prices were a lot higher than they used to be "in the old days."

So, this was Ron McGee, our resident prospector. As I listened to his stories, it sounded like he was one of those people that were always searching around, without ever hitting "the big one." When I asked him about the specific materials that I'd found in disarray at the bookstore, he said that he'd seen them, or some of them at least. He thought the histories and journals were really interesting, being something of a prospector himself. He'd flipped through many of them, he said, but hadn't bought any because Lucy was asking too much money for them.

Driving back to town, having thanked him for his time and taking my leave, I thought about our conversation and judged that he was a likely suspect, given his interest and lack of willingness to pay for the books and journals.

The next day was relatively uneventful. Jennifer was rapidly devouring our backlog of non-confidential typing, and I was trying to figure out how to get her at the confidential pile. News of the bookstore break-in travelled throughout the town rapidly, of course, and by mid-day, I doubt there were many people in town that had not heard something about it. The general reaction was one of surprise that anyone would break into what one coffee shop inhabitant referred to as *"that dusty old place."* Probably the most excited was Jennifer, who was practically sitting on the edge of her chair at the detachment, poised and ready to note down any news or confessions that might come in. Unfortunately for both of us, none of the local chatter prompted any useful tips or leads.

There was, however, some excitement the third day after the break-in.

Laurie Schramm

7 THE LIBRARY

Evening foot patrols. Once our troop had gotten its bearings and settled into our training routine at Depot Division, we started to be assigned security shifts around the training centre.

The "base," was actually quite large. In addition to all of the residence, dining, and lecture facilities, there were many other buildings. One housed an indoor pool, a large gymnasium, and an indoor shooting range in the basement. The drill hall was massive, as was the stables building, which had a large indoor riding arena in its centre, and of course, several large fields for riding and for growing the hay to feed the horses. The base was also home to the administration building for "F" Division, which was concerned with the policing of the province of Saskatchewan, and right in front of that building was a military-style parade ground, beyond which was "The Square."

The Square was an approximately square plot of grass, with a tall flagpole in the centre, ancient field cannons in the two corners adjacent to the parade ground. The Square was surrounded by houses for officers and their families on two sides, and buildings on the remaining fourth side. Among these buildings were a large forensic laboratory building, and a restored, small-town style chapel. There were several other blocks of houses and buildings, but these are the highlights. The whole thing covered a substantial area.

One of the security rotations involved guard duty at one of the three main entrances, but I often seemed to draw foot patrol, which involved an evening walking patrol of the main buildings, the main streets, the square, and the perimeter of the occupied area.

One night, having completed most of my round, I was patrolling the perimeter and was walking along the portion that bordered the top of the bank of Wascana Creek when I heard a muffled sound, followed by a series of 'thumps,' coming from the bushes on the side of the bank. My first thought was that it was an animal in the bushes.

Slowing my pace, I changed my grip on my large flashlight so that I had a finger on the light switch and a grip that would enable me to use the flashlight like a baton for defence, if necessary. As I got closer, I heard more muffled sounds – human. Although I couldn't make out the words, there were two distinctly different voices.

In my own best imitation of a parade ground voice I said "Come on out!" and simultaneously turned on my flashlight. There framed in the bushes, about a foot off the ground, were two faces looking up at me. The faces looked surprised, their eyes squinting in the unexpected light shining on them, and they looked embarrassed rather than threatening.

"You're going to have to come out, I'm afraid," I explained, "You can't stay here on this property."

As they came out, I realized, with a shock that they had good reason to be embarrassed. Jack McDonald was a colleague from my troop, and was mostly dressed – he was pulling his shirt back on and holding a jacket, which had apparently served as a makeshift groundsheet. She had very little on and was mostly using the clothes she was clutching as a shield, in a fairly unsuccessful attempt at preserving a little modesty. I recognized her as the daughter of our Sergeant Major.

"Holy Smokes!" I exclaimed, "If Sergeant Major Walsh finds out about this, we'll have a homicide in our training class!"

If possible, this made both Jack and the young woman look even more sheepish. It was hard to tell by flashlight, but it seemed like the mention of Sergeant Major Walsh's name had made Jack turn a bit green.

As my mind reeled with the implications of what was standing before me, in my outside voice, I said, "Look, you really can't be here, but I'll tell you what. I'm going to continue my patrol until I get to the houses on The Square, and then turn back. If, when I get back here there's nothing to see, then there's nothing I need to report. OK?"

They both silently nodded, heads bowed, and I moved on. When I got to the houses on The Square, I didn't turn back. There was no need. If the Sergeant Major found out about this, I wasn't sure who would be in the most trouble, Jack, or his daughter. As far as I was concerned, they were both old enough, they just needed to find a better place for their romancing than anywhere along my patrol route.

When Jack sought me out to thank me on the next day, I asked him how in the world he found the time to meet her, and advance to that stage! In the middle of our non-stop training, exercise, fatigues, and odd-jobs, I certainly had neither the time nor the energy for such things. He just smiled, looked down at the floor, and said, "Well, you know how it is." I most certainly did not, but I let it go at that.

***

I did evening foot patrols in Radium City as well.

Although I'd learned to respect Mike's police knowledge and experience, he wasn't the most energetic or active person I'd ever met. I already mentioned that he'd basically ordered me to conduct frequent, random patrols around town, and either that fact that I'd diligently followed-up on this or else the fact that I preferred walking patrols to driving, seemed to amuse him for some reason. I harboured a strong suspicion that he mostly viewed walking patrols as being too much work.

"A good officer has to conserve their energy," he would say, followed by his usual "nothing ever happens around here anyway."

If he seemed amused by my foot patrols, he was also serious about the need. I have to admit that I quite enjoyed my foot patrols. They got me out in the fresh air, it was good exercise, and I actually enjoyed the relative autonomy of being somewhat out and on my own. Although I conducted these patrols at different times of day, my preference was to go out in the evenings, when things were otherwise usually fairly quiet. As I walked around the town, I would check windows and doors, keep a weather-eye on vacant properties, and so on.

Apparently, the townspeople weren't used to such diligent patrols, because two nights after the bookstore incident there was another.

It was the library this time. I had chosen a rambling route for my evening patrol and was walking along a side street looking around and testing doors to make sure they were locked. The town library was a single-story building about the size of the bookstore. When I tested the front door, it was secure but my rattling of the latch prompted a muffled exclamation from inside, followed by a series of 'thumps.' *Déjà vu* again – the exclamation and thumps reminded me of the sounds I had heard that night as a recruit on patrol. That made me think of something human as the cause of the first noise, although the latter sounds made me think of something hitting the floor. This time, however, I doubted that I was going to encounter an interrupted romance.

Just like with the bookstore break-in, I ran around to the back of the building and found that the back door of the library had been forced open and was slightly ajar. Turning my flashlight on and drawing my revolver, I crept slowly inside.

Unfortunately, Murphy's Law was in full force. Now that I was moving extremely cautiously, fully alert with all senses on high alert, armed, and with a light, my measured investigation of the library found … nothing. As I looked down each aisle of bookcases and made my way to the front door, I failed to encounter anyone. The front door was now standing wide open and proceeding through it and into the centre of the street, there was nothing to see or hear in any direction.

The Radium City Library

Re-entering the library, I turned on all the lights and proceeded to search for clues. This turned out to be easy. Once again, I found a pile of books scattered on the floor beside one of the bookcases. This was clearly the source of the sounds I had heard from the front door.

Looking through the pile, I found Geological Survey of Canada publications, with names like *Geology of Lake Athabasca Region* (1949), exploration reports like "Preliminary Report - Radiumfields and Martin Lake Area" (1939), and maps, like "Radiumfields – Martin Lake Area Map" (1952). The mineral exploration reports seemed to have appendices full of assay results from core-drilling samples collected from various locations in the areas named.

As I closed up the library, securing the back door to the extent possible, it seemed to me that a pattern was beginning to emerge. The bookstore break-in seemed to involve prospecting and early uranium mine developments, while here at the library it was exploration geology and mineral assay reports. In both cases, mineral exploration maps seemed to have been of interest as well. Although there was some consistency in the targets of both break-ins, it was far from obvious why there should be such interest in old historical documents. Did someone think there was an undeveloped uranium deposit out there?

When I met with Mike at the hospital that night, I gave him my impressions of Radium City's major crime wave, comprising two break-ins within three days, two messy piles of books, nothing seeming to have been stolen, and only minor damage to the doors that had been forced. I would still have to check with the town's librarian to see if anything had been stolen, but for the moment it appeared unlikely. So … not much actual crime, and no motive, yet.

"Try talking all of this over with the bank manager," was Mike's suggestion this time.

"What on earth for?" I asked.

"Andrew actually knows quite a lot about minerals, and metals, and money," he said, "If you show him some of the things that were being searched, he might be able to think of some financial reasons why someone is going to all this trouble."

Andrew Fielding

8 A FIRST LEAD

The next morning, I borrowed the rifled books, journals, and maps from the bookstore, and also the scattered reports and maps from the library, and lugged my cardboard boxes of clues over to the bank, where I had made an appointment to see the manager.

I found Radium City's bank manager, Andrew Fielding, to be quite distinctive. He was very dapper in both dress and manner. Over time, I noticed that he always wore a suit, quite like the way I always wore a uniform on duty, except that Andrew was the only person in Radium City to wear a suit (and I suspected that few other residents even owned a suit).

Andrew explained that among his many duties as manager of the bank, were assessing and approving bank loans to mining companies and (sometimes) to prospectors. Mike must have known this, hence his advice for me to consult with Andrew.

Andrew summarized some of the area's history, much like Horace Best had related to me when I'd first arrived in Radium City.

"In the early 1900s," he said, "there was quite a lot of mineral exploration activity in the Beaverlodge area, mostly focused on base metals like iron and copper and precious metals like silver and gold. The Geological Survey of Canada had sent parties out to determine the mineral potential of the area in 1935, and they found a number of occurrences of gold and also of pitchblende, which is a uranium mineral. That same year, a pretty good quality gold deposit was discovered not too far from Bell Island, about ten miles from here. The ABC Mine went into production in 1938, and produced gold for four years before being abandoned in 1942."

Andrew explained that the pitchblende deposits remained

something of an academic curiosity until the nuclear developments of World War II led to a national strategic interest in uranium and a revisiting of the Beaverlodge area. By the early 1950s, purely academic interest had given way to an all-out uranium exploration boom, with thousands of claims being staked in the Beaverlodge area, ranging from new 'finds' to restakings of old gold and base metal mines, including the former Bell Mine on Bell Island. As a result, several new uranium mines were opened. Some of the old gold mines were re-opened as uranium mines, while others had nothing more to offer and remained abandoned.

"OK," I said, "so what possible interest could anyone have in these old, abandoned mines after all these years?"

Andrew thought for a while, and then said, "Well, possibly in hopes of finding some overlooked uranium deposit in the area, but that seems unlikely given how carefully the area was scoured during the uranium rush. There could be interest in mining the tailings left over from the old mines, but that doesn't explain the break-ins because everyone knows where the old mines and their tailings ponds are – the mines are well documented and the some of the tailings ponds are so large you can easily spot them from an airplane... and more to the point, anyone could just go buy a Geiger Counter and go survey the tailings themselves."

"Wouldn't that be expensive and require a lot of training?" I asked.

"Not in the least," Andrew replied, "used Geiger Counters can be bought pretty cheaply – even the old instruments from the 1950s can still do the job – and they are easy to use. You just turn them on and listen for the ticking noises. On normal ground you get a slow rate of ticking, and if you get near something worthwhile the counter goes crazy. If the counter goes crazy you grab a sample and get it assayed, and you can easily get it assayed without telling anyone where it came from. In this town, with prospectors still prowling around every summer, that would be considered quite normal."

"So, if it's not uranium then what?" I asked. "Would those old assay reports show anything else of interest?"

"Not likely," Andrew mused, "everyone was looking for uranium because of the Cold War and the chance to get rich. Prospecting booms are like that, someone finds something and the next thing you know everyone's running around searching for their own little piece to stake, in fact..." he paused, lost in thought for a few more minutes, then 'whack,' he slapped both hands down on his desk. "Wait a minute, I have an idea!" he said reaching for the reports with the assay result appendices. After flipping through a couple of them, he reached for a pencil and paper and his calculator.

I had noticed his calculator when I sat down in his office. It was the most modern thing I'd yet seen in Radium City. I remembered using one of the first pocket electronic calculators near the end of my university days in 1971. At that time, they were just simple 'adding-machines,' in that they could add, subtract, multiply, and divide. In contrast, Andrew's new one had scientific functions built in and was clearly quite powerful. Andrew started muttering to himself, as he entered data, calculated things and made notes on a pad of paper. Then, he got up, pulled a book from his bookcase and started leafing through it before going back to making more calculations and notes. I tried to sit patiently and not distract him, but his growing energy was becoming infectious. Finally, my patience was rewarded.

"Holy smokes!" he exclaimed, "I think someone's after gold!"

"Gold?" I asked, dubiously.

"Gold!" he repeated. Then, seeing my confused look, he said "Look, we had a couple of gold mines in the old days, like the ABC Mine I told you about earlier. Back then you had to have a high enough ore grade to be worth the time and money it would take to get the gold out. The ore grade for the ABC Mine was about 0.05 ounces per ton – doesn't sound like much does it? - but watch the math here: 0.05 ounces per ton times the 1.5 million tons of ore that they dug out between 1938 and 1942, gives us 75 thousand ounces of gold. At something like $400 dollars per ounce, that means the company earned revenues of about $30 million – not bad for a company in the days of the Second World War!"

"Sounds great," I said, "what's the catch?"

"Two catches, really. First, only a few deposits were ever found that had enough quantity of ore and a high enough grade to be worth mining. Secondly, following the Second World War, the price of gold dropped. By 1965 it had dropped to around $270 per ounce, and by the middle of 1970, it hit a 50-year low of $230 per ounce. Made headlines everywhere it did, in a bad way, of course, because that knocked the stuffing out of any gold mining around here, I can tell you."

"If that's the case then why did you just get all excited about the thought of gold?" I asked.

"Ah," he smiled as he sat back in his chair, "because after that the price of gold started rising again. In 1971, it rose back up to $270 per ounce, then kept on rising to," as he consulted his notes, "over $500 an ounce in 1973, over $600 an ounce by 1973, and last year it rose to over $800 per ounce. The 'buzz' on the 'street' in Toronto is that in a few more years it will hit $1,000 an ounce for the first time in history[12]."

"And that means…" I murmured.

"It means that an ore grade that isn't economic at $200 to $300 per ounce might just be more than economic at $1,000 an ounce."

Andrew went back to the reports I'd shown him. "Look here, he said," handing over one of the opened reports.

"What am I looking at?" I asked.

"These are assay results for core samples drilled back in the 1950s on Bell Island. Look at the part I've marked in pencil."

> During a diamond drilling program in late 1954 and early 1955, hole #FH-25-36 intersected 0.11 oz/ton Au over 38 ft in quartzite and ferruginous quartzite.
>
> Additional samples from holes #FH-25-1 through -3, and -7 yielded spot values ranging from 0.06 to 0.65 oz/ton.

"Where it says 'Au,' that's the chemical language for gold. What they are saying is that they've found zones where the gold assay is actually reasonably high. Some of the zones might be quite small, so the whole deposit might not have such a high grade on average, but suppose that the deposit has an average grade matching the lowest of the samples mentioned in this report. That would be 0.06 ounces per ton. Let's suppose that there are a million tons of such ore in the deposit, which would be quite small for a mine, then the total value would be $60 million if gold goes to $1,000 an ounce. That's twice what they got out of the old ABC gold mine, but mining costs are at least double what they used to be as well. Still, that could be a mine that's well worth developing."

"Gold," I repeated, mostly to myself. "So now we have a possible money angle in all of this. $60 million could be a lot of motive!"

Thanking Andrew for his financial detective work, I swore him to absolute secrecy about all of this, gathered up my boxes of borrowed materials, and took my leave. As I carried them back to the bookstore and library, I thought about what I'd just learned.

Even if I was on track with the gold and old-mine ideas, why would someone take the risks of breaking-and-entering, and why break into the library so soon after almost getting caught at the bookstore?

Either my mystery searcher was really stupid, or maybe they were in a really big hurry for some reason. I remembered my meeting with Ron McGee and wondered if it could have been him. He was certainly the only person I'd met so far that had a clear interest in the kinds of books and journals that had been displaced.

I now had some vague leads on motive and a possible suspect, but still not much crime. I decided that if things remained otherwise quiet around town, I would continue to investigate this whole business, as much out of personal interest as professional.

Laurie Schramm

9 INVESTIGATING

... as the circumstances of each case will vary widely, it is not possible to draft a set of rules that would be adequate for every situation... The constable must have patience, as haste will result in an incomplete and inconclusive investigation... To overcome the danger of forming a preconceived opinion of the case, the constable should try to keep an open mind.

INVESTIGATIONS. "RCMP CONSTABLES' MANUAL." OTTAWA

By now I had many questions but not much useful information. I was trying to keep an open mind, but not too open, as I couldn't possibly pursue every idea. The mining connection seemed like the one clue that warranted further investigation, the rifled journals, maps, and reports mostly focused on the North shore of Lake Athabasca, and my instincts were leaning towards some kind of gold angle. My mystery person had probably learned these same things but may or may not have arrived at specific locations.

I decided to have a look at some of the lakeshore uranium mines that had been mentioned in the bookstore/library materials. This wasn't going to be easy. By 1950, the uranium exploration boom had uncovered uranium occurrences in an area spanning about 200 square miles. These were mostly north of Lake Athabasca, but that's a huge lake, covering an area of over three thousand square miles, and having a northern coastline of nearly 200 miles. For many of the mines, I'd have to go by boat. I did, however, have a list of specific mine names that figured prominently in the bookstore/library materials. Some of them had impressive-sounding names, like Consolidated Athabasca Uranium Mines, some were rather cryptic, like ABC Mines, and still, others had clearly been named for their discoverers or developers. An example was the Bell Mine, which I learned had been named for the prospector that discovered it: Thomas Bell. I decided to start with one of the larger of the mines, Gunnar, which had not only been a mine and a mill but also had an entire townsite associated with it.

Ron McGee had mentioned an interest in the Gunnar Mine when I'd first met with him, so I asked if he'd take me with him the next time he went there "to prospect around." He seemed pleased at my interest, said he'd been thinking about going back there and offered to take me in a couple of days' time. When the time came up, we headed out in his rather small boat – Ron, his cat Ally, and myself.

I think I may have mentioned that Ron and his cat were close, but it was more than that, the two of them seemed to go everywhere together. The feeling must have been mutual because Ally seemed happy enough to go in the boat with us. Ron had even made a little life jacket for her, that seemed to involve sections cut-out from a human's life jacket and attached to a small dog harness of the kind that strapped around the chest and both front legs, leaving the neck and throat free. I wouldn't have expected Ally to put up with the indignity of wearing a bulky harness like that, but she did and without a fuss. Once on the boat, she curled up near Ron's seat in the stern and promptly went to sleep.

We went by boat because there was no road from Radium City to the Gunnar Mine site. Between the small size of Ron's boat and motor, and the mildly rough conditions on Lake Athabasca, it took us about an hour to get here. I could appreciate now why they'd built a town at Gunnar. The site was huge, it was a long way away from Radium City, and the only ways in and out were by air or water (or over the ice in winter-time).

As Ron had explained to me earlier, the Gunnar mine and mill were opened in 1955, and by 1956 it was considered to be the largest uranium producer in the world. It didn't last though, as the uranium ore quickly ran out and the mine was closed in 1964. This killed the Gunnar town-site too, of course, and whereas at one time it boasted over 850 residents, by 1964 it was a ghost town. When we set foot on the site, more than ten years later, everything but the people still seemed to be there. The mine structures, the mill buildings, the houses and apartment buildings, even the school, cafeteria, gymnasium, and a huge shopping centre – but they were all empty.

Over ten years of abandonment had caused some changes to the site. Things were showing signs of weathering and rust, open doors swung on their hinges, quite a lot of the windows had been smashed, and bushes and small trees were beginning to push their way up through the roadways.

It turned out that the site was not completely uninhabited, however. As Ron and I walked around the site (he with Ally tucked inside his jacket), we did encounter a team of exploration geologists that were working the area. They explained that their exploration work was actually some distance away, but that using the abandoned houses as a base of operations was much preferable to their usual mode of accommodations, which comprised tents. I asked Ron if he was worried about the competition, but he said "no," and that the big professional teams tended to be out searching for big deposits of gold.

In addition to the exploration team, there was one other hub of human activity at the mine site. A fish packing co-operative had been established in an old warehouse that was conveniently located next to the mine's old dock at the lakeshore. Every once in a while, a couple of small fishing boats would come in and drop off their loads of fish. Ron explained that the business was pretty marginal, but as a fishermen-owned co-op, and with government subsidies, they were able to make a living. It looked like a lot of hard work to me.

Leaving the warehouse and dock behind, we next walked past the old mine itself and up a small mountain formed from waste-rock that had come out of the mine. Ron explained that they'd separated the uranium ore that was worth processing, from the waste-rock, which was not. When we reached the top of the waste-rock pile (which seemed like a small mountain to me), he pulled a Geiger-counter from his old army surplus rucksack and showed me how it worked.

I had heard of these but only seen them in the movies before this. A Geiger counter consists of a sensing tube that is attached by several feet of wire to an electronics box. The sensing tube has a window at one end so that any radiation coming its way can get in. Once inside the tube, the radiation strikes the molecules of a special gas, which immediately separate into positive ions and negative electrons. The electrons are attracted to a positively charged wire that runs down the center of the tube creating an electrical pulse. The pulse is measured with a meter in the electronics box, which also houses an amplifier and a small speaker. That way, each pulse can be heard as a distinct "click."

Neat, I thought. Seeing a scientist use a Geiger counter in a movie had been one of the things that had inspired me to major in science in university. Now I was seeing one in actual use. For the most part, we could hear about one "click" per second, but once in a while, Ron would hold the sensing tube over a place where the counting rate seemed to double, at least. As the counter clicked away at one of these locations, Ron explained that it was sensing gamma radiation from uranium in the waste-rock, but that the level was not high enough for me to be concerned about safety - as long as we didn't start camping on the waste-rock for days at a time.

Ron said that he'd scoured the whole site, mine, mill, town, waste-rock piles, and tailings areas looking for any sign of a residual 'hot' area, or even possibly a missed vein of ore, but without success. I'd previously told Ron about the library break-in that had followed the bookstore break-in. This was my *segue* to ask him about the old mine histories and prospecting journals, and so on, and whether he thought they'd be of any use to someone looking for places to prospect.

"I suppose so," Ron said, after a moment's thought, "but everyone out here knows where the uranium finds were. Even accounting for the fact that uranium's worth more than it used to be, we all kind of know where to look. Besides, it's not like you need to be a geologist. Anyone with a Geiger-counter can just walk around wherever they like and it will tell them if there's anything radioactive nearby."

Ron didn't seem aware of the gold-in-uranium angle and reminding myself that he was a suspect, I didn't bring it up.

Thinking it over on the boat ride back to Radium City, it seemed to me that Ron was knowledgeable enough to be capable of figuring out the possible gold angle, but he'd given no outward signs of being interested in anything but uranium (and his cat, who had accompanied us on our hike around the Gunnar site).

***

After my trip with Ron, I didn't feel like I was any further ahead. Remembering Norm and his guiding boat, I went to him next. Despite his initial rough manner, my interest in his hobbies had led to a rapid warming up on his part, and we frequently chatted in the café and casual street-side encounters. I had previously shown an appropriate interest in his work boat, and I found him more than willing to take me out.

Norm and I spent a very long day visiting what seemed like the most likely old mines, working our way along the shoreline in the area that seemed to be indicated by the break-in materials. Time after time, though, all we found were derelict old workings whose entrances were blocked with rock or covered with rusty old iron grates. Each site we visited displayed a unique collection of odd bits of bent iron and pipe, and assorted artifacts from their old mining days: an old boot, a broken shovel, some crushed barrels, an old dynamite case, and the like. The only signs I could find of more recent activities were beer bottles, cans, campfire remnants, and related debris that I associated with partiers, picnickers, and hunters having stopped by to rest, look around, and eat.

Inevitably, Norm grew curious at my interest in these mines. I didn't want to divulge too much (everyone is a suspect until demonstrated otherwise), but as we took a break before heading back to Radium City at the end of the day, I told him that I had reason to believe that someone might be looking into old mines in the area. I asked him if he knew of any way any of these old mines could be resurrected.

"That would sure be fine," he sighed. "Most people around here would like the good old days back, but these old mines died when the ore ran out, not because the uranium prices dropped."

"If it had been anything but uranium, there might be the chance that a good vein was missed here or there in the old days, and that with modern know-how someone could maybe find a new vein and restart an old mine. They've done that in the Yukon, with some of the old gold mines over there, and some people are talking about re-mining the tailings left over from the old mines - to get the gold that the original miners left behind. But, with uranium it's different. Uranium is pretty easy to detect with a Geiger Counter, and the uranium boom had so many fortune hunters swarming the hills around here that there's not much chance anything was missed."

"The tailings here aren't worth picking over either," he said. "We only had three mills built and there's too little uranium left in their tailings to be worth anyone's while to go after."

I asked him how he knew so much about uranium mines, and he explained that his father had worked at the old Bell Mine, which was one of the ones we had not had time to visit that day. Apparently, Norm's father had been a part owner of the original mine, long before it and a couple of other mines were bought-up by an investment consortium and renamed Consolidated Bell Mines.

"Dad left me his shares in the company," Norm said, "so if anyone was going to be interested in any chance of re-opening these old mines it would sure be me."

Out of the mouths of babes, I thought. Out loud, I said, "You mean people still own these old mines?"

"Sure they do, they're all owned by companies, and all the companies have shareholders. In some cases, the shares are still valuable because the companies have moved on to other mines in other parts of the country. In other cases, the companies are barely still alive and their share certificates aren't good for much more than wallpaper. Those are the kind I have."

Ah-ha, I thought to myself, so if someone had an idea how to resurrect one of these old mines, they might not want the owners to get wind of it until that someone could first get a piece of the action for themselves. That could be a reason for stealth, and maybe a reason for break-ins and who knows what else.

Watching my face as I took all this in and considered the implications, he shrewdly asked, "Are you sure you don't want to tell me more about what you're really looking for out here?"

"Not now," I replied, "maybe later though, once I learn a bit more."

"Just let me know," he said, "someday you might need my help."

He was right. Someday I would need Norm's help, but by then it would be too late.

10 BELL ISLAND

"DON'T PANIC!"
When had I told myself that before?

* * *

It was 1970. I had been SCUBA diving with a university classmate in the St. Lawrence River, northeast of Québec City. We were exploring what was left of a ship that had grounded in a freshwater inlet so that freshwater and silt were constantly flowing into and mixing with the mostly seawater of the estuary. These conditions created turbid water and years' worth of silt deposited on the wreck. The ship lay at an angle following the sediment as it dropped downwards so that the tip of the bow was exposed at the surface, while the midship and stern sections lay broken at the bottom, at a depth of just over 40 feet. As we sculled around looking for artifacts, we hadn't noticed that our fins and hands were stirring up the fine-grained sediments, reducing visibility from limited to nearly zero. When I finally looked up and around, I couldn't see a thing. Not my buddy, not the wreck, not even my hand held less than a foot from my mask.

As I realized what must have happened, my first thought was: damn, a rookie mistake. As I tried to figure out where I and everything else were, my senses piled-on by becoming alive to the cold of the water, the hiss of the air coming from the second stage of my regulator into my mouthpiece, the bubbling of the air being expelled out the exhaust valves with my breath, and the air ... seemed to be getting harder to breathe. Was I running out of air too? Reaching around, I found my pressure gauge hose by feel and brought it up close to my mask, where I could just barely read the pressure at 300 psi. Damn, another rookie mistake. What had we been thinking not to have watched our air pressures more closely?

My SCUBA instructors had been "old school" type army and police sergeants. They put us through all kinds of elaborate practices designed to make us uncomfortable, if not panicky, in hopes of making us learn how to "deal with it." These exercises were usually peppered with friendly reminders that "panic kills," while pausing for a moment's thought can save. I hadn't taken them all that seriously at the time, but their advice came back to me now. I steadied my thoughts (and nerves). I realized only then that it was feeling hard to breathe because my J-valve, a mechanical reserve valve, had probably kicked-in and was trying to do its job of making it harder to breathe as a warning that my pressure was falling dangerously low. With this spark of recognition, I reached back for the metal rod that ran along the side of my air tank and pulled it sharply down, opening the bypass valve to allow a full flow of air to resume. What a relief! However, I had been warned, and I had little time left.

I needed to surface! I knew better than to try to just swim straight up because we had been searching under an overhanging part of the wreckage and I didn't want to get caught up in the dangling bits of twisted and torn metal of the ship's hull. On the other hand, I had zero visibility so I couldn't tell how to avoid the wreckage and get clear. I knew that I wasn't really deep, only around 25 feet to my position in the wreck. I probably had 4 to 5 minutes of air left, so I did the one thing the right side of my brain kept telling me not to do – I just hung on to a bit of the ship's deck and stayed still, hoping that the sediment would settle out enough for me to see my way clear of the wreck.

I lost all track of time as I focused alternately on my pressure gauge and the visibility. At such a low pressure, the gauge needle swung up and down with my breathing, so that after each breath I would watch to see how high the pressure reading came up to, which was less, and less, and less. As the needle began to swing lower and simply stay near the zero mark, I could just begin to be able to see a dark area where the ship's overhang was and a brighter area beside it – that was my way out! Now that I had something to aim for, I let go of the wreck and swam diagonally up for the surface as fast as I could (thinking "to hell" with the slow ascent we would normally make as a precaution against getting an air embolism, I was less than thirty feet down, I would take the risk).

I finally broke through the surface and gasped a big lung-full of fresh air. It had never tasted sweeter! Looking around, I spotted my dive buddy, who had been watching from our agreed meeting point, and waved. We had both made it back to the surface!

I tore off my mask, snorkel, and regulator and just floated on my back for a few minutes, drinking in that beautiful fresh air and looking up at the sky. Recriminations would come later. For now, I was happy we were both alive. Even so, I did have the grace to spare a thought of thanks for those two crusty sergeants, who had taught me more than I had realized.

* * *

The Bell Mine Headframe

Little did I know that those skills, developed years earlier, would come in handy once more in a completely different context. I hadn't been able to find Norm to take me out on the lake again, but Jim had a boat that he used to guide hunters and sports fishers. I had asked him to take me out to Bell Island, to see the site of the Bell Uranium Mine. Always willing to be helpful, Jim had immediately agreed and then followed-up with what seemed to be his favourite phrase: "It'll cost you though." I'd said, "Fine, make it your standard hourly guide's rate and write me a bill for it."

We had set out in his guide boat, an aluminum 21-foot Lund Tyee Offshore with a 165 hp outboard. Jim was cheap, but he didn't skimp on his equipment. We settled into the two heavily cushioned front seats behind the windshield, under a convertible roof, with his large outboard motor providing a steady roar. Thankfully, the lake was quite calm so it was an uneventful ninety-minute ride, leaving me to lean back and enjoy the beauty of one of Canada's largest and least travelled lakes. It struck me once again what a beautiful part of the country this was. To our right was nothing but water as far as the eye could see – we could just as well have been in the middle of an ocean. To our left, only a mile away was the shoreline with its rocky hills, beaches, and patches of forest, with an occasional trapper's cabin – reminders of the occasional presence of humans in this area. Looking ahead, it was the big wide-open blue sky that commanded my attention, with only a few clouds and the occasional bird or two to add scale to the expansive landscape.

Reaching the island, and making sure the boat was securely tied up, Jim led me into the forest along what looked like an old gravel roadway, now almost lost as mature trees leaned in and over it from each side, and bushes and small young trees resolutely pushed their way up through the gravel. Fifteen or twenty minutes of hiking brought us to a clearing on the far side of which was a fairly large hill with what looked like a cave entrance. As we got closer, it became clear that it wasn't a natural cave but rather a large entrance that had been blasted out from the side of the hill. At some point in the past, someone had installed a metal grate affair across the entrance to seal it off. It was rusty, with rough, reddish-brown surfaces indicating many years of corrosion, but it still looked strong to me.

"This is it?" I asked Jim, "This is the Bell Mine?"

"Not exactly," Jim replied, squinting at the grate as if to see what lay beyond. "This is what they call an adit – a passage that's been blasted into the side of a hill to provide access to the inner workings of the mine. Sometimes these adits were used as emergency exits too. The real mine entrance is higher up and on the other side of this hill. That's where the headframe used to be, where they would have hoisted the miners down into the mine, and lifted the mined ore up and out of the mine... Now that we're here, what are we looking for?"

"I'm interested in any evidence of recent human activity. Any signs someone might have been opening up old entrances, collecting samples, or blasting – anything you wouldn't expect to find around a mine that's been abandoned for ten years," I replied. It was decided that I would investigate this adit, while Jim would go and have a look at another adit that he said was just around the side of the hill. Not without further negotiation, however. Following another "It'll cost you though," from Jim and a "Fine, whatever," from me, we agreed to meet at the main mine entrance on the far side of the hill in an hour.

We found that we could swing the grate out enough from one side for me to be able to squeeze by and get into the adit passageway. Jim said that it was safe for me to go in, but not to go in too far. As he started to hike around the hill to look at the next adit, he called back over his shoulder: "Go straight, don't go too far, don't take any side passages, and ..." The rest was lost to the breeze as I watched his blue plaid jacket waving in the wind as he disappeared around the side of the hill.

I went in. The walls just inside the entrance were extremely rough, as no attempt had been made to smooth the walls or ceiling. The early miners must have just blasted and pickaxed their way in, clearing away just enough rock to provide the access they needed. The floor was fairly smooth, although it was heavily cluttered with rocks and dust. I had had to step carefully around bits of rusty metal that appeared to have come from everything from pipes to machinery. The passageway had been shrinking as I went in deeper, and I had gone in just about as far as I felt comfortable going when I saw a lump of red. A red-ish cloth was either attached to or hanging on a wall a couple of feet off the ground, and it was just a few more yards ahead. I crept forward. Now there were occasional wooden planks on the floor, making it easier to walk. I was looking at the cloth, wondering what it was when there was a loud "crack - snap," and the floor gave way, right below my feet.

"Eeek!" I gave an involuntary squeal as I dropped. In an instant, I had fallen forward and into some kind of open shaft. Fortunately, the shaft was narrow, because some involuntary instinct had induced me to lean quickly forward, just barely in time to get my arms stretched out and over the rock floor on the other side so that I didn't fall in completely. On the other hand, it had left me with my arms out on the floor, my armpits pressed against the lip of the shaft, and all of the rest of me dangling into the abyss.

"*DON'T PANIC!*"

I had told myself that once before.

In my mind, I could once again hear the voices of my two SCUBA sergeants saying *Get a grip! Panic kills!* As I tried to implement this advice, my senses piled-on once more. I became alive to the cold surface of the rock face I was now hugging, the even colder air coming up the mine shaft below me, and the cool, inky darkness in whatever it was that lay before me.

OK, don't panic, I thought. *Take a few slow, calming breaths - and think!* I couldn't move much, but I didn't seem to be in immediate danger of falling in any further, so I took a minute to catch my breath. Time to inventory my surroundings and take stock of the situation.

The sharp edge of the shaft was cutting into my chest just below the armpits, but it was reassuring to feel something solid. I must have fallen into a raise. Jim had explained that vertical, or nearly vertical, openings in an underground mine were called "raises," and that they were usually constructed to provide access from one mining level to another or even all the way to the surface. The miners had clearly taken more care in the construction of this raise because the wall I was hugging was remarkably smooth. Raising one leg at a time as far as I dared, I tried to feel for a toe-hold of some kind but felt nothing. Try as I might, I couldn't feel anything that the toes or the sides of my boots could rest on.

With my arms extended and my armpits wedged tightly against the edge of the raise, I could keep myself from falling the rest of the way in, but I didn't have the strength to pull myself up and over the edge. I couldn't see or feel anything on the floor that I could grip with my hands or forearms and, with nothing to brace my boots on, I had no means of leverage there either.

"Help!" I tried yelling for help every few minutes, in hopes Jim might have wandered back this way, but I could only hear my own echoes. Calling out wasn't helping, and it was making me tire faster, so I eventually gave that up. I hadn't brought my service revolver with me, and I'm not sure I could have released one of my arms to try to get at it anyway.

Tired. I was feeling very tired...

I was beginning to feel that my sergeants were letting me down, as I just couldn't visualize a pathway to saving myself this time.

At this point, I was about ready to try something riskier. If I could shuffle to the left or right maybe I could get to some kind of wall or protrusion that I could get a knee or boot on without loosening my grip on the rock or spending the last of my strength. Before I could try it, the silence of the mine was broken by an ear-splitting sound.

"*Grruph, Grruph, Grruph.*" Suddenly a huge hairy face, with piercing blue-grey eyes and jaws bearing large teeth, appeared. It felt like the eyes and teeth were rushing right at my face.

I involuntarily jumped, and so sharply that I felt like I was going to pop out of my skin, but part of my brain alerted me to keep my arms firmly on the rock so I wouldn't fall down the raise. Struggling to get a grip on this new terror, I realized that I was looking at a wolf. No, on second thought, it wasn't a wolf, it was a large dog – more like a Husky of some kind. Once I got my heart-rate back down (again!), and still staring literally eye-to-eye with this apparition, I got the strangest sense that he (it felt like a "he") wasn't so much threatening me as trying to get my attention.

Now that I could take a moment to examine him, I could see that he wasn't really baring his teeth at me, and he wasn't growling either. He barked a few more times, and then once he clearly had my attention, he lowered his shoulders and put his head down on the rock, almost as if he was bowing or kneeling like a dog does to another dog to signal an invitation to play. I was pretty sure he didn't want to play. The tone of his bark seemed purposeful, serious. I looked into his eyes – I know that the advice books say not to stare directly into a strange dog's eyes but since I couldn't move, and he was right there, literally in my face, I didn't have a lot of other options. Anyway, as I looked into his eyes, I suddenly got the distinct impression that he wanted me to grab his scruff, the fur at the back of his neck.

"You've got to be kidding me," I said out loud.

As we shared a gaze, all I could see in my mind was an image of me grabbing his fur so he could help me get up and over the edge of the raise. I dimly recalled reading somewhere or other that the right half of the brain was good at processing emotions and generating awareness of other people's mental states, but I'd never heard of it serving as a means of communication, certainly not between humans and animals, and I didn't believe in telepathy or the occult. Yet, I was getting weaker by the minute and colder now, too.

The dog was still very intent on me, alternating between barks to get my attention and bowing his head to show that he wasn't being aggressive. I really couldn't think of anything else to do, so I very slowly moved one forearm over to him and lifted my left hand up and on top of his neck. At this, he gave a sniff and kept staring at me, so I grabbed his fur with my left hand and moved my right arm slightly in preparation for a push upward. This produced a distinct snort as if to say "about time," and he braced himself and lifted his head and shoulders.

Unbelievably, he then started to shift his body back and I realized that this was actually a pretty big dog. With him shifting back and me levering up on my right arm I was able to rise up just a bit. At this point, he lowered his head again and this time closed those huge jaws on the collars of my shirt and jacket. Backing up once more with my collars in his jaws, and me holding on to him with my left hand and pushing up on the rock with my right arm, we moved a bit further. Pretty soon, I was able to essentially crawl with my elbows on the ground, while still holding onto his fur, and we continued to inch ever so slowly along the ground. Eventually, I got enough of my chest over the edge that I was able to catch a full breath, without too much fear of falling back over, and soon it was pretty easy to get my waist up and then bent over the edge. With a final swing, the last of me came over the top.

Saved!

Once again, I found myself just lying on my back for a few minutes, drinking in that beautiful fresh air and looking up at ... well, nothing really. The roof was just rough-hewn rock. But at that moment, it was as beautiful a sight as the broad blue sky had been. Maybe I should have been a geologist. *Thanks again, my two sergeants*, I thought. I turned to look at my saviour – who was sitting on his haunches looking at me – and said, "Thank you. I don't know where you came from, but thank you!"

Now, finally, I could go take a look at the lump of red-ish cloth that had drawn me so far into the adit in the first place. I found that it was a red felt jacket, hanging from a bit of protruding rock. As I rummaged through it, looking unsuccessfully for any contents or some means of identification, I detected an unusual odour. The musty lived-in smell of seldom-washed clothing, mixed with the scent I associated with the fur hats and gloves that I had seen the locals wearing. I knew that smell. It was like when I'd visited Norm in his trapper's cabin and he had shown me some of his stuffed-animal trophies.

Norm!

I was pretty sure that Norm had been here, but doing what? Now that I was able to reach the flashlight that I had brought with me, I used it to look around, especially around the place where the ground had given way below me. I could see that there had been wooden beams, set beneath a thin cover of dirt and gravel. Looking closely at the projecting, broken ends of the beams I could see that they were partly smooth and partly fractured. Someone had deliberately set a trap!

Examining further, it looked like the boards covering the shaft had been removed, sawed most of the way through, and then replaced and covered over. If someone had seen the beams, they probably would have looked solid but weren't capable of holding up any significant weight. A deliberate attempt to injure or even kill someone.

Now I had more questions. Why would anyone set a trap here? Was it Norm? If so, it would have been foolish to leave his own jacket behind. If it was someone else that set the trap, then had Norm been shrewd enough, or lucky enough, to avoid the trap? Or had he been here before the trap had been set?

Cautiously advancing to the edge, I shone the beam down the raise I had nearly dropped into. It was a long way down, but the last traces of the beam's light were just able to show that the bottom only looked like more rock. Certainly nobody down there. Sweeping the light around, I failed to find anything else unusual, and I certainly had no intention of going down into the raise.

Meanwhile, where the hell had Jim been while I was living out my last few minutes of upper body strength hanging in that damn mine shaft? It was time to go find Jim. As the dog trotted along - not close, but not far away - I found Jim where we had planned to meet, around the far side of the hill, sitting and smoking next to the ruins of what he called the mine's head-frame.

Jim was surprised to see that I was so tired out and amazed to hear my story. "Why didn't you call me?" he asked, which provoked an "I yelled like there was no tomorrow," from me. He explained that he'd found the next adit to be completely blocked, so he'd come all the way around the hill to the mine's main entrance and hadn't heard a thing. "You've had a lucky escape," he said, "the inner layouts of these old mines are long forgotten, and no two mines seem to be laid out in quite the same way." Jim was so apologetic about not hearing me that I waved it all off and asked about the dog.

"Him? Why that's Silver, one of Norm's sled dogs," he said. "Norm has a whole team of sled dogs, and Silver here is their leader. "I've heard of dogs rescuing small children before, but I never heard of a dog rescuing a Mountie," Jim chuckled. I showed him the jacket that I had found, which he allowed could be Norm's, and certainly looked like his.

"Why would Norm be out here poking around?" I wondered out loud. "Where is he? What is Norm's dog doing out here, all by himself on an island? Could Silver have swum out to the island?"

"He probably did," Jim said, "but I've never seen him in the water before." We searched around and called out several times, but there was no further sign of Norm.

It didn't take long for Jim and I to look at what was left of the mine and the island. The island wasn't very big, the second adit was blocked with rock, and the main shaft was covered with a secure-looking metal grate. With my flashlight, we could see that the shaft was flooded down below. Jim explained that flooding was natural in these old mines when there were no longer pumps running to take the water out.

As we searched around, I noticed that Silver would roam around, seemingly following his own interests, but he never strayed far from us. I would often see him turn to look at us as if making sure that he knew where we were, or perhaps where we were going. By the time we had seen everything, there was to see and had come full-circle back to the boat, I had resolved to try to bring Silver with us.

"Jim, do you think he'll come in the boat with us?" I asked. "I don't like the idea of leaving him marooned here on this island."

"He might come," Jim allowed, "but who's going to look after him until Norm shows up?"

"I will," I said firmly. He'd saved my life and I was not going to turn around and abandon him to the elements in the middle of nowhere.

"OK. It'll cost you though," Jim started to say, and then hastily added as he saw me start to flare up, "Cost you in dog food and whatnot, I mean."

"That's OK," I supplied, "he's earned all the dog food he can ever eat." We eased the bow of the boat into shallow water, I climbed in, turned, and called out "Come Silver, come jump in the boat!" To our surprise, he just padded down to the shore, gave Jim a glance, and jumped into the boat as if he'd been doing it all his life. Which, come to think of it, he probably had. I had expected Silver to be wary of us and wanting to stay behind to wait for his master. Maybe he'd had enough of waiting though because he showed no hesitation at coming with us.

As Jim directed the boat back towards Radium City, I offered Silver some of my lunch. In a flash, it was all gone. Although his demeanour and his coat seemed to be healthy, he was ravenously hungry and ate everything I offered. Eventually, he curled up on the seat behind me and immediately dropped-off to sleep. I had now acquired a marooned dog and a missing person. Being in a remote, almost uninhabited area, I wondered about the probability of encountering three mysteries in the same month. I had no reason to connect Norm or Silver to the two break-ins, beyond my suspicious nature, but I filed them away in my mind as being possibly connected, and I resolved to keep an open mind.

As we journeyed back, I once again gazed raptly out at the huge expanse of water, fully matched by the wide-open sky, and it occurred to me to wonder if the red jacket I'd found could symbolize something else: a red herring?

Silver

11 A NEW PARTNER

I drove out to Norm's place, but there was no trace of Norm. All of his sled dogs, except Silver, were gone. Like most northerners, Norm didn't keep his dogs tied up or fenced in, and the sled dogs could normally be seen prowling around town, playing in their yard, or lying on the tops of their individual dog houses – either napping or surveying their realms. Of course, the dogs could have been off prowling around town, and Norm could have been off hunting, or doing any of a million other things, but my suspicions were aroused now. Otherwise, Norm's house seemed undisturbed.

Driving around town, I saw what looked like some of Norm's dogs hovering around the back of Ruby's café (mooching for food?). When I stopped by the marina, I found that Norm's boat was still moored in its usual berth.

Unsure about what to do with Silver, I decided to keep him with me for the time being. Mike had agreed with me and said he was fine with Silver staying at the detachment as long as I took responsibility for him. This was an easy thing to accomplish as Silver seemed to be sticking with me like glue.

Silver padded around the detachment, sniffing in every nook and cranny, but he seemed satisfied with his new surroundings. That evening, he accompanied me on my foot patrol around town, and I found that I enjoyed his company. Honesty compels me to admit that I also felt safer having him with me, as I had not fully shaken-off the effects of being jumped in the bookstore only two days before, and then nearly dying in a mine shaft the previous day.

Later that night, although he must have been an "outdoor dog," he put up an awful fuss when I tried to leave him in the yard. Still very much feeling indebted to him, I let him stay inside with me, and he quickly claimed the foot of my bed as his own.

The next day, Silver had immediately joined me in a morning run, a habit that was a legacy of all the running I'd had to do in my police training. With no real gym in town, I had developed the habit of jogging around town early in the morning, roughly every second day of the week. By picking more or less random running routes, I had gotten to know the look and feel of the whole town this way, and the townspeople had gotten to know me by sight if nothing else. Another small step forward in building community-police relations. Silver quickly followed suit. I soon found that he would try to join me in everything I did. In this case, he would lope off in his own directions from time to time, to investigate interesting smells - presumably to get a sense of what the other dogs in town had been up to. Finding one, he'd lift a leg to deposit a small scent message to let others know he'd been there too, and then finally run back, catch-up to me, and trot along companionably until the next interesting spot came along. As much as I was used to being alone, I found that I really enjoyed his quiet company.

I had hoped for an early-morning trip to look around the Fish Hook Bay area mine sites, but these could only be accessed by air or water. Unfortunately, it was too rough to go out on the big lake that day, so I had to postpone the trip. As it was too early to be knocking on doors around town, I cleaned-up the Detachment ("fatigues" again!), finished up the day's administrative duties. After that, accompanied by Silver, I tried talking to people around town. By mid-afternoon, my asking around to see whether anyone had seen Norm lately had been spectacularly unsuccessful.

I had just about convinced myself that I was worrying needlessly about Norm and that I should simply wait to see whether he or any news of him turned up when Ruby came running up to me.

"I'm worried about Norm," she exclaimed, "He does odd jobs for me around the café. He was supposed to have done things for me over the past two days but hasn't shown up. I went out to his place several times, but he hasn't been there either. No one around town has seen him, and I'm getting worried."

"What's Silver hanging around here for?" she asked, noticing that he had been sitting nearby, watching us.

I told her that I'd been looking for Norm too, that he hadn't taken his boat out either, and that Silver had been following me around for some reason.

"When did you last see Norm?" I asked.

"Last time I saw him was two days ago, Tuesday morning, at about 11 am, when he came in for lunch at the café."

I took down all the details Ruby could give me, and told her I would file a missing person report. As the two of us walked back to her café, I asked her to let me know right away if she heard anything from anyone else about Norm, and I promised to keep looking and asking around myself. When we got there, Ruby's café was deserted except for Ron McGee, who was sitting in a booth, nursing a cup of coffee. As I went over to join him, I noticed that there was a saucer of milk or cream sitting in front of him, even though he took his coffee black. This mystery, at least, was soon solved as the question forming on my lips was pre-empted by the emergence from his jacket of the small white and black head of his cat, Ally, who stretched herself out to take a few licks of cream before disappearing back into Ron's jacket. Ron may not have been much of a "people person" but he sure was attached to his cat.

"The cat's not really allowed in here," Ron explained, "but no one has ever minded as long as I keep her tucked away."

"She's obsessed with food," Ron continued, "I think she must have been a stray at one time because once they've gone starving they tend to eat every chance that they get... she even wakes me up with her meowing in the middle of the night because she's afraid of going hungry," Ron explained.

I was too worried about Norm to bother with the cat and simply asked Ron if he'd seen Norm around anywhere. Like Ruby, he too had seen Norm two days earlier, in the café, but not since.

I didn't want to over-react, but as I asked around town, it soon became clear that no one else had seen or heard from Norm since Tuesday morning either. Returning to the detachment, I filed a Missing Person report by telex.

```
M
0535 EST+
RCMP PR ALBERT
V
VIA WUI+
RCMP PR ALBERT

RCMP RADCITY

PRIORITY

FM:  RADIUM CITY DET.
TO:  PR ALBERT S/DIV
BT
UNCLAS
```

MISSING PERSON REPORTED BY RUBY GILLESPIE, AGE 45, APPEARS TO
BE SINCERE. REPORTED MISSING IS NORMAN VINCENT POOLE, AGE 40,
AKA NORM, RESIDENT OF RADIUM CITY. LAST SEEN R. CITY, ON 9
SEPT, AT 11 AM. INVESTIGATING.
ELS.
+
RCMP PR ALBERT

RCMP RADCITY
VVV

Received 11 SEP 1975 — Radio Registry R.C.M.P.

***

Talking things over with Mike in the hospital that evening, he remarked that I seemed to have a new partner. I hadn't even noticed that Silver had followed me into the hospital, and the staff had let him get away with it too.

"He won't leave me," I said, "but I have to admit that I do like having him around."

"Well, I feel better knowing that you're not alone on your patrols right now, especially with all your mysteries piling up. A bit of volunteer back-up could be better than none until Dr. Evans lets me out of here."

That night Silver and I did a walking patrol together, and more than one person compared us to Hollywood's Sergeant Preston and his dog, Yukon King. It wasn't that Silver really stuck to me like glue. He would run off and sniff around, keep an eye on any other dogs in range of his senses, and sometimes simply run ahead. On the other hand, he never wandered far away, and never seemed to lose track of where I was, or what I was doing. Catching him gazing up at me with his penetrating blue-grey eyes, I began to wonder whether he was actively protecting me for some reason.

I wasn't sure whether to be relieved or disappointed that there were no more suspicious incidents that night.

The next morning, I went to see Andrew again, in his office at the bank. Silver had slipped in with me, and as I apologized and made to shoo him outside, Andrew waved me off.

"We don't normally allow dogs in the bank, but silver is always welcome here … get it? 'Silver?' …" I'd found another comedian.

Getting down to business, I related some of my investigations and adventures, and my discussion with Norm about mines and stocks. At this, Andrew gave a slow whistle. "So, you think there's gold to be had in the old Bell Mine, and someone's killed off poor Norm to get at it?"

That was exactly what I thought, but I hadn't planned on letting Andrew that far into my confidence, and I was more than a little disconcerted at how quickly he had leaped to the same hypothesis. I hadn't even shared my suspicion that the mine shaft Silver had rescued me from had been a trap set for poor Norm.

In for a penny…, I thought. "What about Norm's father's share certificates?" I asked. "Could someone steal them and cash them in?"

"No. They would have been registered in Norm's father's name or, if Norm inherited them, he probably had the registrations transferred to his name. If someone stole them, they'd be out of luck."

"A dead end then," I mused.

"Yes, unless he had option certificates or stock purchase warrants. Those would allow anyone to buy shares at the prices listed on the certificates, but even if they exist, they would have had expiry dates, and it's unlikely that any would still be valid.'"

"Would you be able to check?"

"Sure, I'll call my broker in Winnipeg. Which Bell mine are you interested in?'"

"WHAT?" I exclaimed, straightening up in my chair. "What do you mean 'which' Bell mine?"

"There were two. People usually just refer to the one on Bell Island, because the island and the old headframe serves as an unofficial navigation marker in the area. But there was a second Bell Mine fairly close by. It was on the mainland, just north of Fish Hook Bay. When both mines were bought out, they became part of

Consolidated Bell Mines and the company referred to them as the Bell-A and Bell-B mines, but most people just refer to 'Bell Mine,' meaning the one on the island with the headframe."

"Can you check on both?" I asked.

"Sure," he replied, picking up his phone and dialing.

While Andrew called his broker, I was mentally replaying my conversations with Norm and Jim. Neither had mentioned a second mine. Now, Norm was missing. I made a mental note to go check on Jim, just to be on the safe side.

When Andrew got off the phone, he looked puzzled. "Well, someone must really have had optimism or faith, because there are still stock purchase warrants outstanding, under the name Consolidated Bell Mines, which still exists and still owns both the Bell-A and Bell-B mines."

"Wow, the plot thickens!"

"Yes, but there's one more thing … the last of the warrants expire on the 30th of this month. I don't know why they allowed them to remain in force for so many years, but whatever the reason, their time is almost up."

"So now we have a reason for someone to be in a rush," I mused. "That could explain a lot... and that rush is probably still on if they're after those warrants. What's involved in exercising them?"

"You'd have to have the physical certificates in hand and deliver them to a registered stock broker's office before the expiry date. I'd suggest two business days before, to allow time for the broker to make all the arrangements."

"OK, so today is the 12th and they'd need to be delivered to somewhere like Saskatoon or Winnipeg by, say, Friday the 26th if the broker needs until the following Monday to make the necessary arrangements. If we're right about all this, that gives our hypothetical mystery person exactly two weeks. This is going to get more interesting before we're done!"

Thanking Andrew, and swearing him to absolute secrecy about all this once again, I took my leave. I wasn't more than five feet outside the bank before Silver silently appeared by my side and brushed up against my leg by way of announcing his presence.

"Well Silver," I said, "it's time to go visit one more abandoned uranium mine."

"Grruph," he said.

"Yes, we'll need to be very careful this time."

Mike didn't want me to go, but I convinced him that we might be running out of time. He couldn't be released from the hospital yet, and we didn't have sufficient basis to ask Prince Albert Sub-Division to send official backup. We also agreed that, while I didn't seriously suspect Jim, we should avoid raising his curiosity any further, and that I'd get someone else to take me out.

"Ask Horace," Mike said.

"The Mayor?"

"Yes, he's not a professional guide, but he's a keen boater, hunter, and fisherman, and he grew up around here, so he knows the geography. He can read the water, and he can read the weather. He'll be a good choice... unless he's our mystery person – so be careful, and promise me you won't go without Silver."

"Silver?"

"Yes, he's a smart dog, he's a leader, and he's obviously attached himself to you." Then, looking over at Silver, who was half-sleeping, curled up in a corner, "I wouldn't like to be in his bad books if I could help it. Right Silver?"

"Grruph," he said, more loudly this time.

"I can't believe we're having these conversations with him... come on deputy Silver. Tomorrow, we hunt!" I only got a few feet towards the hospital ward's door when a sharp word from Mike brought me up short.

"Alex!!" he called, and then as I turned with eyebrows raised,

"Go armed!"

Laurie Schramm

12 THE GUIDE IS FOUND

In my SCUBA diving days, I had once been visiting friends in Halifax and we had all gone out for a boat dive just outside the extreme mouth of the Halifax harbour. If that sounds like a place where the water would have been calm, it wasn't. On this particular day, the water was especially rough. As soon as we had left the relatively protected waters of the inner harbour and passed McNabs Island the swell increased and our dive boat began to bob up and down more and more violently with each wave.

As we continued outward, the boat began to roll as well. It was the twisting motion of the pitching and rolling, that soon had two of my friends turning green and heading for the gunwales in search of a place to throw up.

Our skipper insisted that it was still safe to go on, but he allowed that we could turn back if we wanted to. Being students at the time, we were relatively rich in terms of spare time but not in terms of money, and we were going to have to pay for the boat trip either way – so that provided a reason to keep going. Besides, we were after big game. The goal of this trip was to find the wreck of a World War II fighter plane that was believed to have crashed into the ocean just outside the harbour entrance.

With this in mind, the consensus was to continue. By the time we reached the dive site and dropped anchor, a third friend was down with sea-sickness and I was concentrating on keeping my eyes firmly focused on the horizon while trying to keep my stomach in place. By the time the anchor was set, there were only four of us able to dive. We would go in as pairs, one pair at a time. When my dive buddy and I entered the water and dropped below the waves, we silently rejoiced. The water below the waves almost immediately became relatively calm, and all feelings of pending sickness quickly vanished.

Following the anchor rope to the bottom, we scoured the area around it as best we could in the limited visibility. This was done by swimming in a search pattern of concentric circles, using a separate rope linked to the anchor rope as a guide. When our air ran low we came up to change air tanks (courtesy of our companions who were unable to dive and couldn't use theirs) and searched again without success. When two tanks each had been used up, we had essentially also used up our available "no-decompression" bottom time, so we had to give up the search for the fighter plane.

The trip back to Halifax was slightly less stressful, and the four of us that "survived" were able to joke about being able to use the tanks of our less fortunate companions, but my main takeaway memory was of how close I had come to being violently seasick myself.

***

Now I was experiencing the same thing all over again, this time on Lake Athabasca.

I'd certainly had no trouble convincing Horace to take me out to the Bell-B mine. He was impressed that I knew the difference between the two Bell mines and told me that they had been an important part of Radium City's history, one of them having had the distinction of being the first uranium discovery in all of Saskatchewan. He seemed more than happy to have Silver along too, as I explained that I'd still had no success locating Norm and that in the meantime I was looking after Silver.

This was my third venture out on Lake Athabasca, and it was nothing like the previous two trips. The wind was blowing hard, and even though we stayed close inshore and Horace had us duck around islands every chance he could, the waves were high and angry. I hadn't realized that waves could get so violent on an inland lake. Horace explained that on such large lakes when the wind blew out of the wrong direction, which wasn't very often, it had lots of time and space to build dangerous waves. That's what it was doing now, and with a vengeance.

Silver had curled up in the lowest part of the boat, and very near its centre. *That's a very smart dog*, I thought, not for the first time. Meanwhile, the boat continued to hammer against each wavefront in turn, and I was remembering my Halifax experience. Once again, I tried to use the tricks of concentrating my eyes on the horizon and mentally trying to keep my stomach in place, but memories of having barely pulled this off before were not helping me. As if my stomach wasn't enough, I was starting to worry about my back, which was feeling each and every blow radiate up from my bottom to my neck.

I could see that Horace was doing his best to moderate the effects of the waves. He constantly adjusted the throttle to try to match the speed of the boat to the frequency of the wave crests, but every time he succeeded we'd get only a brief reprieve, lasting a couple of wavefronts at most, before the frequency of the waves changed and he'd have to adjust yet again. This happened over, and over on the two and a half hours, it took us to reach Bell Island and then land and tie-up on the shore of Fish Hook Bay. It was such a relief to beach the boat and escape the waves that we just sat and rested for a while, admiring the beautiful scenery and allowing our internal systems to get back to some kind of balance again.

From the shore, it was a bit of a hike inland. We followed an old road that was barely visible, it was so heavily overgrown with bushes and trees. This made our progress slow and sweaty, despite the fact that we were now into the coolness of early fall, northern weather.

As we trudged along, pausing now and again to consult our map and compass, I was just about ready to call for a rest stop when a loud bark broke the relative stillness of the forest. Silver had gone from padding along slightly ahead of us, to giving out a ringing bark and then taking off at full speed ahead, along the road we'd been following.

"What's got into him?" Horace asked as we heard a furious barking coming from somewhere up ahead of us.

"No idea," I responded. "Maybe he's cornered a skunk, or a bear or something."

As we finally emerged from the forest, we found ourselves looking at the entrance to an old mine adit. Silver was standing in front of a rusty old iron grate that was covering the entrance, and still barking furiously.

"OK Silver. Stay! Calm down, and we'll go take a look together." Silver seemed to understand me because he obediently sat on his haunches and watched us.

The Bell-B Mine

As we examined the iron grate, we found that the whole thing was secured by four bolts that had been driven into the rock.

The rock face itself looked like granite, so we weren't likely to be able to dig the bolts out, and we didn't have the tools to try unscrewing them. There was quite a bit of mine debris laying around, however, and we were able to find an eight-foot length of solid-looking angle-iron we could use as a lever, and a boxy-shaped piece of iron we could use as a fulcrum.

With me holding the makeshift fulcrum, Horace positioned the angle-iron to pry the grate away from its bolts on one side and put all of his strength and energy into a huge push of our makeshift lever toward the rock face. This turned out to have been completely unnecessary, as with a sharp cry he flew into the rock face itself. At the same time, the other end of the lever came away from the grate and would have caught me in the neck or head if not for the fact that the sudden and unexpected motion had caused me to promptly fall to the ground. We both laughed sheepishly as we picked ourselves up, and then we both looked at the mine entrance in wonder. The side of the grate had come completely free!

"Someone's been through here before us," Horace exclaimed. "Look at the bolts."

Both of the large lag bolts on one side had popped out of the rock when the grate came free, and we found that when we tried replacing them in the rock, they just slid right in without having to be turned.

"Someone was through here, and then put the grate back and pushed the bolts into the holes so everything would look normal, even though it wasn't," Horace concluded, as he showed me how he could wiggle each bolt in the holes in the rock.

The other side of the grate seemed secure in the rock, so Horace and I put our weight behind the free edge and pushed the grate more and more open until we were rewarded with a loud scraping sound and a metallic popping sound. This time, the remaining two bolts had stayed in the rock, but the grate had come right off. We laid the grate aside, and I quickly called Silver to stop as he had poised himself to run inside.

Once again, Silver paused, and sat on his hind legs, looking at me expectantly.

"We'll go in together – slowly... OK?"

"Does he really understand what you're saying?" Horace asked.

"I have no idea. Maybe he's very well trained, but sometimes it seems like he can read my mind."

Both Horace and I had brought flashlights with us, so we switched them on and entered carefully, with me holding onto Silver's ruff to remind him not to leap ahead. I wasn't sure that Silver would let me get away with holding on to him, but he seemed content. After my previous Bell Mine experience, it was impossible for me to avoid thinking about falling into an open shaft, giving me a second reason to hang on to Silver, and I wondered if he could sense that.

In we went.

The three of us proceeded cautiously along the narrow, low passageway, being careful not to overstep the illumination from our flashlights. It was dark and damp, and I could feel a current of cold air coming from somewhere ahead - presumably a lower level of the workings. The cold air felt nice after our lengthy hike, but I wondered what the radiation level was, and that we probably shouldn't explore inside for very long without getting it tested first.

We soon came to a three-way junction and paused to consider whether to proceed straight ahead or take one of the side tunnels.

"Which way do you want to go?" Horace asked.

Silver had been sniffing very diligently as we had made our way into the mine, and he now began to make whimpering sounds as he pulled me toward the right-hand tunnel.

"Silver smells something," I replied, "and he wants us to go this way – let's give it a try."

We had only gone about three feet into the side tunnel, when our flashlights illuminated two lines on the floor, spaced about a foot apart, leading ahead. In about fifteen more feet, the lines ended at a pair of boots. The boots had feet in them. We had found poor Norm!

Silver immediately went up to Norm's face and gave him a good sniff and then a couple of licks, before sitting down with a low whine.

"I'm sorry Silver," I said, as even in the poor light of our flashlights I could see that Norm's skin had turned an unhopeful grey colour. I felt for his body temperature – cold, like the rock. I checked for a pulse – nothing. "I'm afraid Norm is gone."

We found that *rigor mortis* was still partially set-in when we turned his body over, revealing the cause of death - the lower back of his skull had been crushed.

"Looks like he'd been hit with something fairly large," I murmured, mostly to myself. "Could have been a rock or a large tree branch..."

"How about the *rigor mortis?*," Horace asked.

There were two answers to this.

"We'll have to ask Dr. Evans," I said out loud. This was the truth, but not the whole truth.

In my own mind, I remembered being taught that *rigor mortis* is usually fully set-in by about 13 hours after death and that it starts relaxing after another 50 to 60 hours. That added up to something like 73 hours. In the cold confines of the mine, I suspected that it would take longer than that. Norm was last seen in town on Tuesday, about 84 hours previously. So, according to my mental math, whenever Norm was killed, it wasn't a lot later than that. He almost certainly died later on the same day that he was last seen. All of this I kept to myself.

"It looks like he's been dragged in here, so I bet he was killed somewhere else," Horace's voice brought my thoughts back to the present.

"Yes, I think so too," I said. "I wonder if he came here from Bell Island," I mused.

"Why Bell Island?"

I told Horace about my adventure on Bell Island, and how I'd found Silver, and a jacket I believed to be Norm's, on the island only a few days earlier.

Horace whistled softly, "So he might have met up with someone here or on Bell lsland."

"Yes, but I'm inclined to suspect Bell Island because otherwise, I can't figure out why Silver was left there." I don't think we'll learn too much more today, but at least we have some new things to go on."

Sure enough, although we searched the other two mine passageways, and then searched back the way we had come, there seemed to be no more clues to find. Certainly, there was no sign of a struggle anywhere, and nothing in the nature of a bloody murder weapon. It took the rest of the afternoon for us to carry Norm out of the mine, and back to the boat, where we covered him with an old blanket of Horace's. It was evening by the time we were able to deliver Norm to the hospital for Dr. Evans to take a look at him.

I still didn't see Horace as a realistic suspect, and the shock on his face when we'd found Norm had seemed genuine. I did, however, take the precaution of swearing him to secrecy for the time being, as I'd done before with Andrew.

Silver came along with me, as always. I think he understood that poor Norm was gone forever.

The next day, I went to see Dr. Evans, and we held an impromptu meeting in the ward, sitting around Mike's bed. He confirmed the cause of death as being massive trauma due to a blunt force injury to the lower back of the head, and he gave me a copy of his death certificate. Given the circumstances, we decided that I should go and search Norm's place for clues, before going to see the town's two lawyers.

Norm's place had not been broken-into the last time I'd been there, but it had certainly been broken-into more recently. While Silver went off to visit with some of Norm's dogs in the yard, I went in. Surveying the various rooms, things seemed more or less intact but in disarray. It seemed like the place had been pretty thoroughly searched, including furniture pulled-out and pictures askew, suggesting a search for a safe or strong-box of some kind. It was a locking four-drawer filing cabinet in a basement office that seemed to have received the most attention. The locked drawers had been forced open, probably with the large crowbar that was lying nearby on the floor. All four drawers had been pulled out and searched, and there was a large folder of stock certificates lying on the floor. Most of the stock certificates were for shares in Consolidated Bell Mines and had Norm's name printed on them. There was also a large, accordion-style file folder lying empty on the floor nearby. I wondered what had been in the empty file folder, especially since it represented the only evidence of anything having actually been stolen.

Not finding anything else, I photographed each part of the house that showed signs of the intruder and then tried dusting the most obvious locations for fingerprints. Places like the door, filing cabinet, and file folders had been wiped clean of fingerprints. I gathered up the file of stock certificates, two more files that seemed to contain legal and broker correspondence regarding Norm's investments, and the crowbar. Making my way out, I secured the entrance to Norm's house and locked the evidence away in the trunk of our detachment's blue and white patrol car. I watched to see if Silver would want to stay behind with his pack mates, but he raced over as soon as he saw me open the car's door, and jumped right in to come with me.

My afternoon plan was to visit Radium City's two lawyers, in hopes of finding a will. The first lawyer was Mervyn J. Crowe, who was very much like the stereotype of a small-town lawyer. He was elderly, slow-moving, slow-speaking, and very reserved - to the point of being disengaged and aloof. His office, which was located at one extreme end of the town's main street, was a perfect match for him. The walls were almost completely covered with wooden bookcases filled with dusty looking books having dull-coloured spines, lettered in small print. The only parts of the walls not covered with bookcases were a small multi-paned window and an antique railway-station clock that was clearly still in working condition, with its pendulum swinging and a regular "tick, tick" on the extreme ends of each swing. The floor was fully covered with a faded carpet, on which were placed two antique hardwood chairs and a large oak desk. You could almost imagine a hush unfolding as you entered, with the carpet silencing even your footsteps. I explained why I was there and, despite receiving a solemn lecture on solicitor-client privilege, I was eventually able to drag out of him that no, Norm had not ever been a client of his. Wow, a classic character for sure. Leaving his office, I re-acquired Silver (who certainly had no chance of being admitted to that office) and we strolled down the main street to visit lawyer #2, whose office was located (really, I'm not making this up) at the extreme other end of the main street.

It was a sign. Not only were the two lawyers' offices located at the opposite ends of the town, they were just about opposite in personality too. Franklin P. Heath, "Please, call me Frank," turned out to be a middle-aged, former big-city corporate lawyer, and an extrovert. Frank explained that he had moved to Radium City several years earlier in an attempt to get away from the "rat race."

"The best decision I ever made was to get away from the rat-eating-rat worlds of Toronto and New York and hide out up here," Frank asserted with a chuckle.

In complete contrast to Mervyn J. Crowe's almost claustrophobia-inducing office, Frank's was very modern, bright, and open. He had several large windows, lots of lighting, and a tiled floor with petal-shaped chairs, and laminated wood office furniture. His decorations were brightly coloured, and he had a nice-looking modern stereo with bookshelf speakers and cassette-deck playing background music. Shortly into our meeting, I realized that he'd been playing Elton John's *Greatest Hits* album, which had just recently been released. He seemed to be quite the modern person, with a sense of humour to match.

I'd asked him if there was enough work in town to support two lawyers, and whereas Mervyn J. Crowe would have been offended by such a question, Frank was amused.

"We lawyers have a saying," Frank answered, "One lawyer in town goes broke. Two lawyers in town get rich!"

I tried but failed to imagine Mervyn J. Crowe espousing such a saying.

When I explained the purpose of my visit, Frank immediately switched to a very helpful and competent-seeming lawyer mode. He'd already heard about Norm going missing and then being found dead. Frank confirmed that yes, Norm had been a client and that yes there was a will. He'd helped Norm revise his will about a year or two ago.

I gave Frank a copy of the death certificate and asked if I could see the will. Frank said that he couldn't give me the will just yet, citing client confidentiality, but that he could tell me what I wanted to know.

"Basically, Norm bequeathed everything to Ruby Gillespie: the house, his truck and boats, his dogs, and everything else, except for instructing that his estate cover his funeral and some minor debts."

"Why Ruby?"

"Well, he had no next of kin, and Norm and Ruby were really quite close, you know. They were more than employer-employee, more than just casual friends. How much more, I don't know. I didn't ever ask. I was curious, naturally, but I didn't need to know so I didn't come right out and ask him. '*Live and let live*,' I always say."

I asked whether Ruby knew about all this, and he said that he assumed so, but didn't know for sure. In any case, he was going to go and see her right away to tell her, so she could start thinking about the decisions she was going to have to make and to see whether she would need any help from him.

I told Frank about the break-in at Norm's house and asked whether he had mentioned specific securities in his will. Frank said he hadn't, that he'd simply referred to having bank accounts and investments, but that a list might show up in Norm's effects somewhere. I gave him the folders of stock certificates and correspondence that I salvaged, for safekeeping, and I promised to get him the break-in report when I had it completed.

Knowing that Frank was heading over to see Ruby right away, I decided that I'd wait until the next day before going to see her.

The next day, it was quiet in Ruby's café after the breakfast rush subsided and we had a chance to sit at a corner table and have a quiet talk.

"Norm and I were very close. We grew up together," she explained, "beginning with going to the old school at the Gunnar mine's town-site, near where our parents worked. Our fathers both worked at the Gunnar mine back then, and our mothers worked at the Gunnar hospital. Our fathers weren't friends, particularly, but our mothers were, and eventually, we were too... just friends, but good friends. After we'd grown up, we stayed friends and looked out for each other. We did some trips together, and Norm was always there to help me with things that needed doing around the café. I paid him for that, but money wasn't the reason he helped me out," she finished, wiping away a tear.

Frank's announcement the day before, that she was going to inherit Norm's estate, had come as a surprise but not a huge surprise once she'd thought about it, since she had known that Norm no longer had any living relatives. She said that Frank had explained everything to her, but "It's all a blur in my mind right now, so I'm going to have to go back in a while and get Frank to explain it all to me again."

Spotting Silver lurking about in front of the café's main bay window, Ruby said she was not a dog person, really, although she did feed them scraps from the back of her kitchen from time to time. She'd also been going out to Norm's place and feeding them every day that Norm had been missing. She didn't want to keep them permanently though, and she thought that she'd probably sell the sled dogs to a musher she knew quite well that lived in Skagway, Alaska.

"Silver too?" I tried to ask casually.

"No," she said. Then, with a kindly smile on her face, and having correctly interpreted my unsuccessful attempt to sound professionally neutral, she said "Norm and Silver got along all right but they were never really very close. Silver was a great lead dog, and that's all Norm wanted from him."

"Silver must be nearly three years old now and in all that time, they never became as close as you two have in less than a week," she said, looking through the window at where Silver had curled up outside on the sidewalk. Something tells me you two need to be together, so I'll tell you what I'll do..."

"Yes?" I asked, in a low voice.

"I'll sign Silver over to you as soon as Frank gets all the legal niceties sorted out. Just promise me one thing."

"What's that?"

"You find Norm's killer and bring him to justice. Do it for Norm, and… for all of us. Shake on it?"

"Ruby, I have to tell you that I'm already resolved to solve this thing anyway, but I'm not going to argue with you!" We shook hands with a solemnity that would have befitted a major business corporation's transaction. "And thank you for Silver, he's become my first real partner."

I was feeling quite whimsical as I took my leave of the café, and for some reason, it reminded me of the ending of the 1942 movie

Casablanca. So, having stepped out onto the sidewalk I stopped, took a serious stance looking down at Silver, with my feet spread apart, and my hands on my hips, and I said,

"Silver, I think this is the beginning of a beautiful friendship!"

Laurie Schramm

13 THE TRAIL GETS WARM

Having met with Ruby right after lunch, I went over to the hospital to meet with Mike in hopes of reviewing the whole case with him. As a preliminary step, I had written out two lists in an attempt to organize my thoughts. So far, I had:

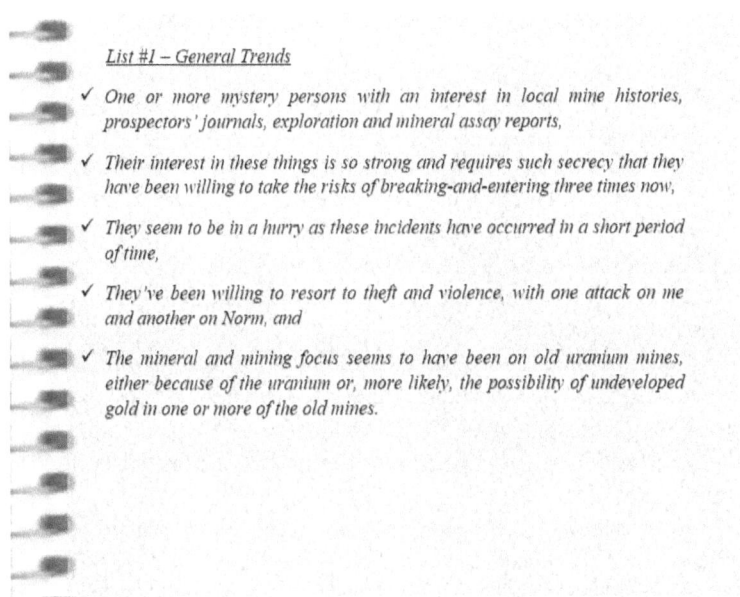

List #1 – General Trends

✓ One or more mystery persons with an interest in local mine histories, prospectors' journals, exploration and mineral assay reports,

✓ Their interest in these things is so strong and requires such secrecy that they have been willing to take the risks of breaking-and-entering three times now,

✓ They seem to be in a hurry as these incidents have occurred in a short period of time,

✓ They've been willing to resort to theft and violence, with one attack on me and another on Norm, and

✓ The mineral and mining focus seems to have been on old uranium mines, either because of the uranium or, more likely, the possibility of undeveloped gold in one or more of the old mines.

List #2 – The "Norm" Connection

✓ Although possibly not the whole story the Norm connection is, at least, quite specific, with actionable leads,

✓ Norm's father had been a part owner of a uranium mine that, together with a couple of other mines, ultimately became Consolidated Bell Mines Ltd.,

✓ Of those mines, I found Norm's jacket and Silver at the old Bell-A mine, and Norm's body at the old Bell-B mine, suggesting that he had been looking around one or both of these before falling victim to foul play,

✓ Norm's father had left him his shares in the company, which was still listed on the stock exchange, although it was trading at a very low share price,

✓ The share certificates at Norm's house had not been stolen, presumably because they were registered with a broker and the stock exchange, making the paper certificates themselves practically worthless,

✓ Norm's father may have also left him stock purchase warrants for Consolidated Bell Mines, but the warrants expire very soon (on Sept. 30th),

✓ It might be these warrants that were stolen from Norm's home, if so, the thief only had until the end of the month to use them to buy shares in the company– that would explain the need for speed,

✓ The share price for exercising the warrants is fixed by the terms on the certificates, but if the same person or persons were also buying shares on the market, then they wouldn't want any news about gold potential to get out until they'd bought their shares, so the stock price wouldn't shoot up until they had their stake secured – that would explain the need for secrecy.

As Mike and I discussed the case, we both thought it probable that our murderer, or murderers, had set the trap in the Bell Island mine specifically for Norm. That trap had been intended to kill, but it hadn't worked. Norm must have avoided it, whether intentionally or accidentally while checking out the adit and left his jacket behind. Instead, the trap had caught me, but I'd survived.

"Why would Norm have gone to the mine in the first place?" I wondered.

"Someone may have started asking questions about the Bell mines, either asking Norm directly or asking others causing rumours to circulate," offered Mike. "That might have been enough to cause him to go and look for any signs of recent activity, like surveying or sampling."

"If so, then our murderer may have seen Norm on the island, gone over to see what he was up to at the Bell-A mine, and taken him over to the Bell-B mine – either dead or alive," I speculated, "and if our murderer was well enough known to Norm he might not have been suspicious of him, and might have willingly gone with the murderer over to the Bell-B mine, possibly leaving Silver behind with the intention of coming back for him later."

"In that case, whoever did it must have killed Norm then gone back for his boat, purposely left Silver marooned, and towed the boat from Bell Island back to its usual mooring in the Radium City marina. It would probably have been done late at night when it would have been unlikely for anyone to notice," mused Mike. "I think you should check his boat again, this time to see if the boat's wheel and controls have been wiped clean of fingerprints."

"Right. Even if the prints have been wiped clean that alone will tell us that we're on the right track."

"You're doing well Alex," Mike concluded, "I think you have a good handle on the What, Where, When, and the Why, so now we need the Who and we'll need some proof!"

Mike's preferred suspect was Ron McGee, and that was certainly a possibility as Ron was very knowledgeable about the mines and the metals they contained, and their values. This made him a natural suspect. I had no reason to eliminate him as a suspect, but something about it didn't feel right. Ron was probably shrewd enough to figure out the gold angle, but I didn't think that he had. In every encounter I'd had with him, he displayed a single-minded focus on uranium. It also occurred to me, rather uncharitably, that Mike might have been a bit biased against Ron - as Mike didn't like cats! But if not Ron, then who?

"Well..." I started to say, thinking it through, "It's probably someone with a boat or at least frequent access to a boat..."

Mike gave me a meaningful look.

"OK, so that narrows it down to most of Radium City," I admitted, "and it could take forever to check everyone out..."

"Unless..." we both said at the same time.

"Unless we set a trap," I finished the thought, "Can we do that?"

"Entrapment – no," said Mike, and then steepled his hands and fingers together, preparatory to delivering a judgement, "but in this case, the trap wouldn't be aimed at tricking someone into committing a crime, it would be aimed at exposing our murderer. I think that kind of trap is quite justified in this case."

"A trap..." I murmured, thoughtfully...

Laurie Schramm

14 A TRAP IS SET

When a Constable has concluded that an arrest should be made, they must proceed with the utmost determination to accomplish that purpose. Nothing short of imminent danger to the Constable's life will excuse failing to effect the arrest and hold the prisoner.

ARRESTS. "RCMP CONSTABLES' MANUAL." OTTAWA

The next morning, I was "chomping at the bit," as they say, to do more investigating, but my top priority now had to be planning, rather than physical activity.

While continuing to ponder our next steps, I still had to look after routine detachment business, and I decided that I should get a licence for Silver as well. This created some high amusement at my expense for our mayor, Horace.

Having gone to the town office, I once again found that Mayor Horace Best was the only one on duty.

"You want what?" he asked, incredulously.

"A dog licence. For Silver."

"You want a dog licence for Silver," he repeated, in wonder, and then he started chuckling, "Have you seen how many dogs there are prowling around this town?" he asked.

"Sure."

"Do you have any idea how many of them are licensed?"

"No, I guess not," I admitted.

"Try none," he said, shifting from chuckling to outright laughter.

"Didn't you have a dog by-law back when Radium City had 5,000 people?" I asked, "There must have been an awful lot of dogs running around back then."

"Well sure, of course we did," Horace asserted, gaining control of himself, "I was just a youngster on the city council back then, but I remember we had a devil of a time controlling all those damn dogs, and we finally had to enact a dog by-law to get things under control."

"And did you ever repeal the by-law?" I asked.

"I guess not. When the city shrunk to the size of a town, and then a small town, I guess somewhere along the way we just stopped enforcing it," he said. "Why, are you planning to go out and arrest all the dogs in town?" he asked, starting to chuckle again.

"No, I have more than enough to do without looking for more work, thank you very much," I retorted, "Here's the thing. You know that Ruby inherited Silver, and has given him to me?"

He nodded. News travelled fast.

"Well, I'm going to want to be able to take Silver with me when I travel beyond Radium City. If I take him to, let's say Fort McMurray or Prince Albert, and we get separated, I might not be able to find him. If that happens, and if someone else finds him, then how will they know that he belongs to someone, or who to call? They might just put him down. But if he has a Radium City licence tag on him, then both questions are answered, and they'll call here first."

"I'm sorry Alex," Horace said, soberly. (We were on a first-name basis now. Finding a dead man together can do that.) "I see that you have thought this through, and that's actually a pretty good idea."

Horace searched through a series of old filing cabinets until finally, with an exclamation of success, he brought out a box containing dog licence forms, and licence tags with matching numbers. Filling out a form I passed it over to him and asked, "How much?"

Scratching his head and looking at the register, he eventually said, "According to this we haven't issued a dog licence since 1962... and the last time the licence fee was raised was in... 1955!" he said, triumphantly.

"And?" I prompted.

"And what?"

"And what does it cost now?"

"Oh, well, in 1955 we raised the licence fee to $5. Caused quite a stir, it did. Some of the people in town were quite incensed about it. Anyway, that means the fee is $5"

"Still?" I asked.

"Until the town council changes it, that's the fee," Horace said.

Now it was my turn to laugh. I paid the fee and went out to the sidewalk to show Silver his new licence. He sniffed at it and gave it a lick, but he didn't look very impressed.

I didn't have a collar for him, and I had a feeling that the general store owner's reaction to asking for a collar would lead to the same kind of vaudeville response I'd received from Horace. Instead, I went back to the detachment and rummaged through a couple of boxes of left-over clothes and other items that had been left behind by previous personnel.

In the end, I was able to make a beautiful collar from an old Sam Browne[13] shoulder strap. With a little polish, the brown leather and brass buckle really shone, and the whole effect had an official RCMP look to it. Silver was fine with wearing the collar and licence tag, and I didn't push my luck by trying to get him on a leash.

Meanwhile, I had been thinking about dates. Not the romantic kind of dates, calendar dates: it was now Tuesday, September the 16th. If I was right that the Consolidated Bell Mines stock-purchase warrant existed, had been stolen by the murderer, and were the reason for the murderer's hurry, then according to Andrew at the bank the murderer would have to have someone physically deliver the certificates to a registered stockbroker's office before they expire on the 30th. Andrew recommended two business days before, to allow time for the broker to make all the arrangements, so that would move the deadline to September 28th. That would be a Sunday, so make it Friday the 26th.

So far so good. Now, either the certificates had already been exercised or they hadn't. Now that it was a murder investigation, I could ask Andrew to check with the closest brokers to see if anyone had brought them in already and to ask them to notify us if they surfaced in the next two weeks. Andrew had agreed to this and promised to alert the brokers in all the major cities between Alberta and Manitoba.

My work would involve assuming that they had not yet been exercised. That assumption meant that sometime in the next week and a half, someone was going to try to get the certificates out of

Radium City. I was guessing that the murderer was unlikely to trust anyone else enough to handle the certificates, and would therefore make the trip in person. Even if I was wrong, if we could catch anyone in possession of the certificates, we'd have another lead. Naturally, however, I hoped to catch the actual murderer directly.

The trouble now was, our murderer could go to any registered broker in any big city, not just the closest one, and we wouldn't be able to watch them all. Furthermore, having found Norm, everyone in town would now know about his death. Of course, I'd made Horace and Dr. Evans swear not to say anything about the manner of his death, or that we police considered it suspicious, but the murderer (or murderers) would know and would be on guard. Would they flee immediately, or lie low and try to avoid notice?

Our murderer would be wary, but so far there would be no reason for them to suspect that anyone knew what was stolen from Norm's house, nor about the way to make money from it.

I returned to the hospital and found Mike eager to discuss the case. I asked him how he would get out of Radium City if he was in a hurry.

"Until the lake freezes and a winter road is plowed, the only ways out are by boat or aircraft," he said, "You can go to Stony Rapids by boat and then drive to Winnipeg – that would take about 24 hours – or you could just fly commercial to Saskatoon and then connect onto a flight to Winnipeg. Depending on the flight connections, that would take about 3 hours to Saskatoon, then another 2 hours to Winnipeg – allowing, say, an hour between flights that would be something like 6 hours all told. Of course, there are only three scheduled flights per week: they fly in and out again every Monday, Wednesday, and Friday. The only other options would be to hire a charter aircraft in from, say Fort McMurray, or to get Vern to make the flight in his plane."

"That's it?"

"The only other way I can think of would be to go out on the barge. That would be chancy though, because it only comes in about once a week, not always on schedule, and when it leaves here it could just as easily be headed for any of the communities on the lake. Even to Waterways, Alberta, which is a very long trip from here."

"So what it comes down to is, to keep someone here we'd have to shut the airport down and prevent all boats from leaving, and hold everything up for ten days," I concluded.

"You're not serious!" Mike said, with eyes wide.

"Maybe not," I relented, "but I'd be tempted to try it if I could," and then, thinking furiously, "If we can't build a trap around our murderer, maybe we can get our murderer to step into a trap."

"What are you thinking?"

"I don't know yet, but I'll think of something. Maybe I'll go do some more research."

I went off to check the commercial flight and barge schedules for the next week and a half. The regular flights were still scheduled, but I got a break on the barge. It turned out that the barge was already out at Waterways, Alberta. It was apparently busy ferrying materials from the railhead up to Fort McMurray for a new oil sands mine, called Syncrude, that was under construction. It would be busy over there for at least the next two weeks. Then, I went to see Vern and his plane.

Vern wasn't at the airport, but the commercial air service people suggested I try the marina. I hadn't received the impression that Vern was interested in boats but dutifully followed up, and sure enough, Vern was there, and so was his plane. He explained that he'd shifted from conventional landing wheels to floats so that he'd be able to do some fly-in fishing with some friends that would be coming up to visit the following month.

Vern explained that he'd put the floats on early so he could go and scout a couple of new fishing lakes he'd heard about from Jim and Horace. I'd brought a thermos of coffee with me in the police truck and offered him a cup in return for answering some more questions I had about flying in the north.

The next day was Wednesday, and I just 'happened' to be at the airport around noon, when the scheduled flight from Saskatoon and Prince Albert came. It had a load of people coming in, but just a couple of teenagers flying out. So far, so good.

Later that afternoon, I dropped into Ruby's café, partly to see how she was bearing up under her grief and partly just to grab a cup of tea and visit.

"Did you hear about the airport?" Ruby asked.

"The airport?"

"Yeah, the airport's going to be closed for a week. Maybe two weeks!"

"Really, what for?" I asked.

"Some kind of work on the runway marker lights. Some federal aviation authority people of some kind are coming up to replace them. They're coming over by boat from Fond-du-Lac with the new lights. Should be here tomorrow or Friday."

I saw that Vern was sitting with Ron (and Ally) and Jim over cups of coffee, in a booth nearby, and called over to him. "Hey, Vern, what's up with the runway?"

"They're finally going to do the lighting upgrades we've been bugging them for," said Vern. "You know those white lights that run along on both sides of the runway?"

I nodded.

"Well, in good visibility conditions those lights are white. In poor visibility conditions, when pilots are flying on instruments only, what we call IFR. The white lights change to yellow when the aircraft gets to the last half of the runway, and then they turn red when the aircraft gets to the end of the runway... kind of important when the visibility's low. You don't want to run off the sides or the end of the runway!"

"Right…"

"Anyway," Vern continued, "The runway lights we have are really old and the technology has improved a lot. We're finally getting an upgrade to HIRL, which stands for 'high-intensity runway lighting.' This is going to make life easier, and safer, for all pilots flying in and out, especially when the winter comes and we have short days and lots of snowstorms."

Ruby chimed in, "The only problem is getting supplies over the next two weeks, but Vern has offered to help out. See," she said, pointing to a typed sheet of paper thumbtacked to her community noticeboard.

I went over and read the notice.

> **<u>NOTICE:</u>**
>
> If anyone has an urgent need for anything over the next two weeks, while our airport is being upgraded, I'm going to be flying south twice and am willing to pick-up things, within reason, and fly them up to Radium City.
>
> My two scheduled trips are:
>
> 1. Friday, Sept. 19, 11 am, to Prince Albert,
> 2. Tuesday, Sept. 30, 11 am, to Fort McMurray.
>
> Vern Schriver

"That's very nice of you Vern. I'm sure people will really appreciate it," I said. "As a matter of fact, I have a small package that I need to send down, would you be willing to take it for me? I can get someone from the Prince Albert detachment to come to the airport to meet you and pick it up."

"Sure Alex, I'd be glad to."

"Do you have other errands to run?"

"Well, I have a fairly long list of small things. I only put the list up a couple of hours ago and it seems like everyone in town knows about it already."

"Sounds great. I'll see you on Friday then, with my package."

Vern simply gave a distracted wave and went back to his coffee. I visited with Ruby a little longer and then headed back to the detachment to catch up on some paperwork.

It was a long wait until Friday, and I was waiting 'on pins and needles' the whole time, but the day and a half eventually did pass.

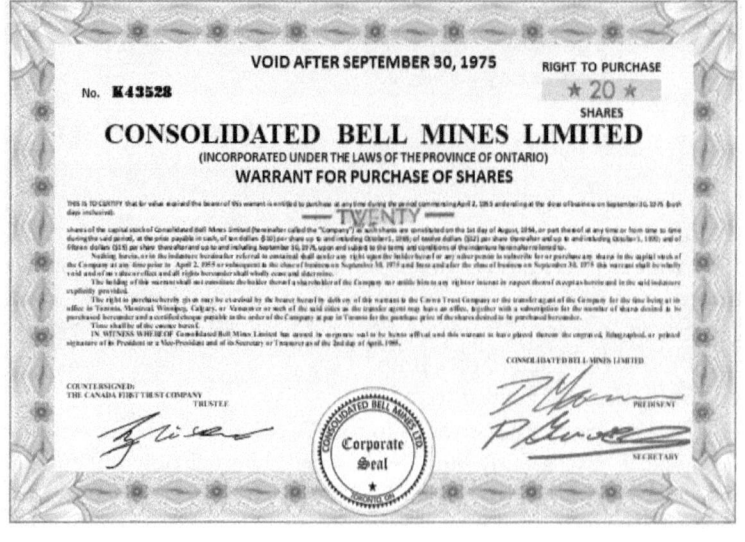

15 "COME INTO MY PARLOUR"

On Friday morning, Silver and I drove to the marina with my package for Prince Albert. I didn't have a specific plan for Silver, but I had taken the precaution of removing his new collar, not wanting to advertise that he'd become anything other than "Norm's dog."

Vern's plane was tied-up at the same pier where I had seen it earlier in the week and he was pulling seats out again, presumably to make room for the parcels he'd be bringing back from Prince Albert.

"Got any passengers coming with you?" I asked, as nonchalantly as I could.

"Not so far, but you never know. Someone may just show up at the last minute," he replied.

These words were no sooner out of his mouth than we heard the sound of a vehicle approaching and Ron's old truck appeared over the crest of the hill, on its way down to us at the marina.

Hmmm, I thought.

Ron asked if he could catch a ride with Vern, who agreed, and the three of us just stood around waiting in silence, each lost in their own thoughts. For my part, I was still having trouble visualizing Ron as our murderer, but by showing up when he did, I was forced to raise him up higher on my mental suspect list.

We waited and waited, but by 11 am, no one else had come. Vern was just saying, "Maybe we should wait a few more minutes and see if …" when two vehicles came down the gravel road to the marina. One was Dr. Evans' bright red Suburban SUV, and the other was an older pickup truck that I didn't recognize right away. They both parked, and then Dr. Evans and Jim got out of their vehicles and walked down to the docks together, the former carrying a cardboard box, and the latter with a shoulder bag slung from one shoulder.

Dr. Evans asked Vern if he had room for one more box.

"You bet," said Vern, "most people want me to pick-up stuff, so I'm pretty much flying down empty."

"Does that mean you have room for a passenger then?" Jim asked.

"Sure thing Jim," Vern said, and then, looking at him shrewdly, "no charge."

I was so surprised that Jim also wanted to fly out, that I hesitated for a moment as a whole bunch of things clicked together in my mind. Ron was strong, but he wasn't big enough to have been the person that had attacked me in the bookstore. But Jim, ...

Instinctively, without conscious thought I found myself taking a step forward and blurting out "Jim! It was you that attacked me in the bookstore that night!"

At this, Jim immediately turned white as a sheet and involuntarily backed-up a step. "Now wait a minute, who says I was ever there?" he began, but the rest of his words were lost as Silver started barking and advancing towards him. In response, Jim backed up another step and started looking around as if trying to decide whether or not to bolt and run.

Meanwhile, Silver continued to advance slowly, barking furiously, to the point of getting his whole shoulders into the movement of his barks. I'd never seen him do that before, and it was clearly enough to frighten Jim, who had slipped his satchel off his shoulder and turned as if to run back up the dock.

Before he'd taken two more steps, Silver lunged forward, grabbed the satchel strap in his jaws and pulled it away from Jim. Then it was Silver that ran to the end of the dock, followed by Jim and the rest of us.

Silver had stopped when he reached the shore and was growling and shaking his head furiously, still with the satchel in his mouth, as if he'd caught a rabbit or something and was trying to snap its neck by violently shaking it back and forth.

Jim seemed to have gotten over his momentary fear of Silver, as he was yelling at him to let go. As he reached Silver, he grabbed the satchel strap too. In the few moments that it took the rest of us to catch up, Jim and Silver had engaged in a violent tug of war, with Jim yelling and Silver growling as they struggled over the satchel.

Just as we caught up to them, the strap tore away from the

satchel, causing Jim to fall back, holding one piece. Silver, being better balanced on four legs was just standing there with another piece hanging out of his jaws. In between them flew a cloud of the papers that had been in the satchel.

As Jim started crawling toward the papers, trying to gather them all up in his arms, Dr. Evans, Vern, Ron, and I each grabbed a few ourselves.

I glanced at the top piece of paper that I had picked up, and read the bold type at its top: "Consolidated Bell Mines Limited," and in smaller type: "Warrant for Purchase of Shares."

"Well Jim, I guess we know what was stolen from Norm's place now don't we?"

As I advanced toward him, he said, "Those are mine. You don't have anything on me," and as I continued to advance, "You wouldn't arrest a friend, would you?"

"Jim, we've been friends, and I'll grant that you might not have known it was me in the bookstore - maybe you just panicked - but the break-ins were no accident. Norm is dead, and that might have been an accident too, although you should have at least reported it and not just left him out there in a cold mine shaft. Anyway, you'll get your chance to tell it all to a judge. For now, my duty comes first and you have to be held to account for your actions."

Saying this, I'd come up close enough to Jim to put my hand on his shoulder and say, as I'd been taught, "James Dumont, I arrest you for the murder of Norman Poole. You need not say anything. You have nothing to hope from any promise or favour, and nothing to fear from any threat, whether or not you say anything. Anything you do or say may be used as evidence against you at your trial."

I handcuffed Jim, led him to our police truck, and seated him in the back, while he muttered darkly about 'damn Mounties and their damn dogs.'

As I did this, Dr. Evans had gone up to his SUV, taken a wheelchair out of the back and helped Mike into it. Mike had been sitting inside, quietly observing the whole incident.

Ron had whistled long and low when he'd read the text printed on the stock purchase warrants, and he explained to the others that anyone could take them to a broker and use them to buy the actual stock – cheap! I could tell from his tone of surprise that he'd been completely unaware of their existence until now.

For myself, on top of everything else, I was amazed to see Mike out of the hospital.

When I asked how Mike had managed to get released early, they explained that Mike had been adamant that he "wasn't going to sit cooped-up in bed and miss this." Conversely, Dr. Evans had been just as adamant that Mike wasn't ready to go "roaming around town" yet. They had compromised on Mike agreeing to use the wheelchair and to having Dr. Evans come along to make sure he didn't overdo it.

At this point, we heard the sound of an approaching aircraft, and we all looked up to see the regular commercial flight from Prince Albert fly over us *en route* to the airport.

"What the Hell??" exclaimed Dr. Evans, "I thought the airport was closed for two weeks!"

"So did everyone," Mike said, grinning, "especially Jim over there."

Jim could be heard all the way from the back of our police truck swearing loudly and sulfurously.

"It was all a trick," Mike explained, exhibiting his Cheshire Cat smile. "Alex here wanted to get the airport shut down. She couldn't manage that, so she did the next best thing and made everyone except Vern here think that it was shut down."

"I had thought of watching the airport and the air service bookings," I explained, "but then I would have had to watch all the boats as well, which would have been too much."

"I got a lucky break with the barge being away, and no one else but Vern had a private plane in town. Even so, I still had to deal with the commercial air service and the boats. So, I got Vern here to help me create the illusion of the airport shutting down, and set-up Vern and his plane as an easy opportunity to quickly get to Prince Albert. From there, it would have been easy to connect to flights to Winnipeg. Our murderer could still have snuck out by boat, but I hoped he take the easier and faster opportunity, especially since Vern would probably have taken him for free!"

"Very smart, and very convincing," Dr. Evans offered, "You certainly had me fooled."

"Me too," offered Ron, scratching his head as he put all the pieces together in his mind.

"I had more than just Mike and Vern's help," I added. "Silver was really the one that prevented Jim from getting away."

"It was a good thing he grabbed at the satchel and, by fighting over it, got it torn-up enough that the certificates fell out," Mike added. "Otherwise, we'd have had to do a lot of fast talking to try to get a search warrant for it, and by then Jim might have simply denied everything and gotten away."

"Yes, he leaped forward at Jim as soon as I accused him of jumping me in the bookstore. I don't know what made him decide to do that, whether it was my tone of voice, or Jim turning pale and looking guilty, or if he somehow knew it had been Jim all along."

"That's a very unusual dog," Mike concluded, not for the first time.

"I was lucky that Jim went for the 'bait,' and I was lucky to have Silver jump in at just the right time," I said, reattaching Silver's fancy leather collar.

"Nonsense," Mike jumped in, "A Mountie doesn't rely on luck!"

Wait for it, I thought to myself, *here comes Mike the professor.*

"A Mountie, plans ahead, is resourceful, is tenacious… and you know what they say…" he paused for effect.

We all looked at him expectantly, as he put on his professorial look and proclaimed:

"A Mountie always gets **her** man!"

James Dumont

16 EPILOGUE

I was able to call a Magistrate in Prince Albert and submit my application for a warrant by telephone. Two hours later, we received a printed search warrant by telex.

My search of Jim's house turned up a small library of materials that were consistent with, but different from, the mine histories, prospecting stories, maps, and journals that had been sifted through in the bookstore, and the government geological reports that had been sifted through in the library. All told, it made for a pretty comprehensive looking collection.

The most telling find, however, was a complete looking set of calculations, among which featured estimates of the gold potential in a wide range of former uranium mines of the area, together with estimates of the dollar value of the gold that could potentially be realized from each of the mines. Looking at Jim's list of final estimates, it was clear that the gold potential of most of the old uranium mines was quite low, except for two mines: The Bell-A and the Bell-B mines!

We had confiscated the stock purchase warrants from Jim's satchel of course. There were lots of them. The warrants were for different numbers of shares, but otherwise, the wording, numbers, and dates were identical.

Here is an example of what the warrants said:

THIS IS TO CERTIFY that for value received the bearer of this warrant is entitled to purchase at any time during the period commencing April 2, 1955, and ending at the close of business on September 30, 1975 (both days inclusive): TWENTY shares of the capital stock of Consolidated Bell Mines Limited (hereinafter called the "Company") as such shares are constituted on the 1st day of August, 1954, or part thereof at any time or from time to time during the said period, at the price payable in cash, of ten dollars ($10) per share up to and including October 1, 1965; of twelve dollars ($12) per share thereafter and up to and including October 1, 1970; and of fifteen dollars ($15) per share thereafter and up to and including September 30, 1975, upon and subject to the terms and conditions of the indenture hereinafter referred to. Nothing herein, or in the indenture hereinafter referred to contained shall confer any right upon the holder hereof or any other person to subscribe for or purchase any shares in the capital stock of the Company at any time prior to April 2, 1955 or subsequent to the close of business on September 30, 1975 and from and after the close of business on September 30, 1975 this warrant shall be wholly void and of no value or effect and all rights hereunder shall wholly cease and determine.

So, there we had it, *"and from and after the close of business on September 30, 1975, this warrant shall be wholly void and of no value or effect and all rights hereunder shall wholly cease and determine."* That set the deadline, just as Andrew had predicted. So now we knew for sure.

I read on:

The right to purchase hereby given may be exercised by the bearer hereof by delivery of this warrant to the Crown Trust Company or the transfer agent of the Company for the time being at its office in Toronto, Montreal, Winnipeg, Calgary, or Vancouver or such of the said cities as the transfer agent may have an office, together with a subscription for the number of shares desired to be purchased hereunder and a certified cheque payable to the order of the Company at par in Toronto for the purchase price of the shares desired to be purchased hereunder.

That fixed the place, *"… may be exercised by the bearer hereof by delivery of this warrant to the Crown Trust Company or the transfer agent of the Company for the time being at its office in Toronto, Montreal, Winnipeg, Calgary, or Vancouver…"* The nearest such office was in Winnipeg.

I'd taken the stock purchase warrants over to show Andrew at the bank. We'd found ninety altogether, fifty for the purchase of twenty shares each, twenty for the purchase of fifty shares each, and thirty for the purchase of one hundred shares each.

"Norm's father must have really believed in the potential of the Bell mines," Andrew concluded, "He probably bought shares in the company when he worked there. Any time the company put new shares out on the market, they would have offered these share purchase warrants as an inducement for people to buy the stock. At the time, the company probably offered something like one or maybe two future share purchases for each actual share purchased. So, if Norm's father bought, say a hundred shares, then he'd get warrants enabling him to purchase another hundred or two hundred at a future date, for the prices we saw listed on the warrants."

"Why so many certificates then?"

"He probably bought different numbers of shares from time to time. Some combination of when they were made available and when he could afford them. Then again, I suppose the company might have given him some warrants directly as a kind of bonus or extra pay. I suspect another thing that happened, though, is that he probably had bought a lot of these warrants from other investors as they lost confidence in the operation over the years."

"How do the numbers add up?" I asked.

"Well, all together these warrants can be used to buy five thousand shares at fifteen dollars a share. If they're used before they expire, then that would cost $75,000, plus a small brokerage fee. In 1970, the shares were trading for twelve dollars a share. At that time, these warrants were completely worthless, but since then the stock price has more than tripled, to thirty-eight dollars a share. So, at the current price, you'd be paying $75,000 for $190,000 worth of shares."

I whistled sharply, "That's not bad, you'd more than double your money. I wonder whether Norm was planning to use them himself. I guess we'll never know."

"Wait, it gets better," Andrew exclaimed. "Let's say someone buys the shares like we just said, and then waits for the news to get out about the gold potential of the mines. That would drive the share price even higher. I could see it easily doubling, or more. If it doubles, then you could sell the shares while the market for them is hot and turn your $75,000 into at least $380,000! Think of what you could do with that kind of money, that's enough …"

"To kill for… yes," I interjected, dampening Andrew's excitement at the numbers.

"Could you take control of the company with those shares?" I asked.

"Probably not. We're talking about five thousand shares here, and my broker says that there are something like a million shares outstanding. But, simply selling them would make someone a lot of money if the mine was reopened and put into production for the gold."

"Well, I guess that will be up to Ruby. We'll have to get some legal advice on how we can preserve the evidence value of the warrants and still let Ruby exercise them before the expiry date, if she wants to," I mused, "I'll let her know what we've figured out so far and suggest that she talk to Frank about it and get his advice."

In training, we'd been taught that peoples' appearances can be deceiving – hardly a stunning revelation - but one that can be difficult to always bear in mind. If I'd needed an object lesson, then it was provided by Norm, and Ron, and Jim. Norm's aggressive and surly manner hid a willingness to help people, and a deep respect for people and nature. Ron's lack of interest in other people made him seem almost rude, and certainly suspicious. Although Jim's preoccupation with money was impossible to miss, his outgoing, friendly, and perennially happy demeanour hid a selfish and ruthless nature. I found that sad.

I've mentioned Jim's love of talking and story-telling. Although I'd warned him about the hazards of saying anything that might be incriminating, after a day in jail he became quite talkative. I'd expected him to continue to plead innocence, but once he started talking the story tumbled out, and he surprised me by confessing to the whole thing.

It was in a casual conversation with Norm that Jim had learned about the gold potential. He hadn't let on to Norm but had secretly done his own planning and research, hoping to maximize the potential payout he could get.

He said that he hadn't planned to kill Norm. He was going to keep everything secret, and simply steal the stock purchase warrants from him. In his own mind, he had rationalized that Norm would still come out of it all ahead of the game because Norm had a lot of actual shares of the company registered in his own name (the ones he'd inherited from his father). The trap in the abandoned mine raise wasn't intended to kill, he insisted, it was to put a big scare into anyone that got interested in the mine and his idea was that it would persuade them to stay away.

It turned out that Norm had gone to look around the Bell-A mine on Bell Island, and Jim said he'd only noticed it by accident. Jim had apparently been headed for a completely different destination that day and had seen Norm's boat pulled-up on Bell Island. Jim had pulled in alongside and gone to see what Norm was up to. Discovering that his trap hadn't worked, Jim had lured Norm (but not Silver) over to the Bell-B mine. In the process, Norm told Jim his ideas about the mineral value left in the two Bell mines, and that he thought there might be enough gold to justify reopening one or both mines. Jim hadn't been too worried at first and had simply pretended ignorant interest. When Norm said that he was planning to bring in a drilling rig to get new samples and have them assayed, Jim panicked, grabbed a large rock when Norm's back was turned, and killed him. He'd then dragged Norm's body into the side passage where Horace and I had found it and left it there thinking that he'd be able to get back and move the body to a better hiding place long before anyone else happened along.

Jim had later gone back to Bell Island, retrieved Norm's boat (once again abandoning Silver to the island), and towed it back to Radium City, timing the journey so that he'd reach the marina at about 3 am, so he could tie-up Norm's boat in its usual berth without much chance of being spotted.

Andrew and I had been right about the financial aspects. Jim admitted that he had just over $75,000 as his life savings. He was planning to simply buy some shares on the market, but then he'd realized that he could make a lot more money if he could get the warrants and use them before word got out about the gold, and before they expired. His big hurry, of course, had been because of the expiry date.

Jim's estimate of the future share value was higher than ours though. He figured that once news of the gold potential became public, that the stock would rise by another 250%, in which case he'd have been able to fairly quickly turn his $75,000 investment into $475,000. With nearly half a million dollars he was going to move south and retire to a "life of ease."

17 LOOSE ENDS

So, that was my first experience with small-town policing.

I'd gotten what I'd asked for, and more. I got my chance to try "real policing." I'd had to face new challenges, and I'd learned a lot. Along the way, a few things had happened that scared the hell out of me, but I'd survived them. In a bizarre set of crises, I'd been able to rescue Mike from one mine floor collapse and then had a strange dog named Silver rescue me from another – and gained two new friends in the process. Looking back, I realized that I'd grown up a bit too.

Four months! It had all happened in four months.

In comparison, the months of October and November were pretty quiet. Mike was allowed out of the hospital, on crutches, a few days after I'd arrested Jim, and it didn't take long for him to get his strength back and leave the crutches behind. That allowed us to ease back into a more sustainable routine. We'd now learned the value of having Jennifer cover the daytime phone and telex, and few other tasks for us. She was still undecided about her long-term future and had loved working with us, so we found a way to keep her on, out of our meagre detachment maintenance budget.

Winter comes early in the North, and we had snow on the ground by mid-October, and a thick snow cover by Halloween.

Halloween! I was remembering Norm and his snarky question about Halloween when I'd landed in Radium City for the very first time when we received an unusual telex. It rather cryptically informed us that Assistant Commissioner MacLeod was going to be flying by police plane the following day, and would make a brief stopover in Radium City. "Unofficial visit. No ceremony," it said.

"Something's up," I said.

"Know him?" asked Mike.

"We've met. He's the one that talked me into leaving Metro Toronto to join the Force."

"Mmmmm. Something tells me you're getting transferred."

"What, already? I've only been here six months!"

Mike steepled his fingers and shifted into professorial mode. "True, but sometimes summer replacements are just that – summer replacements."

"I guess," I said, thinking about it. Mike interrupted my thoughts:

"Speaking of telexes, I saw the telex you sent about my mine accident. Very concise, to the point, and factual. A model telex... In fact, if a person reading that telex didn't know better, they'd be forced to conclude that the ground simply collapsed under my weight. The kind of thing that could have happened to anyone..."

"Well, that's true," I offered.

"What you probably should have added, was that it was caused by my own bloody idiotic, schoolboy theatrics!" he said, having shifted to his gruff expression and peering at me from between his bushy eyebrows and his thick handlebar moustache.

"Maybe," I said, "but there was no harm done, other than to yourself, and I thought that you were going to pay a pretty stiff price already, what with being confined to traction for so long, without having to have it on your record as well."

His face softened at this point, and he dialled his voice down from parade ground to bedside, "Thanks, Alex."

"None needed... but you're welcome."

The next day, Mike and I were both at the airport to greet Assistant Commissioner MacLeod, who disembarked from the police plane in civilian clothes – a plain suit that wouldn't be out of place in any big corporation, anywhere. Following a quick drive around town and coffee with both of us back at the detachment, he eventually shifted to a change in body language that Mike correctly interpreted as a polite signal for him to leave us.

When it was just the two of us, he asked how I now felt about having joined the RCMP, and about my experiences in Radium City. These were clearly more than casual questions, as he quite thoroughly questioned me about specific aspects of my experiences, how I'd handled them, and how I felt about them with the clarity of hindsight. I was surprised to find that he seemed to be as interested in my approaches to policing, and getting to know the area and its people as he was about our murder-robbery case. He also seemed to have already been aware of the Silver connection and had a lot of questions about him too.

After a thorough debriefing, it wouldn't have taken a genius to detect that I was wondering what all this was about, and this was clearly a very intelligent man. He knew what I was thinking, and he also saved me from trying to figure out how to go about interrogating such a senior officer, by smoothly moving the topic of conversation forward.

He explained that earlier in the year he had been transferred from 'Depot' Division to become the new head of the Security Service[14]. He added that, although things there were in pretty good shape, he had some new ideas he wanted to try out, and just like when he was at 'Depot' Division, he intended to launch a few experimental pilot projects.

"Like me?" I asked.

"Exactly," he said, "Although a lot of my experiments don't work out as planned…" He paused, as if in thought for a moment, and then he beamed: "But this one did! You have proven yourself royally. I'd have been happy if you'd done half as well as you have. Following in your bootsteps," he chuckled as his own joke, "the first full troop of women is in training in 'Depot' Division right now, and by next Spring, they'll be getting posted right across the country."

"That's great," I said, "So you don't need me anymore?"

"Hardly," he said sharply, "We have another opportunity now. Most people won't be used to the idea of a woman Mountie for a few years yet. I think there might be a few ways we can use that to our advantage, don't you? … I want you to come and work for me."

"What about Cpl. Morrison, Sir? Shouldn't I stay on here and help him get fully up to speed again first?"

"Cpl. Morrison is as strong as a horse," he replied. "He's back on his feet, and the truth is, he can run this detachment single-handed. That's partly why I got you assigned here in the first place, so you'd have a chance to show what you could do without having been 'set-up to fail' – and it worked beyond anything any of us could have imagined! Besides, he'll be getting a replacement for you anyway."

Before I could respond to this, he continued, "I've already spoken to him about this, but I ordered him not to tell you until I could get here in person. You should know that he fought hard to keep you. I'd worried about sending you to work with such an old traditionalist and hard-liner, but you obviously proved yourself with him, and that's another point in your favour."

I smiled, "His bark was a lot worse than his bite, sir, and I found gold under that crusty, traditionalist outer layer of his. In the end, honour and common sense won out over his prejudices and preconceived notions."

"May that be said of any of us," said the Assistant Commissioner.

Then, as if sensing that the conversation was turning slightly soapy, he pulled himself together with a gruff "Harumph," that would have impressed even Sergeant Major Walsh. "In any case, you've already learned most of what there is to learn in Radium City. It's time to transfer you on to something new, and as I said, I'd like you to come work for me. I could just arrange to have you transferred, but I want you to come willingly, and I'll want you to be totally committed."

And then, just like he'd said over a year previously, in Toronto: "Will you do it?"

Before I could answer, he added, "You'd better bring that dog of yours too. I have a feeling you wouldn't leave without him, and we might just need him. What do you say?"

The man was a mind-reader! All I could do was say "Yes, Sir!"

***

… Alex and Silver return in
An Inconspicuous Mountie.

Laurie Schramm

BOOK 1 ENDNOTES

1. In real life, a first full troop of women began training in the RCMP in 1974, but for this fictional story, it all began with a single-woman pilot test.
2. These movies can be found on the internet.
3. Physical training, outdoors or in the gym.
4. Like a troop leader, but without any real authority. The Right Marker deals with roll call, marching the troop here and there, and serving as a liaison for administrative matters affecting the troop.
5. Equitation was dropped from recruit training in 1965, but for this story, I left it in for another decade.
6. Non-commissioned officer in charge.
7. The telex network was a switched network of teleprinters similar to a telephone network, that enabled text-based messages to be sent and received. It had evolved from the old telegraph systems.
8. Within the RCMP are distinguished "Members," or "Regular Members," meaning official police officers of any rank, and "Civilian Members," meaning non-officer employees.
9. However, of the "open files," a smaller number would actually be considered "active" at any given time.
10. It did eventually become a protected area, as the Athabasca Sand Dunes Provincial Wilderness Park, but not until 1992.
11. A piece of metal looking vaguely like the number eight, but with one end larger than the other. When threaded with a climbing

rope this device creates enough friction to enable a climber to control their rate of descent with a single hand while rappelling.

12. Which it did, in 1979.

13. A Sam Browne belt is a wide leather belt, supported by a narrow leather strap passing diagonally over the (usually) right shoulder. Captain Sam Browne VC, who lost his left arm in combat in India in 1858, needed a way to hold his scabbard in place so he could draw his sword one-handed. He invented this belt, which had hooks for attaching the scabbard on the left side, while the diagonal strap was used to support its weight. His pistol was carried in a flap-style holster on the right side. The RCMP version is made of brown leather.

14. At this point in time it was still part of the RCMP, but in 1984 the Security Service was spun-out to create the present-day Canadian Security Intelligence Service (CSIS).

An Inconspicuous Mountie

Adventures of the First Woman Mountie. Book 2

LAURIE SCHRAMM

Laurie Schramm

The detection of crime is an art, not a science. Therefore, little can be written upon it, but much can be learnt by observation of all that goes on around one by those who have a natural aptitude for investigation. This natural aptitude for investigation is the chief stock-in-trade of a constable, whether in uniform, or a so-called detective in plain clothes. This, together with application to the matter in hand, general knowledge acquired by reading and observation, experience, and personal courage, are the roads to success.

INTRODUCTION. "R.C.M.P. CONSTABLES' MANUAL." OTTAWA

Laurie Schramm

DEDICATION

To Teddy.

Laurie Schramm

BOOK 2 CONTENTS

Laurie Schramm

LIST OF CHARACTERS
(IN ORDER OF APPEARANCE)

- Constable Alexandra (Alex) Houston, RCMP
- Assistant Commissioner George MacLeod, RCMP Security Service
- Silver, an Alaskan Malamute; and Alex's friend and companion
- Staff Sergeant Robert (Bob) G. Simpson, RCMP Security Service
- Inspector Lawrence (Larry) J. Walsh, RCMP Dog Service Training Centre
- Sergeant William (Bill) Preston, RCMP Dog Service Training Centre
- Geoff Laker, GCOS Employee
- Karen Laker, Restaurant Night Manager, Fort McMurray
- Teddy, a Yorkie-Havanese Cross and friend of the Lakers
- Laurie and Ann MacDonald, neighbours in Fort McMurray
- James, Geoff Laker's brother-in-law (Karen's brother)
- Franklin (Frank) D. Stoner, GCOS Safety Supervisor
- Fred, Bucketwheel Excavator Operator, GCOS mining Operations
- Helen, 'Heavy Hauler' Truck Driver, GCOS Mining Operations
- Jack ('JJ,') Johnson, Chemical Engineer GCOS Extraction Operations
- Jason Hill, Salesperson, Electronics City, Fort McMurray
- Larry Hand, Chemical Engineer GCOS Upgrading Operations
- Jack McDonald, former recruit colleague, now with RCMP Fort McMurray
- Dr. Rick Williams, veterinary surgeon, Fort McMurray.

Cst. Alexandra Houston

1 A NEW POSTING

"Will you do it?"

My name is Alexandra Houston. My friends call me Alex.

In the summer of 1974, I'd been 24 years old, and feeling like my career was at a standstill. I'd studied chemistry at university and liked it, but not enough to pursue science as a career. I'd reset my sights on police work next and had joined the Metropolitan Toronto Police force ('Metro'). Although policing seemed like a better fit for me than science, my two years with Metro had mostly comprised routine administrative- and traffic duties. These assignments were important, and needed to be done by somebody, and done well. But for me, they didn't fit the Hollywood vision of policing that I had developed, and I hadn't found them to be very challenging.

They say you should be careful what you wish for.

My life soon changed drastically, beginning with an unexpected meeting. Without explanation, my Captain had sent me to go and see a Royal Canadian Mounted Police (RCMP) officer that wanted to meet me. My reaction to this was apprehension, and I wondered what I could possibly have messed-up so badly that it had caught the notice of our national police force.

That's how I first came to meet Assistant Commissioner George MacLeod. After a lengthy conversation that I belatedly realized was an interview, he told me that he had asked my Captain (his friend) to recommend one of his young officers for a special pilot project he had in mind. He wanted someone who wanted to accomplish things, someone eager *and tenacious, someone chomping at the bit to be allowed to do some 'real' police work, and ... someone female. At this point he had shed his stern 'Mountie look,' relaxed his entire body, chuckled, and said that my Captain had recommended the "biggest pain in the butt" in his Division - **me**.*

Assistant Commissioner MacLeod had explained that the Force had fallen behind the times and that its senior leadership wanted to build a more diverse police force. "We're going to be recruiting immigrants, visible minorities, maybe even people with some kinds of disabilities as well," he said, "But we have to start somewhere, and that somewhere is by engaging women." He wanted to try a first pilot test with a woman, but that the pilot test had to succeed as it would pave the way for an entire first troop of policewomen that would follow. He had thought of using someone that had already qualified as a policewoman, and simply re-train them in the "RCMP way."

That had brought me up to full attention. "Wait a minute! Do basic training all over again?"

"Yes!" he'd replied, "that's the only way you can possibly succeed. In the old days of the Northwest Mounted Police, a person could get appointed straight into the Force, even as a commissioned officer[1], if they had the right political connections. No more. Now everyone starts out the same way, as a Constable, and by going through the same basic training. If you want to have any hope of being accepted, much less respected, that's how you have to begin."

So, that's what I'd done. I'd gone through training at the RCMP's Depot Division training centre in Regina, dealt with the good and the bad issues that came with being the first woman to train there, and survived to become the first woman Mountie[2]. I hadn't intended for it to happen, really. The opportunity just came and found me.

After training, or re-training if you like, I'd been posted to Radium City, a small town in very northern Saskatchewan that, in its early days, had been a great uranium mining centre. Although my new boss, Corporal Morrison, had told me that nothing interesting ever happened around there, he'd been wrong, and I'd had to rescue him from a mine collapse, run our entire detachment single-handed while he was confined to hospital for six weeks, get rescued by a strange dog from near-death, solve a mystery, and find and catch a murderer – all in only four months!

The dog was named Silver. Investigating a mysterious series of break-ins had led me to some unusual places, including several abandoned uranium mines. In one such mine, I'd fallen through a trap and found myself hanging precariously over the sharp edge of a raise, a kind of vertical mine shaft. Unable to get out and tiring fast, I was saved by the almost magical appearance of what I first took to be a wolf, which gave me quite a scare, but turned out to be Silver, an Alaskan Malamute. Silver somehow sensed that I was in danger, had decided to help, and with his assistance I had been able to climb up and out of the raise. To make a long story short[3], while I'd continued to investigate the case, he had attached himself to me, was eventually given to me, and we'd been close friends ever since.

Sometime later I'd found myself in another surprise meeting with the same Assistant Commissioner MacLeod. Once again, a coffee meeting had turned into an interview and, once again, he had something new in mind for me. By this time, he'd become head of the Force's Security Service[4] and, unsurprisingly, he had some ideas he wanted to try out by way of some experimental pilot projects.

"Like me?" I'd asked.

"Exactly," he'd replied. It turned out that he now wanted me to go and work for him in the Security Service. Of course, he could have just ordered me to go, but he wanted me to go willingly, and immerse myself in his new plans.

Then, just like he'd said over a year previously in Toronto, "Will you do it?"

***

It was November 1975. Having wrapped-up things in my former Radium City detachment and having left Silver in the temporary care of Ruby, the local café-owner that had given Silver to me in the first place, I found myself flying off to Ottawa to learn about my next assignment.

Headquarters (HQ) Division in Ottawa comprises several large sprawling buildings on sweeping grounds that lie just outside the downtown-core area. Among these are a huge administration building, a sizeable building for Identification Services (which in any other police force would be called the crime or forensics lab), and another one that contained what at the time were called the Security Service, and the new Canadian Police Information Centre (CPIC). CPIC was just beginning to create and manage computer databases of digitized information like criminal records and even fingerprints. It wasn't all up and running yet, but it held a lot of promise for the future.

While getting acquainted with my new Security Service supervisor, Staff Sergeant Robert ("Call me Bob") G. Simpson, I discovered that he had a fascinating background. He'd grown up in the Okanagan Valley of British Columbia and then moved to northern Alberta. As a young man, he first found work as a deckhand, helping barge prospectors' supplies on the Athabasca, Slave, and Mackenzie Rivers, and later, on Lake Athabasca, spanning both Alberta and Saskatchewan. This exposure had sparked an interest in prospecting, and he next joined-up with a mineral exploration company that was sending prospecting parties across the northern regions of all three prairie provinces, plus the Northwest Territories (NWT) and the Yukon.

One of Bob's fond memories was of spending several summers at prospective mineral resource locations, living in the wilderness, hiking, paddling, and blasting into the mineral showings as they looked for sizable deposits of gold, uranium, and nickel. In 1937 he joined the NWT Gold Rush to search for gold in the Yellowknife area, continuing to work there until 1939, when Germany invaded Poland, effectively beginning the Second World War.

With the outbreak of war in 1939, he'd wanted to do something "more worthwhile" but didn't share quite the same fervour as the teenagers that were rushing to sign-up for overseas military service. Fortunately, there was another option. With the war effort scaling-up, the RCMP had volunteered to create a military police company and send 120 Members overseas to form 1 Provost Company (of the 1st Canadian Infantry Division). This left the Force short-handed and, they'd had to increase their recruiting efforts to find replacements in the face of the active military recruiting campaign, which had also been increased. Simpson, who was by then twenty-four years old, offered his services to the RCMP and was accepted that same year.

Graduating from basic training in 1940, he was posted to a series of small-town detachments in southern Saskatchewan and Alberta. He'd moved to the RCMP security intelligence service in 1945, initially focusing on Cold War-era anti-espionage, then moving to other domestic issues. All his promotions had been during his time in the Security Service, and he'd clearly seen and done a lot in his time there so far.

At this point in his narrative, I'd become really curious. Spies, counter-espionage, anarchists, and terrorists? Surely, we didn't have any of those in Canada? I'd asked.

"We did, and we do," he'd answered, and with that, he started telling me some 'intelligence' stories.

"Like you, most of us thought we were safe here in Canada" he began. "After all, the last war fought on our own soil had taken place nearly 150 years earlier, when we'd beaten the Americans in the War of 1812." He paused then as if considering how best to proceed.

"Our first wake-up call came when the Second World War had just ended. We didn't even realize it yet, but the Cold War had begun immediately after that. In September of 1945, a cipher clerk from the Soviet embassy in Ottawa defected to Canada."

Bob explained that he had sat in on the cipher clerk's first interview with the RCMP, during which it developed that not one, but several Soviet espionage rings were operating in the country and that they had already penetrated some highly sensitive government positions, including the Chalk River Nuclear Laboratories. Apparently, that got everyone's attention. In those days, Canada was one of the leading nations in nuclear research, as much of the U.S.-U.K.-Canada nuclear research had been conducted in Canada during The Second World War.

"The biggest surprise," Bob concluded, "was that the Soviets – our former allies – had been actively spying on us and we'd been caught 'with our pants down' as it were. Naturally, we resolved never to be caught out like that again, and that's how the RCMP got into the counter-intelligence game."

I'd never heard of this before and said so. "Have there been many cases like that?"

"More than you'd guess," Bob sighed, "That first one and a few others made the news, but most of them have remained secret."

Bob said that a few years later, in 1951, a KGB agent had snuck in and settled quietly into Verdun, Quebec. From there he set up a small network of agents to search-out classified information on military projects like the CF-105 Avro Arrow jet fighter program.

"We only found out about him because he fell in love with a

Canadian woman who convinced him to turn himself in – and he actually went ahead and did it!" Bob said, with some satisfaction. "We were able to convert him into a double agent, working for us and sending disinformation back to the Soviet Union... Then, in 1957, we discovered that we had a home-grown spy in our diplomatic service. That case resolved itself, as he committed suicide once he learned that we were on to him."

There was silence for a moment, as Bob was clearly caught-up in old memories. Then, he shook himself and came back to the present, "Anyway, those are just examples. Last year we did a thirty-year retrospective review and found that we'd successfully concluded just over thirty espionage cases, an average of one per year not counting the many files that are still open. Those thirty cases resulted in twenty cases of people being charged with espionage offences under the Official Secrets Act, and forty diplomats being expelled for espionage-related activities, all between 1945 and last year. I'll show you the summary report and a few specific cases, that I think you should read up on. Some of them make spy fiction books look tame," he added, dryly.

"I'm starting to imagine," I said, and then paused as a new thought struck, "So it's all counter-espionage then?"

"Oh no, that's just what got the RCMP involved back in the Cold War, and of course such things continue today, but we have our share of domestic issues to worry about too. Remember the FLQ Crisis?"

"Of course!" I sat up straight.

I'd been immersed in my studies at Carleton University during the FLQ Crisis of 1970, but living in Ottawa at the time, no one could have missed that one. All of Canada had been brought to attention and affected by the events, in which the militant arm of the Front de libération du Québec (FLQ) had kidnapped two prominent politicians and murdered one of them. The federal government had reacted swiftly, invoking the War Measures Act, calling out the army, and temporarily expanding police powers. In the end, the FLQ had been shut down and the kidnappers exiled to Cuba, but it had shattered forever our illusion that terrorist attacks 'couldn't happen here' in Canada.

"That gave the RCMP quite a black eye, didn't it?" I asked, tentatively.

"It sure did," Bob explained, "I want to go through that with you too. We made some mistakes and have tried to learn from them. You can learn from them too, so that's going on your reading list as well."

Bob next moved to modern-day criminal threats which, beyond, counter-intelligence and local anti-government movements, also included a variety of special-interest groups that might be motivated to resort to civil disobedience or worse tactics.

"So, this means spying on our own people?" I'd asked at one point.

"Not in the 'Big Brother' sense," Bob explained. "Don't forget, if someone's thinking about committing a crime, but doesn't do anything illegal, then we don't have the authority to do anything, and we won't. As you know very well, we don't have the time and resources to worry about such people even if we wanted to, and we don't. By the same token, we're not interested in people or groups that have a cause, or an issue, and are lawfully complaining and/or protesting. We **are** interested in the ones that 'cross the line' into law-breaking, but, as you know, it isn't usually very easy to distinguish who's who until it's too late.

"There are some groups that it's obvious we have to keep an eye on, like agents of foreign powers, organized crime groups, self-declared anarchists, and political groups that publicly espouse violence to further their causes. Mostly what it comes down to, though, is simply intelligence gathering. If we can anticipate that someone is going to commit a crime, then we can better position to try to catch them in the act and convict them. Or, in very dangerous situations, we can take steps to prevent the crimes themselves. For example, a pattern of suspicious events might trigger an investigation by us to see if crimes are being committed, or even if they're likely to be committed, and if so, why and by whom. If something major is underway, like a planned bombing, for example, then we'll try to prevent the bombing to save lives, even if it means not catching or convicting the bomber or bombers.

"Finally, there's also a new kind of national security threat. This one isn't international, or military though. As Canada starts to develop more major industries, some of it is happening in small communities that aren't used to all the new people, the new activities, and the changes to their town, the landscape, and their way of life. Some see it as an opportunity and want the economic development, while others see it as a threat and want to prevent or stop the development. Some of these kinds of tensions are building up where there are new or changing industries in different parts of the country. So, we have to keep an eye on those too."

As if all this wasn't enough to set my head spinning, he gave me a bunch of cases to read as a supplement to the other orientation and training I'd be doing for the next few weeks.

The cases were an eye-opener in the sense of so many things having happened in Canada that I'd never heard about on the news, or even imagined. Not all of them were criminal, or anarchist, or foreign-agent type incidents, of course.

One interesting case concerned the heavy water plants in Nova Scotia. Canada's nuclear reactor development program had focused on natural uranium fuel, moderated by heavy water[5]. The reactor designs were called CANDU (for CANadian Deuterium Uranium system). To build CANDU reactors, our nuclear industry needed uranium (which was mined in Saskatchewan and refined in Ontario), and heavy water.

The heavy water was going to come from two large plants on Cape Breton Island in Nova Scotia, one in Glace Bay and one in Port Hawkesbury. The reasons these sites were chosen were partly technical (availability of suitable water and power) and partly political (economic development). The second reason had unintended consequences, because these plants created a lot of jobs for construction workers from the two small towns and their nearby communities, at a time in the late 1960s when their economies were really struggling. They not only provided jobs but relatively high paying jobs, especially when overtime was required, which happened more and more frequently as the projects fell behind schedule. The Port Hawkesbury plant started-up in 1970, not far behind schedule, but the Glace Bay plant continued to suffer setbacks. Ultimately, a series of suspicious construction and equipment failures had caused so much alarm that Atomic Energy of Canada Ltd. (AECL) and the Province of Nova Scotia had both asked the RCMP to investigate the possibility of sabotage. Naturally enough, the RCMP was concerned that this could be a new chapter of Cold War type activity.

It turned out that there had been acts of sabotage, but not from foreign agents. The Glace Bay sabotage was caused by some of the workers themselves, who wanted to keep the construction project alive for as long as they possibly could, to keep their jobs alive. The overtime pay issue hadn't been thought of in advance, but once it had become obvious that there was money for this, it just provided an extra inducement to continue to sabotage things. Ultimately, the RCMP had discovered the people behind the sabotage and foiled their plans but hadn't found enough evidence to be able to press charges. The files on the people concerned were kept open, but otherwise, the saboteurs lost their jobs but avoided prosecution. With construction progress restored, the Glace Bay plant was finally completed and had only just commenced production when I was reading the report (that is, in 1976, eight years behind schedule).

After some of my preliminary orientation and training in procedures had been completed, Bob got around to discussing me and my role. He explained that they were developing a few people that they could send out, inconspicuously, to investigate suspicious circumstances or patterns, in cases for which formal investigations, by regular Members, whether uniformed or plain-clothed, would be unproductive, or even counter-productive. From time to time, he said, I would probably get a chance to meet some of the others.

In my case, both Bob and Assistant Commissioner MacLeod were interested in the possibilities presented by the first female 'Mountie.' They were also interested in, and seemingly amused, by the potential of me having Silver along as a kind of side-kick.

"If that dog is going to go everywhere with you, then we should get him trained too," Assistant Commissioner MacLeod decided, on one of his periodic visits to see how my orientation was coming along.

"First, we'll get him trained as a regular police dog," Bob said. "You too, since we train dogs and their handlers together. But the idea is not for him to serve as a regular police dog. It might be an advantage for us that he doesn't look like a police dog. Despite the Hollywood image, it's pretty well known that all our regular dogs are German Shepherds, so having Silver trained could provide us with an undercover advantage.

"Our dogs usually go into training when they're about a year and a half old," Bob continued, "but, in this case, we'll make an exception. In addition to his regular training, I'd like to see if Silver can be trained to detect explosives. In our line of work that could turn out to be very handy.

"The Dog Service Training Centre is part of Depot Division, but it's located at Innisfail, Alberta, which is about an hour's drive north of Calgary. Basic dog and handler training will take about four months, and along the way, we'll get him tested to see if he meets the requirements for explosives training. If he does, you two can stay on for that too."

Eventually, my orientation and initial training in the Security Service were complete. I wasn't issued a bunch of 'James Bond' or 'CIA-type' gadgets, although I supposed that they had access to such things. I was issued a snub-nosed Smith & Wesson .38 Special revolver, which I hadn't expected. It made sense though. It was much smaller, and easier to conceal than my regular-issue service revolver (which had a 5.5-inch barrel). It sure wasn't very accurate though. It was hard enough to shoot accurately with a long-barrel revolver. The snub-nosed version was lighter and easier to hold steady, but it was a close-range weapon at best. Anyway, Bob had two more surprises in store for me, which he'd held for our last face-to-face meeting before I left to head out west.

"Let's discuss your cover story," he'd said. That was the first surprise.

"My cover story?" I asked, "Do I need a cover story when I'm working with our own people?"

"Sometimes, yes," Bob said, firmly. "The fewer people that know what you're up to when you're working on cases, the better. It's safer for you that way too."

"But I don't even know what I'll be doing after the dog service training, so I can't very well spill the beans to anyone, can I?"

"No, you can't," said Bob, chuckling, "and before you get mad, I don't know what your first real assignment will be either – we'll see what's going on in the world when the time comes. But, let's not give anyone too many ideas about you just yet."

"Here's your cover story: When you go out to Alberta, you can talk about everything up to and including your recent posting in Radium City. If you're pressed, you can say that you've been transferred to HQ Division in Ottawa – that's a bit misleading but still true. You're going to get some questions about the Dog Service training. That's unavoidable because we're shoving you down their throats, outside of their normal selection process for dog handlers, and of course, Silver is obviously not our usual choice of breed. So, when the topic comes up, just say you're a pilot project of Assistant Commissioner MacLeod's, and that the idea is to have you and Silver be trained so that you can be used as an inconspicuous part of our diplomatic protective service."

"Is that what we'll be doing?" I asked.

"Who knows?" Bob replied, chuckling again. "For all I know, it could turn out to be true! Seriously, if you get questioned too closely, just play dumb and refer people to Assistant Commissioner MacLeod, or to me. That should shut them up."

So, my next steps were going to be to head back to Saskatchewan, pack and pick-up Silver, and then the two of us would be ... "*Alberta bound*," as they say.

The second surprise? Oh, yes, Bob also gave me a bunch more historical cases to take away with me and read while travelling to my new posting in Alberta. Since the case summaries were all marked "Top Secret," they were given to me in a special combination-locked briefcase that contained an explosive charge designed to incinerate the contents if anyone tried to force the locks. Bob then dryly suggested to me – really, I'm not making this up - that I take care not to enter the wrong combination, for my own safety!

2 ALBERTA AND THE 'OIL BOOM'

I love all of Canada's provinces and territories, for their similarities, and also for their differences. If you compare Canada to other countries, then many aspects of our culture and geography are similar right across the country. If you look a bit deeper, though, many aspects of culture and geography are different in every single region of the country. Among the many things that are unique to Alberta, was the effects of what would later be called the '*1970s Oil Crisis*,' and the '*1970s Oil Boom*.'

To explain this, I need to back-up a bit. The first major oil discovery in Alberta was in 1947, at Imperial Oil's "Leduc No. 1" well, near the town of Leduc. This got the Alberta oil industry started, but the real frenzy arrived in the mid-1970s, almost thirty years later. The fall of 1973 had marked the beginning of the fourth Arab-Israeli (Yom Kippur) War, and oil, or at least the supply of oil, become a weapon of war. A series of announcements from the Organization of Petroleum Exporting Countries (OPEC) involved oil price increases, production cuts, and an embargo against Israel and countries, like the U.S., that were judged by OPEC to be supporting Israel. This created the 1970s Oil Crisis, and it led to dramatic price increases. Whereas in 1972, the international price for a barrel of light crude oil was about US$3.60, by 1974 it had nearly tripled, to US$9.35, and by now in 1976, it had nearly quadrupled, to US$13.10.

The U.S., like most of the western industrialized countries, was unprepared for the consequences of the oil embargo. As a result, they'd had to impose gas rationing, with gas-rationing stamps, long lines at gas stations, and bizarre practices, like only allowing drivers of vehicles with odd-numbered license plates to buy gasoline on odd-numbered days, and drivers with even-numbered plates on even-numbered days. We in Canada had been spared the rationing because our federal government had imposed export controls to ensure that shipments of oil to the U.S. didn't disrupt our domestic supplies. Not only were we able to keep the oil (and therefore gasoline), flowing in Canada, we were in no danger of running out of oil for generations yet to come. That benefit came courtesy of our huge oil sands deposits, which were only beginning to become developed, and which by themselves contained over six-hundred billion barrels of bitumen (an extra-heavy oil) – more oil than there was in Ghawar, Saudi Arabia, the world's largest conventional oilfield. So, it wasn't really an oil crisis for us.

We weren't immune to market forces though. Down in the U.S., they'd brought-in new fuel economy standards, leading to a series of new domestic- and foreign-built small cars, and this affected vehicles available in Canada as well. Drivers wanting more space and more powerful engines tended to move toward trucks, which were not as strongly affected by the new regulations.

Taken together, the biggest 'Oil Boom' changes being experienced in Alberta were inflation and a boom in oil exploration and oil developments, like the oil sands, and that meant lots of new jobs. For young adults looking for work, Alberta had become 'the' place to be, whether they'd grown up in the prairie provinces, Cape Breton Island, or Newfoundland and Labrador. Having a province full of young adults that suddenly had high-paying jobs had led, in turn, to an entire culture of *'work hard – play hard.'* It's probably not surprising then, that many young men, and some young women, had begun to collect and display 'toys.' These spanned the range from trucks, to boats, to snowmobiles, and almost anything else that was 'noisy, expensive, and unnecessary.' Of all of these, probably the most evident to a new visitor was the proliferation of pickup trucks - big, expensive, gas-guzzling pickup trucks.

For myself, I wasn't drawn into the collecting of expensive toys. I once saw a bumper sticker that read *Whoever has the most toys when he dies – Wins!*

But I did fall prey to the temptation to buy a truck.

***

*"If you should be in Rome, live in the Roman manner;
if you should be elsewhere, live as they do there."*
St. Ambrose, Bishop of Milan, 387 C.E.

The RCMP Police Dog Service Training Centre was a part of Depot Division but located on its own grounds just outside of Innisfail, Alberta, a small, quiet town located a couple of miles south of the city of Red Deer, and about seventy miles north of Calgary. It was not too different from other small towns sprinkled across the Western Prairies, except for its proximity and good highway access to the Rocky Mountains, which lay in plain sight, due west. Being 'ranch country,' with activities like amateur and professional rodeo being highly popular, it felt like 'truck central,' in a province that was full of trucks.

Silver and I had moved to Alberta from Radium City in northern Saskatchewan, where Ruby Gillespie, a friend from my previous posting, had been looking after Silver and some of my clothes and stuff. We'd moved in an old car that had been on its 'last legs' before the trip, and the long highway drive hadn't done the car any favours. So, one of the first things I did in Alberta was to trade-in the car and buy a brand-new pickup truck. Although I wanted the ruggedness of a truck, I also wanted a large truck, so it would have a large, sheltered, heated space.

I may have been influenced in this, by the fact that we'd moved in January, the middle of winter, and southern Alberta had just been hit with a blast of minus forty-degree Celsius weather. Canada was still struggling into the metric system in the 1970s and had only started to change weather reporting the previous year, so the radio stations were often giving weather information in both systems. Minus forty is the one temperature for which the two temperature scales give the same number, and the week we moved all we heard on the radio was announcers having fun with this, saying, for example: "Minus forty-degrees Celsius! That's minus forty-degrees Fahrenheit for all of you old people that have trouble converting to metric!"

Anyway, as I said, I'd wanted a larger truck cab so I'd have room for Silver with the extra enclosed space, and so it would be nice in bad weather and cold winters. To me, that meant getting an extended cab. I chose a 1976 Chevy Cheyenne, 4-door crew-cab, pickup truck.

It was Crimson Red, with white trim. This was a big, heavy, ¾-ton truck, with 4-wheel drive and some key options. Factory installed AM/FM radios had only been available since 1971, but by 1976 most people felt like they were a necessity. The 1976 model had the new dual front lap-and-shoulder safety belts with emergency locking retractors (instead of the old, inadequate lap belts), and the front brakes had been switched from drum brakes to disc brakes, which provided higher performance braking (without the brake-fade that had characterized earlier models).

Silver seemed to get a kick out of the big crew-cab and made a point of going to each of the three passenger doors in turn, pawing for me to open the windows, and then hanging his head out of each one. When we took the truck for a test-drive, he seemed highly amused by his ability to take over the back seat and alternate hanging out of the windows on each side. When I commented to him that he seemed to have enjoyed the test-drive, he gave me a big wolfly grin and one of his meaningful wide-eyed looks that always made me wonder just how much of my thoughts and speech he actually understood.

With my new truck, I seemed to fit right into the Alberta culture. If young men were to ask me about my truck, and they did, I remained silent on the safety features that had impressed me, and instead I would rattle off 'male-interest' features like my 400-cubic inch V-8 engine, 4-by-4 drive drain with manual-locking hubs, and six thousand pounds of towing capacity, which seemed to impress them to no end. (I drew the line, however, at opening beer bottles with my bare teeth, so I did leave some room for macho one-upmanship.)

***

While I was settling into Innisfail, elsewhere in Alberta, and unbeknownst to me, trouble was brewing in Fort McMurray. Someone sent a series of letters to the Presidents of both Great Canadian Oil Sands ('GCOS') and Syncrude Canada Ltd., warning them to shut down their oil sand operations (or construction, in the case of Syncrude), and to leave Alberta. These letters were hand-written - printed really - in a childish script. Here are some of the key phrases that I was shown later, from transcripts of the notes:

"GCOS and Syncrude you have until May 9th of 1976 (Sunday 12:00 NOON) to close down your GCOS operations and your Syncrude construction and leave the area until further notice."

"We will not negotiate with you on tar sand [sic] activities as you keep on endangering our families with crazy expansion of deadly facilities. FULL STOP!!"

"We are done with talking. As you have clearly decided to continue to disrupt our lands and our quality of life we give you this last chance to stop operations volontarily [sic]."

"Don't let yur [sic] pride and greed force us to stop you. DON'T DELAY!!"

Apparently, one of the Presidents had contacted the other and discovered that each company had received similar letters. They didn't react much to these at first, but when several more arrived over a period of six weeks, they contacted the RCMP. I was told later, that when the GCOS President had spoken with my boss, Staff Sergeant Simpson, in Ottawa, he'd said that at first, he didn't take the threats too seriously: "First thing, you say to yourself, okay, now we've got a wing-nut in the area. But later, you start thinking, can I take the chance that this person isn't serious?"

The two company Presidents had asked the RCMP to investigate but otherwise to keep the existence of the letters secret for the time being. So, nothing was made public, but the RCMP Security Service did start an investigation, aided by the closest Detachment, which was in Fort McMurray.

3 K-9 TRAINING FOR TWO

"WHAT THE HELL ARE YOU DOING HERE?"

That's what I'd expected to hear. That had been my greeting when I had reported for training at the RCMP's Depot Division training centre in Regina, and pretty much the same words had greeted me when I had reported for my first posting in Radium City Saskatchewan. In both cases, it had been due to the shock of unexpectedly meeting the first woman Mountie.

Now, as Silver and I reported for training at the RCMP's Police Dog Service (PDS) Training Centre just outside of Innisfail, I'd expected to have to go through this routine once more. Between my being the only female in the Force, and Silver being an Alaskan Malamute rather than a German Shepherd, I thought that we were going to be a novelty at best. But I was wrong.

It was obvious that they'd already received their orders regarding training Silver and me, as we were expected, and I was quickly passed from main reception to the Officer in Charge (OIC), Inspector Lawrence (Larry) J. Walsh. In my Depot Division training, all the commissioned officers I'd encountered were of the 'spit and polish' variety: very formal, very superior, and very correct in all things. Insp. Walsh's demeanour was much more engaging.

"Call me Larry," he'd said as we shook hands. "I know that I can count on you to address me formally in front of others, and especially in public, but when it's just us working together 'Larry' will do me just fine. You'll find that we're a pretty close-knit bunch around here."

"Thank you, Sss… Larry," I replied, "and please call me Alex."

(I'd been introduced to him as Constable Houston, Alexandra, Regimental #15425.)

I was struck by the fact that Insp. Walsh took time to meet and greet Silver, in addition to me, and that he invited me to bring Silver along into his office. I was beginning to realize that we were really going to like it here.

In his introduction to the dog training centre, Insp. Walsh explained that dogs had a long history of being used in the Force, but that an organized police dog selection and training program had only begun in the RCMP in 1935. Nevertheless, it was (and is) the longest standing police dog program in Canada.

"The PDS Centre has four essential functions," he continued, "acquiring the best dogs, acquiring the best handlers, training the dog and handler teams, and regular re-testing and re-training of the teams, as needed."

"Acquiring the best handlers?"

"Absolutely. Just like not all dogs are suitable to be police dogs, not all humans are suitable to be handlers. The first requirement is that they must be interested enough to volunteer for this service. Beyond that, they must be physically fit, highly motivated, require almost no supervision, and have a genuine love for animals. Dogs in particular." Then, looking directly at me for a moment, he added, "I had a long chat with Assistant Commissioner MacLeod ..."

My eyebrows shot up.

"Yes," he smiled, "it's a small world in the Force, and George and I go back a long way. He was in the senior troop when I started training at Depot, and our paths seem to keep crossing as our careers have advanced. In any case, he's convinced that you have what it takes for this, and his judgement is good enough for me."

"Thank you," I said, gratefully.

"You'll still have to prove yourselves to your colleagues though," he warned. "I know the people in my team here, and none of them will hold it against you that you're a woman, or that Silver's not a German Shepherd. What they'll be watching for, is to see how you perform - together. That's all that counts here."

I must have looked a bit worried at this point, because he smiled again, and said, "Look, I'm not trying to scare you. We don't bite here (that's a dog handler's joke by the way). You're going to find that we have a very private group of people that love their animals, have a passion for their work, and take a quiet pride in the work that we do.

"There aren't many dog handlers in the Force, only 62 out of our total strength of over 11,600 Members, not including civilian Members, of course. That sets us apart a bit, and our work is quite different too[6]. A dog handler and dog have to work very independently. It's kind of like Hollywood's *Lone Ranger* stories in that a team gets sent-in somewhere, they do their job, they hopefully 'save the day,' and then they quietly disappear.

"Another thing about this job is that you don't have a boss breathing down your neck all the time. For most of our dog handlers, that independence is part of the job's appeal." Seeing me smiling, he paused at this point, and then continued, "I take it that all this is striking a chord, Alex?"

"Yes, Sirrr… Larry," I responded, "I'm not a fan of paperwork, or of routine work. That's mostly why I left the Metro Toronto Force to join the RCMP."

"There you go. You've got another thing in common with us already."

He paused again, as if gathering his thoughts, and then continued, "We normally look for three- to seven years of street policing before coming to the PDS, and between your Metro Toronto experience and your first year with the Force, you're OK on that score too.

"You'll begin with some PARE testing. PARE stands for Physical Abilities Requirements Exam and is part of the selection process for prospective dog handlers. You won't need to pass it on the first try, but we'll use it to figure out where you need some extra work. You will have to pass it before you're done here. We'll put Silver through some tests as well, but we'll be testing his character more than his physical abilities. From there, you'll go on to the basic police dog and handler training. We also have a whole range of specialty programs, such as narcotics detection, explosives detection, search and rescue, emergency response (tactical, riot, SWAT team), and so on, but I gather it'll be the Explosives Detection course for you two. For that, you'll also need an explosives training course, but we offer that on-site here as well."

Insp. Walsh next took me to meet my trainer, Sergeant William (Bill) Preston. Bill Preston was medium height, lean, and soft-spoken, very much like the Hollywood stereotype of a cowboy. He was perceptive too, and quickly read the expression that crossed my face while we were being introduced.

"I know what you're thinking," he said. "When I was quite young, I saw the TV series *Sergeant Preston of the Yukon*, and I was fascinated with the characters of Sergeant Preston the Mountie, Yukon King his faithful dog - who looked quite a bit like Silver by the way, and his horse Rex."

"With a name like Preston," Bill continued, "I strongly identified with his character and I often imagined myself as the Mountie, chasing the bad guys. Those images always stayed with me, and as I grew up, I resolved to follow the same path." He paused in thought for a moment, then said "Anyway, I joined up as soon as I was old enough, and I transferred to the dog service as soon as I could... I've been a dog-handler ever since."

Sgt. William (Bill) Preston

"And you're even a sergeant now, too," I supplied.

"For my sins, yes, I really am Sergeant Preston now. I really got everything I wanted, except the horse," he laughed. "It's probably just as well, because I've always gotten along well with dogs, but I never really connected with any of the horses during my equitation training at Depot Division. Talking about it still reminds me of how many times those horses bucked me off, and it makes my back ache."

"What do you like best about being a dog-handler?" I'd asked.

Without hesitation, he responded, "I like the action. I like independence. I like the hunt. Before I transferred to PDS, I was always chomping at the bit for opportunities to do 'real police work' and I'd start moving as soon as a call came in. With the dog service, it's often less excitement and more about 'the hunt' though. The most heart-wrenching are the searches for lost children, even when we're successful, but for me, the most challenging, and the most rewarding, are hunting for criminals that are fleeing, but cunning. There's a famous quote from Hemingway about hunting humans, especially armed humans: they are the riskiest, the most difficult, and ultimately, the most rewarding of the hunts."

As I moved into my new training phase and met the rest of the staff, I found that the other dog handlers had very similar stories. They all loved dogs, and I would hear comments like "I always enjoyed being around dogs," and "Dogs always seem to like me." Although they were a pretty soft-spoken bunch, they all seemed to share Bill's interests in the job, and they all exuded a quiet camaraderie and professionalism that I found to be very engaging.

I had thought that I was still in pretty good physical condition. Wrong again. I failed the PARE testing, although thankfully I came pretty close to passing. They took it in good humour, and simply added more exercise into my routine. I hadn't taken it in particularly good humour, but I'll admit that I did cheer-up when I discovered that the other three dog-handler trainees hadn't passed yet either.

Other than the extra exercises we now needed to do, Silver and I launched into our training program, which comprised a combination of skills and teamwork development. For most of these, we worked with a trainer and a 'quarry.' A quarry is essentially a future dog-handler in training. It was the quarry that would lay scent tracks and hide search articles for Silver and me to find. A quarry would also role-play a 'criminal' to be tracked, or apprehended, or that might turn and try to attack us.

Although Hollywood portrayals of police dogs sometimes involve them vigorously attacking and injuring people, RCMP dogs, at least, are trained only to grab and hold a quarry, never to attack with intent to injure. Similarly, RCMP dogs are trained to defend their handler, but only to use the amount of force necessary for defence, not attack. These matched Silver's natural instincts very well, and in any case, I'm sure that he would have flat-out refused any attempt to train him to be vicious.

I had been worried about how well Silver would do at detecting and following scents, but I clearly need not have worried. In tracking practice, I was amazed at how well Silver could perform based on small amounts of scented material: a few drops of blood, a worn piece of clothing or shoe, and sometimes even items that had been burned in an attempt to disguise the scent. Similarly, he could track with a fairly strong wind blowing, although he would slow down and gather more input at every location he tried to sniff, and sometimes he could even track in the pouring rain. Bill told me that Silver's 'nose' and tracking instincts weren't the best he'd ever seen, but that they were more than sufficient. That was a relief. I suppose he'd inherited enough of his wolf ancestry.

As our training advanced, and as Bill and I became better acquainted, he would sometimes allow himself to be drawn into telling police dog stories from the past. These stories were always fascinating, and sometimes quite humorous.

In one episode, an off-duty dog-handler and his partner were walking along the side of a farmer's field when they encountered a man searching for something in the ditch between the road and the field. Upon asking him what he was doing, the man replied that he had lost his wallet while walking along this route earlier that same day, and that he had returned to search for it. The dog-handler decided to help the man out, and use the opportunity as a training practice, so he let his dog sniff the man to 'catch the scent,' and the two of them proceeded to search. Before long, the dog found what the man had really lost: not his wallet, but a complete set of (illegal) burglar's tools. The man was arrested, charged, and convicted.

Being true to life, some of the stories were very sad of course … I'll spare you those.

Some of the other stories were of the kind you would probably expect, success stories, but they usually contained a twist of some kind. In one story, for example, a dog and dog-handler had tracked a suspected drug-dealer deep into the Rocky Mountain forests of Northern British Columbia. Not only had they found the suspect after an exhausting search through the forest, but they also recovered a substantial quantity of illegal drugs on the suspect's person. But the story wasn't over yet. It turned out that the chase had been more than just exhausting for the suspect, and he was suffering from hypothermia when they'd finally tracked him down. So, they didn't just find him, and the evidence, they rescued him too and ended up saving the suspect's life. Naturally, I liked these kinds of stories the best, and I often thought that Silver did too – as his intelligent, glowing eyes would so closely watch Bill's face as he told these stories. I remember wondering, and not for the first time, just how much of our speech and thoughts Silver could understand.

***

Lick, lick, lick …

I was afraid of big dogs when I was a little girl. I was probably about five- or six years old when a new family moved in next door to us with what, to my young self, looked like a huge brown, furry elephant. It was a St. Bernard, and it was certainly much larger than I was at the time.

I know now that it was really just a very friendly dog (in the shape of a monster), but it had a very deep and loud "Woof, Woof, Woof" kind of bark, that frightened me. When the dog got close, it would slobber all over me … 'Yuck.' It would even slobber on me just by shaking its huge head – in which case streams of slobber would come right through the spaces between the boards in our backyard fence. Did I mention 'Yuck!' ?

***

Silver

Lick, lick, lick.

Here I was again with a big dog, his forepaws up on my lap, arching his body up to lick every part of my face that he could get at. But there were differences. This was Silver, who had once saved my life and was now a close friend and constant companion.

Another difference was that I was much older now, at age 25, and I realized that that huge, scary, St. Bernard of my youth was probably just trying to make friends in the only noisy, bumbling way that he knew how. Even with this revelation, I still much preferred Silver, with whom I'd developed such a special bond.

Now, Silver and I were nearing the end of our mutual K-9 training.

Pictures of police dog training courses often show a dog navigating a complicated obstacle course while their handler stands nearby, so it looks like the dog is learning how to make all the right maneuvers. This conjures up the Hollywood movie images of a bunch of army recruits working their way through an obstacle course. In this case, though, the obstacle course isn't there to teach dogs how to climb up and over, or through various obstacles: they instinctively know how to do those things. In our case, the course was there so that the dog and handler could practice working together in distracting terrain. An example would be having the handler send the dog in to search for something, having both handler and dog maintain awareness of each other's location, and have the dog return promptly when recalled.

The strange thing with Silver was that he seemed to learn almost all the commands and exercises as fast as they could be introduced, and he seldom needed to repeat a training exercise more than once. This mystified our instructors, but I'd gotten so used to him that I hadn't really noticed. From our very first meeting, I'd had the sense that he could sense my thoughts. I'd guessed that he was sensing mental images rather than words, of course, and I had no idea how he was doing it, but there was a consistent pattern with him that I could not explain. I certainly didn't discuss it with anyone else, lest I be thought crazy and kicked off the Force! I told our trainers that I was just lucky that he'd been so well trained before we took the course, but they still looked at him strangely and wondered.

Anyway, in our training exercises, by the time the two of us were taught the proper commands and the exercise sequences, he'd already know what to do. In fact, I'd developed an uneasy feeling that the rate-limiting factor in our training was my rate of learning rather than his. The commands themselves seemed to serve, at best, as a way of getting his attention and making sure we were both on the same page.

The modern fashion of dog training was to use positive reinforcement for good behaviour and particularly for obeying commands and successfully completing tasks. For this, effusive praise and treats were used, the idea being that the dogs would eventually connect the desired behaviours with the rewards so much that they would continue the behaviours even without the praise and treats. I couldn't help feeling that this was a bit of an insult to Silver's intelligence, but he seemed to respond to these methods every bit as eagerly as the other dogs in our class.

After a while, though, I became suspicious that he was playing at being a bit slow on the uptake now and again, in order to get more repetitive training, which would produce extra treats. Sure enough, one day we'd been practising an exercise that really wasn't difficult but which he'd not been getting quite right, and in exasperation I looked at him and said, "Silver, if I'd didn't know any better, I'd think you were playing dumb just to get extra treats!"

At this, he stopped what he was doing, sat on his haunches, and looked up at me with those piercing blue-grey eyes of his, then opened his mouth and let his tongue loll out in a big toothy grin as if to say: "*Heh, heh, heh* ..." Our discussion degenerated from there.

It's a good thing we'd been out of sight and hearing of anyone else. When our instructor and quarry did approach over a nearby hill, they were amused to see the two of us play-wrestling and rolling around in the sand and January snow of the training course.

Beyond skills training, we did lots of scenario training too. One night, we were woken up in the middle of the night, at my apartment. We were given only a few minutes to get ready, and then taken out and walked far into the bush somewhere out of town. There was no need for blindfolds, as it was pitch black outside. We didn't know the area, and I couldn't see anything anyway. We were simply told to wait ten minutes, then find our way back! The ten-minute wait gave me time to 'take stock,' but our stocks were meagre. I had my tactical uniform on, with parka, boots, and gloves (it was late February, so winter had not yet given up). Other than that, I had my watch and a Swiss-Army combination knife that I almost always carried with me, but that was about all. I had no compass, no visible moon, and no wind or even breeze, any of which might have given us some clue about direction, or at least a means of not walking around in circles.

At least I had Silver with me, and as the two of us slowly walked around the small clearing into which we had been dropped, I saw that there were many pathways out, and each of them had been well trampled so it wasn't going to be as easy as following someone's boot-prints. With no obvious clues as to which way to go, I decided that I'd have to trust Silver's nose and instincts. I thought back to the advice our trainers and quarries had uniformly given me:

"Pay attention to what the dog is trying to tell you."

"Be patient. Force yourself to work at the dog's speed."

Kneeling down beside Silver, I looked deep into his eyes and said: "Find the way home, Silver, we need to go home."

Several times in the past year that I'd known him, we'd 'had a moment' where our thoughts met and aligned in mutual recognition. This was another of those times. There was a kind of mental spark or connection, and then he lifted-up from where he'd been sitting and led me forward. He re-traced our circuit of the clearing, but this time stopped at each pathway and sniffed all around it, the path itself, the nearby bushes and weeds, and the occasional tree. Then he would advance to the next pathway and do it again, pushing his muzzle down into the trampled snow when he needed to. As he repeated this process at each of the pathways, in turn, I realized that our trainers must have purposely trampled them to remove any visible markers, and confuse me, and to create multiple scent trails at each, to confuse Silver.

"Clever," I said out loud. "They've created a maze for us, and they've laid false scent trails," and then to Silver: "Follow the strongest scent, Silver, … the strongest scent."

Without hesitation, Silver padded diagonally across the clearing from where we were, paused at one of the pathways, looked straight at me and barked twice, "Gruphh, Gruphh."

"OK," I said, "lead on," and automatically gave the hand-signal for 'track,' even though he didn't really need it.

From then on, it was fairly easy. I let Silver set the pace and gave him the time he needed to carefully sniff-out each fork in the path, after which he'd pick one and look up at me. I'd nod OK, and we'd proceed to the next. After what seemed like a couple of hours, but was really only about thirty minutes, we emerged to find Bill and several other trainers and quarries waiting for us with a congratulatory thermos of hot chocolate for me, and a bowl of water for Silver. We passed, of course. The time to find our way out wasn't considered important, only that we'd worked together as a team and hadn't needed to be rescued. Apparently, not all prospective teams succeeded at the 'forest maze' test.

More difficult was explosives training.

***

I'd been interested in science since the age of about twelve, and I had been influenced by the Hollywood depictions of scientists as being intelligent, knowledgeable, logical, and of course, able to save the day. This interest remained with me in later years, and I eventually majored in chemistry in university. While I was mostly interested in learning what made things work the way they did, a few of my student colleagues seemed mostly interested in making explosives (and later went on to join the military), while another colleague was mostly interested in making drugs (and later ended up in jail).

Most of us enjoyed learning to synthesize familiar things, like acetylsalicylic acid (better known under the trade-name 'Aspirin'), and ascorbic acid (Vitamin C), and even some minor explosives, like nitrogen tri-iodide. Nitrogen tri-iodide is interesting because in its normal crystalline form it is a very sensitive contact explosive – some people call it 'touch-powder.' Even quite small amounts of it will explode with a satisfyingly loud 'pop' when touched lightly, and the subsequent reaction produces an impressive, purple-coloured cloud of iodine vapour.

One of the ways to make nitrogen tri-iodide involves iodine, ammonia, and water. The resulting solution in water can be spread over a surface, like a petri dish, and when the water evaporates, it leaves behind a layer of nitrogen tri-iodide crystals. A popular 'chemical magic show' trick is to take a feather and touch it to the crystals, producing the explosion and purple vapour cloud. This was fun to watch, and fun to perform.

One of my colleagues with the explosives interests, however, took this to the extreme. Reasoning that if a little bit was fun, a lot of it would be a lot of fun, he made a huge batch in the lab one Sunday afternoon when the Chemistry Building was quiet. - Don't do this, by the way, it's very dangerous, which is why I'm not providing the instructions here. – Anyway, he then proceeded to paint the final solution along the main stairways and hallways of the Chemistry Building and then waited for Monday morning, by which time the crystals would be in place and the morning rush of students would provide the detonation contacts.

As I entered the building that morning, I heard bursts of loud popping noises, accompanied by squeals of surprise from several women students. My suspicions about the nature of the pops were confirmed when I saw that the floor in the hallway where I had entered, was covered in purple blotches. Needless to say, this episode was the source of much merriment on the part of the students, quiet amusement on the part of the faculty, and anger and condemnation on the part of the department's administration. The custodial staff would have been angry too, except that the administration rather quickly identified the amateur bomb maker, and for many days thereafter we would encounter him crouched in the stairwells and hallways, scrubbing out the purple iodine stains with a small brush and a bucket of sodium thiosulfate solution. A little chemical research of my own proved that this was more about punishment than clean-up because a simpler way to remove the stains is to do nothing and wait – the iodine would have eventually all sublimed, that is, changed form from a solid to a gas and simply diffused away leaving the floors clean. The last I heard, my colleague had joined the military, in search of a more legitimate way to pursue his explosive interests.

***

All that's needed to make an explosive device is to mix a suitable oxidizer with a suitable fuel, and then add a detonator. Once the device has been placed, the detonator just needs to be triggered to start the reaction going, and it should go 'boom.'

My university chemistry training had taught me several ways to make things explode, but we had well-equipped chemistry labs at our disposal. When I took the RCMP's explosives training course, we learned how people made them at home and I was surprised at the variety of explosives that can be made from materials that are fairly easy to obtain from pharmacies and hardware stores. I'd never given much thought to detonators before, but it turns out that they're pretty easy to make too.

The biggest shock for me was learning that with a bit of training and diligence, and quite a lot of luck, even amateurs can make what can only be described as 'military grade' explosives. I mention luck here because doing this 'at home,' with crude equipment and materials is incredibly dangerous.

My explosives training focused on three areas: the kinds of explosives and detonators that can be made, their destructive nature and power, and the kinds of raw materials for making them that can be acquired and used by amateurs. This last component, the raw materials, was taught so we'd know what to look for if we were ever searching for an explosives-making operation.

Silver's training was focused on learning the scents of the explosive materials, and their post-blast residues.

***

In May, while Silver and I were completing our explosives training, the trouble that had been brewing in Fort McMurray reached the boiling point. Someone (presumably the same someone that had sent the threatening letters to the two oil sand company Presidents), set off a bomb at an exposed section of the product pipeline (containing synthetic crude oil, SCO) that ran between the GCOS plant (where it was produced) and refineries in Edmonton. The explosion ruptured the pipeline and created an oil spill until the flow could be shut off, but fortunately, the leaked oil did not catch fire. The explosion was, however, powerful enough to create a blast hole about ten feet wide by eight feet deep.

This incident did make the news, causing media reporters and some members of the public to question the safety of these giant bitumen processing installations in Canada, especially with a second such plant currently under construction by Syncrude. The next day, the local RCMP

*called a press conference to state that they believed that the public was safe,
while at the same time admitting that it would be very difficult to protect
the huge expanse of area covered by the north-south pipeline. The RCMP
spokesperson also stated that they believed that it was an isolated act of
sabotage by a single, unknown person or group.*

*A week later, and once again unknown to the public, another series of
threatening letters was sent to the two companies' Presidents. There were
very similar in style and message to the previous letters, leading my
(Ottawa) boss, Staff Sergeant Simpson, to conclude that they were the
work of the same person or persons as before. They were sent to the same
Presidents as before, were hand-printed in the same or similar childish
script, chided them for failing to heed the previous warnings, re-stated the
warnings, and promised dire consequences for continuing to operate. These
latest letters also contained a new deadline for ceasing operations, saying
"GCOS and Syncrude you have until September 5th of 1976 (Sunday
12:00 NOON) to close down your operations and leave the area."*

*That gave the RCMP until the Labour Day Weekend to try to find,
and stop, our saboteur.*

***

Silver and I were about to head out for a day of quarry-hunting
when the office received a rush telex instructing me to call-in
immediately. When I called Staff Sergeant Simpson in Ottawa, he
filled me in on what had been going on with the oil sands sites.
Reaching the end of his summary, he concluded by saying, "The
official investigation is underway, and we're checking for any
possible connection to foreign agencies or extremist groups, but it's
time for us to send someone inside as well."

"You think it's an inside job?" I asked, surprised.

"Probably not, but we have to consider all of the possibilities."

"That will be like looking for a needle in a haystack, they must
have hundreds of employees working up there."

"More like a thousand, between the operating plant and the one
that's under construction, but I want you to go in and sniff around
anyway. Both sites are potential targets, and both have been
threatened, but an operating plant will get more attention than one
that is only under construction, so the odds are higher that GCOS

will be the one our saboteur chooses. Even if you don't come up with any suspects, I want an independent view of the operation, culture, and vulnerabilities, so I want you to go in undercover."

"OK, when do I start?" I'd asked.

"Right away! Pack up now and drive up there tomorrow. Get yourself a place in Fort McMurray, and within a day or two we'll have a job lined up for you with GCOS."

"That's quick work," I commented.

"All the machinery is in motion around here," he replied. "The GCOS and Syncrude Presidents know we're sending someone in, but not who or where. The only person that will know about you specifically, is the GCOS Vice President responsible for personnel. 'Human Resources,' they call it now. Anyway, they'd already been recruiting for a job in their safety department, so they're going to call me every time they receive an application for it. When you've applied, I'll tell them to hire you."

"Wow!"

"Wow is right, so write up a spontaneous application for a job. Tell them that you heard from a friend that they're hiring in the safety area. Include your actual resume, right up to the point where you left the Metro Toronto Police. Instead of joining the Force, we'll say that you went to work for a security company in Toronto. Right after this call I'll send you a telex with a reference name and phone number at a large, well-known security company. If anyone should call that number and name, they will reach a duty officer here in Ottawa, who will have a script handy, so they can role-play your 'former supervisor,' 'confirm' your employment at the security firm and give a good reference for your work there."

My mind was now racing as I tried to keep up and think it all through. "What reason will they give for my leaving?" I asked.

Bob laughed, "We're going to say that your security job involved sitting at a front desk on the main floor of a downtown Toronto high-rise office building for a Bay Street accounting firm. You found it boring, so you decided to try something new and went off to Alberta to look for something more interesting. Somewhere out of the big city. Now," he added, still chuckling, "does that sound like you?"

"It sounds like me," I agreed, smiling to myself.

"It gets better," he added. "You can list your former Captain at Metro Toronto as a reference. If they call him, he's been sworn to secrecy and briefed on the story to give if he's called. He was very pleased to learn how well you've been doing and 'tickled' to be able to play a small role in what he calls our 'cloak and dagger' affair."

"What do I say about the safety job?"

"Always stay as close to the truth as you can," he advised. "It's easier to remember and easier to seem genuine. Just say that you don't know anything about the oil industry, or oil sands, or even safety, but that you're willing to learn and willing to relocate. That's all true, as far as it goes, and you'll be like hundreds of young people from across the country, flooding out to Alberta looking for a job and an adventure. Tell them you heard that GCOS was hiring, and offering to train people on the job, so you decided to take a chance. I'll send you the name and address to apply to. Meanwhile, get yourself up there and find a place to stay," he paused. "Are you still driving that old piece of junk you had when you were here in Ottawa?"

"No way!" I said and told him about the new truck.

"Better and better," he said, amused again. "You and Silver will fit right in. When you get the job at GCOS they'll put you on payroll and start paying you. You'll have to accept the pay, so it won't look suspicious." I could imagine him smiling his 'Cheshire Cat' grin.

"By the way," he concluded, "No one else will know about you, not even our Members in the Fort McMurray Detachment. If you need to convince someone who you really are, get them to call the same Ottawa number as your imaginary job reference, but have them give your name, Regimental Number, and a phone number to call back. The number is monitored continuously, day and night. The duty officer will find me, and I'll call back. If you need to reach me yourself, do the same thing... good luck!"

Laurie Schramm

4 FORT MCMURRAY

Fort McMurray is in Northern Alberta, about 270 miles north of Edmonton. Although the area had been used by Aboriginal people thousands of years earlier, the community of Fort McMurray itself had been launched much more recently, in the late 1700s. The European settlement had begun life as a trading-post and way-station for the Voyageurs of the Northwest Trading Company, as they and other adventurers passed by in their search for furs and adventure in the area. As the fur trading business waned in the late 1800s, the Hudson's Bay Company trading post endured, and Fort McMurray itself became an important transportation hub, with paddle-wheeled steamships and barges delivering freight and passengers headed for the Arctic, the northern territories, and northern parts of the prairie provinces. These activities increased when the railroad was extended to the nearby town of Waterways, in about 1920, and when the first commercial air services began, with Bush Planes in the 1930s.

In later years, several local industries had sprung up, including a commercial fishery, a salt plant, and numerous sawmills. Soon, it was well-served by highway, railways, and airlines. Although its population was relatively constant at about a thousand people throughout most of the 1950s and early '60s, it more than doubled in the late 1960s. It was over fifteen thousand now (in 1976) and still rapidly growing, with no obvious end to the boom in sight.

The nearby oil sands deposits had been well known to the local Aboriginal peoples, who had famously used the bitumen (an extremely viscous oil, much like asphalt) to waterproof canoes. Some of the first Europeans on the scene had drilled for oil, hoping to find conventional oil underneath the oil sand deposits. These 'business explorers' were disappointed, but others that came in the 1910s and 1920s sought to learn whether the oil sands themselves could be developed commercially. These latter pioneers, mostly geologists, chemists, and engineers, were somewhat more successful in that they proved that the bitumen could be extracted from the sand fairly easily. Nevertheless, commercial development would not occur until 1963, when Sun Oil had begun the Great Canadian Oil Sands[7] (GCOS) project at 'Tar Island,' about 25 miles north of Fort McMurray. GCOS was launched with an initial investment of almost a quarter of a billion dollars, and what some in the media had referred to as "the biggest gamble in history."

Construction at the GCOS site had begun in 1964, and continued through most of 1967, producing an open-pit oil sands mine, bitumen extraction plant, and an upgrading plant that was capable of producing 45,000 barrels per day of synthetic crude oil (SCO). By 1968, the first SCO had been produced and was being sent down the Interprovincial Pipe Line past Fort McMurray, to Edmonton, and all the way to Sarnia, Ontario, for refining. By 1972, the plant was producing 51,000 barrels per day, and further expansions were currently under development.

Although the massive construction workforce was long gone, the operating mine and processing plants employed over 450 permanent employees, with a host of maintenance and other jobs being provided by contractors. Adding to the workforce recruiting and retention challenges, was the fact that another company, Syncrude Canada Ltd., had been given the approval to construct a 125,000 barrel per day mine and processing operation at their 'Mildred Lake' site, which was literally just across the highway from the GCOS mine.

It wasn't long before GCOS, Fort McMurray, and essentially all of Alberta and Saskatchewan were to benefit from the famous 1970s oil boom, that I described earlier, and which drove expansions in exploration and developments of conventional crude oil, what Canada calls "heavy crude oil," and oil sands.

***

Having driven up to Fort McMurray with Silver, we set about getting acquainted with our new surroundings and looking for a place to stay. It was hard for me to avoid the normal protocol of promptly 'checking-in' with the local RCMP Detachment, but of course, we needed to remain anonymous.

I did fairly quickly luck out in my search for a place to rent. I found a condominium town-house that one of the oil sands workers had built as a source of rental income while also being a long-term investment. Geoff Laker seemed like a really nice guy and was particularly pleased to be renting to a fellow GCOS employee (I guessed that this helped ensure regular rent payments). He and his wife Karen had built two adjacent units, lived in one, and rented out the other.

The town-houses were somewhat unusual, in that they were very narrow but tall, three-stories tall. This meant that they only had a couple of rooms on each floor, and a LOT of stairs, but altogether they were quite spacious. Importantly, they had a little bit of yard and attached garage out front (important in the winter!), and a medium-size fenced yard in the back (great for Silver). Silver seemed to really like the stairs for some reason. He'd bound up one staircase, sniff around each room on that floor, then race up to the next floor and repeat the process, then go back down again and start over, as if he was on some kind of giant treasure hunt.

The best news was that Geoff and Karen were also dog lovers, had a dog of their own, and didn't mind their tenant having one. It turned out that Geoff was going to start working rotating shifts in the Upgrading plant, and they wanted someone to help look after their dog when he was working the evening (4 pm to midnight) shifts because Karen worked evenings as a restaurant manager in town. In return, Geoff offered to help look after Silver during the daytime on those days.

It was amusing to watch the two dogs get introduced. I had a big dog in the form of Silver, who was an Alaskan Malamute. Karen and Geoff had a Yorkie[8]-Havanese cross named Teddy, who was very small. Although Geoff said that Teddy wasn't too sure about most other dogs, especially other males, he and Silver seemed to connect immediately. Watching the two of them together reminded me of the Saturday morning cartoons of my youth, in which a tiny, hyperactive dog would run in circles around the large, more sedate dog. Within a few days, their mutual goodwill had developed into a positive friendship, to the surprise and pleasure of Geoff, Karen, and I.

The dogs' friendship included another amusing side. Teddy was a bit of a nervous dog, and he would sometimes take offence at some movement or signal on the part of Silver. At this, Teddy would 'yap' rather aggressively at Silver, as if 'telling him off' in no uncertain terms about whatever may have been the perceived transgression. This was like 'water off a duck's back' for Silver though, who would simply look calmly and patiently at Teddy, while wearing a bit of a mystified-looking expression – as if wondering what all the fuss was about. The 'fuss' would invariably die off after a few moments, and the two of them would resume whatever they'd be doing. We were to see this little drama played out fairly frequently, but it never seemed to get in the way of their friendship, and Silver was always extremely patient with his feisty little friend.

Geoff and Karen also introduced me to some of the sights and people of Fort McMurray. I quickly discovered that it was mostly a city of young adults that had grown up in other parts of Canada, mostly Newfoundland and Cape Breton Island, who had been drawn by the prospect of jobs. There were genuine 'locals' of course, but it was rare to meet someone that had actually grown up in the area.

Two consequences of the influx of so many young people with good jobs and no roots in the area were that there were lots of parties, and it was incredibly easy to meet people and feel welcome. Although Geoff and Karen took me to some parties to meet people, I think that a stranger could simply have walked in, unaccompanied, to the larger parties and said, "I'm new here," to be welcomed.

There were also lots of recreational opportunities in Fort McMurray. The growing community had a large recreation complex under construction (as well as new schools and plans to build a hospital and a college). Being in the north meant that there was also an abundance of opportunities for hiking, boating, hunting and fishing, and the most recent craze: mountain biking. There were no mountains nearby, of course, but these 'go anywhere' bicycles were extremely popular. With their rugged yet lightweight construction and their large, wide tires, a favourite activity was riding them on walking and hiking trails in the hills and valleys that crisscrossed the city, and beyond.

It wasn't long before Geoff had persuaded me to try one out, so he loaned me Karen's bike and we went out with the two dogs along a winding path that dropped into a small river valley on one edge of the city. I say path, but it was rough going. The path seemed to mostly comprise bits of dirt between a profusion of rocks and tree roots of varying sizes and shapes. This wouldn't have been so bad except that another aspect of the local 'work hard, play hard' culture was to do everything at break-neck speed, and I nearly broke my neck - literally!

To be fair, Geoff probably felt like he was riding at a painfully slow pace to accommodate me. But for me, who wasn't used to biking, much less at high speed on rough terrain, it took my full concentration to navigate over the smaller obstructions and around the larger ones. Although I was in the best physical shape of my life after the dog training course, I didn't have mountain biking skills. We took a long route, and it was exhausting. All things considered, I suppose it was inevitable that, just when I started to feel like I was getting the 'hang' of it all, I ran straight into a big rock. The front wheel then stopped immediately, and momentum lifted my body straight up and over the handlebars.

I had apparently done a cartwheel over the handlebars because the next thing I remembered was landing flat on my back ahead of the bike and feeling Silver and Teddy both licking my face while a wave of shock coursed through my body. As Geoff rode back to see what had happened to me, I was trying to ride out the effects of my body going into shock, and at the same time mentally reconstructing what must have happened. By the time Geoff appeared out of the bush ahead of us, I'd pulled myself up to a sitting position and was concentrating on measured breathing.

"Are you alright?" he asked.

"I will be," I said, somewhat sheepishly. "Lucky for me I landed mostly on dirt and tree roots, rather than a big rock."

"Do you feel like you broke anything?"

"No, no breaks," I said, as I tried stretching and moving various parts of my body, "But I must have landed on my left shoulder and side – they don't feel very good." I judged.

"Well then, they're going to feel worse before they get better." He thought for a moment, then said, "Tell you what, a friend of mine near here has a big hot tub in his backyard. Let's try a slow ride back a ways, and we'll get over to his place and drop you in the tub. You'll find it works wonders for sore muscles."

We found that I could stand and move around. Despite my

injuries, the mountain bike seemed to be completely unscathed. Seeing my expression, Geoff said, "What's wrong, are you too hurt to bike?"

"No, it's not that," I replied, shaking my head, "It's the bike. I hit that rock straight-on. I feel like hell, and the front wheel should be a twisted mess but look at it – it's not even bent!" I said, feeling somewhat offended.

He laughed, "If you can joke about it and get back on, then you're really going to fit in around here Alex. Now come and see how we do First Aid, 'Fort Mac' style."

What followed was a classic tale of 'Fort Mac' culture. As we slowly made our way over to Geoff's friend's house, I asked whether he'd even be there.

"Doesn't matter," Geoff said. "Laurie's probably working 'shift,' but the house won't be locked, and he won't mind us just going in and using the hot tub. Besides, I'll need to phone him anyway, to ask him to pick up some supplies on his way home from work."

"Supplies?"

"You'll see," he said, mysteriously.

So, we eventually got to the house. Sure enough, it was empty but unlocked. Geoff showed me where the towels were, and we went out and opened-up the large hot tub in his friend's backyard. It was huge! All I had with me for clothes was the rather sweaty T-shirt and shorts I'd been cycling in, but Geoff said, "Just hop in dressed like you are. When Laurie gets here, he'll find you something you can change into for going home later. I'm going to go and raid his fridge for something for us to drink."

By the time I'd eased my aching body into the hot tub, Geoff had returned with two glasses and two bottles of champagne. "This is part of the cure," he explained, brandishing the bottles, "Laurie only had two in his fridge, but we'll get more delivered later."

"Delivered?"

"You'll see," he replied, with a smile.

I'd thought easing myself into the hot tub was doing wonders for my side, shoulder, and arm bruising, but the hot tub plus a glass of champagne really did hit home. "You know, this is pretty darn civilized," I commented, sipping my champagne and looking around at the forest of trees that framed the perimeter of the back-yard.

Geoff obviously agreed, and we lounged companionably in silence, enjoying the surroundings, while our two dogs lapped-up the water and munched on the dog food that Geoff had found somewhere.

"Where did you find dog food?" I asked, not seeing any dogs around.

"I found some hot dogs in the fridge and cut them up," Geoff admitted. "They're not good for a small-breed dog like Teddy but they make for a nice treat for him."

Teddy obviously agreed, as he'd made a bee-line for the dish as soon as Geoff had brought it out, followed only a half-pace behind by Silver, who hadn't had hot dogs before (as far as I knew), but was clearly enjoying his first tastes.

Geoff had phoned his friend Laurie MacDonald, and by the time we'd had our second glass of champagne both he and his wife, Ann, had arrived with several more bottles of champagne – the 'supplies' that Geoff had mentioned earlier.

Next thing you know, Laurie and Ann were in the tub as well, joining us in a glass, and we alternated between getting acquainted and relating our mountain biking tale. By this time, it was getting late in the afternoon, probably close to 5 pm, and Geoff said, "Anybody hungry?"

Everyone was hungry. I was starting to feel sufficiently recovered and hydrated that food was rising-up on my hierarchy of needs. Once again, Geoff took the lead. "OK. My brother-in-law, James should be getting off work soon, I'll call him and invite him to join us in the tub."

I held back from asking the obvious question at this point, but it was soon answered anyway.

"Hello, James," we heard, as he spoke into the cordless extension phone he'd liberated from the kitchen. "Yeah, we're over in Laurie and Ann's hot tub, why don't you come over and join us? ... You can, great. Now, before you do, we need you to drop by the liquor store and get a few bottles of champagne, and then we need you to pick up a bunch of take-out fried chicken, enough for, ... (counting) ... five people, OK? ... OK, see you," and then, after hanging up the phone he turned to me, "and that's how we do it in 'Fort Mac'"

Within an hour, James had joined us, along with the 'supplies,' which we drank and ate while still in the hot tub. The only times anyone got out of the tub were to go into the house to use the bathroom. The hot tub manufacturers recommend only staying in hot tubs for about twenty minutes, and they usually recommend not drinking alcohol. Geoff and I'd already been in for close to two hours, drinking and eating and visiting, and it felt wonderful, although I was wondering at what point we'd shrivel up into prunes. But the evening wasn't over yet. As the clock passed 6:30 pm, someone said, "Hey, what about the hockey game?" Apparently 'Hockey Night in Canada' was going to be coming on the TV at 7 pm.

"No problem." It was Laurie this time. He launched himself out of the hot tub and returned shortly with a small table, which he placed on the lawn beside the hot tub. As fast as I could say, "You're not serious ...." he'd dashed back to the house and returned with a colour TV and an extension cord. With the former placed on the table and the latter connected to the house, he tossed the remote control over to Geoff, saying "Fire it up."

So, there we were for the next two hours, with the evening darkness coming on, the hockey game running, the conversation flowing in and around the game, and the champagne continuing to flow. I remember thinking to myself, "This is a very different kind of community!"

By the time the game was over, we really had had enough – of everything - and the party was about to break up, but with one more surprise in store for me. I'd begun to wonder how I was going to get home because wet clothes and injuries aside, I'd clearly had far too much to drink to be able to safely ride the mountain bike home. Before I could raise the subject, Geoff again rose to the occasion, this time by phoning his wife Karen to ask her to bring their van over to collect all the inebriated people that needed to get home: Geoff, James, and I. Meanwhile, Ann guided me into the house to find some dry clothes I could borrow.

Soon Karen arrived, immediately took stock of all the empty champagne bottles that were lying around the yard and put on a pretense of disapproval, although I could tell she was far more amused than upset. We said our goodbyes, and I thanked Laurie and Ann profusely for their hospitality, but they seemed to think it was nothing worthy of comment. As we loaded everybody into the van, including the two dogs, I did seem to detect a disapproving gaze from Silver, and I really couldn't tell whether he was disapproving or teasing. Do dogs tease? I know now, but I didn't know then.

The final chapter came the next morning (late the next morning) when both Geoff and I drove our respective trucks over to Laurie and Ann's house to help clean up the place. This included picking up all the empties from the yard. As we picked up the empties, I counted them and did the math on the average quantities consumed per person the night before.

I think I'll just quietly blush and leave the answer unstated.

My favourite takeaway from the whole episode is the welcoming hospitality I experienced on '*The Day of the Mountain Bike Accident*.' It was the first of many, many examples of such welcoming openness and generosity that I was to experience during my relatively short time living in Fort McMurray.

Meanwhile, the people at GCOS did their reference checks with both my fictitious former boss at the security company and my real former Captain on the Metro Toronto force, who had apparently advised that I was a quick study and would "learn the ropes" quickly. Apparently, they were sufficiently satisfied, because I promptly received a call from them, and was asked to report for work immediately.

Laurie Schramm

5 THE 'WILD, WILD, WEST' OF NORTHERN ALBERTA

Leaving Silver at home, in the care of Geoff and Karen, I headed off for my first day of work at the GCOS mine.

While driving north from the city to the GCOS site, I experienced another taste of the wild-frontier character of Fort McMurray. At first, I was simply driving along Highway 63, a standard two-lane highway, along with any number of other drivers, all of whom were headed to the same place for their next shift in the mine or the plant in which they worked.

The first things I noticed were how many vehicles there were, that they all seemed to have only one occupant each – the driver – and that they all seemed to be in a huge rush. Watching so many vehicles rush furiously past my pace, of slightly over the 60 miles per hour speed limit, I thought it strange at the time that everyone would be in such a rush to get to work. When I'd lived in Toronto, I'd gotten used to driving on congested freeways, but the real rush was always when people were going home from work, not the other way around. I learned later that it was quite common for the Fort McMurray people to be in a rush to get anywhere, at any time. This fit in with their full throttle approach to life and driving to work was no exception.

As surprising as I found this to be, I apparently hadn't seen anything yet. Before long, our convoy of vehicles was headed up the rising slope of a very long hill, which I later learned was known locally as 'Super-Test Hill,' because of the challenge of maintaining a speeding pace all the way up. I had no trouble maintaining my speed, with the 400-cubic-inch V8 engine in my truck, but I was amazed that so many of the other vehicles were able to not only maintain higher speeds but to increase them as they went up the hill. Clearly, this was a signature place to demonstrate the power of each driver's vehicle (mostly trucks).

It soon became clear that it was a place to demonstrate foolishness as well, because while I was just taking note of the acceleration of the masses of vehicles, I could see a pecking order beginning to be established, with vehicles passing each other and jostling for position. Soon, the passing lane was a solid line of vehicles, all passing the ones in the normal lane. We were only halfway up the hill, when one driver, clearly frustrated with his inability to pass on the left, pulled over onto the shoulder of the highway and began passing vehicles on their right-hand sides. As my police training was cataloging the offences (crossing a solid line to pass on the right, driving on the shoulder), another driver pulled-out to do the same, and then another. Soon, there were three lines of vehicles headed up the hill, and the convoy began to take on the appearance of a drag race. It occurred to me that a drag-race was exactly what I was watching.

As the vehicles reached two-thirds of the way up the hill, the centre line of the highway changed from a broken line to a double solid line, to prevent any more vehicles from passing and potentially running into unseen, southbound vehicles, that might soon make an appearance over the crest of the hill. To my amazement, nothing changed as the leftmost line of vehicles remained in place, giving me more offences to catalogue (crossing a double-solid line, passing in a no-passing zone). Now my attention was focused on the top of the hill, thinking that if a line of workers coming off from their shifts started appearing in the southbound lane, probably all in a hurry to get home, we'd have the makings of a spectacular accident.

I'd no sooner formed this thought in my mind than the first of a series of vehicles appeared over the crest of the hill and began their descent towards us. Powerless to do anything but watch, I had just become convinced that a catastrophe was inevitable when, magically, the drivers in the normal lane all eased up to create room, and the entire left-hand line of vehicles merged back where they belonged. It was as if it had all been choreographed. All, that is, but one maniac, who stayed put, and was seemingly daring the first oncoming vehicle to hit him.

The only thing the southbound drivers could do was shift to the shoulder of the highway on their side, and this they quickly did – the entire line of them!

As I breathed a huge sigh of relief, it became clear to me that they'd all done all this before, both the drivers heading to the mine and those heading home. Clearly, the maniac had won, and I noticed that he tapped on his brakes quickly, twice, just before disappearing over the top of the hill. Clearly, this was a '*Look at me!*' signal. Meanwhile, the drivers in the right-hand shoulder lane seemed to be the second-place winners, as they hadn't had to slow down for all this, and soon the entire pack disappeared over the top of the hill.

With the amateur drag-racers out of my sight for the moment, the smaller numbers of minor speeders, like myself, who were comparatively sedately making their way up the last of the hill were able to relax a bit. As I took stock of this new experience, I thought: *This can't be the polite, "no, please, you go first," law-abiding Canada that I'd grown up in. I wondered, not for the first time, what had happened to quiet, old, "nothing much happens around here" Alberta.*

Arriving at the GCOS site I checked-in with security at the front gate and was directed to a large administration where my new boss, Franklin D. Stoner, came down to meet me. Frank was a very friendly guy and suggested we begin by heading to the cafeteria for coffee.

"What did you think of the drive up here from town?" he asked.

"Unbelievable, I'm glad I didn't buy one of those new little import cars or I'd get blown off the road. Is it always like that?"

"Every day. It's all part of the 'Work Hard – Play Hard' culture up here," he said, "I blame all these kids. For most of them, this is their first time living on their own, away from their parents' homes and influence, and making lots of money – so they've gone a bit wild." Then, after a pause, "I blame them, but the truth is that sometimes even us old-timers get caught up in it all."

"Doesn't anyone ever get hurt?" I asked, in amazement.

"Oh, sure! Every couple of months there's a bad accident and people get injured. A couple of people died earlier this year."

Franklin (Frank) D. Stoner

"What about the highway patrol?" I asked, thinking to myself that if I'd been on highway patrol that morning, I'd have had a field-day issuing well-deserved tickets.

"The RCMP detachment here is small. In a normal town, they'd probably be OK, but in a wild place like this, they're understaffed. They patrol the highway when they can, but what you saw this morning is constant. Our plant and mine run three shifts per day, seven days a week. Across the highway at Syncrude, their construction is mostly running a single shift per day, plus overtime sometimes, and they're also operating seven days a week. The highway patrol mostly watches the highway when the 4 pm shift changes. That's the worst one, and they do random checks when the other shifts change... of course, there's a game there too," he added thoughtfully.

"What do you mean?"

"Avoiding the police is another game. You know what a CB radio is?"

"Sure," I replied. Citizens' Band radio was another fad that had begun in the U.S. as a result of the oil crisis. What had happened was, along with the oil shortages and rationing, the U.S. also reduced highway speed limits, most famously bringing-in their country-wide 55 mph speed limit on interstate highways. The CB radio craze began with commercial truckers, who used them to advise each other of weather and traffic conditions, identify gas stations that hadn't run out of fuel, alert each other to highway patrol speed traps, and to organize convoys. It wasn't long before CB radios became popular with young drivers of sports cars and pickup trucks. One of the popular novelty songs of the previous year (1975) had been C.W. McCall's *"Convoy,"* which popularized free-spirits, CB radios, and avoiding the police. From the U.S., it had been a short step to Canada, where Citizens' Band radio was officially called the General Radio Service (GRS), but due to the impact of American 'pop culture,' almost everyone referred to "CB radios."

"Well, many of the vehicles up here have CB radios in them, especially the trucks. By the time the highway patrol arrives on the highway, everyone knows they're there and settles down – but only until the highway patrol gives up and heads back to town."

I shook my head. "Does that mean everyone is crazy on the mine and plant sites too?"

"Actually, no," he replied. "We're very strict on safety here. These young kids we're hiring here still think they're invincible, ..." he paused and looked at me, "no offence."

"None taken," I replied, pleased to still be included in his 'young kids' demographic.

"These young kids think they're invincible, so although we preach to them about hazards and the risks of getting injured or killed, they don't really take it to heart until they've seen a friend or colleague actually get hurt. So, although we still try to teach them all the right things, at the end of the day we basically pound it into their heads in ways they can understand."

"What does that mean?"

"It means that they have to follow our safety rules or lose their job. That, they can understand! For a minor infraction, we'll call it a mistake, and coach them a bit. For a second infraction, it goes on their record, and we re-train them. Three strikes and they're subject to dismissal."

"Does that put the safety people more in the nature of 'safety police' than 'safety advisors and coaches'?" I asked.

"Very good question!" he answered approvingly, "If you're thinking that's wrong, then you're right... What I mean is, we want our safety people to be a safety resource, and to be coaches and advisors, as well as trainers, but we're not there yet. First, we need to get a strong safety culture in place, then we can advance to something better. If I had my way, our motto would be 'Nobody Moves – Nobody Gets Hurt,' but that's not practical, so we need to find ways to let people do their jobs while managing things so that they don't get hurt in the process."

"Sounds good to me," I said, and meant it.

Frank went on, "Look, I understand what they're thinking. When I was their age, the Second World War was on. At 18 years of age, I joined the Royal Canadian Air Force (RCAF) and went overseas as a tail-gunner in a Lancaster bomber. At first, it seemed like an adventure, and none of us really thought much about death. Soon, my buddies were dying all around me. The tail-gunner was the most exposed member of a Lancaster's crew, and the enemy fighters tried to take out the gunners first, to give them more time to bring the bombers down. The survival rate for tail-gunners was only about one in five," his voice weakened a bit at his point. "We learned very quickly how lucky we are to be alive, and how quickly a life can be lost – and I don't want to see us lose anyone on this site," he concluded, picking up energy again.

"Wow, I don't know what to say," I offered, "but I agree with trying not to lose anyone, and I much prefer the thought of aiming to be coaches and advisors rather than company police."

"Good, and you don't need to say anything," he said, with a smile, "and you shouldn't have to spend your time listening to old fossils like me telling war stories either. Let's go get you started."

So, after a quick tour of the Safety and Security area and having spent some time in Human Resources (HR) doing all the standard employee paperwork, Frank and I discussed what I'd actually be doing for the next couple of weeks.

"First off," he started, "we'll put you through the same basic safety courses everyone else gets, plus a few that you'll need in order to be able to access some of the more dangerous areas. You'll also have some studying to do, so you're up on the government safety regulations, our own company's safety policies, and you'll need to become familiar with the safety committees we have in each major area of the site. You'll also need to get to know the site itself and meet as many of our people as possible, so they'll know you, what your job is, and why you'll be showing up without warning in areas you don't normally work in. Eventually, we'll want you to work some late shifts, so you become familiar with the same operations as they're carried on at night, and the shift workers too, but we can leave that until later."

I raised an eyebrow, "That's just to begin with?"

He laughed. "Don't worry, '*Rome wasn't built in a day.*' There's no panic, and it will become easier as time goes on. You can do the courses one at a time, and as for the studying and touring, you can do those in parallel, so the studying and paperwork parts don't get you down. It's up to you, but I'd suggest that if you're a morning person then do the studying and paperwork in the morning and do the touring in the afternoons as a reward or reverse it if you're an afternoon person."

"I'm a morning person as long as I get my morning coffee," I laughed.

"Then you'll fit in just fine," he chuckled, "there's not a single part of this operation that operates without coffee near at hand, not even the mine or the tailings areas. For now, get yourself over to Central Stores, and they'll issue you with a hard-hat, safety glasses, gloves and coveralls. That will form the core of your personal protective equipment (PPE). You'll get other stuff issued to you as you need it.

"I need hardly remind you that as a safety specialist you're expected to not only preach safety ('*talking the talk*') but also practise safety ('*walking the walk*'). Later, when you're back in town, get yourself a pair of CSA[9]-approved, steel-toed boots. Not the low ones, they need to be tall enough to support and protect your ankles. After you get your PPE, we'll have lunch, and after that, I'll drive you around the site to give you the big picture."

Lunch provided another revelation. I'd hear that northern mine sites had to have good food in order to keep their employees, but I wasn't prepared for the diversity and quantities of food that would be available. Although it was only lunchtime, it seemed like you could eat almost anything, and in unlimited quantities. It was very good too, and I could see that I was either going to have to be very active or watch my food intake very carefully.

After lunch, I was introduced to the way safety was managed at GCOS. Frank explained that all employers have a common-law duty to take reasonable care of the safety of their employees and that, in addition, the Alberta government had recently announced that a new Occupational Health and Safety (OH&S) Act and regulations would become law by December[10]. On top of that, the company's policy was to do better than what was required and to strive to be an industry leader in OH&S.

What it boiled down to, was that our OH&S goals were to obey the laws and regulations and foster a safe and healthy work environment. This brought us back to our morning's conversation, as the new direction on site was to move from a compliance ('obey the rules') culture, to a participative (positive, shared-values, 'we're all in this together') culture. So, our OH&S work comprised several elements, including a safety management system, statements of OH&S principles and policies, training policies and practises, promoting an effective safety culture, of course, and so on.

This certainly made sense to me, and as I found myself getting excited about my 'new job,' I realized that I would have to be careful not to get so drawn into this that I lost sight of the real reason I was there. One thing was certain. The timing of the company's move to change their approach to safety could not have come a better time for me, as now I had licence to roam about the site and try to be seen as a roving helper, rather than some kind of 'safety police' that might be resented and/or shunned.

Frank drove me on a tour of the whole site, which covered a huge geographic area. Their infrastructure – mostly buildings, processing plants, and pipelines - was very concentrated in some spots (like the extraction and froth treatment plants, upgrading facility, and an associated maze of pipelines), but it was almost desolate in other spots (like the mine and tailings-pond areas).

Three days after my initial briefings, I had all my PPE together, had completed my basic safety training, and was ready for more detailed tours and orientations of the operations. There are entire books written about the GCOS operation (and Frank had given me several to read), but I'll try to give you some idea of the scale of the operation as it was shown to me.

For my first detailed tour, a mine-site geologist named Tom Peters took me in tow. Tom was a sandy-haired, wiry figure of modest height that was more than compensated for by an exuberant personality. His energy and enthusiasm were infectious.

"The oil sand deposit on the GCOS lease comprises a layer of oil sand that is about 150 feet thick, sandwiched between layers of muskeg and sand above, and a bed of limestone below," he explained. "First, the muskeg has to be drained. We're doing this by digging ditches and letting the water drain out naturally," he added, as we drove over to see this part of the operation underway.

"Doesn't that take a long time?" I asked.

He grinned, "Two years, but it's easy, cheap, and works like a charm. We started draining sections years ago and are always working about a year ahead of the next step in the operation, so there's no reason to rush it. After the excess water has drained off, the muskeg is still wet, so we wait for winter and dig it out when it's frozen. That way, nature freezes it for free and then we just use power shovels and trucks to take it out."

By now, we were able to see the shovels and trucks in operation, and we stopped to watch for a while before driving over to see the overburden removal process.

Arriving at the current site of overburden removal, he went on, "The next step is to remove the overburden layer, using power shovels or front-end loaders, and trucks. We have to remove about a half ton of overburden for every ton of oil sand that we expose. That's a lot of overburden, but in this case, we use almost all of it to build walls for the ponds we create with the tailings from the extraction process. As we produce more tailings, we just keep increasing the height of the walls to contain them."

Very neat and tidy, I thought. *The waste from one part of the process gets used in another.*

I was already marvelling at the sheer number of heavy equipment units in continuous operation. "How long does this go on?" I asked.

"Forever," he said. "As long as we're on schedule, we only need to remove the muskeg and the overburden during daylight hours, so we work one shift per day, seven days a week, and our current plan is to continue this for the next thirty years." He paused in thought, then added, "Of course, that's only for the company's current leases. If more leases (new areas to develop) are taken up, then theoretically we could keep doing this for the next several hundred years – that's how large these oil sand deposits are!"

"Amazing." I began to get a glimmering of the magnitude of the operation – not just in size, but in time-scale as well.

"Finally, we get to the next layer: the oil sand itself," he continued, as we'd driven to an area in which all the muskeg and overburden had already been removed. Here the ground looked inky black and almost shiny, and I realized with a shock that I was seeing oil sand for the first time.

Correctly interpreting my thoughts, Tom said: "Yes, the colour is from the bitumen, and when it's been fairly freshly exposed it's usually quite shiny." He went on to explain that depending on the oil content – the 'grade' – oil sand's appearance could range from that of ordinary sand to a darker brown, to a dull grey-black, or to a very shiny black. "The best grade is fourteen or fifteen percent," he went on, "and that's the black shiny stuff."

My next surprise came as we turned a corner around a tall hill of oil sand. There in front of me was some kind of machine that was taller than a ten-storey building.

"This is a bucketwheel excavator!" he said proudly.

"The oil sand layer here is generally about 150 feet thick, and we have two bucketwheel excavators. You can see over there," he pointed to one side, "there is another bucketwheel operating ahead of us."

On one end of the machine, a thirty-five-foot diameter wheel was slowly turning. On the outer edge of the wheel, ten large buckets with big teeth were spaced at intervals. Each bucket had a two-ton capacity and was about three feet by four feet at the mouth, and about six feet deep. You could place four miners, standing, inside a single bucket.

As the wheel turned, the buckets cut into the oil sand, carrying it up and over the wheel, and then on the other side dumping it out so it fell into a hopper feeding a conveyor belt.

At this point, we got out of the truck and walked over to a just-mined area, and Tom showed me the sandy-coloured surface of the limestone rock that had been underneath the oil sand. Prying a lump of oil sand ore out from the freshly exposed mine face, he showed me a few spots where the bitumen was literally oozing out of the sand. When he tossed the lump back and showed me his hands, they were stained black with bitumen residue.

The bucketwheel extractors were built so that the bucketwheel fed one conveyor, which then fed another, which in turn fed another. The bucketwheel machinery, and each of these individual conveyors were attached to each other but individually mounted on legs, which were in turn mounted on large caterpillar tracks. Four such (twelve-foot high) tracks were under the bucketwheel part alone. The articulated conveyor system allowed the bucketwheel operator to move the wheel as needed while constantly rearranging the articulated conveyors so that the machine was always in reach of a fixed conveyor system that ran along the length of the mine and over to a large building off in the distance. The other bucketwheel was similarly connected to its own conveyor system, and the two of them looked like large snakes sprawled across the mine.

Tom drove me over to the closest bucketwheel, parked nearby, and he radioed to the operator that he was coming up to say "Hi." As we walked over to it I was struck by the size. What had looked from a distance like the toys in a child's sandbox, now looked, up-close, like mechanized giants. At Tom's urging, we walked over to a ladder secured to one side and climbed up. Walking along several catwalks and climbing up more ladders, we eventually came to the operator's cabin and went in.

Fred, the operator, was sitting in a very well-padded chair that, at first glance, looked like a living room recliner. A second look brought out some differences though. Attached to the front of each of the chair's arms was a joystick that would not have looked out of place on the most modern video game in an amusement centre. Directly in front of the chair were large wrap-around windows giving him a great view of the mine face and the swinging buckets. Surrounding the windows was an array of closed-circuit TV monitors, dials, gauges, switches and flashing lights of various colours that would have made a jet airline pilot jealous. Fred explained that the windows and cameras let him see exactly what he was digging, as he had to avoid areas that were simply sand and shale (without any bitumen), and he had to avoid the occasional band of solid rock. Meanwhile, the instruments let him know how much stress was being placed on the various moving parts. Sure enough, as we watched for a while, I could see that he was not only adjusting the position of the big wheel but also its cutting angle and speed. Fred proudly explained that his bucketwheel could mine as much as 10,000 tons in an hour, but that the average mining rate was "only" 5,000 tons per hour.

At first, I thought he was joking when he explained that each tooth on the buckets weighed over 100 pounds and that a set of teeth could be worn down in as little as four hours of digging in the wintertime when the bitumen-oil was almost rock-hard! There were 120 such teeth on his bucketwheel, ten buckets, each with twelve teeth. Huge, like everything else in this operation. I found it mesmerizing, but the best was yet to come. After a few minutes, Fred said that he was about to "walk the wheel," at which point Tom led me outside the operator's cabin to a spot on one of the catwalks.

"Watch," Tom said.

No sooner had he said this, then there were three blasts of a loud horn, just like a large ship will sound before leaving its dock in a busy harbour. Sure enough, after a pause, the entire bucketwheel mechanism began to move as the operator engaged the six caterpillar tracks below us to relocate the wheel.

I was amazed! It was as if we were standing on a balcony on a downtown Toronto high-rise building that had suddenly decided to 'lift its skirts' and walk. It was hard to believe that such a massive piece of machinery could move, much less propel itself. As Tom led me over to another catwalk, we could see that Fred was also 'walking' the articulated, five-foot wide conveyor systems, repositioning them so that they were properly placed to feed the mined ore to the six-foot-wide fixed conveyor system.

The bucketwheel excavators fed two such fixed conveyor systems, which at full mining capacity delivered 140,000 tons per day of oil sand out of the mine and dropped it all into a single, 5,000 ton-capacity feed bin, which in turn fed a single conveyor belt that carried it to the extraction plant. Tom explained that the contents of one bin-full of oil sand would only keep the extraction plant running for thirty minutes, so their challenge was to keep the entire mining operation running continuously.

I marvelled at the size and the engineering of it all. Remembering why I was really there, I tried to review what I had seen through the eyes of a saboteur. There were some obvious vulnerabilities. Not only was the equipment spread out over a large area, but there were also really very few people around, so access might not be difficult. In addition, although the bucketwheels might make attractive targets, there were two 'pinch-points,' that, if incapacitated, would bring the entire operation to a halt: the main feed bin and the single conveyor following it. Everything else had two or more parallel process elements. It would bear thinking about.

If the huge bucketwheel excavators and their chains of conveyers were the main attraction of the mine, then the secondary players were surely the army of bulldozers, power shovels, front-end loaders, and 75-ton 'heavy-hauler' trucks that could be seen crawling about everywhere. Tom explained that these were employed cutting away regions of sand that didn't have enough bitumen content to be worth mining and picking-up any oil sand from the mine face that had been spilled or missed by the bucketwheels.

On our way back from the mine we stopped at one of the heavy haulers that was jacked-up at the side of the pathway and having one of its great tires changed. Tom introduced me to the truck's driver, Helen. She explained that some people weren't used to the sight of women driving such massive industrial equipment, but that on this site it was normal.

"The nice thing about the shortage of workers up here," she explained, "is that the company will hire anyone capable of relocating to Fort McMurray and learning to do a job. If you can do the job, they treat you the same or better than the men."

"Better?" I asked.

"It's turned out that women are better, on average, at driving these heavy haulers than the men are. Less testosterone, less reckless, and all that, which has meant fewer accidents in the mine, and less wear and tear on the trucks themselves – so the company actually prefers to have women drivers. That's created job opportunities, and there are already more women driving heavy haulers in the mine than there are men."

"Neat," I said, "A win for the women's movement."

"Sure thing," she agreed, "The next thing you know there'll be women Mounties!"

I just smiled, and said, "I hope you're right..."

6 SMOKE AND FIRE TRAINING

It can be hard not to panic when you can't see anything and have lost your sense of direction.

It was 1969, I was in my second year studying chemistry at Carleton University in Ottawa, and to get a break from academics I had enrolled in a SCUBA diving course. My SCUBA instructors had been 'old school' type army and police sergeants. They put us through all kinds of elaborate practices designed to make us uncomfortable, if not panicky, in hopes of making us learn how to "deal with it." These exercises were usually peppered with friendly reminders that "panic kills," while pausing for a moment's thought can save.

In one of these exercises, they wanted us to practice 'buddy breathing,' in which two divers would share the air from a single compressed-air tank by sharing the mouthpiece from its single regulator. So as not to make it "too easy" for us, we had been made to enter the water with our masks blacked-out by covering the insides with aluminum foil. This was very unnerving. We rely so much on our eyesight, that having it suddenly taken away, and needing to rely instead on other senses, like touch and sound, takes getting used to. That's what made the foil-in-mask exercise so effective.

Once we'd reached a depth of about twenty-five feet, the instructors had rotated each of us a couple of times to disorient us. We were each then handed one end of a short 'buddy-line,' so we'd be able to find each other, and left to "deal with it."

The secret, of course, was to hold-off panic, pause, and think things through. This was not easy! We each had to just stop everything, calm our thoughts, get oriented as best we could, and find each other. Then, my buddy had to hand over his regulator mouthpiece and hold his breath while trusting me not to take too long with it. For my part, I had to get a first rush of air into my starving lungs, take just one more breath, and then hand it back over trusting him not to hog it either. My classmate buddy and I managed to do this, more or less, but it wasn't easy until we'd passed the regulator back and forth a few times and our hearts and lungs had calmed down somewhat. Our discussion over beers later touched on the Nietzsche quote: "That which does not kill us makes us stronger." Although we learned a valuable skill, and a valuable lesson, it seemed to us that there must be a better way to learn these things. (If there is, I've yet to discover it.)

***

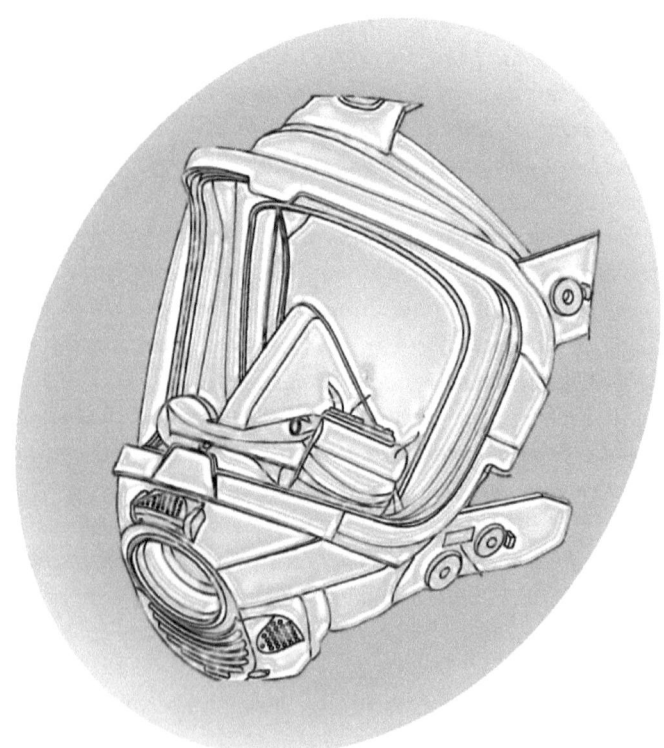

Déjà vu.

Now here I was, once again with an aluminum foil darkened mask on, disoriented, and trying hard not to panic.

As part of the training for my GCOS job, I'd been sent for the 'smoke and fire' version of Scott air-pack training and certification. "Scott," was the brand of self-contained breathing apparatus (SCBA) that GCOS used in its plants and fire department. Similar but different from SCUBA, these units had smaller tanks, were not designed to handle the higher ambient pressures of diving, and had full-face masks rather than just mouthpieces. These were designed to keep smoke, soot, and hazardous vapours away from the nose and mouth while providing clean air to breathe. A benefit of the full-face mask was that you could talk to people (although you kind of had to yell, really) and they could even be fitted with two-way radios for easier communication with others.

Our class had completed the theory portion and were now working on the practical part. There were two stages to this. Part one involved two 'buddies' entering a maze to search for and locate a body (a mannequin, heavily weighted to simulate that of a fairly heavy-set adult), check it for vital signs, not find any, get a few good puffs of air into its simulated lungs, and carry (or drag) it out of there, together, without getting lost or separated in the process. They would then time us, and there was a maximum time associated with a passing grade. It didn't sound all that bad when they first explained it to us until we found out that we'd be doing it blind – with air packs on and aluminum foil inserted into our masks to black them out. If we survived that, then part two involved doing it all over again in a different maze, with no foil this time, but real smoke and fire so we'd still be effectively blind but now would have to demonstrate that we could keep a perfect seal on our masks while heaving, sweating, and contorting our way through the maze.

My assigned buddy and I were in the middle of part one. In clambering over some obstacles no one had bothered to warn us about, we'd lost contact with the wall we'd been following (a cardinal sin), so the two of us had gotten twisted- and turned around, then disoriented. Great!

At some level, we both knew that it was only an exercise, that we were being monitored by people who could see, and we could always just stop and remove our masks, but that would be admitting defeat.

On the other hand, we were lost in the maze and the clock was literally ticking. We'd agreed to stop for a moment to catch our breath, and the advice of those two crusty sergeants from my SCUBA-training days belatedly came back to me: *pause and think*. I paused, calmed the urge to panic, and started to think.

"Look," I yelled to my buddy. "Let's just pick a direction, crawl to the nearest wall, I'll stick to it like glue while you search out with your free arm. We'll have to choose right or left, but at least we have a 50:50 chance of being right and even if we're wrong we'll at least get ourselves out properly."

"OK," he said. "Let's say whoever hits a wall first picks a direction and the other follows."

"Agreed," I yelled back, and we struck out blindly. As we crept forward, I was the first to feel a wall. I called this out and said, "Let's go to the right!"

That's what we did, and for a wonder, it worked! My buddy soon encountered the mannequin. We did the obligatory checks and simulated breathing assist and together started to carry it out, back the way we had come. We knew now not to lose touch with the guide wall we'd chosen but using one hand to follow the wall and the rest of me to help carry the unreasonably heavy mannequin was almost too much. I was amazed at how slowly we had to proceed, and only at the last second did the two of us remember to support the mannequin's head and treat it like a real person. (Our instructors later showed us a video of a pair of rescuers dragging a mannequin along a maze-way with its head bumping and bouncing on the floor the whole way. They'd later informed those particular rescuers that they'd successfully located the subject, but then 'killed' him during the 'rescue.') Anyway, we got out, mannequin intact and were judged to have saved him, but only barely within the allowable time limit.

I offered up a silent "thanks" to my two crusty instructor sergeants from my SCUBA days.

After this experience, the more realistic one, in the maze with real fire and smoke, was somewhat more dangerous, but we carried out the exercise with relative ease because we knew what to do, we'd conquered our fears, and we simply went about it in a slow and methodical fashion that may not have looked elegant but got the job done. Overall, I looked back on it as a pretty cool experience – but only after I had survived it.

***

With the advent of another new day, and with my new SCBA certification in-hand, I presented myself for an introduction and tour of the extraction plants that picked-up where the mine tour had left-off.

A chemical engineer named Jack Johnson, "Call me 'JJ,' everyone does," took me over to see the extraction plants. JJ was tall and slim, with an air of complete technical competence, and a quiet sense of humour. He checked my personal protective equipment (PPE), decided I needed hearing protection and took me over to get huge ear-protecting earmuffs that clipped-into each side of my hard-hat. "You're going to be glad to have these once we get into the plants," he commented, as he showed me how they could be placed up and out of the way on the hard hat, but then quickly swivelled down and over the ears when needed.

Thus armed, we entered Plant 4, the extraction plant and began to follow the natural process flow, beginning with the main conveyor bringing oil sand in from the feed bin in the mine, that I had seen in the mine tour a few days earlier. Once the oil sand entered the plant, it was divided among three of four smaller conveyor systems. JJ explained that there were four independent extraction processing streams and that they normally operated only three of them at a time, while a fourth was undergoing maintenance and/or repairs.

At the front of each process stream was a mammoth rotating drum-cylinder, called a tumbler, into the front-end of which oil sand was fed by a conveyor. It was hard to see this clearly due to the huge cloud of steam that enveloped the front-end. JJ explained that this was because hot water, process chemicals, and steam were all added to the front-end at the same time and that it all got mixed together as it journeyed down the length of the tumbler. At the outlet end, the conditioned mass was passed over a screen and diluted with more hot water to form a slurry that could be pumped to the next processing stage.

As we walked along, JJ first showed me the bottoms of four huge cone-shaped vessels that he called separation cells, one for each tumbler. The bottoms of them made me think of giant-sized, steel versions of funnels, but as we climbed what seemed like an endless series of stairs to see the top of one, I could see that the funnel shape was just the bottom of a very tall and broad vertical cylinder. When we reached the top of it, we could see that its open surface was covered in a bubbling, inky black mass of bitumen that JJ called froth.

"The bitumen comes off from the sand, and picks-up air when it's in the tumbler," JJ explained, "then in this vessel, the bitumen droplets float up to the top. This froth layer that you can see is mostly made up of bitumen and air. Some of the bitumen droplets don't rise very quickly, and they are pumped out from the middle of the vessel (we call them 'middlings'), and they are treated further down the line. Most of the solids get pumped out the bottom (we call them 'tailings'), and they are pumped to the tailings ponds."

We next walked down some stairs and entered a new section of the plant. Here, I could see rows of differently shaped process vessels that JJ called scavenger cells. There were 36 of them. JJ explained that these too were flotation vessels, but in this case the middlings streams from each separation cell were divided among nine scavenger cells and treated with more air in order to get more bitumen to float and be recovered. Sure enough, as we got closer, I could see that they had bubbling froth layers, but they looked rather brownish-black rather than the bright, shiny black I'd just seen at the top of the separation cell.

"That's because this froth contains less bitumen and more fine solids than the other one," JJ explained. "This secondary froth isn't as high quality, but it's still worth recovering. Everything else goes to the tailings pond."

This was clearly the plant in which JJ mostly worked, because he then went into a lengthy discussion of process chemicals and process optimization, that I could barely follow, even with my chemistry background. Eventually, I got completely lost in the details, and to slow him down a bit, I asked whether he'd helped develop the process.

"Not me, that was all done in our Research and Development (R&D) department. People had been working on a suitable process for decades, but our scientists in R&D still had to make adjustments so it would work on this particular site, and then our R&D engineers had to scale-up the process, design and build a pilot plant to prove that it would still work at larger scale, and then we built the real plant that you're seeing here."

"A lot of work," I commented.

That was clearly the right thing to say as he beamed. "Yes, and a lot of people over a lot of years. We all have a lot personally invested in making this project a success," he said, with obvious pride.

As I listened to JJ, I began to perceive that malcontents would not last long in this culture and wondered whether that meant that our saboteur was an outside agent. At the risk of triggering another lecture, I couldn't help commenting once again on the sheer size of everything.

"Well, it takes a lot of material handling just to get to this point, not to mention the water, steam, chemicals, and electrical power involved," he said, "but in order to produce a single barrel of synthetic crude oil at the very end, we have to remove about 1.1 tons of overburden, then mine and ship 2.2 tons of oil sand! Most of the separation then takes place in this plant."

We continued into the next building, called the froth treatment plant. As we entered it, JJ explained that anyone entering this building had to be certified for Scott air-pack use and be clean-shaven (if male) so that the full-face mask could properly seal. He said he'd explain why presently, but that if we needed to use them to follow him and we'd grab air-packs from ready-use racks spaced along the length of the building and use them to escape. This was what I had survived the 'smoke and fire' test for!

The froth treatment plant was comparatively quiet compared with the almost deafening sounds that characterized every moment of our time in the extraction plant, and we swung our hearing protection muffs up and away from our ears. Another difference was that, whereas the extraction plant smelled strongly of heavy oil (the bitumen), this plant smelled strongly but different. My chemistry training returned, and I said "This plant smells of some kind of solvent. I can't make it out, but it smells aromatic, almost like benzene or toluene but not quite."

"No, but those are pretty good guesses," JJ responded. "What you're smelling is naphtha. It's a hydrocarbon fraction we pull off the distillation towers in the upgrading plant, so it's a mixture of high molecular weight compounds, but they're all highly aromatic. What happens, is that we take the froth, still hot (160 °F), from the extraction plant, run it through deaerating columns to get the air out, and then dilute it with naphtha to lower the viscosity enough to be able to use the centrifuges that you see here to spin the water and fine solids out."

"So, you keep it hot because otherwise the viscosity would rise and interfere with the centrifuging," I said, catching on to the concept.

"Right," he said, approvingly. "We can let it cool down later but at this stage, we still need to keep it hot. Otherwise, we'd need to add a lot more naphtha. This way is easier and cheaper."

I might have known. I was learning that at every stage, someone had worked out not just what to do and how to do it, but how to do it all for the lowest possible cost.

"There's a problem though," said JJ, breaking into my thoughts. "The naphtha is hazardous to breathe at concentrations higher than we're breathing right now, and it's VERY flammable."

"Those are two good reasons to be able to use the Scott air-packs" I observed.

"Right again," said JJ. "See those two over there?" He pointed to two air-pack clad workers doing something to a machine that was shaped somewhat like a child's spinnable top: it made me think of an overgrown laboratory centrifuge, which turned out to be a good guess.

"They're repairing a centrifuge that's still running. If one of the seals breaks they'll get a face full of naphtha at a concentration that could cause them to drop."

"And if it caught fire, they'd want to have their air-packs already on, so they could either make their escape or stay to help fight the fire," I reasoned out loud.

"Right. So, back to the process. Froths from the separation cells and the scavenger cells in the last plant are combined, deaerated, diluted and sent here, where we have forty high-speed centrifuges driving the water and fine solids out. The water and solids get sent to the tailings ponds. When the diluted bitumen product leaves this plant, it goes to two distillation towers that strip the naphtha out (at about 600 °F) for recycling. Then the 'dry' bitumen is sent to holding tanks to wait for upgrading."

"How much of the original bitumen in the feed has been recovered after all of this?" I asked.

"The design basis is ninety-seven percent, and that's still our target, but so far we're still learning how to optimize everything, and we're only getting ninety percent."

"Isn't that pretty great?" I asked.

"Oh, sure," he laughed, "people used to say the company was out of its mind to even try to develop the oil sands. The oil crisis has helped us too because, with the run-up in oil prices, we've suddenly become profitable. But we're still trying to get the recovery factors up higher, mostly so that we'll still be OK if the higher oil prices don't last."

Laurie Schramm

7 SHAKING AND SWAYING

It was while living in Fort McMurray that I first experienced the phenomenon that I had always thought of as *Man Spaces*.

The term *Man Cave* wouldn't actually be invented for another twenty years yet, but the concept of a dedicated, special *Man Space* in the home, where guys could relax and hang out, had certainly already been invented by somebody. In Fort McMurray, one of the latest fads was to renovate the garage into a multi-purpose *Man Space* that provided utilitarian and social amenities.

The utilitarian function was usually to provide a place for the home workshop which, would be well suited to carpentry, auto-mechanics, and potentially other hobbies. In an ideal case, the garage would be well supplied with an array of noisy, expensive, and largely unnecessary power tools.

The social function was to provide a place to 'hang out' with friends. In an ideal case, the garage would be equipped with comfortable chairs, a stereo, TV, and some life-support aids. The latter might comprise a refrigerator (for beer), a space heater (to counter the cold winters), and a coffee maker. The coffee and beer would mostly be needed to support long sessions of socializing.

Each such garage was equipped to the owner's personal tastes, and there was some competition among the guys to see who could create the nicest (and most expensive) garage space. Needless to say, the ideally equipped garage would have everything except one thing – space to park a vehicle. The cars and trucks lived outside, on the driveways, even at minus forty degrees in the winter.

Although I have referred to them as *Man Spaces*, women didn't seem to be specifically excluded, it was just that they seemed only to be created by men – I guess the women must have been expected to be content to have had the rest of the house at their command. In any case, I was certainly always made to feel welcome in any *Man Spaces* that I visited, and in most cases, an introduction would immediately be followed by an elaborate tour of the entire operation by its proud owner.

As an example, Silver and I were out for a walk fairly early one Saturday morning. We would often walk different routes, and while walking down a new street I was surprised to hear my name being called. Looking around, I spotted Geoff sitting with a few other guys in an open garage. He beckoned us over to join them and introduced us to the owner, Jason Hill, and the others. Jason seemed quite outgoing and friendly. He was of medium height and build, and wore a full beard, which was unusual in Fort McMurray.

Seeing me look at his garage in awe, Jason quickly pointed out the highlights, beginning with handing me a big mug of coffee from the large pot that had already been made and pointing out the comfortable sitting area with a TV and an impressively large and elaborate component stereo system with huge tower-style speakers. They were playing Queen's *Bohemian Rhapsody*, one of the top hits of the year (1976). The rest of the garage was taken up with two workbenches, one for wood- and metal-working, and the other for electronics. The electronics bench was covered in partially disassembled garage door openers and radio remote controls.

In short order, I learned that Jason worked in town at 'Electronics City,' a store that dealt in stereos, TVs, radios, and other household electronics. One of the hot products was a new generation of remote-control garage door openers, and when I arrived the guys had been discussing ways to extend the range of the remote controls. Jason immediately launched into a crash course on the new systems. He explained that these early garage door opener remote controls involved a simple transmitter (the 'remote'), which would transmit a fixed code, on a specific frequency. The code could be set by the user, by way of matching 'DIP Switches' ('Dual Inline Package' switches) on each of the remote and the receiver. A fancy model allowed any of 4,096 possible combinations to be set. The radio receiver would listen for the correct signal and then open or close the garage.

Cradling my coffee mug in both hands, I continued to gaze around the garage as Jason resumed the demonstration I'd interrupted of something he called a 'Curtain Antenna,' which seemed to involve extending the radio receiver's antenna with an arrangement of wires that looked like a long fork (a long wire) with only two tines (two wires stretching out perpendicularly, at first, and then allowed to hang downwards – forming the 'curtain'). Apparently, the idea had been borrowed from something 'Ham' radio enthusiasts used to increase the sensitivity of their radio receivers, and Jason was hoping to use it to get a two-hundred-foot range for his garage door remote.

I didn't listen to the technical discussions very closely. The gist of it all seemed to be that the guys were unsatisfied with a system that only opened the garage door for them when they were on their driveways. What they really wanted, was a system that would do the job from some distance down the block. I didn't say so, but I wondered why bother with all this when the *Man Space* garages were so full of stuff that their vehicles were going to be left parked out on the driveways anyway. This was doubly the case for Jason, who was the proud owner of a big black truck that had been modified with lift-kits to give it an extra foot of ground clearance. This, of course, made it too tall to fit into his garage.

I thought it was all pretty silly, but I wanted to be accepted by the people I was meeting. Fortunately, I had the presence of mind to keep a straight face and just listen. Eventually, full of coffee, I thanked Jason, said goodbye to everyone, and Silver and I went off to continue our walk before the guys' conversation turned from technology to intellectual discussions surrounding important matters of the day, i.e., gossiping.

***

Back at the GCOS site and following a morning of paperwork and more studying of safety policies and procedures, the afternoon brought an opportunity to continue my detailed touring of the site. The next stage of the processing was called upgrading, and for this, I was introduced to Larry Hand, a chemical engineer that worked in the Upgrading Maintenance group.

Larry was a bit unusual, in that he was actually born and raised in Alberta. He'd grown up in 'cattle country,' Alberta's south-west foothills region. He was fair-haired and medium height, but otherwise a lot like JJ (my extraction guide of the previous day). Like

JJ, Larry was slim, had an air of complete technical competence, and a quiet sense of humour. He reminded me of cowboys I had met when Silver and I'd been in Innisfail.

As we headed out in his truck, Larry explained that after extraction and froth treatment, the bitumen had been separated from the sand and water, but it wasn't yet in a form that could be sold to refineries. It still needed to have the naphtha stripped back out, and then be upgraded to synthetic crude oil (SCO). As the name suggests, SCO is similar enough to conventional crude oil, that some refineries can accept it for further processing into consumer and industrial products, like gasoline and diesel.

Although the upgrading 'plant' was really a maze of process units of varying types, and it took us the whole day to walk through it all, I'll just mention a few features that really stood out for me. Once again, the upgrading process comprised parallel process streams, three of them this time, and at the core of each was a thirty-foot diameter coking tower. In these 'coker' vessels, the large molecules that make up the bitumen would be fractured (at over 900 °F), into a whole range of smaller hydrocarbon molecules.

From there, a virtual maze of piping and vessels carried process streams to vessels that separated the components by molecular size, and from there on to other vessels that either removed unwanted components, like sulphur, or added components, like hydrogen.

Once again, the first impressions I received were the huge size of everything, the petroleum odours, and the noise. It was the noise that struck me as odd, because, unlike the mine and extraction plants, nothing here seemed to be moving. Yet, there was a fairly loud, undulating noise. Larry explained that the noise came from a variety of sources, including pumps, compressors, the process vessels themselves, and even the sounds of things like steam and other fluids surging down the pipes and making them vibrate.

At one point, Larry led me on an upwards tour, in which we climbed up a seemingly endless series of vertical, steel ladders along the side of a tall fractionation vessel. Larry had clearly done this a lot as he had the stamina and balance to be able to climb them effortlessly, like a monkey. The people that maintained the upgrading vessels and processes not only had to climb all these ladders, but to do so laden-down with heavy tool belts, extra safety gear, and often equipment, like replacement valves or instruments. Like the inexperienced tourist that I was, I had to stop and catch my breath every few ladders, and I wasn't burdened with any of the extra paraphernalia that regular workers would have had to carry along. Larry, on the other hand, could probably have done the whole thing continuously, without stopping at all, burdened-down or not.

Finally, after what seemed like forever, we reached the top of the tower. From that point, we had a sweeping, panoramic view overlooking the entire site. Now that I had had my detailed tours of the mine, extraction plants, and most of the upgrading facilities, I could not only see the whole site but understand what was happening at each point in the mining and processing sequence. It was fantastic, but I also had to keep my mind on hanging tightly to the railing of the small catwalk upon which we were standing. The reason for this was the intense vibration and swaying of the tower itself.

Our climb up the various ladders had been complicated by the strong vibrations permeating the entire tower, but only now, at the top, did I realize that the entire tower was swaying. I estimated that the top was swinging back and forth by at least six feet! Larry assured me that this was safe and normal, but I had to remain focused on hanging on tightly as I was looking around.

After this adventure, the climb down was anti-climactic. I was used to the worst of the swaying and vibrating by then and climbing down was more of an exercise in coordination than strength, so it was much easier for me.

When we reached the bottom of the tower, the noise level was lower, and we could speak without yelling. "The smaller hydrocarbons resulting from the thermal cracking process in the cokers are sent to these fractionating towers," Larry said, as he continued the tour. "The fractionating towers separate the hydrocarbons into different streams. The lightest fractions are drawn off for naphtha, kerosene, and gas oil. The gas oil and naphtha get hydrotreated, and then turned into the SCO. The heaviest fraction, coke, is used to fuel the power plant."

"So, there's no waste?"

"Actually, there is," he said. "Most of the product streams other than the coke have to be treated to remove sulphur. We don't have any use for the sulphur so, for now, we are just stockpiling it."

"Ah. Those are the huge, bright yellow piles I saw off to the side," I said. "Aren't you worried about the fire hazard?"

"Yes, we are. That's partly why the sulphur is kept well away from the rest of the upgrading plant, and even then, we still have to keep a close eye on them."

As we concluded our tour and were walking towards Larry's truck, a piercing shriek filled the air as a series of undulating alarms sounded.

"Emergency alarm!" we both said, in unison. We paused to look around and listen, but we'd heard no explosions and didn't see any smoke.

"Let's hop in the truck and stay out of the way until we know what's going on, and where," Larry suggested. "We can use the truck's radio to listen in on the emergency channel."

Sitting in the truck, we heard a series of radio bursts, from which it rapidly became clear that there was an incident somewhere in the upgrading facility. Apparently, someone engaged in repairs to a large vessel had not been responding to their radio. It was some kind of work that required a 'Buddy System,' and their supervisor had also been unable to reach the worker's 'buddy.' The supervisor was way over on the far side of the plant site, and he had followed protocol by calling an emergency before venturing over himself to investigate further.

The next thing we knew, a red pickup truck with red lights flashing and siren blaring burst around a corner, crossed right in front of us, and screeched to a halt in front of a large vessel that was right across the access-way in front of us. As we watched, an emergency responder – I couldn't tell whether it was a man or a woman - wearing a firefighter's coat and helmet hopped out of the truck then reached back in to drag out a Scott air pack with a full-face mask attached. Hoisting the air pack onto their shoulders and clipping the mask to the harness while on the run, the rescue worker dashed into an open hatch that I hadn't previously noticed.

Having only just been certified for SCBA air pack use, the training was still quite fresh in my mind. "Shouldn't that mask be on?" I asked.

"It sure should," Larry replied, getting out of the truck. "Come on!"

Exiting the truck, Larry opened-up a compartment along the side and began to pull out an air pack. "There's one like this on your side too," he yelled. Part of our air pack training had involved relentless practising of the art of donning such gear quickly, but properly, and in next to no time we were both suited up and jogging across the access-way. Reaching the vessel's large hatch, we could see that some kind of paper sign was attached to the vessel by a single corner, and otherwise flapping in the breeze.

When we straightened out the sign and pressed it against the vessel wall, we read "DANGER | CONFINED SPACE | HAZARDOUS ATMOSPHERE | ENTRY BY PERMIT ONLY."

"My God, they've gone into a vessel that's being purged. It's probably full of nitrogen," said Larry. With an abrupt, "Hang-on a second," Larry used his radio to quickly call the emergency coordination centre, to inform them that we were at the specified vessel, and that a rescuer had just gone in alone, but without a mask on, and that we two were about to follow but with masks on.

Then, he looked me in the eye and said, "Are you OK to do this?"

"Let's do it," I responded, with a nod of my head, "You lead."

"OK, let's go. Whatever happens, stick to me like glue."

Donning our masks, we each took a quick breath to make sure our air supplies were feeding us properly, we each switched on the flashlights that we'd also grabbed from Larry's truck, and in we went.

As we entered, it suddenly became quieter and, of course, pitch black. There was some kind of fine mist or dust in the vessel – I never found out which – so our flashlight beams only penetrated a short distance and there was a lot of backscatters. Even the partial light was a comfort compared to what I'd trained in, though, and I had no trouble keeping visual track of Larry. Nevertheless, we advanced to the left, following the inner wall of the vessel, Larry with his left hand on the wall, and me with my left hand hanging on to the corner of his jacket, both of us holding our flashlights in our right hands.

On we went: step, step, pause, swing our lights around, call out for anyone to respond. Every time, we heard nothing, so we'd repeat the process...

We repeated this pattern over, and over again. At each pause, our flashlights only reflected light back from suspended droplets or particles (whatever they were), and the predominant sounds were the hissing of our regulators as they reduced the air pressure from our tanks and delivered it to our masks at a pressure we could breathe.

Finally, Larry tripped over something, felt around, and called out to me. Crouching down myself, I saw that he'd stumbled over the rescuer that we'd first seen entering the vessel. As Larry and I rolled him over onto his back, we could see that he still had no mask on, we had no way of knowing whether his breathing air system was functional or not, and he didn't appear to be breathing. Larry immediately whipped his mask off, placed it over our victim's face and hit the manual 'positive flow' button, causing his regulator to deliver a blast of air into the mask. Meanwhile, I tried a few quick chest compressions in hopes of getting some of that air into the victim's lungs.

Next, I pulled my own mask off, held my breath, and placed the mask over Larry's face so he could get a couple of restorative breaths of air in too. After gulping a few breaths, he passed my mask back to me and replaced his own. Then he yelled through his mask: "Let's not waste time checking for pulse and respiration. Let's just get him the hell out of here!"

"OK," I agreed.

As I replaced my mask on my own face, Larry picked our victim up, air tank and all, and heaved him over his shoulders to a 'fireman's carry' position. "Lead on," was all he said.

Not stopping to argue, I simply nodded, turned around and started towards the hatch. Now our positions were reversed, with me following the inner wall of the vessel back with my right hand on the wall, and Larry close behind with his right hand hanging on to the corner of my jacket.

This time we moved faster, and soon the light from my flashlight was overtaken by a beam of light shining out just up ahead. Clearly, someone else had arrived and had thought to create a beacon of light for us!

Eventually, we reached the hatch, and as the two of us laboured to get our victim through the hatch, there were many hands reaching out to help us. Still, others appeared to help Larry and me too, as we made our way through the hatch. As we were assisted over to one side, out of the way, I could see an array of emergency vehicles with flashing lights, including an ambulance. Two paramedics took control of our victim, and immediately re-commenced first aid.

With a single glance at each other, we each gave a curt nod, and Larry and I simultaneously rose and turned back towards the hatch.

"Hey, where do you think you're going?" an authoritative voice yelled.

"Back in! There should be at least one more person back in there somewhere!" Larry exclaimed.

"Take it easy," the authoritative voice (who turned out to be a supervisor) said, walking up to us. "There's a fresh team going in right now... see for yourself."

Looking toward the vessel's main hatch, we could see another pair of emergency responders in firefighting gear and air packs entering the hatch, just like we had done only a few minutes earlier.

"You've done your part. Let the professionals take it from here. There's another ambulance on its way. When it gets here, I want you two checked out. If they say you're OK, then you can leave. We'll debrief everything tomorrow."

Relieved, we both stepped aside to strip off our heavy gear and wait for the next ambulance. This whole thing, having come on the heels of a full day of work, had left us both exhausted – mentally and physically.

"Hey!" the supervisor yelled over his shoulder. He had started to jog over to another group of emergency responders, but paused, lowered his radio, and said "Great work you two! I'll thank you properly tomorrow," Then the supervisor ran off, continuing to bark commands into his radio.

By this point, our adrenaline was waning, and a wave of exhaustion was starting to set in, so Larry and I both just collapsed into sitting positions beside a fire truck and watched as a larger rescue effort was mobilized to find the remaining one or two victims.

It wasn't long before one of the first two paramedics ran over to us. "I just thought you would like to know. Your victim's got a pulse and he's breathing again. His pulse is weak, and so is his breathing, but we think he's going to make it. We're going to go set a speed record down Super-Test Hill to the hospital," and then over his shoulder as he ran back to the ambulance, "I thought you'd want to know!!"

As the ambulance sped off at many times the plant site's speed limit, Larry and I looked at each other and said, simultaneously, "I hope there's no brain damage."

"It felt like it took us forever to do that. How long do you think he was without oxygen?" I asked.

"Good question," Larry said, "It felt like forever to me too, but we saw him go in, and we almost immediately suited up and went in ourselves. Then we had to search." He paused, thinking, then "he may only have been down for five minutes I suppose."

"It's going to be close, then," I sighed, too tired to think much more.

It wasn't long before the second ambulance arrived. The new paramedics judged that Larry and I were both exhausted but otherwise fine and released us.

As we were stowing our gear back into Larry's truck, the supervisor-type jogged over again, looked us over himself, and said, "Leave your truck here. I'll have someone drive you both all the way back home. Get a good night's rest and take taxis back to the site tomorrow morning." Then he smiled at us, "If your bosses won't pay for the taxi fares let me know, and when I'm through yelling at them, I'll pay the fares myself. Now get out of here."

At this point, he looked up, waved the latest emergency vehicle to arrive over and told the driver that they had more than enough resources on hand now and that he wanted them to take these two 'sorry-looking' people wherever they wanted to go.

As a little girl, I'd always wanted to ride in a fire truck …

That afternoon, at age 26, I got my wish, as a full-size rescue engine drove Larry and me all the way home, siren off, but red lights flashing all the way. Unfortunately, I just sat in a daze, grateful that we might have saved a life, and worried about the one or two left behind that others were trying to save. I was even too exhausted to remind the fire engine driver that he was breaking the law by speeding with his emergency lights on, just to get us home.

Halfway home I fell asleep.

**

The next morning there was a debriefing in a large meeting room, involving safety people (including my GCOS boss, Frank), upgrading-plant people of various kinds (including Larry and his boss), the supervisor of the night before (who turned out to be the emergency response team's shift-supervisor at the time everything had happened), and several managers.

One of the managers led the initial discussion. He first made it emphatically clear that this was not going to be about assigning blame, using rather colourful language to make his points clear.

"What we are all here to do," he said, "is to figure out what happened so we can make sure it never happens again."

Next, he led a narration of the sequence of events as it had been pieced together overnight, interspersed with comments from various people that had been involved at each stage. Apparently, several things had gone wrong more or less simultaneously. Isn't that always the way?

The big vessel had been shut-down for maintenance, and it was being purged with nitrogen gas to remove all of the flammable gases that it normally contained. The maintenance procedure had been properly posted in advance and warning signs were placed near the big hatch and a few other places. The signs were intended to alert people that the interior might not contain breathable air, meaning that it might be full of flammable gases, or nitrogen, or both, but possibly not oxygen. As I already knew, the warning sign by the hatch had become dislodged and, depending on how the wind was gusting, was not always even recognizable as a warning sign, much less visibly showing what the warning was.

It was at this point that we were told that there had been casualties. Two people had died. As most of us sat, riveted to the fronts of our seats, you could hear a pin drop in the room as we were told what happened next. It was thought that the first worker had gone into the vessel, wearing an SCBA air pack but without his mask on, apparently not realizing that there was no breathable air inside. He had collapsed in the middle of the vessel.

His buddy probably became concerned when, after a few minutes, he had not been able to see or hear him. In any case, the buddy radioed for help, as he was supposed to do, and then went in on his own – which he was not supposed to do. He must not have put his mask on either, because he was found with no mask on, collapsed on top of his buddy, in the centre of the vessel.

The next steps Larry and I already knew. The first emergency responder had arrived, took in the situation, concluded that at least one person needed rescuing, and plunged into the vessel, also without his mask on. He had later confirmed, from his hospital bed, that he had not seen the warning sign, thought worker number two might have just wandered off, and went in to see about worker number one. Although he had been trained in both air pack use and confined-space entry procedures, he'd simply "not thought about" the risk that the atmosphere inside might not be breathable. That mistake had nearly gotten him killed. The prognosis at the time was that the physicians felt he'd been rescued just in time, and he would live. The physicians were more guarded when it came to making predictions, but the consensus was that there was probably some minor brain damage, but almost certainly nothing really serious. Only time would tell.

That was our cue, and Larry took up the narrative of how we had happened to be on the scene and our actions. Larry did a good job of summarizing our story, so I really didn't have to do much beyond nodding from time to time, in support. As our part of the story came to an end, one of the other managers pointed out that we had failed to follow proper procedures by going into rescue mode, and that "as amateurs," we should have stayed put and let the emergency responders handle it.

That brought all semblance of decorum to an end. Larry and I had barely had time to sit up straight and bristle at this criticism, before a cascade of voices rose to our defence, prime among those being the voices of our two supervisors, and even the emergency-response shift-supervisor of the night before. The latter, in the loudest voice of all, pointed out in sulphurous language that the first *'professional'* emergency responder had already arrived on the scene and made an ass of himself by stupidly rushing-in, single-handedly and wrongly, to try to effect the rescue. Furthermore, had not the two of us 'amateurs' gone in and done the job quickly and properly, there would have been three deaths, rather than two.

This brought about another cascade of yelling and finger-pointing and it was decided to take a break, so everyone could calm down.

Sick of it all, Larry and I simply left, followed by our respective supervisors who congratulated us on our quick thinking and actions, reminded us that we'd saved a life, told us that they were proud of us, that everyone else was too, and that we should ignore the one asshole who was the exception.

They felt that the nit-picky and accusing manager was just worried that he'd be blamed for everything and was looking for a scapegoat. "Don't worry about the asshole's rank either," they said. The emergency services people themselves were embarrassed but could be counted on to be professional. More than that, apparently the emergency services people were very pleased with our performance. We had saved one of their own after all, and they were also pleased that we had demonstrated the virtues of training all employees in safety skills and preparedness. Besides, our supervisors concluded with contentment, word had spread quickly, and the entire mine and plant site were now fans of ours.

Our supervisors suggested that Larry and I go home and take another day off, but we each said we'd rather stay at work and try to get back to normal. They understood and didn't press the matter.

I went back to the office with my own supervisor, Frank. I was mostly feeling bad for the two workers that had lost their lives. While Frank sympathized, he counselled me not to take it all on myself, that I'd done everything that I could, more than I should (*"according to some"*), and that he was very proud of me.

Frank said that his war-time experiences had taught him a couple of things, one was that every organization had a few assholes (who should be ignored), and the other was that a person could only *"do so much to save the world"* (and had to let the rest go). We talked it through a bit more, but that was the gist of it. I could feel Frank's pride in my actions, and I reluctantly decided that the life we'd saved was going to have to be enough for me.

As a small post-script to this incident, we were later told that all of the other managers and the head of the union had, in a rare display of unanimity, taken on the offending manager in force, demanding that if he didn't "smarten-up, change his tune, and give Larry and I some kind of medals," the union would call for a general strike and be supported in this (!) by the rest of management.

"It's unheard of, eh?" Frank, chortled. "A strike call that's supported by management?"

We didn't get any medals, of course, and didn't want any either, and we never heard another word, positive or negative, from the offending manager either. It's interesting how things work themselves out sometimes. Do you suppose that it was a coincidence that that manager was transferred to Chicago the following month?

Anyway, in the afternoon of the debriefing day, I met another young engineer, who took me through the tailings area, where the various water-based tailings streams were all collected together in pipeline-gathering systems, and ultimately released into a massive tailings pond. This also was all very impressive, but a bit of an anticlimax after everything I'd just been through, and I have to admit that I didn't pay as much attention as I could have. I don't even remember the young engineer's name.

It was a relief to finally get home and spend some quiet-time playing with Silver, who seemed to sense that I needed both consoling and distraction for a while.

8 VULNERABILITIES

The detection of crime is an art, not a science. Therefore, little can be written upon it, but much can be learnt by observation of all that goes on around one by those who have a natural aptitude for investigation. This natural aptitude for investigation is the chief stock-in-trade of a constable, whether in uniform, or a so-called detective in plain clothes. This, together with application to the matter in hand, general knowledge acquired by reading and observation, experience, and personal courage, are the roads to success.

INTRODUCTION. "R.C.M.P. CONSTABLES' MANUAL." OTTAWA

Another weekend had arrived, bringing with it another Saturday night yard party. We were in the last week of August, now, and the evenings were still warm, but with some cooling as the sunset, which seemed to be a signal that fall would be coming soon.

As often happened with these yard parties I was able to bring Silver and could visit with several people I knew, while meeting others at the same time. This particular party included almost everyone from the community that I'd met so far, including my landlords (Geoff and Karen Laker and their dog, Teddy), the rest of the crew from the infamous hot-tub party (Laurie and Ann

MacDonald, and Geoff and Karen's brother-in-law/brother James). There were also several people from the Man Space introduction, including Jason, plus a few from GCOS and Syncrude, including JJ and Larry.

It was interesting, and a bit surprising, to see how Silver reacted to some of these people. For the most part, he was just calm and obliging if someone was introduced to him and wanted to talk to him and pet him. For other people, though, he was a bit 'growly,' while for still others he was almost affectionate to the point of cuddly (which wasn't like him at all). Eventually, I began to see a pattern.

In the various interactions at these parties, it was natural that some people would be searching for possible romantic interests. In most cases, if a guy walked up and seemed to be showing more than a casual interest in me, Silver would start inserting himself between us and looking at the new entry with a gaze that bordered on fierce. Jason, the architect of the Man Space I'd recently been introduced to, was a case in point. At this party, and others, Jason made no pretense of hiding his interest, and was behaving in a very attentive and somewhat forward manner towards me. I was less than interested in him, and Silver was positively rude to him – pushing himself between us and giving out low growls, from time to time, from the back of his throat. I wondered whether this rebuffing of Jason was over-protectiveness on the part of Silver, who seemed to sense my complete lack of romantic interest in Jason.

If that was strange, Silver's response to Larry was downright embarrassing. I didn't have any romantic interest in Larry either, but he was a very genuine and down-to-earth kind of guy and I liked him. That and the rescue experience we'd been through together really brought us together as fast friends. In this case, Silver was almost cat-like and pretty darn cuddly in his attentiveness to Larry, practically rubbing up against his leg. I remember thinking '*Who needs a dating service?*' After all, I had the Fort McMurray parties to provide easy opportunities to meet new people, and I had Silver to not only help screen the prospects but do his best to either repel or attract them as either he judged them or sensed I was judging them, or both.

***

Sunday, the day after the big party, I was lounging over a mug of coffee in my little kitchen nook. I was pondering everything I had seen and learned at the oil sands site, while at the same time being very aware that the Sept 5 deadline was rapidly approaching.

The problems were not only the lack of obvious suspects but my discovery that the GCOS site was like a saboteur's dream. Every stage of the process could be fairly easily disrupted, and most processing units beyond the mine seemed to have things that could burn and/or explode!

Searching for inspiration, Silver and I took a drive up to the site and stopped along the highway, where we could pull-over and look at the mine. Up close, the machines and other equipment had all looked immense and invulnerable. Now, from my more distant perspective on the highway, I could better visualize how everything followed a linear process order: remove muskeg and overburden, then mine the ore, then move the ore through the feed bin, then extract the bitumen as a froth, then treat the froth to clean it, then pass it on for upgrading. Linked to the treatment plants were the side-streams: extraction tailings, froth treatment tailings, vented steam and gases, and upgrading side-products. Finally, the ultimate product, synthetic crude oil, emerged and went into the transportation pipeline.

It all seemed so huge, and so organized. Unassailable. Unstoppable.

As I continued to look on from afar, I tried to turn my thoughts around and think about it from the other direction. Assume that the process could be interrupted. Think like a saboteur, or more specifically, like a saboteur that wanted to create attention and make a point. In my notebook, I started noting what seemed to me to be the key points:

Clearly, a strike at any link in the chain, up to and including upgrading, would bring the entire process to a halt as long as all parallel processes at that point were hit. Since almost everything was designed to allow at least one processing unit to continue while another was off-line for maintenance, one would have to hit all such parallel units to bring the whole operation to a halt.

Links in the chain with the least number of parallel processes would be the easiest to disrupt. In the extraction plant, one would have to disrupt all four process streams, the three operating ones, plus the standby one. In the froth treatment plant, it would have to be all of the scroll centrifuges, or else all of the disc-nozzle centrifuges. It was a similar situation in the upgrading plant, which had three parallel 'trains.' Any of these would be extremely difficult, short of blowing up entire plants.

So. The further upstream the better, then. That would limit any attempts to bypass a disruption too. Taking an extreme example, *disrupting a tailings pipeline would be less harmful than disrupting a bucketwheel excavator*, I thought.

Next, the more visible from the outside world the better. That way, more people, including television crews, reporters, and photographers would be able to see, record, and broadcast it all. Striking at something like an extraction vessel or centrifuge inside a large building, for example, wouldn't have much public impact. But imagine the media attention that would be paid to visible destruction in the mine, or to a huge fireball from an explosion in the upgrading plant! I shuddered at the thought.

Looked at in this way, it seemed to me that there were several key vulnerabilities and that a saboteur's approach would depend a lot on the options available.

If, for example, it was an insider, someone with access to the operation, then they might be able to get at the upgrading plant and create an explosion that would cause a cascade of further explosions. This could easily wreak havoc with the entire plant, create a visible sensation of explosions, fireballs, flames, and smoke, while creating a level of destruction that could take years to rebuild. This was the nightmare scenario. I really didn't see how I could help guard against an inside job beyond patrolling the site as frequently as I could and maintaining a general vigilance.

If, on the other hand, it was an outsider, someone with no easy access to the operation, then they had a more limited range of points of entry. The easiest, would be to simply drive up the highway to a point alongside the operation, as I had just done, pick their time, and then simply drive overland: (1) into the mine, (2) over to the pipeline that carried the synthetic crude oil south to the refineries in Edmonton, or (3) close to one of the two tailings ponds, or the big pipelines that fed them. Any of these three options seemed feasible.

Of the three options, number two seemed unlikely as the synthetic crude oil pipeline had already been hit once, although at a point some distance away from the plant site. That event had received some attention, but the company had demonstrated that they could get pipelines back into operation quite quickly, and it was logical to conclude that the company, and the police, would now be watching the SCO pipeline fairly closely. It seemed to me that a second strike would be in a different location.

Of the other two options, number one would be attractive. Someone could drive into the mine, and strike at any point in the articulated, bucketwheel reclaimer trains, from the machinery driving the bucketwheel itself, to the conveyors or their transfer points. There were only the two bucketwheel trains, so only two places need be hit to bring the entire operation to a standstill. Alternatively, the main feed bin provided a single strike-point that wouldn't be as easy to approach by stealth, but a single blast would halt everything.

Option number three seemed less attractive, but possibly easier, since the tailings area was least populated with workers, probably not closely watched, and probably not watched at all at night. I'd have to keep this option in mind.

"I think that it's time to call Ottawa," I said to Silver.

As Silver and I returned to town, I resolved to increase my tours of inspection around the plant site and to see if I could get away with bringing Silver with me. Back at home, I dialled the Ottawa number that Staff Sergeant Simpson, my RCMP boss, had given me, and said, "Constable Houston, Alexandra, Regimental Number 15425," to the duty officer that answered.

"Phone number?" was the reply.

I provided my home number and was told I would be contacted.

Given that it was a Saturday evening, Ottawa time, I expected to have to wait a while, but the call-back came within an hour.

"Alex? Bob here. How are things going?"

I told him everything that I'd learned so far, and most of what I thought, including my assessment of vulnerabilities and probabilities. It took a while.

"Excellent!" he enthused, "That's fantastic progress."

"I thought you'd be disappointed," I responded. "It still feels like searching for a needle in a haystack, and I'm no closer to identifying suspects."

"Patience," he counselled. "Besides, you're not alone. We have uniformed Members keeping an eye on the main pipeline, and we have two official investigators interviewing people in the city and at the two plant sites. We're also going through all the personnel records at both companies. You just keep on doing what you're doing. ... What are you planning next?"

"I want to make sweeping patrols of the areas that seem like high probability targets, but if I overdo it my cover might get blown. I also want to ask more questions when I meet people at parties and such in town, but that also may start to look suspicious."

"Follow your instincts," Bob said, firmly. "If people get suspicious, so be it. At this stage of the game, we need to take some calculated risks. In the worst-case scenario, if your cover is completely blown, then we can take advantage of your insider knowledge and have you conduct patrols on the plant sites - in full uniform if need be – so don't get stressed about it. ... Are you wearing your gun when you go up there?"

"No, but with the saboteur's deadline approaching, I've been thinking about it. I think that I'm going to see if I can get away with Silver coming along with me now, though."

"It's your call but think about doing both. We don't want to lose you."

And that was that. It was time to take a few more risks.

9 THE CLOCK IS TICKING

"It's a small world," they say.

One of an undercover agent's fears is that they'll encounter someone they knew in their former life. I suppose that it was inevitable that it would happen eventually.

In addition to going for walks around our neighbourhood, Silver and I often went for walks downtown and along the Athabasca River, which bordered the downtown area. Going downtown meant using a leash with Silver, but he was quite OK with a leash. He had been able to roam free quite a lot in his former life in Radium City, but he had also been a lead sled dog so I figured that he must have been comfortable being in harnesses and the dog-sled traces, as well. We were well into one of these walks downtown when I heard someone call my name.

"Alex, is that you?"

I'd been walking downtown one day when I heard my name called. I turned to see a wide-eyed Jack McDonald. Jack and I had been recruits together at the RCMP Depot Division training centre in Regina. I hadn't just met Jack while in training, there was also the 'Sergeant-Major's Daughter' incident. Although the circumstances of that incident were quite awkward, and I wasn't personally interested in the 'Don Juan type,' which is what I'd put him down as, I really had found him to be a nice guy to have as a colleague. I hadn't seen him since we'd graduated and received our first postings though, which had taken us to different parts of Canada. Now, there he was coming down the sidewalk towards me.

"Jack! How are you?"

"Great... but I'd walked right past you before I realized who you were. What are you doing in Fort McMurray?"

Not knowing what else to do, I quickly rushed up to him and gave him a hug. While doing so, I whispered in his ear, "I'm undercover. Don't give me away."

Although he was surprised to get a hug from me, he was quick enough to take in what I'd whispered and to play along. "It feels like I haven't seen you in forever," he said. "How about a coffee?"

"Sure," I said. "Somewhere that Silver here can come with us."

We walked to the nearest coffee shop where Jack could go in and get us something, while Silver and I waited outside. When he emerged with two coffees, and a cup of water for Silver (a nice gesture, I thought), we walked to a small park on the edge of town, near the river, and found a bench.

"What's going on, and when did you get a dog?" he asked. I quickly explained what I'd been up to over the past year, and the story of how Silver had come into my life, all the way up to the two of us being sent to Fort McMurray undercover. Jack was impressed with the idea of using me for undercover work, and he thought it was pretty funny that Silver would be undercover too.

"How about you?" I asked.

"I'm posted to the detachment here," he said. "I've been here all year, ever since graduating... and I'm working on the same case you are, in a small way." He explained that he wasn't one of the official investigators on the case, but that he'd done a few of the interviews in town and had been helping to keep an eye on the main pipeline.

When I explained that I'd been ordered not to contact the local detachment, except in an emergency, he agreed to keep my secret. I shared my cover story, and we agreed to pretend that we'd met in Regina while he was in training (which was true enough) and I was there visiting a friend from university days. That way, we'd both be able to improvise if we met again, especially at one of the city's ubiquitous parties.

When we finished our coffees, we strolled along the river bank, where I'd been idly throwing sticks into the river thinking that Silver would like to jump in and fetch them, but he didn't seem to want to go into the water.

"That's funny," I said. "I wonder what that's all about."

"What do you mean?" Jack asked.

"Well, Silver's been in boats lots of times before, with no

concern, even in rough water. But, now that I think about it, I don't think I've ever seen him go into the water."

"I'd have expected a big dog like him to jump in at the first chance he gets," Jack offered. "Do you think something scared him when he was little?"

"Maybe. I originally found Silver marooned on an island. In fact, now that I think about it I did wonder why he hadn't tried swimming to the mainland. It wasn't all that far from the island. I wonder what that's all about." I made a mental note to pursue this 'no swimming' business some time, but let it go for the moment.

Before parting, Jack and I exchanged our home and office phone numbers, and he said to call him if I ever needed anything. Meeting Jack wasn't supposed to have happened, but I felt a bit better knowing I had an ally in town.

***

Now that I'd had my in-depth tours of all the major parts of the GCOS site, a lot of my job was to rove around the site and check-in with the various shift supervisors in each area at the beginning and ending of their shifts. As Frank had explained it to me, this 'checking-in' was a combination of what he called "Waving the flag," and genuinely interacting with the supervisors to show them that Safety was more interested in assisting them with safety than in being a form of 'Safety Police.' When the supervisors identified things they wanted help with, such as equipment, training, or coaching for their teams, then that's what I would work on in the middle of the shifts – between patrols, as it were.

This, of course, was almost perfect in terms of my undercover job, as it allowed me to roam fairly freely, and often, around the site. I quickly became well known and well received around the site. Frequent exposure, plus the reputation I'd gained as a result of the confined-space rescue, meant that I could go almost anywhere without raising eyebrows. One thing that was reinforced by my interactions with the workforce was that they really did seem to be quite happy with, and very committed to, their jobs. As time went on, I became more and more convinced that our saboteur was either not a plant worker or was really well hidden.

When a day approached that I knew Geoff and Karen would be out of town, I took advantage of the opportunity to ask Frank if I could bring Silver on-site with me. Frank had said sure, as long as I kept him in the truck that they'd issued me for on-site work. I said thanks and kept to myself the obvious question about why he shouldn't be allowed in the offices. Keeping my mouth shut turned out to be wise, in hindsight, because I discovered Frank's concern soon enough on my own.

The first time I brought Silver along to the site, we went out for a tour of the mine area, and it wasn't until we'd completed our first stop and the two of us had hopped back into my truck, that I noticed his paws were shiny black.

We'd been walking around heavy equipment in the mine, an oil sand mine. That is, an oil sand mine in which bitumen oozed from the higher-grade oil sand and coated almost everything else. My boots and Silver's paws were no exception. We all removed our boots when we entered the office trailers and buildings, and then walked around in socks, or slippers or little felt booties. I didn't have anything like that for Silver. It was a good thing that there was no-one there to see me blushing as I looked at Silver's paws after that first mine-walk together.

As an aside, when we got back home, it took me a long time to get the bitumen out of the fur on Silver's paws, and out from between the pads on the bottoms of his paws. Long enough that I resolved to not have to do that again. However, I did want to be able to have Silver come with me and not have to stay in the truck all the time. In the end, I solved this by sewing little cloth booties for him, like the ones people buy for little dogs to use in the winter except that these had to be for a big dog in the fall. I made them out of the nylon from an old rain jacket and, although it took Silver a bit of time to get used to them, they worked quite well. I put them on him when we got to the GCOS site in the mornings and removed them when we changed from my work truck to 'Big Red,' my personal truck, at the end of the workday. On-site, people laughed when they first saw them on Silver's paws, but anyone that spent any time in the mine quickly realized that they were a very practical innovation.

Another issue with driving around in the mine was that there were patches of fairly boggy ground. These seemed to be residual legacies of the muskeg and overburden that had been mostly, but not completely, removed earlier. On one of my days driving through the mine, I inadvertently got stuck in one of the patches. When I say stuck I mean really stuck. I'd been issued with a four-wheel drive work truck that could handle most of the rugged terrain of the site, but not on this occasion. At first, it seemed like a small thing. The truck had bogged down, so I put it into four-wheel drive and tried again. No luck, either forward or backwards. Next, I tried to slowly rock the truck back and forth, trying to build up enough momentum to get free. Worse than no luck, instead of getting free, this just settled the truck in deeper. With all four wheels deep in the muck, I realized that I'd been defeated. Fortunately, I was able to get help – with the aid of hard hat stickers.

This takes a bit of explaining. One of the things I'd learned early on in my orientation to the GCOS site, was that there was kind of a fad related to hard hat stickers. I imagined that it had probably started innocently enough, when employees were given stickers to display on their hard hats, showing that they'd received training certifications in things like basic safety, first aid, SCBA, and confined-space entry. I had a number of these on my own hard hat already. Next, individual work units started making up stickers that illustrated the part of the company they worked for. I had one of these too, representing the Safety and Security group. Similarly, Tom wore one for Mining, JJ had one for Extraction, and so on.

It didn't take long for the competitive spirits in the company to get the idea of trying to have the best-looking stickers. So, whereas the Extraction Department stayed with a simple red sticker with the word "Extraction" on it, other groups added drawings and more colours, such as the one for Mining, which had the outline of a bucketwheel excavator on a bright background. Another group added a cartoon figure wearing a hard hat, and so on.

The next level of escalation involved collecting hard-hat stickers, and that's when the company's suppliers got into the act. The marketing and sales people from the various supplier companies were always looking for a way to get name recognition and beat out their competition. These companies stood to make a lot of money on big sales contracts, so they were able to afford commercial artists and graphic designers. Before long, there was a wide array of stickers for everything from centrifuges, to pumps, to chemicals, and it was around this time that the collectible stickers became an underground currency. That is, you could trade unique or popular stickers for other stickers, or other stuff, or, … favours.

This had a very practical application for me on the day when I'd managed to get my truck well and truly stuck in the mine. I'd first radioed Tom, who happened to be 'on shift' that day in the mine and explained what had happened. He'd driven over to take a look and agreed that his truck wasn't going to be able to pull me out. He next tried calling a couple of supervisors in the area to see if we could get a bulldozer to come over and help but was told that all of them were busily occupied with other work right then. Tom said, "Well, we'll just have to wait, unless … you wouldn't happen to have any good hard hat stickers with you, would you?"

Actually, I did. The fact that I'd been roaming all around the site talking to so many people in so many different areas meant that I'd been given quite a pile of them. I wasn't collecting them, people just gave them to me, and I'd taken to throwing them into a small cardboard box in the truck. When I showed them to Tom, his jaw dropped. "You're sitting on a gold mine!" he exclaimed, "and you're sure you're willing to give some of them up?"

"Sure," I replied. I didn't mention that I wasn't interested in them and had only hung on to them because it seemed a shame to throw them out.

Well, the next thing you know, Tom was on the radio again promising a handful of collectible hard-hat stickers to the first bulldozer or power shovel that came to my rescue.

It worked, sort of. Before long a power shovel on caterpillar tracks came crunching and squeaking over to us, and its operator, after a quick look, attached a chain to my truck and started pulling. Unfortunately, this resulting in him getting stuck too. It was amazing to see those large tracks going around and around, as the entire machine sunk lower and lower into the muck. As the operator finally admitted defeat, we now had two vehicles stuck.

Back on the radio again, this time Tom was more specific, and called out for help from a D9 'cat.' The D9 Caterpillar bulldozer is a giant among bulldozers, with huge tracks and weighing in at about 50 tons. In less than half an hour we could hear the clanking and rattling of a D9 cat working its way towards us. When it arrived, and the operator got out to look things over, he had a great laugh. "Looks like you need me all right," he said.

Whereas the power shovel operator had come over for hard hat stickers, the D9 cat operator wasn't interested in those at all. He was proud of the capabilities, and the raw power, of his machine, and was eager to demonstrate them. Although he was more than happy to help us out, he did jokingly say he'd pull us out for the price of a photograph of him doing it. I had a camera with me as part of my safety work, so I readily agreed.

With the big D9 cat, it didn't take long to pull the power shovel out, although it took both machines under power with each of their big sets of tracks churning muck out everywhere. After getting the power shovel out, getting my truck out was easier. I took some good pictures of both rescues.

***

By day three of bringing Silver along, I got caught. I suppose it was inevitable.

I'd been out touring around and checking in with some of the shift-supervisors when I received a radio call from Frank, asking me to drop by his office once I'd finished my rounds.

When I arrived in his office, Frank got me seated, got me a coffee, and then shut his office door.

"What's up, Alex?"

"What do you mean?"

"What I mean is, you're doing a great job, and you're getting everything on your plate done faster than anyone I've ever had in your job before, so I'm not complaining, but it's strange." He paused, ... "You're spending much more time patrolling the site than you need to, and you're covering the entire site twice a day – at the beginning and the end of each shift."

"But, ..." I began.

"Let me finish," he jumped in. "Anyone else doing this job would make it easier on themselves by picking one area to do at the beginning of a shift, then another at the end, then two more the next day. Say it was the mine and extraction on a Monday, then froth treatment and upgrading on a Tuesday, then tailings on Wednesday morning, then repeat it all for the rest of the week. By the end of the week, every major unit has been visited twice, and once each at shift-start and shift-ending ... but not you, you're hitting every area fourteen times a week."

"At first, I thought it was just that you're keen to do a good job and working extra hard to show that you're serious and have a future here. That would be natural enough, but you've been going way beyond that, ..." he paused again. "Then there's that dog of yours. You've stretched my permission to bring him on-site to the limit."

I started to speak again, but he waved me down.

"I'm not done yet Alex. Now look, I don't mind you bringing the dog along either, even if you do it every single day, and everyone around here likes you so much that no one's going to complain about you either, so it's not that." He sighed. "But when I see the two of you prowling the entire production line twice a day, when I know that you don't need to, and I know that you don't need the dog, then it makes me wonder, and I can't help remembering things."

"Things?" I asked.

"When I was in the war, the combined RAF/RCAF bases I was posted to had security guards with dogs patrolling the perimeters all the time, night and day, seven days a week. That's what I keep remembering when I see you. So, here it is. What are you two really up to?"

"What are we up to?" I repeated as I took a sip of my coffee. Thinking furiously, I was running through the various fairy tales I could think up, trying to decide which one to tell, when I made the mistake of looking at him, straight in the eye.

I deflated, maybe I really wasn't cut out for 'cloak and dagger' work. Time to take another risk.

"OK," I said. "I'm not really a safety person, … Well, I guess I am now, but what I mean is, that I'm also something else. I'm a police officer, RCMP, and I'm hoping to prevent a bombing here at the site." Before he could speak, I rushed on, "We don't know that there will be a bomb, and we don't know where, when, or from whom, but there have been threats. Your President is worried, the Syncrude President is worried, and so is the RCMP. There is an official investigation underway, but they also sent me in, to the inside, mostly just to sniff around and be available, but I'd like to stop it if I can!"

He thought for a moment, "The pipeline bomb that went off three months ago?"

I nodded, "Same person or persons."

"F***! I mean, sorry, but F***!"

"That's OK," I said, "I feel more or less the same way."

He thought for another moment, "But you're a woman!"

I raised an eyebrow.

"There aren't any women in the RCMP!"

"There are now," I said. "They started a pilot project. I'm it. But there are more women in training already."

"And the dog?"

"Long story, but Silver and I became attached when I was posted to Radium City, then we both got trained to serve as a dog service team, and then we were sent here."

This was coming pretty fast, but Frank didn't seem to have any trouble keeping up. "You two wouldn't happen to have had any special training, would you?" he asked.

In for a penny, ..., I thought. "Explosives," I said.

"Wow, what a story!" he said, "I knew you were up to something, but I could never have made all this up."

"I can give you a number to call, to get confirmation, ..." I started to say, but he waved me off.

"No, I believe you. It's just that this is stranger than fiction." Then he dropped his feet from where they had been perched on his desk-top, sat up straight, and said: "Well, what do you need from me?"

Grateful, I gave him my first thoughts: "Silence and moral support, for now." Then my second thought, "And let me give you that phone number anyway so you can use it in case I get into trouble."

"OK, and if anyone else asks questions about your behaviour, I'll cover for you."

"Thanks, Frank," I said and meant it.

"Oh, and tell me how all this came about someday, OK? I'll provide the Scotch."

"I promise, Frank."

10 ACTION

With Frank in the know, it was easier for Silver and me to patrol the site, but everything seemed quiet for the next week. When the threatened deadline of Sunday, September 5th came and went without incident, I became more concerned, feeling that if the bomber was going to strike, it would be soon.

I suppose 'soon' is a relative term. More days came and went, still with nothing happening. By Friday, I was going crazy. Based on the pattern of the previous bombing, I was pretty sure that our saboteur would wait several days past the deadline before acting, but we were now five days past. I still had no doubts that the threat was real, and it seemed to me that time was running out.

I'd had another quiet coffee meeting with Jack McDonald, who told me that the official investigation was continuing but without useful results. The threatening letters had contained no useful clues. The envelopes had some partial fingerprints, but nothing that matched the Canadian Police Information Centre records, and in any case, such prints could have come from anyone that had handled the envelopes and didn't necessarily belong to the saboteur(s). Like me, they felt that they were searching for a needle in a haystack, without even knowing what a needle looks like.

When I was invited to another yard party for the Saturday night, I decided that it was time for a mental health break and agreed to attend. This time, when Silver and I arrived, I discovered that I knew almost everyone there. That was a change, and I remember thinking that I'd really begun to settle into the community, which was bittersweet considering that one way or another, I'd probably be leaving before long.

I'd volunteered to help the hosts set things up and get the initial snacks and drinks going, so it was some time before I could wander around the yard and chat with people. I spent some time talking to Geoff and Karen, while the three of us played with our dogs. After that, Silver and I had strolled over to the next cluster of people. As we approached, I could hear raised voices. Some kind of animated discussion was underway, and I was able to pick out Jason's voice. Just before we reached the group, Silver suddenly stiffened and stopped in his tracks. This was fairly unusual for him, so it caught my attention. He seemed to sense something, and he cast his head up and around, as if he heard, or sensed, or smelled something but wasn't sure what it was.

I didn't pay too much attention and was about to say "Hi" to the closest member of the little group when Silver suddenly walked purposely up to Jason. Jason, in turn, immediately held out his hand for Silver to sniff, by way of introduction. Silver walked right up to sniff the proffered hand, and then immediately sat right down on his haunches, and turned to stare directly at me, with wide penetrating eyes.

I knew that look!

Holy Smokes! I thought. Clearly, Silver had detected explosives residue of some kind and had immediately sat on his haunches to signal me.

As alarm bells went off in my mind, I quickly turned my head to avoid having any facial expression give me away (and to attempt to slow my suddenly elevated pulse rate). With my thoughts racing, I tried to casually turn to one side and stroll to the house, where I asked one of the hosts the way to their bathroom. Entering the house, I avoided the bathroom and walked straight out the front door and over to my truck. I hadn't had to say or signal anything to Silver, who had immediately followed me.

We drove home, and I immediately made three phone calls: one to Bob in Ottawa, one to Frank, and one to Jack. I told them all the same thing: that Silver had detected explosive materials or residues on Jason, that I suspected him of being the saboteur, and that I was concerned that tonight could be the night. His appearance at the party could either be arrogance, or part of a weak attempt to create an alibi.

Bob said that he would call the Fort McMurray detachment to alert them to the possibilities and that he would tell them about me but instruct them not to contact me or blow my cover unless I called them first. I had previously told him about my discovery by Frank, and my encounter with Jack, and I told Bob that I was about to warn both of them.

When I called Frank and Jack, they had each asked me what I was planning to do next, and I told them. Frank said he'd drive up to the site and 'hang around' the office, just in case, and that I could call or radio him there. Jack said that he was about to start a shift on highway patrol and would just 'happen' to be in the area where the highway ran close to the mine and tailings areas, but more or less out of sight. Jack also said that if I'd wait a few minutes, he'd drop by my townhouse and loan me a hand-held radio that was set for the local RCMP Detachment's regular and tactical frequencies.

My next call was to the home of the yard party. I asked one of the hosts if Jason was still there and was told that he'd left early, right after I had left, in fact. No, they didn't know where he had gone.

Feeling like the time for subterfuge was over, I changed into my tactical uniform for the first time since moving to Fort McMurray. The snub-nosed revolver fit into the standard holster, but I now wished that I'd brought my regular issue, longer-barrelled revolver with me. Too late for that now.

I already had a hand-held radio set for the GCOS mine and other plant-site frequencies, so by the time Jack dropped by, I was as ready as I was going to get. I described Jason's truck, and Jack said he'd keep an eye out for it. It was time to go.

Jack was already in uniform and driving a highway patrol car, and the two of us took the precaution of driving by the home of the yard party. With its lifted chassis, Jason's truck would have been easy to spot, but it was nowhere to be seen. We next drove by Jason's house, but it wasn't there either.

"I think it's going to be tonight, and that he planted the explosives earlier or is going to plant them now," I said.

"If he planted them earlier, why didn't he trigger them already?" Jack wondered.

"I don't know, maybe he was interrupted, or maybe something broke, or ..." I paused as a new idea came to mind. "Maybe he doesn't want to kill anyone. The daytime shift has the most people swarming around the site, the evening shift has less, but the graveyard shift is almost deserted, with only the bare minimum of employees on duty."

"A bomber with a conscience?" Jack scoffed.

"I've seen the transcripts of the letters," I said. "They're always about stopping the oil sand developments, and they always provide warnings in advance. When he last struck, he even allowed a bit of time after the deadline, so maybe he's simply on some kind of social- or environmental crusade," I mused.

"Sounds crazy to me," Jack said.

"No argument there. Anyway, I'm going to go check out the tailings areas and the mine site – I think it's going to be one of those."

"OK," Jack said. "I'll be on the highway, somewhere along the GCOS stretch. Radio if you need me."

Then, with a "Thanks Jack," we were both off.

***

"Certainly, there is no hunting like the hunting of man and those who have hunted armed men long enough and liked it, never really care for anything else thereafter."

Ernest Hemingway,
"On the Blue Water," *Esquire*, April 1936

Driving along the highway by the GCOS mine and tailings areas, I didn't see any sign of the black truck, so I continued onwards. When I drove up to the security gate, the guard recognized me but was surprised at my uniform.

"Alex?" he asked.

"Surprise!" I said, and then, "It's a long story. I'll come by later and tell you about it, OK? ... If you have any questions, just call Frank Stoner."

Between my GCOS ID, the fact that he recognized me, and my police uniform, he really had no reason to delay or detain me, so he let me in, shaking his head.

We parked my personal truck, got into my GCOS truck, and I radioed Frank to advise him that we were on site and heading over to scout the tailings pond area.

"Is that where you think he'll strike?" Frank asked.

"Actually, I don't, but I want to have a quick look before heading out to the mine. If I've assessed things properly, it will be the mine."

"OK. I still don't have enough certainty to raise an alarm, much less shut down any of the operations, but I'll be ready."

"I think that's all you can do for now Frank. I have a radio link to some backup out on the highway now too. This fellow is very knowledgeable about technology, so we'll have to bear in mind that he might be able to monitor our radio calls with a scanner."

"Be careful," he warned.

"Always," I said out loud.

'Usually,' I said to myself.

Silver and I drove all around the tailings pond area. Silver was perched on one side, with half of his body hanging out the window, like dogs often do, but in this case, I could tell he was probing with all his senses. Nothing seemed amiss there. It was quiet, and I didn't see any workers around, but that was normal. It was past midnight, and this part of the site was generally deserted during the graveyard shift.

As we drove away from the main tailings pond, the RCMP radio crackled. It was Jack.

"I've found the black truck," he said. "It's just off the highway, but far enough off that it isn't obvious unless you're looking for it, ... and the dark night doesn't help. Anyway, it's near where the forest fringe comes up to the fenced mine area."

"It's the mine, then," I said, "I think he's going to try to shut the entire operation down."

"Can he do that?"

"If he hits the right spot he can," I replied. "I'm heading for the dump pocket area, where the two big conveyors meet and dump all the oil sand into the feed bin. That's the big framework you can see where the two big conveyors meet, and just before the Extraction Plant, which is that big first building you can see. If you can stay out of sight where you are, he should be in between us, somewhere."

"Roger that," was all that came back.

As Silver and I reached the mine, I radioed Frank to give him the latest news. I didn't think Jason would try to strike at the two bucketwheel excavators or their feeder conveyors, but I wanted to be methodical, so we took a slow drive around them anyway. Both bucketwheels were operating as usual, with their methodical cutting-away of oil sand from their assigned areas, and the sights and smells of heavy equipment operating. Nothing seemed out of the ordinary at those ends.

This time, Silver and I got out of the truck at each bucketwheel in turn and walked 'the line' from the giant buckets, along the connecting conveyors and drop chutes, to the main conveyors. Neither of us sensed anything out of the ordinary.

Next, we turned our attention to the main conveyors and drove slowly along each one, stopping and getting out now and again for a closer look. It was quieter here, with mostly just the sound of the heavily laden conveyor belt moving over the many sets of idlers, which are basically rollers that support the belt. Nothing.

Well, I hadn't expected to find anything until we got to the main feed bin, and that was where we next took our search. This part of the operation involved the two main conveyors dumping their oil sand loads through a large container called a dump pocket that was suspended up off the ground by a framework of steel beams. From this point, the collected oil sand dropped through the feed bin onto a single conveyor that took it to the extraction plant. Although the conveyor could be a target, I'd always felt that the first-choice target would be right where we already were.

I wasn't excited about the prospect of waving a flashlight around and giving away my position, so I instead tried to let my eyes adjust to the darkness and prowled cautiously around the steel framework structure. As I moved along, Silver conducted his own search. Slightly ahead of me, Silver had been sniffing around in a seemingly random pattern, but his searches soon seemed to converge on a path that led to the side of the feed bin that faced the highway.

Suddenly, Silver sat down and pointedly looked upward.

"What is it Silver?" I asked, as I walked over to him and peered around. I couldn't see anything unusual as I peered around, but when I started to look up and around the structure, I noticed a thin wire hanging down, vertically, from one of the steel cross-beams, about eight feet off the ground.

Whistling softly to myself, I continued to look up and around and spotted a second thin wire nearby. It was about ten feet away, seemingly coming from the same cross-beam, and hanging down, vertically, like the first one. These wires seemed unusual to me, although I supposed that they could have been signal lines from some kind of strain sensors on the framework. On previous visits to the mine, I had occasionally encountered engineers from the Research and Development Department crawling over virtually every piece of the system. Monitoring the stresses and strains in the mechanical systems so that they could learn how to predict, and eventually avoid material failures, they'd said.

Suspicious, but unsure, I decided to climb up and investigate. Telling Silver to 'stay,' I found the closest access ladder and started climbing. Once I was able to get up and basically inside the steel framework, I carefully walked along horizontal beams, heading for where we'd seen one of the vertical wires. I hadn't been particularly good on the balance beam in high school gym class, but these beams were about ten inches wide, so it was mostly a case of proceeding slowly, with one or both hands placed on the many vertically and diagonally oriented cross-beams for support.

I took a few wrong turns, but I eventually found one of the vertical wires and I then saw that it was attached to a horizontal wire. Following the latter, I came to a branch point, at which one wire went off towards the centre of the structure somewhere and the other seemed to lead towards another part of the front face of the structure. I followed this second branch first and found that it led to the other vertical wire, that Silver and I had seen from the ground.

Before going back to follow the other branch, I sat down on the beam for a moment to think. Something about this arrangement seemed familiar for some reason, but what? Then it hit me – a cage antenna. "Son of a bitch!" I exclaimed, to no one in particular, as an image of the whole thing flooded into my mind.

First things first. Before going any further, and while I was positioned near the front face of the framework structure, I got on the RCMP radio. "Jack," I called, "There's a bomb up here somewhere, and I think Jason plans to use a remote-control garage-door opener to trigger the detonator."

"OK," Jack replied, "I'm searching for him with binoculars, but haven't found him yet. Be careful!"

I had just started to reply "OK," when there was a sharp metallic 'ping' sound, followed by a rifle crack.

"What the hell was that?"

"Someone took a shot at me. Sounds like a rifle," I said, as I tried my best to crouch down behind some big steel beams. "I don't know what direction the shot came from," I added, over the radio.

"I thought he didn't want to hurt anyone?!"

"Maybe I was wrong," I replied. "Maybe he's panicking, ... or getting desperate!"

"I'll radio for more backup," Jack shot back. "I still think he's between us, so I'm going to leave the highway and work my way in a bit closer towards you. If he takes another shot, I may be able to locate him."

"See if you can get him off my back so Silver and I can look for the bomb."

"Give me one moment to call this in, then I'll start in."

With Jack occupied, and me still crouched down behind the large steel supports, I took a moment to call Frank on the radio.

"Frank! He's out here in the mine. I think I've found antenna wires from a detonator, and someone's already taken a shot at me. I think it's time to shut the whole operation down and evacuate the mine."

"That's enough for me, I'll sound the alarm ... you be careful!!"

"I will, Frank, thanks," and then, "you stay clear too!"

I set the GCOS radio aside. I didn't think I'd be needing it anymore, and I was going to need to be as nimble as I could. From my crouching position, I tried to look up and around for the bomb, and also look out and around for the shooter. Neither was very easy, and neither worked. I'd have to try something else.

Still waiting for Jack, I yelled out from my hiding place, "Jason! I know that you're out there. There's still time to stop this and back away!"

Before I could say anything more, two things happened almost simultaneously. Another shot pinged off the steel somewhere nearby, and the GCOS site-wide emergency evacuation alarms went off, making a massive racket that could be heard everywhere across the entire operation.

Thinking this might give me the distraction I needed, I called down to remind Silver to stay put, and left my cover to creep back to the junction I'd found in the wires and follow the third wire deeper into the steel framework. It led up somewhere.

I couldn't go everywhere the wire went so I had to find another access ladder. As I was doing this, I heard the siren from Jack's highway patrol car in between the shrieks of the evacuation alarm. Jack had obviously turned on the siren to announce his presence, in an attempt to distract Jason from shooting at me. I didn't have time to worry about Jack, though and, hoping that the double distractions would confuse Jason, or at least make him pause, I started up a ladder to the next level. Now I was deeper into the upper support structure for the feed bin, and I had to hunt around again for the wire. Nothing. I must have gone the wrong way.

Retracing my path, I went back down the ladder, crossed to the other side of the structure, found another ladder, and went up again. Once again, I searched around for the wire, sometimes having to crawl around and feel around for the wire by touch. While doing this, I tried to remember to be careful not to lose my balance and fall, but it was hard to remain focused with multiple sirens adding to my already elevated adrenaline level. Backing up again, a stray flash of light from somewhere showed me an in-between level that I hadn't noticed before. I'd no sooner climbed down the half-level and crawled forward a bit when I nearly ran right into it. It was just an electrical wire, but for a moment I imagined it was a trip-wire, and my heart nearly exploded.

A moment's pause with no explosion demonstrated that it wasn't a trip-wire, and I reminded myself that it was just a piece of fancy antenna wire. This realization led to another flash of the obvious – an antenna wire!

Of course!

Still crouched down, I reached for my trusty Swiss Army knife, pulled out the 'saw' blade and started cutting. It took a few moments but at last the saw blade cut completely through and I pushed the part that connected to the other two branches away from me. That destroyed the 'curtain' part of the curtain antenna, but Jason might still be within range, there was no way to tell. I'd have to follow the rest of the wire back until I found the receiver.

I foolishly stood up to turn around and - 'ping,' another sharp metallic sound, followed by a rifle crack. "Son of a bitch!" I exclaimed, mad at myself for being stupid. But I had an idea of direction now, as my exposure had been quite limited.

"Jack," I radioed, "he's taken another shot at me. He must be on the west side of my position somewhere. I can see the forest fringe from here, and from his position, he must be able to see where the conveyors end, and the entrance to the first large plant building."

Not waiting for a reply, I didn't even know if he could hear me over the noise of the sirens, I went back to following what was left of the antenna wire. Now I could follow it by crawling in and around beams, and every six or eight feet, I'd stop, get my knife out, and cut the wire, making the antenna shorter and shorter.

Finally, I came to a box. Not pausing to congratulate myself, I hastily cut the rest of the antenna wire. *Jason shouldn't be able to trigger it now*, I thought to myself, *unless he's really close*. But I didn't know where Jason was, maybe he was really close!

Chancing the use of my flashlight for the first time, I tried illuminating the box I'd found. It was a smallish metal box, about the size of a milk bottle. Now, with the aid of the flashlight, I could see that a bunch of really thick wires ran out of one side of the box and away into the dark in at least six different directions. There was no way my little knife was going to be able to cut those wires!

Inspecting the metal box more closely, I saw that one face-plate was secured with Robertson (square-slotted) screws.

Smiling for the first time, I thought *Only in Canada, eh?*

This I was prepared for, and I quickly switched blades on my multi-tool, selecting the smallest flat screwdriver blade, which I knew from experience could be used in a Robertson-head if it was inserted diagonally into the square slot. This doesn't work for all screw sizes, but in this case, it did – the flat blade could be nicely wedged into the screws and used to unscrew them.

Unscrewing the screws from the box's faceplate seemed to take forever, but it was probably only a couple of minutes until finally, the last one was out and, switching blades again, I was able to pry the face plate off the box. This was the radio receiver! I recognized the exposed circuit board from the ones I'd seen in Jason's garage, where several of them had been lying around on his workbench.

I'd already cut away the antenna, and I didn't think I'd be able to cut away the big thick wires that I was certain went to the various explosives Jason had placed, probably each with its own detonator at the end of each wire. The box in front of me was clearly the trigger-signal receiver and it was also the mechanism that would send the 'detonate' pulse to the detonators.

Now what? I'm not an explosive expert, I'd only been trained in the chemistry of explosives, and in the various ways amateurs could make them 'at home.' It seemed to me that when the radio receiver got its coded signal, that it either closed an open electrical circuit or opened a closed circuit. But which? There was no way to tell.

People later asked me why I didn't just move away and leave it all to blow up. My problem was that I wasn't sure how quickly the evacuation was proceeding, and I was afraid that there might still be people working nearby. Anyway, rightly or wrongly, I couldn't just leave it for fear that Jason either was close, or could get close, to the device and trigger it so I felt that I needed to at least try disable the receiver - somehow.

As I was thinking it all through, the beam of my flashlight fell on the stack of batteries in retaining clips. If I pulled the batteries out, I reasoned, then I'd either defuse the bomb or trigger the bomb. But which?

I felt time ticking away on me. I had a 50:50 chance. *Flip a coin,* I said to myself, but first I had to get Silver away from me.

"Silver, go find Jack!" I yelled down. "Silver, go find Jack!" I yelled again.

I couldn't see down to the ground from my position, so I didn't know whether he heard me or not. Or if he did, whether he obeyed me or not. I hoped so. I wanted him as far away as possible if the bomb went off.

I gave him a slow count of thirty to hopefully get away, then held my breath. *Fools rush in where angels fear to tread,* I thought. I grabbed one of the batteries and pulled it up and out of its restraining clip. That should have broken the power circuit.

Nothing happened. *Whew!*

Not wanting to push my luck any further, I decided to leave the wires, detonators, and bomb packages alone, wherever they were, and backed away.

When I'd crawled, and then climbed, back down to ground level, Silver was there waiting for me, his large eyes not giving me any clue as to whether he'd failed to hear or failed to heed my instructions to go and find Jack. It was too late to worry about it, and I was glad to see him.

When we got into my truck I radioed, first Jack, and then Frank, to let them know that I'd found and disconnected the trigger mechanism but left the detonators and bombs alone.

To Frank, I advised continuing to keep the mine clear, as the explosives needed to be properly deactivated by a professional, and we still had a shooter on the loose.

Jack said that backup was on its way, but that it would take time for others to arrive on the scene. He added that when he arrived on the scene, he'd seen someone between the woods and all those conveyors, and that someone had later run off into the woods, carrying a rife.

We weren't done yet.

***

Silver and I drove towards the highway and met Jack near Jason's big black truck, which was well off the highway and close to the forest fringe that bordered the mine. Rather than risk a long delay, we decided that Jack should stay on guard there, in case Jason doubled back, and also to watch for the backup when it arrived. Meanwhile, Silver and I would go hunt for Jason. Jack was understandably concerned for our safety, but he was reluctantly persuaded that we had limited options available to us.

Jason would have been well aware that his bomb had been deactivated. I didn't want to wait for reinforcements to arrive because I was concerned that he might now be a danger to any workers he might encounter.

"Besides," I'd added, "Silver and I have a better chance of finding him and catching him by surprise if it's just the two of us."

Jason's truck wasn't locked, so we opened it up and let Silver in, so he could register Jason's scent. Then, Jack showed us where he saw Jason go into the woods. It looked like a game trail.

It was late in the evening now, I was later told it was about 10 pm. It was still very dark, of course, and now it was distinctly cold, too.

Silver and I went in to search for Jason.

Tracking him was mechanically like our exercises, I suppose, but it did not feel remotely like an exercise to me. This was real, and our quarry was armed, and desperate, or panicky, or both. He had already shot at me several times (I hadn't been counting), and regardless of whether he was trying to hit me or just scare me off, I knew that he'd be willing to shoot again. That meant that not only was he trying to evade us for real, we had to try not to give our position away while we were tracking. I turned my radio off.

As always, I made sure that Silver understood what we needed to do and then let him take the lead and go about the tracking in his own way. I don't know exactly how his senses and thinking went but watching him was like watching a series of successive approximations. He would catch the scent and slowly proceed in a given direction, then he'd go a bit too far before deciding that the direction had changed, after which he'd drift back until the scent was stronger, then set a new direction and follow it, and so on, and so on.

This led us in a kind of zig-zag pattern, sometimes along a game trail, sometimes through the brush, then back along a game trail, and inevitably back into the brush again. After doing this for over half an hour, I decided that Jason had struck out blindly, without a clear sense of where he was going. Judging from the path we'd taken to that point, *he must be lost by now*, I thought. I certainly was, although I knew that Silver could get us back out again.

It also was not at all like I'd seen in movies, where you see a bunch of tracking dogs barking and howling, and making a huge amount of noise, so the person fleeing knows where the dogs are at all times and gets even more panicky. In our case, we were in 'stealth mode,' proceeding as quietly as we could. We weren't trying to scare him or warn him. We wanted to detect Jason before he spotted us, and of course, I didn't want either Silver or myself to get shot!

Sometimes, when the trail took a turn, Silver would first detect it, then check around to be sure, and then he'd pause and look up at me that penetrating gaze of his, that I knew so well. It was if he was trying to say: "This way." I'd whisper "OK," and we'd go a little further. On, and on, and on.

Shortly after I'd checked my watch and discovered that we'd been tracking for over an hour and a half, Silver suddenly froze and gave out a low and prolonged growl.

As I crept up to kneel beside him, there was Jason, standing at the far edge of a clearing and peering away from us, into the forest, as if trying to decide which way to go next.

"Police! Jason! Stop where you are. Police!" I yelled out across the clearing.

"Alex?" he said, in a confused-sounding voice.

"Yes, it's me, Alex, but I'm a police officer, RCMP."

"Just back away and leave me alone, and you won't get hurt," he said.

"Jason, I'm a Mountie … you have to know that I can't do that."

At this, he lifted his rifle and pointed it at us.

I drew my revolver and yelled out "Drop the rifle!"

Jason just remained standing, with his rifle pointed at me. I motioned Silver to sweep around to one side, and tried to keep him talking, asking him to drop the rifle, pointing out that it didn't have to end like this, and so on.

Jason didn't really reply, or not much at least, that I can recall. I do remember that as Silver silently moved away from me, to begin his sweep to the side, Jason had to split his attention back and forth between the two of us. Once Silver was well away from me, he turned and the two of us took a few steps towards Jason at the same time. I'm not sure how we did that, we hadn't practised it, and I hadn't given him any specific commands, we both just instinctively took a few slow steps forward, simultaneously.

"Drop the rifle!" I yelled out again, with my revolver pointed at him, as we took those first few steps.

"No! You need to walk away!" Jason yelled back at us.

We took a couple more steps forward. As we did so, Jason alternated, first starting to point his rifle at me, then towards Silver, then back towards me again, as if undecided which of us posed the greater threat. Silver was still giving out a low growl that would have worried me if I didn't know him well. Of course, I had my revolver pointed dead-centre at Jason, so I would have thought it was no contest who posed the greater threat. Perhaps he thought that a dog was likely to attack whereas a woman would hesitate. If so, he didn't know me well enough. Apparently, Jason decided the same thing, because he eventually swung his rifle back at me and then tensed, as if he was going to pull the trigger.

I actually did hesitate, wanting to give him every possible chance to surrender.

Silver decided otherwise, however, and must have judged that Jason was about to fire at me because he suddenly accelerated to top speed towards Jason.

Hearing, or sensing, this Jason swung back to face Silver and fired.

"No!!!" I yelled and then fired at Jason in turn.

I must have hit Jason, somewhere, as his leg seemed to collapse, and he dropped to one knee, still holding his rifle up.

Silver was down and clearly injured, but he was snarling now, and crawling forward towards Jason. He was now very close, and I don't know whether he'd have had the strength to jump Jason, but there was no mistaking the fact that he was intent on trying to.

Jason obviously thought so too, as he raised his gun and aimed it at Silver again. His body shifted, and I sensed that he was going to fire again.

I yelled "Don't do it!" but this time I didn't wait for him to fire first. I fired before Jason could get off another shot.

I must have hit him again, somewhere, because his other leg collapsed this time, and his whole body dropped prone to the ground. This time he let go of the rifle. As I approached him, my revolver still up and aimed at him, I could see that he was out of the fight. His attention was now completely focused on trying to use both hands to stop the bleeding from wounds in both thighs.

I left him to it for a moment, grabbed his rifle and ran to Silver, who was lying on his side, in an expanding pool of blood. It looked like he had been shot high up on one leg. I'd had a bandanna in one pocket, which I quickly turned into a bandage, and with one hand pressing the bandage down to stem the bleeding, I used the other to turn my radio back on and call Jack.

Jack came on the air immediately, and I told him that we'd found and subdued the suspect and that the area was clear, but we had two injuries and needed ambulances.

Jack said he'd heard the shots, help was on the way, and that we should stay put.

It took them a while to find us, but not as long as I'd expected. Apparently, Jason had circled a bit in his attempt to escape in the woods, and Silver and I had been too intent on the hunt to really notice. The backup Jack had requested had clearly arrived, as there were soon lots of helping hands for us. We let the others bandage Jason and carry him and his rifle out. Jack and another Member helped me bandage and carry Silver out.

"Nice work, Alex," Jack had said.

When we emerged from the forest, two teams of paramedics, and two ambulances, all from the GCOS site, had just arrived and were waiting for us. They put Jason in one ambulance and raced off to the Fort McMurray hospital.

I climbed into the second ambulance with Silver, which raced off to the veterinary clinic in Fort McMurray, with Jack providing a high-speed escort down the highway.

Jack and my paramedic driver weren't wasting any time: we passed the first ambulance before we even got to Super-Test Hill.

The vet, Dr. Rick Williams, was understanding, and he let me sit by Silver's head in the surgery, where I was able to try to comfort him while we waited for an anesthetic to take effect. Once it did, Dr. Williams pushed and probed around for a while in Silver's leg, which worried me even more because it led to a lot more blood loss. After what seemed like an eternity, but was probably only five or ten minutes, he stepped back from the operating table and announced the good news: the bullet had gone right through the fleshy part of the leg and hadn't hit anything major along the way.

What a relief! As the crisis was now behind us, I could feel fatigue setting in, and I barely heard the next part.

Dr. Williams concluded that fortunately for Silver, he was a big, healthy dog. He explained that Silver would be walking with a limp for a while and that he would need some time "off the job," but he expected him to recover completely. On the other hand, he wanted to keep him for observation overnight, "Just to be on the safe side."

I didn't argue with that, but I did object to them locking Silver up in one of the clinic's large animal cages overnight, so we compromised. Silver would be allowed to curl up on a blanket in the clinic's waiting room, and I would be allowed to stay with him and sleep in one of the big, upholstered chairs.

When we carried Silver out to the waiting room, Jack was still there waiting for news, which I really appreciated. As he took his leave, Dr. Williams and I got Silver settled on a blanket. He was still drowsy from the anesthetic and I remember seeing his eyes droop as I fell into a deep sleep myself.

When Jack and Frank came over to check on us at dawn the next morning, they found the two of us curled up together on the waiting room floor, sound asleep.

11 EPILOGUE

Innisfail, Alberta.

Silver and I had been invited to come and tell some of the stories of our Fort McMurray adventures at the Police Dog Service (PDS) Training Centre. As I understood it, the idea was to have a bit of a debriefing session in which we shared and discussed what went right and what went wrong with the trainers and the dog handlers that were available, so everyone could learn.

They couldn't order me to attend, of course, since I worked in a different division, but the invitation was polite and sincere, and it seemed like a sensible practice. Besides, Silver and I had enjoyed working with the PDS people and I looked forward to seeing them again before driving back to Ottawa.

We'd just completed a very thorough accounting of the various events, and a back-and-forth discussion of the dog handling aspects of the case when the Officer in Charge, Insp. Larry Walsh rose. He congratulated Silver and I on the successful completion of a difficult case and commiserated with me over the pain he was sure I must have felt at having to shoot Jason and having Silver get shot. "Not necessarily in that order," he'd said. He also thanked me for coming and spending the time with them discussing the case and said they were all very proud of the two of us, especially since we hadn't had as much dog handling training or experience as he would have liked to see before we were thrown into the whole thing. After a nice round of applause and kind words from Sergeant Preston, our PDS trainer, and a few others, Insp. Walsh had one more thing to say.

"There's one more order of business for today. We have planned a small ceremony. If everyone would please come outside to the training grounds, we'll begin immediately."

Not knowing what to expect, Silver and I just followed everyone out.

The next thing that I knew, there we were, standing out in the training grounds on a beautiful fall day, with a somewhat larger group in attendance. In addition to Insp. Walsh and Sergeant Preston were all the other trainers and their dogs, the other dog and handler teams that had been available to come for the debriefing session, all the quarries, all the rest of the PDS staff, and the greatest surprise of all. There, to one side, were Assistant Commissioner MacLeod and Staff Sergeant Simpson, who I learned later had flown out for the occasion. They'd come out in stealth, having only informed Insp. Walsh in advance, which I thought was both funny and appropriate for two senior Security Service officers.

All the dog and handler teams lined-up in a PDS version of parade ground order, and with the rest forming an audience, Insp. Walsh called Silver and me to step forward. As I marched forward a few steps and stood to attention, Silver limped along beside me and struck a fine pose. Silver seemed quite aware of what was going on, and it occurred to me, as it has so very often, that I have never seen or heard of a dog with such a keen understanding of human speech and behaviour – or was it more than that? I wasn't sure.

Anyway, after repeating for the broader audience some of the kind things he'd said at our debriefing, Insp. Walsh looked directly at Silver, and said, "Silver, I'm very sorry for your injury, and I hope that you make a full recovery very quickly. I'm afraid that in the RCMP, we don't have anything like the military 'Purple Heart,' for Members that are injured in the line of duty, but we do have something for Police Service dogs that demonstrate outstanding service while on duty."

With that, he motioned to an aide that I noticed was carrying something that looked somehow familiar.

He called out "Constable Houston!" and I stepped forward. He opened it up and held out to me a dog jacket that had been sewn in the style and colours of an RCMP shabrack[11] (horse blanket), complete with a yellow stripe around the border and the famous yellow 'MP' brand in the lower back corner on each side.

"The honours go to you," he said, handing it to me.

With shaking hands, I took it from him and put it on Silver, who stood proudly with his head erect, and as the applause broke out all I could do was fall to my knees, throw my arms around him, and bury my face in his side to hide the tears that were welling up in my eyes.

I think I mentioned before that the RCMP dog handlers tend to be a reserved, quiet-spoken bunch, but no one should ever underestimate their silent pride in the work they do or their love for their animal partner-friends. They all understood. They gave Silver and I a minute of silence to ourselves, but when Silver lifted his head to give me a huge lick, running from my chin to my eyebrows, they erupted into a huge cheer that even got all of the dogs barking.

All semblance of discipline dissolved at that point, and to this day, I have never again seen such a rowdy display from such normally well-trained and well-behaved dogs. It was as if they all understood, Silver included.

If discipline lost a bit of ground that day, it certainly helped me, as it got everyone laughing, even the senior officers, and it enabled me to get a grip on myself and get back to a more professional demeanour.

Silver and His Shabrack

For myself, I was content. Most importantly, Silver was recovering. I didn't need any medals or special ceremonies. Like the dog and handler team we'd become, Silver and I had been sent in to a situation, we'd done our job, we'd even saved the day, and then we'd quietly disappeared.

Just like the Lone Ranger.

It was enough.

12 LOOSE ENDS

After the big ceremony, Assistant Commissioner Macleod and Staff Sergeant Simpson met separately with Silver and me.

The biggest question Assistant Commissioner Macleod had, was why I'd shot Jason in the legs and hadn't aimed for the heart? Bob, for his part, marvelled at my shooting accuracy, considering that I'd only been armed with a snub-nose revolver and had been shooting under extreme duress!

Sheepishly, I explained the awful truth, which was that in reality, I'd aimed for his torso, the centre of his torso in fact. I wasn't trying to kill him, I was trying to stop him, and aiming dead-centre was simply so that I'd have the best odds of actually hitting him at all, which was the way I'd been taught. This was fortunate for me because I really wasn't that good a shot, and it was just a fluke - two flukes, in fact - that I'd ended up shooting him in both legs.

This admission produced howls of laughter from Bob and the Assistant Commissioner, but they clearly approved, and both hastened to tell me that they were still impressed that I'd been able to stop Jason before he hurt or killed anyone else.

Still chuckling, the Assistant Commissioner advised that I should be prepared for the possibility of the news media picking up the story as an example of how a Mountie came under direct fire, and still only returned fire when absolutely necessary and even then, only shot to incapacitate the suspect. As an undercover officer, the Force would seek to protect my identity when I was called to testify in court, but investigative reporters wouldn't have much trouble finding out who I was.

We reviewed the rest of the case together, but that was the highlight of our debriefing.

"Take some time off," they'd said. When it was over.

"Get Silver better, get yourself rested, and then we'll meet in Ottawa and discuss your next assignment," they'd said.

"Don't rush into getting yourself a permanent place to stay in Ottawa," Assistant Commissioner MacLeod had added. When I raised an eyebrow, he went on, "We're not going to waste you in a desk job, you're too valuable to us in the field."

Then, looking at me narrowly, he added, "Seems to me that the Metro Toronto force tried something like that, and they lost you as a result. So, report back in two or three weeks and we'll have figured out …"

"Another pilot project!" Bob and I said in unison.

"Probably so," he went on, unperturbed. "Do you know what you're going to do?"

"I think we'll go spend some time in Radium City," I said. "It's beautiful and quiet up there, and Corporal Morrison and a few of the others were always after me to try fishing when I was posted there. Maybe I'll give it a try."

It might have been my imagination, but I thought I detected a twinkle in the Assistant Commissioner's eye. "Corporal Morrison, hmmm, … he isn't married, is he?"

"Not that I know of, Sir," I said, with a straight face, and not blushing (I think).

Chuckling, "Go rest-up and have some fun. You've earned it."

Then, looking directly at Silver in his new coat, "You both have. We'll see you later in Ottawa."

***

Silver made a complete recovery, although he wasn't above milking his convalescence for extra care and attention from me. I didn't mind.

I'd taken Frank and Jack out for dinner, at the fanciest restaurant in town, to explain everything that had been going on, provide Frank with the promised Scotch (single malt), and to thank them both for their support. Both of them had stretched the boundaries of their jobs to help me, and I wanted to make sure that they knew how much it meant to me. I'd made two new friends and leaving them behind was hard.

Speaking of new friends, I'd wanted to take Geoff and Karen Laker out for dinner as well, to thank them for their friendship and to apologize for having to shortly break their lease and return to Ottawa. But they wouldn't hear of it. Instead, they insisted on banding together with Laurie and Ann, hosts of the famous Fort McMurray hot tub party, and throwing a huge yard party. There was no hot tubbing this time, it was just that their yard was larger, and they could have a larger crowd of friends, acquaintances, co-workers from the GCOS site, and our favourite two dogs, Silver and Teddy (who were once again spoiled with hot dogs).

There aren't many secrets in a small community, and everyone seemed to be familiar with what had happened at the mine, and Silver and my roles in it all. Frank and Jack, who were both there, enjoyed telling their versions of the story. I didn't have much to say, but Silver seemed to both understand and appreciate all the attention. Between his role in the story and his very visible bandages, he was practically the centre of attention.

Leaving so many other new friends was hard as well.

∗∗∗

Jason lived to survive his wounds. I was glad about that. I'd wanted to stop him, but I hadn't wanted to kill him, despite what he'd done to Silver, and what he'd tried to do to me.

I had mixed feelings about the three shots Jason had taken at me out in the mine. I was never able to make up my mind on whether he'd just been trying to scare me away, or whether I was fortunate that he wasn't a very good shot. It may have been both.

Jason was, however, charged with an impressive list of offenses, including attempted murder of a police officer, attempted murder with regard to the bomb, "injuring or endangering other animals" (which was the closest offense listed in the Criminal Code for what I would call attempted murder of a police dog), attempted arson, uttering threats, and so on. He was quite open about what he had done, and his defence was basically that the mine developments were invasive, that they were harming both animals and the natural environment, and that, therefore, his actions had been justified.

His pattern of civil disobedience would have continued if Silver and I had not tracked him down and stopped him.

The local detachment's investigators had obtained a warrant and searched Jason's home. When they did, they found more than just the remote controls I'd seen in his garage. Hidden in his basement and in a backyard shed, they found the ingredients for many more detonators and many more bombs.

I'd had to testify, of course, but the judge placed a publication ban on my identity. This meant that, although I was too well known in Fort McMurray, I could probably work undercover in other parts of the country. For a while at least.

During the trial, it came out that Jason had been born and raised in Fort McMurray, and he was one of the people that had been firmly against the new oil sand developments. With one oil sand plant running, another under construction, and more being considered, he wanted to not only stop the developments but to "turn back the clock." It seemed to be a bit of concern for the environment, and the wildlife, as his lawyer had argued in court, but I think it was mostly just that he wanted a return to the earlier, slower, quieter ways that he'd grown up with.

I could understand that, but not his methods.

Speaking of methods, I had wondered why he had attempted to use a remote control to detonate the explosives rather than a simple timer. He'd explained that there were two reasons, both of which came down to control. He'd wanted to be able to control the precise moment when the explosives were triggered, and he hadn't liked the idea of setting an arbitrary time on a timer.

Secondly, he wanted to be able to get to a safe distance and then be able to have the satisfaction of triggering and watching the explosion first-hand. It seemed like an unnecessary complication to me, and I guessed that there was a third reason: his love of electronic gadgetry.

To this day I'm also not sure whether he may have wanted to make sure that there no people working nearby when the bomb was triggered. I'd like to think this was another of his reasons, but of course, he'd taken a rifle with him and he'd been willing to shoot at Silver and I.

It was just as well though. If he'd used a simple timer, we might not have found it in time. We might even have been caught in the blast!

There weren't many grey areas as far as the court was concerned, however. He was convicted of the most serious of the charges and given a life sentence.

That's what I'd learned from the newspapers, anyway.

Silver and I had gone fishing.

***

Laurie Schramm

… Alex and Silver return in
An Indestructible Mountie.

Laurie Schramm

BOOK 2 ENDNOTES

1. For example, Francis Dickens, son of British novelist Charles Dickens, was able to join the North West Mounted Police as a Sub Inspector in 1874, courtesy of political influence from his family.

2. In real life, a first full troop of women began training in the RCMP in 1974, but for this fictional series, it all began with a single-woman pilot test.

3. See *An Inconvenient Mountie* (ISBN: 978-1-9994940-0-1).

4. At this point in time, it was still part of the RCMP. Years later, in 1984, the Security Service was spun-out to create the present-day Canadian Security Intelligence Service (C.S.I.S.).

5. Heavy water meaning water composed of deuterium (an isotope of hydrogen containing one proton and one neutron) and oxygen atoms rather than hydrogen and oxygen atoms.

6. For factual background on the RCMP's Police Dog Service, I recommend the following non-fiction source:
   Aimoe, L.D., "An Examination of the Skills and Characteristics of Successful Royal Canadian Mounted Police Dog Handlers," M.A.Ed. Thesis, St. Francis Xavier University, Antigonish, NS, 7 May 2009, http://www.rcmp-grc.gc.ca/depot/pdstc-cdcp/publications/handler-characteristics-caracteristiques-dun-maitre-chien/index-eng.htm.

7. In 1979, all the Canadian operations of Sun Oil were amalgamated with Great Canadian Oil Sands, and the new,

integrated company, was renamed Suncor Inc.

8. Yorkshire Terrier.

9. Canadian Standards Association.

10. The Alberta OH&S Act and regulations did become law in December 1976.

11. Dating back to at least the 18th century, the shabrack (or shabraque) was originally a large cloth placed over, or under, the saddles of European cavalry. At some point it became traditional to add a border of contrasting colour, and to display a crest or other symbol in the lower-rear corner. The RCMP shabrack, which is placed under the saddle, seems to have originated in 1887, at about the same time as "MP" was registered as the horse brand of the North West Mounted Police. It is black with yellow trim and displays the MP brand, topped by the Royal Crown, displayed (also in yellow) in the lower-rear corner on each side.

An Indestructible Mountie

Adventures of the First Woman Mountie. Book 3

LAURIE SCHRAMM

Laurie Schramm

DEDICATION

To Kent,
who served as a CELE Officer in the Royal Canadian Air Force

Laurie Schramm

BOOK 3 CONTENTS

Laurie Schramm

LIST OF CHARACTERS
(IN ORDER OF APPEARANCE)

- Max Lichte, graduate student (atmospheric physics), Heidelberg University
- Corporal Leonard (Lenny) Dwyer, radio technician, 14 Wing, Canadian Forces
- Sharon Sanders, graduate student (biochemistry), Dalhousie University
- Dr. David Keen, physicist, DREA, Canadian Forces
- Constable Alexandra (Alex) Houston, RCMP
- Assistant Commissioner George MacLeod, RCMP Security Service
- Silver, an Alaskan Malamute; and Alex's friend and companion
- Staff Sergeant Robert (Bob) G. Simpson, RCMP Security Service
- Dr. Parke, Chemistry Professor, Dalhousie University
- Sergeant Ian (Scotty) Scott, Quartermaster, RCMP HQ Division
- Dr. Alan Grey, Chemistry Professor, Carleton University
- Captain Donald (Don) Harrison, Military Intelligence, Canadian Forces
- Marcus Light, Co-Owner, Oceanside Antiques, Ingonish
- Anna Miller, Manager, Ingonish Beach restaurant/bakery
- Henry Miller, Chef and Baker, Ingonish Beach restaurant/bakery
- Wilma Light, Co-Owner, Oceanside Antiques, Ingonish
- Constable Jack McDonald, former recruit colleague, RCMP.

Cst. Alexandra Houston

1 FIRST PRELUDE: 1942

October 25, 1942

Max Lichte (the Englishers always pronounced it, incorrectly, as 'Lite') was standing on the bridge, looking out at the rocky cliffs that could just barely be seen through the thick fog and low-hanging clouds. Everything looked cold, and grey, and barren. "What brought people to such a forbidding place?" he wondered. As a teenager, he had visited North American cities like New York and Montreal and had arrived by steamship in a civilized fashion. This was something completely different.

The first thing he'd noticed had been the fog and clouds, which blanketed the churning sea down below. The second thing was the rock. Now and then a bit of fog, or cloud, or both, cleared providing a glimpse of a wall of rock rising vertically up from the crashing waves on the shore. He knew from his briefing that there was a bit of beach there – somewhere - and a way to climb up the rocky cliff, but at the moment he could see neither, making the cliff appear forbidding and unassailable.

The third and fourth things he noticed simultaneously. One was the cold. It wasn't just the cold, or the wind, it was the dampness in the cold and the wind. Dampness that seemed to penetrate through his parka and uniform clothes. The other thing was the pitching and rolling. Although it was a great relief and privilege to be granted a few minutes on the bridge, breathing in the fresh air, the damp cold exacted a heavy price.

Unlike the relative luxury of his previous trips on ocean liners to this continent, this trip, which had been on a U-boat, had been miserable. U-687 was one of the newest submarines. Referred to as Type VIIC/41, it was based on the "workhorse" design that characterized most of the U-boats in the fleet but had a few significant improvements over earlier models, particularly its active sonar and stronger pressure hull, giving it a deeper crush depth of well over 300 metres. This latter feature was important for a U-boat that was to be used for secret missions and, to help maintain security, U-687 had been listed on the official register as never having been deployed[1].

Although it was the most modern submarine in the fleet, it was not built for comfort. They had left their base at Kiel in September of 1942, in high spirits, with everyone looking forward to the adventure, and to their chance to prove themselves against the Allies. Inside the pressure hull, the submarine's effective size was only 50 metres in length by less than 5 metres in width[2] – not a lot of space to share on a long-duration voyage with fifty-one officers and crew. After a week of life in the confinement of U-687, the adventure had been stripped of its glamour, and the journey had simply become a burden to be endured. By four such weeks, it had become unbearable.

Max had been plucked out of university, Ruprecht-Karls-Universität Heidelberg (Heidelberg University), where he had been studying atmospheric physics. He had been attracted to the idea of becoming a scientist and learning to do scientific research, but it had been the development of applications of science that had interested him the most. Of the many applications of physics, it was the world of atmospheric physics and the relatively new field of radio-wave transmission that interested him the most. The former had become his scientific specialty, and the latter his hobby. In fact, he had just finished building his latest, and best, short-wave radio transmitting and receiving set when he'd been called into Herr Professor's office to meet with two strangers. The strangers were obviously military men, despite their civilian clothes.

Herr Professor had a name, of course, but everyone in the university simply referred to him as "Herr Professor," and there was an uncharitable rumour going around that his wife referred to him as Herr Professor as well.

Herr Professor had originally built his reputation in meteorology, the physics of weather, and in recent years had shifted his focus to the development of weather-monitoring instruments. For some reason, this had brought him to the attention of the military, and Max knew that a secret project had been underway in a locked laboratory in the attic of their Physics Building. It appeared that Max was finally going to be brought into Herr Professor's confidence.

"You know my interest in weather and weather-monitoring stations?" This was a rhetorical question, of course. "Then you should also know that we have been working on ways to make automatic weather stations — stations that can monitor the weather and transmit the weather information by radio signal, all without the need for human hands!" Herr Professor had then sat back, complacently as if awaiting applause.

Max had tried not to disappoint him and launched a volley of questions about how it could be done, how to automate the data gathering, how to assemble it for transmission, and of course, how the radio transmission would be done and what transmission distance would be needed. Max's focus on the technical aspects had clearly pleased Herr Professor as they provided him with an opportunity to deliver a lengthy lecture on such aspects. It did not, at first, occur to Max to wonder why someone would actually want an automatic weather station.

The strangers answered this last question first. The military wanted automatic weather stations so that they could be placed in strategic locations around the world and used to deliver precise weather information for the air force and navy. Especially the navy. The military men explained that weather information was particularly difficult to obtain in remote locations that might be of interest for future invasion landings, ship movements, and … U-boats hunting convoys.

In the North-Atlantic Ocean, weather forecasts were important for both sides, as they had a profound influence on the planning of naval convoys and the U-boats that hunted them. For the Allies, bad weather meant opportunities to conceal convoys and hinder enemy aircraft. For the Germans, bad weather meant good hunting. Weather forecasting was straightforward for the Allies, who had a large network of ground-based weather stations that could take advantage of the general trend for weather fronts to move from west to east. In contrast, the Germans had to do what they could with specially equipped aircraft and ships, which was both inefficient and dangerous. A better option might be for Germany to have their own weather stations on the North American East Coast.

At the military's urging, Herr Professor had secretly developed a new kind of weather station, one that was quite small, self-contained in terms of power and processes, and automatic in function. If successful, such stations could be secretly set-up wherever they might be needed, from which point they could send coded weather information to offshore U-boats for as long as the batteries lasted, or until the batteries were replaced. Other than the battery replacement issue, the stations should not need human intervention once they'd been landed and set-up. It was at this point in the narrative that all three men looked straight at Max.

"What has all this to do with me?" Max had asked.

One of the military men said that Herr Professor had done the Fatherland a great service by developing the automatic weather station, which had been successfully tested, not only in our attic laboratory but also near one of our own naval bases on the coast. Now it was time to send one out into real service. What it had to do with Max, they explained, was that it would have to be shipped in pieces by U-boat, taken ashore at the right spot, re-assembled in place, and set into operation. For this, they needed a specialist, someone who could not only deliver and set-up the station but who could, if necessary, make any last-minute adjustments or repairs that might prove to be necessary. "With all respect to Herr Professor," they explained, "this is a job for a younger man." They all had looked at Max again.

Max had agreed to do it, of course. It was his duty to the Fatherland, it sounded interesting, and it sounded like an adventure.

It had felt like an adventure too when they'd assembled the two large, inflatable rubber rafts on the forward deck of the U-boat, but an adventure of the terrifying kind. The Captain, an Oberleutnant zur See (Naval Lieutenant), was under orders to find a desolate place on Canada's East Coast, to conceal the weather station. Accordingly, the U-boat had anchored near Cape Breton Island, offshore the south end of Broad Cove, near Red Head. This was well north of Ingonish, the nearest town, and well away from the closest inhabitants.

The weather had not improved, the cold was damp and bitter at the same time, and the submarine was pitching and swaying. The two inflatable rubber boats were not very large, but they took up about half of the forward deck, with the boat crews and equipment taking up the rest. One had to move carefully to avoid being swept overboard!

Eventually, they had launched the two boats and their crews had paddled them to shore. Once there, everyone pitched in and helped to carry the components across the narrow beach, and all the way up about a hundred feet to the top of the rocky cliff. They carried everything on their backs, the ten cannisters, the masts, the instruments, and the stakes, wires, and cables. Fortunately, they had enough people to do it in one trip as each boat carried eight sailors, one with an officer, and the other with Max and a Coxswain.

In the forest fringe at the top of the cliff, Max assembled Wetter-Funkgerät Land (Weather Radio for Land) number one, or WFL-1. The primary canister contained the measuring instruments, a telemetry system, and a radio transmitter. There was also a ten-metre-high antenna mast and a shorter mast that held an anemometer and a wind vane. By placing WFL-1 well back from the cliff's edge, at the edge of the forest fringe, it was hoped that it would avoid detection. The rest of WFL-1 comprised nine more canisters, each of which was about 1.5 metres tall and about a half metre in diameter, and each of which housed sets of heavy nickel-cadmium batteries to power the station.

They'd waited for evening to surface and anchor the submarine, so by the time Max was able to begin assembly, it was in near darkness. When it was done, Max set the station to broadcast weather readings every six hours, using a two-minute transmission at 3940 kHz and made sure that it was operating. The station was designed to operate for six months using three-hour intervals, but Max had reduced the frequency of transmissions in order to have enough power for the "secret within a secret" package in battery canister number nine. This was the special secret that he should not have referred to in his letter to his girlfriend Wilhelmina (Willie).

With their cargo disembarked, the submarine left for home. They had spent less than twelve hours near the Canadian coast and had carried out their mission undetected. They didn't have much opportunity to celebrate, however - U-687 never made it home. It was sunk by an RAF bomber in late November, near the Norwegian coast.

2 SECOND PRELUDE: AN ODD COINCIDENCE

March 16, 1977 – 34 years and 4.5 months later.

The Canadian Forces (CF) CP-107 Argus reduced altitude for another pass along Cape Breton's eastern shore. The Argus was on a mission: to seek out and identify a British submarine that was acting the role of the hunted in a NATO[3] hide and seek exercise. The submarine's mission was to approach Canada's East Coast by stealth and fire a dummy torpedo at an old Second-World-War observation point near the mouth of the Halifax Harbour.

Designed specifically for marine reconnaissance, the CF Argus was widely regarded as the best anti-submarine warfare (ASW) aircraft in the world. Its mission, along with five other Argus aircraft that were spaced-out along Nova Scotia's eastern coast, was to find and identify the sub before it could get into position to attack. If they were successful in locating the sub, then the exercise would shift to that of capture or destroy. If U.S. or Canadian surface ships from the exercise happened to be in the target area, then the mission would be turned over to them. If not, then the Argus was well equipped to handle the job itself. It was only carrying dummy weapons today, but in a potential combat situation, its forward and aft bomb bays could carry eight thousand pounds of torpedoes, bombs, mines and depth charges.

Although the Argus was capable of carrying a flight crew of fifteen, today it held fourteen: three pilots, three navigators, two flight engineers, and six radio technicians (radio techs). Four of the crew were resting or sleeping in bunks near the galley. The remaining ten crewmembers were at their posts, intent on their mission.

In the belly of the Argus, Corporal Leonard (Lenny) Dwyer was hunched over his console trying to concentrate on his readings over the constant, roaring drone of the aircraft's four large turbo-compound engines. The noise, long hours, uncomfortable seat, and sickly greens and blues of his meter readouts and CRT[4] monitor screens made concentrating difficult. They had already been airborne for nearly ten hours since taking off from Canadian Forces Base (CFB) Greenwood, which was in southwest Nova Scotia – diagonally all the way across the province from where they were now.

Their flight plan called for a twenty-hour reconnaissance[5], so Lenny's shift was about to end, and he was looking forward to being relieved, so he could take a nap in one of the bunks. Scanning his instruments for what seemed like the millionth time, everything looked normal: search radar, signals from the sono-buoys they'd dropped, the magnetic anomaly detector (MAD), and the relay from the shore-based SOSUS station[6].

Canadian Forces CP-107 Argus

He was just about to request an explosives-drop, to try another go at explosive echo ranging (EER) when he heard a soft buzz and a light flashed on the instrument panel to his right.

"What's up?" asked his replacement, who had come forward to be ready for their shift change.

"Not sure," replied Lenny, "the new BS detector just went off."

This was properly called BSRFDET (Broad Spectrum Radio Frequency Detector), and it was an experimental radio scanner they'd been carrying for the past week. It was the brainchild of DREA[7] and was designed to scan a broad spectrum of radio frequencies in hopes of detecting any submerged submarine that was incautious enough to be sending a message ashore or to another vessel. Like everything military, the machine had an acronym, and like many things military, there was a slang term for it. Inevitably, BSRFDET was known as the "BS Detector," and there was talk of installing one in the mess hall.

Lenny's complete attention was now focused on BSRFDET and, having thrown the switch to relay the sounds it had detected to his headphones, he manually fine-tuned the frequency detector.

"That's odd," he muttered. "There's a signal coming in on shortwave at 3940 kHz. It's not voice, it's not Morse, and … [continuing to listen] … it sounds like a telex signal."

"A target, you think?" his replacement asked.

"No, it's in the wrong frequency range, it's the wrong signal type, and … there, it's gone."

"Did you grab it?"

"Got it!" Lenny said, looking up above the instrument panel where a reel-to-reel tape recorder had automatically begun recording as soon as the warning light and buzzer had been triggered.

Lenny continued to listen, but the signal did not reappear.

"Well, time for me to relieve you," said Lenny's replacement. "I'll keep an eye on the BS Detector and let you know if it comes back."

"OK, thanks," said Lenny, as he levered himself out of his station's jump-seat and ambled aft for a snack in the galley. As his replacement was donning his headset, Lenny called back to him, "Keep the tape, will you?"

Later, lying in his bunk, Lenny was having trouble getting to sleep. Usually, the drone of the engines and the vibration of the aircraft, coupled with the fatigue from concentrating on his instruments for a full shift helped him to fall asleep, but he was still thinking about the strange radio signal. "It doesn't make any sense," he thought. "It sounded like a telex signal, but it wasn't on any of the usual telex frequencies for weather data or communications."

Lenny eventually fell into a light sleep as the Argus, having found nothing actionable, rumbled off to search another map quadrant.

The next day, and still thinking about the mysterious radio signal, Lenny decided to make a copy of his notes and the tape recording and, together with a brief explanatory note, sent them off to the Electromagnetic and Acoustics Laboratory at DREA – Dartmouth. This made him feel a bit better about it all, but he was sure that nothing would ever come of it.

Lenny was wrong.

***

April 16, 1977.

Sharon Sanders was not, at first, having a great day. Her research project in biochemistry at Dalhousie University had stalled, again, and it was beginning to feel like she would never be able to complete her master's degree. As a result, her stress level had risen to the point where she was having trouble sleeping.

Thinking that a complete break might help, she'd taken a day off and driven north from Halifax for a trip to scenic Cape Breton Island. Following a surprisingly relaxing five-hour drive, she'd stopped at the famous Keltic Lodge resort and treated herself to lunch. Although great for lunch, the lodge was too expensive for her, so she checked in at a small bed-and-breakfast in nearby Ingonish Beach. Then, with time for a brief hike, she debated where she should go and pulled a topographic map of the area from her backpack.

Having been to this area several times before, she'd already done the well-travelled trails just north of the nearby town of Ingonish, one to Middle Head, and the other to Lakies Head. The map showed another point of land, however, that might be interesting. Halfway between Middle Head and Lakies Head was something called Red Head. There might not be much of a trail, but according to the map, it was only about a 1 mile from the highway. It shouldn't be too difficult to reach, she reasoned, and it should offer good views of the ocean and of the coastline in both directions.

Deciding to give Red Head a try, Sharon drove the short distance up the highway, parked off to the side, grabbed her backpack and headed east towards what the topo map suggested would be a cliff rising about a hundred feet above sea level.

At first, it was much more difficult than she'd imagined. The trees were surrounded by thick, shoulder-height brush, and she had to pull, elbow, and push her way forward. Every twenty or thirty feet she had to stop and catch her breath, which may have been just as well since it prompted her to check her compass each time. This, in turn, directed her to make slight course changes at almost every stop, so they at least served to keep her from going in circles, she thought to herself.

After the sixth such stop, it seemed like she'd been struggling through the forest forever, and it felt like she must soon be in danger of reaching the cliff face if she wasn't careful. Pausing to reflect though, convinced her that six stops must only add up to something like 120 to 180 feet – meaning that she had something like five thousand feet still to go. That was discouraging!

"Maybe this wasn't a good idea after all," she thought.

Sharon wasn't the type to give up easily, however, and she decided to try a few more segments of bush-whacking and then re-evaluate.

Red Head, Cape Breton, Nova Scotia

The next four such segments were no different from the last, and although she was pretty sure she knew exactly where she was, she was rapidly becoming convinced that this particular stretch of forest, was basically impenetrable.

"Maybe just a little more," she thought.

Pressing on, nothing seemed to be changing, and she was finally ready to admit defeat and turn back when the brush cleared, just a little, and she found herself standing on what looked like a game trail. It was narrow and moderately overgrown, but it was definitely a trail and it appeared to head more or less east, toward the cliff. Thinking that this seemed promising, she followed the trail.

Now Sharon was able to increase her pace and decrease the frequency with which she checked her compass. Stopping about every two hundred feet, her compass indicated that the path meandered a bit, but she judged that it deviated about equally to the northeast, then the southeast, then back again, and so on so that she was pretty sure that the trail was still taking her where she wanted to go.

Eventually, Sharon's persistence was rewarded with the slow brightening of her surroundings that meant that the tree density was thinning out and allowing more sunlight to penetrate the forest. Accordingly, she slowed her pace a bit and was glad she did as the forest finally came to an abrupt halt about twenty feet from the edge of the cliff.

Finally!

Approaching as close to the edge of the cliff as she dared, she judged that she was about a hundred feet up from the ocean, and roughly at the broad summit of this particular stretch of cliff. Her orienteering skills had clearly served her well, as she was almost exactly at the position she'd intended to reach.

With a happy sigh, Sharon sat down near the edge, took her pack off and pulled out her water bottle and a plastic bag of GORP[8] for a well-deserved snack while she enjoyed the fantastic views of the ocean below, and coastlines to the north and south. Munching away, and consulting her topo map again, she relished the thought that not many people would have fought their way to this particular spot. Other than the trek though the dense forest, a person could probably hike up along the ocean-facing ridge from the north or the south, where in both cases the cliff eventually and gradually sloped downwards towards the ocean. Either of those would be a long, and possibly treacherous hike though. On balance, she decided, the route she'd taken was probably the easiest of the three.

Fortified by her snack, and having reveled in the unspoiled location, fresh ocean breeze, and scenic views, Sharon decided that she should start back as she still had to preserve some energy and alertness for the long drive back to Halifax.

Shrugging her daypack onto her shoulders as she was about to re-enter the forest, she momentarily lost her balance just enough to cause her to step to one side of the game trail. This was also just enough for her hiking boot to catch on something unseen in the long grass, and just enough to cause her to fall to that same side.

"What the hell was that?" Sharon thought as she picked herself up. She wasn't hurt but she was annoyed at herself for tripping, and fully prepared to take it out on whatever her boot had gotten caught on. Crouching back down, she pushed the long grass, first one way and then another, until a glint of dull metal appeared. Continuing to push the grass around she discovered a rusty length of stranded wire rope attached to a ring, which in turn ran through a hole at the top of a metal stake that just barely protruded above the ground.

"Someone must have pitched a tent up here," was Sharon's first thought. "But who in their right mind would carry wire ropes up here just to tie down a tent?" was her second thought.

Her natural curiosity aroused, Sharon instinctively pulled on the other end of the wire rope, expecting to see a frayed end snake its way toward her out of the grass. Except that instead of coming free, the wire rope immediately pulled tight and lifted out of the grass, at about a 45 degree-angle. Getting up, she followed the rope. It seemed to go a short length to just inside the edge of the forest.

Sharon just stood there, staring, with her mouth open.

***

May 2, 1977,
Defence Research Establishment Atlantic (DREA),
Dartmouth, Nova Scotia

It was a cloudy, foggy, and rainy Monday morning, … again.

As Dr. David (Dave) Keen jogged from the parking lot to the rather ordinary-looking brown-brick building in which his Electromagnetic and Acoustics Laboratory (EAL) was housed.

311

Entering through the main doors, he gave his raincoat a shake to dislodge the worst of the water it was carrying and headed for the stairs. Despite its official name, EAL comprised not just a laboratory, but three laboratories, several offices, and a high-head engineering area, in the latter of which were assembled instruments and prototypes before deployment on ships or submarines for field testing and demonstration.

Reaching his office, he shed his raincoat, dropped his briefcase on a side chair, and headed for his main lab, which served as the nerve centre for his little research group because it housed the coffee machine. With coffee in-hand and having said "good morning" to his lab technologists, he returned to his office and immersed himself in a continuation of his previous week's intensive study of the latest results from their experimental anti-sonar technology. Pausing only occasionally to make a circuit of the bathroom and then the main lab for more coffee ("You didn't buy coffee – You only borrowed it" he always thought), Dave remained single-mindedly focused on trying to make sense of the latest data until he heard a distinct "plop" sound, at 11:30. The plop sound announced the arrival of the morning's incoming mail in his wire 'In' basket.

Happy now, to have an excuse for a mental break, Dave got up to check out the fresh mail. On the top of the pile of inter-office mail envelopes and fresh technical journals was a large, brown envelope. Picking up the envelope, his eyes went to the return address on the label:

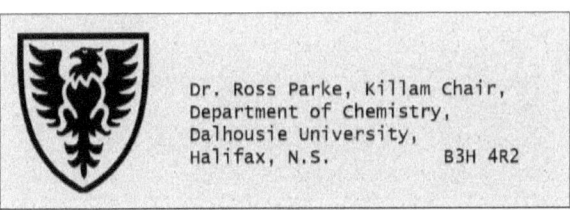

Dr. Ross Parke, Killam Chair,
Department of Chemistry,
Dalhousie University,
Halifax, N.S.   B3H 4R2

Ross was a friend and former fellow Dal[9] graduate student from days gone by. Suppressing the urge to revisit old memories from his grad school era, Dave opened and then shook the envelope, and picked up the note and photograph that fell out.

The photo showed what looked like a radio mast surrounded by dense forest and bushes. Nearby were what looked like miniature oil drums poking their heads up above the tall grass. Old ones if he was any judge, as they seemed to be covered in rust.

The note from Ross said that one of his graduate students had encountered this strange looking apparatus, surrounded by trees and bushes, but close to the edge of a high cliff overlooking the ocean. She had taken a picture of it and shown it to Ross who, knowing Dave's interest in things related to radio waves, had thought to pass it on to him.

Dave really did have some interest in radio waves and had done research on acoustics for his Ph.D. in Physics, but he mostly maintained an illusion of continuing interest in conventional radio to provide cover for the nature of his real military research on torpedo detection and evasion systems, which had more to do with sonar than radio. As a result of this slight misdirection on his part, Dave received a fair number of leads on things he wasn't really interested in, like this one... except that, in this case, the location seemed to ring a bell.

Cape Breton, Dave thought, *and on the east coast, ... hmmm.*

Walking to the back of another of his labs, Dave went to a bank of filing cabinets, one of which was labelled "Dead Files." This was where he kept the odd things Dave's various colleagues occasionally sent him. Unless they truly interested him, he generally kept such files for a year and then, if nothing else related to them arose, they were either destroyed or sent elsewhere for deep storage, just in case. The package from Maritime Patrol Squadron was easily found as it was the most recent of the odd referrals. Pulling out the file, his eyes again went to the return address label:

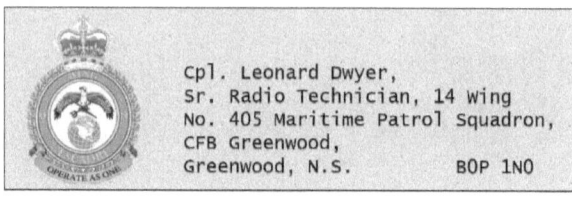

Cpl. Leonard Dwyer,
Sr. Radio Technician, 14 Wing
No. 405 Maritime Patrol Squadron,
CFB Greenwood,
Greenwood, N.S.   B0P 1N0

"Lenny," he thought, as he re-opened the package. Shaking the package, a reel of magnetic tape, some photocopies, and a hand-written note fell out. He'd looked at all this when he'd received it the previous month. It was unusual, but not rare, for operational techs to send him recordings of strange signals. Usually, they were odd radio or sonar signals, and they generally ended up being classified as instrument malfunctions, or noise, or simply "unidentified." In any of those cases, the incident would be logged and forgotten. Re-reading the note and the copy of the signals log from Lenny, Dave was inclined to think that this one would fall into the latter category, but he thought he may as well re-play the tape anyway.

Walking over to one of his other labs, he spooled the tape onto one of the compatible taper recorder/players and put a set of headphones on to listen. It definitely sounded like Lenny's description: something made by a machine, definitely not Morse, something more like telex.

"A short burst of telex on an odd frequency," Dave muttered to himself. "Nothing to do with the sub-hunting exercise Lenny had been on," he'd decided when he first listened to it in March and listening to it again didn't change that opinion. It certainly had nothing to do with his own sonar work, of course. Contrary to what a lot of people thought, or assumed, sonar and radio had little in common with each other beyond the fact that waves were involved.

According to Lenny's log, it had been a very weak signal too. Dave's original conclusion had been that it was probably some kind of private-sector transmission, and most likely a ham radio operator[10] playing around. He'd scribbled a note to that effect and put it all away in the Dead Files cabinet. The log also contained the aircraft's coordinates at the time they'd picked-up the strange signal.

Walking back to another of his labs Dave pulled open a chart drawer and, flipping through the contents, removed the Canadian Hydrographic Service nautical chart that covered northeastern Cape Breton, #4363 "Cape Smoky to St. Paul Island." Taking it over to a large table, Dave spread out the chart and identified Red Head, near Ingonish, just like Ross had said in his note. Dave placed the end of a ballpoint pen over the location of Red Head.

Now, picking up the note and log Lenny had sent, he ran the forefinger of each hand along the approximate latitude and longitude noted in Lenny's log.

More interested now, Dave grabbed a ruler and fine-tuned his identification of the location at which Lenny and the Argus had received the strange radio signal. Placing the end of a mechanical pencil at this point he stood up and looked again at the chart with its two makeshift markers.

"I'll be damned …"

3 CALL TO ACTION

"Will you do it?"

"Arrgh! This again."

My name is Alexandra Houston. My friends call me Alex.

In the summer of 1974, I'd been 24 years old, and feeling like my career was at a standstill. I'd studied chemistry at university and liked it, but not enough to pursue science as a career. I'd reset my sights on police work next and joined the Metropolitan Toronto Police force (Metro). Although policing seemed like a better fit for me than science, my two years with Metro had mostly comprised routine administrative- and traffic duties. These assignments were important, and needed to be done by somebody, and done well. But for me, they didn't fit the Hollywood vision of policing that I had developed, and I hadn't found them to be very challenging.

They say you should be careful what you wish for.

My life soon changed drastically, beginning with an unexpected meeting. Without explanation, my Captain had sent me to go and see a Royal Canadian Mounted Police (RCMP) officer that wanted to meet me. My reaction to this was apprehension, and I wondered what I could possibly have messed-up so badly that it had caught the notice of our national police force.

That's how I first came to meet Assistant Commissioner George MacLeod. After a lengthy conversation that I belatedly realized was an *interview, he told me that he had asked my Captain (his friend) to recommend one of his young officers for a special pilot project he had in mind. He wanted someone who wanted to accomplish things, someone eager and tenacious, someone chomping at the bit to be allowed to do some 'real' police work, and ... someone female. At this point he had shed his stern 'Mountie look,' relaxed his entire body, chuckled, and said that my Captain had recommended the "biggest pain in the butt" in his Division - **me**.*

Assistant Commissioner MacLeod had explained that the 'Force' had fallen behind the times and that its senior leadership wanted to build a more diverse police force. "We're going to be recruiting immigrants, visible minorities, maybe even people with some kinds of disabilities as well," he said, "But we have to start somewhere, and that somewhere is by engaging women." He wanted to try a first "pilot test" with a woman, but that pilot test had to succeed as it would pave the way for an entire first troop of policewomen that would follow. He had thought of using someone that had already qualified as a policewoman, and simply re-train them in the "RCMP way."

That had brought me up to full attention. "Wait a minute! Do basic training all over again?"

"Yes!" he'd replied, "that's the only way you can possibly succeed. In the old days of the Northwest Mounted Police, a person could get appointed straight into the Force, even as a commissioned officer, if they had the right political connections. No more. Now everyone starts out the same way, as a Constable, and by going through the same basic training. If you want to have any hope of being accepted, much less respected, that's how you have to begin."

So, that's what I'd done. I went through training at the RCMP's Depot Division training centre in Regina, dealt with the good and the bad issues that came with being the first woman to train there, and survived to become the first woman Mountie. I hadn't intended for it to happen, really. The opportunity just came and found me.

After training, or re-training if you like, I'd been posted to Radium City, a small town in very northern Saskatchewan that, in its early days, had been a great uranium mining centre. Although my new boss, Corporal Morrison, had told me that nothing interesting ever happened around there, he'd been wrong, and I'd had to rescue him from a mine collapse, run our entire detachment single-handed while he was confined to hospital for six weeks, get rescued by a strange dog from near-death, solve a mystery, and find and catch a murderer – all in only four months!

The dog was named Silver. Investigating a mysterious series of break-ins had led me to some unusual places, including several abandoned uranium mines. In one such mine, I'd fallen through a trap and found myself hanging precariously over the sharp edge of a raise, a kind of vertical mine shaft. Unable to get out and tiring fast, I was saved by the almost magical appearance of what I first took to be a wolf, which gave me quite a scare, but turned out to be Silver, an Alaskan Malamute. Silver somehow sensed that I was in danger, had decided to help, and with his assistance I had been able to climb up and out of the raise. To make a long story short[11], while I'd continued to investigate the case, he had attached himself to me, was eventually given to me, and we'd been close friends ever since.

Sometime later I'd found myself in another surprise meeting with the same Assistant Commissioner MacLeod. Once again, a 'coffee meeting' had turned into an interview and, once again, he had something new in mind for me. By this time, he'd become head of the Force's Security Service[12] and, unsurprisingly, he had some ideas he wanted to try out by way of some experimental pilot projects.

"Like me?" I'd asked.

"Exactly," he'd replied. It turned out that he now wanted me to go and work for him in the Security Service. Of course, he could have just ordered me to go, but he wanted me to go willingly, and immerse myself in his new plans.

And then, just like he'd said over a year previously in Toronto, "Will you do it?" and just like at our previous meeting, I'd said, "Yes, Sir."

That had taken me to Ottawa in November of 1975. I'd met my new supervisor in the Security Service, Staff Sergeant Robert ("Call me Bob") G. Simpson, and been introduced to the shady worlds of spies, counter-espionage, anarchists, and terrorists.

"Surely, we don't have any of those in Canada?" I'd asked.

"We did, and we do," Bob had answered and had illuminated me with a number of fascinating, yet somewhat discouraging 'intelligence' stories.

"Like you, most of us thought we were safe here in Canada" Bob had

begun. It went downhill from there, from the Second World War, through to the Cold War. Despite Bob's chilling stories, my first Security Service assignment hadn't been counter-espionage but a domestic threat. A series of bomb threats directed at two oil sands companies in northern Alberta had led to Silver and I being sent undercover to investigate.

Our path to the oil sands was indirect, however, as Silver and I were first sent to Innisfail, Alberta, to be trained as a police dog and handler team. "If that dog is going to go everywhere with you, then we should get him trained too," Assistant Commissioner MacLeod had announced, on one of his periodic visits to see how my orientation was coming along. Both Bob and Assistant Commissioner MacLeod had been interested in the possibilities presented by the first female Mountie, especially undercover possibilities, and they were also interested in, and seemingly amused by, the notion of me having Silver along as a kind of side-kick.

After training in Innisfail, Silver had officially joined the Mounties too and we were sent up to Fort McMurray, undercover. We'd made an interesting pair. At that time, I was the first and only woman Mountie, while Silver was the first and only Alaskan Malamute police dog in the RCMP. The notion that no one would suspect us as being undercover police succeeded pretty well and had at least held up for long enough for us to identify and apprehend the bomber, although not before a few more adventures. In one of those adventures, I'd been able to save Silver's life, which evened up the score and reinforced the feeling I'd long had that our destinies were inter-twined.

***

May 10, 1977,
Security Service offices,
RCMP "HQ" Division, Ottawa, Ontario

"Hi, Bob. What's up?"

Staff Sergeant Robert G. Simpson, my boss, had summoned me to his office.

"Morning Alex," he replied. "I want to show you something. Have a look at these." He motioned with his hand to several objects that were spread out across the front of his desk: some hand-written notes, some photocopies, a photograph, and a reel of magnetic tape.

I read the notes first, then glanced at the photocopies, and looked more carefully at the photograph. Knowing there would be more to come, I looked up at him and raised an eyebrow inquisitively.

"There are a few people scattered here and there around the country that know that I'm in the Security Service and that I have an interest in odd coincidences," he said.

I nodded knowingly.

"These arrived Friday from a colleague in defence research, who's based in Dartmouth," Bob explained. "People send him odd things too. These arrived at his labs within a few weeks of each other. He didn't see any reason for the military to be interested but noted the geographical connection and sent them to me."

"OK," I said. "Do we have any reason to be interested?"

"Well, we have one or two additional pieces of information," Bob said, leaning back in his chair. "Have a look at this," he said, pulling another photograph out of his desk drawer.

What he'd handed over was an 8 x 10" black and white, glossy photograph of a bunch of cannisters that looked a bit like miniature oil drums, arranged in some kind of obscure pattern and connected by what looked like a bunch of guy-wires. Near the centre of the pattern were two masts, one taller than the other.

"What's this?" I asked.

"First take another look with this," said Bob, handing me a large magnifying glass.

Scanning the picture with the magnifying glass, I could now see that the guy-wires were supporting the two masts, the taller of which had some kind of box attached to it partway up its length, and the shorter of which had two little devices mounted at the top.

"Is that an arrow on top?" I said, and then before Bob could say anything, "no wait, it looks more like a wind vane."

"A wind vane and an anemometer," agreed Bob. You are looking at a picture of a small automatic weather station."

"It looks old," I commented, voicing my first thought.

"Very old, in fact," confirmed Bob. "It's a Second World War era German *Wetter-Funkgerät Land*, or WFL, automatic weather station. During the war, the Germans set up a few of them here and there in the North Atlantic to provide weather information for their ships and submarines. This one was discovered earlier this year on the east coast of Labrador[13]. Now compare the two photographs."

Reaching for the smaller photograph, I could see in a glance that they were pictures of the same thing. "You can't see very much of this one with all the trees and bushes in the way," I commented, "but now that I know what to look for, they look the same. Did it get moved?"

"No, I think this is another one."

"Are we interested in old German weather stations?" I asked.

"Not by themselves, no. But I wonder whether this one has been put back into use."

"The batteries would have died long ago, and if it's been reactivated, it wouldn't be for weather information," I muttered, still looking at the photographs.

"I agree," said Bob, "but there's something intriguing about a hidden radio transmitter sending low power transmissions in code, don't you think?"

"In code!" I exclaimed, sitting up straight.

Bob grinned his Cheshire Cat grin that I knew so well. He loved to let these little secrets of his out, bit by bit. I didn't mind. I sensed that it was his way of coaching my thinking processes.

"In code," he said firmly. "Our signals people are working on the transmission that the Argus picked up. All they've been able to determine so far it that it's in some kind of code – they don't even know what language has been coded, although English or German are high on their list of possibilities."

"Any idea what's going on then?" I asked.

"One or two. Give me your thoughts first," said Bob, still in coaching mode.

"OK," I said, thinking about it. "Suppose someone has access to an old war-time weather station and transmitter. They don't need the weather part because they can just listen to any radio station for that."

Bob nodded.

"They could use the transmitter to send messages if they replace the batteries and feed their own signal in – is that hard to do?" I asked.

"I'm told that these old stations took the signals from the weather instruments and fed them to some kind of converter that turned them into telex messages and sent them out. Our people think that you could type new messages on a teleprinter machine and have them come out as a series of dots punched onto a strip of paper. They say that you could then take the paper strip, plus a handheld paper reader, and read the data into the relay circuit of the weather station, and have the station send the signal out. Apparently, it would only require a bit of rewiring in the relay circuit."

"OK, so it can be done," I said. "The next question is why go to all this trouble just to send telex messages by radio? Presumably to avoid detection…"

"That's what I think," said Bob. "According to the military, the signal they received was weak. If it came from this old station, then we have someone sending coded messages, at low power, from a hidden location, and I'd like to know why."

"Yes," I agreed. "Of course, it could be legitimate. Some kind of hobbyist or history buff maybe, or some kind of industrial secrets?"

"What do you think?" Bob asked, with the Cheshire Cat grin back on his face.

"No, I don't really think so either," I admitted.

"You're right that whatever it is could be perfectly legal," Bob, changed tack. "Or the signal and the weather station may not be connected at all, but I want to be sure." Bob paused, and then said, "There's another reason… do you remember the reading you did last year on the construction delays at the Cape Breton heavy water plants?"

I did remember. Canada's nuclear reactor development program was focused on natural uranium fuel, moderated by heavy water[14]. The reactor designs were called CANDU (CANadian Deuterium Uranium system). In order to build CANDU reactors, our nuclear industry needed uranium (which was mined in Saskatchewan and refined in Ontario), and heavy water. The heavy water came from two large plants in Cape Breton, one in Glace Bay and one in Port Hawkesbury.

The reasons these sites were chosen were partly technical (availability of suitable water and power) and partly political (economic development). The second reason had unintended consequences, because these plants created a lot of jobs for construction workers from the two small towns and their nearby communities, at a time in the late 1960s when their economies were really struggling. They not only provided jobs but relatively high paying jobs, especially when overtime was required, which happened more and more frequently as the projects fell behind schedule. The Port Hawkesbury plant started-up in 1970, not far behind schedule, but the Glace Bay plant continued to suffer set-backs. Ultimately, a series of suspicious construction and equipment failures had caused so much alarm that Atomic Energy of Canada Ltd. (AECL) and the Province of Nova Scotia had both asked the RCMP to investigate the possibility of sabotage. Naturally enough, the RCMP was concerned that this could be a new chapter of Cold War activity.

It turned out that there *had* been acts of sabotage, and the RCMP had discovered that the Glace Bay sabotage was caused by some of the workers themselves, who wanted to keep the construction project alive for as long as they possibly could, to keep their jobs alive. The overtime pay issue hadn't been thought of in advance, but once it had become obvious that there was money for this, it just provided an extra inducement to continue to sabotage things. Ultimately, the RCMP had discovered the people behind the sabotage and foiled their plans but hadn't found enough evidence to be able to press charges. The files on the people concerned were kept 'open,' but otherwise, the saboteurs lost their jobs but avoided prosecution. With construction progress restored the Glace Bay plant was finally completed and had only just commenced production the previous year (that is, in 1976, some eight years behind schedule!).

"I thought that the conclusion was that the sabotage was due to workers wanting to continue working, and not from foreign agents?" I asked, shaking myself back in to the present.

"That's the official conclusion, yes." Bob agreed. "But I've always wondered whether there was foreign influence behind the scenes. We know, from other sources, that the Soviets are interested in the heavy water technologies – both the CANDU reactor technology and the heavy water production technology. We suspected that there may have been a plot, not only to delay our construction program but to use the delay to try to steal our know-how."

Bob sighed. "There were indications of a shadowy presence behind the scenes but nothing definitive, and we eventually had to let it go, but I've always wondered if there was an agent in-place somewhere."

"Or is still in place?" I asked.

"Could be," Bob replied. "I'd like to send someone in, under cover, to snoop around and find out ... will you do it?"

There was the perennial question. "Sure," I replied.

"Not so fast," Bob cautioned. "We've just strung together a whole series of 'what ifs,' so you might discover that it's all just our overactive imaginations, or something innocent, or at least something legal..., but if it's really some kind of espionage game then it could get dangerous."

"Dangerous how?" I asked.

"If we have an agent in place, it could be a civilian that's been suborned, or it could be someone better trained. Either way, if your cover gets blown and you scare them enough or corner them, they may strike at you without warning, and strike to kill. So, if you go in you'll be going alone. If you get into a situation and don't have the time or resources to call in for help, then you'll have to look after yourself. I have confidence in you, but I want you going in with your eyes wide open."

"I can bring Silver?" I asked.

"I wouldn't have it any other way," Bob laughed.

Bob's concern had gotten me thinking about personal security, so before leaving Ottawa, I paid a visit to the "HQ" Division's Quartermaster and explained in very general terms what I was going to be up to.

"So, what do you want from me?" Sergeant Ian Scott growled. He was clearly another of the Force's ubiquitous crusty Sergeants.

I explained that I'd been issued a snub-nosed Smith & Wesson '.38 Special' revolver when I'd gone undercover in Alberta and that it had been reasonably easy to conceal in the clothing I'd worn in northern Alberta's cold Fall through Spring seasons, but now I'd be working in the summer and was interested in something smaller.

"Huh," he'd said. "Did you ever shoot the snub nose?"

I had, and I related the tale of my close brush with a bomber armed with a rifle against my little revolver, but with which I'd managed to bring him down after he'd shot Silver and was about to do so again."

"So, you know from experience how inaccurate a snub nose is," he growled, "and now you want something even smaller?" My brush with death had softened his attitude a little, but not by very much.

"I do," I replied firmly. "I need something I can carry securely, and conceal, even if I'm only wearing a T-shirt and shorts."

"You don't ask for much!" he growled again, but I could tell he was thinking about it as he looked me up and down as if examining every contour of my body.

Being examined so closely made me feel uncomfortable, but I held my ground, glared at him, and tried not to blush.

Seeing my reaction, he relented further. "Call me Scotty," he said with a sigh, "and don't worry, I'm not leering, I'm thinking …"

Finally, he shook his head, and said, "I think this is crazy, but you're the one that has to survive in the field, not me."

"Come along," he said with a wave, motioning me to follow him to the back of the armory. There, he opened a cabinet and rummaged around a bit before giving a satisfied grunt and pulling out a small cloth bag, which he handed over to me."

Opening the bag, I discovered a fancy looking silver derringer with pink hand grips. As I looked back up at Scotty, he smiled for the first time, saying "We confiscated that from an American fraudster who was plying his trade out in Alberta. He used to wear cowboy boots, and he had the habit of carrying the derringer in his boot. Sounds like a tale out of the Wild West of the last century, doesn't it?"

"He obviously got caught," I observed.

"Caught yes, but the fraud charges didn't stick, and he was acquitted." There was a pause, and he grinned, "But he was convicted of carrying, and concealing, a restricted weapon – the one you're holding now. We usually collect up this kind of confiscated junk and send it out in batches to be melted down for scrap, but I like to keep the odd thing around just in case."

"Does it actually work?" I asked, looking at it dubiously.

Scotty chuckled, "Now you're starting to sound like me," he said. "Yes, it works. What you're holding there is a Remington Derringer. This model is called the 'Mama Bear,' and it was designed specifically for women. The idea is to be easily concealed in a purse or stocking[15].

As I continued to examine the little gun, Scotty showed me how the two barrels pivoted upwards for reloading, and how a cam on the hammer alternated, when fired, between the top and bottom barrels.

"It looks like a toy," Scotty continued, "especially with the fancy silver plating and the pink pearl hand grips but looks are deceiving. It has a trigger guard, which is unusual in a derringer, but I like that for safety. It's about as small as you can get, with only a 2.5" barrel, and this particular model takes .38 Special rounds, the same as your snub-nose and your regular-issue revolvers, so you only need to carry one kind of ammunition. It's only effective at close range, but at close range it can easily kill."

"Thanks, Scotty," I said gratefully, "I'll figure out some way of carrying it."

"Tape it!" he said.

"What?"

"Tape it. Forget holsters and purses. If you want to conceal it get some first aid tape, pick a likely spot on an arm or leg, and tape it there. You'll always be able to carry it and find it easily, no matter how many… or how few, clothes you're wearing. If you get into a tight spot and get searched, chances are it will be overlooked as a bandaged injury. If you need to draw it, just tear away the tape."

Ouch, I thought.

Scotty smiled, correctly reading my mind. "Lesser of the evils…"

"OK," I said, "I'd never think to look for something like that on a suspect, so maybe no one else will either."

I hesitated.

"Yes?" Scotty, asked, with an air of extended patience.

"Since you obviously have an eye for this kind of thing, I was wondering about a knife."

"A knife?"

"Well, kind of a survival knife, but small, and concealable, and something that could also be used for self-defence in a pinch."

"You don't ask for much do you?" The gruff tone was back, but I could see that he was thinking, so I just waited silently.

After a moment, he went back to another cabinet at the back of the armory and rummaged around for a while before appearing with another cloth bag, which he was about to hand-over when he thought better of it and opened it himself. "I'd better show you this one first," he said.

Opening the bag, he withdrew what looked like a very small, black, rectangular box made of metal. It was only about five inches long and very narrow and thin.

"Watch," he said, as he pressed a tiny button that I hadn't noticed at first. As soon as he did, there was a "click," and a blade hissed straight out from one end.

I jumped involuntarily.

Grinning, he said, "This is a small, modified version of a military UDT knife[16]."

"Like a switch-blade," I observed.

"Something like that," he agreed, "except that with a switch-blade the blade swings down and around on a pivot. They were popular with street gangs in the 1960s because the swinging blade alone could be an intimidating sight. This one is more functional than fancy. As you can see, it's automatic – you push the release and the blade springs out from the front-end. The blade is stainless steel and partially serrated, so it will cut through almost anything. The blade is only two and a half inches long, but you can still cut with it... or kill with it," he added grimly. "The handle is made from aircraft-grade aluminum so its light but strong. The whole thing only weighs one ounce."

"You said it had been modified," I prompted.

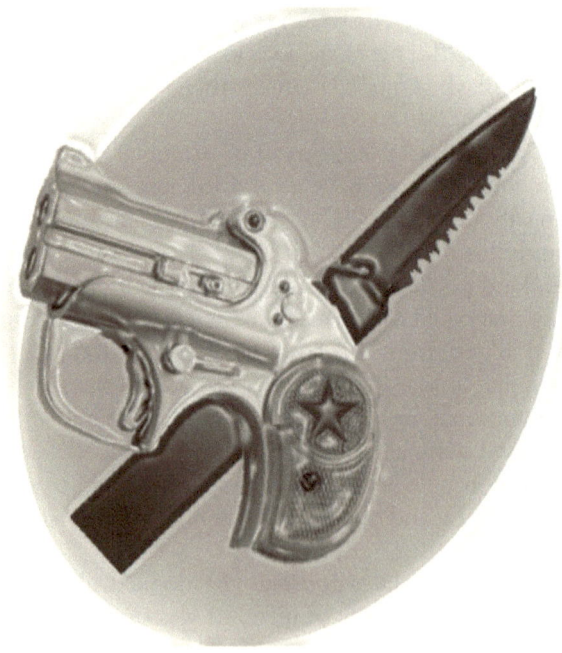

"Yes, in fact, the only reason I kept it is that I've never seen one like this before. Look here," he said, turning the knife around. "Someone made an entirely new handle for this. It's very much like the factory original, except that it's a bit longer so that right behind the spring mechanism there's just enough room for this."

With a flourish, he twisted and pulled on the handle's end cap, which popped-out to reveal a piece of dull grey metal protruding from the inside of the cap.

"Magnesium!" I said.

"Ferrocerium," Scotty corrected. "Same idea though. Ferrocerium is a metal alloy you can strike with a knife blade to create extremely hot sparks." He seemed a bit taken-back by my close guess at the nature of the metal.

"I originally trained as a chemist," I explained. "So, you strike the ferrocerium with the knife blade and you get sparks to start a fire?"

"Right. Like its name, it's mostly iron and cerium, but it also contains a few other metals, one of which is magnesium, like your first guess. The advantage is that you can make sparks even in cold, damp conditions. That makes it better than flint. Better yet is to use the knife to scrape some ferrocerium shavings onto some tinder then strike it to produce the sparks. Try practising it a few times and you'll never forget the trick."

"And I should tape it somewhere, just like with the gun?"

"Exactly, it's small, light, won't rust and could save your life. My father used to tell me to always carry a knife and to always carry a way to make a fire. I used to think it was a quaint old notion, but maybe the old advice still applies where you're going."

"Thank you, Scotty, I really appreciate this. You obviously kept these for a reason, are you sure you're willing to part with them?"

Sergeant Scott peered out at me again for a moment, from under his bushy eyebrows, and then shrugged. "I have two daughters that I'd never want anything bad to happen to" he said, pausing in thought... "I think maybe I kept them for you."

I was saved from having to come up with any kind of appropriate reply to this as he immediately turned, went back to the front of the armoury, and sat down at his desk. Selecting a form from a rack, he inserted it in to the typewriter and began to type while issuing a string of brusque questions: full name, regimental number, home address, and so on. Finishing one, he inserted another form and started typing on it as well. When he was done, he carefully tore the perforated tops off from each form, removed the carbon-copies from the backs, and handed the two originals over to me.

"Restricted weapons permits," he said. "These show that they were officially issued to you. If you lose the originals or need to clear yourself with other authorities, have someone call this office – the copies will be on file right here."

As I turned to go, he added, "Do me one favour. When it's all over, come back and tell me what it was really all about, will you?"

"I promise, Scotty."

4 NOVA SCOTIA BOUND

I still had the big red and white '76 Chevy Cheyenne, 4-door crew-cab, pickup truck that I'd purchased when posted to Alberta the previous year. It was great for long road trips, and Silver always seemed highly amused by his ability to take over the back seat and alternate hanging his head out of the windows on each side. Any time that I teased him about this, he'd give me a big wolfly grin and one of his meaningful wide-eyed looks, that always made me wonder just how much of my thoughts and speech he actually understood.

Silver's cover story was easy. He was supposed to be my dog and best friend. That was true, although he and I were much closer than that – kind of like the brother that I'd never had. My cover story was a bit more complex.

"The fewer the number of people that know what you're up to when you're working on cases, the better. It improves your chances of success, and it's safer for you that way," Bob always insisted. We did have to bring a few people into our confidence, however.

Since the woman that had originally discovered the old weather station was a biochemist working in a Chemistry Department and given that contacting her would be one of my first tasks, Bob decided I should go back to my roots and go out as a chemist myself. This wasn't as much of a stretch as it might seem since I had originally trained at Carleton University to become an analytical chemist. Bob wanted my old analytical chemistry professor at Carleton to 'hire' me back as a Research Associate, and then send me out to Nova Scotia to study something that would require travelling around and taking samples, and therefore a good excuse to snoop around. I'd liked my prof at Carleton but wondered out loud why in the world he should agree to take me on to do an imaginary job that he probably wouldn't have any real interest in.

"Patriotism maybe?" Bob had replied, but the Cheshire Cat grin was back on his face. I had to laugh when I discovered the real answer, which was simplicity itself. Bob just offered him a healthy research grant, saying that the prof was free to use the money to do whatever kind of research he wanted, as long as he'd act the role of my employer and supervisor if anyone started asking questions.

"You know, to be fair, he might go along with all this for free," I'd suggested to Bob before the two of us had headed over to Carleton to broach the subject with my former prof.

"I'd like to think so," said Bob, "but this is a small price to pay to get his complete cooperation. If little annoyances should come up while you're out east, I want him fully on-board with us, and not irritated enough to make mistakes or opt out without warning."

My old prof, Dr. Alan Grey, had found the whole thing interesting and amusing, was very appreciative of the research grant and seemed genuinely taken with the notion of playing a small role in a 'cloak and dagger' affair, as he called it. With his help, we decided that I'd go out to collect samples for a study of possible connections between heavy metal concentrations and the 'Red Tide' phenomenon that occasionally played havoc with the East Coast fishery.

"Is there such a connection?" I'd asked. I knew about heavy metal analyses but not much biochemistry.

"Who knows? That's why they call it research!" said Dr. Grey. "Maybe there's an inverse correlation if the heavy metals are toxic to the algae." He paused, thinking it over. "Tell you what, let's make it a real research project and find out. If you're sampling before the Red Tide hits, then we'll say you're collecting baseline samples. If the Red Tide actually strikes while you're out there, then you'll take the comparison samples. We'll go ahead and analyze the samples back here and if we spot anything interesting, we might even be able to publish the results," he said, starting to smile his own kind of satisfied inner smile as the notion began to appeal to his professional interests.

So that settled the first part. Alex Houston, B.Sc. would re-enter the world of science.

***

Silver and I had a great trip driving from Ottawa to Halifax. The nine hundred-mile trip along the Trans-Canada Highway took us through Montreal to Quebec City, where we stopped overnight, and then through Fredericton and Moncton, New Brunswick, and from there to Truro, Nova Scotia. From Truro, it was only another hour's drive south to Halifax.

Our office staff in Ottawa had rented a nice, unassuming old house for us in Halifax. It had a small yard in the back, but it was large enough for me to park the truck there with about two-thirds left over for grass, on which Silver could roll around and play, and on which I could install a Bar-B-Que and a couple of chairs. We didn't need a lot of outdoor room for Silver, because the house was just off Robie Street, which put us only a block away from the Halifax Commons. If asked, I was to say that we'd gotten a great deal on the house from a local owner/investor that mostly just wanted the house lived-in and looked-after, while they waited for a hoped-for economic recovery that was supposed to drive prices up and create a selling opportunity. Nova Scotians always seemed to be waiting for an economic recovery that never seemed to materialize. Anyway, the idea was that with a house, I'd have enough room to deal with storing supplies and organizing all the samples I'd be collecting for shipment back to Ottawa.

The Commons is a large inner-city park. It is bounded on one side by a big hill, on top of which sits The Citadel, a partly restored 18th-century fortress. The Commons was a great place for Silver and I to go for runs and walks, and from there it was only a short distance to the downtown core and the harbour-front.

One of our favourite routes was to head up to the fortress, with its sweeping, panoramic views of the harbour, and then to drop down and stroll along the harbour-front area. As we discovered more of the city, another favourite became Point Pleasant Park, near the mouth of the harbour, which contains a virtual maze of harbour and forest pathways that were great for walks and runs.

Silver seemed to enjoy the city as much as I did, although he continued to display his curious habit of avoiding water. He didn't mind getting wet, so Halifax's frequent periods of fog and rain didn't bother him, but I could never coax him to jump into the ocean – not to walk and splash, not to chase a stick, and not even to join me in a refreshing swim (in Halifax, that's a euphemism for a freezing cold swim). It didn't bother me, and I could tell that there was something going on behind that penetrating gaze that he so often directed at me, but I simply filed it away in the back of my mind with the many other things I didn't understand about him.

Once Silver and I had settled in to the house and gotten our bearings in the city, it was time to approach Sharon at the university. I'd suggested simply contacting Sharon openly and directly, but Bob had vetoed that, feeling that she had no "need to know." In similar fashion, Bob didn't want me to approach his colleague at national defence or any of the crew from the Argus patrol aircraft, on the grounds that they'd already passed on everything they had, and they likewise had no need to know about Silver or me.

Instead, my Carleton prof had been asked to contact Sharon's Dal (Dalhousie University) professor, whom he knew slightly, and ask whether he could host me in his lab from spring through summer. My prof had relayed the gist of our research project and suggested that I'd only need occasional access to some lab bench and fume hood space in order to prepare my sample bottles and sampling reagents. Since we were going to be assaying samples for heavy metals back in Ottawa, I would need to carefully clean some of the sample bottles with an acid mixture, and I'd also need to treat some of the samples themselves with acids, and/or oxidizing or reducing media in order to preserve or change the oxidation states of the heavy metals in the samples. Sharon's prof, Dr. Ross Parke, had agreed, so that was my next destination.

Silver and I first did a walking reconnaissance of the Dal campus. As befits one of Canada's oldest cities, the Dal campus was beautiful and showed its age to advantage. Some of Canada's university campuses don't really stand out to the uninitiated observer as campuses, *per se*, in that they are so well distributed around the downtown cores of their respective host cities that one can't easily discern where the city ends, and the campus begins. Carleton and Dal's campuses appear more like the storybook image of universities, with fairly clear borders, a scattering of broad, treed grassy areas, and a heavy concentration of academic buildings of various sorts. That is where the similarities end though because whereas Carleton has a modern campus, with modern architecture, Dalhousie has an old-style campus. I don't mean this in a negative way. In fact, I found it charming. Its low stone fences, classical arrangement of ivy-covered brick buildings, and huge old trees created an old-world atmosphere that refused to be overwhelmed by the numerous more modern buildings that were tucked away here and there. Founded nearly 160 years previously, in 1818, Dal wore its age with style.

In the same vein, the two universities' Chemistry Buildings were certainly a study in contrasts. Whereas Carleton's was modern in every way, Dal's was a prime exemplar of its long history. I don't know whether the building was one of the first to have been built, but it certainly looked like it from the outside – a large, four-story brick building, covered in ivy and facing the campus's central quad area. It was flanked by the old Administration Building to one side, and by a massive, modern library on the other.

Having left Silver at home one day, while I went off for my first meeting with Dr. Parke, I found that the interior of the Chemistry Building didn't disappoint either. With its broad staircases, high ceilings, large pane-glass windows, and stately wooden doors and fittings, it struck me as the kind of building one might expect to find at Oxford or Cambridge in Britain, which I supposed made historical sense in a former British Colony.

Most of the faculty offices and research laboratories were on higher floors, and I eventually found Dr. Parke's office by the simple expedient of reading the name-plate on each door in turn. In this case, the office door was wide open, and the office itself unoccupied. Guessing that the nearest laboratory might be his, I tried walking in through its wide-open door and found a middle-aged man in rumpled clothes engaged in conversation with what was clearly a graduate student, or research assistant, of some kind. My first impressions of the lab itself were another contrast with the way I'd been trained. Beyond the sense of great space, with an impressively high ceiling, and equally impressive pane-glass windows, was wood! Wooden walls, wooden shelves, wooden lab benches, wooden fume hoods, and a hardwood floor!

I think it was the floor that dumbfounded me the most. At Carleton, I'd twice seen accidental mercury spills in the labs. Liquid metal mercury, that is, just like in a mercury thermometer but in larger quantities. Once spilled, the mercury would immediately break up into hundreds or thousands of tiny droplets and go racing off in all directions, reflecting light from their shiny, "silvery" surfaces. In this case, clean-up wasn't as difficult as you might imagine because the designers had foreseen this kind of accident and specified solid poured-epoxy floors that had no cracks and even curved upwards at the walls so that spilled liquids of any kind could be contained and dealt with. Not so in this lab, was my first thought. A mercury spill here would have all those little droplets speeding into the cracks between the hardwood slats and underneath the baseboards at the junctures with the walls. Realizing that the building itself was probably a hundred years old[17], I apprehensively wondered just how much mercury had fallen and accumulated 'between the cracks,' as it were, over all those years.

Such dark thoughts were quickly suspended when I heard a friendly "Hello!"

Introducing myself, I was immediately assured that this was, in fact, Dr. Parke's lab – he introduced himself, with a smile, as Ross, and then introduced me to his graduate student, who turned out to be Sharon Sanders.

"Wow, that was quick!" I thought to myself, appreciating the quick gift of a natural introduction to Sharon.

"Coffee?" Ross asked. Nodding in the affirmative, it took effort to keep my jaw from dropping at what came next.

Ross had picked up a coffee mug from the rack of pegs over the lab's main sink, where it had been nestled in among a variety of lab beakers and flasks that had presumably been cleaned and put up to dry. This was normal practice in many chemistry labs, as it avoided the possibility of contamination from cloth or paper drying towels. What wasn't normal, was having food or drink containers in the same place, or even in the lab at all.

This was only the beginning, however, as Ross took the coffee mug over to a central lab bench which I now saw was crowned by a large hollow glass figure of Obelix, a well-known comic book character[18]. The glass Obelix figure had been made in a classic pose with his body erect, his head lifted, and one arm raised about his shoulder. The hand of the raised arm held a large hollow war hammer, the head of which was positioned directly over a large filter funnel. The funnel had a cone of filter paper in it, and the filter paper must have held ground coffee because connected underneath the funnel was a large, inverted-cone-shaped Erlenmeyer flask sitting on the surface of a standard laboratory hot plate. Near the bottom of the flask, which was half-full of coffee, a small bent-glass tube led coffee to a rubber hose with a pinch-clamp. Placing the coffee mug under the rubber hose, Ross released the pinch-clamp to allow coffee to pour out, then closed it again, and turned to offer me the mug with a very nonchalant "Cream or sugar?"

He was a good actor, but the glint in his eyes gave him away. They were obviously very proud of their drip-coffee machine.

"Black is great thanks," I said, taking the mug. "Where in the world did you get this?"

"We have a very skilled scientific glassblower in the department. He makes all kinds of intricate glassware for us and, like our coffee machine here, he can make them out of Pyrex[19]."

I didn't even attempt to hide my amazement and, encouraged by this, he showed me how they filled and heated the water for it. A rubber hose was fitted to the side of the cartoon figure, with the other end connected to a lab-bench water tap, so that fresh water could be added by simply turning on the tap. As I watched, he turned on the tap and filled the figure half full of fresh water. The glass figure itself was clamped to the vertical post of a large ring-stand and held in place over the top of a Meker burner, which is basically a very high-heat version of the kind of natural gas-fuelled burners that you see in laboratories in movies or TV shows. A separate rubber hose led from the burner to the gas tap and placed very close to the top of the burner was the tip of an electrode.

It was Sharon's turn next.

"You're kidding," I exclaimed when she pointed to the electrode, but no, they weren't kidding. They had wired up the electrode to a high-voltage power supply, so that if you turned on the gas and then quickly punched a small push-button switch that was conveniently secured to the edge of the lab bench, a spark arced from the electrode the top of the burner, which ignited the gas to heat the water, which she briefly demonstrated. The high-intensity flame was directly below the glass figure's two hollow feet, and I could see that it would not take long to bring the water to a boil.

Ross was clearly pleased with my reactions to all this, saying, "Well, it's not all hard work and suffering around here."

I was pretty sure I was going to like these two, so I avoided making any comments about people that have watched too many 'mad scientist' movies. Besides, I was genuinely amazed and intrigued by their coffee machine. I kept my other surprise to myself, though. The lab culture here was very relaxed and friendly, which was a welcome contrast to the much more formal environment I had trained in at Carleton – but the safety standards were clearly more relaxed here as well. If any of us had been foolish enough to bring a cup of coffee into one of the labs there, much less make it, drink it, and clean and store the utensils in it, we'd have been figuratively taken out and shot! Similarly, whereas I'd trained in an atmosphere of mandatory lab coats, covered limbs and toes, and safety glasses, if not goggles, in this lab, it was T-shirts, shorts and sandals except when doing something that was clearly highly hazardous. "This was going to take some getting used to," I thought to myself, although I wasn't planning on spending much time in the lab.

Over coffee, I briefly reiterated the 'cover story' purpose of my arriving in Nova Scotia. This was news to Sharon but simply a repeat for Ross. I'd done some research on the Red Tide phenomenon before leaving Ottawa, and I gave them a summary of what I'd learned.

"I'm sure you two know more about the first part than me," I began, "but here goes. 'Red Tide' refers to periods of rapid marine algae growth, or 'blooms,' in which the algae can replicate themselves a million times in as little as two weeks. There are actually cycles of such growth, followed by decay periods, and the algae blooms usually occur in spring and summer when there are favourable conditions of light intensity and available nutrients in the ocean. The name itself comes from the fact that having many millions of coloured algae in the water causes the water to appear to take on their colour, the most common of which is red." Ross and Sharon nodded their heads. This, they knew.

"OK then, the public concern comes from the fact that some of these algae are poisonous for humans, but are eaten by filter-feeding shellfish, such as mussels, clams, and oysters. The toxins produced by the poisonous algae then accumulate in the shellfish. Depending on the strain and concentration of the toxins, the results of eating such contaminated shellfish have ranged from stomach upset and diarrhea, to amnesia, to paralysis, to death. To counter this threat, government agencies regularly monitor shellfish toxicity, and when they detect dangerous concentrations, they close the affected areas to shellfish harvesting. The reason that the government has to constantly do sampling and testing is that sometimes the Red Tide effect is severely toxic for humans, sometimes it's only mildly uncomfortable, and sometimes there is no noticeable effect on humans at all." Ross and Sharon kept nodding. This too, was familiar to them.

"So, people in your field are trying to work out whether it's a case of different strains of algae causing different effects, which is the conventional theory. Our team is interested in whether the toxic algae are sometimes being deactivated by heavy metals – either metals in the ocean itself, or metals that also concentrate in the shellfish. The idea is that certain metals, or maybe certain concentrations of certain metals, might be dampening or eliminating the toxic effects of the algae." I paused, expectantly, but they continued to nod their heads and simply asked me a few questions about which metals and which oxidation states we thought might be involved, and how we were going to analyze for them. This was more familiar territory for me, and I could hear my voice gain confidence as I listed some of the kinds and forms of heavy metals that, frankly, are almost always the ones of concern in any environmental chemistry issue, and the various methods and instruments we had in our labs for analyzing for them. This, we discussed a bit more over our coffees.

Thankfully, they seemed to accept my story at face value, didn't press me for many more details, and if they thought our research project was a bit of a shot in the dark, they were polite enough not to say so or to challenge me on it.

Getting down to the business at hand, Ross said that he'd just had a Ph.D. student graduate and was trying to find a new one to start in September. This meant that there was a vacant desk in the lab that I was welcome to use between then and now. It made for perfect timing for me, and I gratefully accepted and thanked him. Not only would this be convenient for my cover work, but it also made Sharon and I 'lab-mates,' or "fellow lab rats," as she called us, in keeping with the biological aspects of her own research project, which I was to learn about later.

Ross had provided me with an account number so that I could charge chemicals and sample bottles from the department's Stores, which was extremely helpful for me. He'd waved off my thanks, saying that it was no problem and that if the costs added-up to anything serious he'd just send my own prof a bill for them, but in any case, "Not to worry." This allowed me to get started right away, and for the rest of the week, I divided my time among getting things sorted out in the lab, getting to know Sharon and the campus, and getting to know Halifax.

I think my Fort McMurray yard-party experiences must have left a lasting impression on me because, although the rented house was officially fully-furnished, it was not furnished with a backyard Bar-B-Que. Accordingly, that became one of my first Halifax purchases. The only other thing a Bar-B-Que calls for is company, so by the end of that first week, I'd invited Sharon over for a Saturday dinner in my small backyard.

Sharon's arrival at my place marked her first introduction to Silver. She'd noticed my tendency to disappear every lunch-time during the week, and I'd explained that I went home every day to feed and visit with Silver, so he wasn't just stuck alone in the house by himself all day.

The topic of Silver's breed hadn't come up, as Sharon wasn't much into dogs, and I rather suspect that she imagined that he might be something small, like a Yorkie or possibly a Miniature Poodle. Sharon is quite petite, which may have had something to do with her ideas, but whatever she expected it wasn't what she met.

I hadn't heard her ring the front doorbell, although Silver clearly did, as his head immediately popped-up and he went into his high-alert, sensing mode. With my hands full, I couldn't head for the front door right away. Before I could break away to go to the door, Sharon had quite reasonably just walked around to the back of the house to see if we were there. She reached the fence gate just before Silver did, and the sight of what she first took to be a huge wolf bounding up caused her to take a big step back and raise her hands in the air with a loud "Whoa!"

For his part, Silver had given a single bark at her approach, and now was simply interested in seeing if she was going to pass his careful "sniff test," but Sharon didn't know that. She was initially reluctant to advance a step and hold out her hand for him to sniff, but with some encouragement from me, gathered up her courage and gave it a try. She quickly relaxed, however, after Silver gave her a series of deep sniffs, took a long, deep gaze into her eyes and then, satisfied, gave her hand a quick lick. Only then did he turn to look at me in a meaningful way that seemed to say, "This one's OK." It never ceased to amaze me how his penetrating looks seemed to plant message-images in my head.

With Silver's approval having been granted, we poured ourselves drinks, water for Silver and wine for Sharon and I, and settled into a great dinner and evening of visiting. By the end of the evening I couldn't help but smile as I noticed that the two of them were comfortably sitting together on the sofa, Silver curled up with his back nestled against her leg, and Sharon unconsciously stroking his fur with her left hand. "That didn't take long," I thought to myself, wondering which of them was actually the larger and heavier. I suspected it might be Silver, but it didn't matter as Sharon had quickly gotten over her first apprehensions, and they'd already become friends.

Our evening discussions covered a range of topics including Sharon's research project, which involved chemical interactions between seawater and ocean sediments, and was a combination of chemistry, biochemistry, and chemical oceanography. As she described her research Sharon mentioned, in passing, that she was going to need to plan a few dives to get water and sediment samples from a few locations.

Discovering in this way that we both had an interest in SCUBA diving sparked an entire discussion about freshwater diving (which was all I'd done to that point) and saltwater diving (which was all Sharon had done). It further came out that Sharon didn't have any regular dive buddies, but simply joined the university SCUBA club when they planned group outings. Sensing an unstated plea for help, I volunteered to go and help with her sampling if she wanted. It was the right thing to say as she gave me a huge smile and gratefully accepted.

I had left my diving gear with my parents in Ottawa, so the next day I called and asked them to ship it all out by air cargo the following week.

5 EAST COAST DIVING

The following weekend, Sharon was visiting Silver and I in the backyard of my house again, this time examining my SCUBA gear. Sharon approved everything that I had but warned me that I'd need to add a couple of pounds of lead weight to my weight belt to allow for the increased buoyancy I'd have in saltwater versus the freshwater that I'd been used to.

Since I'd never been in the ocean before, we decided that Sharon would take me out for an orientation dive before we started on any sample-collecting dives for her.

"Can we go see a shipwreck?" I asked.

"That's easy," Sharon laughed. "There are more shipwrecks per mile of coastline here than anywhere else in the world. Partly because of all the wars, from the war with the Americans in 1812, all the way through the First and Second World Wars, and there are more recent wrecks too."

"Sounds exciting!" I exclaimed, my imagination taking off.

Seeing this, Sharon felt compelled to lower my expectations a bit, saying, "I should tell you that most of the wrecks look more like junk yards than ships. It's not just because of their age, though. The pounding of rough seas against wrecks that are up against big rocks means that even modern wrecks get torn to shreds very quickly."

"They're still worth seeing though," Sharon hastily added, seeing my face drop.

Sharon suggested that we start with the wreck of the Humboldt, and that's where we found ourselves a week later.

The nice thing about diving in Nova Scotia is that there are so many great spots that can be reached by hiking, rather than requiring a boat. The not so nice thing is that those hikes always seem to be over rough terrain, and they often involve hiking down narrow pathways from a cliff, and all this while carrying all the diving gear: compressed air tank, regulator, gauges, mask, snorkel, fins, diving knife, full wetsuit, weight belt with twenty pounds of lead weights, towel, plus a thermos of something hot, for later.

As we were finally getting our gear assembled near the water's edge, we could at least appreciate that we'd picked a fine day for diving. The sky was clear, with only the occasional cloud, and there was very little wind. This meant that the ocean, for once, was calm, with only a gentle swell causing small waves to break-up on the near-shore rocks. The water itself was a deep blue colour in the distance, but a lighter, greenish blue near the shore – indicating that the sediment below was unlikely to have been recently stirred-up, and underwater visibility should be quite good.

During the preceding week, Sharon had brought a book on local shipwrecks in to the lab. According to the book, the Humboldt had been an American steam-driven, paddle-wheel ocean liner. On December 5, 1853, it had been crossing the Atlantic Ocean, on its way from Southampton to New York, when rough weather and a shortage of coal had apparently led its captain to decide to divert to Halifax. Unfortunately, they never made it. Hampered by poor visibility, the ship ran aground on shoals near Sambro Island. They were able to get the ship off the rocks, but that only delayed the inevitable as it was rapidly taking on water. The captain then purposely ran the ship aground in Portuguese Cove, just twelve miles south of Halifax, in an attempt to save the lives of the ninety passengers and crew. Although all but one of the people on board were saved, the ship was torn apart by intense waves and sank, along with most of its cargo. Now, I was going to observe what was left of the wreck, over 120 years later.

We geared up and I told Silver that I would be back soon and that he should stay near our gear bags on the shore and wait for us. As always, he showed absolutely zero interest in going anywhere near the water. Also, as always, he seemed to understand what I was asking him to do. I took both for granted, but Sharon thought that both were very odd.

"I don't know which is stranger," she remarked, looking at us. "I've never heard of a large dog being afraid of the water before, and I can't get over how you two seem to be able to actually communicate with each other."

"I think something must have happened to him when he was younger, to make him dislike going in the water, but I can't imagine what it would have been," I replied.

"We have always been able to understand each other though," I added, thoughtfully. "If I speak slowly and carefully, and directly to him, he seems to be able to get a sense of what I'm thinking, even if he only understands a few of the actual words. I don't usually talk about it because I used to think that I didn't believe in psychic things – it goes against my scientific training and instincts after all. Another reason is that I don't want people to think I'm crazy, … but there's something there all the same. It works both ways, too. Sometimes he'll give me that penetrating stare of his, and I'll get a sense in my mind of what he's thinking. More like pictures or emotions than words, but very real. He saved my life that way once, and it happens so often between the two of us that I tend to take it for granted now. Please keep it to yourself, OK?"

"Fine with me," Sharon agreed. "Whatever it is, it's pretty cool."

With a last word of reminder to Silver, we carefully entered the water with all our gear on, excepting our fins. The cold water immediately began to work its way through our wetsuits. That hit me like a shock wave, and I chomped down on the mouthpiece of my snorkel as I waited out the few minutes it took for my body heat to warm the water to something reasonable, if not comfortable.

Once we were past most of the big rocks, we donned our fins and moved to slightly deeper water, so I could test my buoyancy. I mentioned earlier that Sharon had recommended an adjustment to my weight belt to compensate for the increased buoyancy of seawater over the freshwater that I'd been used to. I'd added just a bit too much weight and compensated for it by releasing a bit of air into my buoyancy compensator[20] – which is like an inflatable life vest, but more sophisticated and with a compressed air line and a dump-valve, so air could be easily added or released as needed. Later, I would note all this in my dive log and reduce the weight on my belt for the next dive.

Finally, ready to proceed, Sharon showed me the landmarks on the shore that local divers used to estimate their heading to the wreck site, and with these in mind, we headed for deeper water. To save air, we snorkeled out for a while before switching to our regulators and diving down. I don't know how much of it was following

Sharon's bearings and how much just good luck, but we found the right spot almost right away. As we descended the water colour shifted from greenish blue to blue, and as we crossed the thermocline at just over 30 feet of depth, the water instantly became much colder and a darker blue.

We found part of the wreck at a depth of 40 feet – with several ribs from the hull and some long spikes sticking up from the bottom. Continuing to follow the downward slope of the ocean floor we soon found what the local divers called the 'Button Hole,' at a depth of 50 feet. At this depth, there was much less light. Everything was rendered in shades of dark blue, but the visibility was still pretty good. Pretty good that is, until we started to stir up the sediment.

Sharon motioned me to dig around in the sand, in between the rocks and boulders, and sure enough, I found several buttons and nails. The digging stirred up a cloud of fine-grained sediment, however, and I soon couldn't see a thing in front of me. I kept on searching, though, working by feel alone, and I was rewarded by finding a few more things. Lifting a few feet off the bottom took me out of the sediment cloud and, able to see again, I found that I'd been rewarded by finding a couple of small, shiny medallions or charms of some kind. I'd never found artifacts on a shipwreck before and didn't want to lose them, so I slipped them one by one under the cuff and into my left wetsuit mitt, having nowhere else to put them.

Looking up, I caught Sharon's eyes and waved my pressure gauge at her. She used her hands and fins to move closer to me, so we could see each other's gauges. Mine read 900 psi, while hers read 1500psi. "Damn," I thought, "she's in better diving shape than I am!" On second thought though, this had been my first ocean dive so maybe I was entitled to a bit faster air consumption. In any case, low pressure meant time to head back and I gave the 'let's go up' hand signal to her. She nodded agreement and we slowly ascended straight up.

Breaking the surface and inflating my buoyancy compensator to keep me floating with my head up, I saw that we were now quite far from shore. Sharon had warned me to save more reserve air than I would have done in fresh water diving. She explained that it was common to surface from a dive to find that the sea was rougher than it had been when we entered, and it could make life a lot easier if we had enough air left to use our regulators rather than have to revert to snorkels.

"Why?" I'd asked, naively.

"If the sea is rough, we'll have waves crashing over our heads every once in a while. It's no fun having a wave push your head under water and then fill your snorkel to boot. The first time isn't so bad, but pretty soon you get very tired and you'll need your energy to watch the waves as we near the shore, so we can make the final dash for shore in between wave crests. Otherwise, we get slammed into the rocks for good measure.

This prompted me to retort "Why are we doing this again?" but she knew that I was joking.

As it turned out, we were lucky on this day, as the sea was just as beautifully tranquil as it had been when we first entered the water. Nevertheless, it was a long swim back. On top of that we were now both becoming chilled from the cold water, and tired from our exertions, and it really was easier to be able to keep breathing air from my regulator than from my snorkel.

The relatively calm sea made exiting the water easy as well, and we were soon carrying our gear back to where Silver had been lying in comfort across our two large gear bags. Our adventure wasn't quite over yet, though. Coming out of the water chilled and tired, I was surprised at the additional chill contributed by the moist, onshore wind that had come up from out of nowhere. This, however, I was prepared for. Unzipping my huge gear bag, I quickly extracted a blanket into which I'd long ago cut a head-sized hole, right in the centre. Pulling it over my head created a kind of tent that blocked the wind and absorbed some of the water while I stripped off the rest of my wetsuit and my bathing suit. As I started to use my towel to dry myself off, under the blanket, I heard a sharp exclamation from Sharon.

"Where in the world did you get that?" she asked, sounding amazed.

"I made it myself, from an old blanket," I replied, still towelling myself vigorously. "When I was diving in Ontario and Quebec, it was generally with one of two other girls and a bunch of guys. The blanket-poncho idea was originally just for privacy while changing, but my first winter ice-dive in an old Quebec limestone quarry taught me that it was a great way to warm up too. Now, I've just learned that it also makes a great wind break. When we get back to town we can make you one too."

"Thank you, that would be so great." Sharon seemed genuinely appreciative of such a small thing, and I realized that sharing a lab and a first adventure together were bringing us close together. This provoked a flash of shame that I was in Nova Scotia under false pretenses, and even as I immediately suppressed such thoughts, I already knew deep down that I was going to have to tell her at least some of the truth before long.

"Not yet," though, I told myself as I dug into my dive bag for my final surprise. Pulling out a thermos flask, with its cup-lid and a spare cup, I quickly filled each cup and passed one over to her. "Try this now, but carefully – it's very hot" was all I said.

Taking the steaming cup from my hand, Sharon sniffed at it suspiciously and then tried a sip. "Wow, that's hot," and then, after a second sip, "what is this stuff? It's tomato soup, but something's different about it."

"You got it. Hot cream of tomato soup with powdered red pepper added. It's hot from the heat, loaded with calories, and the red peppers make it taste hotter than it really is. Some of the hot taste is an illusion, but when I'm really cold I find that it works for me."

"Me too," said Sharon draining her cup at a rate that should have burned her mouth and tongue. "Got any more?"

Laughing, I poured her another cup.

Warmer now, we chatted about the dive as we finished changing into dry clothes. Finally, armed with our last cup of hot soup, we sat on our filled dive bags and filled out our dive logs: average depth 40 feet, maximum depth 50 feet, visibility 30 feet (vertical) and 15 to 30 feet (horizontal), air pressure in: 3100 psi, pressure out: 900 psi, and total bottom time[21] 60 minutes.

"Not bad at all," I thought. Out loud, I said, "I'm surprised that there are still buttons and things to be found in the sand if this is such a popular diving spot."

"That's partly why the 'Button Hole' is famous among divers around here. Apparently, the ship was carrying a fortune in dry goods and a lot of stuff just happened to sink into that nice little spot where it is protected on all sides by lots of big rocks. Also, the storms churn up the bottom, so every once in a while, a fresh batch of things to find seems to get churned up. It has to run out someday, but it hasn't yet. Did I see you finding some things down there?' she asked.

"I did," I said excitedly and emptied my wetsuit mitt into one hand to show her. "I found some buttons and nails, and some kind of medallions or charms."

Taking them into her hand for a closer look, she said "These aren't jewelry; they're pocket watch winding keys. Most people, certainly most men, had pocket watches in 1853, and at that time most of them had to be wound with a separate key. The keys were usually attached to the pocket watch chain, so they wouldn't get lost, and they were often decorated to look nice when hanging on the chain." Then, peering more closely, "I think these are brass. If so, they'll look really nice if you polish them up."

"Did you find anything down there?" I asked, suddenly concerned that I might have had all the fun of discovery.

"Just one thing," she said mysteriously. Nonchalantly, she then up-ended a wetsuit glove, and out fell ..."

"A pocket watch cover," I exclaimed.

"Look again," she retorted.

Taking the cover, I turned it over. "I think it's the whole watch," I said, amazed. "Are you going to open it?"

"Not here," replied Sharon, "I'm going to soak it in distilled water for a few days when we get back to the lab, and then I'll dry it and take it to a watch repair shop," and then, after a pause, she added the clincher: "I think it might be gold."

"Gold!"

"I'm not sure, but I've seen a lot of brass come up from shipwrecks and this looks shinier to me. Anyway, gold or brass, I'm going to get it cleaned up either way. If it can't be fixed, then I'll get it mounted so it can sit on a shelf or mantelpiece."

There was one final chapter to this adventure, and that came as we were just finishing our gear packing and getting ready for the trek back to my truck.

"By the way," Sharon asked, "when we were following the bottom to the Button Hole, why did you keep turning to look behind you? It wasn't to keep an eye on me because I was right beside you."

"Oh that," I looked at her directly, but I felt the flush of my cheeks reddening, "I was hoping you hadn't noticed that."

"What gives?"

"I'm embarrassed to admit this, but here goes ... do you remember how the Spielberg movie *Jaws* was the big movie to see when it came out two years ago?"

"No!" she exclaimed, but she clearly did remember and meant no to what I was about to admit.

"Yes!" I nodded, "you remember how the great white shark terrorized a small American town?" She nodded. "And the shark was huge?" More nods. "And in the movie, there'd be this thumping music that would slowly increase in volume, and then the shark would suddenly loom right out of the dark blue water to attack people?"

Sharon was still nodding, her mouth open. She knew what was coming now.

"Well, this was my first experience diving in the ocean, and there we were at 50 feet down, suddenly surrounded by dark, blue water, and in the back of my mind I imagined I could hear that music again, and I kept involuntarily looking over my shoulder …"

"Trying to spot the shark," Sharon finished for me.

She didn't say a thing at first. I expected her to laugh and make a joke, but she surprised me by dropping her gear bag and coming close, so she could give me a big hug. Now, I'm not generally big on hugs, but Sharon's instinctive warmth really touched me, as did the hug itself.

"I would never have thought of that," she said, "maybe I'm not the imaginative type. But I understand fear well enough. My first check-out dives after SCUBA training were in the ocean and, on the first two, I was terrified the whole time. If we hadn't been required to do three check-out dives, and if I hadn't been too stubborn to back out of a dive I'd already paid for I probably wouldn't have even gone in for the third dive. I was lucky I did though, because everything finally went right for me on the third dive, and I learned to get over my fears and enjoy diving on that one 'last' dive. So there – we're even on embarrassing stories."

"For now," I laughed, as we picked up our gear and walked with Silver back to my truck for the drive back to Halifax and my sort-of home. Silver had seemed to pay close attention to our exchange of stories, and emotions, and it seemed to somehow draw he and Sharon closer together as well. Driving back to town, I noticed that he'd abandoned his traditional habit of commanding the back seat and had instead planted himself firmly in Sharon's lap where he promptly fell into a doze, likely aided by Sharon's constant, gentle stroking of his fur.

The driving and a companionable silence got me back to thinking about my mission. The diving had been a great change of pace, and now I had to help Sharon with some dives of her own, but with a fresh new week around the corner, I was also going to have to find a way to check out the Cape Breton discovery that had led to my real assignment.

***

In the week that followed, I found that I was able to combine helping Sharon with dives she needed to make for her research project with collecting samples for my own cover-story research project. Sharon had picked three sites for her work, one down south by Lunenburg, one near Peggy's Cove, and one – I couldn't believe my luck – in Cape Breton. All three were beautiful and historic locations that made for great sight-seeing while we were there. The Lunenburg dive was uneventful, and we each collected the samples we needed without difficulty. Getting the water samples was easy, Sharon needed some sediment samples from a moderate depth, so I grabbed a couple for myself, just in case they might be useful later, and Sharon helped me find a few mussels and clams which we shucked on the spot since I didn't need the shells.

The dive near Peggy's Cove was a bit more exciting.

The dive site Sharon had selected wasn't literally Peggy's Cove, the famous tourist site, but about a mile away, at a spot called Polly's Cove. Whereas Peggy's Cove was well marked with huge signs aimed at inviting the tourists, Polly's Cove is completely unmarked. Fortunately, Sharon knew where she was going and directed me onto an almost invisible dirt road that shortly came to an abrupt stop in front of boulders that were nearly the size of my truck. From there we had to hike with our gear, and our bags of sample bottles, along an almost imperceptible trail that led along a tall cliff.

Compared to the great weather and calm seas of our previous two dives, this day looked miserable. It was cloudy and grey with a touch of fog, plus a light drizzle that made the rocks wet and slippery. As we marched along the top of the cliff, I could see that the sea was quite rough, with lots of whitecaps in evidence. Sharon seemed quite unconcerned about all this, however. I'd learned that her judgement was sound, so Silver and I followed along.

One thing that Polly's Cove and Peggy's Cove had in common were incredible views of Nova Scotia's rugged coastline beauty. The only thing preventing it from being a potentially favourite hike was that we soon had to carefully make our way along a series of switchbacks as the path led down to the ocean. Going down was hard enough; I wasn't looking forward to the return trip!

As we followed the path down to the water, I learned why Sharon hadn't been worried about the rough sea. Polly's Cove is a small cove that is well protected by a long, curving spit of rock, forming a natural breakwater. On the seaward side, we could see water being constantly thrown up as waves hammered into the rocks, but on the landward side, the water was relatively calm, with only a gentle swell rising and falling. As we paused about halfway down, to catch our breath, Sharon explained that the Hulda had broken up over the spit of rock, leaving about half of the wreck lying in the sheltered part and about half lying on the seaward side. It was near high tide when we got there, but Sharon said that at low tide part of the wreck could be seen projecting out of the water. Despite the miserable weather, I couldn't help admiring the dive site: a naturally protected cove with part of a shipwreck neatly provided in its care. Sharon said I should expect to see lots of marine life taking shelter in and around the wreck.

As we sat on the path to rest, Sharon pulled out a photocopy of a few pages from her book of Nova Scotia shipwreck descriptions and began to read aloud. Compared with the 120-year-old Humboldt that we'd visited the previous week, this was a much more recent wreck. A small cargo ship, the Hulda had run aground on the curving spit of rock almost exactly six years previously. That is, in late May of 1971. Since the ship had been damaged beyond recovery, everything that was considered salvageable was removed from the ship over the following several months, leaving the remnants for divers and marine life alike to enjoy.

Having rested, we gathered up our gear and finished our hike down to the water's edge. In what was now our standard pattern, we checked and donned our gear, I asked Silver to stay and wait for us, and we carefully made our way into the water. Finding the wreck was easy, we simply snorkeled to the centre of the cove, switched to regulators, dove for the bottom, and there it was.

Work was our top priority, so we first collected our water and sediment samples, and then Sharon once again helped me to find some shellfish. Just mussels this time, but that was enough for me, I thought. We had each brought rope-mesh bags with us to carry our sample bottles in, and our filled sample bottles and my shellfish out.

Once they were filled, we used a piece of rope to tie them together and connect them to a small inflatable lift-bag that Sharon always kept attached to her weight belt. She held the lift-bag with its open end facing down, clipped the rope to a set of straps that hung down from the bag, then filled the lift-bag with air by holding her regulator under the open end and depressing the constant-flow button of her regulator. Once the bag was about two-thirds full of air, she released it and it shot up to the surface to wait for us at the end of our dive.

Now that the work part was over, we still had lots of compressed air left for an exploration of the wreck, which lay upright on the bottom, at a depth of about 40 feet. Some of the ship's compartments had been cut and/or torn wide open so that two divers could enter together and without fear of becoming trapped inside the wreck. It quickly became obvious that it was the stern half of the ship, as we found ourselves in what was left of the engine room. Leaving the engine room and swimming a circuit around the outside of the wreck showed us a variety of unrecognizable, rusting machinery scattered here and there.

It was cold and impending tiredness this time, rather than low air pressure, that caused us to halt our explorations and ascend to the surface. As we did, I mentally compiled the vital statistics that I'd later enter into my dive log: average and maximum depth both 40 feet, visibility 30 feet (vertical and horizontal), air pressure in: 3200 psi, pressure out: 1400 psi, and total bottom time 40 minutes. Another great dive, I thought, and Sharon had been right about the marine life: I'd seen lots of ocean perch, sea anemones of different colours, and even a couple of crabs lying on the bottom watching me to see whether they'd need to scuttle away or not.

Once we'd surfaced, we spotted Sharon's bright orange lift bag floating nearby, collected it and our samples and turned to swim for shore thinking our adventure for the day was complete.

Except that it wasn't.

At the same time as we were retrieving our sample bags, I could hear the sound of Silver barking at someone who was standing on the beach not far from our gear bags. We had to first focus on reaching the shore, getting our fins off, and dragging our bags of samples up out of the water. As soon as we had that accomplished, I could see that Silver had been barking at a very angry looking, elderly man that could only have been a fisherman.

As I looked more closely at the man, he raised his left arm and with it a double-barreled shotgun that he had been holding out of our sight behind his left leg. As I softly called Sharon's name to get her attention, she raised her eyes from what she'd been doing to join me in the uncomfortable position of looking at the muzzle of the shotgun.

"What the hell do you two think you're doing raiding my traps?" the man asked.

"Traps?" I asked, genuinely puzzled.

"He means lobster traps, Alex," explained Sharon. "He thinks we've been raiding his lobster traps." Then, speaking to the angry man, "Look, mister, we haven't touched your traps. We're scientists, collecting water and sediment samples. If you put that gun down, we'll show you."

"Not so fast," retorted the fisherman, "I don't trust city people."

By this time, I was getting concerned, not because I was afraid that this guy was going to shoot us, but because I could see that Silver had been carefully watching this guy and was now slinking along in a flanking maneuver. Any moment now he was going to be in a position that was just outside of the fisherman's peripheral vision, but within range for a leap for the arm that was attached to his trigger finger. He'd been trained not to disarm a suspect until I gave the command, but I wasn't sure he'd heed that training if he thought I was in imminent danger.

"Please," I added my voice to Sharon's, "Put the gun down and give us a chance to convince you that we're innocent."

The fisherman still looked angry, did not at all seem disposed to listen to us, was still pointing the shotgun at us, and at fairly close range too. I knew what a shotgun could do to us at that range, and I didn't like our odds if his trigger finger got shaky. I was debating whether to identify Silver as a police dog and warn him that he might have more to fear from Silver than we did from him, but I had an uneasy feeling that I wouldn't be believed and also that he might just turn and shoot Silver first, leaving a second barrel ready for us.

Fortunately, I was saved from making a final decision by a loud, commanding voice that suddenly filled the air.

"That's enough of that Angus. Put the gun down." This from a largish man, in some kind of uniform, who was picking his way toward us over and around the rocks.

The fisherman obviously knew this voice, because he immediately lowered his weapon and turned to face the newcomer.

"I'm in the right, Stephen. I've a right to protect my traps."

"That's right, Angus, you do, although I don't think a judge would think you were justified in shooting two unarmed girls even if they did disturb your traps … do you?"

"Girls?" said the fisherman, his anger turning to amazement.

"Girls," said the uniformed man definitively. "Listen to their voices and, if you'll pardon me, ladies, look at the curve of their hips!"

Trying to play along, Sharon and I both pulled off our wetsuit hoods and shook our hair out, emphasizing our gender.

"Well, I don't hear or see so well anymore," grumbled the fisherman sounding, and looking, confused.

"What do you say we have a look at what's in their catch-bags, hmmm? That should clear things up one way or the other." As he was saying this he purposefully strode over to our catch-bags, grabbed one end, and looked up at Sharon and me.

"Go ahead," we said, nearly in unison. I could see now that his uniform identified him as a Fisheries Officer.

Separating the bags from the rope he opened and fished around in each one with his hand. Then, setting them both back down on the sand he straightened up and looked over to the fisherman.

"Well, Angus, I see bottles of water, bottles of sand, and a handful of mussels, but I don't see any stolen lobsters. Do you want to come see for yourself?"

"No, not if you say so," grumbled the fisherman, subdued now and almost shuffling his feet.

"Well then, why don't we walk back up together and you can buy me a rum and coke?"

The fisherman's reply was lost in the wind, but he shuffled around and started back up the path to the top of the cliff.

Stephen, the Fisheries Officer, then turned to us and said, "Sorry about Angus. The fishermen around here have had several incidences of sport divers stealing lobsters out of their traps, and it's making them cranky. That's no excuse for pointing a gun at you, even if – as I suspect – it wasn't loaded, but they're trying to protect their livelihood."

"Thank you for coming to our rescue," Sharon said. "We're sure glad you came along when you did."

"I don't think Angus would have done you any harm, but when I saw him headed this way with his shotgun, I had a feeling he was going to cause trouble. I'm glad you weren't taking any lobsters though because although I wouldn't have let him shoot you, I would have had to charge you. Under the new regulations, taking lobsters without a licence carries a hefty fine and confiscation of all your diving gear. You're welcome to the mussels though, no matter what you want them for."

Bidding us a good day, the Fisheries Officer turned up the trail, presumably to collect his unofficial fine of a glass of rum from the fisherman and leaving us to pack up.

"That felt like a close one," remarked Sharon, "but you seemed more concerned about Silver than yourself. Was I seeing things, or was he positioning himself to attack that guy before he could shoot?"

"It's a long story," I sighed. Things were getting complicated. "Would you be willing to trust me to tell you about it sometime, but just not right now?" I asked.

"A mystery woman," Sharon shrewdly observed. "OK, fine, but you have to promise to tell me eventually."

"I promise," was all I could say.

6 CAPE BRETON ISLAND

Cape Breton may or may not really be an island anymore, depending on your point of view. It once was an island, of course, being completely surrounded by water and requiring a ferry trip to get to mainland Nova Scotia. Between 1952 and 1955, however, a land-bridge, called the Canso Causeway, had been constructed to create a more efficient, higher traffic-volume, all-weather connection. It was still technically an island, because a narrow canal (the Canso Canal), with a swing-bridge, had been included to allow ship traffic to pass through. To the older generations, however, the land-bridge had turned the island into a peninsula.

Shortly after crossing the Causeway, the highway began to more closely follow the coastline and I was exposed to the incredible beauty and scenic vistas of the Cabot Trail.

When I had been briefly posted to Innisfail, Alberta the previous year[22], we had been so close to the Rocky Mountains that it had seemed natural for Silver and I to head off to explore them almost every weekend, and especially any time we had the opportunity of a three-day weekend. This had introduced us to what I thought must be the most beautiful highway drive in all of Canada: the Columbia Icefields Parkway. This judgement was severely tested by the beauty of the Cabot Trail, with its winding path alternating between forests and ocean-side vistas, and with the excitement that comes with a coastal highway that your left-brain (the rational, logical side) tells you must be safe, but your right-brain (the colourful and more interesting emotional side) keeps telling you is way too close to the edge, especially when, as often happens, the edge of the road is also the edge of a very high cliff above the ocean. Setting aside the meaningless debate about which drive was the more beautiful, I quickly resolved that I would come back to Cape Breton and explore it further. Little did I know.

***

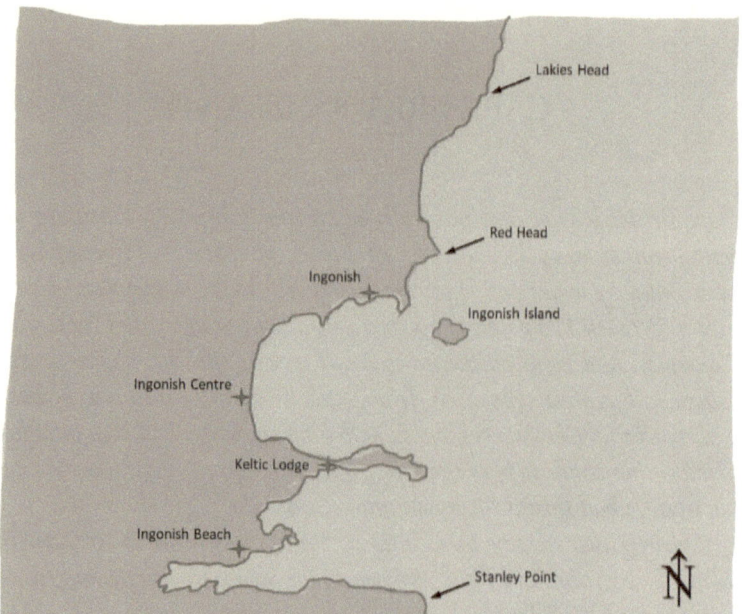

I think I read somewhere that you have to make choices as you proceed along life's journey, that there are seldom easy answers, and that you need to make the best choices that you can in the circumstances, and then move on and hope for the best. My next choice had to do with Sharon.

My instructions had been clear. What I was supposed to do was to find a way to get her to either describe for me or actually guide me to, the location of the mysterious apparatus she'd discovered on her Cape Breton hike the previous month. How I was supposed to pull that off without revealing my true identity or mission was up to me.

The problem was my conscience. Sharon had been so open, so helpful, and such a good friend, that I just couldn't keep on deceiving her. So, I decided to take the risk of filling her in.

Maybe the real lesson for me was that I just wasn't cut out for undercover work. I hadn't liked deceiving people when I'd been undercover in Fort McMurray[22], and I was even less happy about it now in Nova Scotia. In the end, I resolved that if I survived this mission, I'd tell Bob about it and take the consequences, but for now, I'd bring Sharon 'into the fold.'

So, it was a few days later, on the first Saturday of June, that Sharon was over for another of my backyard Bar-B-Ques. While she was playing with Silver, and I was tending to the grill, I told her the truth about me being a Mountie and Silver being a police dog, and that we'd been sent to follow-up on her strange discovery that she'd mentioned to her prof who had, in turn, contacted his colleague at National Defense.

Sharon hadn't been as surprised about Silver's and my real identities as she was that anyone thought her discovery was worth following up on. Although she was keen to see my badge and Silver's ID. I explained that a Canadian Forces Argus patrol aircraft had picked up unusual radio signals from roughly the same location just a month before she had made her discovery. The radio technician on the patrol aircraft had thought the signals were strange enough to send a copy to Dr. Keen at the Defence Research labs in Dartmouth. Dr. Keen, in turn, had been struck by the coincidence of the location being essentially the same as the one Sharon's supervisor had reported to him, and so he'd sent everything off to my boss in the RCMP Security Service. My boss thought it was worth following up on, hence Silver and I were snooping around.

Sharon whistled softly, "That's quite a chain of coincidences and suspicions! What makes it a police business? ... Wait, don't tell me. It's got to be spies? Right?"

Now I was starting to appreciate Bob's instructions about secrecy and questioning the wisdom of bringing Sharon into the loop. It was difficult to tell only part of a story, especially an interesting story. "In for a penny..." I thought to myself. Out loud I said, "It might be nothing, but if it *is* something, then it could be part of a covert messaging system for some kind of illegal activity. That probably means either organized crime or espionage."

"Does that really happen in Canada?"

"Organized crime, yes, constantly. Espionage, yes, sometimes. Not often, but sometimes."

"So, what do we do next?"

"We?" I responded. "There's no we. If you'll draw me a sketch-map and write out some directions, Silver and I will go check it out."

"I think I should come along and show you," Sharon asserted. "There shouldn't be any danger, right? No one else knows why you're here, and if we do run into anyone, we'll just be two girls and a dog out for a day-hike, just like the thousands of tourists that swarm all over the province this time of year."

"Besides," she said, with a flash of inspiration, "with me along, I can arrange for our hike to take us directly to the site. Without me, you and Silver will have to search around to find it, and *that* would look suspicious, right?"

I had to laugh at her plotting. "All right, all right, you win. We'll go together. When could we go?"

"Tomorrow's Sunday. What better day for a day hike in Cape Breton?"

So, it was agreed, and as I already mentioned, the beautiful drive along Cape Breton's Cabot Trail almost made me forget why we were really there. Not completely, of course, but almost.

Although I agreed with Sharon that there wouldn't be much danger for the three of us doing the first reconnaissance, I'd taken the precaution of going armed. Since we were going to be hiking in T-shirts and shorts, I tried Scotty's suggestion of taping my Derringer and UDT knife to my inner thighs. With their lowest points about three inches above my knees, they were well hidden behind the Bermuda-style shorts that I was wearing. I had done some experimenting on previous weekends and found that they wouldn't stay in place if simply applied tape like for a bandage on a cut. Instead, I had to wrap the tape around my leg multiple times; more like you might with a small splint. It turned out that regular first-aid tape worked well but hurt like hell when it was removed. On the other hand, most other tapes didn't hurt coming off but didn't hold well either. Eventually, I did what I should have done in the first place: I went and asked a pharmacist for advice on tape for fragile skin. The pharmacist had suggested a kind of sensitive-skin tape that he said provided good adhesion, relatively pain-free removal, water resistance, and best of all, tears easily by hand. I tried it out, including in the shower, and it was perfect.

Just like Sharon had done on her earlier trip, we stopped at the Keltic Lodge resort for lunch (take-out, so we could eat outside, with Silver). On her advice, we had booked a cabin to share, near Ingonish Beach. Being early June, we were still in what was considered low season so the cost was reasonable, and Silver was allowed in the cabin (the real influx of tourists would begin just before the July long weekend). After checking in to the cabin, we drove north, past Ingonish, to the same place Sharon had previously parked off to the side of the highway. Although we wouldn't need them, we each put on a small backpack and Sharon took out her topographic map of the area. Sharon had already told me about the indistinct trail that she thought might be a game trail, and she now knew where it came out, so that's where we headed.

The one-mile hike must have been a lot easier for us than Sharon's original bush-whacking and somewhat meandering route, and we made good time getting to the cliff at Red Head. Just like Sharon had described, all of a sudden, the forest came to an abrupt halt about twenty feet from the edge of the cliff. The cliff itself was about a hundred feet above sea level, and it offered quite stunning views of the ocean and of the coastline in both directions.

Like me, Sharon was on a mission, however, and she immediately said, "Over here!" and led me to the spot where she'd previously tripped over a rusty length of stranded wire rope attached to the top of a metal stake in the ground. Continuing past the stake, she pointed proudly at the strange assortment of rusty metal canisters and the two masts.

"Wow," I said, stepping carefully in among the tall grasses and bushes that were overgrowing the site.

"Do you know what it is?' Sharon asked.

"Well, I know what it was. It was an automatic weather station placed here by the German navy during the Second World War. Another one was found in Labrador earlier this year, and when it was taken apart, our military people figured out that they were used to collect weather information and then radio it out for the benefit of U-boats that would have been sneaking down the coast to prepare to attack convoys leaving from Halifax."

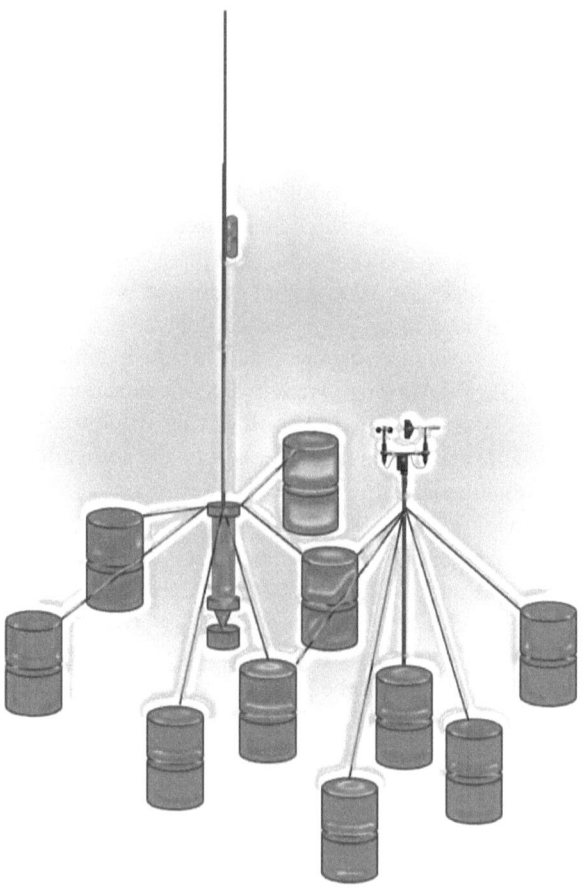

Continuing to step carefully around the site I pointed out the radio antenna attached to the tallest mast and the shorter mast that held the wind vane and anemometer. "I was told that these canisters mostly held batteries to power it all, but one or two of them must have held the measuring parts, a coding machine, and the radio itself," I continued.

At this point, Silver, who had been interestedly sniffing around sounded a low "Yip," to get my attention, and we moved over to see what he'd found. Sure enough, the canister he'd been sniffing at had bright scratches near the latches that held its cover in place.

"Let's not touch it but have a look around and see if any more of these cannisters have scratches on them," I suggested.

The next two cannisters that I inspected just looked rusty and untouched, but a third had scratches, just like the first one.

"Here's another one!" Sharon motioned me over to the canister that stood closest to the one that Silver had found. This one had scratches around its latches too, and it also had a name plate on it that was so weathered, we could barely read it.

"Canadian Meteorological Instruments," Sharon read out, "and some kind of company logo." She sounded disappointed. "Looks like it's been a wild goose chase – this is just some kind of old research station."

"Not so fast," I disagreed. "You haven't seen the pictures of the one they found in Labrador but was identical to this one. I think that the name plate is a decoy, put there to avoid suspicion. Let's back up a bit." Saying this, I took a 35 mm camera from my daypack and started taking pictures, up close for the name plate and the various scratches, then from further back to take-in all the various components of the overall system.

"Aren't you going to open them up?" Sharon asked.

"No. I think someone has put the radio transmitter back into use, and not to send weather information out. Let's not give whomever it is any warning just yet. I think we should just leave everything alone and continue our hike as if we'd simply come across an interesting artifact and then moved along."

"If you say so," shrugged Sharon. "Ready to move on then? We can continue south along the ridge and then cut across to the highway and circle back to the truck."

"One last thing," I said and motioned Silver to come with me back to the first canister he'd found for us. Pointing at the scratched latches, I looked into his eyes and said "Scent, Silver. Remember the scent."

As Silver advanced his nose for a serious session of snuffling around the indicated cannister, Sharon chuckled "I thought dog trainers used commands like Sit, Stay, and Heel, but you seem to have your own language."

"You're right, we both had to learn all the standard commands and hand signals during our police dog and handler training, but when it's just the two of us on our own I've been finding that Silver understands a lot more words than he's supposed to, and it means we can communicate much better with each other. In fact, sometimes I find myself using hand signals just to disguise the fact that he understands so much."

"I still think you two make the oddest pair," she said, shaking her head with a grin.

"No argument there," I agreed, and we all set off. The rest of our hike was beautiful but uneventful. I kept my camera out and used it to take some pictures of the stunning coastal vistas that were laid out before us, one to the south and one to the north. Eventually, we turned east into the forest and endured tough going until finally, we emerged at the highway. From there it was an easy walk back to where we'd parked.

"How about stopping for coffee at that last town we came through on the way here," I suggested nonchalantly, I thought, but Sharon wasn't fooled.

"You mean so you can snoop around some more," she accused, smiling.

"Snooping is such a strong word. Let's say taking in the tourist amenities," I countered.

The nearest town was Ingonish, which turned out to be a small village rather than a town. Its main features were an assortment of well-spaced houses, a breakwater protecting a couple of piers to which were tied-up a number of Cape Islander[23] fishing boats, and a quiet, protected beach. It was just large enough, however, to include a small café/gift shop and a full restaurant, both in restored former homes and both with fantastic views of the ocean. We chose the café, partly because it had a couple of tables on a small outside deck and that let us sit and order while Silver lounged on the grass right beside us.

The woman that came to take our order had the traditional Maritimer's ability to spot people who were "from away[24]" and immediately asked me where I was from. "Ottawa, originally, but staying in Halifax for the summer," I replied truthfully, and used the segue to ask her what kinds of things there were to do in the area.

"Hiking, golfing, whale-watching, swimming, lying in the sun on the beach," rolled smoothly off her tongue as if she'd repeated this list a million times before, which I supposed that she had. "The restaurant down the lane is good if you're staying for dinner, but shopping is limited to our gift shop next door and an antique shop that you'll see at the edge of the village on your way back to Halifax.

There were other tourists seated at a nearby table, so we avoided talking about the weather station and simply enjoyed the location and each other's company. Our waitress was kind enough to spontaneously appear with a bowl of water and a soup bone for Silver, who very contentedly laid in the grass working away at the large bone.

There was one other interesting thing about Ingonish, and I almost missed it.

We still had some time before dinner, and Sharon was telling me a story about something or other as we drove through the village on our way to do some more sightseeing. We were just about to turn onto the highway when I suddenly hit the brakes. "Do you mind if we stop in that antique store that we just passed?" I asked.

"Sure, I mean no, I don't mind, why?"

"Just a feeling. I'm curious about it. Besides, it might have some interesting things to see."

"OK, but beware, shops around here price things high for the American tourists. You can get better deals in Halifax," she warned.

"Right," I said, slowly. "I hadn't thought of that. OK, if I get starry-eyed about something, then drag me out of there, OK?"

"Deal," she said.

Turning around, we drove back to the antique store that we'd just passed, Oceanside Antiques, and parked in front. Leaving Silver in the truck, we got out and strolled in.

The store was amazing. It had everything from oil lamps, to furniture, to pictures and books. As we looked around, I noticed that there were a large number of old radios and TVs near the back of the store, all of them in handsome, heavy-looking wooden cabinets.

"Are you interested in vintage radios?" a voice asked.

Startled, I turned to see that a thin, elderly man had quietly appeared at my side.

"I'm not sure," I said, honestly. "I was just thinking that the cabinets made the radios look more like pieces of fine furniture, and how heavy they must be."

"When radio shows became popular, these were intended to be shown off as pieces of fine furniture," the man said. "See how the really old sets, the ones from the 1930s I mean, are just machines, with their tubes sticking up into the air. But in the 1940s and '50s, all across America, and Canada too, families would gather around their radio in the evenings and listen to the news and the popular radio shows. 'Soap Operas' they were called, because the early radio dramas and comedy shows were often sponsored by companies that made soap, and you had to listen to their soap commercials if you wanted to hear the shows."

He paused then, lost in thought, or more likely memories I thought. "Anyway," he continued, "in those days the family radio was a prized piece of furniture … not like today with our plastics and our transistors," he added, dismissively.

"Are they hard to fix? I asked.

"Not really," he said, conspiratorially. "The only thing that ever went wrong with radios of this vintage was the vacuum tubes would either burn out or spring a leak and lose their vacuum. All you have to do is find out which tubes have gone bad and replace them.

"But where do you get the tubes then?" I asked, getting more interested now.

"Mostly by swapping tubes from other sets. As you can see, I have a pretty good supply right here," he said, sweeping his arms to the left and right to emphasize just how many of these old radios he had piled up in his shop. "I have a small radio and TV repair shop in the back of the store, and outside of tourist season that's where most of my business comes from," he explained.

I was getting very interested but didn't want to let it show. To change the topic, I asked the first thing that popped into my head: "Do you have any nautical artifacts?"

"Nautical?" he asked, taken off-guard by the sudden change of topic.

"Sorry, I guess that's a stupid question to ask in an antique store, but we were diving on a couple of shipwrecks last week and it's gotten me interested in things nautical."

"There are no stupid questions," he retorted automatically, "only people that are too stupid to ask questions," but I could see that he was thinking.

"Well, I don't have anything off ships, but diving now… I used to have a replica of an old-style diver's helmet, let's see if we can find it, hmm?" Without waiting for an answer, he shuffled off to another corner of his store and started rummaging around behind a large collection of old table and floor lamps, all of which I thought looked quite hideous. I could see that Sharon did too, as I caught a glimpse of her trying to stifle a laugh.

Thinking it was time to move on I had started to move away when the old man said "Here we are. I haven't entirely lost my memory yet!" and he gingerly stepped around his various tables and lamps carrying, as advertised, a replica of an old diver's helmet. Except that it wasn't a life-size replica, it was more like a model. Whereas a real diving helmet is huge and weighs nearly sixty pounds, this one was only about eight inches high and only weighed about two pounds. It was beautiful though! Made of copper and brass, it still had an upper helmet attached to a corselet piece that would sit on a diver's shoulders. The upper helmet had the three porthole-style windows, and the handle on top, to which the tether from the surface would be attached.

"How much is it?" I asked, almost involuntarily.

"Sixty-five dollars," he replied.

"Hmm, that's a bit much for me right now." As I hesitated, Sharon jumped in and said that we'd better get going since we had to make our own dinner yet.

I told the old man that I'd think about it and that we'd probably be back the next week to do some diving for our university projects, so I would come back and see him again.

"Any time," he said. He was used to this.

Driving back to the cottage, I thanked Sharon for providing an excuse for us to leave.

"Were you really so interested in old radios?" she asked. You seemed very focused and then suddenly changed the subject and sent him off to find that model diving helmet.

"Radio receivers, no, but I'm very interested in radio transmitters."

"Transmitters!"

"Exactly, transmitters. That guy must have thought we were just a couple of stupid females, but you have to know more than how to swap vacuum tubes to be able to repair radios and TVs," I said, rather hotly. "Anyway, if he knows how to repair radios, maybe he knows how to fix and use transmitters too."

"Wow, so he's a suspect?"

"I don't know," I said, mulling it over in my mind. "Let's just say that I'm interested in the coincidence of finding someone knowledgeable about old radios that lives so close to a reactivated old radio transmitter."

"And the diving helmet?"

"Now that, I am interested in! I really do want to buy that helmet, but I don't want him to think that I can afford it on a student's stipend. What's more, I really wanted to have an excuse to go back to that shop again, and now we have one."

"We?"

"Well, you still have a Cape Breton dive to do and I may as well do one more as well, so that gives us a couple of excuses to come back up here again."

"Sounds great," Sharon sat back contentedly, and we both enjoyed a quiet drive back to Halifax. I thought that we'd be safe for at least one more trip to the Inverness area and that after that I'd have to take care not to get her involved any deeper.

We drove back to Halifax, and then it took a couple of days to get my pictures developed. I'd ordered two sets of prints, so I could send one set along with the original negatives to Bob in Ottawa and keep the other set for myself. I also wrote out an account of what I'd learned so far, which wasn't much, but I did include the company name from the weather station and asking him to find out anything he could. I sent everything off to him by airmail.

Meanwhile, I tried to do a little digging of my own via the university and city libraries too. I couldn't find any record of a company called Canadian Meteorological Instruments Ltd.

Other than my library research, I spent the rest of the week processing the samples I had collected from our Lunenburg and Polly's Cove dives and getting new sample bottles ready for my upcoming dive in Cape Breton.

It was hard trying to be patient, but by Saturday I was rewarded with a flashing message light on my answering machine. Bob had left a message to call him at his home in Ottawa. When I called him back, he had mixed news.

"There's no trace of a company called Canadian Meteorological Instruments Ltd.," he began.

"So, it's pretty obscure?"

"No, I mean no such company has ever existed in Canada. We even did a trademark search of the logo design you sent the picture of, and we even talked to some people at Environment Canada. Nothing."

"A red herring then," I hissed. "I thought so."

"Yes, the plot thickens," said Bob.

"So, someone's secretly transmitting something from a hidden location, with a low-power transmitter, but what?" I wondered out loud.

"That's what we're going to find out next," said Bob. "You keep on with what you're doing, cover story and all, while I see if I can find someone that can help you out on the radio transmitting side. I'll be in touch."

***

Naval Lieutenant Don Harrison

7 A NEW COLLEAGUE

I thought things must be getting serious for Bob to be arranging for extra help, and this was confirmed by the speed with which it came together. It was only two days later that I received a message to call Bob, and when I got hold of him he said he'd arranged a meeting for me with someone from the military that knew a lot about radio transmissions.

We were to meet at a Harvey's™ restaurant in Dartmouth, part of a Canadian fast-food restaurant chain that specialized in charbroiled hamburgers and fresh-cut fries. I loved going to Harvey's and had spent a lot of time at the one near Carleton in my university days. If this character liked Harvey's, maybe working with him wouldn't be too bad, I thought.

Leaving Silver behind in the truck, I went in. I'd been told to walk in at 7 pm, past the rush hour so it should be quiet, to look for a military-looking person, and to ask him for the time of day. The proper response was to give me an absurdly wrong time. The only other thing I'd been told was that if asked, he'd give his first name as Don. It all struck me as a bit elaborate but being a rookie at this cloak and dagger stuff, I tried to take it seriously.

As I walked into the restaurant, it was quiet all right. I think I must have been looking for someone like Humphrey Bogart in the movie *Casablanca*, with a fedora hat and trench-coat with the lapels pulled up. Fortunately for me, there was only one customer in sight, sitting on a booth at the back. He looked like an actor all right, but more like a young version of Rock Hudson than Humphrey Bogart, and instead of hiding under a hat and trench-coat, he was very conspicuously dressed in a naval officer's uniform and still wearing his peaked cap. This was definitely not what I'd expected, but with no one else in sight, I was pretty sure that I'd found my contact.

Strolling over to him, I said: "Excuse me, but could you tell me the time?"

"Eleven thirty," he replied with a straight face.

"Don?" he nodded.

"Alexandra?" I nodded in turn and said, "Call me Alex."

"Pleased to meet you, Alex," he said, "Naval Lieutenant Donald Harrison at your service, please call me Don." Then he smiled at me for the first time and I suddenly felt... *interested* in this new acquaintance. I've always thought that I'm more interested in substance than appearances, but this dreamy face and the engaging first impression made me wonder whether I was really a lot shallower than I wanted to admit. Trying hard to maintain a professional outward appearance, I put on a polite smile and shook hands.

"Please join me," he offered. "Or would you like to grab something to eat first? I didn't know exactly when you'd arrive, and I was famished, so I've already started," he said, pointing down at the partially eaten burger and fries sitting in front of him.

"I'm starving too," I replied. "Be back in a second."

Moving back to the counter to place my order and wait for it to be prepared gave me a few minutes to get my thoughts and questions straight in my mind (and my emotions under control too, if I'm going to be completely honest here). Then, supplied with my own tray of burger, fries, and a vanilla shake I went back to join Don in the booth.

"Come here often?" I asked, and then suddenly felt awkward, realizing that I'd unintentionally blurted out a cheesy come-on line.

Don smiled again, to show he appreciated the joke, but saved me with a very genuine-sounding response. "Believe it or not," he said, "I actually do come here a lot. This is my favourite restaurant in the whole area." Waving towards his own food, he added: "it's not fancy but I love these burgers and you can't beat the prices."

I was going to like this guy. "Me too," I supplied, "and I have a hard time not overdoing it on their fries too!"

"I'm glad we're off to a good start... Alex." He'd almost but not quite forgotten my name. "I work alone...," there was an awkward pause, "What I mean is, my work is usually pretty solitary, sitting at a desk and doing paper studies. I'm not used to working with a partner."

Brief aside: At this point, my inner voice was saying: *"This fellow looks like a god, sounds like someone with real character, and he's solitary and shy? Why can't I ever meet someone like this when I'm off duty?"*

"No problem," I said, passing his awkwardness off with a wave. "I get it. I often work kind of alone too, except that now I kind of have a dog as a partner."

"A dog?" he asked, raising his eyebrows and looking around.

"He's in my truck, outside. You can meet him later if you want," I made it sound like a question.

"I always wanted to have a dog," Don mused. "Sure, I'd like to meet him. Where'd you find him?"

"Long story. Ask me another time. Is Don your real name?" I countered.

"Look for yourself," he countered, pulling out his wallet and extracting a card, which he passed over to me.

It was a military identification card, with his picture on it, plus a name rank and serial number. "Lieutenant (N) Donald Harrison," I read out loud. "Naval Lieutenant, that's like a Captain in the Army or Air Force, right?" He nodded. "Looks authentic," I added, handing it back.

"Good, since it's not," Don replied in a very low voice, and then, raising his voice back to a normal volume, "Ask me about it another time, but my name really is Don." Once again, he countered any possible offense with a disarming smile and a genuine-sounding tone of voice.

"OK, answer me this then," I said. "Is this your idea of maintaining a low profile?" I asked looking pointedly at the dress uniform he was wearing.

That got another chuckle. "I know what you mean, but actually, it is. I gather you're not from around here?" I shook my head. "Well, around here naval uniforms are so common that no one gives me a second look. Anyone walking in on us right now would simply assume that it's Friday night, probably date night, and that I just got off work and have popped in to have a quick dinner in the company of a pretty girl. Besides, who's going to be interested in a junior officer? Junior officers like me are a dime-a-dozen around here!"

Ignoring the 'pretty girl' remark, I was trying to come up with a snappy reply when the restaurant door opened, and four people came in. Two guys and two girls, and obviously university students given the textbooks and binders of notes they were all carrying. They dumped the books onto a table and lined-up to place their orders, talking about profs and unfair deadlines, and none of them giving us more than the barest of uninterested glances.

"See?" Don said with a smile.

"OK, fine," I relented, "so where do we go from here?"

"You tell me," Don countered. He was quick though. Before I could retort he'd seen me start to bristle and quickly continued: "Look, all I know is that I was ordered to meet you, find out what I could from you about these mysterious radio signals, and then go out myself with a receiver and try to intercept some more of them."

"How are you going to do that? It'll take forever! And why?"

"Well, first of all, I need to find out where this transmitter is that you've found. Then, I need to find a place where I can work without raising suspicions because I'll have a radio scanner and a recorder. Then, I need to sit tight and listen-in for more signals. If I can record a bunch of signals, then our cryptology people can try to figure out what kind of code is being used, break the code, and then maybe we'll have a better idea of what's going on," he finished, as if it was the most logical and natural thing to be doing.

"But that could take forever," I said, as I tried to picture it in my mind. "What if the signals only go out once in a week, or a month, or several months?"

"I don't know," Don replied frankly, showing some worry for the first time, "but I have my orders, so I guess I'll have to give it a try and see what happens."

"Wow," I gave a low whistle. "I think I'd rather have my job than yours. Is your work always like this?"

"Tedious? Working in the dark, only knowing a little bit about what's really going on?" he asked. "I suppose so," he replied, thoughtfully. "I started out as a CELE[25] Officer in the air force, so I know something about radios. But nowadays…" he drifted off, thinking. "You know what branch of the service I'm really in?"

"I wasn't told, but all of sudden I think I do," I nodded.

"There you go then," he nodded in reply. "It's like being a fire fighter or a police officer," he said, looking at me meaningfully. "They spend a lot of time sitting around or doing boring, repetitive work, and then all of a sudden all hell breaks loose and sometimes a lifetime's worth of action and experiences get packed into a few days or weeks."

"Now your job sounds exactly like mine," I exclaimed. Impulsively I reached over the table, offering to shake his hand again. "I'm glad to meet you Don, or whatever your name really is, I think we're going to get along just fine."

For a while, I brought him up to date on how I'd come into the case and what little I knew so far. Since Bob had essentially vouched for him, I didn't hold back and basically told everything. For his part, Don showed himself to be intelligent, a good listener, and able to interject good questions.

"You said that you were in communications engineering?" I'd asked.

"Originally, yes."

"Can you tell me more about this automatic telex business then?"

"You know about telegraphs and Morse code, right?"

I nodded.

"OK, well then, telegraphy didn't completely go away when radio came in," Don explained. "Teletypewriters were invented to eliminate the need for operators trained in the use of Morse code. That automated the message encoding, and they used pulse-code dialing to send telex messages over phone lines and *voilà*, "telex." A similar thing was done for radio. Telex systems were adapted to short-wave radio by sending tones over a single sideband. It's called telex-on-radio, or TOR. It's not very common in North America, but it's still being used in some third-world countries because it's cheap and reliable."

"What's it used for?" I asked.

"One use is to broadcast short weather or news updates. You've heard of organizations like Associated Press and Reuters?"

"Sure."

"Well, at one time that's how news flashes were sent out around the country. The signals would be received on simple, receive-only teleprinters - with no keyboards or dials or anything - and when the teleprinters started hammering away printing something, people would know that there was a news flash and come and tear off the printed paper to see what it was."

"So then, if people thought it was newsworthy they'd print it in a newspaper or read it out over the radio news," I said, catching on.

"Exactly," Don said. "Sending telegrams works the same way, except that there are sending and receiving machines on each end, and message switching systems to route the messages to their target destinations. That's how Western Union works."

"Can it be done in any language?"

"As long as the sending and receiving machines use the same characters. Most teleprinters use English and some special keys, like to signal the beginning and end of messages, and for starting new lines and paragraphs. There even special keys for weather symbols. All of the characters get coded on a simple DC (that's direct current) circuit and sent by turning the current on and off. It's just like the dialing clicks you hear on a rotary telephone. Telex is the same thing but with a lot more characters to send. Big companies like Western Union have computers now, which lets them use fancier coding and faster speeds, but it still comes down to little on/off electrical pulses."

"OK, so then how would you automate the message sending from our mystery station – its small and pretty remote."

"Ah hah!" he responded. "Even in big offices, the teleprinter circuit is usually linked to a 5-bit paper-tape punch and reader, allowing messages to be received and then stored or even resent, on another circuit."

"So," I mused. "If you had the right equipment you could type out a message on one of these paper tapes, at home, say. Then, you could carry the paper tape to another location and read the message in through a paper tape reader, which could then send the coded message out by radio. Right?"

"Right. The military still has systems like that for sending messages out to ships, and bombers, and so on. A really important message might have a special code on it that means Flash-Priority to indicate that the message needs to be read and delivered to the Captain right away."

When we'd gone through everything and finished our dinners, Don thought for another moment, and then said, "OK, I think I've got it. I already had the frequency and now you've given me the location of the transmitter. Give me some time to scout the place and get set up, and then I'll call you to set up another meeting... it will take about a week. Here's my number at work, it has an answering machine in case you want to leave me a message," he said, writing a phone number on the back of his dinner receipt.

"OK," I agreed and did the same for him. "The lab I'm working out of at Dal is too public, so this is my number at home. I have an answering machine too, so my boss can leave me messages."

"I don't think I've ever met a girl and gotten her number so quickly," he smiled again. Where in the world had he acquired such an attentive manner and such a disarming smile, I wondered?

"Don't get carried away in your role," I warned, archly, but he could tell that my heart wasn't in it. I was going to have to watch myself with this one.

Surprisingly, I didn't get any help whatsoever from the normally over-protective Silver.

As we walked out of the restaurant together, I indicated my truck and offered to introduce Don to Silver, as promised.

Don was clearly impressed by the truck and must have momentarily forgotten about the dog because he walked up close to the driver-side door to peer into the window. I'm not sure what he wanted to see, but what he got was a huge white face showing a lot of big teeth, and a volley of loud barking.

Don started and pushed back so violently that he fell backwards to the ground. He was pretty agile though, and recovered himself quickly, turned to me, and said: "That's a wolf!"

"Not a wolf, an Alaskan Malamute, but I have to admit that he does look the part. The first time we met, he nearly gave me a heart attack too!"

Telling Silver to relax, I opened the front door, gave him a vigourous rub on the head, and said, "Silver, I'd like you to meet Don. We're going to be working together now and then."

Don instinctively offered his right hand to be sniffed, which Silver accepted as an appropriate peace offering and gave him a thorough sniffing. Pulling back a bit, Silver looked Don straight in the eyes with that penetrating gaze he could switch on, then he shifted his gaze and looked pointedly at Don's left hand.

"He's smart," Don commented. "Is it OK if I give him a bit of a burger?"

Surprised at both his foresight and his manners I nodded yes, and Don held out his opened hand to reveal several chunks that had obviously been saved from his burger.

Silver 'wolfed' them down in a flash, and then looked up at me as if to say: "I like him!"

***

377

8 ANOTHER SUSPECT?

The Monday after the weekend, Sharon, Silver, and I drove back up to Cape Breton again. Our first task was going to be the last of the three dives that we'd planned together for our respective research projects. Assuming, of course, that the sea was calm enough. Naturally, I wanted to take a look at (or, as Sharon phrased it, "snoop around") more of the small villages that populated the Cabot Trail every few miles in the Ingonish area.

We'd booked the same cabin near Ingonish Beach as before and, after checking in, we used the time to drive through all the nearby communities. In the 14-mile drive north from the summit of Cape Smokey to where we'd be diving the next day, there are five small communities. Six if you count the small community at the Keltic Lodge resort. These include Ingonish Ferry, Ingonish Harbour, Ingonish Beach, Ingonish Centre, and Ingonish itself. Some of these have only a scattering of homes and a couple of docks for the local fishing boats, while a couple have one or two small restaurants or cafes, and there was an occasional store or gas station.

Ingonish Centre, for example, had a pizzeria, while Ingonish Beach had a restaurant/bakery and a liquor store. We drove through them all, but I didn't spot much beyond houses and fishing boats. Stopping at the few stores and gas station in the area, we met more of the local people, but none aroused any suspicions on my part, or on Silver's. After making our own dinner again, and going for an evening walk, we made it an early night, so we'd be ready for diving the next day.

Sharon wanted to try diving in the bay off Ingonish, which was just south of Bear Cove and the Red Head cliffs where she'd found the old weather station. A small point of land, appropriately named 'The Point' provided some protection from the open sea, but we knew that we were going to have to watch out for rip tides.

This dive was relatively uneventful, compared with our two previous ones. It was another cloudy, grey day. We were able to park near the shore, which was a blessing as that allowed us to avoid a long hike each way, with all of our gear, and we were away from the tall cliffs that were so beautiful but such hard work to carry our gear down and up.

Leaving Silver to lounge on top of our gear bags, we entered the water and swum out a good distance before switching from snorkels to regulators and diving down to the bottom. When we reached the bottom, we were already at 30 feet of depth, and we were almost immediately greeted by lots of marine life. Sharon wanted to collect her sediment samples from below the thermocline, so we followed the bottom out until it kind of plateaued at 55 feet. There had been a strong current pulling at us initially, but at this depth, the water was very calm and fairly clear, about 30-foot visibility. As a result, we had no trouble getting our water and sediment samples.

With our sample bottles in our mesh carry-bags, we each looked around but there wasn't much more to see, so Sharon signaled that we may as well head back for shore. The current had moved us off our intended course a bit, so it was a new route heading back that brought us over some very rocky areas where we had to be careful not to become tangled up in a couple of lost fishing nets. These did not pose a significant danger, as long as we still had lots of air left plus a way to cut them away if one of us got caught on one. In this case, our air supplies were still in good shape, and it was for situations like this that we carried large diving knives strapped to our legs.

In my Ontario and Quebec freshwater-diving days I used to have visions of getting tangled up in an underwater fishing net or line in such a way that I might not be able to actually reach down for the knife strapped to my calf. So, being the worrier that I am, I had adopted the habit of diving with a second knife attached to either my upper arm or to the hose with my pressure gauge on it. As a result, I wasn't worried about the nets we encountered, but we avoided contact with them anyway.

Rather than surfacing, we stayed on compressed air and followed the rising bottom all the way back in to shore, and I was rewarded by finding a bed of Bar Clams[26], tucked in around the base of a sand bar that we later decided would have been just below the low tide level. This enabled me to grab a bunch of clam samples.

Sharon and I each had a steaming mug of my signature tomato soup while we were changing and packing away our gear and our samples but were still left feeling hungry, so we stopped in at the Ingonish Beach restaurant/bakery for coffee and fresh, hot cinnamon buns. Once again, the restaurant had a small deck outside, so Silver could lie on the grass nearby and keep us company.

We were served by a nice, older lady who stopped to chat a bit every time she came to our table. In this way, we discovered that she and her husband owned and managed the restaurant/bakery, with him being the cook and baker and her the front manager and occasional pitch-in waitress, when needed, to help their one full-time waitress.

The more we spoke, the more I became convinced that I was hearing a very slight German accent in her voice. Curiosity aroused, I was wondering about the husband when Sharon mentioned how much she enjoyed the fresh cinnamon buns. When I added my genuine endorsement of Sharon's praises, she said she'd tell her husband and went off to the kitchen.

Sure enough, when we'd gone inside to pay the bill, he came out of the kitchen.

"So, you like my rolls?" he asked.

We did, and we asked where he'd learned to bake so well. He credited his mother for teaching him. Like so many people for whom English is a second language, the more he talked about his parents and his childhood, the more a very slight accent from his native language set in. German, it sounded like.

My mind was alive with possibilities as we began our drive back to Halifax.

"What are you thinking?" Sharon asked.

"That couple we just met, Henry and Anna Miller – I thought that I detected slight German accents from each of them and I was wondering about their names."

"What about them?"

"Well, a lot of immigrants anglicize their names when they move to Canada or the U.S., and I was wondering whether Henry and Anna Miller might have been Heinrich and Johanna Müller, or something like that."

"Isn't that a bit of a stretch? Why suspect them?"

"I'm not sure that I suspect them, exactly, but there were a few too many coincidences there."

"Like their names and accents?"

"Those, yes, but did you notice the large, floor-model antique radio in the corner of the main restaurant? It was actually working; with those big speakers they used to use the sound quality was actually pretty good."

"No, I heard some music but didn't see where it was coming from. I hadn't thought to look. Is that all?"

"Almost. As we were pulling away, did you happen to notice that tall pole standing behind the closest house to the restaurant? I think that was a ham radio operator's antenna."

"My God, I must be blind!"

"Not blind, it's just that I've been looking for things like that every time we've passed through a village. That was the only one that I've seen. I think I'll ask Ottawa to do some digging for us."

"Us! I like that," Sharon said, excitedly.

Damn, damn, damn. "Promise me that you'll back out of this when I ask you, OK? I don't want to expose you to danger."

"You think there'll be danger?" Sharon asked, still excited.

"I hope not, but I'm getting a bad feeling about all this… Promise me?"

"OK, I promise," Sharon said, giving the Girl Guides' salute. I hoped that she was the type to keep her promises.

The next morning, I called Bob and asked him to please check into the names Henry and Anna Miller, when they'd emigrated to Canada, whether their original names might have been different, whether Henry had a ham radio licence, whether either of them had a criminal record and anything else they could dig up.

Once again, his people were quick. By Thursday I'd received a message to call Bob. I'd been close on the names. Henry and Anna Miller's immigration records showed them to have entered Canada from West Germany, as a married couple, in 1957 - twenty years earlier. Their original names had been Herbert and Angela Müller. Neither had a criminal record, but Henry had a Class A Amateur Radio Operator Certificate and a radio station licence, both issued in 1966.

Now I had a suspect or two in the Millers and some vague suspicions about the owner of the antique store. It felt like progress.

The following day (Friday) we cleaned our gear and worked in the lab with our new samples. Neither Sharon nor I were quite ready for our next dive or dives, and Don was still off somewhere doing something secret, so Silver and I simply took the weekend off and enjoyed sleeping-in in the mornings and going for long walks. Our new favourite was walking along the many pathways in Point Pleasant Park, which lies at the mouth of Halifax Harbour. Many of the paths eventually led to the harbour-front, with great views, a couple of beaches (although Silver still refused to put more than a paw in the seawater), and a few historical monuments – like the huge anchor from the HMCS Bonaventure, Canada's last aircraft carrier, which had been decommissioned in 1970.

Fortified by our weekend off, it felt like good timing when Sharon showed me the Fisheries Notice on Monday morning. I was in the lab finishing my work with the samples from my last dive when Sharon rushed in excitedly waving a fisheries department notice at me.

"Read," was all she said.

Red Tide Prompts Shellfish Closures

News Release

DARTMOUTH, N.S. – The Department of Fisheries and Oceans (DFO) is advising the public that the levels of paralytic shellfish poisoning toxin (PSP or red tide) are high in numerous locations throughout the coast. Many areas are now closed to harvesting bivalve shellfish due to unacceptable PSP levels. Coordinates of the latest closed areas are outlined below.

Shellfish closures can change frequently, therefore harvesters also are encouraged to call local DFO offices for information on current PSP closures prior to fishing.

- 30 -

I'd been wondering what I'd do next but now, as luck would have it, we had an actual Red Tide alert out. Although she now knew that my research project wasn't strictly real, Sharon thought I would want to head out the next day and get some samples while the Red Tide levels were high.

With nothing better to do, I agreed. Looking at the list of affected areas, I saw that one of them was the entire Ingonish area. It seemed like a sign, so I jumped at the chance to get some Red Tide samples and, more importantly, do a bit more snooping around in Cape Breton. With three sample-collecting dives behind us, we had a system now, so it didn't take us long to prepare. I was looking forward to the dive with Sharon, knowing that it might be my last. With samples collected before and during the Red Tide, there would be no excuse for me to go back again, and no real motivation to collect more samples further south.

That night, I found a message from Jack McDonald waiting on my answering machine. Jack and I had been recruits together at the RCMP Depot Division training centre in Regina, Saskatchewan, and then our paths had crossed again the previous year, when I was on an undercover assignment in Fort McMurray, Alberta. We'd worked well together, and I'd learned that I could trust him. The phone number he'd left had a Nova Scotia area code, and when I returned his call he explained that he was on a temporary assignment to the Baddeck Detachment, where he was filling-in for a constable that was sick and not expected back to work for a couple of months. Apparently, Jack had only just arrived the day before.

I told him that his timing was great because I was going to be driving to Cape Breton the next day and that although I'd be going up with a friend, she knew about my real job and we'd be able to talk reasonably freely.

I thought I knew the answer, but I did ask Jack how it was that he knew where I was and how to reach me.

"Staff Sergeant Simpson called me and asked me to call you," Jack replied. "He seemed to feel that since we'd be in the same neighborhood for a while, we might enjoy a chance to get together over coffee."

"Mmmm hmmm… more like he's found some way to engineer your temporary transfer out here in case I need your help, like I did in Alberta last year."

"All he said was that you were on another undercover mission, and since I'd be coming out here anyway, he thought it would be good for you to have someone nearby that you could call if needed. Someone that would understand what you're doing and not waste time with a lot of damn-fool questions."

"That sounds like a direct quote."

"It is. He didn't give me any details about the operation, but you know you can count on me."

"I do Jack, thank you. By the way, I'm not mad at my boss, things are starting to heat up a bit out here and I might very well need your help before long. I just don't want you getting involved without knowing what you might be getting yourself into."

For the next few minutes, I summarized what I'd been sent out to do and the progress I'd made to date. To his credit, none of this fazed Jack in the least.

"Look, Alex, I'm not one for undercover work, much less all this cloak-and-dagger stuff, so I'm happy to leave that to you. But with all your focus on this part of the province, I don't have any doubts about your boss having found some sneaky way to get me transferred out here. As I said, you can count on me."

I sighed. "Thanks, Jack, I really appreciate this."

It was arranged that Jack and I, and Sharon, would meet at a coffee shop in Baddeck the next day before Sharon and I continued to Ingonish.

The coffee shop Jack had recommended was on Water Street, giving us a great view of the inland sea[27] called Bras d'Or Lake. I introduced Sharon to Jack, who'd had the presence of mind to come in plain clothes. Having spent time together the previous year, Silver and Jack recognized each other immediately. Once again, we were able to sit outside so Silver could keep us company, and our server was nice enough to bring out a bowl of water for him.

"He looks like a wolf," she said, as she cautiously set the bowl on the ground a few feet from him.

To this, Silver immediately smiled up at her, with his tongue lolling out.

"It's like he heard me!" she exclaimed.

"I think he really appreciates getting the water. Thank you," I said, to change the topic.

With introductions made and drinks acquired, and with no one else within earshot, I sketched-in the details of Sharon's discovery and my investigation to date. I mentioned that someone from military intelligence was also involved but didn't identify him or provide any details of what he was up to.

Before parting, Jack and I exchanged our home and office telephone numbers, and I told him that I also had a police radio. Following my first undercover assignment in Alberta, a year earlier,

I'd asked to have a radio installed in my truck. What I'd wanted was one that looked like a CB radio[28] but that actually worked on the police band.

The radio technician that installed it for me had done me one better. The radio inside the cab and the antennas that were conspicuously attached to my oversized rear-view mirrors on each of the front doors not only looked like a CB radio system but if anyone were to turn the system on, they would find that it worked like any other CB radio. Almost, that is. The radio technician had explained that he'd tuned the antennas to optimize sending and receiving on the police band, so the signal strength on the CB frequencies wouldn't be as good as it should be. I thought that was unlikely to be a problem. As far as the police band went, the RCMP has a standard frequency that is used by the dispatchers and highway patrol right across the country, plus several tactical frequencies. A hidden switch on my radio allowed me to access these using the ordinary pre-set buttons on the front panel.

Jack said that he was about to start a shift on highway patrol and would just 'happen' to be in the area where the highway ran from Ingonish through to Ingonish Beach and gave me his car number in case we should need to make contact by radio. We made up a fictitious car number for me to use as well. We also agreed that in future, I would call Jack before going to Cape Breton and again on the way out or failing that when back in Halifax. I have to admit that I felt better knowing I had a local ally.

Between the long drive north and our visit with Jack, it was too late in the day and we were too tired for our dive, so we put that off until the next day. After checking into our rented cabin at Ingonish Beach, we had time to spare before dinner and went back to the Oceanside Antiques store in Ingonish. Nosing around the store, I was still fascinated by the old tube-style radios. The man I'd met on our previous visit wasn't there this time, and an elderly lady introduced herself as his wife, Wilma.

Wilma had noticed me looking at a table model radio in a handsome wooden cabinet and had come over to talk to me about it.

"Are you interested in old radios?"

"Well, I didn't think so, but when I visited your store a few weeks ago I noticed these beautiful old radios, and your husband had explained a bit about them to me. I guess I still find them fascinating.

Why do they seem to have so many frequency bands on them?" I asked pointing to the radio I'd been looking at, which had four frequency bands on its main dial.

"This one is a 1947 RCA Victor model," she explained. "In those days people were used to listening to the AM band for music stations, and the short-wave bands for news reports and this radio had the new frequency modulation band, what we now call FM, and which was brand new at the time. The AM and FM bands were popular for local music radio stations, and the short-wave bands were popular for getting new reports from far away stations in the US and Europe. You can see that this model also had the special 'Magic Eye' feature, which was a vacuum tube that you would look at to help get the stations tuned just right. It had a dark centre that would shrink from a circle to a narrow band when a station was properly tuned. The changing shape reminded people of a cat's eye, which is where the name came from."

"Was it that difficult to tune then?" I asked.

"Not for the AM or FM stations, but the signals were much weaker for short-wave stations that were far away, like on the continent in Europe, so the Magic Eye tube really made a difference. Come, let me show you," and with that, she led to way to the back of the store where they had a similar old, multi-band radio that was plugged in. Turning it on she waited a minute for the tubes to warm up and then began turning the tuning dial.

Sure enough, as she slowly moved the tuning indicator, we could begin to hear a station come in. The sound was fuzzy at first, then it became clear that someone was talking, and then when the Magic Eye displayed its narrow cats-eye image the voice became clear – it was a man reading a news report.

"There, you see? That's probably a radio station in England or Western Europe transmitting on short wave."

Another working short-wave radio..., I thought to myself. *Oh no.*

To cover my racing thoughts, I tried to show a polite interest and then change the conversation. The only idea that popped into my head was the model diving helmet I'd seen on my previous visit, so I asked whether they still had it in the store. It turned out that they did, so I looked it over again and decided to buy it. This provided the distraction that I needed and covered my exit from the store. As a bonus, I really had wanted to buy the model helmet so it all worked out well.

As Sharon and I drove to a restaurant for dinner I resolved to send a new message to Bob in Ottawa, asking him for more information on the owners of Oceanside Antiques. Over the previous six weeks, I'd driven and/or walked through every village in the Ingonish area and had looked inside every one of their stores and restaurants. Everything had seemed peaceful and innocent-looking except for the two places in Ingonish that had made my danger-sense tingle.

The next day we did our Red Tide sampling dive at the same location as our previous dive near Ingonish Beach. The main difference this time was that a pretty violent storm had just passed through the area. Its aftermath was a mixed blessing for us. On one hand, the ocean was very calm, so it was easy to get into the water, swim out, and do our dive. On the other hand, the storm had stirred the sediment up so much that visibility was very poor. In fact, in order to make sure we didn't get separated we'd had to use a short piece of rope, about ten feet in length, that had a loop to go over one wrist at each end. This reminded me of my student-era's diving days, in which we'd had to do this in some lakes and rivers, but it was the first time I'd had to do this in an ocean. Despite the visibility issues, we eventually got to the location we wanted and collected the samples we'd needed. It all just took a lot more time and energy than it otherwise would have.

When we emerged from the water, tired but content, Silver was happy to see us, as always, and we took some time to play with him and enjoy the beautiful location. As we packed away our gear and loaded everything into my truck, I reflected that I now had my Red Tide samples, so the minimum results needed to lend credence to my cover story were in good shape regardless of whether I did any more dives or not. That was not only convenient but, as we made the long drive home to Halifax, I reflected that I'd genuinely enjoyed Sharon's company and each of the dives I'd done with her.

Sharon's professional instincts led her to convince me that we should do one more dive, so I could get a second set of 'Red Tide' samples for comparison while the Red Tide notices were still in effect. I didn't really have anything better to do, so the next day we drove south along the coast for what would become our last dive together.

We had a choice of the two previous sites: the one down by Lunenburg, and the one at Polly's Cove, near Peggy's Cove. Although neither of us had fond memories of our previous experience at Polly's Cove, it was a shorter drive so that decided it. I'm glad that we decided to back there because the weather was beautiful, the sea was calm and relatively clear, and we got our samples with no difficulty. Later, at the restaurant at nearby Peggy's Cove, as we sat with Silver in the box of my pickup truck eating seafood chowder and enjoying the views of the famous lighthouse, amazing rocks, and the ocean swell, I felt the most amazing sense of peace and contentment.

When Silver and I got home in Halifax that evening, there was a message from Don on my answering machine, asking me to call him as soon as I could.

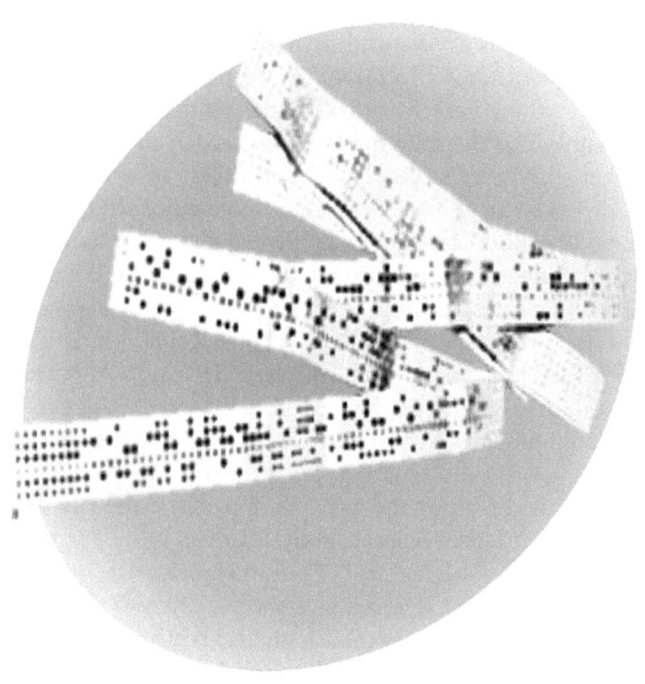

9 DISASTER

When I returned Don's call, I told him about my experiences since our restaurant meeting.

"It feels like I'm making some progress," I summarized, as I wound up my narrative.

"I'm making progress too," he'd said, "do you want to come and see for yourself."

"Sure!"

"OK, how about meeting me tomorrow afternoon at the docks, at Neil's Harbour. That's a small village just north of Ingonish. I have a boat there, and we can cast off at about 4 pm."

I'd readily agreed and the next day Silver and I made the drive back to Cape Breton, and up to Neil's Harbour. All these long drives were making me wish we'd dreamt up a Cape Breton-based cover story.

Parking in a public lot near the docks, Silver and I quickly found Don, who was watching for us. He had rented an older-looking Cape Islander boat.

"The boat is sound," Don said, rather defensively, when he noticed my skeptical gaze scanning the boat. "From the outside, she looks like an ordinary fishing boat, just like the fifty or so others in this area. The owner has been converting her into a touring and diving boat for his own use and started out by completely overhauling all the mechanical systems, so everything inside is in top working condition. The coffee is already on in the galley. Hop in, and we'll get underway."

Silver and I boarded the boat and Don cast off, and expertly navigated his way out of the harbor and south towards the Ingonish area.

"We're heading for Red Head, but not in a direct line. My cover story is that I'm taking hyper-accurate soundings for the Canadian Hydrographic Service. It's nonsense, of course, but it offers an explanation for all the fancy looking electronics that I've had to lug aboard and install. Did you see the long antennas mounted along each side of the boat?"

"Yes, they look a bit like the fishing-net booms that some boats have. The kind that swing out from the sides to support the nets in position when they're fishing."

"Good," Don said with a smile. "That's what they're supposed to look like, or at least to a casual glance. In fact, they are my radio antennas, and they swing up rather than out. You'll see when we get there."

As we continued along, Don explained that he'd been cruising around the area trying to pick-up short-wave radio signals and then triangulating them back to pinpoint their origins.

"How many have you found so far?" I asked.

"Lots of signals of all kinds, of course, but only three that are being transmitted from Nova Scotia. Two of them are ham radio operators."

"Both from people in the Ingonish area?"

"That's right! How did you know?"

I explained about Sharon's and my visit to Ingonish Beach, our meeting with the Millers, and the information I'd received from Ottawa, including Henry Miller's ham radio licence. Clearly, there was a second ham radio operator and I began to wonder whether that might turn out to be Wilma's husband in the antique store, although I'd so far only spotted one tall antenna in the entire area.

"Well, could be, but I have to tell you that so far there's been nothing suspicious about either of their transmissions. One or the other seems to go on the air most evenings after their businesses close, I guess. But when they do, everything is strictly correct. Their transmissions are in plain language, properly identified, and they're pretty typical sounding chatter – mostly with other hams down the coast and in the New England states."

"Rats," I muttered. "That doesn't sound very promising after all."

"Well, the third signal is certainly interesting," Don said proudly. "It's your mystery station!"

"Really? You heard it?"

"Only at first. I was lucky, and just after I got out here it started sending a fairly short message of some kind, in code. It repeated itself every six hours for 24 hours then went silent. There's been nothing in the past week, and I've been snooping around in the area every day!"

"Isn't that a lot of transmitting for our suspect to have do, working from a supposedly secret location?" I asked.

"Not really," Don said. "He only has to go there once, to check that the batteries are OK, then feed in his pre-prepared paper tape loop. Do you remember my explanation of the paper tape recording and re-playing business?" I nodded. "Well, there you are then. They make up the message tape in advance, then feed it in to the machine. The machine is probably preset to transmit the message at intervals for 24 hours and then stop. Our suspect only has to visit the transmitter when there's a new message to be sent, and I somehow doubt that happens very often."

"Simple. Frighteningly simple," I remarked. "How many recordings do you need before the cryptographers can work their magic and decode them?"

"I don't really know," Don replied, thoughtfully. "From what I can understand, it depends on how complex the messages are, whether they repeat enough common words, and so on. I imagine that they are assuming that the language is German, but they would have to bear in mind that it might be some other language, so I don't know what that does to their puzzle-solving. Today, we were lucky again, because when I was out here about three hours ago, it was transmitting again. I only caught the end of the message, but if it repeats itself when we're out there now, we should be able to get the whole thing. That would give us two new messages, plus the first one that started all this."

We were both alone with our thoughts for much of the rest of the trip. It turned out to be the calm before the storm.

As we passed Lakies Head, Don took us out to deeper water but still running parallel to the shore.

It wasn't long before we were passing Broad Cove. As we continued past Red Head and its cliffs, I pointed out the place where we'd found the weather station.

"Should we be hearing something?"

Don laughed. "Not to worry, let's just keep cruising towards Bear Cove." Then, after consulting his logbook, "We're here a bit early.

Let's keep going as far as Ingonish Island then circle back and we should be able to catch the repeated message. Then we can call it a day."

As we passed Bear Cove and The Point, I pointed out where Sharon and I had done our most recent SCUBA dive. Don seemed very interested in diving, so this led me to describing some of our earlier dives as well. With stories to tell, the time passed quickly, and soon it was time for Don to take us around the southern shore of Ingonish Island and turn northwest and back to the waters off Red Head. As we did, I mentioned to Don that Ingonish Island looked like a nice place to visit sometime.

Someday, I really should learn to be careful what I wish for.

As we came around the island, Don reduced speed and said, "Here, you take the wheel." As I did, he raised the two big antennas on each side of the boat, switched on his scanning receiver[29], and started his tape recorder running, with its two large reels slowly turning around and around. He had no sooner done this than there was a squawk, and then the sounds of a bunch of pulse tones coming out of the speaker in one of Don's myriad pieces of electronics. Don focused on his equipment, started turning dials and making notes in his logbook, then gave a sharp "Yes!"

Returning to take over the helm, he quickly said, "Let's just troll very slowly around here a bit."

"Is it our mystery station?" I asked, getting excited.

"It sure is, you must be good luck!" Don exclaimed. Within two minutes, the signal abruptly stopped.

"You were saying," I prompted.

"That was it. The messages are only two minutes long, and we just got the latest one!"

Handing me the wheel again, Don went to lower the antennas. He was just in the process of doing this when there was a 'beep' sound from another piece of equipment.

"What's that?" I asked.

"Radar," Don said, turning to look. "It must be a malfunction because it's scanning forward and there's nothing but ocean ahead of us right now."

I could see now that the beep sound had come from a round display screen that had a bright line sweeping around it, like the hour-hand of a clock. As the line swept around, the machine beeped again, and a spot on the screen flared brightly for a moment and then dimmed again.

"Alex," Don said in a measured tone that sounded forced, "Please go back to the stern of the boat, put a life jacket on, grab a second one for Silver, and keep Silver close to you."

Something in his tone commanded instant action, but I did ask "What's going on?" as I passed by him, heading for the stern.

"Something's out there that should not be there, and I think it's heading for us," Don said, "and I have a very bad feeling about it."

"What about you?" I asked, but there was no reply, and I didn't want to distract him.

Reaching the stern, I pulled out two life jackets from one of the storage bins under the aft gunwales. Saying, "Stay with me Silver," I pulled one over my head, put an arm through the armhole of the second, and was trying to find the straps to tie the first one when I heard a loud "Brace yourself!" from Don. Before I could do anything more, I felt and then heard a heart-stopping crash. Either we had run aground, or something had hit us, I couldn't tell which, and the next thing I remember was the deck being tipped up and me falling backwards into the sea.

Did I mention that the northern Atlantic Ocean is cold? I thought it was bad with a wetsuit to protect me, but with only light clothes and a light pullover on it felt like it must be near freezing. The shock of the cold and the dark of the water completely disoriented me at first, but my instinct to kick for the surface coupled with the lift from the two life jackets soon had my head breaching the surface.

Shaking my head to get the water out of my ears, I looked around. To my left was the shore, I thought. To my right was the boat, but it looked like it had been broken roughly in half, with the broken parts sticking up out of the water and the bow and stern underwater. Calling out Silver's name, I heard a 'yelp' and, turning around, there he was behind me, dog paddling.

So, he could swim after all! That was a relief.

Turning back, I tried to spot Don, but couldn't see anything but the boat. It was surreal, because there was no sound, really. The engine had stopped or been destroyed, there were no explosions, or fires or anything, just a very broken boat that was rapidly settling lower in the water. Then, just ahead and beyond the bow of the boat,

I did see something. Something dark – black, or maybe a dark grey in colour – and low in the water. I thought it might be another part of the boat at first, but it was the wrong colour, it was moving away from us, and the shape was wrong.

Taking stock, I tried calling for Don, while struggling to find the straps for my lifejacket and tie them roughly around me. That done, I was able to paddle over to Silver. He seemed OK, but he had a wild look in his eyes that I didn't like. He surely hated being in the water! Eventually, I decided that the best way to help him was by putting the lifejacket under his chest, putting each of his front legs through the armholes of the jacket, and then tying the straps over his back. That way, his chest and abdomen got most of the lift, he could easily keep his head out of the water, his front legs could paddle a bit, and his back legs could still paddle freely.

With one hand on Silver's lifejacket and the other arm stretched out in front of me, I side-stroked as best I could and headed us toward the shore. It seemed to take forever, but eventually my shoulder and hip brushed over some rocks, then the swell pounded us against some other rocks, and I was eventually able to stand up and tow Silver to the shallows. Then, finally, we both kind of crawled up onto the beach.

There was good news and bad news on the beach.

The good news was that we found Don. Not far away from where we'd landed, he was lying in a crumpled heap, exhausted but breathing. He said that he hadn't had time to get a lifejacket, had been partially submersed while still in the boat, and it had taken all his strength to extricate himself from the wreck and swim to shore. With no lifejacket on, his head had been low in the water, so that he hadn't seen me, nor me him.

The bad news was that what I'd taken to be the shore was the shore of Ingonish Island, not the mainland. With hindsight it was obvious, of course. We hadn't had to swim all that far to get to it. As I was considering what to do next, I noticed Don staring out at the ocean – but there was nothing in sight.

"All gone," Don said, softly, between shivers. "So quickly, too."

"What happened?" I asked, and then before he could answer, "Never mind, we need to warm up first or we'll freeze to death. I think we're on the island, what do you want to do? As I see it, we can try to build a fire here, try walking around to the other side of the island and build one there, or go around and then try to swim for the mainland."

"That's a one-mile swim, and it's a half-mile to get around the island according to the chart. If you'll excuse me not being very macho right now," he said, between shivers, "I vote for building a fire right here on the island, but on the other side. That way we'll be sheltered from the worst of the wind."

So that's what we did. Fortunately, none of us were actually injured in the wreck. We were just exhausted and cold. The short hike got the blood flowing well enough, but with soaked clothing, it didn't seem to warm me up at all. One blessing was that we found a fire pit on the other side of the island. It even had a large pile of wood to one side, that had been split and covered with a tarp to keep most of the wood more-or-less dry.

"This must be a picnic site for boaters in the area," Don said, looking it over in approval. But we still need a way to make a fire and I don't have any matches on me. How are you at rubbing sticks together?" he asked me, trying to lighten the mood.

"Terrible! But if we can find some dry kindling, I might have a trick left up my sleeve," I replied.

He raised an eyebrow at this but didn't comment further and set about looking for dry kindling. There wasn't much to be found.

"You know, in Girl Guides, we were taught that dead branches that are still attached to their trees stay dry and make good kindling," I said as I reflected on moments from my youth.

"That we have," said Don, briskly, and the two of us set about stripping all the nearby trees of their dead branches. These were actually quite plentiful and in a wide range of sizes so that we soon had two large piles of dry kindling, roughly sorted by size.

"I guess the people around here don't know that trick," said Don, appreciatively. "OK, Miss Magician, what's your idea for starting the fire?"

"Don't get the wrong idea now," I said, and proceeded to pull off my wet pants.

"I'm all eyes!"

"I can see that," I said, dryly, "It's your thoughts I'm worried about."

If Don was about to continue the banter, he was cut short by the sight of the bandage on my leg. "You're hurt," he exclaimed, the concern plain in his voice.

"Not hurt. Watch," I said and, gritting my teeth, I ripped-off the bandage that had been concealing my UDT knife. Then, having built a small pile of the smallest bits of kindling wood, I used the knife to add a cluster of shavings from some of the larger kindling, then twisted the end cap to release it.

"A fire starter," Don whistled. Actually, he was shivering too hard to whistle, so it came out more like a wheeze, but I knew what he meant.

"It's called ferrocerium," I said, repeating what Scotty had told me so long ago (*was it only a month ago?* I thought). "It's a metal alloy that you're supposed to be able to strike with a knife blade to create extremely hot sparks. I haven't had a chance to try it before, but this seems like the time."

As Don watched, fascinated, I used the knife blade to carefully scrape some shavings of metal onto the top of my little tinder pile, and then reversed the blade and tried striking it against the ferrocerium rod with a downward, glancing motion. I was rewarded with a few small sparks that were quickly extinguished. I sighed.

"Don't give up now Alex, you've got this," encouraged Don.

I tried again, this time with much more force, and was rewarded with several small showers of sparks that eventually ignited some of the metal shavings. Those shavings burned hot, as the exposed pieces of metal oxidized vigorously in the air. At this, I set the knife down and started to gently blow on the glowing strips of metal as, one by one, they ignited and began to glow white hot. Their heat gradually produced a few slender streamers of smoke from the wood kindling, and with constant, careful blowing I could eventually see some reddish glow coming from the wood itself.

It got easier from there. As the wood began to catch, I carefully added some more small twigs and branches, and then built a teepee of medium-sized pieces over top.

"Girl Guides again?" asked Don, admiring my little teepee of firewood.

"Yes, this part I've done before. Once the fire picks up a bit more, we can start adding the larger branches, and when we have a solid bed of coals we can start putting the split logs on."

After carefully blowing and feeding the fledgling fire some more, I eventually decided it wasn't going to go out on me and stood up. It was a relief to be able to catch my breath and stretch my back, but I was shivering pretty strongly now. We were going to need heat, and soon.

Fortunately, Don was starting to feel better, despite his shivering, which hadn't relented since we'd met on the beach in the first place. With a brusque "My turn to help," he rose and went over to the tarp-covered pile of split wood. Removing the tarp, he started taking the wood pile apart and moving the split firewood closer to us and then began to construct a wall with it.

As he built it up, layer by layer, I asked "A wall?"

"A wall," he confirmed. There's enough wood here to make a very nice wind-break, and once the fire builds up it will reflect some of the heat back to us if we sit right in front of it.

"I don't think I would have ever thought of that," I commended him.

"Well, fair's fair. You got the fire going in the first place," he said, helping me to put some larger pieces of wood on the fire, which was really taking hold now. We could finally feel some warmth from it seeping into our hands as we fed it with the larger branches.

Once Don had the wall built up about three feet high, he decided that was enough for now and retrieved the tarp, which he shook out and then laid over the wall so part of it hung from the top of the wall down to the ground, and then about three feet towards the fire. Underneath the horizontal part, he placed the two lifejackets I had brought with me. They were soaking wet, but the tarp kept the water away from us.

"Seating for two!" he said with a flourish, and when I moved over to sit, he busied himself with putting the first of the large pieces of split wood onto the collapsed, burning remnants of my firewood teepee, saying over his shoulder "I think you should get out of the rest of those wet clothes."

He was right, of course, so I peeled off my wet clothes and sat huddled in front of the growing fire, feeling warmth starting to enter the rest of my body. "At last," I sighed.

Don stripped off his wet clothes too, but not before making another pile of wood near the side of the fire, over which he draped my wet clothes to dry. He made another makeshift drying rack for himself on the other side of the fire, and his clothes soon followed.

Sitting side by side, but not touching, we could both feel the warmth from the fire seep into our bodies, and we were each able to wrap a bit of the tarp around our outward-facing shoulders, which cut more of the wind off.

Then, glancing over at me for the first time since unclothing, his face immediately went back to concern again.

"Is that other bandage a knife too, or are you really are injured after all?' he asked.

"I'm fine now that this fire's going," I assured him. "There's a Derringer under that other bandage."

"Really?" Don exclaimed, amazed again. "You're serious, aren't you?"

"I'll show it to you if you keep on staring at me like that," I said, without a smile, but just barely. He knew I was joking.

"Another time then," Don laughed. "Your first miracle is more than enough for me, for one night anyway."

Then, before the conversation could get awkward, we were interrupted by Silver who had long since shaken the excess water out of his fur, and who had been sitting close to the fire from the moment it had taken hold. Now, however, he had decided it was time to make himself a bit more comfortable, and he weaseled and squeezed his way in between Don and I and settled down in the warmest spot in the whole site, with the windbreak behind him, the fire in front, and two human bodies radiating warmth from either side.

"He's either chaperoning us, or he's the smartest one here," Don chuckled.

"Probably both," I agreed.

With our survival assured, for the moment, we finally had a chance to discuss our adventure.

"Something hit us!" I exclaimed, "and afterward I thought I saw something moving away from us, low in the water."

"Right on both counts," agreed Don, morosely. "I'm sorry, Alex, but I truly did not see that coming or I'd never have asked you to come along with me today."

"What was it? At first, I thought it must be a whale or something, but it didn't look round, it looked angular."

"Mmmm hmmmm, and a whale would have given us a shock, but it wouldn't have sunk us... I think it was a sub."

"What? No! Things like that don't happen anymore," I asserted.

Don was silent, letting the thought sink in.

"Right?" I asked, less certain now.

"I'm afraid we made somebody feel very worried. Worried enough to take the risk of sinking us and possibly getting spotted. That means this is no small thing that we're prying into Alex."

"So, the sub was here to receive the coded message," I said out loud, thinking it through. "That's why the message gets sent out repeatedly over a 24-hour period because they can't predict exactly when the sub will be waiting offshore."

I started ticking things off then, lining them up in my mind. "Low power, coded messages are being sent out to where a ship or a submarine can receive them. It's about something important, something secret, but the messages are brief. At least so far, right?"

"Right," Don agreed. "I think you're on the right track, but my guess is that the messages are simply providing dates and times and places for people to meet to exchange something bigger."

"And it's probably whoever is on land that is setting those dates, times, and places. If it was a ship or sub, they could just transmit them and the person on shore could listen in on any short-wave radio set."

"That would be my guess," agreed Don.

"But who?"

"Who?" Don echoed.

"Whose sub was that?"

"Ah. Well, it's the cold war, right? My guess would be East Germany, the Soviet Union, or another of the Soviet satellite countries. It doesn't matter, really. It all comes to the same thing."

"So, it's espionage after all," I mused. I explained to Don that we had considered that the messages might have had to do with organized crime in some way.

"Seems unlikely, now."

"What do you think will happen next?"

"Well, I imagine that our masters will ask us to keep digging. No one is going to declare war over the mystery sinking of a fishing boat. We don't know whom to accuse, and even if we did, they'd deny it, claim the boat sank for some other reason, and that if we think we saw a sub we must have been drunk or delusional. Who would contradict them? ... Besides us, of course."

"Damn and damn," I cursed.

"Yeah," was all Don said.

"If we're right, then they won, didn't they? They sunk us to prevent you from intercepting their message. All three of us came up to the surface between our boat and the island, so they may not have seen us in the water, but they didn't even bother to check to see if anyone survived. Did they? That must mean that they didn't care, as long as the message remained secret."

"I'm afraid so. On the other hand, if they thought we had the message, and if they knew or suspected that we have more of their messages, then they'd be worried about us breaking the code and breaking up their meetings, whatever they are. In that case, they'd probably just shift their operations to another place, maybe use other methods, and other people. Their agent here could just retreat back into hiding for a while, or forever if necessary."

"But how does that help us?" I asked. "They're probably thinking that they're safe for the moment, but we don't have any of your tapes." Then I looked at him more closely. "We don't have the tapes... do we?"

"Well, I wouldn't say that..." In the fire light, I could see that Don's eyes were twinkling now. Then he reached over to his bundle of wet clothes, rummaged around a bit, and produced a cloth bag with long straps dangling from it. "This is the reason you didn't see me for a while when the boat was hit. I grabbed my earlier tapes, ripped the new one off the front of the recorder, stuffed them all into this bag and tied the drawstrings around my waist."

"Are you crazy? You're lucky you didn't get trapped and go down with the boat!"

"Well, actually, I did. By the time I had the bag tied around my waist, the bow section was almost completely under water. Since it was settling slowly, I decided to wait until the water reached the ceiling, then held my breath for a bit longer. When it felt like my lungs were going to burst, I swam out and up to the surface. When I got there, I used some floating debris to hide behind. I heard you call for me and tried to answer back, but I guess you didn't hear me. From the sound of your voice I judged that you were closer to shore than I was, so instead of using up my strength yelling I decided to follow you in."

"You took an awful chance, Don, but I'm glad you made it. Are the tapes any good now?" I asked, looking at the wet bag dubiously.

"I think so. I'll send them in so someone who knows what they're doing can deal with them, but a short dunk in the water won't erase a magnetic tape. I broke the reel tearing the new one away from the recorder, but they'll be able to wind the tape onto a new reel easily enough."

"So that means we'll have three different recordings all told," I said excitedly. "I hope that's enough to break the code."

"We'll see."

"Seems like I'm not the only magician around here," I said, leaning back against our wooden wall and feeling the heat from the fire course through me. We were each alone with our own thoughts for a moment, and it occurred to me that I had rarely met a man who was so comfortable with silences. I liked it.

We both jumped, then, as a log in the fire suddenly popped and cracked. Don reached over to throw a couple more logs on the fire. Bigger pieces now.

"Don," I said tentatively. Then when he turned to look me in the eyes, "you didn't build this wall just to keep the wind out, did you?"

"No. I'm sorry Alex. I'd hoped you wouldn't notice, but I think it would be safer if no one saw a light coming from this spot tonight. Don't you?"

"I'm glad you're here," I replied. "I don't like this cloak and dagger business. I don't have the mind for it."

"Are you kidding? Look at you. You've survived a shipwreck, looked after Silver there, looked after me, got a fire started when everything's wet and we have no lighter or matches. You know that someone very nasty has just tried to kill us and you're sitting here with me, naked and shivering, but you're holding your own in thinking everything through, and I bet there's more, isn't there?" he challenged.

"What do you mean?" I asked, but I knew what was coming.

"You're not going to give up, are you? No matter what anyone says tomorrow, you're going to keep on until you get to the bottom of this thing, aren't you?"

"I suppose I am…" I said. I hadn't framed it quite so explicitly in my mind as Don had just laid out but, examining my feelings, I found that I couldn't disagree with him either.

"Do me one favour?" he asked. "Let me help…" then he put his hand out, palm up. "Partners?"

I sighed because he was right again. My first instincts were to try to keep him out of danger, as they would now with Sharon. But, after hesitating a moment, I realized that in his case I was being foolish. Resolved, I put my hand over his, palm down. "Partners," I agreed.

Silver surprised us both then, by standing up and placing one of his forepaws on top of mine, then he raised his head to the sky and let out a defiant howl that would have made his wolf ancestors proud.

"The Three Musketeers, '*All for one, and one for all*,'" quipped Don. "Does he actually understand what we were just talking about?" he asked, in amazement, watching Silver as he sat back down and snuggled up between us.

"I really don't know," I said, thoughtfully. "But… and I know this is crazy, I think he understands exactly. Not the words or the details, but the big picture and the emotions… he always seems to understand the important parts."

"This is a very strange dog."

"You don't know the half of it," I confirmed.

"Rrrrrrrr," growled Silver, low and contented.

***

We didn't talk much after that. There was no need, and we were exhausted. Eventually, our clothes dried out and we were able to get dressed, which added a bit more warmth and comfort. We didn't need to worry about posting a lookout, as Silver would detect an intruder sooner and more reliably than either of us could, but we did resolve to take turns sleeping versus tending to the fire. You'd think we'd have been famished, but I think our adrenaline levels were still up and we were both mostly just sleepy. That would change soon enough.

I was to take the first shift sleeping, and the last things I remember saying to Don before I fell asleep was "What a way to celebrate Canada Day!"[30]

Don, by the way, cheated and let me sleep through the whole night. I awoke with the dawning sun, ravenous but alive!

As it turned out, we were able to attract the attention of an early morning fisherman. Don told him that our boat had struck a shoal and sunk, but otherwise stuck to the truth. The fisherman was sympathetic.

"These kinds of things happen all too often," the man asserted. He kindly agreed to take us all the way back to Neil's Harbour.

It was Saturday morning. Amazingly, we both still had our keys: Don in his pants pocket and me in the jogger's belt-pouch that I had worn instead of taking a purse. Our vehicles were still where we had left them. Although we needed food, I had no intention of letting us be seen in any of the Ingonish area villages, so we drove sixty miles further south, and pulled in at a restaurant in Baddeck.

The nice thing about small towns and villages is that dogs don't have to be tied up or on leashes – at least, not if they are well behaved. I always kept dog food, water, and dishes for them in the truck, so we were able to set Silver up with everything he needed in the box of my truck before Don and I went into the restaurant to eat. The food and surroundings weren't fancy, but I think it was probably the best meal of my life. Silver probably thought so too!

Neither of us had the energy for the long drive back to Halifax so we got rooms at a local motel for the night. Baddeck had a liquor store, so we also made an important stop there. It's not what you're thinking. The fisherman that had so generously taken us all the way back to Neil's Harbour, had absolutely refused to consider taking any kind of payment from us, saying that we'd have done the same for him. That was true but beside the point. We did manage to get his name, at least, and later thought of another, alcohol-based, way to thank him.

Since we were in Baddeck, I gave Jack a call. Jack was staying in dormitory-style accommodation at the local Detachment office, so he didn't have a place, as such, and suggested we meet at a local restaurant for dinner. When we had all converged at the restaurant, I introduced Jack with a few words about our training days and my Alberta adventure. Don introduced himself as a Captain in the Military Police and handed Jack a business card that stated the same. I raised a questioning eyebrow at this change in identification, but all I got I return was a broad, mischievous smile, so I filed my questions away for another time.

Jack was suitably amazed at our story and promised to keep it to himself as I still had to report it all to Ottawa, and we suspected that Bob and his military counterpart would want to keep it all secret. We had a nice dinner together, but Don and I were pretty exhausted, so we made it an early night and headed to our motel rooms for the night. For my part, I called in a lengthy verbal report for Bob in Ottawa. Once I'd contacted his special number I just gave the whole verbal dump – I knew it would all be recorded – and asked the desk officer to make sure it got to Bob the next morning, and then I dropped into bed with Silver curled up beside me and immediately fell asleep.

After sleeping in late the next morning, Don and I met for breakfast, then searched out where our rescuer lived, snuck up, and left a case of rum and a thank you note on his back doorstep. Only then did we each drive our vehicles home to Halifax. As I was driving back, I mentally reviewed everything that had happened to date and then my thoughts turned to Jack and Don. They'd seemed to get along well the previous evening over dinner, but I didn't have a read yet on what they actually thought of each other. I found that I liked them both, but in different ways.

Appearances can be so deceiving, I thought. Jack looked quite plain but was a compulsive Don-Juan-type when it came to women. As early as basic training together, I'd learned that his motto could easily have been "Love 'em and leave 'em," as the old saying went. In other ways, he was fun to be with and our previous experience together in Alberta had demonstrated that I could trust him. Don, on the other hand, looked like a young Rock Hudson, always acted like a perfect gentleman, to use an old-fashioned term, and his strengths seemed to somehow complement mine.

Anyway, once we made it back to Halifax, we agreed that we'd each file our proper reports, he'd pass along his magnetic tapes, and that we'd wait for developments. It was a Sunday, so it was decided that in the absence of anything else happening, he'd come over to my place the next evening for dinner.

For my part, I retreated to a long, hot bath accompanied by a restorative glass (OK, two glasses) of brandy. I'd no sooner gotten out of the tub, finally feeling genuinely warm, when Bob phoned from his home in Ottawa.

I'd begun with "Sorry to disturb your Sunday evening," but he quickly brushed that aside and asked what was up. I didn't repeat the details of the report I'd already filed, but I supplemented the things I knew with everything I thought I knew, and some of what I suspected.

Bob didn't interrupt a single time, and when I was finished, the line remained silent for a while as he thought it all over. He expressed suitable amazement at my adventure and our narrow escape from drowning, freezing, or starving. I expected that, but his next remark came as a surprise.

"I'll pull you out if you want Alex. I didn't expect things to go this far."

"That's one of the things Don and I talked about over the last couple of days," I replied. "By the way, is his name really Don? He always seems to be pretending to be a different person."

That got a chuckle. "Yes, his name's really Don, but he certainly is more than he seems on the surface. I'm glad he was there with you, and that you looked after each other so well."

"Well, that's a relief. Anyway, Don and I decided we both want to see this thing through. Right about now he's probably having a similar conversation with his boss, although I don't know whether he'll have a choice about staying on."

"He'll have a choice, but he'll stick to this thing like glue. I know Don and his boss, my counterpart, quite well, and they're both solid." In Bob's book, good dependable people were 'solid.'

As he was saying this, I began to think of the whole thing as a chess game, with Bob and his counterpart at Military Intelligence (or wherever) moving their pieces around the board, with Don and I as rooks, sneaking around corners, while supporting and protecting each other, and people like Jack and the cryptographers in important but narrower supporting roles, like pawns in some greater game.

Realizing that Bob had finished speaking, I came alert with a start. "Well, for my part, I want to see this thing through. I think my cover's still intact, although Don's might not be… Anyway, I'd like to stay on."

"Cover not blown? Are you aware how much people talk in those small villages of yours? How many red-headed women with a dog that looks like a wolf do you suppose there are in all of Cape Breton right now?"

"Oh…"

"Yes, 'Oh.' Anyway, you might be right about your cover being intact. Maybe they're only talking about the crazy people that wrecked their fishing boat and had to be rescued." Bob's good humour was back.

"In any case, you're no longer inconspicuous, and it's best if we assume that your cover's blown. My advice is to lie low in Halifax for now. If the cryptology people can crack the code and give us a date, time, and place, then maybe we can arrange to eavesdrop on them. We'll have to wait and see. Meanwhile, I'm still working on what I can find out about your antique people."

I'd just like to say right here that I did try to follow his advice.

Laurie Schramm

10 THE GAME IS AFOOT

As planned, Don came over the next day, and since it was only late morning, we decided to take Silver for a walk down to the waterfront. As we walked across the Halifax Commons and past the Citadel, we reviewed everything that had happened over the previous 48 hours. Don agreed that our covers had most likely been exposed and that he too was supposed to 'keep his head down.' While Bob's people were trying to learn more about the Oceanside Antiques people, Don's people had retrieved the messages from his tapes and were trying to figure out how to decode them.

There didn't seem to be much either of us could do for the moment, so we decided to just enjoy our walk and what had developed into quite a nice afternoon. When we reached the waterfront, we turned and followed the docks as closely as we could, walking towards the mouth of the harbor. Being next to the downtown core, there were lots of people out for strolls and just sitting on benches along the way – business people, locals, and tourists alike – all brought out by the nice weather. Well behind us were the navy yards, with a few destroyers tied up, and well ahead of us were the container-ship piers, with their container yards and huge rolling cranes for loading and unloading the containers.

In contrast to the military and commercial sections, most of the boats tied up along these piers comprised pleasure craft, tour boats, and an assortment of tugboats. Most people were looking interestedly at the various boats as they strolled by. I was one of these, so it was while I was eyeing a medium-sized tugboat and wondering whether it could be converted into a floating recreational vehicle of sorts when I realized that someone other than Don was addressing me.

"Excuse me," said a voice, "but aren't you the young lady that bought a model diving helmet from me recently?"

Turning, I saw that it was the couple from the antique store in Ingonish. "Why yes, I am. It's sitting on the mantle in my house right now."

"Well, I'm glad to hear that you're happy with it. My wife tells me that you're interested in old radios too."

"Only because they're so different from what people use now, and I really like the big wooden cabinets and the glow of the tuning band panels."

"You must come to see us again sometime, and I'll show you some more. Do you come to Cape Breton often?"

"I was up several times SCUBA diving with a colleague, but I think it may be a while before we're up again." All my danger senses were screaming at me, but I did my best to keep a straight face and a relaxed tone of voice. I was trying so hard to be nonchalant, that I didn't at first notice what Silver was doing. He had slowly gone up and sniffed all around Wilma, who had nervously backed up a step.

"He won't hurt you," I said, "by sniffing you he's trying to learn about you. Try offering him your hand."

As she slowly held one hand out, Silver sniffed it closely and then gave it a tiny lick with his tongue, which provoked a tiny smile from Wilma.

"Here boy," the man said, holding out his hand to be sniffed.

In this case, though, Silver gave his hand two sniffs and then immediately sat down and stared back at me.

I knew that look! It was time for us to move along.

"Well, it was nice seeing you again," was the best I could manage to say. "I'll drop by the next time I'm in Cape Breton," and with that, I took Don's arm in mine and moved forward to continue our walk, with Silver following close behind.

Don had remained silent and seemed to have barely been noticed during this entire exchange. He was quick to follow my lead though and seemed to enjoy having the two of us walking arm-in-arm. When we were at least a quarter mile further along the docks, I spotted a café with a waterfront deck and suggested we stop there for coffee. We were able to get an outside table on the deck and were the only ones there. With our backs to the café's main window and facing the water I thought it would be safe for us to talk. Since it was so quiet, the waiter said that Silver could stay with us as long as he curled up down around our feet and didn't disturb anyone that might come along.

"What was that all about?" asked Don as soon as the waiter had taken our order and left.

"That was the couple I met at Oceanside Antiques in Ingonish. The man is the one I met the first time I was there, and the woman – Wilma – is his wife. I think that they are the owners of the place."

"OK, so?"

"So, the first time I went up to Cape Breton it was so Sharon could show me where she'd stumbled across the old weather transmitting station. Silver found a couple of cannisters that showed signs of being recently opened and I asked him to remember the scent."

"You asked him to remember the scent," Don said, in a neutral voice.

"Don't look at me like that. I'm not crazy." Don kept looking at me. "OK, well I'm not completely crazy," I modified. That provoked a smile from him.

"Do you remember when I told you that I had a dog as a partner?"

Don nodded. "As a friend too."

"Right, well it's the literal truth in this case. Last year Silver and I were trained to function as a police dog and handler team. When we're tracking a scent, Silver's signal that he's found what we're looking for is to immediately sit at attention and look directly at me."

"I saw that," said Don, getting interested now. "But that was, what, a month ago, can he remember scents that long?"

"It was just over three weeks ago, and I don't know how long he can remember scents, but the one at the weather station is the only one I've asked him to remember while we've been out here, and I know that look that he gave me."

"So, you think he's the one that's maintaining the station and sending the messages?"

"I do. My only real suspects so far have been the couple that run the café/gift shop and these two. All four of them live in Ingonish."

"You think they know who you are?"

"I think so. I think when they spotted me they came up to talk to us purposely, to see if I'd give myself away."

"Do you think they know who I am?" Don asked.

"My guess is that they heard the stories of a man and a woman and a big dog having their boat sunk and being rescued. They probably put two and two together as far as Silver and I but it didn't seem like they paid much attention to you."

"If you're right then they'll now be guessing that it was me with you and Silver on that boat. So... if the sub radioed in that they'd sunk a boat they suspected of monitoring their communications..."

"... and if they felt secure thinking that any recordings had gone down with the boat..." I supplied.

"Then these two would now know that we survived the wreck." Don nodded, thoughtfully.

"Would they suspect that we have the tapes too?" I asked.

"I think so," concluded Don. "These are cautious people that have probably been in this game for a very long time. If so, they've survived without detection by being very careful. If I were them, I would now assume that we have recordings, and I'd assume that we have enough to have broken the code by now too."

"Then if the last message was to set up some kind of meeting they would want to call it off or change it."

"I think so. That's what I would do."

"We have to stop them!"

"Just the two of us?"

"Three of us," I said, looking pointedly at Silver.

"Right," Don said, chuckling. "OK, if we assume that they've headed for home it will still take them awhile to drive, then write and code a new message, print it on tape, and then get the tape over to the transmitting station. That should give us just enough time to call in to our bosses and then hightail it up there."

***

We took a taxi back to my house, to save time, and then took turns calling in to our bosses. It was still early afternoon, Ottawa time, and I was able to reach Bob right away. We each had news.

"First of all, we're going to remain silent about that submarine you encountered. We don't know how much they know about what we know, and they may think that you and Don are dead, so there won't be any news flashes or diplomatic protests."

"We don't really know very much yet, do we? I mean, who would you even protest to?"

"Well, we're making progress on a number of fronts and I suspect that the sub was East German. I thought you and Don might like to know that you've made a little bit of Canadian history. The last time German submarines attacked ships in Canadian waters was off the Newfoundland coast in 1942[31]."

"That's kind of cool, actually. I'll tell Don."

"OK, and we've done some research on Oceanside Antiques. The business is owned and operated by a Marcus and Wilma Light."

"So, the man I met there the first time is probably Marcus Light," I supplied.

"Sounds like it, and Marcus...."

"Has a Ham Radio Licence?" I supplied.

"It's not polite to steal my revelations," admonished Bob, but I could tell from his tone that he was amused rather than upset. "Fine then, you were right, it turns out that Marcus Light has a ham radio licence. Do you want to guess when he first got licensed?"

"Judging by all the old radios and TVs in his shop I'd say the 1960s?" I guessed.

"Earlier than that! He received a Class A Amateur Radio Operator Certificate and a radio station licence in 1947."

"1947! Isn't that about when the Cold War started?"

"Go to the head of the class," Bob said approvingly. "I think you've found our mystery man. We even have his Call Sign, and it matches some of the transmissions that Don intercepted, although I doubt that we'll learn anything useful from transmissions made from his store."

"No, Don said the same thing to me a few days ago."

"I'm trying to get a photograph of Marcus for you, but this is where it gets really interesting because there are some things we haven't found for this Marcus Light: there is no passport, no birth record, and no record of him entering the country."

"Nothing?"

"Nothing. Now that isn't conclusive, because most government departments are still in the middle of computerizing their paper records. It could be that we just haven't found them yet. The records might be missing, or maybe the reason we can't find any birth or entry records is that they don't exist for that name."

"You mean he's a spy?"

"Well, not like James Bond, but yes he could be an agent of some kind. This kind of thing has happened before. Not often, but occasionally[32]. Anyway, we'll keep digging."

"Well, I suspect he has a driver's licence because Don and I just ran into him here in Halifax," I supplied. When I'd related the story of our encounter Bob agreed that we seemed to have found our mystery message transmitter.

"Be careful Alex, they're certainly on to you both now."

"I know, but if Marcus Light is going to try to send a warning message out, Don and I need to get up there right away if we're going to stop it."

"OK then, I'll contact the Baddeck Detachment and get them to have Jack meet you on the way up. If the situation warrants it, he'll be able to call for additional backup."

"Thanks, Bob. I'll call in later tonight whichever way this plays out."

"Good luck."

"Thanks, I hope we won't need it."

Handing the phone over to Don so he could call his boss, I made some coffee to take with us and grabbed a jacket to toss into my truck.

When Don got off the phone, he found me rummaging through a briefcase in the spare bedroom that I'd been using as an office.

"Ready to go?"

"I am now," I answered, showing him my badge and Silver's official police identity card. "Do you still have that military ID of yours?"

"Right here," Don said, patting his wallet. "Think we'll need it?"

"Who knows, but I don't think we have time for anything else."

As we made our way out, Don asked which vehicle I wanted to take.

"How about mine," I replied. "I have one more trick to show you." As we reached the truck, I reached for a cloth bag that I had hidden under the front seat. In it were a softball-sized red flashing light with a magnetic roof mount base and a cigarette-lighter power adapter.

"Cool," said Don. "Just like on *The Streets of San Francisco*[33]."

"The same. Let's go." With that, we loaded Silver into my truck, positioned the roof light and took off for Cape Breton. As we drove, I explained that my boss was going to try to have Jack meet us along the way. I didn't use the flashing light the whole way, just here and there to keep us moving through traffic congestion and make sure we could make good time on the road. When I did, given that my truck was also a bright red colour, I imagine that people probably took us to be from a volunteer fire department and responding to a rural call.

We continued to discuss the case as I drove north, and when that dried up Don asked about our police dog training experiences, which naturally led to our work on the Fort McMurray bomb threats the previous year. By the time we crossed the causeway from the mainland onto Cape Breton, I realized that Don had not only done a good job of helping pass the time, but a good job getting me to open up and tell him more about myself. I, on the other hand, had so far learned very little about him. I resolved to change that when I got a chance.

I had thought we might see Jack as we crossed the causeway, as it would be a natural spot from which to watch for us, but there was no sign of him. I tried raising him on the police radio but was only able to contact a confused dispatcher who wondered who I was and what I was doing on a police radio frequency. My explanation that I was an out-of-province officer trying to contact Jack wasn't very convincing, apparently, so I settled for asking them to get Jack to contact me as soon as possible and that in the meantime they could phone my boss in Ottawa for confirmation of my legitimacy.

We'd kept driving through this process, and I eventually learned from the dispatcher that Jack was on another call somewhere. Twenty minutes later this was confirmed by Jack himself, who came on the radio to explain that he'd been on his way to meet me when he'd encountered a serious highway accident and had had to stop to deal with it because there were injured people involved. Apparently, we'd hit one of those periodic surges in which the quiet tedium of rural policing is interrupted by a rash of events that suddenly have all available officers out on one kind of call or another. In other words, there was no one available to relieve him yet, and he wouldn't be able to leave the scene of the accident for another half hour or so.

I couldn't say too much on the radio - it had only just occurred to me that a radio expert would have no trouble tuning in on our police band if he wanted to. Fortunately, Jack knew what I'd been up to, so I was able to cryptically get across that 'the game is afoot' as Sherlock Holmes used to say, and that my partner and I were heading for the scene of interest. I said that I'd park by the side of the highway and leave my flashing red light on the roof, so he'd be able to find us.

"Seems like we're on our own again," I said to Don as we passed Ingonish Centre. The next village was Ingonish itself.

"What do you want to do?"

"Let's take a quick look at the antique shop and see if anyone is there. If both Marcus and Wilma Light are in town, then I think we should probably just stay well back and observe until we can get reinforcements."

Don agreed and when we entered the village, I stopped well back from the Oceanside Antiques Store. It was early evening now, but there was no light on outside the store, no vehicles parked in front, and it wasn't obvious that any inside lights were on.

We decided that, with a hooded jacket on, Don would be the least identifiable of us, so he pulled on his jacket and strolled up to the store, walked right by it without appearing to even look at it, then crossed the road and came back to the truck.

"That was quick," I commented, "and from my line of sight you didn't even notice the store as you went by."

"I'm going to choose to take that as a compliment," said Don with a grin. "A compliment, because I saw everything there was to see, including…" he rushed on before I could get another word out, "the piece of paper tacked onto the front door."

"Saying they're closed," I guessed.

"Saying they're closed, and written in a rather hasty scrawl if I'm any judge," said Don, with satisfaction.

"So, they've been here and left already. I guess we'd better go see if they're at the weather station."

Just to be thorough, we took a slow drive down the back lane behind the antique store, but everything seemed closed-up, unlighted, and quiet there too. There were no vehicles parked in the vicinity, so we continued on through the village and along the north road. When we reached the usual pull-off spot for hiking to Red Head, there was an older model brown car parked by the side of the road. Pulling up behind it, I made a note of the licence plate number before turning off my headlights. Switching off the engine, I left its parking lights on and then turned on the flashing red light on the roof.

"I guess the time for secrecy is over," I commented as we all got out of the truck. "If they give us the slip, I have their licence plate number and I think we have enough to get a search warrant for their place if we need it."

"My guess is that they can't be more than minutes ahead of us now, so I think we're going to find them at the weather station itself," judged Don.

Don, Silver, and I headed into the woods along the path that Sharon and I had followed almost a month earlier. We were pretty quiet as we carefully hiked along, and when I'd judged that we were getting close to the edge of the woods to the cliff at Red Head, I whispered to Don that I thought we should slow down and approach carefully. At the same time, I patted Silver on the shoulder, and he seemed to understand that we were going to take the last 50 yards or so very carefully.

We covered this last stretch uneventfully, but just before we exited the forest Silver suddenly perked up, sniffed the air a bit, then turned to look at me and gave a very low growl. It wasn't an angry or defensive growl, but rather had a tone of warning.

At this Don and I spread out a bit, but otherwise just kept on approaching as cautiously and silently as we could.

When we reached the clearing, and just before the edge of the cliff, I motioned to Don that the weather station was situated to our left. Don immediately moved ahead and to the left, motioning me to fall back a bit. As he did, I signaled Silver to stay close to me, and the two of us followed.

We weren't far from the weather station at this point and I could soon see that someone was crouched down by one of the cannisters, with their back facing us.

Neither Don nor I said anything, but it was inevitable that one of us would eventually be heard.

I was a bit surprised that, showing no shock or surprise, the figure slowly stood up and calmly turned to face us. Then came the second surprise: it was Wilma!

"We had a feeling that you would come," she said.

Laurie Schramm

11 CONFRONTATION

In order to carry out the duties assigned to them constables are permitted by law to use the minimum amount of force necessary to cope with a given situation. Still, the discharge of firearms in the line of duty amounts to such violent force that they must only be resorted to in the most extreme cases... A constable may use a weapon in self-defence, if in carrying out their legal duty, their life is endangered by the unlawful act of another person and no less violent defence is adequate or available.

"R.C.M.P. CONSTABLES' MANUAL." OTTAWA

I shot a man once. Shot him twice actually.

I hadn't wanted to. I'd been trying to talk him down, wanting to give him every possible chance to surrender, but he'd already taken several shots at me. When he had shot Silver, I'd fired in return. Recovering, he'd raised his rifle again and aimed it at Silver. Then his body shifted, and I sensed that he was going to fire again. Once again, I'd yelled "Don't do it!" but this time I didn't wait for him to fire first. I fired before he could get off another shot and kill Silver.

My shots hit him both times, once in each leg, which is what had finally grounded him and caused him to drop his weapon. The biggest question Assistant Commissioner Macleod had, was why I'd shot this fellow in the legs and hadn't aimed for the heart? Bob, for his part, had marvelled at my shooting accuracy, considering that I'd only been armed with a snub-nose revolver and had been shooting under extreme duress!

Sheepishly, I'd explained the embarrassing truth, which was that I'd actually aimed for his torso. The centre of his torso in fact. I really wasn't trying to kill him, I was trying to stop him. Aiming dead-centre was simply so that I'd have the best odds of actually hitting him at all, which was the way I'd been taught. It was fortunate for me because I really wasn't that good a shot, and it was just a fluke - two flukes, in fact - that I'd ended up shooting him in both legs. My explanation had produced howls of laughter from Bob and the Assistant Commissioner, but they clearly approved, and both hastened to tell me that they were still impressed that I'd been able to stop our suspect before he'd been able to hurt or kill anyone else. Our suspect was convicted on several charges and is serving a life sentence in prison.

The episode left me with distinctly mixed feelings about easy-to-conceal but inaccurate weapons.

***

Now, roughly a year later, here I was in a somewhat similar situation.

"Where's Marcus?"

I said it loudly enough for Wilma to hear, but it was Don that I'd wanted to warn. If Wilma was here, I was suddenly certain that Marcus would not be far away.

Don had heard me, but he was clearly on the same page I was, and he'd immediately drawn a small pistol of some kind that he must previously have had concealed in his clothing somewhere. As he was drawing his gun, he repeated my question. "Where is Marcus, Wilma? He wouldn't have left you to do this by himself!"

"You are quite correct, young man," came a voice from behind me. It was Marcus.

"Everyone should move very slowly as I am feeling a bit nervous right now," continued Marcus, raising an ugly looking Luger and pointing it in Don's and my general direction. I suppose that "ugly looking" is an odd description to apply to a gun, but that's how it seemed to me at the time.

Although Marcus had said he was feeling nervous, his voice was entirely calm and his diction was precise.

"… and where is that rather large dog of yours?" Marcus continued.

"I don't know," I answered truthfully. Silver had quietly faded away into the forest, but I knew that he wouldn't be far away.

"It would be best for both of you if you drop the gun and surrender to us," said Don.

"You would be from some part of the military – am I right?"

Don nodded.

"And you are?" Marcus asked, looking at me.

"Police, RCMP," I replied, "Don's right, it would be best for both of you to drop that gun. I honestly don't know whether either of you would even be charged with anything, but you can't point a gun at us, and we can't let you send that message out."

"I am afraid that it is too late for us, my dear. I have been working in the service of the Fatherland since 1942… thirty-five years now, and I'm afraid that I'm too old to change my ways now. Besides, we haven't even lost yet. We can just send our message out and then leave the country as quietly as we entered so many years ago."

"Alex is right, Marcus," said Don, raising both his voice and his pistol and aiming the gun in Marcus' direction. "You need to drop that gun – right now."

BLAM!

Without blinking, Marcus had immediately fired. I startled and simultaneously realized that I hadn't been hit, so I turned to look back at Don, who had dropped his gun and was trying to hold back the blood that was oozing between the fingers he had clasped around his right arm.

I think I sensed Silver's motion, even before I heard the sounds of him running nearby in the forest.

"Stop your dog or I will shoot him too," said Marcus, still very calm and precise.

"Silver!" I exclaimed loudly. Sure enough, he hadn't missed a thing and was in the woods directly in line with Marcus. He'd already started running towards Marcus, probably as soon as he heard the gunshot, and we could all hear the sound of him sliding as he immediately halted his running motion. I told Silver to stay where he was, and thankfully he listened to me.

"I don't know how long I can keep him at bay Marcus, but if you shoot me, he'll tear your arm off, and if you shoot him, I'll throw you over the cliff myself."

"I believe you," said Marcus. "Just stand where you are for now and no one else needs to get hurt." Then, "Wilma! Pick up that little gun of his and throw it over the cliff."

Wilma, who had quietly approached, just nodded, picked up Don's gun, and did as Marcus had instructed.

"Now then, here's what we're all going to do. You two just stand still and you, young lady, keep that dog where he is. Wilma will go back and send our message out. We almost had everything ready when you came along, and it won't take long to send the message out, then – if you cooperate - we can all leave peacefully."

"Why should we believe you?" I asked. "Are you just going to let us go after shooting Don and threatening Silver and I?"

"Now, now," Marcus admonished, "the very fact that you are here means our cover here is compromised. That means our work here is ended. As long as Wilma and I can walk away, we will quietly leave the country and you will never see or hear of us again, and that will be the end of it."

"You sound pretty confident," I commented.

"Of course. As you now know, I have been working in your country for a very long time. It was inevitable that I would be discovered some day, and I have done my best to prepare accordingly. I have several contingency plans for our exit, which I won't disclose to you. I noted that your friend here failed to identify himself, but I judge him to be a soldier ..."

Then, looking directly at Don, "don't bother to deny it, it shows plainly on your face. As a soldier, you will appreciate that when my mission is accomplished it is my duty to return home. In my situation, you would do the same. I have no desire to hurt either of you any further, so if you're prepared to be civilized about all this then we can soon all go on our way, and you will be able to go and tell your superiors that you have eliminated the enemy's transmitting station, but that the clever spies got away. They will be sufficiently pleased, I think."

"You're very clever," I replied. "If we're all going to be so civilized about this, do you mind if I help tend to my friend's bleeding arm? I have a bandage on my leg that will do him more good than it will me right now."

"Go right ahead," said Marcus, expansively. He felt that he was in complete control now, and clearly enjoying it. "Wilma, you go and send our message, while I keep an eye on these three."

Other than reminding Silver to stay put, I didn't waste any time going over to Don and prying his hand away from his arm, so I could have a look at his arm. There was a small, bleeding hole where the bullet had gone in, of course and a larger and ragged exit hole on the other side of his arm. It was the exit hole that was really bleeding badly.

"The bullet's gone right through Don, but we're still going to need to put your arm in a sling." Don had brought his light cotton pullover with him, tied around his waist, and I usually carried a woman's handkerchief in my pocket. Pulling out my handkerchief, I placed it over Don's entrance wound and got him to hold it in place while I pulled off the bandage I'd been wearing on one leg – the one that held my Derringer. Quickly slipping the Derringer into the pocket of my Bermuda Shorts, I used the tape to secure my makeshift bandage on Don's arm, then used his pullover to build a makeshift sling to support his arm. This done I turned to face Marcus and took my Derringer out in the same motion.

"Last warning Marcus – drop the gun!"

He laughed, of course. I knew he would.

So… there we were, and just like in my *déjà vu* moment, I was outgunned. Just like a high-powered rifle had had the advantage over my snub-nose revolver back in Alberta a year earlier, now Max's 9-mm semi-automatic Luger pistol had the advantage over my two-chamber Derringer.

Except that it was worse than that.

It would have been somewhat of a standoff, except that the only advantage I had left was surprise - so I used it. I aimed and pulled the trigger.

There was an audible 'click' sound.

If Marcus laughed politely before, he was even more amused now. "You went to all the trouble to hide and carry that thing all this time and didn't even remember to load it? No wonder there aren't any other women in the RCMP!" he exclaimed.

While Marcus had his little joke and final comments, I'd continued to point the Derringer at him, with what I'd hoped was a suitably rueful, embarrassed expression.

Now, as Marcus tensed to pull the Luger's trigger, I pulled the trigger of my Derringer again and fired. It may have been a tiny little gun, but a .38 Special bullet fired at short range can easily kill.

Marcus dropped like a rock, having immediately dropped his Luger so he could press both hands over his chest on a spot centred on, and to the right of his breastbone.

Not bad, I thought, clinically, *serious but probably not life-threatening.*

On the ground, writhing in pain, Marcus had to force his next words out: "What happened?"

"It wasn't that I didn't load the gun," I explained, "but it only had two chambers. I was taught to always leave the chamber with the hammer over it empty, to make sure that the gun doesn't go off accidentally if it's ever dropped. In this case, that made a two-shot Derringer into a one-shot Derringer."

As I said this I'd run over to Marcus, not to help with his wound – not yet anyway – but to recover his Luger, which I immediately tossed to Don. Silver had immediately come to my side to make sure I was OK, and I gave him a reassuring pat on the shoulder.

"Can you shoot with your left hand?" I asked Don.

"Well enough," he replied, grimly, and turned to go pull Wilma away from the transmitting station.

"The message hadn't been sent yet," he called back over his shoulder. "She'd just lined up the perforated tape though, so it was a close call."

While Don kept an eye on Wilma, I helped with first aid for Marcus. As I was working on stopping the bleeding from his chest, I heard a dull sound in the distance that eventually resolved itself into the '*thump, thump, thump*' sounds of a large helicopter approaching.

Before long, what started out as a barely discernable thumping had developed into a blasting roar as a Sea King[34] helicopter suddenly popped-up into sight over the edge of the cliff. It had clearly come along the coast, low and out of our sight and mostly out of hearing as it approached. As the helicopter rose up above cliff level, its crew switched on a powerful searchlight. It had been getting quite dark before this, but now we were all bathed in an intense, broad beam of light. Without bothering to land, the helicopter pilot simply hovered a foot from the ground and several MPs in combat fatigues hopped out, with their sidearms drawn.

The MPs naturally went to Don first, and after a few words the senior among them, a Sergeant, came over to me and told me that they were there to provide any assistance I might need. Thanking him, I asked for whatever first aid supplies they might have so we could get Don and Marcus properly bandaged.

By the time that was taken care of, Jack appeared from the forest path, also with his gun drawn. He had seen my truck parked with its red light flashing and had just pulled-up behind it when he heard the first gunshot. Hearing that, he'd first called for backup, and then come running.

We found out later that the timing of the helicopter's arrival had been a bit of a fluke. Don's call to his boss before we'd left Halifax had set in motion a chain of events that led to a helicopter being detached from a navy frigate. It had picked up the MPs and headed directly for our area. They were originally going to land on one of the nearby beaches, but Jack's call for backup had also been relayed to the military, who had alerted the helicopter crew.

With the hammering sound of the nearby helicopter, we couldn't really talk much – it was more like terse yelling at each other, but I was able to satisfy myself that Don was going to be OK.

"The bullet wound is nothing," Don had yelled. "I just about had heart failure when I heard the hammer go 'click' on the empty chamber in your Derringer. I thought it was a misfire, and we were all going to either be shot or pushed over the cliff!"

Telling him that I'd come and see him in Halifax as soon as I could, I stepped back so the MPs could take Don and Marcus by helicopter to one of the hospitals in Halifax. Meanwhile, Jack and Silver and I took charge of Wilma and headed back through the forest to our vehicles.

Before we left Red Head, however, I went back to the old weather station. I wanted to disable it without destroying anything, so in the end, I simply used my UDT knife to cut the cables running to and from the cannister that contained the tape-reading machine and carried Marcus and Wilma's tape and the entire cannister out with me.

When we reached our vehicles where they'd been parked alongside the highway, Jack radioed in and learned that instructions had come from Ottawa to arrest and hold both Marcus and Wilma on charges under the Official Secrets Act. Jack took care of that part, leaving Silver and I free for the moment.

I'd wanted to head back to Halifax to see Don, but recognizing the early signs of exhaustion in myself, and knowing that after all the excitement there would be a low following the adrenalin surge I'd been operating on, Jack wisely talked me into coming back to the detachment with him to get some food and sleep first.

I thought it was ironic that while our efforts had led to the capture and arrest of Marcus and Wilma, Silver and I had spent the night sleeping in a cell at the Baddeck RCMP detachment.

At least the door to our cell wasn't locked.

12 AFTERMATH

By the time Silver and I got back to Halifax the next day, Don had been treated and released from the hospital with orders to stay home and rest for the day. We visited him at his apartment, and it was a relief to learn that the bullet had only grazed the bone before it had gone the rest of the way through his arm. Whereas I had expected to see his arm in a cast and supported by a sling, he was simply bandaged and still taking pain killers. Not bad, considering what might have happened.

I'd been wondering what I'd do for however long it took the military cryptology people to decode the intercepted messages, but I needn't have worried. While we were discussing the previous day's adventure – our second life-or-death adventure already, Don received a phone call from one of his colleagues in military intelligence. Once he found out what it was about, he put it on his speakerphone, so we could both listen. Don's cryptology colleagues had finally broken Marcus' code!

Since Don still had trouble writing, due to his injury, I reached for a pen and paper and took notes. The intercepted messages were short and simple, containing only the dates, times, and places for meetings. The implication was that there was a foreign agent, or agents, in place in the region, and/or coming and going through Halifax. The current working assumption was that Marcus was not actively involved in such meetings, but simply a messaging relay. That should mean that the meeting referred in to the latest message should still go ahead.

The next news was about the latest message, the one that Don had intercepted while we were on the boat together. It specified that the meeting would be "15:00, 06.07.1977, by the anchor, Point Pleasant Park." In other words, at 3 pm July 6th in Point Pleasant Park.

"'By the anchor' can only mean somewhere close to that huge anchor monument from the aircraft carrier[35]," I concluded.

"That's what we think too," confirmed Don's colleague on the phone.

"But July 6th is tomorrow!" Don exclaimed. "That's not much time to prepare anything."

"Right, I'm supposed to tell both of you to call your bosses ASAP for instructions," concluded Don's colleague.

Thanking him, I hung up the phone and stared at Don for a few moments.

"What would you do if you were in our bosses' shoes?" I asked Don.

"Depends on whether they want to arrest these people or just follow them, I guess. Sometimes the game is to learn who the agents are and then just keep an eye on them, sometimes it's to grab them and try to turn them in to double agents, and other times it's just to arrest them before they flee and try to get them convicted and put away."

There was little point in speculating any further, so we decided I should call Bob first. I reached Bob right away and let him know that we were on speakerphone and that Don was with me.

"Excellent," said Bob. "Hi, Don."

"Hello, Sir."

"I'm glad you're both together because I just got off the phone with Don's boss and we have come up with a plan. Congratulations on foiling Marcus' attempt to send a new message. We're going to work on the assumption that the previous message is still valid, and that Marcus wasn't going to be part of the meeting itself. Unfortunately, that doesn't give us much time to organize a reception committee!"

"We were thinking the same thing here."

"OK then, here's the thing: under other circumstances, we might just put a surveillance team on each of the people that meet. It will likely be just two people. In this case, however, we want to know what they're exchanging at these meetings. What we want to do is have a surveillance team ready to follow the sender, wherever they go. For that person we have time on our side, so we'll use a plainclothes team and have them just follow and report. The recipient we want to be arrested so we can find out who they are, where they came from, and what they're receiving. For that person, we need an arrest team."

"Can we help?" Don and I both asked at the same time.

"That's the spirit!" said Bob, approvingly. "Yes, you can. We don't have time to organize a big team, and we have to send in the smallest team we can anyway to minimize the risk that our two suspects spot something unusual, get spooked, and abort the meeting. We have three Security Service people attached to H Division[36], and we'll have them be the surveillance team for the sender. You two can go meet them at H Division headquarters tomorrow morning."

"That's it?" I asked.

"Oh no," replied Bob. "I'm detaching Jack from the pretense of his temporary assignment at the Baddeck Detachment and sending him down to act as a liaison between you two and the Halifax Regional Police. He'll be driving down tomorrow morning and you'll be able to meet him in the afternoon sometime. He'll have his highway patrol car, so you can contact him by radio. Now, Don doesn't have the authority to make a civilian arrest, but I've formally requested his assistance from the Canadian Forces which gives him fairly wide latitude in how he assists you and Jack. What I want you, Alex, or Jack to do is arrest the recipient and seize whatever it is that the sender passes to him, OK?"

"OK," echoed Don and I together.

"All right then, one more thing. I want you to go in uniform. The surveillance team will go in plain clothes, and their job is to watch, not to interfere with anything. If we're lucky, our two suspects will meet, exchange something, then separate. When they're out of sight of each other the surveillance team can shadow, and the arrest team can move in. The arrest team will be Jack and a couple of people from H Division. I want you two there as a backup for the arrest team. If things go wrong and there's a chase, I want you to be instantly recognizable to police and civilians alike, OK?"

"OK," we repeated.

"Right then, when you meet up with Jack he can introduce you to the H Division people. Good luck!"

After hanging-up Don and I looked at each other for a moment.

"Wow, this could get dangerous again Alex," said Don.

"Well, so far in my career I've been sexually harassed, trapped in a mine shaft, shot at, and shipwrecked. Silver here has been marooned, left to die, shot, and dumped into the ocean – which he hates with a passion. We've survived a lot together. Maybe we'll survive this too. Besides, what else could possibly go wrong?"

"Bite your tongue!" responded Don. The words and his tone sounded so much like me that we both had a good laugh. With nothing else to do but wait for the moment, we decided to go out for dinner and then to meet the next day for lunch.

***

The next day was the day of the 'big spy meeting,' as Don and I thought of it. Our lunch *rendezvous* meeting was at the same Harvey's Restaurant in Dartmouth at which we'd originally met. This time I was in uniform, my black tactical uniform – which I favoured for working in the field with Silver – and my service revolver, which made a change from the little Derringer I'd been carrying around all summer.

"Now you look like a police officer – and serious business too!" Don quipped half-admiringly and half-teasingly.

"You don't look like anyone to trifle with yourself," I observed, noting that Don was in uniform again, but this time, instead of a Naval Lieutenant's dress uniform he had on camouflage fatigues with Captain's bars, an MP armband, and a sidearm. "I see that you're a Captain again today… who are you really?"

Don sighed and thought for a moment. "I have a strange job and sometimes I get confused myself. I started out as a CELE officer like I told you, but it was originally in the Air Force, not the Navy. I really am a Captain, but other than that I'm often whatever I need to be depending on what mission I've been assigned. I lose track of who I really am sometimes, but when we were on the island trying to survive together, that was the real me. It was scary, but I felt grounded, if you know what I mean, for the first time in a long time. Seems strange to say it out loud, but I'm glad we went through that together."

"I am too, but let's not do it again for a while, OK?"

"OK by me," Don agreed – "let's eat."

By unspoken agreement, we avoided talking about work for a while and just enjoyed munching on our burgers together. It struck me, while we were eating how comfortable I had become with Don. I'd been on dates before and had a boyfriend for several years in high school, but this was different. We'd evolved from being colleagues to partners, to friends and it occurred to me that Don was rapidly becoming best-friend material. This was a new experience for me and I wondered where it might lead.

***

After lunch, I was able to raise Jack on the police radio and we arranged to meet him and the other Security Service people at H Division headquarters. I found them pretty reserved, almost secretive, and quite aloof, but I didn't have to like them I just had to be able to work with them. I did, however, take the precaution of introducing them to Silver so he could register their scent and know that they were on our side. The briefing was fairly straightforward, since the plan was for Don, Jack, Silver, and I to stay in the background but be available to help catch our 'recipient suspect' if necessary, while the others covertly tailed the 'sender suspect.'

After the briefing, there wasn't a lot of time for waiting as we had to be in position long before the specified meeting time of 3 pm.

We'd been issued hand-held VHF radios, and Don, Jack, Silver and I took position hiding out in my big red truck in a back corner of one of the upper-level parking lots. There were closer places to park down by the harbor-front, but we didn't want to be spotted by either of our suspects.

When 3 pm arrived, it wasn't long before we heard "someone's approaching the bench" over the radio, presumably referring to one of the park benches that was near the anchor memorial. It seemed like an eternity but was probably only a couple of minutes before this was followed by "here comes number two."

After that, the pace of events picked-up considerably.

"Shit!" we heard someone say. "Did someone break cover?" then "Damn."

"Jack are you there?"

"Right here," Jack confirmed.

"Our two suspects met all right, but only briefly. Something spooked them, and they've bolted. They did exchange something, and most of our team is going to follow the sender. The other guy left a sweater behind, so we'll leave someone here to show you in case your dog can get the scent and track him."

"OK," Jack replied, "we're coming now."

With the need for secrecy gone, I threw my red flashing light up on the roof of my truck, hit the gas, and simply drove down the walking path towards the monument. You weren't supposed to drive on the walking path, of course, but it was wide enough for the park maintenance vehicles, so it was wide enough for me. There weren't many people on the path, so I made good time getting down to the monument and we quickly spotted one of my Security Service colleagues standing by a nearby park bench.

Sure enough, in his rush to get away, our recipient had conveniently left a grey sweater behind. I let Silver register a good series of sniffs while Don and Jack wrote down the suspect's description. It sounded like it was a middle-aged male wearing everyday clothes - browns and beiges in colour - that could just as easily denote a tourist or Halifax resident. The key news for us was that he was carrying a significantly heavy gym bag – so that, at least, would stand out.

It was Silver's turn now, and he led us along the beaches, across the waterfront parking lot, and past the container ship terminal, heading in the direction of downtown. As we followed, Jack radioed in the recent events and asked to have the Halifax police keep an eye out for anyone in the harbor-front area matching our suspect's description.

Silver did his usual tracking routine, sweeping left and right, frequently stopping to sniff around. He didn't seem to have much trouble following the scent through, as he only occasionally lost the track and had to sweep more broadly before finding it again. As he continued to lead us towards the downtown area, we passed the big grain elevators, the historic Pier 21 Immigration Dock, and then a small marina and the docks for tug boats and the Harbor Pilot boats. Now we were in the most popular walking area for tourists and locals alike, and it became much harder for Silver to keep track of the scent while navigating around all the people that were out for a stroll and the inevitable children and other dogs that wanted to approach and say "hi" to him. We all persevered as best we could, however, and something like forty minutes into our tracking, Jack suddenly exclaimed "Look there," and pointed straight ahead.

Sure enough, we could just make out the back of someone matching our suspect's description and carrying a bag of some kind.

Jack volunteered to break off to our left and try to run up ahead along Lower Water Street, in parallel with our suspect's current heading. Jack was the runner among us, so it made sense for him to break away while Don stayed with Silver and I in direct pursuit.

Our suspect hadn't noticed us yet and apparently knew better than to frequently turn and look back over his shoulder. Jack would need some time to sweep up along the parallel street, so we let Silver continue with his tracking. Since our suspect was trying to blend in with the crowd he was walking at the rate of a leisurely stroll, so we were able to narrow the gap between us.

If it was indeed our recipient, then it was inevitable that he would eventually look behind him. Sure enough, he soon stopped to look at a local vendor's display and gave a very casual glance back the way he had come. His body language immediately changed, showing that he'd spotted us and correctly interpreted our presence. He was good though. Without otherwise seeming to show any alarm, he simply resumed his former route, but he increased his pace. Silver was ready to race on ahead, but I told him to stay and keep pace with Don and me.

"Where will he go?" I asked Don. "He could try for the ferry, but we'd just get on it too."

"Watch for a tour boat or a sailboat that's about to leave the dock," Don suggested. "He might try jumping on one that's just leaving!"

Don and I increased our pace now, to make sure that we could keep our suspect in sight, and Don radioed a warning to Jack, telling him that our suspect was nearing the Queen's Landing Market and might get lost in the crowd. Jack said "OK," and that he'd approach the market from the north side, while we approached from the south side. With the harbor to our right, that would still leave the west side unguarded, however.

We'd no sooner agreed to this than our suspect reached the market and melted into the crowd. At this Don and I broke into an all-out run and, as we hadn't been far away, reached the market only about thirty seconds behind our suspect. Forced to slow down by the crowd, I was able to catch my breath and suggest that Don stay with me and let Silver find him.

Silver, for his part, knew exactly what we were doing and led us on a zig-zag route through the crowd. He couldn't have had much scent to go on, but he seemed always to find a rough trail to follow, led us to the east side of the market square, and then came to a halt looking directly ahead to a market stall that was selling brightly coloured scarves. At first, I didn't see why he had stopped, but on second glance there was our suspect holding a woman in front of him. He had one arm around her, with the gym bag still clutched in his hand. His other hand held a gun, and the gun was aimed at us.

"That's close enough," the man said.

Silver and I had already stopped. I wondered at first why Don had stepped behind me, but I was answered by the sound of him quietly relaying information to Jack on his radio.

Our suspect guessed at the truth as well, saying "Tell your colleague to come out where I can see him and to drop the radio." Don came and stood beside me and placed his radio on the ground.

"Good. Now, here's what we're going to do. This lady and I are going to find a boat to take us out in the harbor. If you stay out of our way, I'll release her further along the harbor and no one needs to get hurt. OK?"

"You'll never get away with this." As I said this, I realized that the words could have come out of a Hollywood movie, but they needed to be said.

"I'll take my chances, thank you," replied our suspect, and nudged into motion the woman he'd grabbed.

As the two of them moved back towards the docks, Jack arrived at the edge of the crowd to our suspect's left. Telling him to stop, our suspect repeated the instructions he'd just given us. Seeing that he was momentarily distracted, I made a sweeping motion with my arm and Silver melted into the crowd to our right.

Keeping a grip on the gym bag and the woman from the market, our suspect backed the two of them slowly but surely towards the docks while trying to keep an eye on Jack, Don, and I. He seemed to have forgotten about Silver, or maybe he hadn't realized that Silver was with us. A hush had fallen over the other shoppers, who seemed to have melted away with the sudden appearance of a man brandishing a gun. That was just as well, as it cleared the field for us.

To the onlookers, it must have seemed like a movie set, but Jack, Don, and I were all too aware of the potential for people to get hurt or killed if someone made a wrong move.

As luck would have it, no sooner had our suspect and his hostage reached the docks again than an empty tour boat swung alongside, probably in preparation for another load of sight-seers. As a deck-hand hopped onto the pier to tie up the boat, our suspect yelled to him to stay where he was. Our suspect was close enough that by the time the deck-hand had completed a double-take, there was a gun waving in his face, causing him to hesitate even further.

The deck-hand's confusion worked to our advantage, as our suspect now had to slow down and explain what he wanted to be done.

This was our chance!

I yelled "Run to the Mountie!" to the woman, pointing to Jack who was off to one side.

Fortunately, she had the courage and presence of mind to pull away and run for Jack, causing a moment of confusion for our suspect. We would have only another second before he decided that the deck-hand could just as well be his new hostage, and I used that second to yell, "Silver, get the gun!"

Silver heard the urgency in my voice and, almost instantaneously, there was a greyish-white blur and a yell of pain from our suspect. In the blink of an eye, Silver had his jaws clamped on our suspect's arm, between the forearm and wrist. Our suspect was still gamely holding onto the gun, but with Silver's jaws fully engaged on his arm and all of Silver's considerable weight dragging it down, he wasn't likely to be able to shoot at anything vulnerable. Only a few seconds behind Silver, Don and I grabbed our suspect as well, just as he was trying to use his other arm to toss the gym bag out into the harbour.

It didn't take long for us to disarm and arrest him. Jack had called for reinforcements, who took him into custody for us. Jack also took down the names and addresses of the woman from the market and the man from the tour boat, and he made sure that they were both OK.

When we opened the gym bag, we found several reels of black and white 35-mm film and a bunch of pieces of metal in varying sizes and shapes.

"Any idea what these are?" I asked Don.

"No, but if I had to guess, I'd say that they are samples of metal alloys from one of the Cape Breton heavy water plants. There really isn't anything else in this region that would interest a foreign country in our metallurgy – but nuclear secrets are always a hot commodity. The DREA[37] folks will be able to tell us for sure."

So, that was it. It was a bit of an anticlimax after Don's and Silver's and my adventure on the cliff at Red Head, but still quite exciting. We had accomplished at least part of our objective by capturing one of the suspects and his stuff and, of course, we had uncovered Marcus' and Wilma's operation as well.

Later that day we learned that the 'sending suspect' had raced deep into the park and managed to elude the officers that were chasing him. The Security Service would continue working to figure out who he was and probably start watching him for a while to get a better sense of the extent of his activities.

13 LOOSE ENDS

The receiving suspect that Don, Jack, Silver, and I had caught was debriefed by a combined team from Military Intelligence and the RCMP Security Service. He admitted to being an East German agent and provided more insight into how their message transfers worked. When one of their locally-based sources was ready with new industrial materials to sell, they would get a message to Marcus, who would, in turn, send out meeting dates from his hidden, low-power transmitter. The messages could be received on any shortwave radio receiver that was in the general area of the Atlantic Provinces or U.S. New England States, as long as the receiving person had a means of decoding, or at least recording, the message burst. Such receivers were sometimes on military vessels, like submarines, but were more often on innocuous vessels like commercial freighters.

In the case of our receiving suspect, he had come to Canada only the day before our meeting, on a container ship, and had received the message with the meeting particulars while still at sea. The container ships generally only docked for a day – just long enough to unload/load their cargo – then left port the next day. This is why careful coordination of the meetings was needed. They also had to be flexible, because the container ships don't follow a rigid schedule – sometimes they arrived every week, but sometimes only every other week. If we hadn't intercepted him, he would have boarded the same container ship the night of the hand-off and the ship would have been gone the following morning.

I hadn't realized that container ships carried passengers but, apparently, they do – usually up to ten passengers at a time – in nice, but not luxurious accommodations. After leaving Halifax, a typical itinerary would have the ship go, in succession, to New York, Norfolk, Savannah, Charleston, and through the Suez Canal to various ports in Asia. Our suspect could disembark in any of those cities. If in a hurry it would be New York, but to avoid having a regular pattern it would often be one of the other U.S. ports, after which he'd simply board a regular passenger liner for the transatlantic crossing home. The reason for choosing ships was simple: no metal detectors or X-raying of passenger baggage, and generally lax customs and immigration checks compared with other means of crossing in and out of Canada.

He admitted that the Soviet Bloc nations were keenly interested in Canada's CANDU[38] nuclear reactor and heavy water production technologies and had been acquiring pieces of the technology for several years. They already had the necessary scientific knowledge of course. What they wanted was the practical know-how, hence their interest in operating plant specifications and procedures, specific equipment, and specific material requirements such as specialized metal alloys – thus the metal samples he had been trying to smuggle out.

In the end, he was threatened but not charged with any crimes. Bob and his counterpart talked him into becoming a double-agent for them. After making a copy of the spools of film and photographing the pieces of metal alloy, they let him take them home with him. I didn't ever hear how it all turned out in the end. That is, whether our suspect continued to work as a double-agent, was eventually turned into a triple-agent by the other side, or whether something worse happened to him.

I did ask Bob why they bothered with such elaborate measures when they could just send films and samples out in diplomatic bags from their embassy in Ottawa (even though this kind of use of diplomatic bags was forbidden). Bob explained that many of the foreign embassies in Ottawa have intelligence agents, who could be anyone from a military attaché to the Ambassador, but it was complicated.

"We generally know who the intelligence agents are, and we watch them carefully," Bob explained. "By the same token, they know that we know who they are, and we know that they know. So, they have to be very careful about the risks that they take, and sometimes we intercept their diplomatic bags and search them, even though that too is forbidden by diplomatic convention."

This conversation with Bob did not inspire me to get further involved in foreign intelligence work!

***

The story of our sending suspect was later resolved by the Security Service. The plain-clothes officers had never found him in Point Pleasant Park, but the spools of the film contained images of plans and specifications for parts of our heavy water plants. As secret-classified documents, they were individually numbered, so it didn't take long to figure out who had access to them, and of those people who made periodic trips to Halifax – including the date of the most recent meeting, which we had interrupted.

Bob and his Military Intelligence counterpart had some fun with this suspect, who they also convinced to work for them, and through whom they sent years-worth of slightly altered plans, specifications, and operating instructions. I don't know if it's true or not, but I was told by a colleague that if another country followed all those altered plans and instructions, that critical parts of the processing plant would spin out of balance until they self-destructed.

***

Marcus and Wilma seemed almost relieved to be done with their espionage activities and told us a fascinating story. Marcus Light's real name had been Max Lichte, and on October 25, 1942, he had been put ashore by German Navy U-boat – number U-687. Along with the crew, he had helped carry the components for *Wetter-Funkgerät Land (Weather Radio for Land) number one, or WFL-1,* the automated weather station, up to the top of the cliff at Red Head, where he assembled it and got everything working. After that was done, the U-boat moved south along the coast, and one of the submarine's dinghies put Marcus and his suitcases ashore on Ingonish Beach at 3 am. After waiting by the side of the road until dawn, he had been able to hitch a ride with local fisherman, claiming to be a travelling salesman. He briefly established himself at Keltic Lodge and later moved to Ingonish. During the war, his mission was simply to remain under cover and maintain the weather station – nothing more.

After the end of the Second World War, however, the East

German government had asked Marcus to stay in place, convert the weather station to a message sending station, and be available to transmit encrypted messages for them from time to time. Feeling that such was his duty, he had agreed and later sent for his girlfriend Willie (Wilhelmina). Willie had agreed, and the East German government had arranged for her to be smuggled into the country. They were provided with forged documents showing their names to be Marcus and Wilma Light and had set-up a home, and base of operations, in their antique store in Ingonish. Meanwhile, the official records back in Germany were altered to show that Max and Wilhelmina had gone missing during the war and were presumed dead.

Marcus had certainly been successful in that his careful sending of short-burst, low-power messages from the former automatic weather station had worked well and without detection for nearly 35 years! I learned that Military Intelligence had previously tracked foreign agents to Halifax but then their trails had always run cold. They had suspected that someone must have been radioing signals to ships approaching the harbour. They had assumed the source would be in Halifax but had never intercepted any such signals, leaving them mystified. No one had considered that the transmitter might be as far away as Cape Breton, much less a hold-over from the Second World War.

I had mixed feelings about Marcus and Wilma. When I first knew them, they seemed to be genuinely nice people. Wilma, in particular, reminded me of one of my favourite Aunts: always cheerful, friendly, and welcoming. I had experienced another side of their characters on the cliff at Red Head, where they had shot Don, threatened to shoot Silver and I, and I really don't think either one of them would have hesitated to throw us all over the cliff. Even during the debriefing with our Security Service and Military Intelligence colleagues, Marcus failed to show any remorse whatsoever, and Wilma's only regret was that the two of them had never really gotten married so many years before.

They were charged with attempted murder and a few other things, but in the end, our government simply deported them to Germany with the suggestion that they focus on retirement in the 'old country' and a stern warning to count themselves lucky. As far as I know, that's exactly what they did.

I still have the brass model diver's helmet that I had bought from them.

***

Before leaving Halifax, I visited Sharon and her boss to thank them for their help and support – especially Sharon, who had become a friend. Her boss was gracious and fascinated rather than irritated by my deception, and I told him as much of the truth as I could about my adventure – which wasn't much, really, but seemed to satisfy him.

Just before Jack left to return to his main posting in Alberta, I had Sharon over for dinner one day, so she could visit with all of us: Jack, Don, and of course Silver and I. It was brief but very nice. A lot, in fact, like a family reunion and it gave me another of my *déjà vu* remembrances, recalling to my mind how hard it had been to leave the new friends I had made on my previous three assignments – the most recent ones in Fort McMurray and Innisfail, Alberta, and the one before that in Radium City, Saskatchewan. I resolved to stay in touch with all these new friends as best I could.

I knew that I didn't have to thank Jack for his help, but I did anyway. He said that he'd enjoyed his time as a 'spook' in Atlantic Canada but that he was looking forward to getting back to regular policing back in Alberta. We were both sure that our paths would cross again, so we only had to say: "Good-bye for now."

And Don?

I had to clean everything out of the lab I'd been using at Dalhousie, and after all our adventures there was a bunch of paperwork to do of course, so Silver and I had to stay on in Halifax for several more days. On the first of these, after our capture of the recipient suspect, Don had come over to my place for a visit and supper, which had become a familiar pattern with us, but this time he seemed unaccountably nervous.

"What's eating you, anyway?" I eventually asked.

"Well, I want to ask you something, but I'm feeling a bit embarrassed," he replied, rather sheepishly, which wasn't like Don at all.

"Embarrassed? Don, we've faced death together and seen each other naked, what could possibly be embarrassing?"

"Well… I was wondering if you would like to go out for dinner with me tomorrow night… but not as colleagues… on a date?"

"A date?"

I pretended to think it over – girls can be cruel sometimes. "Can Silver come along?" Girls can be teases, too.

"Of course!" he replied.

"Then the answer is yes, silly," I replied. That's about when the kissing started.

We went out on dates every night for the rest of the week that I was in Halifax.

***

When Silver and I got back to Ottawa I fulfilled my promise to Scotty and told him what my mission had really been all about, and how his weapons had saved my life – probably twice. He didn't say too much, but I could tell he was pleased.

I also paid a visit to Dr. Alan Grey, my former professor at Carleton University, to thank him for his role in my cover story. When I did, I was surprised and pleased to learn that all my Nova Scotia diving with Sharon had served a greater purpose than just my cover story.

Dr. Grey had had one of his students do the analytical work on my samples and then did all the data analysis himself. It was already known that bivalve molluscs, like mussels and clams, accumulate heavy metals in their soft body tissues. What our measurements showed, was evidence for an inverse correlation between the incidence of heavy metals, particularly cadmium and copper, and the levels of Red Tide toxins in the shellfish tissues. We speculated that the heavy metals were toxic to the algae. Of course, high concentrations of heavy metals in the shellfish tissues would be toxic to humans all by themselves, but our work showed that small heavy metal concentrations could be beneficial, by killing the dangerous algae.

Not only that, but based on all this work, Dr. Grey wrote a scientific paper titled "*The Influence of Red Tide Algae on Heavy Metal Concentrations in Edible Bivalves Found in Coastal Atlantic Canada.*" In the paper, he described our work and its results, proposed a set of mechanisms, recommended further research, and got it all past the journal's referees and editor. That was one pleasant surprise. The second was that he included me as a co-author on the paper! So, I got my first (and probably only) scientific paper publication out of the experience.

Pretty cool!

Reprinted from:

Canadian Journal of Chemistry

The Influence of Red Tide Algae on Heavy Metal Concentrations in Edible Bivalves Found in Coastal Atlantic Canada

ALAN GREY AND ALEXANDRA HOUSTON

Volume 56 • Number 4 • 1978
Pages 567-575

National Research
Council Canada

While back in Ottawa, I had a few debriefings and conversations with my boss, Bob, and others, which kind of closed the book on my Nova Scotia adventure. At one of the last ones, we were joined by Assistant Commissioner MacLeod, the person that had lured me into the RCMP in the first place. It never ceased to amaze me how the Assistant Commissioner would pop-up, seemingly out of nowhere, just before and just after one of these special projects that I was given. He even hinted that he had another "special assignment" in mind for me but wouldn't disclose it yet.

"You have some annual leave[39] due, so go take a break and we'll talk when you get back to Ottawa," he'd said.

"Where do you think you'll go?"

"I'm a bit tempted to just stay here, relax, and enjoy the National Capitol Region a bit, but I've also been thinking about driving to Alaska. It's supposed to be beautiful, and I think that I might try to see if I can discover where Silver was born."

"Well, whatever you decide, give yourself a break from your adventures and decompress a bit," said Bob. "You need to look after yourself, especially since you keep getting into gun battles. If you don't have your wits about you, I'm afraid that one of these times you're going to get hurt!

"I'm not too worried about her," said Assistant Commissioner Macleod. "She's indestructible."

"Hmmm," said Bob, "An Indestructible Mountie!"

… Alex and Silver return in
An International Mountie.

Laurie Schramm

BOOK 3 ENDNOTES

1. In fact, official records still list U-687 as never having been deployed.
2. In exterior dimensions, the submarine was approximately 67 metres in length by just over 6 metres in width.
3. North Atlantic Treaty Organization. A defense alliance of the U.S., Canada, and a number of other countries, formed in 1949.
4. Cathode-ray tube. Very similar in appearance to black and white television screens of the time, except that the displayed images were green on black.
5. The CF Argus was capable of long-range patrols of just over 26 hours when fully armed and loaded.
6. Sound System Underwater Surveillance (SOSUS) was a secret chain of U.S. underwater listening devices placed at strategic locations on the ocean floor. The data was transmitted to shore stations, including one in Nova Scotia.
7. Defence Research Establishment Atlantic (DREA), part of the Canadian Forces' Research and Development Branch, which was reorganized into Defence Research and Development Canada (DRDC) in 2000.
8. "Good Old Raisins and Peanuts," a traditional backpacker's snack, which in Sharon's case was supplemented with candy-covered chocolates.
9. Dalhousie University.
10. A slang term for a licensed amateur radio operator. The term 'ham' seems to have originally been coined by analogy with ham

versus professional actors.

11. See *An Inconvenient Mountie* (ISBN: 978-1-9994940-0-1).

12. At this point in time, it was still part of the RCMP. Years later, in 1984, the Security Service was spun-out to create the present-day Canadian Security Intelligence Service (C.S.I.S.).

13. An actual Second-World-War era German *Wetter-Funkgerät Land* automatic weather station, denoted as WFL- 26, was discovered on the Labrador coast in 1977. It is on display in the Canadian War Museum.

14. Heavy water meaning water composed of deuterium and oxygen atoms rather than hydrogen and oxygen atoms.

15. Such weapons were originally called "muff pistols", because their small size enabled them to be carried in a woman's muff.

16. Underwater Demolition Team.

17. Being first occupied in 1915, it was actually 62 years old in 1977.

18. From the French comic series *Astérix le Gaulois*, by R. Goscinny and A. Uderzo.

19. Pyrex™ was a Corning Inc. brand of clear, low-thermal-expansion borosilicate glass that was very popular for laboratory use because it could be heated, cooled, and even handled quite vigorously, without breaking.

20. Buoyancy compensator, or BC, was the prevailing terminology in the 1970s. Eventually, the terms buoyancy compensator device, or BCD, became more common.

21. For SCUBA divers, 'bottom time' is the elapsed time from starting the descent, to the moment of starting the final ascent back to the surface. This does not include the time for the ascent itself, nor decompression stops along the way, if any.

22. See *An Inconspicuous Mountie* (ISBN: 978-1-9994940-2-5).

23. The Cape Islander is Atlantic Canada's signature fishing boat, with its distinctively high, sweeping bow, and a low, flat stern. They are known for their ability to handle rough, rolling seas.

24. Anyone that wasn't born and raised in the Maritimes is considered to be "from away," no matter how long they might

stay or live in the Maritimes.

25. Communications and Electronics Engineering.

26. "Bar Clam" is the local name for the Atlantic Surf Clam, *Spisula solidissima.*

27. A large body of mixed fresh and salt water that lies roughly in the centre of Cape Breton Island.

28. Citizens' Band radio. This was officially called the General Radio Service (GRS), but due to the impact of American pop culture of the 1970s, almost everyone referred to CB radios.

29. The same kind of radio scanner that Lenny had used three months earlier on the Canadian Forces CP-107 Argus.

30. It was Friday, July 1, 1977.

31. German U-boats attacked four freighters near Bell Island, Newfoundland. The *SS Saganaga* and *SS Lord Strathcona* were sunk by U-513 on September 5, 1942, and the *SS Rosecastle* and PLM 27 were sunk by U-518 on November 2 of the same year.

32. On November 9, 1942, a German spy was dropped off near New Carlisle, Quebec, by submarine U-518. He was almost immediately caught. His suitcase, which housed a complete radio transmitter, is on display in the RCMP Museum in Regina.

33. A popular police-drama TV series that had just finished its final season.

34. Sikorsky CH-124 Sea Kings are twin-engine, anti-submarine warfare helicopters that were used by Canadian Forces for over 50 years, and which were usually housed on and deployed from destroyers and frigates of the Royal Canadian Navy. Sea Kings were a familiar sight to people in Canada's Atlantic provinces in those days, partly because they frequently assisted with maritime search and rescue operations.

35. The anchor is from *HMCS Bonaventure.*

36. The RCMP Division responsible for federal and provincial policing in Nova Scotia.

37. Defence Research Establishment Atlantic (DREA).

38. CANDU (CANada Deuterium Uranium) is a Canadian

pressurized heavy water reactor design used to generate electric power. The word deuterium refers to the deuterium oxide (heavy water) that is used to moderate the nuclear fission reaction, and the word uranium refers to the uranium that is used as the fuel.

39. Vacation.

An International Mountie

Adventures of the First Woman Mountie. Book 4

LAURIE SCHRAMM

Miners and packers ascending the summit of the Chilkoot Pass in the winter of 1898. Photo by E.A. Hegg, courtesy of Library and Archives Canada, C-005142.

DEDICATION

To Max

Laurie Schramm

BOOK 4 CONTENTS

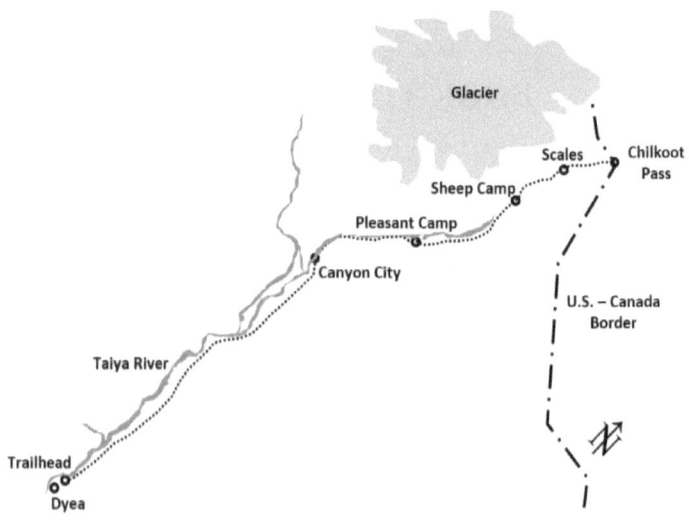

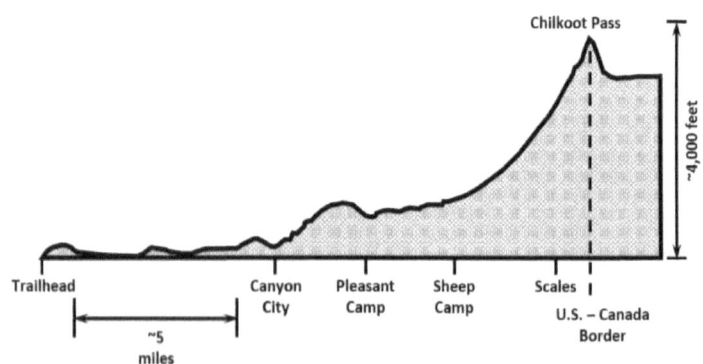

LIST OF CHARACTERS
(IN ORDER OF APPEARANCE)

- Inspector Stone, NWMP
- Corporal Frank Pool, NWMP
- Lucy Lake, a Girl Guide Pathfinder
- Allison Smith, a Girl Guide Pathfinder. Lucy's best friend
- Max, an orange Mackerel Tabby Cat
- Constable Alexandra (Alex) Houston, RCMP
- Assistant Commissioner George MacLeod, RCMP Security Service
- Silver, an Alaskan Malamute. Alex's friend and companion
- Ross and Sally Peake, Owner/Operators of Alaskan Malamute Adventures, Dyea, AK.
- Goldie, an Alaskan Malamute. Silver's sister
- King and Queenie, Alaskan Malamutes. Silver's parents
- Norm Poole, Hunting and Fishing Guide
- Jim Dumont, Hunting and Fishing Guide
- George Carter, Chief of Police, Skagway, AK
- Staff Sergeant Robert (Bob) G. Simpson, RCMP Security Service
- Mark Johnston, Search and Rescue Coordinator, Skagway, AK
- Julie Sawyer, Seasonal Park Ranger, Klondike Gold Rush National Historic Park, AK
- Captain Donald (Don) Harrison, Military Intelligence, Canadian Forces

1 PRELUDE: THE CHILKOOT

April 12, 1898
Chilkoot Trail, Alaska,
Two miles north of the Canyon City camp.

Sitting in the snow, huddled-up against a tree trunk, bleeding, and nearing complete exhaustion Corporal Frank Pool, of the North West Mounted Police[1], knew he was in trouble. He had faced danger many times in his first year of being posted to the Klondike but now, for the first time, he had to face the practical reality that he might not survive the day.

It had, at first, seemed like just another day when Superintendent Sam Steele[2] had assigned Inspector Stone, Frank, and five constables to transport some 150,000 dollars in gold and notes over the Chilkoot Pass, down the mountain to Skagway, Alaska, and from there on to Victoria, British Columbia. The gold had been collected as customs duties, mining lease registrations, and production royalties from miners and others that had joined the Klondike Gold Rush.

The gold rush had been triggered by the discovery, nineteen months earlier (in August, 1896), of placer gold at Bonanza Creek, which is a tributary of the Klondike River. As the news permeated North America, and then the rest of the world, the Klondike became – almost overnight – the scene of the greatest gold rush in North American history. It began with prospectors, but then spread to anyone willing to travel and risk their lives in the pursuit of potentially striking it rich, whether by mining, providing services to the miners, or simply stealing from the miners.

Determined to keep the peace, at least on the Canadian side of the border, Mounted Police reinforcements and supplies were almost immediately sent into the Yukon to bolster the small detachment that had already been in place.

Now, with the long 1897/98 winter finally beginning to retreat, it was time to begin escorting batches of gold ingots out of the territory. Although it was considered 'safe' to transport valuables on the Canadian side of the border, the same could not be said of travel on the American side, which had already fully earned the reputation of being a completely lawless part of the "Wild, Wild West." The portion of Alaska stretching from Skagway to the summit of the Chilkoot Pass, in particular, had become controlled in its entirety by the infamous Soapy Smith[3] and his huge gang of thieves and accomplices.

The Mounties' main concern was not for the rigors of the trail, the mud and snow, the likelihood of avalanches and premature river-ice breakup, or the virtual certainty of bad weather along the way, but rather how to get the gold past Soapy and his gang.

Soapy had so many spies and accomplices that the maintenance of secrecy was viewed as sheer fantasy. Instead, Superintendent Steele and Inspector Stone had quietly let it be known that Stone was being transferred to the prairies, specifically Regina, and was taking with him only his baggage. The men, in turn, each carried on their horses one large box or trunk, plus their ordinary Mounted Police kit bag. The boxes and trunks were empty – simply part of the illusion. The gold ingots were hidden in the kit bags beneath layers of clothing and pemmican[4].

As the group set out, there was no immediate danger from Soapy Smith or his gang. Steele and his Mounties had done such a good job of enforcing peace on the Canadian side that it was rare indeed that any member of Soapy's gang crossed the border to test the Mounties' mettle. So, it was natural for Stone's patrol to expect a quiet journey to the summit of Chilkoot Pass. Trouble, if there was to be trouble, was expected on their descent from the summit on the American side, particularly as they descended the steepest section that led to The Scales, during which they could be simultaneously assailed by rough terrain, bad weather, and well-hidden attackers. If they were going to be ambushed, they thought, that is where they would have to have their wits about them. This was a very reasonable, and time-tested, rationale.

Unfortunately, they were only partly right.

The first sixteen and a half miles of their journey were completely uneventful. On the first day, they proceeded from their headquarters at Lake Bennett, past Lindemann City, and then above the tree-line to Happy Camp, where they spent the night. The second day, they proceeded past Stone Crib and up the short but steep section to the summit of the Chilkoot Pass. Here the Mounties had a permanent camp and Customs Post that was equipped with men, provisions, two Maxim machine guns, and ammunition. At this exposed but secure post they paused for a rest, and to ensure that their water bottles were full, before embarking on the great descent that was to come.

The next phase of their journey was to carefully descend some 3,500 feet, of which the first section – from the summit to The Scales – was the steepest, involving the descent of a thousand feet in just over half of a mile. This was arduous going, as the entire slope was still covered in snow and, although there was a well-travelled path, the men had to proceed on foot, each leading their horse behind him.

Experienced mountaineers know well that, regardless of whether one is ascending or descending a mountain, there is a psychological tendency to relax at the end of a strenuous and/or hazardous segment. None of the Mounties were particularly experienced at mountaineering, so they may not have been aware of this, and whether such was part of Soapy's calculations or not will probably never be known. When the Mounties had reached The Scales, Inspector Stone gave a huge sigh of relief and allowed his men to take a break to rest and relax, after which they resumed their downward travel. When they reached Sheep Camp, and had put most of the steep decline behind them, the Inspector let out an even greater sigh of relief and ordered his men to remount their horses. They should now be able to relax somewhat, he thought, as they rode the much gentler terrain for the rest of the way.

The ambush came two miles further ahead, as the Mounties were passing Pleasant Camp and riding up a short rise on the west side of the valley. It was here that Soapy Smith and his gang had positioned themselves. Soapy had brought twenty of his men, every one of them armed with pistols and some of them carrying repeating rifles. Here, they had hidden themselves. The location was well chosen. In addition to having the element of surprise, they were below the tree-line at this point, so Soapy and his men were able to take cover among the plentiful supply of trees and dull grey boulders. From their hiding places, when the time came, and completely without warning, they suddenly unleashed a blistering volley of gunfire.

Although caught completely off-guard, the Mounties were quick enough to respond. At the first sounds of shots Inspector Stone had ordered his men to dismount, spread out, take cover, and return fire. There was no need for any of these orders, however, as to a man they had immediately leapt from their horses and spread out. Having established what cover they could, each Mountie returned fire on their own.

Although outnumbered four-to-one, and with hastily chosen cover, the Mounties soon gained the advantage in the gun battle that ensued. This was because, although Soapy and his men had chosen their location and their cover with care, their shooting was both undisciplined and generally poorly aimed. The Mounties, on the other hand were well-trained, disciplined, and much better shots. They took their time, conserved their ammunition, and carefully squeezed off their shots only at the most favourable, if fleeting, exposures of Soapy's men. As a result, after what seemed like an eternity but was in fact only about fifteen minutes, more than half of Soapy's men's guns had been silenced, whether because their owners had become incapacitated or killed, or because they had rashly expended their ammunition and were no longer able to participate in the ambush.

At this point in the battle only about half of Soapy's men were still firing, but the survivors had learned their lesson. They were now conserving their remaining ammunition, and were finally choosing their shots with greater care – although their accuracy had not noticeably improved.

Correctly guessing that these were the more skilled and experienced members of Soapy's gang, and not wanting to press the providential luck that had so far enabled all of his men to avoid being shot, Stone made the difficult decision to order his men to run for their horses.

Here was another difference between these opposing forces. Whereas Soapy and his men had ridden whatever horses they could conveniently borrow or steal in Skagway, all Mountie horses had been chosen with great care and carefully trained to stand fast under fire. As a result, every one of them was to be found patiently standing nearby, waiting for their human masters and partners. Had Soapy been a better strategist he would have had his men shoot the horses first, thus effectively trapping his quarry where they had taken cover. Perhaps he had thought it unnecessary. Amazingly, however, none of the Mounties' horses had yet been injured – or worse – in the gun battle.

As the Mounties ran for their horses, Stone yelled out his orders to disperse and "make a run for it as best they could" straight down the trail, through the centre of Soapy and his men, and on to Finnegan's Point, where they would regroup.

Stone was taking a dangerous, calculated risk with this manoeuvre but he judged it to be less risky than remaining in place with declining ammunition and against a superior, if diminished, force.

For the most part his plan was successful.

Seeing the Mounties break from cover and run for their horses, Soapy and the remainder of his men immediately knew that their targets were about to "make a run for it," and they all stood up in plain sight and attempted to shoot the fleeing Mounties, and/or their horses before they could escape.

Fortunately for the Mounties, their zig-zag run for their horses coupled with the gang's lack of coordination and poor marksmanship soon took them right through Soapy and his men. Up the rest of the hill they raced, quickly moving beyond the range of the pistols, and leaving only the few attackers that were equipped with repeating rifles to worry about. Soon, however, they gained the crest of the hill, and disappeared over the other side, taking them out of sight of the rifles as well.

Unfortunately for Frank, who was the last to reach his horse, two of the repeating rifles had been aimed at him throughout the final phase of the battle. For his part, he'd quickly mounted his horse and spurred him ahead, but no sooner had he passed the gang than one bullet hit him and another struck his horse.

Frank had immediately fallen from his saddle, but his horse stood firm. Reaching up for his saddle and reins, he was just barely able to remount. Then, leaning far forward over his saddle horn, he urged his horse forward, and they managed to slowly ride off in the direction of their comrades, who were already over the crest of the hill and far ahead along the trail, well out of sight.

Left behind were Soapy Smith and ten very angry and vocal gang members, several of whom continued to fire in the direction of the escaping Mounties notwithstanding the fact that there was no longer anyone in sight at whom to actually aim. Although none of the gang were motivated to jump on their horses in pursuit, their continued shooting had the unfortunate effect of convincing the fleeing Mounties that they were being actively pursued. As a result, they continued their retreat without taking time to assess whether or not all of their detail was still intact.

For his part, Frank didn't feel very intact. It was all he could do to hang on and remain in the saddle. As a result, he made it most of the way down the hill towards Canyon City before he realized that, like him, his horse Angel had been shot. He'd been so concerned with staying on the trail and stemming his bleeding wound that he didn't even notice the first few times that Angel had stumbled, but eventually it became clear that something was wrong. Quickly dismounting to check, he noticed two things simultaneously. One was that there was a long trail of blood behind him; and the other was that Angel was trembling violently. He no sooner found the entrance wound and began an attempt to stop the bleeding than Angel raised his head, gave out a huge sigh, collapsed, and died. Brave and loyal to the end, Mounted Police Horse Angel had lived up to his name and given everything he'd had to get his master away from the gun battle.

Mentally attempting to set aside mourning for a more appropriate time, Frank removed the saddle, placed the horse blanket over Angel's head, and whispered a few words of thanks and good-bye. Then he wearily grabbed his kit bag, forced himself to stand, and trudged ahead on foot.

As Frank determinedly kept moving forward, it wasn't long before pain, loss of blood, and the encroaching cold began to take their toll. Frank eventually fell into a kind of delirium that caused him to lose the proper trail and follow a game trail that branched off to the west, thus missing the canyon, and Canyon City, completely.

Most of the snow had melted away at this elevation so that a mile along the game trail, Frank encountered a creek. Mistaking this for the Taiya River, rather than one of its tributaries, he followed it further west. Four miles later the creek abruptly ended, and while trying to understand what had happened, Frank collapsed at the base of a youngish balsam fir tree. He was now cold, exhausted, still bleeding, disoriented, and completely lost. Realizing that his chances of survival were now running very low,

Frank forced himself to eat a few bites of his pemmican, then used his sheath knife to scrape a shallow depression in the ground near the base of the tree. He placed his kit bag into the depression and covered it with the earth that he'd removed. On top of this, he built a broad but low cairn of rocks to mark the spot.

With his load lightened, he struggled to his feet and staggered back the way he had come, retracing his steps in hopes of regaining the proper trail back to his post. It was impossible to lose his way back because of the bright red trail of blood, but stamina was another matter. Sheer determination was all that kept him moving at this point and, amazingly, he managed three of the miles back, but only three.

Corporal Frank Pool of the North West Mounted Police collapsed and died where his searching colleagues later found him, just two miles west of the Chilkoot Trail, and slightly north of Canyon City. Although they searched until dusk made further searching impossible, they never found the buried kit bag.

Laurie Schramm

2 ALASKA BOUND

My name is Alexandra Houston. My friends call me Alex.

In the summer of 1974, I'd been 24 years old, and feeling like my career was at a standstill. I'd studied chemistry at university and liked it, but not enough to pursue science as a career. I'd reset my sights on police work next, and had joined the Metropolitan Toronto Police force (Metro). Although policing seemed like a better fit for me than science, my two years with Metro had mostly comprised routine administrative- and traffic duties. These assignments were important, and needed to be done by somebody, and done well. But for me, they didn't fit the Hollywood vision of policing that I had developed, and I hadn't found them to be very challenging.

They say you should be careful what you wish for.

My life soon changed drastically, beginning with an unexpected meeting. Without explanation, my Captain had sent me to go and see a Royal Canadian Mounted Police (RCMP) officer that wanted to meet me. My reaction to this was apprehension, and I wondered what I could possibly have messed-up so badly that it had caught the notice of our national police force.

That's how I first came to meet Assistant Commissioner George MacLeod. After a lengthy conversation that I belatedly realized was an interview, he told me that he had asked my Captain (his friend) to recommend one of his young officers for a special pilot project he had in mind. He wanted someone who wanted to accomplish things, someone eager and tenacious, someone chomping at the bit to be allowed to do some 'real' police work, and... someone female. At this point he had shed his stern 'Mountie look,' relaxed his entire body, chuckled, and said that my Captain had recommended the "biggest pain in the butt" in his Division - me.

Assistant Commissioner MacLeod had explained that the 'Force' had fallen behind the times, and that its senior leadership wanted to build a more diverse police force. "We're going to be recruiting immigrants, visible minorities, maybe even people with some kinds of disabilities as well," he said, "But we have to start somewhere, and that somewhere is by engaging women." He wanted to try a first 'pilot test' with a woman, but that pilot test had to succeed as it would pave the way for an entire first troop of policewomen that would follow. He had thought of using someone that had already qualified as a policewoman, and simply re-train them in the 'RCMP way.'

That had brought me up to full attention. "Wait a minute! Do basic training all over again?"

"Yes!" he'd replied, "that's the only way you can possibly succeed. In the old days of the Northwest Mounted Police, a person could get appointed straight into the Force, even as a commissioned officer, if they had the right political connections. No more. Now everyone starts out the same way, as a Constable, and by going through the same basic training. If you want to have any hope of being accepted, much less respected, that's how you have to begin."

So, in the fall of 1974, I went through training at the RCMP's 'Depot' Division training centre in Regina, dealt with the good and the bad issues that came with being the first woman to train there, and survived to become the first woman Mountie. I hadn't intended for it to happen, really. The opportunity just came and found me.

After training, or re-training if you like, I'd been posted to Radium City, a small town in very northern Saskatchewan that, in its early days, had been a great uranium mining centre.

Although my new boss, Corporal Morrison, had told me that nothing interesting ever happened around there, he'd been wrong, and I'd had to rescue him from a mine collapse, run our entire detachment single-handed while he was confined to hospital for six weeks, get rescued by a strange dog from near-death, solve a mystery, and find and catch a murderer – all in only four months!

The dog was named Silver. Investigating a mysterious series of break-ins had led me to some unusual places, including several abandoned uranium mines. In one such mine I'd fallen through a trap and found myself hanging precariously over the sharp edge of a vertical mine shaft. Unable to get out and tiring fast, I was saved by the almost magical appearance of what I first took to be a wolf, which gave me quite a scare, but turned out to be Silver, an Alaskan Malamute. Silver somehow sensed that I was in danger, had decided to help, and with his assistance I had been able to climb up and out of the raise. To make a long story short[5], while I'd continued to investigate the case, he had attached himself to me, was eventually given to me, and we'd been close friends ever since.

Sometime later I'd found myself in another surprise meeting with the same Assistant Commissioner MacLeod. Once again, a "coffee meeting" had turned into an interview and, once again, he had something new in mind for me. By this time, he'd become head of the Force's Security Service[6] and, unsurprisingly, he had some new ideas he wanted to try out by way of some experimental pilot projects. One of them involved me.

That had taken me to Ottawa in November of 1975, where I joined the Security Service. My new boss, Staff Sergeant Robert ("Call me Bob") G. Simpson, introduced me to the shady worlds of spies, counter-espionage, anarchists, and terrorists, and then sent Silver and I to Northern Alberta, undercover, to help look into a series of bomb threats directed at oil sands companies.

Our path to the oil sands was indirect, however, as Silver and I were first sent to Innisfail, Alberta, to be trained as a police dog and handler team. "If that dog is going to go everywhere with you, then we should get him trained too," I'd been told. Both Bob and Assistant Commissioner MacLeod had been interested in, and seemingly amused by, the undercover possibilities presented by the first female Mountie and her canine partner. So in that way, Silver had officially joined the Mounties too and we were sent to Fort McMurray, undercover to investigate the bomb threats. Our cover stories had held up just long enough for us to identify and apprehend the bomber, although not before a few more adventures. In one of those adventures I'd been able to save Silver's life, which evened up the score and reinforced the feeling I'd long had that our destinies were inter-twined. That had been 1976.

In the Spring of 1977, Silver and I were sent, undercover again, to Nova Scotia to look into a mysterious weather station on Cape Breton Island. This had involved a lot of SCUBA diving, which was a lot of fun, and a peek inside the shadowy world of international espionage, which had at times been downright terrifying. By the end of July, the case had been wrapped-up, and Silver and I had been ordered to go off on vacation and get some rest.

Through our adventures together I'd often wondered about Silver's origins, particularly since he was such an unusual dog. So, with the gift of free time, I decided to go explore Silver's past. *That should be restful*, I had thought.

I was wrong.

***

August, 1977

Having put things in order back in Ottawa, Silver and I drove west and made brief stops in Saskatchewan and Alberta to visit with colleague-friends along the way. That part alone saw us drive over 2,150 miles in five days.

It was so great to be back out west again! Most people just see the flat prairie that characterizes south-central Saskatchewan, without realizing that there is a huge proliferation of gorgeous lakes in the northern half of the province. Alberta, of course has the grandeur of the Rocky Mountains.

Our Alaska adventure began in earnest when we left Edmonton for the drive to Skagway, which involved driving another 1,300 miles. That drive was more fun for me because it was all new. Driving northwest from Edmonton took us through a lot of sparsely populated, wide open spaces. Two days' driving took us well past Fort Saint John and Fort Nelson, to an oasis at Liard River. This was a hot oasis, as Liard River's claim to fame is a large natural hot spring beautifully positioned in boreal forest.

I'd had no idea that the hot springs even existed, but once we got there, I immediately decided that it was an ideal spot for a break and stayed there for the night and all the next morning. The most memorable part for me was the morning soak in the springs when the entire area was covered in a low fog bank, and the fact that the springs had been developed into two huge pools connected by a modest waterfall. One pool was formed by the source water flowing up from underground, so it was very hot! The second pool was cooler, so you could practically pick your desired water temperature by moving around in the pools. It also turned out that you could swim underneath the waterfall, come up behind it, and sit there with rock behind you and a solid curtain of hot water falling right in front of you. It was a natural steam chamber. It was gorgeous, and it was very relaxing.

Silver, with his natural aversion to water had, of course, refused to enter the hot spring and simply watched my antics from a safe distance, while managing to project an attitude of amused tolerance.

Departing from Liard River, we were well along the famous Alaska Highway route. It was exciting to drive a highway that I'd heard and read so much about, although I was a bit concerned about all the stories of rough road patches and the hazards to vehicles. Bearing those stories in mind, I hoped that being in a four-wheel-drive truck, with good ground clearance, would enable us to make the trip without serious mishaps.

It turned out that the highway wasn't as bad as I feared, although it did call for cautious driving. This was brought home to me by a chance meeting with a fellow traveler, in the

coffee shop of a roadside gas station. He had been travelling in the opposite direction, driving a medium-sized RV and told me that he had hit a 'rough patch' that left him with a broken axle. His RV had been towed to the gas station and he had already been waiting for a week for the garage to get the parts they needed to fix it! His hard-won advice to me was to pay close attention to the changing road conditions, and to drive slowly. Taking his advice, and with a more rugged vehicle, I had no real problems with the highway.

An afternoon's drive took us over the border into the Yukon Territory and Watson Lake. Following an overnight stay there, an easy day's driving took us further northwest through changing terrain and scenery until we reached Whitehorse. On day 5, we had an early morning look around Whitehorse, where I paid a quick visit to the RCMP Detachment and borrowed a locker in which to deposit my gun. After that, we back-tracked a bit, and then drove more or less due west, up and over the mountains, across the border and into the United States. We made it down the mountains to Skagway by mid-day.

***

All I knew about Silver's background was that he had been born and raised in Skagway, Alaska, and that he had been sold to Norm Poole, a Radium City hunting and fishing guide, for his dogsled team. This had apparently worked out so well that, at some point, Silver had become Norm's lead dog.

Although Silver had attached himself to me[5] shortly before he (Norm) had died, under the terms of Norm's will his legal ownership had passed to Ruby Gillespie, the owner/manager of Radium City's Coffee Shop. Fortunately, before I was transferred out to another assignment, Ruby had kindly transferred Silver's ownership to me. Ruby had even found the original bill of sale in Norm's files, so I knew the name and address of the Skagway sled-dog breeders. Their place turned out to be just West of Skagway – across the Skagway River and along the route to the neighbouring ghost-town of Dyea. The town had hosted a busy port during the Klondike Gold Rush, but it was eventually overtaken by the deeper water port of Skagway, and the final straw for Dyea had come when Skagway became the terminus for the White Pass and Yukon Route Railroad (which had decided to follow the White Pass Trail rather than the Chilkoot Trail for its ascent up the mountain and to the Yukon).

Now, nearly 80 years later, my travel guide explained that only a few people still lived on small homesteads in the valley near Dyea. Apparently, the main local tourist attraction was the late-summer salmon-spawning run, which attracted bears (black bears and brown bears) and eagles. After a few false turns, we were able to find *Alaskan Malamute Adventures*, the homestead of Ross Peake, who had been listed as Silver's breeder and seller.

Ross Peake

As we turned into the yard, we were greeted by Ross himself, who was a bit frightening at first glance. He had rather wild-looking, longish grey hair, and a very full grey and white beard, but friendly and incredibly clear, penetrating eyes. Those eyes didn't miss much: with only the briefest glance at me he took one look at my companion and yelled: "Silver!"

In the same instant, Silver had recognized and rushed up to him, stood straight up on his hind legs, with his forepaws on Ross' chest, his tail wagging, and proceeded to lick every part of Ross' face that he could get at – which was essentially all of it, although it was mostly beard.

I had stepped back to give Silver room, and was watching bemusedly as Ross peered through Silver's frantic licking to take a second look at me.

"Alex Houston," I said, by way of introduction. "I wanted to see where Silver grew up and it looks like we've found the right place."

"Well I'll say that you have. My name's Ross Peake, and any friend of Silver's is a friend of ours!"

"Ours?"

"My sister, Sally, and I run this place," Ross answered. "She's around somewhere. Why don't you come for a look around then, once we find Sally, we can all go inside for a chat?"

I readily agreed, and Ross showed Silver and I around the place.

The first thing that struck me was the huge yard full of dog houses. Each dog seemed to have their own house, which resembled a rectangular box on short legs. Raising the dog houses up on legs presumably provided an easy way to keep the dog houses warmer and drier than if they sat on the ground. Each dog house had an open, square door and a flat roof that projected out over the door. I had seen sled-dog houses like this in Radium City, Saskatchewan and I wondered whether the design may have originated here in Alaska, or possibly in the Northern Canadian territories. Certainly, the dogs seemed to appreciate the flat roofs as many of them were sprawled on the tops of their dog houses, lounging and either looking lazily around or napping.

The second thing that struck me, was the apparent variety of breeds. "I had the impression that northern sled dogs were usually Siberian Huskies or Alaskan Malamutes," I said.

"That was true in the beginning," agreed Ross. "Alaskan Malamutes and Siberian Huskies are the traditional sled-dogs, going way back in history. They are well adapted to the cold, and they're strong enough to be able to pull heavy loads over great distances. When dog-sledding was the only practical way to get around, and when it was necessary for hunting, then the Alaskan Malamutes and Siberian Huskies were the breeds of choice. Nowadays though, most dog-sledding is for fun or sport, like the dog-sled races that are put on in different countries."

"Like the Iditarod[7]," I suggested.

"Exactly," said Ross, clearly pleased that I was familiar with the name. "That's the most famous dog-sled race in North America, but there are also some great races in the Yukon, and in the Scandinavian countries. In fact, some mushers take their teams all around the world."

"So now you just need speed?" I asked.

"It's not quite that simple. The dogs still need to be able to handle the cold, and they still need to have endurance, and there are a few other things too. For example, we look for dogs that are curious, friendly, flexible, and co-operative team-players."

"Just like picking people for human teams," I commented.

"Exactly," he said, again sounding pleased. "But for the competitive racers, speed has become a larger factor. Speed and gait."

"Gait?"

"Gait! The ability to run efficiently and consistently at different speeds, and the ability to switch smoothly from one speed to another – particularly in 'synch' with the rest of the team."

"Wow, it's a lot more complicated than I'd imagined."

"Things have certainly progressed," Ross agreed. "The

winner of the first Iditarod took almost three weeks to reach Nome, but modern racers can do it in close to ten days – that's a big change! Anyway, the sled-dogs that have been specifically bred to produce all these qualities are called Alaskan Huskies. They're still descended from Siberian Huskies and Alaskan Malamutes, but with other breeds mixed-in as well."

"I'd never heard of Alaskan Huskies before," I commented.

"Well, Alaskan Huskies will probably never be recognized by the Kennel Club, but they're a real breed to the rest of us!"

"Are there any Alaskan Huskies here?"

"Sure. I'll introduce you to some a bit later. You can call us traditionalists, but we also still breed Siberian Huskies and Alaskan Malamutes – like Silver here," he said, reaching out to tussle Silver's fur. "Of course, Silver's grey-blue eyes are unusual among Alaskan Malamutes, and he'd be disqualified as a purebred, but we're not interested in 'show dogs' here."

"Do you race though?" I asked.

"Oh, we race alright. Each season we do the race here, and then some of the Klondike races too. The difference is that we race for fun, and to keep the old spirit alive. So, we don't need the fastest dogs, and we don't push ourselves or our dogs to the limits. It's a big tradition around here. We enjoy the people that come to watch and run the races… and, like I said, I guess we just race for fun and to maintain the spirit of the thing. After all," he laughed, "dog mushing is the Alaska State Sport!"

By this time, we had walked around the large kennel area and the just-as-large training area. Some of the dog runs and jumps reminded me a bit of the RCMP Dog Service Training Centre that Silver and I had trained at in Innisfail, Alberta. The next part of the compound comprised a couple of large Quonset-style huts. Ross explained that these buildings contained a workshop and storage area for dog sleds and summer sleds.

We were walking towards the Quonset huts when Silver suddenly lifted his head, took a big sniff, gave out a distinct "Yip," and darted ahead of us. After only running about five yards though, he suddenly came to an abrupt stop, at which point he lowered his shoulders, placed his two front legs out on the ground in front of him, and lowered his head to the ground in a very deliberate 'bow'. I had seen dogs do that as a signal of non-aggression and wanting to play with another dog, but I'd never seen Silver do it before.

No sooner had I taken in this strange behavior than I noticed that a reddish-gold-coloured dog had come out of one of the buildings and was running full-tilt towards Silver. Other than the colouring, this dog looked quite a lot like Silver, and I began to have some suspicions at that point. I wasn't able to get a close look at this new dog right away, because the meeting of the two dogs immediately turned into a kind of wrestling match in which their bodies twisted and turned in all directions, accompanied by a bunch of growling sounds that sounded fairly loud but happy. You might have to be a 'dog person' to appreciate this, but there's a distinct difference in tone between dogs' happy growling and their angry or defensive growling.

Ross immediately began to chuckle. "It warms the heart to see those two back together again," he said.

"I take it that they know each other?"

"I should say they do! They're brother and sister after all. Her name's Goldie. Let's give them a moment and then I'll call her over for introductions."

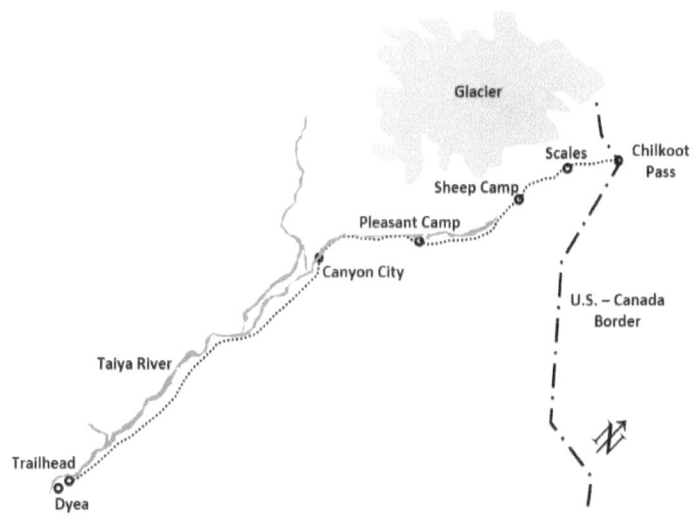

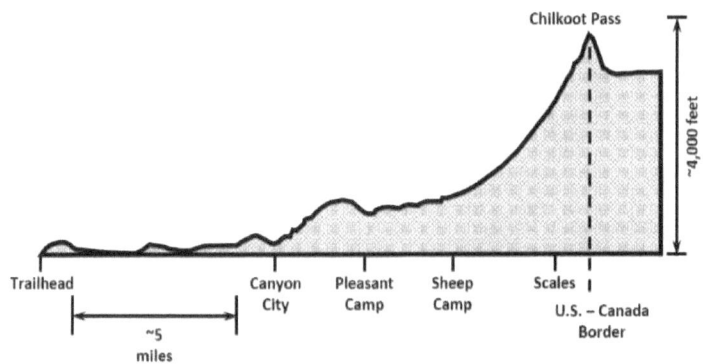

3 THE CHILKOOT REVISITED

August, 1977
Chilkoot Trail, Alaska,
Two miles north of the Canyon City camp.

It had all started out as such a grand, grown-up type adventure.

Lucy Lake was twelve years old. She had been part of the Canadian Girl Guides since starting out as a 'Brownie' at age seven[8]. As the years had gone by, she had been proud to graduate to 'Guides' the previous year (in 1976).

Something Lucy enjoyed about getting older was being able to do more interesting things, and one of the things the older Guides got to do was go on outdoor, or even international, trips. This trip had been both: a chance for her entire patrol to go to Skagway, Alaska and backpack the Chilkoot Trail all the way back to Canada. Back in 1897 and 1898, most of the prospectors and miners had made their way to Skagway, then to nearby Dyea, and from there had hiked and climbed the 17-mile trail to the summit, crossed into Canada, and then hiked another 16 miles to Lake Bennett. Lucy and her patrol were travelling that very same route.

On their first day Lucy, her five patrol-mates, and their two adult leaders had shouldered their heavy backpacks and started out from Dyea – just like the miners had done some 80 years earlier. Those early miners would have been amazed to see their patrol hiking along in their blue uniform shirts and shorts, wearing their traditional navy-blue berets, their bandanna-like ties (white, with red maple leaves and blue border), and their modern, aluminum-frame backpacks. The miners would have been even more impressed with the contents of those packs, which included lightweight freeze-dried foods and down sleeping bags.

The patrol felt a bit of the pain of the prospectors almost immediately as there was a quarter-mile section of the trail that felt like it was almost straight up. Between not having had a chance to really warm up on the hike and the burden of their heavy backpacks, it was hard going and soon had them all huffing and puffing. Their leaders assured them that this was like an initiation, and that the rest of the day would be much easier, but Lucy was in good company in thinking that maybe this hike wasn't such a great idea after all.

No one had wanted to be the one to give up, however, and after pausing to catch their breath the patrol had continued. The next seven miles of the trail to Canyon City had alternated up and down but had seemed quite easy in comparison with the initial stretch. As they hiked along beside the Taiya River they had marveled at the rugged beauty of their surroundings. Along each side of the river were scattered huge boulders and piles of sand and gravel, beyond that were groves of willow, poplar, and birch trees, and further out beyond that a range of steep and towering mountains. There were wild flowers growing here and there, among the rocks, squirrels running around and chattering in the trees, and even a few bald eagles sitting up high in the trees. Along the way they passed the ruins of an old sawmill, several shacks, and the odd bit of machinery rusting away.

As they passed Canyon City, the numbers of boulders lying about increased dramatically. These ranged in size from small to huge and, in many cases, they had one or more nearly-flat sides – indicating that they had been broken away from larger boulders rather than simply eroded down in size.

The forest started to change too. In some areas, a small

number of brave-looking, individual trees raised their heads here and there among the rocks. Their leaders explained that these were survivors of avalanches and rockslides that had come racing down the mountainside sometime in the past. Some slopes were even more stark, with no tress on them at all. The leaders explained that, in these areas, frequent avalanches and rock slides had completely wiped out the trees and prevented new ones from growing. At the bottoms of the barren slopes were piled masses of rock interspersed with the remnants of shattered trees that had been uprooted and carried down with the rocks and/or snow. The most impressive thing, to some of the girls, was how huge some of the fractured tree trunks were!

Beyond Canyon City they'd crossed a suspension bridge and then passed more ruins of old cabins and other artifacts, like cooking utensils and even a large iron stove – all lying scattered about here and there, continuing to rust away as they had been for nearly eighty years. The sense of hiking in a virtual museum continued as they progressed, passing more artifacts and even long lengths of downed telegraph wire.

Although the air was cool, the weather had been good and the trail dry, so they'd had little difficulty making it to their planned first campsite at Mile 10: Pleasant Camp. After a long day of backpacking it had been a relief to ditch their packs, eat a hot supper, relax around their camp-stoves, and finally crawl into their tents for the night.

Lucy shared a tent with her best friend, Allison Smith. Once they were both safely inside, Lucy opened her pack and released her secret passenger: Max, a Mackerel Tabby cat. He had orange, tiger-striped short hair and a bob tail, making him look somewhat like a small, domesticated version of a wildcat. Despite his appearance, Max was actually very social and playful, and Lucy considered him to be her second-best friend. It was for this reason that she had smuggled Max into the Guides' trip by the simple expedient of hiding him in the top of her backpack.

Although he was an exceptionally patient cat, Max did have

to be let out from time to time, of course. For this purpose, he had to wear a light harness to which Lucy could attach a thin but strong leash. With Allison's help Lucy had been able to be fairly discreet so far. Most of the other girls knew about Max, of course, and they considered him to be something in the nature of a trip mascot. Together, and unaware that they were acting foolishly, they had successfully concealed Max's presence from their adult patrol-leaders.

As the evening chill permeated their tent, Max prudently curled up inside Lucy's sleeping bag with his back nestled between the back of her head and the top of one shoulder. As Lucy and Allison continued to discuss the day's adventure in whispers, Max promptly fell asleep.

The next morning, everyone had risen early – without too much grumbling – and made their breakfast. They'd been tired, so breakfast had vanished quickly, but all the girls were looking forward to making their way to the summit and the leaders hadn't had to do much prodding to get them to pack up and get ready for day two on the trail. After that, and with Max safely tucked away in Lucy's pack, the first few miles were over gentle terrain and the next two hours of backpacking passed pleasantly.

The rock slide, when it came, was terrifying.

It had started innocently enough, very high up - above The Scales, and near the summit of the mountain. In the stillness of the morning, a marmot had scurried along, looking for food. It had a regular routine for this, and knew this part of the mountain very well. On this particular day, however, as it scrambled over a rock that was not much larger than itself, the rock tipped to one side and began to slide. The rock only tipped by about thirty degrees, and it only slid about an inch and a half, but it was enough for it to collide with another rock.

In the short few moments that this took, the marmot had already moved along but, had it remained to watch – and had it been able to observe in slow motion – it would have been able to see a kind of rock ballet.

The second rock, which had also been rather precariously balanced, tipped to one side and slid just enough to encounter a third rock. The third rock tipped in a slightly different direction, slid and collided with two rocks. Of these, one rock as well situated and absorbed the blow without moving. The second one, however, slid into an inukshuk[9]. That's where the trouble really began.

The inukshuk, probably having been made by a passing backpacker that had stopped for a rest, had not been particularly well constructed so that, although it looked nice, when the third rock slid into it the whole structure collapsed, setting its other rocks into motion – all twenty of them. All of the rocks began to roll downhill, gathering momentum.

Even these rocks were quite unassuming. Only three or four of them were much larger than the passing marmot, and none of them rolled or slid more than half a foot downhill. Of the twenty rocks, only six or seven of them actually collided with others. It was, however, just enough to create a cascade.

Soon, more rocks were dislodging more rocks, and as the cascade continued, larger and larger rocks came into play. Their momentum increased, and the moving rocks took on the appearance of an opening fan.

The trickle of rocks had become a wave of rocks.

It would have ended there had not just enough rocks been moving just fast enough to cause a layer of shale to break free and begin to slide in a sheet that quickly broke up into dozens of rocks.

The wave of rocks had become a torrent!

What had begun as a modest sheet of rock and scree breaking away had become a torrent that gained speed and broadened its path as it continued downward. As it did so, clouds of dust were created and billowed up, and the sound of it all changed and increased in volume. Compared with the first few, slight clicking sounds of one rock sliding into another, the collective sounds of many rocks, tipping over, sliding, and crashing into each other took on the sound of a rushing waterfall.

The original marmot and all the other animals in the immediate area sensed it now, and instinctively fled.

Although some of the dislodged rocks careened off in more or less random directions, the majority of them followed a combination of the pull of gravity and the path of least resistance.

The path of least resistance was the Chilkoot Trail. For the same reason that the backpackers followed the trail upwards, most of the rocks now followed it downwards.

They were heading for The Scales!

The girls had been enjoying a rest break where they broke-out above the tree-line at Mile 14.5 (1.5 miles beyond Sheep Camp). After their break, Lucy had surreptitiously slipped Max back in to her pack, all of the girls had shouldered their packs, and they had just been about to resume their hike when they had heard a noise that sounded like the rumble of distant thunder. Then the sound had increased to a roar, and they'd realized it was something bad: an avalanche of snow, or rock, or both.

Almost immediately, the noise was accompanied by dust clouds so they could see where it was and where it might be headed.

That got them running!

The patrol immediately abandoned their backpacks and started running. Since the rockslide noises were coming from ahead of them and to their left, they ran to their right (heading approximately south) and they navigated their way over and around the rocky terrain until they reached the edge of the forest. They continued into the forest in the reasonable hope that the trees might protect them from the rocks. Some ran almost blindly through the brush, which slowed them down considerably and frequently leading to falls, while others – whether through luck or a greater degree of control and observation – followed game trails, which allowed them to run faster and generally without tripping. As a result, the patrol became more and more separated from each other the longer they ran.

Being unfamiliar with the area in general, and with avalanches and rockslides in particular, none of the group knew how far to go, they just knew they had to run. As a result, they ran as far as they could.

By the time the rock slide reached Sheep Camp it had finally expended the last of its kinetic energy and come to a halt, some of the rocks and debris having passed through right where the girls had been resting! They didn't know this at the time though, as the patrol had kept on scrambling through the forest until they couldn't run any longer. When they did stop, the eerie silence signaled that the rock slide was over.

Unwilling to trust the sudden silence, the two leaders quickly decided to stay where they were for a while, in a small clearing, and to use the time to collect their patrol together. Since they had purposely not overtaken any of the running girls, they hoped that they would be able to simply remain in place and wait for the girls to backtrack to them. For the most part, this worked out quite well. After much calling out, the first two arrived almost immediately, followed by the stragglers, one, then another, then another.

Five of the girls, once they'd calmed down enough to provide coherent self-assessments seemed to be OK – they were bruised, tired, shaken, and scared, but bravely declared themselves to be "OK." That, however, was only five of the original patrol of six Guides.

"Has anyone seen Lucy?" Brown Owl[10] asked.

Silence.

It turned out that no one had seen Lucy since they'd all dropped their packs and started running.

They'd tried calling out for Lucy, but received no response. The leaders next tried sending the girls out in various directions, each heading along a different path or trail but always remaining in sight of another Guide or one of the leaders. This was a very smart thing to do, and a testament to the quality of the Guide leaders that they had come up with this plan without any prior training[11]. Unfortunately, this tactic didn't produce any results either.

Their next decision was to range forward, in case Lucy had outrun them all. In this case the two leaders had the girls stay together in the clearing, and went forward together, again calling out Lucy's name. This was also unsuccessful.

Running out of options, their next decision was to backtrack. With the girls spread out in a rough line, but such that each could see a patrol-member on each side of her, they worked their way back to the Chilkoot Trail. When they arrived, they found all of their backpacks were still where they had left them, dust-covered but intact, but there was still no sign of Lucy.

Where is she? they wondered.

Laurie Schramm

4 SILVER'S REUNION

Goldie, was about the same size as Silver, but had golden eyes, and reddish-golden colouring. It was easy to see how she had earned her name.

As we watched the vigorous reunion, Ross continued his explanation. "Goldie was born a few minutes before Silver here, but that was enough to establish her as the head of the litter. There were six puppies originally. We sold off the rest of them but had intended to keep Goldie and Silver for ourselves."

By this time, Silver and Goldie had stopped tussling and were simply standing, virtually nose-to-nose, gazing intently into each other's eyes. It was uncanny seeing them silently stare at each other like that. It reminded me of all the times that I'd looked into Silver's eyes and felt like I could tell what he was thinking, and for a moment... I had the sense that they were communicating in some way. This feeling was reinforced when they broke off and I felt – not just saw but felt – Goldie's penetrating gaze on me.

"Ross..." I began, still watching her intently.

"Yeah," Ross said, somewhat sheepishly. "We don't talk about that..."

Goldie padded forward to greet me, and I went down on my knees to meet her. I offered my hand for her to sniff, which she did, and then she surprised me by reaching up and licking my face.

As she was doing this I glanced over at Silver, who was looking at me very intently and I couldn't escape the feeling that I was being welcomed into a larger pack. My mind was filling with questions now but, before I could ask, a woman somewhat younger than Ross had come out of one of the buildings and walked up meet us.

"Hi! I'm Sally," was all she had time to say before Silver was there standing upright on his two back legs and licking her face.

It took a while for both dogs to decide that they'd completed enough licking for now, but eventually I was able to stand up, shake hands with Sally, and reiterate that I'd wanted to come and see where Silver had grown up.

It was decided that we should head back to the house and exchange some stories. As we walked back, Ross and Sally pointed out some other features of their place including a dog training run that looked a lot like a racetrack for horses, buggies, or even race cars, except that it was smaller. As we went by, I noticed that they even had summer sleds – dog sleds with wheels instead of skis, and which were clearly designed for dog team training in the summer months.

Reaching the house and being shown into their living room, I quickly discovered that the reunions weren't over yet. Two older dogs immediately rose from their blankets on the floor and together met with Silver. Whereas Silver and Goldie's reunion had mostly resembled a friendly wrestling match, Silver's meeting with what turned out to be his parents was more like a meeting of diplomats. As the three of them stood together, gazing intently at each other, nose to nose to nose I was reminded of childhood storybooks in which a King and Queen's knightly son would return home after a long absence in which he had grown to manhood.

I don't know exactly what put this thought into my head but it was quite prophetic, as Ross told me that these were Silver's parents: King and Queenie.

I immediately put my hand to my mouth in an attempt to

hide my instinctive smile, but this turned out to be a futile gesture as I couldn't help breaking out into laughter as well: "King and Queenie, and Goldie and Silver?"

"Sure, what's wrong with that?" asked Sally, looking a bit mystified, and possibly wondering whether to be offended or not.

"It's just all too much," I said, still chuckling, "the coincidences I mean."

Now both Ross and Sally looked mystified. "Maybe I should tell you a bit of our story," I offered. With Silver still visiting with his parents, we all sat down and I told them a bit about my background and how I'd come to join the Mounted Police, then my first posting and how Silver and I had come to meet[5].

"Later on, Silver and I trained in the RCMP's dog service, so he's now a police dog and we're a team – both on the job and off," I concluded. "The reason I was laughing, was that part of the Mounties' Hollywood legacy is a whole series of shows and books about a fictional character known as Sergeant Preston of the Mounties and his faithful side-kick and ally, Yukon King, who was an Alaskan Malamute. Not only that – I don't know if you've ever seen any of the TV or book pictures of Yukon King, but he was the spitting image of your own dog King!"

Putting my two hands out, both King and Queenie padded over and each commandeered a hand for a prolonged sniffing session, after which they curled up at my feet looking quite contented.

Ross and Sally had heard of the Sergeant Preston character but weren't familiar with the stories, or his famous dog. They did, however, appreciate the multiple coincidences. Although they were naturally curious about Silver's and my adventures together, they also wanted to know about Norm.

"Norman Poole came to see us in 1974," Ross explained. "He told us that he was a hunting and fishing guide in Northern Saskatchewan, and that he was building a dogsled team and wanted a young dog that could lead the team."

"We hadn't been planning to sell Silver at all, but Norm seemed so dedicated to the spirit of dog-sledding, and like he'd be a good and considerate owner, that our resolve weakened. We couldn't keep all of our dogs, of course, so in the end we'd reluctantly agreed to sell Silver to him. Silver was only four years old then, but he'd already shown great promise, had been trained to pull a sled, and enjoyed it so much that he'd become a lead dog. Even most of the older dogs had already accepted his leadership in the harness traces. I think he enjoyed the relative independence of being in the front, and he was certainly the best I've ever seen at understanding the commands of the musher."

That had been the last time Ross and Sally had seen Norm or Silver.

"I think Norm would have been a good owner," I offered, explaining that I'd heard good things about the two of them, and that I'd gotten to know Norm fairly well during my posting to Radium City, where he'd lived. I also briefly related the sad tale of Norm's death, and how Silver's ownership had passed to Norm's friend, Ruby Gillespie, and then to me.

"Of course, by that time Silver had already attached himself to me and we'd become friends and partners," I finished.

Although they were saddened to hear of Norm's fate, they were pleased with the tale of Silver's and my history together, and especially pleased to be able to see Silver again. It was on this note that they made me an offer I couldn't refuse.

"Where are you staying?" Sally had asked.

"I don't really know," I responded. "I was actually going to ask you for a recommendation."

"Look, we have several tourist cabins here. We're normally full, but we just had a cancellation so we have an empty cabin available for tonight and tomorrow night. You're welcome to stay here for free if you want – meals included."

"Thank you, that sounds great! But I'm happy to pay for it."

"Tell you what," put in Ross. "Tell us some more stories while you're here, maybe pick up a bottle of wine or two for tomorrow, and we'll call it even – OK?"

I'd readily agreed, and Silver and I had spent two really enjoyable, and relaxing days with them during which a couple of really significant things happened. The first came up over dinner when Ross had been talking about why they loved Alaska and all the outdoor activities that were available. This provided my cue to ask about one of the things I'd always wondered about Silver.

"Do you know why he doesn't like to go into the water?"

This produced chuckling and a simultaneous "Yes" from both Ross and Sally.

"We laugh about it now," Ross explained, "but it was a serious thing at the time.

"It was a gorgeous Spring day and I was out with a team practising for a dog-sled race. Silver and Goldie were matched-up together, behind our most senior lead dog. Behind them were some of our younger, and less experienced, dogs. Things had been going well, and we had turned around and were on our way back home. About a mile from here we crossed the river, like we always do.

"With hindsight, there were more pressure ridges and cracks than normal for the time of year, but they were hidden under a light covering of snow. We learned later that there was also some kind of rise in the water level up-stream that caused another pressure surge. In any case, we were almost across the river. In fact, the lead dog, and Silver and Goldie, were already fully across when all of a sudden there was a tremendous 'crack' and the ice broke-up in large pieces, right underneath the sled. The sled twisted upwards and began to sink, putting even more pressure on an uplifted sheet of ice, which promptly broke apart, and before I could react, the sled dropped right down into the water, dragging the whole dog team with it.

"It took me a long time to get at all the dogs and cut them free and, in every case, a terrified dog had been completely immersed for at least a moment before I was able to get them out. Silver and Goldie had the worst of it. They never forgot and neither of them would ever go in the water again!"

"Wow," I remarked. "That must have been terrifying for

all of you. I always found it odd that Silver really doesn't mind getting wet but never wants to go in the water – now I can understand why."

At this point Silver gave a grave sort of "yip," as if in agreement.

"But now I need to tell you a new story that involved Silver being thrown into the water again," I continued.

Although I left out some of the most interesting details, which were either national security, or highly personal secrets, I related the essence of the story[12] of how Silver, and a colleague, and I had been out on a converted fishing boat off Cape Breton Island, Nova Scotia. The boat had struck something in the water and immediately begun to sink. This had the effect of dumping us all into the frigid Atlantic Ocean and requiring us to swim to a nearby island, find some rudimentary shelter, and survive a highly uncomfortable night before being rescued by a fisherman the following morning.

Even without the juicy details, Ross and Sally were suitably impressed and sympathetic. Once again, Silver and Goldie had been watching closely during the telling of this story, which provided the segue to the second really significant thing.

"By the way," I began, "is it just me, or have you ever had the impression that Silver understands more about human speech than can really be possible?"

There was a long silence. I waited, as Ross turned to look at Sally, who gave him a significant but indecipherable (to me) look. With a sigh, Ross shifted in his chair, seemed to struggle with how to begin, and then clearly decided to just let it out.

"You asked me something like this when we were watching Silver's reunion with Goldie," he began.

"Yes, and then you said something to the effect that you don't talk about it."

"Well, yes, that's right. We don't talk about it because we don't want people to think we're crazy." Then, thinking about what he'd just said, he amended, "or, at least any crazier than they already think we are." This produced smiles all around, and I let another silence play out – waiting for him to continue.

"Well," Ross sighed, "it all started when Queenie had the litter of pups that produced Goldie, Silver, and their siblings. Everything seemed normal at first, but over time it often seemed like Goldie and Silver could communicate with each other somehow. In addition to all the usual playing, sometimes we'd notice them staring intently at each other, after which they'd go off and do something together. There was no way to be sure, but we eventually got the distinct impression that they were communicating – or at least had a remarkable understanding of each other."

"You'd never seen this before?" I asked.

"Not like this, and we've raised over 60 sled-dogs here. There are always dogs that bond with some more closely than with others, and some that learn faster than others, but something always seemed different with these two... and then there was the time they tried it on me!"

"On you?"

"Yes. I'd been out on a practice run with a sled and a team that included Goldie and Silver. Once again, I had matched the two of them up, right behind the lead dog. On the way back home, I'd decided to try following a game trail through the forest, which I really should not have done since it was late in the day."

Ross paused and sighed. "Anyway, I lost my way in the forest and eventually came to a fork in the trail. It was late in the day, and the sky was cloudy, so the light was poor, and I hadn't brought a compass with me. I wasn't sure which way to turn, but my instinct was to follow the fork to the right. As I tried to get the team moving in that direction, both Goldie and Silver dug their paws in, and refused to mush. As I yelled at them to get going, they simply stood there straining at their harnesses.

"At this point, I was mystified more than angry. Nothing like this had ever happened before with these two dogs. When I finally hesitated, unsure what to do next, both of them turned to stare at me with incredibly penetrating gazes that seemed to say 'Not this way!' I wondered whether I was just imagining things, but some inner instinct persuaded me to pay attention and follow their lead.

"They were right, of course. The trail my instincts wanted me to follow led completely the wrong way and, I later discovered, would have led to an impassable ridge of rock that would have left us far from home, with darkness falling. To this day, I have no idea how they knew which trail to take, nor how they were able to communicate that to me... Anyway, that was the first time, but there have been others. It's always subtle, so subtle that you can easily convince yourself that it's only your imagination, but I've come to believe that there are times when they can sense my thoughts, and times when they can communicate simple thoughts to me – only Goldie and Silver, never any of the other dogs. I think they somehow inherited some abilities that may have been more common in their ancestors.

"The aboriginal tribes have some interesting traditional stories about wolves. In some of those stories, wolves are fierce, unpredictable rulers of the forests that humans need to beware. But in other stories wolves were pinnacles of courage, strength, hunting skill, and loyalty. One of my favourite stories is about how one wolf, back at the dawn of human evolution, was the original brother and best friend of the first man. That wolf, is said to have had powerful instincts, keen intuition, high intelligence, and a rudimentary ability to communicate with humans as well as other wolves.

"I like that one because you can tell just by looking at them that Alaskan Malamutes, like Silver here, aren't far removed from their Arctic Wolf ancestors, and they have a heritage as sled dogs that goes back at least two thousand years. What's more, the best of our dogs have been true best friends of ours."

"You said communicate. Communicate how?"

"I don't really know. The traditional knowledge stories only say that the original man and the original wolf had ways of understanding each other. I asked an elder, from one of our local aboriginal communities, about that once and she said it was probably a version of what people now call telepathy. Now do you get why we don't talk about this? No one believes in the occult anymore!"

"No," I said slowly, "but everything you've said matches my experiences with Silver. When he first saved my life, his sudden appearance scared the hell out of me, but as I gazed into his eyes, he seemed to want me to reach out and grab on to him. Fortunately, I was desperate enough to try it, and he saved me. Ever since then there have been many times when he has seemed to know what I'm thinking or saying, or that I seem to know what he's thinking."

"There you are then," said Ross, sounding relieved. "You're just as crazy as we are."

"What do you think?" I asked, turning to face Silver, who seemed to have been intently observing our conversation, "Are we all crazy?"

At this, Silver promptly rose up, padded over to me and placed his head in my lap. As I stroked behind his ears and looked into his eyes, I could feel a wave of emotion I can only describe as kinship. Looking back at Ross and Sally, I said, "I'm just so grateful that we found each other. Thank you for sharing your stories with me."

A very distinct stomach rumbling from Ross broke the spell, and Ross tried to defend himself against Sally's and my laughter by explaining that he was hungry and we should eat. At this, he and Sally promptly got up to start preparing dinner. They refused to hear of me pitching in to help, but with four dogs to visit with I was well occupied.

We finished the evening sitting outdoors, in companionable intervals of light conversation interspersed by periods of silence that allowed me to soak in the rugged Alaskan mountain beauty.

5 AN INHUMAN MOUNTIE

Here is Silver's story[13]:

My Beginnings. *It was cold where I grew up. Even the summers had chilly nights, especially when the wind was up. The winters, however, were what defined the true meaning of cold...*

When it was well beyond the point when water would freeze solid, you learned early not to put your tongue on bare metal. Not more than once, anyway. The pain of feeling a layer of skin tear off of your tongue is the kind of pain that you never, ever, forget.

Our immediate family: my father, mother, sister and I, were all close. Unnaturally close, some said. At first, I had no idea what that meant. Later, I took it to be a jealous response to how happy our little family was together. It was much later, as I began to grow in maturity as well as size, that it dawned on me that my family communicated with each other somewhat differently than we did with others. It was a subtle thing with my parents, but something much stronger with my sister.

From my very first memories as a youngster, I remember being able to gaze into my sister Goldie's eyes and get − not her actual thoughts − but an image in my mind of what she was thinking. The same thing seemed to work for her too, but in reverse. For example, I might gaze into her eyes and get a clear image of a field with a ball lying in the centre of it. **She wants to go play with the ball**, *I would think. Then, if I thought about the field and the ball, she would know that I was agreeing and we'd both simply get up and go play.*

I soon realized that when playing with others of my age, I couldn't understand them in the same way that I could my sister or parents. It's not that I couldn't communicate with others. It was more that our communications weren't as detailed, or as rich. Like the difference between looking out over a forested valley in the bluish illumination of twilight compared with looking at the same scene with the illumination of the late morning sun on a clear day. Like the difference between seeing a single colour compared with a rainbow. I didn't think much of it for the longest time.

***

Home, when I was growing up, was a large, fenced-in area with a large house, a barn, and quite a few smaller houses. My parents were servants, basically, and we lived in one of the small houses. We had a master and a mistress, who lived in the big house. They were kind to us, and I think we all liked them.

One of the other humans was a very old man. I never quite figured out what his duties were supposed to be, but there was no question about his place in our social structure. He was the Elder. He wasn't in charge of anything, such was the province of the master and mistress, but everyone treated him with respect. Even the master and the mistress. Even my playmates, and my sister, and I instinctively deferred to him. At the time I didn't clearly understand why that should be so. He had no authority over us, and even if he had, we were an immature and disrespectful bunch of children. But not to the Elder.

Although my playmates treated the Elder with respect, their relationship went no further. The Elder spoke to us all, but my playmates were never interested in what he had to say. They did not understand him.

For some reason, it was different for my sister and I. We would listen to him and, at first, we did not understand him either, but as time went on, we understood more and more and became ever more captivated. Just like between Goldie and I, we both found that we could understand more of the Elder's stories if we gazed directly into his eyes as he told them. As we came to understand what he was saying to us, we learned that he was descended from the very first peoples to have inhabited the area where I grew up. It hadn't occurred to me that there might have been a time before people.

There was something beyond our growing ability to understand him, however. Looking back, I think now that my sister and I sensed in him something special, something desirable, something that seemed elusive and unreachable. It was more than knowledge, although he certainly had that in abundance. I think we sensed wisdom.

It was his stories that called out to my sister and I. We would gather around him at every opportunity when he was in the mood to tell us stories – which, to be fair, was most of the time. We would sit at his feet and listen as he told us stories. These were stories from the past, some from the very distant past, and they were filled with interesting characters and adventures.

As time went on, I began to perceive that each of the Elder's stories also contained knowledge, and very often a moral or some kind of wisdom. As the last two were of no interest to us at that age, it was a testament to the Elder's storytelling ability that we were drawn into the stories despite our growing awareness that he wasn't entertaining us, he was teaching us. By the time I knew this to be true, it was nowhere near enough to keep me away. I loved to hear his stories, and to watch them unfold in my mind's eye as each story was told.

The 'knowledge stories' told us about the environment in which we lived, and often focused on the different kinds of animals that surrounded us: birds, fish, deer, bears, and so on. Our instincts already told us which we could ignore, which we could hunt, and which to fear. He taught us to look deeper than that. The Elder's favourite stories involved the raven, which he identified as the creator of all things, the one that taught humans and animals alike to hunt. Above all, the raven was the most adventurous of beings.

Most of the Elder's stories took us into the relationships among the animals. In one story for example, the Elder described how wolves would hunt and kill the weaker members of a herd of deer. Without the weak to slow them down, the herd was then faster – and more nimble - enabling the bulk of the herd to better avoid predators of all kinds and therefore survive and reproduce. In this way both species could not only co-exist but benefit from each other. I liked stories like that.

My favourite stories, in fact, involved the wolves.

The wolves of the Elder's stories were mythological, of course. Even at a young age I understood that. Nevertheless, my imagination soared with the ebb and flow of the stories as the best of the wolves exhibited, not just great hunting abilities, but courage, strength, and loyalty. The Elder's stories also taught that wolves and humans are closely related to each other, and that humans and dogs actually descended from wolves long, long ago. In several of the very best stories, a wolf and a human were siblings and/or each other's best friend, and their adventures were strongly overlain by concepts like honour, wisdom, and destiny. These latter were new ideas for me, they sent my imagination racing.

When these stories were told I always wanted to be the wolf, of course, and as more and more of these stories were told they developed in me a yearning to have a destiny like the best of wolves. Like the best of wolves, I would be courageous, strong, loyal, wise, and honourable. The Elder surely intended something like this to happen, although I doubt that he'd have expected the depths to which such concepts would take root in my developing mind. Regardless, he was surely effective.

To this day, after all these years, I still strive to be like the best of the wolves in the Elder's stories. Even so, it's aspirational rather than real. That's because I'm not actually a wolf.

I'm told that I look like a wolf though, so perhaps I'm not so far removed after all.

You wouldn't be able to pronounce the name my parents gave me.

Our master named me Silver.

My sister Goldie and I spent so much time listening to the Elder's stories that, as time progressed, we eventually gained a better understanding of what our master and mistress (whose human names were Ross and Sally) were trying to communicate when they spoke to us. I don't mean their language, exactly, although we did learn quite a few of their words. It was more that we somehow understood more and more of the meaning of what they were trying to say to us.

*If, for example, one of them were to say: "Silver, go get your toy," I could understand that as "**Silver ??? get ??? toy**," because I understood those three words out of the five. This was not remarkable, as any of our other playmates would also have had the same understanding* *of this command.*

If, on the other hand, one of them were to say to the other: "The barometer is falling and I think we're in for a storm. I'm worried about it because we might get caught in a fierce downpour. I think we should take our raincoats with us and keep an eye on the weather while we're out in the fields," I might only recognize the words "storm" and "fields," but I would also have felt the apprehension conveyed and somehow understand the warning to be watchful of the weather. Our playmates would have caught the same two words and some sense of the emotion involved, but they would not have gained the other nuances. Goldie and I didn't know what to make of this, but it must have made our lives richer, more colourful in a sense, and it seems to have accelerated our learning of more and more of our human's words.

I think I was just about fully grown when Goldie and I learned that we could convey much more than growls, whines, and barks back to our humans. This came about quite unexpectedly but at a very important time.

Our master and mistress had begun to train us to join with other dogs in pulling a heavy thing made mostly of wood from trees. They called it a sled, and it was supported on long strips of wood called skis. Each of us would wear a harness connected to a central lead that was, in turn, connected to the sled. Then, working together, we could pull the sled over the snow even if it had things loaded on it and a human standing on the back of it. Pulling our share of the load was work, but it was also exhilarating to be part of a team, to be able to run, and to be able to get out and away from our familiar surroundings and out into wilder country.

Anyway, one day we were out with the master, pulling the sled. Goldie and I were positioned side-by side, as we had been promoted to the two positions immediately following the lead dog. This was a big step for us, but the lead dog was very experienced, demanding but even tempered, and all we had to do was watch him carefully and follow his lead. I thought that our run had gone very well, and we had clearly reached its limit and had turned around, back towards home. When we were part of the way back, our master decided to try following a game trail through the forest.

It was late in the day, and the sky was cloudy, so the light was poor. Maybe that contributed to the problem, but for whatever reason, when we came to a fork in the trail our master signalled for us to turn towards the right and take that path. Our lead dog seemed fine with this and began to pull in that direction, but Goldie suddenly flashed an image into my mind: this was not the path that led towards home. We both remembered being there before, and knew that the path to the right led off in almost exactly the wrong direction and would have led to an impassable ridge of rock that would have left us far from home, with darkness falling. Since my sense of direction, and of what lie ahead on each fork in the trail, matched Goldie's I sent a confirming image back to her.

Now what?

It was winter. It was cold. We both knew that we couldn't afford to take the wrong trail. Not knowing what else to do, we both dug our paws into the snow and refused to mush.

That wasn't fun. Our master started yelling at us, and the lead dog started barking and snapping at us, but we both had the strongest feeling that it was the left-hand path that would take us home. Caught between our senses and our duty to obey, we both stood there frozen, straining at our harnesses. This seemed to catch our master by surprise. He stopped yelling and stared at us, looking more puzzled than angry. It was as if he was trying to understand what was bothering us.

*Not knowing what else to do, Goldie and I simply stood there and stared directly at our master, trying to see into his eyes and to communicate the sense of danger we sensed. We tried to use our minds to project a sense of what we would say to him, if we could, which would have been: "***Not this way!***"*

Unbelievable as it may seem, he seemed to get the essence of what we were trying to communicate.

What an amazing thing, I thought.

To make a long story short, our master decided to try the fork that Goldie and I wanted to take, gave the appropriate instructions to our lead dog, and we made it home, safe and sound. Our master was good enough to recognize that we'd been right, and was very appreciative. Goldie and I were able to lounge in front of the big fireplace in the great house, and soak up the restoring warmth, water, food, and treats.

The master must have told the Elder about our adventure, because the next time we sat at his feet to listen, he told stories about the ancestry of dogs like Alaskan Malamutes, which was the humans' name for our family. The Elder taught us that we had a long heritage that spanned a multitude of generations, that we were descended from the Arctic Wolves, and that our ancestors were the original siblings and best friends of the very first humans. Those original wolves, the Elder taught, had the ability to communicate – or at least to be able to exchange understandings - with humans, as well as with other wolves.

I don't know about Goldie, but these stories inspired in me a desire to push the boundaries and see how far this communication thing with humans could be developed.

There was another sled-pulling trip with our master that was to have a life-long effect on me, and on my attitude towards water.

Once again, we were out with the master and working together to pull the sled. As before, Goldie and I were positioned side-by-side, and immediately following the lead dog. We'd had another good run and we had clearly reached its limit and had turned around, back towards home. When we were most of the way back there was a frozen river we had to cross. This we had done many times before, and I thought nothing of it beyond the fact that the pads on my paws didn't grip as well on ice as they did in snow. This caused a certain amount of slipping around, but I'd learned to keep my balance well enough to avoid running into any of my companions. What happened next was a complete surprise, however.

We were crossing a river when all of a sudden there was a tremendous 'crack' and the ice broke-up in large pieces, right underneath the sled. Almost immediately, the sled dropped right down into the water, dragging the whole dog team with it.

We'd almost made it across the river, and the lead dog, and Goldie and I had even managed to reach the shore when we felt a massive pull from behind us. As I yelped and turned my head, I could see that the ice had broken open, the sled was twisted upwards in to the air, and some of it was already well underwater. Despite our best efforts to move forward, the pull on our harnesses was too great to overcome and we were all pulled back from the shore, back across the ice, and back toward the hole. It was terrifying.

Our master had jumped off the sled and started cutting the other dogs free, but it took a long time. By the time he got to Goldie and I, we'd been repeatedly pulled under the water and each time had to struggle up to get our heads beck up above water so we could breathe. He worked on Goldie's harness before mine, and he was helping to keep her nose and mouth above water at the same time. I approved but, if anything, that made it worse for me, as I was repeatedly being either dragged or pushed under water for longer and longer periods of time.

I don't know how anyone can describe the feeling of drowning without actually experiencing it. My feelings were a combination of horror and panic. I had an overwhelming urge to open my mouth and take in air, but I knew that to open my mouth would only bring in water. My chest and throat would spasm in a desperate, instinctive attempt to get air. At the same time, I would have to clamp my mouth shut in a similarly desperate attempt to prevent me from inhaling water. These roughly equal but opposite forces had me heaving back and forth at the same time as a sense of panic rose up in me. It... was... horrible.

I kept struggling, of course, and I'm sure my eyes were wild with fright, but I knew that our master was doing his best to save us, so I tried to avoid panicking long enough for him to get Goldie and I free. Eventually, and just about when I'd been so starved for air that I was on the verge of blacking out, he got my harness cut and gave me a huge push up onto the ice.

All I could do, for a while, was lie there taking in huge gulps of air.

A few minutes after that, and it was all over.

By the time our master had released the lead dog and dragged himself up onto the shore, our team had mostly calmed down and shaken ourselves out. After that, we all just walked home - shivering all the way. When we got there, our master and mistress were sufficiently worried about us that they let us all into the great room of the main house, wet fur and all, so we could curl up in front of their roaring fireplace.

What a contrast that was to the icy water in which we'd all nearly drowned!

Most of my companions shrugged the experience off. Maybe none of them had spent as much time fully immersed as I had. I don't know. What I do know is that the experience left me with a perpetual fear of drowning. I never forgot, I never shed the horror, and as I re-live these memories again, I find myself shuddering.

I never willingly went into the water again.

Now, I need to explain my relationships with two other humans that changed my world forever.

While growing up, I noticed that as others of our pack had become full grown and had learned to work as part of a team pulling sleds, then strangers would come and look them over. Sooner or later, one of the strangers would make some kind of arrangement with the master and mistress such that the stranger was to become their new master and they would go off with them, never to be seen again.

There was a day when this happened to me.

I'd been lounging on the roof of our family's small house when another stranger showed up to look over all of us that were young but full grown, of which we numbered five at that particular time. Our master didn't introduce him to me at first, only the other four, but the stranger didn't seem impressed with any of them for some reason and kept looking over at me and pointing. Initially, my master just shook his head, as if to say "no" but as they continued their discussion he eventually relented and brought him over to introduce us.

"Silver, this is Norm. Come down and say hello," my master said, by way of introduction.

I jumped down from my rooftop perch and padded over. The male named Norm held out his hand for inspection and I gave him a careful sniff and then looked deeply into his eyes. I didn't sense anything concerning in his scent, or his manner, or his mind, but I didn't find anything very interesting there either. As we stood there, Norm and my master continued what was obviously a prior conversation that had them both talking in animated fashion. I could tell that they were discussing sleds, sled-pulling, and sled racing, and I immediately sensed that they were kindred spirits – in sled racing at least.

I couldn't understand everything they were saying, of course, but when Norm spoke, I got an image of a sled racing through beautiful snow-covered country, a team of dogs, and- to my amazement – he clearly imagined me at the head of the team as lead dog.

That sounded interesting. I'd never been put in the lead position before, although I'd watched enough other lead dogs to have some understanding of the job.

Eventually the master, with some reluctance, seemed to reach an agreement with Norm. They shook hands, and then the master knelt-down by my head and said: "Silver, you're going to be going away with Norm here. He'll be your new master now."

And that was that.

I travelled to a new home with Norm in his 'truck' machine. The journey took many, many cycles of the sun and moon — more cycles than I have claws on my two front paws. Norm's home was not only far away but in a place of quite different geography. There were no mountains, for one thing, just hills. The waters were different, too. Instead of one huge body of undrinkable water — what my former masters had referred to as ocean — there were many smaller bodies of drinkable water, called lakes. Some of them were quite large, but nothing on the scale of the ocean. Also, the forests were quite sparse compared with what I was used to.

Norm's place was similar to that of my previous master and mistress except that everything was smaller. There were quite a few dogs already there, and I was given my own little house with a roof I could lounge on. I kind of liked having my own house, but it was lonely being away from my sister and parents. Not far away from Norm's place was a whole community of human houses. Norm and the other humans referred to it as Radium City.

As a master, Norm was fine. His voice and manner often sounded rough, but he treated his dogs well. The other dogs were fine too. There was no real pack leader when I arrived, but I think there must have been one before. The other dogs accepted me and I them. We had time to play, time to lounge, and then there was the sledding.

If there was one thing we had in common, it was the enjoyment of sledding. Norm dropped me into the leader's traces right from the start. None of the other dogs did more than grumble a bit, and I was somewhat surprised to find that leading worked out just fine. I had to be vigilant, and keep my team-mates in line, but this didn't usually require more than sharp barks, the odd growl, and the occasional nip. I had no trouble at all in understanding Norm's commands as the musher. I didn't understand all of his words, of course, but I always seemed to be able to read the image in his mind, so the two of us were almost always in perfect alignment. Our sled runs, as a result, were amazing fun.

It was through Norm that I was introduced to a way to explore the larger bodies of water without getting wet. Norm called it a boat. In the warmer months, when the water was ice-free, Norm would take people out – one or two at a time – across the big lake to places where they could hunt for larger animals or fish. For some reason, he fell into the habit of bringing me along on such trips. Although I was initially nervous of the possibility of falling into the water, or of the boat sinking, my fears turned out to be groundless, and I learned to enjoy the experience. As the boat made its way over the water, I found that I could observe the changing scenery, smell the complex smells brought by the wind, and relish the freedom of being able to do it all from the comfort of the boat. All without having to do any work!

One day, when Norm went out on the lake, it was just the two of us. After some time, we reached land and Norm pulled the boat up on shore. From there we went for a walk that brought us to a hill, a hill with a cave.

It was obvious that the cave had been made by humans. The floor was smooth and flat, the roof and walls looked un-natural, and it had the smell of machinery. Norm had brought a light with him, and we walked deep inside. Norm called it a mine.

It was cool and damp in the mine. From somewhere up ahead I could hear water dripping. Eventually, the floor changed to wood - something like my master had in his house. Just beyond that, the mine widened and came to an end. Norm took off his outer layer of clothing and hung it from a piece of rock that stuck out from one wall, then he sat down. He seemed to be thinking, so I sat down beside him and curled up to rest.

After a few minutes, my head instinctively popped up as I heard noises coming from the entrance to the mine. I smelled a familiar scent: it was the human named Jim. Jim lived in the same general area that we did, he also had a boat, and I had observed that he spent a lot of his time out on the lake taking other humans – mostly males – out on the big lake.

Jim, I did not like. Until now, I've described relationships with humans that varied from good, such as with Norm, to great, such as with my former master and mistress, to reverent, such as with the Elder. All of my senses and abilities that came together in my head to produce the welcome, colourful impressions of these people, turned against me with certain other humans. Jim is an example. From my very first meeting with him my senses were in conflict. My eyes provided information, but nothing negative or concerning. My ears heard a pleasant voice, and again, nothing in the parts of Jim's speech that I could understand caused me concern. If anything, his conversations with Norm seemed to be very amicable. All of my other senses, however, rebelled at the notion of any kind of contact with Jim. I sensed… a brooding anger, resentment even. Against what, I have never known. I sensed… a darkness in his mind that worried me.

When Jim came into view and greeted Norm, they talked for a while. As nearly as I could judge, they were talking about searching for something valuable. The images in both of their minds seemed to be of a kind of shiny metal that could be broken out of a special kind of rock.

Although prudence advised caution and an outward display of indifference, if not polite companionship, I did not – and to some extent still do not – have enough control over my instincts to prevent my ears from flattening back and a low growl from emerging. This, of course, was promptly noticed by both Norm and Jim, with the former instructing me to back-off and the latter taking a step back and keeping his distance from me. For my part, I did my best to stay close to Norm and be alert for trouble.

When Norm and Jim's conversation concluded, they began walking out of the mine. When we emerged into the light, we walked down to the water. There, beside Norm's boat, was Jim's larger boat. Jim climbed into his boat and motioned for Norm to join him. Then, some kind of argument began, in which they raised their voices and waved their hands, with Jim pointing at me. The core of it seemed to be that Jim wanted Norm to get into the boat without me.

Norm then knelt down beside me and said something like: "Silver… boat… stay." He looked directly into my eyes as he spoke, and the image I received in my mind was that he was trying to tell me that he would come back for me. Then, reminding me to "stay," he got into Jim's boat and they headed out on the lake.

As ordered, I curled up by the shore and waited for Norm to return, but I never saw Norm alive again.

It was a long wait, and when the sun had moved across a significant portion of the sky, I trotted up the big hill with the mine in it, so I could get a better view. From my vantage point on top of the hill, I could also see that the land I was on was surrounded on all sides by water. I was trapped!

Where was Norm?, I wondered.

I know now that I could have tried swimming. I've seen other dogs and wolves swim in water, but at that age I didn't know whether I could swim or not. That, added to my horror of water, plus the fact that I couldn't actually see land anywhere - even from the top of the hill - made me think I should stay put.

For most of the rest of the day, I went back to the top of the hill and resumed my vigil, watching for Norm's return. Although there was no food, there was water, and I occasionally trotted down to the lake for a drink. By the time the sun was beginning to disappear into the distance it was becoming cool and windy, so I went back into the mine and curled up near Norm's clothing, hoping that he would return.

When the sun rose into the sky again, I went out and back down to the water. There was still no sign of Norm. Once again, I went to the top of the hill to watch and wait for Norm. When the sun was high in the sky, I went back to the mine and curled up for a nap near Norm's clothing.

I was woken from my nap by the sounds of someone coming into the mine. There were flashes of light from a hand-held light, and I caught the scent of an unfamiliar human female. She had an interesting scent. Not sensing any danger, and curious about this stranger, I stayed curled-up where I was and waited.

As the woman came slowly forward, I began to sense fragments of her thought. She was being careful, she was searching for something, and I began to detect indications of compassion and a fine mind. As I remained curled up, with my ears up and pointing forward, and my nose doing the same, my sense gathering was interrupted by a loud "crack - snap" sound of wood breaking. At almost the same instant, the woman came into my sight and gave out a sharp "Eeek!" sound as the floor below her gave way and most of her dropped out of sight into a large hole that had opened-up in the floor.

As I blinked in surprise, I saw that she had not completely fallen into the hole. Her head and arms were visible at the top edge of the hole. The rest of her body must have been hanging straight down in to the hole because she was trying to use small movements of her arms to prevent herself from falling completely.

I'm sure she didn't see me yet, that came later, but I could see straight into her eyes. That, combined with the intensity of her thoughts, gave me startlingly clear impressions of her thoughts.

She was afraid, trying to avoid panic, and trying to control her breathing. At the same time, she was trying to figure out how to escape the hole. This reminded me so much of my experience when I was dragged into the water when my former master's sled fell through the ice, that I felt strong surges of empathy and sympathy for her.

Continuing to watch – and sense - the drama before me, I was fascinated by her attempts to stay in control of her emotions and think her way out of trouble. My eyes, ears, nose, and mental perceptions all combined to give me a deep understanding of her efforts. Although my eyes could only see a small amount of her, I could sense through her mind's eye her efforts to find supports for her feet or other parts of her body, trying to find something she could grab with her hands, and trying to shift here self to one side or the other, but nothing worked. It wasn't long before I detected new emotions from her: she was getting tired.

She called "Help!" several times, so there was apparently another human outside the mine somewhere, but whoever it was, they never came. I could tell that she was continuing to tire.

There was something compelling about this person, I sensed intelligence, persistence, a spirit of adventure, and a spirit of purpose about her. I was suddenly reminded of the Elder's stories of the first human and the first wolf and I realized with a start that I could not just lie there and let her fall, possibly to her death.

At the same time as I sensed that she was bracing herself to try something desperate, I leapt to my paws. In two bounds, I was right in front of her, and I called out: "Grruph, grruph, grruph."

That got her attention! She was so startled that she nearly lost her balance on the edge of the hole. I could sense that I had unintentionally frightened her, but she recovered herself quickly.

I stared straight onto her eyes, and gave a couple of neutral barks, trying to get her attention. When I could see her examining me with a puzzled, but wary, look on her face I lowered my shoulders and put my head down on the rock floor, between my front legs and paws, in the universal sign – among dogs and wolves at least – of non-aggression.

Although this behaviour continued to mystify her, she did get the message that she needn't be afraid of me. She also looked straight into my eyes. That was the opportunity I wanted, and I tried to send her an image of grabbing the loose fur at the back of my neck, so I could try to help pull her out.

"You ??? ??? me," she said out loud. I don't know all the words she said, but I got the message of amazement and almost amused disbelief.

As we continued to share our gaze, I kept trying to send an image of her grabbing my fur so I could help her get up and over the edge of the hole. At the same time, I received clearer impressions from her mind that I have ever received from any human. It was amazing!

Although I knew that she was having trouble believing what was happening to her, she was tiring rapidly now and I could feel the exact moment when she decided that she had no other options, and nothing to lose by taking the risk of grabbing me. And that's exactly what she did. She slowly moved one arm over to me and lifted her hand up and on top of my neck. At this, I gave a sniff and kept staring at her, so she grabbed my fur and moved her other arm slightly in preparation for a push upward. At this, I gave a snort, meaning "about time," braced myself, and lifted my head and shoulders. She held on tight, so I next started to shift my body back a bit.

I could sense that she was fully with me now, and the two of us alternately shifted this way and that so she could use her free arm to rise up a bit. That allowed me to lower my head again and use my jaws to grab her clothing. Now that we each had a solid grip on the other, I did my best to back up while she worked at levering more and more of her body up and over the edge of the hole. It wasn't long before we got her upper body over the edge, and after that she was able to swing the lower part of her body up and over the edge.

I could feel waves of relief coming from her, as she let go of my fur, rolled onto her back, and lay there taking in large breaths. After a moment she rolled over onto her side, looked straight into my eyes and said, "Thank you. I ??? know ??? came from ??? thank you!" I only got some of the words, but it was very clear what she was thinking.

When she got her breath back, and her heart rate had slowed, it was interesting to watch what she did next. Rather than quickly leave, she carefully stepped around the big hole and examined our surroundings. She found, and seemed to be very interested, in Norm's clothing. She even smelled it and I could sense her identify the scent as belonging to someone she knew. It reminded her of a home she had been in. Her mental image of that home, and the home's smells, was so clear that I knew without doubt that she had identified the clothing's owner as Norm.

This was amazing. Not only was this the first human I'd ever encountered that used all of her senses, but she had identified the clothing's scent as belonging to Norm! A woman with wolf-like qualities!

Next, she recovered her light and used it to carefully examine the hole. Again, I was able to follow the gist of her thoughts. These ranged from curious, as she investigated, to surprise and anger, as she realized that she had fallen into a trap. This produced so many questions in her mind that I could no longer isolate and identify any of them, but one thing came through clearly: she was determined to find out more. Accordingly, she started walking back out of the mine. Curious, and strangely attracted, I followed along.

Exiting the mine, the woman walked around the hill until she came across a man sitting near the second mine. It was Jim!

Jim seemed surprised to see the woman, and as they talked to each other I sensed frustration and suspicion in her. At some point their conversation came around to me, and I heard my name mentioned.

"Him ??? Silver ??? Norm ??? sled dogs," I heard Jim say.

The woman and Jim continued to talk, and I eventually heard Jim say her human name: Alex. Then they went around everywhere, as if searching for something. I heard Norm's name mentioned so often that I decided they must be searching for him. I thought that was strange, since Norm had gone away with Jim to begin with. My suspicions of Jim deepened.

As they searched around, I more or less followed along, keeping an eye on them. When they reached Jim's boat, it was clear that they were planning to leave. I sensed that Alex wanted to bring me with them. I would have stayed and hoped for Norm's return, but I was reluctant to leave Alex, partly because she fascinated me, and partly because I felt the need to protect her from Jim. The final thing was my sense that she was actually intent on finding Norm. This gave us a common cause, so when she turned to me and said: "Come Silver, ??? boat!" I simply, walked down to the shore, gave Jim a glance, and jumped into the boat.

As Jim directed the boat out across the big lake, Alex offered me some of her food. Feeling starved, I didn't hesitate, and the food quickly vanished. I took the fact that she was willing to share her food with me as another good sign. The rapid infusion of food made me sleepy and, not sensing any immediate action or threat, I curled up on the seat behind Alex and dropped-off to sleep.

When it was time to leave the boat, Alex signaled for me to join her in a truck like Norm's, but which was clearly hers. I hopped in. She drove me home, but there was no one there. Not Norm, and not even any of the other dogs. I thought that was strange, and so did Alex: I could sense that she felt suspicious. I stayed with her as she drove to where other humans often collected, and to where Norm's boat was tied, and finally to where Alex lived. She let me explore her house, and as I sniffed around, I realized that I found her scent strike some kind of chord in me. Something about being with her felt right and, since we were both looking for Norm, I decided that I would continue to stay with her if I could.

When the sun went down, she went for a long walk around the area of the human's houses and I stayed close. I enjoyed being with her and I sensed that she felt appreciative of my company. After that, she tried to leave me outside for the night, but I made it clear that I was unhappy with that idea. I wanted to be inside with her. I had a feeling that I should be protecting her, so I definitely didn't want to be left outside. Fortunately, she relented and let me in, and I lost no time in establishing myself at the foot of her bed for the night.

When the sun next rose, Alex went around the area again, but running this time. That was more fun!

I found that I could run off on my own from time to time, to investigate interesting smells, then run back to catch-up with her, accompany her for a while, and then head off again to other interesting spots. I enjoyed being with her, and I sensed that she enjoyed my company as well. Later, I followed her to various places where she talked to other people, and I sensed that she was still on the hunt for Norm.

For more rising and settings of the sun I followed Alex as she talked to more and more humans in her search for information about Norm. At one point, she looked at me and said: "??? Silver, ??? go visit ??? more ???" In her mind I sensed a trip over waters and more caves or mines: she was planning to search further away for Norm.

"Grruph," I said.

"Yes, we ??? be careful ..." she said. I agreed.

We took one more boat trip out on the big lake to see a different cave, or mine, this time. This time, working together, we found Norm – but Norm was dead. I sat down with a low whine. Poor Norm, *I thought.*

"I??? sorry Silver," Alex said, as she did her own checks to verify that Norm was dead. Then she sat back on her heels and gave me a hug, saying "I??? afraid Norm ??? gone."

Then she did a strange thing. Alex turned Norm's body over and continued to check him over as if looking for something. I sensed that she was trying to discover the cause of his death. When she found a large wound at the back of Norm's head, I could tell that she had found out what she wanted. Anger radiated from her mind. She clearly believed that some other human had killed Norm. I didn't fully understand what she was thinking, but her mind radiated sadness, anger, and an overwhelming desire to find the killer. What surprised me was that, although she was angry, she wasn't thinking about vengeance – she was thinking about justice.

Justice! That was the word I'd been looking for. The Elder had told us stories to illustrate the human concept of justice, and the special class of ancient warriors that were seekers of justice. These special warriors were often aided by their wolf siblings. Now I began to perceive Alex's destiny ... and maybe mine too. We could be seekers of justice and protectors of the weak, like the special warrior-wolf teams of the long past.

What a thought...

On the next rising of the sun, I went with Alex as she met with various humans in different structures. Along the way, we stopped at Norm's home, which was previously mine as well. Alex spent quite a bit of time searching around Norm's home and seemed to find several things that interested her. I could tell that she still had a lot of questions in her mind.

Some of the other sled-pulling dogs had returned, and I visited with them while Alex was busy in Norm's home. When she emerged, carrying some things that she had found, she stood by her truck with the door open and looked directly at me. I knew what she was thinking: did I want to stay with the other dogs or to continue along with her. That was an interesting question. My former master was dead and I had not been given a new master yet. Did that mean I was free? Did I want to be?

I searched my feelings. I wanted to be with her. I didn't know where it would lead, but there was no doubt in my mind. I felt that my place was with her. I raced over and jumped right in. She didn't say anything, but her mind radiated surprise and pleasure.

We visited more humans that day. Sometimes I was able to go into their structures with her, while other times I had to wait outside. As a result, Alex seemed to learn new things, but I didn't. Except for one thing. Other humans seemed to refer to Alex as a "Mountie." I didn't know what that was although, when the word was used, people seemed to be thinking about justice, and Alex seemed to be thinking about helping others. This matched my impressions during the previous cycle of the sun.

On the next rising of the sun we visited more humans, the most interesting of which was Ruby. This was the Ruby that had been a friend of Norm's and of our entire pack of sled-pulling dogs. I wasn't allowed into Ruby's place, but by staying near the entrance I was able to follow bits and pieces of their meeting. As Alex and Ruby spoke to each other, I heard Norm's name mentioned often and it seemed that Ruby was talking about her friendship with Norm. Alex seemed mostly to be sympathetic.

Then I heard my name being mentioned several times, and Ruby seemed to be explaining something about Norm and me. Something Ruby said made Alex's mind jump with a start of excitement and pleasure, and the two of them seemed to reach an agreement about something.

When Alex came out of Ruby's home, her mind was racing so much that I had trouble identifying her thoughts. There was surprise, relief, pleasure, and she was thinking about the future. Then I had it! She was imagining her future, and all of her mental images of her future had me in them with her.

I wondered whether she had just become my new master, but that's not what was in her mind. In her mind she saw me more as a . . . **friend***.*

I've already explained that my knowledge of human words was improving with every cycle of the sun, but still very limited, so when a human spoke to me — even a human that I'd come to know fairly well — I would only get fragments of their speech. I would hear them as understandable words separated by a kind of mumbling. It was only by adding the understandable words to the human's mental images that I was able to understand the thoughts that were behind them. So, what I'm going to tell you next contains words that I understand now but did not at the time they were spoken to me. Even then, however, there was no mistaking Alex's meaning.

As she stepped out of Ruby's place she stopped, adopted a serious body position and tone of voice and said:

"Silver, I think this is the beginning of a beautiful friendship!"

6 CHILKOOT AFTERMATH

The U.S. National Park Service had a backcountry ranger station at Sheep Camp, so the Guide leaders decided to take everyone the mile and a half down the trail to Sheep Camp so they could report in and get help. Once they arrived at Sheep Camp, it took a while to find anyone to report to.

The two park rangers had been out surveying the extent of the damage from the rockslide, and they were relieved to see them - but concerned about Lucy. Apparently, there had been no hikers aiming for the summit ahead of them, but another group had been camped behind them at Canyon City. This other group had turned back to Dyea as soon as they'd heard the roar of the rockslide and seen the huge dust clouds, and all of them had made it back safely, without further incident.

The Parks Canada Wardens on the Canadian side were now holding back hikers from crossing the summit until the slope was judged to be safe, and until at least some of the covered trail could be restored. The only outstanding concern had been for the patrol of Girl Guides, which now focused to the case of the one missing Guide, Lucy.

Although the patrol naturally wanted to stay and help search for Lucy, the rangers convinced them that they had done everything that they could, and that it was time to leave the search to the professionals.

It was decided that the leaders would take the patrol back

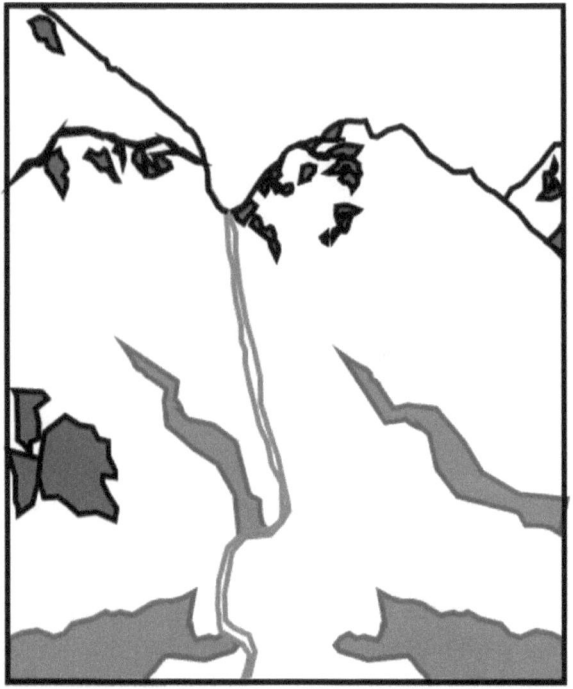

Beyond Sheep Camp

to Skagway and await further developments. Having provided the rangers with a description of Lucy, the Guides set out on the rather disheartening hike back. Although they had risen early, at 06:30, it was now well past noon, meaning that they would have to camp one more night on the way back. As they set out on the trail two thoughts were uppermost in their minds:

I hope they find Lucy! and
I hope she's OK.

Meanwhile, the two park rangers had radioed in a situation report and advised their base that they were going to try to retrace the guides' original escape route in hopes of finding Lucy. This took the rest of the afternoon so that, by the time they had returned to the backcountry ranger station to report their lack of success, it was too late in the day for anyone to do any further searching.

That evening, the Chief Ranger decided that it was time for a better organized and more comprehensive search and started making calls for help from other agencies in Skagway. All of the local emergency service organizations, including police and fire, immediately committed to sending personnel, as did the Alaska State Troopers. Parks Canada had immediately volunteered some Canadian park wardens but, being on the other side of the now-blocked Chilkoot Pass, they would be delayed by having to drive around the mountains to Skagway.

The U.S. Park Service itself had the necessary supporting equipment in storage just outside the Skagway townsite because, sadly, this kind of thing happened all too often in a wilderness park. The local flight-seeing helicopter company immediately agreed to make two of their four helicopters available (the other two were grounded for repairs). Although each would carry a "spotter," their priority task would be to ferry equipment up to Sheep Camp, where the command centre would be established.

The search personnel would meet at dawn the next morning for a briefing, after which everyone would have to hike up the Chilkoot Trail just like everybody else did.

For the rest of the evening all they could do was prepare themselves and wait.

There is a certain amount of excitement involved in participating in a rescue mission, but every one of the searchers-to-be, whether amateur or professional, went to sleep that night thinking some version of:

I hope she's OK.

Laurie Schramm

7 SKAGWAY AND A CALL FOR HELP

The third significant Skagway event occurred on our second day there. While Silver and I were exploring Skagway's downtown area. Having spent most of the morning wandering around the town, I'd been sitting out on the front porch/deck of a coffee shop with Silver when I heard my name called.

"Constable Houston?" said a voice.

Looking up, I saw a medium-sized, middle-aged man that immediately reminded me of James Arness the actor in the popular television series *Gunsmoke*.

"Yes?"

"I'm George Carter, the Chief of Police here in Skagway. I just wanted to meet you and say hello."

"Alex Houston," I replied standing up and offering my hand to shake. "How is it that you know my name?"

"Welcome to small-town America, Alex. Ross and Sally Peake are friends of mine, and they couldn't help talking about the red-haired woman Mountie they'd met and the fact that Silver had become a police dog. They were so proud of Silver, and so pleased to see him again, that I hope you won't mind if they talked a lot more about Silver than they did about you?"

Laughing, I said "Not at all. Would you like to join me in a cup of coffee?"

"Don't mind if I do," George replied, as he took a seat at my table. "Now then, I was pleased to hear about Silver here, but if a woman Mountie is a rarity, then you must be just about the only one that's also a dog handler!"

"Right on both counts," I supplied. "I was kind of a pilot project for the Force, but an entire troop of women Mounties graduated near the end of 1975 plus two more troops of women last year. With nearly a hundred women in the Force I'm not so unique any more, although I'm still the only woman dog handler in the Force… so far, anyway."

For his part, George explained that he'd started out as a U.S. Marine but that after a while he'd wanted a change and had joined the Alaska State Troopers. That also worked out for a period of time, but then he'd switched again – this time to the quieter life of a small-town police chief. That led him into some stories about the challenges of policing a small town that is normally isolated and quiet but that, in tourist season, mushrooms to several times its normal population.

George Carter

"Now we have cruise ships coming in as well. At least two at a time coming in every three or four days!" he'd concluded.

As we continued to chat, I explained how Silver and I had chanced to meet and eventually become friends and partners and that, having learned that he'd been born in Skagway, I'd come to learn more about his origins, which had led to meeting Ross and Sally. I also mentioned that I was thinking of backpacking the Chilkoot Trail with Silver.

George highly recommended hiking the famous Chilkoot Trail, and emphasized that it was best hiked in the same direction as the original prospectors. That is, beginning near Dyea, going up over the pass and into Canada near the summit, and then down to eventually meet the highway. He also warned me that it can be rough going, and to be careful at the higher elevations where, even in the summertime, hypothermia was a serious risk. His advice was to go talk to the park rangers first for advice, and since I'd have to register with them to hike the trail anyway.

After George had taken his leave of us, Silver and I continued strolling around town. The U.S. had just created the Klondike Gold Rush National Historic Park the previous year[14] and they had built a great visitor centre right downtown in the centre of Skagway. The park rangers were extremely friendly and helpful when I explained that I wanted to hike the Chilkoot Trail, and they fussed over Silver a lot – which endeared them to him as well. We left well supplied with advice, trail guides, and topographic maps. The local stores were well prepared for backpacking tourists as well, so we were fully outfitted in next to no time at all.

Notwithstanding my little bit of running around, my first two days in Skagway had been filled with fresh air, beautiful scenery, and wonderful people. It was all so relaxing - especially after our most recent adventures in Nova Scotia[12], and I was starting to daydream about just hanging around and relaxing forever...

I really should have known better than to even think thoughts like that. I was sitting back, relaxing with Silver on the front porch of Ross and Sally's house when a rugged-looking police truck pulled up – it was George.

***

"Hi George," I offered, when he came up to the porch. "Here to see Ross and Sally?"

"No, I'm actually here to see you," he said. That got my antennae twitching.

"What's up?"

"Did you hear about the rockslide up on the Chilkoot Trail yesterday morning?"

"Yes, I did. Ross was just telling me about it. Was anyone hurt?"

"Well, that's kind of the thing. You see there's a young girl missing. Seems a bunch of Girl Scouts were backpacking the trail together when the slide started. The girls were quite a ways down the mountain from the slide, but they were right in line with it so they immediately scattered. When the slide ended and the dust settled, they collected themselves up and found that one of their group was missing."

"Uh oh."

"Uh oh is right. They searched for her but couldn't find her so they eventually went back to a backcountry ranger station and reported in. The rangers there sent them down the rest of the way to town while they went out to search for her themselves. They couldn't find her either."

"What do you think happened?"

"I don't know. She probably ran off somewhere and either had an accident or is just lost in the woods."

"Could she have been caught in the slide itself?" I asked, thinking how horrible that could be.

"It's possible, but according to the rangers, the slide had lost most of its energy by the time it reached the girls, so it would have been more like a dust cloud with some rocks rolling around – nothing that could have covered or buried a person. We think she's out there somewhere, hurt or lost," he paused for a moment of thought, "or both."

I was pretty sure I knew what was coming now. "So, I imagine the rangers conducted a more careful search today?"

"That's right. The Chief Ranger put out a call for help last night. This morning they had two helicopters ferrying supplies up the trail, while a horde of volunteers hiked in to do another search. Between the rangers, police, and fire volunteers they had about as many searchers as they could properly use in that area and they did a careful grid search throughout the whole day and… nothing. That means three failed searches in a row, the two quick and dirty searches made by the leaders and then two of the rangers yesterday, and then the full-out grid-search all day today, and none of them found a damn thing!"

"So, if she's still alive, then she's been out there for a day and a half, and now she'll have a second overnight to deal with. I take it that you're planning one more search tomorrow, and you want Silver and I to come?"

"That's right too. We're worried that time is running out on us. Will you do it?"

Now where had I heard that before?

"Of course we will, but I have to tell you that the odds are not going to be very good."

This prompted Sally, who had been listening through the front-screen door to step out and exclaim: "But I've heard of bloodhounds that can follow a trail after several weeks!"

"I've heard stories like that too, but I really doubt that there is much truth in them. I'm not really an expert on tracking. I can tell you that I have heard some believable stories of police dogs being able to track things after two or three days, but I have an uneasy feeling that that's been under ideal conditions."

"Oh," said Sally, disappointed.

"I just don't want to get anyone's hopes up," I continued. "We won't be searching under ideal conditions. It hasn't rained in the past two days, so that's a blessing. On the other hand, it's not just the time that has passed, we've now had all those hordes of searchers trampling everything down and adding their own scents on top of everything. There's another thing, too… Silver and I have practised tracking people but that's not our specialty. Silver's real training was for explosives."

Sally sighed. "So, it's hopeless then?"

"Oh no, it's not hopeless. Not yet, anyway. We'll go give it a try. Only Silver will know if the girl's scent is still present, so we'll have to trust him on this one. I'm just saying the odds are not good, not good at all." Then, turning back to George, "I'll have to call this in to Ottawa, but we'll do whatever we can to help you." Then, to Sally: "Can I borrow your phone to make a collect call?"

"Of course, but will you be able to get hold of him this late? With the three-hour time-zone difference it will be past midnight in Ottawa."

"I can get a message in any time of the day or night, but there's no telling how long it will take to get an answer back, or what they'll think about it all. I don't know how this cross-border stuff works, but we can count on my boss. He'll either give me an official OK, or he'll know that I'm just going to do it anyway and give me some advice on whether there's a way to do it without getting fired. But just so you know, we're going out with George here no matter what."

"He'll support you," chimed in George, "he won't have any choice."

I just stared at George, knowing there was more to come.

"Didn't I mention it before? She's Canadian!"

"No, you didn't mention that before," I said, looking at him narrowly. "I thought you said they were Girl Scouts?"

"My mistake, they were Canadian Girl Guides. In Alaska we call them Girl Scouts." There was a pause, as George held my gaze for a moment before relenting. "OK, it was a small test."

I raised an eyebrow. "A test?"

He didn't flinch. "Look Alex, I like you, but I don't really know you. Now that things have turned serious, and the going may get tough, I like to know what kind of people I'm dealing with. So yes, a small test."

"Fair enough, I suppose" I said, thinking about it. I wasn't impressed with his 'small test,' but I supposed that he was under stress and worried about who he could count on. I was a stranger, after all, so I decided to let it pass, and simply added: "Let's make the call."

So, I called the phone number that I knew would be constantly monitored, 24 hours per day, and the duty officer in Ottawa carefully took my message to Staff Sergeant Bob Simpson, my boss.

As it happened, I received a call back within fifteen minutes, while George was still there. It was Bob himself.

I briefly explained what had happened, and what I was planning to do. Bob asked a few more questions, gave me some advice, and signed off.

"Permission granted," I said to everyone, "but only if it's clear that I'm volunteering, and George here has to send him a formal request in writing. Since I'll be back on duty, I also have be in uniform."

George reacted instinctively. "Bureaucratic red tape!"

"It's OK," I counseled. "We can count on my boss. Besides, he has his troubles too. He'll have to run this through the Department of External Affairs, and who knows what other departments. If you send in an official-sounding request that will help him. In an emergency, I think they can just grant us the approval and sort out the paperwork later."

"Besides," I concluded, "Silver and I will come with you no matter what they say. If you send the request in by Telex first thing in the morning, you'll get something positive but cautious back from Bob right away. If the bureaucracy gets upset, we'll be out on the trail before anyone can order us to stop – OK?"

"Do you even have your uniform with you?"

"Sure, I always have my tactical uniform in my truck because I never know when we'll be called out on something…" I paused for a moment. "Of course, I don't have my gun with me. I didn't want to bring it across the border, so I left it back in Whitehorse for safekeeping. I'd planned to pick it up again after we leave Alaska."

"That was probably wise. We're pretty relaxed about guns here in Alaska, but it can get sticky at the border crossing. The feds can be a real pain in the ass sometimes…" Then, realizing what he had just said, "No offense."

"None taken, I know what you meant."

"I thought you'd most likely have left your gun on the other side, so I brought you one that I'd like to give you."

I raised my eyebrows at that. "Do you think I need a gun?"

"Probably not, but I'll feel better. Call it a matter of professional courtesy," and with that he reached into a briefcase he'd been carrying and brought out a Smith & Wesson, .357 Magnum-calibre revolver. This was a more powerful revolver than I was used to.

"Do you think I'm going to run up against Soapy Smith[3]?" I joked.

"Not Smith, Alex, bears!"

"Oh, OK," I said, abashed. "Will it stop a bear?"

"Probably not, but it will sure scare the hell out of one! I'm thinking of your dog here, as well. You shouldn't have any trouble in the wilderness with a well-trained dog, but sometimes a dog will go chase a bear, upset it, and then the bear follows the dog right back to its owner. I don't think that's going to happen in your case, but it's possible. Just don't make the mistake of getting caught between a mother bear and her cubs. If you do that, nothing will save you!"

"You're starting to make me think this isn't such a crazy idea after all," I murmured, looking the gun over. Then, looking back up, "You brought this for me, but you also wanted to try your 'small test.' Are you sure about this?"

"Absolutely. I thought I'd read you right when we met yesterday, but I needed to be sure. As far as the gun goes, we just switched out all of our .357 Magnum guns for .44 Magnum – just like in *Dirty Harry*[15] – making the older ones redundant, so I can spare it. Sometime, give one of the new .44 Magnums a try, they can penetrate the door of a truck!"

"OK then… thank you."

"Don't mention it," he said. "One more thing. Gun permits aren't generally required here in Alaska, but some people aren't very keen on foreigners carrying guns here. No offense."

"None taken, I can understand that."

"So, here's what we're going to do, I'm going to issue you a permit, two permits in fact." Then, rummaging through his briefcase, he pulled out two multiple-copy forms that he helped me fill out – one was a gun permit, the other a carry permit. When they were done, he signed them and tore off a copy of each for me to keep.

Just as he was about to leave, George paused and looked at me rather narrowly. "I may be just the small-town police chief you see before you, but I've served in larger organizations too. How is it that a young Constable such as yourself can call Ottawa in what for them is the dead of night, reach a phone number that is staffed around the clock, and then get a call back from your boss within less than an hour?"

"*Uh oh*," my inner voice said. "Just lucky, I guess," I said in what I hoped was an innocent-sounding evasion.

George was clearly no dummy, and he continued to look at me narrowly and let silence be his response.

"Look, I'm not supposed to advertise what branch of the Force I really work for. Can you ask me about it another time?"

"I think you just answered my question anyway," replied George, "but sure, as long as it doesn't interfere with you helping us with the search. Tell me about it some other time."

"Thanks George, I promise." As I said those words, it dawned on me, and not for the first time, that my days of usefulness with the Security Service were surely limited if I kept blabbing my identity all over the place. On the other hand, I needed George to trust me so I'd taken the risk.

After George left, I needed to get some sleep myself and said good night to Ross and Sally.

"Do you think you'll be able to find her?" asked Sally. She was repeating herself, but we were all worried now.

"Like I said, it's not very likely but we can't just abandon her. We'll just have to do the best we can and hope for the best."

"If she isn't injured, how many days can a person survive without food?"

This was more Ross's area of expertise than mine. "Most people should be able to survive for two weeks without food if they're healthy enough, and if it's not too cold," Ross explained.

"How cold does it get at night up there?" I asked.

"It varies a lot. In these mountains the weather can change quickly from great to terrible. Even now, in summer, we can get anything from wet, cold, and windy conditions, all the way to serious rain or snow storms and whiteouts. Why, I remember a few years ago we had an early fall blizzard snow come and hit us that began with gale-force winds, and ended by dropping five feet of snow on us!"

Sally and I must have looked a bit shell-shocked at this, so Ross relented. "Of course, the weather is actually very good right now," he quickly added. "The low tonight shouldn't be worse than 43 degrees and tomorrow's high is forecast to be 54."

"So, down to six degrees Celsius tonight," I said, mentally converting Ross's Fahrenheit temperatures into metric, "and up to twelve tomorrow."

"What's Celsius?" Ross asked.

"Canada is switching over to the metric system. All our weather reporting changed to metric three years ago, and most Canadians are still struggling with it."

"You don't seem to be having any trouble," Ross observed.

"You can blame that on the fact that I majored in chemistry in university, and all scientists use the metric system. So, I got a bit of a jump-start, you might say."

"Seems strange to me," Ross supplied. "Anyway, as long as the good weather holds, the big survival concern is going to be water. Your Lucy should be able to survive for two to three days without water, but three days is probably the limit."

"But she's already been out there for a day and a half!" Sally exclaimed.

"That's why we need to find her," I chimed in, and with that cheery thought we all went to bed.

8 LUCY

Lucy was strong-willed and intelligent. Both of these qualities were about to be tested. When the Guide Patrol had heard the rockslide, dropped their backpacks and started running, Lucy had dropped her pack, reached in to grab Max, and then hesitated.

Which way should I run? she wondered.

Although everyone else was running to the right of the trail, it sounded to Lucy like the dust cloud might be moving towards the right as it approached, so she naturally crossed the trail and ran to her left, heading for the trees on that side.

Everything seemed to be happening at once. The patrol leaders had tried to keep all of the girls in sight, and it was just bad luck that each leader had stopped to assist stumbling Guides at the same time, so that when they looked up Lucy had already run in the opposite direction. Seeing no other girls nearby or behind them, they naturally assumed everyone else was out in front and had made it to the forest, and they followed in turn. As the leaders and the bulk of the patrol ran onward, none of them noticed that Lucy was not with them.

Meanwhile, Lucy had tucked Max inside the front of her shirt and run in the opposite direction. Having started in that direction, and seeing that the ground ahead of her sloped upwards towards forest, she reasoned that the combination of trees and elevation gain might save her from the approaching rockslide.

When she reached the forest, she found a game trail that seemed to be heading in more or less the direction that she wanted to go, and she just kept on running for as long as she could hear the roaring sounds. This took her up and over the hill, deep into the forest. Although she didn't realize it at the time, this continued to lead her in a generally southwest direction.

Once deep into the forest, she couldn't hear the avalanche any longer, but assumed (incorrectly) that it was because the forest was dampening out the sound. She kept on running, pausing only now and again to catch her breath and make sure Max was safe. Occasionally she stumbled and fell, sometimes due to tripping over a rock or tree root, but then more often because she was running out of energy. During one such fall Max was thrown out of her shirt, but she'd been able to scoop him up and slip him back in place before he'd had a chance to scamper away.

One game trail led to another, but Lucy didn't really take much note of her surroundings, other than to make sure that there was still a fairly clear direction in which to run. Eventually, she stumbled upon a creek. Without conscious thought she followed the creek for a while, until it suddenly ended. Unsure what to do next, and too tired to do much of anything anyway, Lucy collapsed in a heap at the base of a very large and old-looking balsam fir tree.

She would have been surprised to learn that she had run for four miles.

Now that she was no longer running, and as she slowly caught her breath, Lucy moved Max from inside her shirt to sitting in her lap, and her mind turned to thinking about what to do next.

"Where is everyone?" she asked Max, rhetorically. She tried calling out, and yelling for help, but there was no reply. She hadn't seen or heard anyone since she started running, and she remembered now that she'd seen the others running in the opposite direction.

"Did everyone else run in the opposite direction?" she wondered, continuing to talk to Max. There was no way to know.

"Don't panic, Max" Lucy told both Max and herself. "Be prepared."

Some of her Guide training began to come back to her. Their motto, '*Be Prepared*,' meant to be ready, prepared in skills and knowledge for whatever might come. This remembrance provided some comfort and gave her a way to focus her thoughts. They'd been taught that taking time to stop and think was the best thing to do, so that's what she tried to do now.

Take a deep breath, stay calm, and think, she thought to herself. On previous hiking trips the Guides had been taught to find a safe place to stay put if they get lost.

"OK," she said to Max, "we're lost." That was a scary thought, but she pushed it to the back of her mind.

Looking around, she saw that she had collapsed under quite a nice old tree. It had lost its lower branches so that not only was she sitting on a nice piece of ground with a solid back support, her head was just underneath a very thick layer of large branches. It occurred to her that the tree would nicely protect from rain, should a storm come along.

"This might not be a bad place to stay put, Max."

The second thing they had taught the Guides to do was take stock of their surroundings and their gear. Unfortunately, she had lost her pack, having dropped it like everyone else when the rockslide had started. That was too bad, as her pack had held clothes, snacks, and water.

"Well Max, I like this tree, and there's water in the stream that I followed."

She next discovered that her Guides' lanyard and tie were both still around her neck! The tie was actually a fairly large, square piece of nylon fabric, like a bandanna. *That could be handy*, she thought.

Early in her Guiding years, Lucy had learned how to weave a Guide's lanyard. These lanyards could be worn comfortably around the neck and were fitted with a key ring, to which they were taught to attach a 'Swiss Army'-type knife, a small compass, and a whistle. Lucy's key ring also had a small waterproof container of matches attached to it. So, she did have some tools after all. That made her feel a bit better.

The woven lanyard was about four feet in length, when untied, and was made of four strands of fabric rope. After untying and unwinding it she had four lengths of rope. By tying three of them together she had 12 feet of rope, which she used as a makeshift leash, tying one end to the cat-harness that Max wore and tying a hand-loop in the other end. That left the fourth length of rope, which she set aside in case she needed it for something else.

Next, there were the tools that had been attached to the lanyard. Looking at the key ring, the orange whistle really stood out.

"That was silly of me, Max" she said, "there I was yelling away and tiring myself out when I should have been blowing my whistle!" She tried that next, blowing the whistle like she had been taught: three sharp blasts, wait a bit, three sharp blasts, wait, repeat…

There was still no response to her whistle-blowing, but she was starting to feel a little more in control of things and went back to thinking her way through her situation.

"OK, I can try the whistle again later," she decided, and went back to thinking about water and food.

She had water – that was good. Was it safe to drink it straight from the stream? She didn't know, but she hoped so. Walking back to the stream she saw that it was a bit silty.

"I wish I still had a cup or my water bottle," she said. She could have used her Guide hat as a cup, but had lost it somewhere. She didn't remember it falling off, but it was certainly gone. Still thinking, she absentmindedly began to untie her waterproof jacket, the arms of which had been used to tie it around her waist back when they'd been getting ready to resume their hike. As she untied the sleeves, she was still thinking about what she could use to hold water when she paused and realized what was in her hands.

"Sleeves!" she exclaimed, and immediately tied a knot in the end of one sleeve, plunged the whole jacket into the stream, and then brought it out being careful to use the tied sleeve as if it were a long, narrow pot. *Voilà*, she thought, *a makeshift pot full of water.*

Lucy decided she'd have to risk the quality of the silty water, but she wasn't sure about the silt. Dumping the water out she refilled the sleeve, but this time she covered the open end with her fabric tie-bandanna. This made it slow and trickier to fill, but she found that it did a good job of filtering-out most of the silt from the water. With her sleeve full of filtered water, she carefully took a long refreshing drink. That felt much better, and she held the water-filled sleeve out for Max to drink as well.

Her confidence growing, Lucy went back to thinking: *OK now, what about food?* She did have some food for Max. She had stuffed a package of cat treats into one of the breast-pockets of her uniform shirt and, taking it out, she shook out a single treat for Max to eat.

"We'll have to conserve your food I'm afraid," she said to Max.

"Now, what about me?" she mused. Looking around, she didn't see anything encouraging. She thought she had read somewhere that you can eat dandelions, but there were none around this late in the year. *Bears eat berries*, she thought, but she didn't see any berries either.

She knew not to try eating mushrooms, but she had no idea how to decide what plants might be safe to eat. She'd heard that a person could eat some kinds of bugs, but she didn't know which, and the idea of trying any made her feel faintly nauseous.

No bugs then, she thought. *What else?*

Looking back at the stream, she wondered about fish. She wasn't sure if she could catch a fish. There were minnows in the stream but she wasn't sure they'd be safe to eat. *I might try that though*, she thought, *if I get desperate enough*.

"What next, Max?" she wondered out loud. "Shelter and fire."

The fir tree would be her shelter, and she had matches so she could make a fire. Although she hoped someone would find her soon, Lucy decided that building a fire pit would help occupy her mind, so walking back to her tree she started collecting rocks to make a fire circle just in front of where she had previously been sitting. Finding suitable rocks was easy, as everywhere she'd been since the previous day seemed to be covered in rocks of various sizes.

Having built a nice-looking fire circle, Lucy tried a couple more series of blasts on her whistle, and then went to work collecting firewood. On family camping trips her parents had shown her the trick of looking for dead branches on trees, which were guaranteed to be nice and dry, and which could be easily broken off. Soon, she had an impressive-looking pile of kindling.

For her main fuel, Lucy wandered a bit – but not too far from her new campsite – picking up larger branches that had fallen from trees. Max didn't appreciate being on a leash, but he was surprisingly cooperative and behaved himself quite well, she thought.

There were lots of fallen branches, and Lucy soon had a big pile of larger-sized firewood. Some of the larger, and longer branches she dragged back to her tree, where she stacked them to make two rough walls. They actually looked quite nice, although the gaps between the branches were easily as large, if not larger, than the diameters of the branches themselves. "Those walls aren't going to block a lot of wind, Max" she said, "but maybe they'll at least reflect some heat from the fire."

As she and Max scouted the area looking for firewood, she kept an eye out for anything else that might be useful – like an old tin can she could heat water in, but without success. "Oh well," she said, "at least I can have water, fire, and a bit of shelter."

With her stockpiles of wood in place, Lucy decided she was worn out and, as she kneeled down by her fire circle, she noticed that the light was beginning to fade.

"Just in time, Max," she said. "It will be getting dark soon. I'm glad we started collecting wood when we did."

Lucy tried some more blasts on her whistle, but with no better success than earlier. With a loud sigh of resignation, she tied Max's leash to a low-hanging tree branch and set about trying to build a fire. This, at least, she knew how to do and she confidently set about selecting the tiniest of twigs and branches to use as tinder, then added layers of slightly larger branches, making loose log-cabin-style boxes of them in ever increasing sizes. Selecting some medium-sized branches, she laid these beside her to use in constructing a teepee-shape over the boxes, but later, once the first was started.

Next, it was time for the big moment and she carefully opened her container of matches and took one out. Holding the match so its head was pointing at the roughened surface along the side of the match holder, she gave the match a vigorous swipe.

"*Snap!*" the match promptly broke, right near the head.

"Rats," she said, and she took out another match and tried it again.

"*Snap*" went the next match, as it too broke without igniting.

"Arrgh," said Lucy, disgusted, and all too aware that a container of matches wasn't going to help if she broke them all.

"I know how to do this," Lucy said to Max.

Think, she said, to herself.

"Ok, Max" she said, "the broken matches will now be tinder," and she placed the broken matches inside her little box of kindling. Next, she took a few calming breaths and selected another match. This time, she held the match right next to its head – willing to risk burning her fingers if only she could get the match to light.

She was right on both counts. The match ignited and started to burn her fingertips. Easing her fingers back just a bit, she held the burning match down beside the broken matches and her kindling, and the two broken match heads immediately ignited as well, followed by a wisp of smoke from the smallest of her twigs of kindling.

"It's not lit yet, Max" she reminded both herself and Max, and she bent low and directed little puffs of breath at the smoking twig and burning match pieces. Trying to find the balance between feeding the glowing bits and extinguishing them, Lucy kept on giving cautious little puffs of air. Just when she thought she'd put the fire out, one of the larger twigs caught fire, then another, and then another. Soon, she had a small but distinct fire burning, smoke was rising, and the occasional little "crack" from the wood could be heard.

Continuing to blow on the fire, but a bit harder now, Lucy started feeding more small twigs into the fire until it was clear that the next larger-sized branches were going to ignite as well. When they did, she built her teepee of medium-sized branches over the fire, and sat back to watch the fire grow.

Lucy knew better than to build a huge fire that would be hard to maintain and might get out of control, so she kept it to what she felt was a modest, manageable size, but it was still a warming and comforting fire, and she smiled for the first time since the rockslide.

Lucy's smile faded as it once again occurred to her that she and Max might have to spend the night in her little campsite. Her makeshift shelter looked nice, with what she now thought of as 'their' tree and the two walls – more like fences really – that she had built.

"That's not going to be very comfortable," she said. Looking at her lanyard again, it was her knife that caught her attention this time, and she promptly got up and started cutting green branches. This time she selected the longest branches that she could cut with her little knife and, carrying them back to her shelter, used them to fill in the gaps in her shelter's walls, and to make a bed. This turned out to be a lot of work as well, especially since she had to keep building the fire at intervals as well, but eventually she had a thick bed of green branches she could lie on.

Trying out the bed, her first discovery was that it was NOT comfortable. "Oh well," she said, "at least it will keep us off the ground."

As the light continued to fade, Lucy went back to the stream to give Max and herself another drink of water, then spread her jacket out, on a teepee of longish branches, near the fire to dry out. She was going to need that to stay warm at night. The temperature was dropping rapidly now. It was going to be another cold night, but with no sleeping bag or foam mattress this time! Thinking these thoughts, Lucy was suddenly extra grateful for the fire, whose flames rather cheerfully danced in front of her.

Sitting down on her bed of green branches, she watched the evening sky begin to materialize, thinking, and feeding the odd branch into her fire. Now she had too much time to think, and her mind turned to animals. She knew that most animals wouldn't approach her, especially with a fire burning, but it was hard not to worry about them all the same – especially when, from time to time, she'd hear the odd strange noise coming from somewhere out in the forest.

"Sigh," she said, out loud. "I wonder where the others are. I hope they're all OK."

After a while, she put on her jacket – which had been dried by the fire – and stretched out on her bed of branches to try to sleep. By this time, Lucy was so tired that neither hunger nor the strange surroundings could keep her awake, and she fell into a deep sleep, with Max curled up beside her.

***

The next day was the hardest.

Lucy knew she should stay put and wait to be rescued. The park rangers would surely be searching by now, but as the hours went by, it was just her and her tree, and the stream, and the forest.

If breakfast-time without food was hard, lunch-time with no food was even harder, and by dinner-time a slight stomach-ache had developed into a full-fledged pain in her stomach. She did her best to ignore her hunger though, and spent her time collecting more wood, keeping her fire going, and blowing three blasts on her whistle every now and again. *It is very discouraging*, she thought, *that there is never any reply*.

Where is everybody?

With lots of time on her hands, Lucy also made several forays out to find and cut more green, leafy branches in hopes of building a slightly less uncomfortable bed than she'd suffered on the night before. It was late in the afternoon, when she had dragged her latest batch of branches back to her shelter and she'd thought to use some of them to try to build a reflector wall on the other side of the fire from her shelter. She hoped this would reflect a bit of heat into her shelter at night.

Finally, she decided to use the smaller green branches, she had collected, to plug more of the gaps in her shelter's walls. It was while working at this that she noticed a small cairn of rocks near her tree and just outside of one of the walls.

"That's funny," she said to Max and herself, "I don't remember noticing that when we built this wall yesterday. I must have been too busy to look around."

Cairns, she remembered from stories that she'd read, had been used for generations as trail markers and/or as markers of supply caches.

"It can't be a trail marker, Max" she reasoned, "who would put a trail marker in the middle of a forest? Someone must have buried something here!"

Lucy had a sudden fear that the cairn might be some kind of grave marker, but it was so close to the tree that she decided to risk having a look and she moved the rocks to one side. Then, using one of her larger firewood branches as a shovel, she started to dig. It was more like scraping a pit than digging but, again, having lots of time and nothing better to do she continued to scrape away at the soil.

Some of the soil was too hard-packed to move, but there was an oval-shaped area where it wasn't so hard to dig – that suggested to her that something might really be buried there. As she worked away on that area, a small pit began to take shape.

The next issue, was that she had no idea how deep she should dig. Having to scrape the soil out with a branch meant that it took a lot of scraping, and a lot of time and effort for each inch of soil that she got out. However, her persistence was rewarded when, after only digging down about two inches, she struck something.

"This is exciting!" she explained to Max and herself, forgetting for the moment her aching stomach.

Working carefully now, she continued to scrape until she had exposed what looked like the top of some kind of canvas satchel or duffel bag. It wasn't very large on top, less than a foot wide and perhaps a foot and a half long, and her scraping exposed the top of a canvas strap on one side. Digging around the strap, she tried inserting her fingers under the strap and tried pulling it up.

The strap, of course, promptly broke.

"OK, that wasn't very smart," she admonished herself, "I guess it's back to digging."

The bag had a flap with buttons, rather than a zipper, on its top so this time she tried digging all around the bag until she had exposed the whole top, and tried undoing the buttons.

That worked, but not in the way she'd intended. The canvas bag was, if anything, more fragile than the strap had been. The buttons gave way easily for the simple reason that the fabric tore at each button point. Tugging on each button in turn allowed her to easily open the bag along its entire length.

Eagerly, Lucy removed the top item: a fragile looking pouch that looked rather like a large, leather envelope. A leather string held a fold-over flap in place. She couldn't untie the string, but her knife took care of that. Opening the pouch, she found a thin sheaf of folded papers. They were faded, and looked very fragile, but she was able to very carefully open them up.

"They look like letters!" exclaimed Lucy. Holding the pile up in the late afternoon sunlight, Lucy found that she could just make out some of the faded, spidery writing. The top one was a letter addressed to a "Corporal Frank Pool, North West Mounted Police."

"Wow, what a find Max!" Lucy said. "North West Mounted Police, the RCMP hasn't been called that for years. I wonder how old these are."

Peering closely, she could just make out the date on the top letter. It read "February 1, 1898."

"1898!" she exclaimed. "These letters are 79 years old! I suppose this whole case must be too." Setting the pouch of letters aside, Lucy went back to the buried bag and found that the next item was again leathery-feeling, but this one seemed to fill the rest of the bag. She took it out, set it aside, and reached back in to feel around the bag. All she could feel was a smooth, hard surface covered in what again felt like leather.

"Must be the bottom of the bag," she concluded.

Turning to the item she had set aside; she saw that it was another leather pouch tied shut with leather cord. She couldn't untie this one either, so she cut the cord and opened the pouch. Inside was a block of something she didn't recognize. It felt waxy, was greyish-brown in colour, and it looked grainy. The first thing that came to her mind was that it looked like someone had compressed a huge brownie, or a large piece of meatloaf.

"I wonder why the first things I thought of were food?" she asked Max. At this her stomach immediately gave a sharp pang and she groaned out loud. "Because I'm hungry," she answered.

Looking at it the block more closely, she could see that one edge was bevelled. It looked like someone had cut a piece away for some reason.

The next thing Lucy tried was sniffing at it. It smelled like meat that was starting to go bad.

"Meat!" Lucy's stomach gave another sharp pang. This time it was more like the stomach cramps she'd once gotten from playing soccer right after having eaten dinner. Her brain now switched into high gear.

"An early Mountie, travelling from the Yukon to Alaska a long time ago would have had to carry some kind of food. They didn't have freeze-dried food in those days, so it would have had to be something else," she reasoned.

"OK, Max, so what did they carry for food in those days?" Lucy wracked her brain. They had learned about something about this in school, but it didn't have anything to do with police, it had to do with... what? she thought, while turning the waxy block over and over in her hands. Then, suddenly she sat up straight, her eyes wide open.

"Pemmican!" the early English and German settlers in Canada's prairies had learned about pemmican from the Blackfoot Confederacy, Cree, Ojibwa, and the Sioux. She remembered now. She had done an essay on the original plains-peoples for her history class, and had gotten an 'A' on it.

Could this be pemmican? she wondered. That could explain why a piece, or pieces, had been cut away. Her stomach gave another wrenching cramp. Lucy had been without food for a day and a half now, and she'd fed Max all of his cat treats by now too. The water they'd been drinking had not caused either of them any troubles, yet, but she sure was hungry, and she imagined that Max must be too.

Am I hungry enough to try this? she asked herself.

Her stomach said *Yes!*

Her brain wasn't so sure.

She used her knife to cut a thick slice. It cut quite easily. *It's like cutting a soft candle*, she thought. She sniffed at the freshly cut surface. It still smelled like meat that was on the edge of going bad, but it smelled even more like food now.

Wrench! her stomach agreed!

Cautiously, Lucy tried nibbling at the slice that she had cut away from the block. It tasted like, what? "Kind of like a waxy, dried, meatloaf taste, Max" she concluded. She took a few more nibbles.

Needs salt! she said to herself, then started giggling, then admonished herself. *Here I am starving. I find the first thing I might be able to eat, and now I'm being picky about the taste! Some Girl Guide I am.* Suitably chastised, she used her knife to cut another slice, which she instantly devoured. Finding that she could eat it, whatever it was, she next decided to limit her intake to those first two slices.

If I feel OK in the morning then I'll eat some more of this, she decided.

Next, she cut some thin slices and set them out in front of Max. Sniffing them carefully, Max seemed unimpressed as well. *He probably doesn't like the smell of it either*, thought Lucy.

"Come on Max, give some a try," she encouraged. "It tastes better than it smells!"

Max looked up at her and then, whether it was because of her encouragement or his own nagging hunger, or both, he took a small bite. Finding that the taste itself was acceptable, he then gobbled down the rest in a flash.

Feeling somewhat better for both of them now, Lucy went back to stoking her fire, and then set about collecting more dead branches so she'd have enough fuel to see her through the night.

As darkness began to fall at the end of their second day in the woods, she wondered whether anyone was ever going to come and find them, and whether they were going to survive.

The next morning, Lucy got up and looked around. Although she'd tried to wake up from time to time to tend the fire, her tired body had betrayed her and insisted that she sleep. Although she now felt a bit better, their fire had gone out.

"Oh well," she said to Max, "We'll just re-light the fire later in the afternoon instead of wasting any more matches and firewood on it right now."

By way of aches and pains, her stomach informed her that it was still very hungry. The pemmican (at least she hoped it was pemmican) hadn't made either Max or her sick, so she decided it was safe to eat and cut off several fresh slices for each of them for breakfast. It still didn't taste very good, but it was kind of satisfying and she began to feel a bit better.

Max, now that he was used to the taste, had no such reservations. He gobbled his share immediately, and then settled back to lick his paws free of any last lingering traces.

"I wonder what my parents are doing right now, Max, and if they even know what's happened to me," she said. She would have been surprised to learn that her parents had been contacted by leader Brown Owl the previous afternoon, and were at that very moment, boarding a plane to fly to Skagway, via Juneau.

Thinking of her parents brought Lucy a pang of homesickness, but then another thought caused her to lift her chin a bit higher.

"Wouldn't they be surprised to see their little Lucy now, with my shelter, and my water and food, and my… not panicking!"

Later in afternoon, with her firewood re-stocked and more branches added to bolster the walls of her shelter, she decided to take Max for a walk along the stream and explore. A short distance along the way, she found a spot where the stream opened up a bit, and looked like it might be fairly deep in the centre.

"I wonder if there are fish in there?" she said, and she took a few steps out into the stream so she could peer into the deeper water.

She was just considering whether she had any way of trying to catch a fish when there was a rustle in the bushes across the stream, and a little black bear cub walked right up to the other edge of the stream.

What a cute little bear cub, she thought. Lucy watched it intently for a moment and then years of advice about bears in the mountains suddenly flooded into her mind.

Where is the mother?

It's mother probably wasn't too far away, she reasoned, looking to the left and then to the right. She certainly didn't see any other bears... then there was a crashing sound from the forest and she heard a mighty roar.

Lucy screamed.

Max fled.

9 THE THIRD SEARCH

In the morning of our third day in Skagway, I'd wanted to begin by meeting the Guides to see what we could learn from them. The Guide Leaders and Guides had returned to Skagway at around mid-day the day before, which was the day after the rockslide, and were staying at a local motel. George had agreed to meet me there.

Overnight, everyone's worries had magnified, of course, so our meeting was a bit sombre – although the girls clearly enjoyed meeting Silver. Nevertheless, it was interesting to meet leader Brown Owl and the rest, and to hear their story first-hand. The two leaders had contacted all of the girls' parents (back in Alberta), some of whom were flying in later that day. For their part, the girls all wanted to stay in Skagway until Lucy was found, and the whole patrol had decided to stay for at least another day or two. The most vocal of the girls turned out to be Lucy's best friend, Allison Smith, who had apparently been almost frantic ever since realizing that Lucy was no longer with them after the rockslide.

I got a good description of Lucy from Allison and the others, and asked whether they had any of her clothes I could borrow to give Silver her scent. This produced blank stares at first, until Allison piped up: "Hey, wait a minute, we found her backpack, remember?"

Allison immediately dashed off and soon returned with Lucy's heavy-looking backpack. Opening it up I searched through it, looking for clothes that looked recently worn, as opposed to freshly laundered, and I settled on a tee-shirt and a light, fleecy pullover. Allison said that Lucy had worn the tee-shirt for the entire day before the rockslide, and the pullover when she'd been sitting around camp in the previous evenings. I said that I'd like to borrow both for the search.

"You'll be able to find Lucy, won't you?" asked Allison, in a pleading tone.

"Silver and I will both do our very best. I'm sure she's fine, and that we'll find her soon," I said, trying to sound as confident as I could, despite the lump in my throat.

"She's been lost a long time already though, and she's all alone out there…"

"Well, we'll just have to keep our hopes up," I responded. "Sometimes people don't know what they're capable of until they're really tested. She's probably just fine, sitting somewhere waiting for us to find her."

With that, there really wasn't much more to say, and George, Silver, and I drove to the trail-head at Dyea.

The first five miles of the Chilkoot Trail follow an old wagon road. Normally, vehicles were banned from the trail, but in our case, we were able to travel in four-wheel-drive Jeeps. This part was very pleasant. Breathing-in the moist, early morning air, we passed through meadows and forest, and crisscrossed shallow sections of the Dyea River. The forest too, was interesting with its unusual (for me) mixture of trees: birches, spruces, willows, and cottonwoods. Five miles in, the wagon road came to an end at Finnegan's Point and we continued forward by foot, on the trail proper.

As we walked along, it began to feel like real hiking as we followed a three-mile stretch along the river into a narrow canyon for that took us past Canyon City. The first part of the trail followed the river so closely that it had to be forded quite a few times. It was shallow enough at such places that I could pick my way across by stepping on protruding rocks, and in that way, I was able to keep my boots reasonably dry. Silver, however, had to cross in the water each time, leaving him wet, muddy, and probably a bit chilled.

After this the trail started to gain elevation, and I was immediately glad that we only carried medium-sized daypacks, rather than the fifty or sixty-pound packs that a backpacker would have had to carry – or the hundred-pound packs that the original prospectors shouldered in the gold rush days. Three miles of this took us to Pleasant Camp, and then after two more miles we finally exited the forest fringe and into the open (and windy!) part of the trail. This was at Mile 13: Sheep Camp.

At Sheep Camp, standing in an open, rock-covered basin, we were able to take in the stunning views of the ring of mountains that surrounded us. It was beautiful. We had a clear morning, and the sun was reflected by the many glaciers that hung like curtains from the peaks of the mountains that encircled us. I felt that the mountains had a way of looking beautiful and dangerous, all at the same time. The summit was now only four miles away, but a long, long way up. I was suddenly glad we weren't going to make the ascent, at least not that day.

Here also, were the many reminders of why we had come. In addition to the backcountry ranger station, Sheep Camp was where the park rangers had set-up their base of operations for the search. The helicopters had ferried up large prospector-type tents, including several that were clearly kitchen, dining, and storage tents. There was quite a large contingent of searchers, wearing a variety of uniforms, bustling about everywhere. It appeared that another grid-search was about to be launched.

George took Silver and I over to meet Mark Johnston, the SAR[16] coordinator, who was standing over a picnic table that was covered in maps. Mark seemed quite cranky and distracted, although to be fair, he was probably frustrated and worried by their lack of success so far. When I asked if he could assign someone to show me the trails that the escaping Guides had followed, he initially bristled and I thought for a moment that he was going to refuse. He caught himself, however, just long enough for me to hurriedly explain that if I could go out ahead of the searchers, it would give Silver a better chance of catching Lucy's scent. Mark was able to see the sense in that, so he calmed down and called over two young rangers.

The two rangers were introduced as the ones that the Guides had first encountered after recovering from the rock slide, and who had done the first, hasty search, two days earlier. They were eager to see Silver and I at work, and happy to show us where to start. After giving Silver time to sniff away at the pieces of Lucy's clothing that I'd brought along, he started out and the three of us followed. Silver did his usual thing, darting around here and there, pausing every now and again for some deep sniffing of the ground, plants and shrubs, but it was obvious to me that he wasn't detecting anything related to Lucy.

With the assistance of the rangers, Silver and I tried each of the four game trails thought to have been travelled by the escaping Guides and their leaders. We took our time, and I gave Silver his lead, except when we needed the rangers to start us off on a new trail. It took hours and it was incredibly frustrating, because Silver found no trace of Lucy whatsoever, not anywhere.

Eventually, we decided to return to base and as we did, we passed the main search force, which in the meantime had re-started the grid-search from the previous day. When we reported-in to George and Mark, who were still standing by the improvised map table, they wanted to know what was wrong.

"I really don't know," I'd answered. "Silver has searched everywhere around the trails your rangers showed us, and a few other spots as well, but he hasn't picked up a single trace of Lucy's scent. It's possible that there wasn't much scent to begin with, or that what there was has been masked by other scents by now."

"Are you sure you're any good at this?" Mark had asked.

That was offensive, and I instinctively bristled and became

defensive.

"Look, we're doing our best, but Silver can't track a scent that isn't there. Sometimes people don't leave much to follow, and sometimes – I motioned vaguely in the direction of the searchers – the scent gets masked by other scents."

I would have gone on, but George interjected at this point. "Mark, give her a break, she volunteered to come help us and she's doing her best."

"Thanks George," I said, gratefully.

Mark relented a bit. "OK, I apologize, but time's running short and things are about to get worse around here. There's bad weather blowing in from the coast. It's going to be overcast, rainy, and cold by late afternoon. If we don't find her by then, she's likely to get very wet and cold, and hypothermia's going to be a major concern. We can't afford to waste time."

"Look," I said, "I've been thinking about this as we walked back here. Is there any chance at all that we've been searching in the wrong direction?"

That brought Mark all the way back up to a boil. "Look, Missy, I talked to every one of the leaders and girls that were up here and they are all adamant that they ran where we've been searching. We didn't find any trace of the missing girl yesterday, but we were looking in the right place, so now we're going to do it all again."

"Fine, but what if Lucy didn't run the same way as the others? I'd like to try a few other directions, just in case. If she went back down the main trail, she should have reached the ranger station, but what if she ran in another direction? Who knows?"

This just made Mark angry again, of course, but once again George jumped in.

"Let her go Mark. We asked for her help, let's let her do it her way, OK?" George encouraged. "It can't hurt."

"Whatever! Bringing you two in was a waste of time anyway," stormed Mark.

"Bark!!"

We were interrupted at that point by Silver. While I was

arguing with Mark, I'd left Silver off-leash, and had been watching him from the corner of my eye. He'd been wandering around the trail and campsite, pausing occasionally to sniff and look around. Eventually, he'd circled one particular area, given it a second careful sniff, and then promptly sat down and signaled to me with a sharp bark.

He was sitting on the other side of the trail and debris pile! That meant that the rangers and other searchers had been searching the wrong area.

Trying for once to be diplomatic, I turned to Mark and said, "I think we may have been searching in the wrong direction."

He disagreed, of course, calling me "Missy" when he really did know my name, and using colourful language that I'd just as soon not repeat. The gist of his remarks was that he wasn't going to let some "stupid dog and a girl," or perhaps it was "some stupid girl and a dog," distract a professional search.

"Fine, then," I said. "You go your way and I'll go mine. I have just one request: could you spare one person to go with me and make sure I don't get lost too?"

"Mark…" George warned.

"All right. All right. Anything to get you out of my hair," replied Mark, exasperated. Then he straightened up and looked at someone that was behind me and yelled out in a parade-ground roar, "Sawyer! Get your butt over here… Now!"

'Sawyer' turned out to be Julie Sawyer, a Seasonal Park Ranger, working in the park for the summer. Julie appeared to be in her early twenties, was slender but not willowy, had a sparkle in her blue eyes, and a blond ponytail sticking out of the back of her National Park Service Cap. She seemed very alive and energetic as she jogged over to where we were standing.

"You called?" she said.

"I want you to babysit this woman and her dog. Make sure they don't get lost too - and keep them out of my hair!" With that he stormed off.

"He's usually not that bad," explained George, "but he's seriously worried about his lack of success in finding Lucy."

"Well, thanks for backing me up with him. I appreciate it," I replied.

"No problem Alex... To tell you the truth, I actually think that you're wrong about searching that way, but there's one thing I am sure of."

"What's that?"

"I asked for your help, and you should be able to do it your own way. Good luck!" and with that, he shook my hand and walked back to help Mark coordinate the grid-search.

Turning to Julie, I apologized for her getting stuck babysitting us, but she surprised me.

"Are you kidding?" she exclaimed. "I want to do something useful, around here, but someone put an MCP in charge and all I've been allowed to do around here so far is organize coffee and doughnuts!"

"MCP?"

"Male Chauvinist Pig."

"Sounds like he's not your favourite person," I put in. So much for appearances, I thought to myself. Mark was good looking: tall, blond, blue-eyed, and muscular. Odd, I thought, that he and Julie didn't hit it off well, as they were almost stereotypical California beach boy/girl types in appearance. On the other hand, he wasn't my type either, so each to their own.

"Thank god he's not my regular boss or I'd have quit long ago," Julie added with some heat.

I laughed. "OK then, let's go. Come and let me introduce you to Silver."

Silver seemed to take an interest in Julie who, for her part was very excited to meet him. A good beginning, I thought. I brought out the two pieces of Lucy's clothing that I'd brought along, gave Silver a 'refresher' sniff, and told him to track.

He immediately led us off to the southwest, away from the main trail and debris pile, and in completely the opposite direction to that of the organized grid-search. As we approached the forest on that side, I turned my head just in time to see Mark shake his head in obvious disgust and turn away.

Julie had noticed as well. "We're going to hear about this if we don't succeed," she warned.

"Worried?"

"Not me," she returned, with a bright smile. "I'm only a 'useless woman.' Besides that, I'm on the bottom of the totem pole around here. I have nowhere to go but up. So, what do we do?"

"That's the spirit! What we do is we follow Silver wherever he wants to take us. I'll watch him. If you can keep me out of trouble, we'll see what kind of scent he's picked up."

"You really think he's caught the girl's scent?"

"I do. This is kind of hard to explain, but Silver and I have worked for nearly two years now. He knows why we're here, and what we're looking for. If he thinks he's found Lucy's scent, then I really would not bet against him."

Silver, for his part, was clearly 'on the hunt.'

The one common thread in Silver's and my tracking stories is that, while the most intense part is in the tracking itself, when trying to relate the stories later there really isn't that much to tell. Silver would walk in broad, sweeping arcs, sometimes a zig-zag, and sometimes he'd backtrack or circle – always sniffing at everything, the ground, the bushes, the tree trunks, everything. Watching him though, I noticed that in this case his average path always seemed to follow established game trails. That made sense. I assumed that, consciously or not, Lucy would have taken the easiest, fastest way possible to make her escape.

It was slow going for us though, and we'd gone along like this for about three miles, when he stopped for longer than usual on the game trail that we happened to be on at the time. For a few moments, he just stood there with his head up, looking around. As I came up to him, he looked up at me and I had a sudden impression that he had lost the scent.

Before I could say anything, Silver retreated about five yards, back the way we had come. With his nose so close to the ground I wondered that it didn't fill with dirt, he regained the scent and commenced another zig-zag course, but more slowly this time. Now, the scent led him off the game trail to our right, through the bush and around some large trees. After about ten yards of very difficult slogging through heavy brush, Silver led us back onto the game trail and his pace increased.

"What was all that about?" asked Julie.

"I think he lost the scent, then reacquired it. Something must have scared Lucy off of the trail through the bush, and then she came back to the trail again, I guess."

No sooner had I said this than Julie and I came up against Silver, who had stopped again, but this time with his head down in some long grasses to one side of the game trail. When his head emerged, he immediately sat down.

"Now what?" asked Julie.

"He's found something... What did you find Silver?" I asked, as I walked over to him. Sitting beside one paw was a piece of blue cloth. When I picked it up and opened it up, it was immediately recognizable.

"It's a Girl Guides camp hat!" I exclaimed, "I had one like this when I was in Guides. We're on the right track!"

"We should tell the others," Julie said, excitedly. "Even if we find Lucy, she might need medical help."

"I agree. Do you have a radio?"

"Are you kidding? We just got some of the new Motorolas[17], but they've only been issued to the 'big shots', not the 'little people' like me."

We had a quick conference and ultimately decided to split up. Silver and I would forge ahead and try to find Lucy, while Julie would go back to the search coordination centre and get more help. As we had followed Silver along the game trails, Julie had been blazing our trail by periodically tying pieces of bright orange flagging tape to tree branches, always at about shoulder height.

The wisdom of this was strongly brought home to me as Julie handed me the roll of tape so I could do the same thing as Silver and I made our way forward. She, in turn, would have no trouble retuning to base or bringing help back, with the way so clearly marked.

"Julie, I'm impressed," I said. "You are way undervalued in the park ranger business."

"All in a day's rangering," she said, brightly. "See you soon," and with that, she set off back to the search base to report in and get more help.

Silver and I continued on with our tracking and blazing. We had another setback when we encountered a shallow stream. It wasn't even shallow, exactly, it was more like a rippling layer of water running along in such a way that it just covered the largest rocks. It was broad though, at least nine feet across. The problem was that as we crossed the stream, Silver lost the scent again. Had Lucy simply crossed the water, like we did, it wouldn't have caused Silver any trouble, as he'd have picked up the scent again on the other side. That didn't happen though.

Lucy must have followed the water in one direction or the other, I thought, as Silver padded around sniffing here and there along the far side of the bubbling waterway. Eventually Silver stopped and looked up at me, as if to say: "*It's gone.*"

We were going to have to search along the far side of the

waterway, it was just a question of whether to search upstream or downstream. *Fifty-fifty odds*, I thought. "Let's go that way Silver," I said, motioning that we should try upstream.

Silver said "Grruph," and headed upstream. It was a bad choice. It was slow going, as we had to maneuver around bushes and branches everywhere. On the other hand, the bushes were quite thick between the big trees of the forest and the stream, so wherever Lucy exited it seemed like there should be a reasonable scent trail. Eventually, however, I thought we'd gone far enough and Silver and turned around a retraced our steps all the way back to the starting point.

When we reached it, I motioned down-stream, and asked Silver to resume the search. Going in that direction was no easier, so it was slow going, and I have to admit that I was starting to wonder whether we needed to back up again and re-evaluate our strategy.

Finally, after what seemed forever, Silver gave a short "Yip." He had found the scent again, right in front of what looked like another game trail.

"Good Boy, Silver!" I praised. "Let's go find her!"

With another "Grruph," Silver was off. Thankfully, this time the scent was obviously easier to follow, as our pace increased considerably.

We had travelled about another mile when we heard a scream.

Silver immediately barked.

"I hear it too Silver. Let's go, but stay close to me, OK?"

Silver went off in the lead, but stopped at intervals to make sure I was keeping up and hadn't lost track of him.

Silver and I both now had a pretty good idea where Lucy was so we were able to pick up our speed. Any chance of us losing the track vanished when we heard a second scream, but closer now. It was loud! *We're close now*, I thought.

Eventually, we burst into a clearing and saw a girl standing in a stream, facing away from us towards a full-sized, angry-looking black bear.

Silver started to growl.

"Lucy?" I called.

"Yes!" There was a pause. "A little bear cub came along and now her mother thinks I'm a threat."

"Silver. Stay!" I ordered, seeing that Silver was beginning to advance toward the bear.

"OK Lucy. My name's Alex, and this is Silver. We're going to help you... Just stay where you are and stand still, OK?"

"OK, I'll try."

"Where's the cub now?"

"I think it ran back behind its mother somewhere."

"That's good. That's where we want it to be. Hang on a second." If the cub was behind its mother, that was a good thing for us. I certainly didn't want us to find ourselves in between the two bears.

Silver and I moved slowly up to the shore, and there we all were for a moment. The bear, or bears, were on one side of the stream, Silver and I were on the other shore, and dead-centre in the middle of the stream stood Lucy. The moment was soon broken, however. The mother bear, who had been growling and shaking her head and shoulders from side to side, suddenly stood up on her hind legs and gave an almighty, great roar.

At this, Lucy screamed again, and Silver let out another menacing growl. I felt like screaming too, but was focused on the bear.

"Lucy. I want you to try taking a very slow step backwards towards us. OK?"

She was scared but she was brave, and very carefully did what I asked. As she did, I slowly moved to my right while motioning Silver to move to the left.

This seemed to mystify the bear, who went back to shaking her head and shoulders and growling.

"OK Lucy. Try taking one more, slow step backwards towards us." This time, as Lucy took her second step backwards, the bear stopped shaking and swaying and actually advanced on Lucy.

I didn't like the look at this, and my 'spider-sense' shifted from tingling to overdrive. I had previously learned to listen to my 'spider sense' and I did so then.

"Silver. Guard Lucy!" I ordered.

At this, Silver looked at me, then at the water, then back to me again. Then I suddenly understood his quandary. Oh no! I thought, Silver's perennial aversion to going into water wasn't going to help us.

As it turned out, I needn't have worried. After a moment's thought, Silver gave a low growl that sounded exactly like a human groan, and then shrugged and leapt into the stream. In a few bounds he had positioned himself in front of Lucy and started barking at the bear in a ferocious way that would have given any rational human pause. It gave the bear pause too, which gave me the time I needed to take a step into the water – a couple of paces to the right. That gave me a clear line of sight to the bear as I drew the heavy revolver George had given me.

Things were tense now. The bear, having taken one step in the water was shaking its head and growling. Silver was standing protectively in front of Lucy, and growling menacingly. Lucy was standing still, with both hands up and over her mouth, trying to maintain her composure. For my part, I had my gun up and aimed at the bear, and was wondering if I should risk shooting it.

"Lucy. Take one more, slow, step backwards towards shore, OK?"

Lucy was shaking, but bravely said, "I'll try," and took the step.

At this, the bear seemed to instinctively take another step towards us, so I changed my aim and fired two shots in succession at the water, about a foot or two in front of the bear.

The loud sounds of the shots, coupled with the splashes of water right in front of it startled and confused the bear, which halted and reared up on its hind legs again.

"Take another step back," I called over to Lucy.

That next step brought her to the shore, with Silver keeping pace but keeping himself in front of her. I stayed where I was. Lucy was now behind both Silver and I, which was where I wanted her.

The bear seemed thoroughly confused now, and it dropped back down on all four legs to think.

I tried firing one more shot. This time the bullet struck much closer to the bear than I had intended, causing a splash of water that was only about an inch from one paw. That caused the bear to involuntarily take a step backward for the first time, which was just as well because that was going to be my last warning shot. There had only been five rounds in my revolver[18] and I was then down to two. I was going to save those last two in case the bear decided to charge us.

Now time slowed, and for a moment everything went quiet.

Silver had reduced his barking to a low, menacing growl. It was as if he was preparing himself for a very uneven fight, having sensed that the bear was trying to decide what to do next.

The momentary silence was broken by a completely unexpected sound: the long, plaintive whine of the bear cub who, in the woods somewhere behind its mother, was feeling frightened and alone.

That broke the tension. The mother bear had her priorities right: her cub was behind her in the forest, she had an escape route behind her, and we were all over on the far side of the stream. With a very decisive sounding snort, the mother bear simply turned back to the forest and tramped off with her cub.

As I holstered my gun and walked out of the stream, Lucy ran up and threw her arms around me in a big hug.

"Thank you!"

"You're very welcome. I'm glad we found you! Everyone's been very worried – are you hurt at all?"

"No, not really, just wet… and hungry and I've lost Max!"

"Max! Who is Max?"

"Max is my cat. I had him tucked into the front of my shirt but, when the bear scared us, he jumped out and went running off somewhere."

"You brought a cat with you to backpack in Alaska?" I asked, amazed.

"He's my friend. I couldn't leave him behind," said Lucy, as if bringing him along had been the most obvious and logical thing in the world to do. And to her, I supposed, it probably was.

"Max must be terrified. We have to find him!"

"OK, Lucy, we'll go look for him, but first things first. I have some granola bars in my pack," I said, reaching for a couple as I spoke.

While Lucy was munching on the granola bars, I called Silver over and knelt down to give him a great big hug. "Good boy Silver! I can't believe you actually jumped into the water!"

"What do you mean?" asked Lucy, between chews.

"When I called for Silver to protect you, I wasn't sure exactly what he'd do. Silver has a terrible fear of going into the water, especially cold water. On the other hand, he knew he had to get between you and the bear. That meant that he had to overcome his fear of the water in order to be able to jump in and protect you, and I'm very proud of him."

"Can I thank him too?"

"Of course, you can. Come on over."

As Lucy knelt beside me to pet Silver, she had lots of questions, beginning with whether all of the others from her patrol were OK. When I reassured her that everyone else was safe and sound but worried about her, she moved on to questions about Silver and I.

"How long have you been a Mountie? How many women Mounties are there? How did you and Silver meet, or were you just assigned to each other? ..."

While answering the barrage of questions as best I could, I was watching Lucy carefully. I noticed that she was making short work of my granola bars, while breaking off some bits to feed to Silver. I would not have expected Silver to eat granola, but he did. Maybe our adventure had made him hungry too.

"Have you been starving the whole time?"

"Well, not starving exactly. I had some cat treats for Max, but they got used up. I didn't have anything to eat at first, but then I found something that I think is pemmican and Max and I have been eating that. It isn't very good, though, and I'm still feeling starved."

That was a surprise. "Where in the world did you find pemmican?"

"I'll show you," Lucy volunteered, "but can we please go look for Max now? I'm really worried about him."

"Sure, we can. He probably climbed up a tree somewhere, so he might not be very far away," I answered, trying to sound more confident than I felt. "Do you have anything with you that would have his scent on it?"

"Scent?"

"Right, something that smells like Max, so Silver will know what to look for."

"Can Silver track cats too?" asked Lucy, sounding more encouraged.

"I don't know Lucy, but I hope so."

"Well," said Lucy doubtfully, "Max spent most of his time in my pack, but I lost that when the rocks came flying down the mountain."

"Well, we found your pack and I brought a tee-shirt and a fleece pullover from it. That's what Silver used to get your scent. It was him that found you here."

"I've been carrying Max around in the front of my shirt. Would that have Max's scent on it too?"

"It will. Kneel down and let's try putting them all together, and we'll see what Silver can do."

Calling Silver to come closer, I pulled Lucy's tee-shirt and a fleece pullover out of my own pack and held them up together, next to the front of Lucy's shirt.

As Silver came over to see what I was holding, I said: "Cat, Silver, track the cat!"

Silver appeared startled, and immediately looked deep into

my eyes, as if trying to make sure that he understood what I was asking him to do.

He'd understood me, all right, and I suddenly had the clearest image in my mind of his reaction. If he could speak English, it would have been: "*Me, track a cat? You have got to be kidding me!*"

I suddenly sat down and started laughing.

"What's so funny?" asked Lucy.

"Well, Silver's a terrific tracker, but I seriously doubt that anyone's ever asked him to track a cat before, and I think he's trying to understand why anyone would even want to."

"He understands what we want him to do?"

"Oh, yes."

"And he's questioning your orders?"

"Oh, yes."

"But, aren't you his master?"

"In the human world, yes, I'm his owner and his master. But, in Silver and my special world, he and I are partners and very, very good friends."

I could see that Lucy was clearly trying to get her mind around this, so I tried again. "How about you and Max? He's your cat, right? But are you two master and servant, or are you two very special friends?"

Now Lucy laughed. "Friends, of course. Max hardly ever does what I tell him to do."

"There you go then. Let's just see whether our friend Silver here can help us out." Then looking back into Silver's eyes: "Silver, we need to find Lucy's cat. OK?"

Silver took a long look into my eyes, then gave Lucy a long look, and then I swear he sighed, and stuck his nose into Lucy's clothing and gave each piece the sniffing of a lifetime. He took more time at this than I'd ever seen him do on a tracking hunt before, and at first, I wondered why. Then, I realized that it was because he was working to separate Lucy's scent from Max's.

Eventually, seeming satisfied, he took a step back and began sweeping the area behind us, away from the river.

"How does he know what to do?" asked Lucy.

"I don't know, Lucy. All I can tell you is that he's the smartest dog I've ever met in my life, and he and I communicate so well that I often feel like he can see into my mind. Let's let him do his thing and see what happens."

As we watched, Silver swept a complete arc on our side of the river, then turned around and swept it again, but going in the opposite direction. He'd retraced his steps about three-quarters of the way back before he began to veer off towards the forest, heading for the same game trail that we'd originally walked in on.

"He's found Max's trail," I said. "Now we'll see if he can track it."

With Silver in the lead and Lucy and I following, we headed back the way we had come, but only for perhaps thirty feet, after which Silver abruptly made a sharp turn to the left and pushed his way into the bush where there was no path at all.

We advanced, but slowly. Silver's pace slowed to a crawl as he thoroughly sniffed everything that was low to the ground. It was just as well, because Lucy and I could only make our way with great difficulty due to dense growth of bushes between the trees.

It seemed to take a long time, but we'd probably only gone through another twenty or thirty feet before I heard Silver give out a distinctive snort.

"I think he's found something," I said to Lucy, as I pushed the last couple of branches out of our way before we could see him.

"Where's Max?" asked Lucy.

Silver was sitting beside a very large tree. Sitting exactly the way he'd been taught to sit after finding his quarry in a hunt. The only thing was, we didn't see any sign of a cat.

"Where is it Silver?" I asked.

Silver had been looking at us and panting with his tongue out, giving that wolfy grin he sometimes did. Then, he closed his mouth and meaningfully looked up. Up at the tree.

Lucy and I looked up, and there, on a branch about twenty

feet off the ground, was Max.

"Max!" squealed Lucy, delightedly.

"Good boy Silver," I said, going over to pet him, "very well done."

"Come down Max, its safe now" called Lucy, but Max gave no sign of moving. "How do we get him down," asked Lucy, turning to me expectantly.

Now it was my turn to groan: I was going to have to climb that tree and get him.

To add insult to injury, I happened to glance into Silver's eyes at that moment and he gave me a look. It was a look of amusement. I could interpret that look: he'd done his part and actually helped rescue a cat, of all things. The rest, his look said, was going to be up to me.

With a sigh, I removed my hat and pack, and took off my gun-belt. Taking a pair of gloves from my pack, I put them on and started to climb the tree.

It had been more than ten years since I'd climbed a tree, but as a young girl I'd done it quite often. Some of my childhood memories flooded back into my mind as I slowly worked my way higher and higher, all the while trying not to think about falling. When I'd made it up about fifteen feet, there were two stout branches under my feet and I paused to catch my breath and make sure Max hadn't moved. I also looked down and found that both Lucy and Silver had backed up several feet to give themselves a clear view and there they were: Silver sitting on his haunches and Lucy kneeling beside him, with both of her arms wrapped around his neck. Both of them were staring up at me as if I was the day's prime entertainment which, in a way, I supposed that I was.

Fortunately, Max hadn't moved an inch so, with a deep breath, I continued my climb. It wasn't long before I had climbed that final five feet. Now for the tricky part. Max, of course, was sitting far enough out on the branch as to be beyond my reach. The question now, was how far out along the branch I could go before it broke under my weight. The branch was too narrow for crawling, so I stepped out on it, using both hands to hang on to higher branches for support.

Max, for his part, had seen me coming and, although he didn't leave the branch, he did turn around to face me so that he could watch whatever I might be up to. He was watching very intently and, not wanting to spook him, I moved as slowly as I possibly could while trying to talk to him in a soothing voice.

I won't try to relate exactly what I said. It was just baby talk really. The only things I was trying to communicate to him were reassurance and patience. When I got close to him, I tried squatting down so I could get a hand over to him.

He promptly backed up a foot and resettled himself to watch me.

I moved a foot closer. He moved a foot further away.

I judged that I could attempt one more foot out from the trunk of the tree and very slowly did so. Max stood up to back up another foot, but then encountered a problem. He'd moved far enough out that there were no other branches close enough for him to jump to, he was too high off the ground to be willing to jump down, and he'd reached a point on the branch we were on where it split into three very narrow branches. He no sooner stretched a tentative paw further out on one of the narrower branches than it began to wobble dangerously and he sucked the paw back in a flash. Trapped!

Unsure what to do next, Max said "Meow," and I was just able to grab him by the scruff of the neck before he had time to do anything desperate. I held Max at arm's length for a moment, trying to judge whether he was going to come quietly or come at me with his claws bared. Fortunately, he seemed to judge that he'd had enough excitement for one day and he allowed his body to go limp. Taking that as a sign of surrender, I brought him in and tucked him into my own shirt front.

"You got him!" squealed Lucy, clapping excitedly.

"He seems fine," I said, "we're coming down."

At this point another childhood memory came back to me: trees tended to be easier to climb up than they were down. I'm sure that Max would have seconded that sentiment. Making my way back to the tree trunk was easy. Climbing back down without either falling or squishing Max in my shirt wasn't so easy, but I eventually made it back down to *terra firma* without further incident and extracted Max from my shirt.

While Lucy and Max conducted a joyous but tearful reunion, I put on my gun-belt and pack and received a wave of commiserating licks from Silver.

I'd continued my practice of tying pieces of the colourful flagging tape onto trees as we'd followed Silver into the woods, so it was a simple matter to retrace our steps to the original game trail, and once there I asked Lucy where she'd been sleeping.

"My campsite is near here and I have a fire burning that we should put out before we leave. Besides, we could sit by it for a minute and get warmed up too."

"Sure. Show me the way and I'll keep tying these pieces of flagging tape onto trees as we go so the rangers can find us."

Just like Lucy said, her campsite was close by, near the end of the stream. As we walked there, she described her adventure, including how she had built a makeshift shelter around a big, old tree, and how she'd built a fire circle, and improvised a way to drink water from her jacket.

"You're an impressive young lady!" I exclaimed.

"Wait until you see this," she said, and showed me the packet of letters.

As I carefully opened them up, Lucy attached her makeshift leash to Max and put more wood on the fire.

"These are amazing," I said, leafing through them. Letters to a North West Mounted Policeman, and all dated in the early months of 1898. That means he was here during the Klondike Gold Rush and might have been one of Sam Steele's force."

"Who's Sam Steele?" She asked.

"Probably one of the most famous Mounties ever[2]. He was sent to help maintain law and order on the Canadian side of the pass, but he and his force often travelled down the Chilkoot Trail to get to Skagway and the ships that could take them to Vancouver and connect with the Trans-Canada

Railway.

"Now look at this," said Lucy, passing me a leather-wrapped packet. Inside was a block of waxy-looking solid. "Would you like to try some?"

Well, I certainly did not, but she was so eager to share her experience with me that I didn't have the heart to disappoint her. She used her knife to cut a small piece for me and I tried it.

"Tastes kind of waxy and bland," I offered. "I think you're right about it being pemmican though. I tried pemmican once when I was in Saskatchewan. It tasted a bit like this, but with berries in it."

"I wasn't sure if it was food a first," Lucy said, "and then I worried about it being seventy years old, but I was so desperate for food that I decided to try a little bit. Max did too. Then, when I woke up yesterday morning and neither of us was sick, I decided we could eat some more. The two of us have been eating it ever since."

"Well, I've read that really well-made pemmican can last for decades, but I've never heard about it lasting seven decades. I suppose that it had something to do with being well wrapped, buried, and stored in such a cold climate. You were very lucky to find it." Then, looking at the letters again, I asked "Where did you say you found these things?"

"They were in an old canvas case or bag of some kind, buried underneath a cairn of stones, and right beside my tree... Here, I'll show you," she said, getting up from the fire.

Sure enough. In a shallow excavation close to 'her' tree, Lucy had exposed the opened top of a canvas bag or case.

"The bottom feels solid, so I figured that I'd pulled out everything that was in it, and I just left the rest in the ground," she explained.

"That would make it an awfully small bag," I mused, bending down to look more closely and feel around inside. "I wonder if there's more there to see..."

So that's how it came about that George, Julie, two other park rangers, and a paramedic emerged from the forest trail to find a dog and a cat watching Lucy and I use tree branches to dig in the ground near a big, old, balsam fir tree.

"What in the world are you doing?" George asked.

"Anyone got a shovel?" I responded, looking up at them.

One of the rangers actually had a small, collapsible shovel tied to the side of his pack, and we soon had the canvas bag fully exposed, and Lucy and I put our hands in to lift it out.

"It's heavy!" we both said, in unison, as we lifted it out and placed it on the ground in front of us.

"It's an old kit bag," George exclaimed, "and look at the marking on it."

The bag was dirty and faded, but on one side of it we could clearly make out a stenciled symbol – that of capital letter 'P' superimposed on the right-hand side of a capital letter 'M.'

"MP," I said. "This was a North West Mounted Police kit bag... but let's see why it's still so heavy. Lucy, since you found it why don't you see what else is in there."

"OK," she said and, reaching on with both hands, she carefully lifted out yet another leather-wrapped object. This one was about seven inches long, by four inches wide, by two inches tall.

"Lucy, why don't you go ahead and unwrap it for us?" When she did, we all got a surprise.

"Gold!" we all said. It was a solid-looking gold bar.

I hefted it, experimentally, in my hands, then put it back down. "It must weigh close to twenty-five pounds[19]," I said.

George and I looked at each other. "A gold bar in an 1898 Mountie's kit bag would have come from the Klondike," I reasoned.

"It was probably on its way to the Bank of Canada," said George. "They would have brought them down through the pass to Skagway and then by boat to one of the cities along the coast, probably Vancouver, and then caught a train east. I'm going to have to hang onto that bar for a while, so we can see if we can identify it and its proper owner."

"Awww," spoke up Lucy.

"He's right Lucy," I agreed. "I think it's probably Canadian gold, but it's been found on U.S. soil, so the local police have to check it out first. But don't worry, we'll take some pictures of it and George here will give you a receipt for it. If they can discover who actually owns it then I'm sure the owner will pay you some kind of salvage or recovery – right George."

"Right," said George. "Besides, if we can't find the legal owner within ninety days, then we'll give the bar back to you."

"The whole thing?" Lucy exclaimed.

"The whole thing." George confirmed. "After all, you found it, right?"

"Not really," Lucy said, losing some of her excitement, "It was Alex here that suggested we dig the bag out and look inside. I thought it was empty."

"Oh no!" I said, "Thank you for trying to be honest, but you found the cairn, you found the bag, and you found everything that was in it. I only helped you."

George and I exchanged another long look.

"Well, that's that then," said George, with a twinkle in his eye. "Why don't you let me carry it for now, and we'll take some pictures of it and I'll write you a receipt when we're back in town?

The paramedic checked Lucy over and declared her fit for travel. Lucy, however, wouldn't budge until the paramedic had checked Max over too. With a chuckle, the paramedic agreed, checked Max over, and then with a completely serious expression and tone of voice declared Max fit to travel as well.

I flashed a grateful smile at the paramedic, who winked in reply.

Next, we turned to extinguishing Lucy's fire. The rangers were very impressed that she'd built a proper fire circle to help keep her fire contained, and said so.

"We heard shots," said Julie. "What happened?"

"There was a bear!" said Lucy, before I could utter a word. "Two bears, a little cub and its mother, and the mother must have been worried about its cub. Max ran off, and I thought the bear was going to attack me but Alex and Silver jumped in to save me!"

As the others looked my way, I filled in the rest of the story, including the part about firing the warning shots. "Turns out you were right about having the gun George... Thank you," I concluded.

"When you said you were planning to hike the trail alone, it gave me an uncomfortable feeling," George explained. "I'm glad I paid attention to it."

The rangers, for their part had visibly relaxed during this exchange, and I could tell that they were relieved that I hadn't actually shot the bear, and particularly relieved that they weren't going to have to take on the dangerous task of trying to locate a potentially injured bear. I wouldn't have wanted to try that myself.

Eventually, with a last look at Lucy's campsite, it was time to leave. Before we did, I impulsively performed a small ceremony with Lucy.

"Lucy," I said, rather formally, "you did a fantastic job of looking after yourself out here and as one Guide to another, I can tell you that Girl Guides and Girl Scouts everywhere would be proud of you!" Saying that, I extended my left hand and offered her the Guides' handshake.

"Hear, hear," announced Julie, "I was a Girl Scout myself and I couldn't agree more," as she straightened up and offered her the Guides salute.

At this, Silver sat up straight with his eyes shining. George and the other park rangers, for their part, silently stood to attention and saluted her as well. As we all held position for a few moments, it made for a very touching moment – one that I will always cherish.

Then, we headed out with the rangers in the lead and the paramedic walking alongside Lucy, Lucy with Max in her shirt, and George, Silver, and I bringing up the rear.

When the others were far enough ahead of us to be out of earshot, George said, in a low voice, "About the gold. Stretching the truth a bit back there weren't you?"

"What do you mean"" I asked, trying to sound innocent.

George just looked at me.

"OK, well, maybe just a little. But I think she's been through enough, and I'd like to see her get all the credit for the discovery, and if there's a reward at the end of it all, then I'd like to see her get that too."

"Hmmm, hmmm, and the fact that since you're on duty you wouldn't have been able to claim any reward anyway?"

"Just one more reason to do the right thing, wouldn't you say George?"

"I would indeed. I knew you were going to turn out to be one of the good ones. It's been a pleasure to meet you Alex."

"You too George. You too."

We walked the rest of the way back to Sheep Camp in companionable silence.

To cap the day off, Mark, the SAR coordinator, even apologized and thanked me for finding Lucy!

Julie loved seeing that.

Mark's contrition surprised me a bit, at first, because I was sure that he wasn't pleased to have been wrong about Lucy's whereabouts. Thinking about it, though, I suspected that he was smart enough to realize that a successful search looked better for him, and his record, than an unsuccessful one. Anyway, the important things had worked out well, so I let it go.

As a result, everyone was in good humour as we all hiked back to Finnegan's Point, and from there the Jeeps took us back to the trail-head and on to Skagway.

10 DUTY CALLS

News had travelled fast, and there was a crowd of people waiting to meet us at the Dyea trail-head. In addition to the park rangers and other searchers, the Girl Guides and their leaders were conspicuous in their uniforms. Others in the crowd ranged from the parents of many of the Guides, to local citizens and, of course, the media.

At first, all of the attention was on Lucy's reunion with her Guide friends and leaders, with her parents, who had just flown in from Alberta, and with her best friend Allison. Allison, in particular, had been frantic with worry, upset at being separated from Lucy and, of course, horrified at the thought that Lucy might have been injured or killed. Seeing Lucy return relatively unscathed, and with Max intact, had produced relief and whales of tears.

Silver and I were able to meet Lucy's parents, Glen and Vicky, who were naturally very relieved and thankful to have her found and returned safely. I replied with the simple truth: that I was just glad we'd been able to find her. Julie, who was standing nearby didn't let me get away with that, however.

"But it was you!" she interjected. Then, addressing the group of people around us, "Everyone else was searching in the wrong direction. It was Alex that wanted to search another way, but no one would listen to her, so in the end she told off Mark and went her own way! Right George?"

"She sure did!" agreed George, who had been standing at the edge of the crowd, quietly listening. "If Alex here hadn't stood up for her instincts, I'm not sure we would have found Lucy in time."

That sobered everyone up in a hurry, and I hastened to fill the sudden silence.

"It wasn't just me. Silver had found a scent where there shouldn't have been one. It was both of us that wanted to search in another direction... Like always, Silver and I did it together."

That made Silver the centre of attention, and brought everyone back to a celebratory mood. Knowing that he wasn't particularly used to crowds, I thought that Silver was very patient with so many people wanting to come up and pet him. At one point, after this had been going one for a while, he looked up at me with what I thought was a very martyred—looking expression.

Partly to give Silver a break and partly to give Lucy credit, where credit was due, I turned back to her parents. "You should be very proud of Lucy. A lot of people would have panicked and hurt themselves. She had to run from the rock-slide, of course, but she kept her head and controlled her fears, and she was very resourceful. In a very real way, she saved herself out there. Also, you're probably not very pleased with her for smuggling Max along for the trip, but in the end, she saved his life too. If the Guides have a merit badge for lifesaving, I think she more than earned it."

Glen and Vicky were too relieved to have their daughter back, and too proud of her as well, to be upset about the cat.

The celebrations continued for a while, but inevitably the days of stress coupled with the emotions of a successful conclusion brought a wave of exhaustion over everyone and the reunion broke up with the usual thanks, congratulations, and promises to keep in touch in the future.

Ross and Sally had invited George and I to their place for dinner, and both of us gratefully accepted. As we all separated to our respective vehicles and went our various ways, I found myself in a reflective mood. In this adventure, like in my most recent assignment since joining the RCMP, I had experienced more than my fair share of mystery, challenges, danger, and excitement. Along the way, I had once again made some interesting new friends, but friends that I would soon have to leave behind when Silver and I moved on.

Of course, I had no idea at the time how soon that time was going to come.

***

Dinner conversation with Ross, Sally, and George, never strayed too far from our adventure, and at one point I got the opportunity to fill them in on a few loose ends.

"Lucy says she's going to donate those letters she found to the RCMP Museum at Depot Division in Regina. That's good of her," I reflected. "I remember spending quite a bit of time in the museum when I was a recruit in training there. There might be something of historical value in the letters, and I think I'd like to have a look at them myself if I get a chance."

"What about the gold?" Sally asked.

"Well, did you notice that I snuck off to make a phone call at one point?"

"I did," said George, who never seemed to miss much. "I assumed that you were calling your boss to fill him in on the results of our search."

"Ah, well, yes, I probably should have done that," I said, a bit sheepishly. "I'll do that tomorrow, I think… What I actually did was call a banking friend in Radium City[5]. I asked my friend about the gold. He said that if the Bank of Canada's ownership is established, they'll probably pay Lucy a recovery fee of 10 or 15%."

"So…"

"So, he said that in 1898 gold was worth slightly over twenty dollars an ounce, but now it's worth about $170 an ounce."

"And a bar of the stuff?"

"Well, apparently a standard bar, he called it a gold ingot, is worth about seventy thousand dollars."

"Holy smokes!" said Ross, "that means Lucy could get as much as ten thousand dollars!"

I nodded. "Pretty cool, huh. I think she earned it!"

As we were all sharing our surprise and pleasure at Lucy's good fortune, the phone rang, and Sally went off to answer it. When she came back, she had a strange look on her face.

"It's for you Alex. There's an Air Force Captain Harrison calling for you."

"Uh oh," George raised his eyebrows and gave me a knowing look.

"Yes, I think you might be right," I said, getting up to go to the phone. Sure enough, it was Don calling, from somewhere…

"I hear your vacation was short-lived?" Don began.

"How'd you hear about that already?"

"I've been talking to Bob, your boss. He says that you've become an '*International Mountie.*' How did things work out on the search?"

"Everything worked out well. I made some new friends and we were able to save a young girl, but…"

"But what?"

"Nothing, it's just that I'm like the Lone Ranger all over again."

"The what?"

"*The Lone Ranger.* You know, the Texas Ranger and his horse Silver, from fiction, from the movies and television. Anyway, never mind. It's just my own little joke."

There was a pause on the line, as Don thought about what I'd said, then:

"I get it!" he said. "You get called into town, save the day, and then while everyone else is celebrating you quietly move on again, just you and your best friend, Silver. Right?"

That was Don, smart, perceptive, and well grounded. No wonder I'd missed him so much.

I sighed contentedly. "You're one in a million, Don, you

really are... So, what's so important that you tracked me down?"

"We need your help."

"What's up?"

"I can't tell you on an open phone line. Let's just say that it's not too dangerous, but we really need your and Silver's special talents. It's important enough that my boss called your boss, to make the request, and Bob agreed immediately. That's why I was talking to him and heard about your aborted vacation."

"Ok then. When and where do we meet?"

"Yesterday!"

"What? Seriously, Don, ..."

"Well, right away then. We're sending a chopper to pick you up at the Skagway airport. It should be there in an hour. I won't be on it, but I'll see you soon. OK?"

"OK Don, we'll be there."

After saying goodbye to Don and hanging up, I told George, Ross, and Sally that something had come up and Silver and I were needed somewhere else. I explained that a helicopter would be coming to get us at the airport, and could I leave my truck somewhere for a while?

George gave me that penetrating stare he always seemed to be able to switch on, but his eyes were twinkling. "Things seem to happen around you, don't they? I seem to recall that yesterday you were able to call Ottawa in the middle of the night and not only reach a constantly monitored phone number, but to have your boss call you back within an hour. Now, your government is able to reach out and find you in the middle of nowhere, and there's a helicopter on its way to come get you. Something tells me it's not going to be an everyday civilian helicopter, is it?"

"Probably not," I allowed.

"And this Captain Harrison of yours might not be a real Air Force Captain?"

"Actually, I think he really is," I said, and then I frowned, "Although he's a bit more than that."

"Hah, I thought so. Do you want to tell me?"

Oh well, in for a penny, I thought.

"I can't say anything more about Don, but everything I told you about Silver and I is true - it's just not the whole truth. As you've probably figured out, I work for the RCMP Security Service and have been for nearly two years now. Having a woman Mountie and a highly unusual-looking police dog working for them was like a double cover, and I guess they couldn't resist taking advantage of it. So, they just send us wherever they need us, whenever they need us. Usually undercover."

"So, you're kind of a female James Bond then?"

I laughed. "I've never really thought about it that way, but if you take away Bond's licence to kill and just focus on criminal matters, then I suppose so. Maybe I should try drinking martinis – shaken, not stirred?"

"Tell you what. Come back for another visit sometime and I'll buy you one."

"Deal."

"And thanks Alex, I really mean that. You and Silver saved a life here today – and save your breath," George rushed on before I could object. "I know you'll tell me that you were just trying to do the right thing, but we'd never have found her alive if it hadn't been for you. Everyone here knows it, and everyone really appreciates it – even Mark!"

He laughed at that. "In fact, it was a good lesson in humility for him. Mark is a better fellow than the one you saw in action, but he still has some growing up to do, and you and Silver just helped him. Thank you for that too."

"Well, you're welcome. I'm just glad it all worked out."

"Come on, I'll drive you to the airport and then I'll put your truck in our police compound where it will be safe until you can come back and pick it up, along with those martinis we're going to have."

So, I went and packed-up, and then thanked Ross and Sally for their hospitality, and for the chance to meet Silver's family too. We had an emotional goodbye, culminating in them making me promise to go back and visit again, with Silver, of course, to which I readily agreed.

***

It wasn't long after George, Silver, and I reached Skagway's airport, that we could hear the heavy 'Thump, Thump, Thump' sound of a large helicopter approaching. Next, we saw the approaching lights, and finally the unmistakable appearance and blasting roar of a Canadian Forces Sea King[20] helicopter.

"Like I said," observed George, "not your everyday little civilian helicopter."

I just shrugged and grinned.

I had shown George the place in my truck where I stowed my red flashing light with magnetic roof mount base and with that in place, flashing on the roof, George simply drove my truck out onto the tarmac and right over to the helicopter. When we got there, a Lieutenant in a flight suit hopped out to meet us.

"Constable Houston?" he said.

"That's me," I agreed.

"My name's Sandy. Captain Harrison said to look for a fiery woman with red hair, and a grey-white dog that looks like a wolf!"

"I am not a fiery woman!" I instinctively retorted. Then, having listened to what I'd just said, and hearing George burst out laughing, I grinned sheepishly. "Maybe Don knows me better than I know myself," I allowed.

Sandy laughed as well. "Hop in!"

A crewmember took my two duffel bags and a third for Silver. Over the whine of the pilot re-starting his engines, I said goodbye to George and I jumped in, with Silver following close behind me.

The big helicopter took off as soon as the SAR Tech[21] signaled that I was belted-in and that Silver was reasonably secure beside me.

After that, all any of us could hear was:

"Thump, Thump, Thump…"

… Alex and Silver will return,
in *An Inseparable Mountie*.

Laurie Schramm

BOOK 4 ENDNOTES

1. Later renamed Royal North West Mounted Police, and later yet the Royal Canadian Mounted Police.
2. Superintendent S.B. (Sam) Steele, was one of the heroes of the Klondike Gold Rush (where he was referred to variously as *Steele of the Mounted*, or the *Lion of the Yukon*), and one of the most famous Mounted Police officers of all time.
3. Jefferson Randolph Smith II, commonly known as *Soapy Smith*, was a notorious confidence artist and gangster-boss in the late 1800s American West, principally in Texas, then in Colorado, and finally in Skagway, Alaska. He was killed in a famous Skagway shoot-out during the 1898 gold rush.
4. Invented by Indigenous Peoples, and a staple of pioneer travelers in Canada's West, pemmican was made from dried, finely pounded bison meat mixed with melted fat and sometimes other ingredients, such as bison bone marrow. Well prepared and stored pemmican has been known to last for more than fifty years.
5. See *An Inconvenient Mountie* (ISBN: 978-1-9994940-0-1).
6. At this point in time, it was still part of the RCMP Years later, in 1984, the Security Service was spun-out to create the present-day Canadian Security Intelligence Service (C.S.I.S.).
7. Although dog teams originally played critical roles in Alaska's and Northern Canada's evolution, snowmobiles (the 'iron dogs')

had almost completely replaced them by the 1960s. The 'Iditarod' was conceived as way to celebrate Alaskan history. A first, two-heat, race was held on part of the Iditarod Trail in 1967 and 1969 (there was a lack of snow in 1968). After completion of the entire trail, all the way from Anchorage to Nome, the first full-length *Iditarod Trail Sled Dog Race®* was held in 1973.

8. It wasn't until 1988 that younger girls could join the Guiding movement (at age five), and not until 1989 that they got their own name: 'Sparks.'

9. Inukshuk is derived from an Inuktitut word, and refers to a human-built stone marker (cairn). They are characteristically found in the Arctic, Canada's northern territories, and Alaska.

10. Girl Guide leaders generally adopt fun names, which can vary widely in nature. In this case the girls' leader had advanced from Brownies to Guides with the same group of girls and had, for simplicity, kept the name she had used as a Brownie leader: 'Brown Owl.' (Brownie Leaders traditionally adopt the names of Owls.)

11. In avalanche training, mountaineers are taught that if some of their expedition is caught in an avalanche, then they should first conduct a 'hasty search' in what seems like the most likely location for their colleagues to be buried. If that fails, then they are to re-start the search but this time over a wider area, and with a careful grid-search methodology – which can be extremely time consuming.

12. See *An Indestructible Mountie* (ISBN: 978-1-9994940-4-9).

13. This chapter, in slightly longer form, has also appeared as the short story "An Inhuman Mountie" on www.laurieschramm.ca, 2019.

14. In June, 1976.

15. *Dirty Harry* was released in 1971, the first in a series of American action/crime movies in which the central character famously carried the powerful .44 Magnum revolver.

16. Search and Rescue.

17. When Motorola launched their MX300 hand-held VHF radios, in 1975, they set a new standard in portability and performance, and the radios were quickly adopted by police, fire, military, and other forces.

18. Although the revolver held six rounds, I was taught to only chamber five, leaving an empty cylinder under the gun's hammer. That way if the gun was ever dropped, it couldn't accidentally fire.

19. It later turned out to be a standard 400-ounce gold bar, 7" x 3⅝" x 1¾", and it weighed exactly 25 lb.

20. Sikorsky CH-124 Sea Kings are twin-engine, anti-submarine warfare helicopters that were used by Canadian Forces for over 50 years. They were usually housed on and deployed from destroyers and frigates of the Royal Canadian Navy. Sea Kings were a familiar sight to people on Canada's Pacific and Atlantic coasts in the 1970s, partly because they frequently assisted with maritime search and rescue operations.

21. Search and Rescue Technician.

Laurie Schramm

BOOK 1 – 4 SUMMARIES

An Inconvenient Mountie (Book 1). It is 1975, and the RCMP needs to modernize. The Force decides to experiment by allowing its first woman to enter training and serve as a pilot project. Alexandra Houston accepts the challenge and embarks on a journey to fulfil her dream of doing "some real policing," not realizing that she should be careful what she asks for. Her first posting is to a remote part of Northern Saskatchewan, where no one is used to dealing with a female Mountie and her adventures in small-town policing are compounded by crises, crime, and mystery.

An Inconspicuous Mountie (Book 2). The year is 1976. RCMP Constable Alex Houston and her dog Silver are training to work as an undercover team. They are an unlikely pair since Alex is the first woman Mountie and Silver, an Alaskan Malamute, looks nothing like a police dog. Meanwhile, trouble is brewing north of Fort McMurray, Alberta. Not everyone is happy with the development of the massive oil sands mines and tensions are running high. Before their training is complete, a pipeline is bombed, and new threats emerge. As Alex and Silver are sent in, this time they need to be … inconspicuous.

An Indestructible Mountie (Book 3). It is 1977, and a hiker on Canada's Cape Breton Island has discovered a strange-looking installation hidden in the forest, on an oceanside cliff. Word of her discovery makes its circuitous way to military intelligence and the RCMP Security Service, where it sets off alarm bells, and Constable Alex Houston and her dog Silver are sent in. As they investigate, a technological curiosity from the Second World War turns out to be the centrepiece of something current, and sinister. As Alex and Silver investigate, this time they will need to be… indestructible.

An International Mountie (Book 4). RCMP Constable Alexandra Houston finally gets a break from a series of hair-raising assignments and heads for Alaska on vacation. While there she hopes to investigate the origins of Silver, her best friend and police-dog partner, and hike the famous Chilkoot Trail. Meanwhile, a young Girl Guide gets lost in the wilds of Alaska and experiences, first-hand, the meaning of the Guides and Scouts motto: *"Be Prepared."*

Laurie Schramm

ABOUT THE AUTHOR

Laurie Schramm comes from an RCMP family, grew up while living in the RCMP Barracks (Depot Division) in Regina, Saskatchewan, and spent several summers working as a civilian for the RCMP while in high school and university. Early personal influences included not only the real-life RCMP culture but also Hollywood's versions via such classics as Rose Marie, and Susannah of the Mounties. Many of the events described in this novel are based on the author's real life, although not necessarily within an RCMP context.

For more information, see Laurier L. Schramm on **Linked**in

and:

www.laurieschramm.ca

or

www.facebook.com/LaurieSchrammBooks

Laurie Schramm

ADVENTURES OF THE FIRST WOMAN MOUNTIE

Book 1: *An Inconvenient Mountie*
Book 2: *An Inconspicuous Mountie*
Book 3: *An Indestructible Mountie*
Book 4: *An International Mountie*
Book 5: *An Inseparable Mountie*
Book 6: *An Indispensable Mountie*
Book 7: *An Inexorable Mountie*

www.laurieschramm.ca

www.facebook.com/LaurieSchrammBooks

Laurie Schramm

Adventures of the First
Woman Mountie